THE BLUE Q
- The World As I See It -

By

Dennis Avelar

First published in the United States of America by Dennis Avelar

ISBN 978-1-7356647-0-5

Summary: In the Land of Eternal Spring, a teenage orphan is forced to
undergo a major transformation which enables him to understand the
importance of the natural balance of the Earth.

I dedicate this story to the many women who made a difference in my life. From the woman who dreamed of me before I came into this world, to the women who have afforded me opportunities which — if given thousands of years to do so — I could never repay.

I would not be the person I am without you, and no written words will ever be enough to express my true gratitude for what each of you have done for me.

To you who laughed with me, cried with me, educated me, escalated me to my greatest triumphs and were present at the time of my fiercest falls, these words I solemnly dedicate.

With love, now and always,

- Dennis

Chapter One

High in the mountains of Canada there once lived a pair of golden eagles. They were young eagles, and they loved soaring high above the land and exploring the mountainsides together; they were as inseparable as two golden eagles could be. These two birds, though fierce in sight and superior to almost all others, were more tame and more gentle than they seemed. To one another, they were birds of a feather – never too far from one another yet distant enough to keep a sense of mystery between them. To the rest of the birds of the mountains, they were the rulers of the skies, and they soared unlike any other.

As with most young families that begin with two individuals, the time had come for the young golden eagles to create a home of their own. They found a perfect location on a steep cliff, one that overlooked the beauty of the Canadian wilderness and which was far enough away from poachers or hunters. They worked tirelessly for days, swooping below their normal flying altitudes to gather whatever twigs, branches, rocks, and other strong materials they could find. They lifted their collection of items and created a nest along a high cliff which oversaw Banff National Park; their view of nature was greater than even the most beautiful of dreams.

As the greening spring approached, and as the days grew slightly longer and the nights slightly shorter, the eagles spent more time apart than was normal. The male hunted, working tirelessly to find the perfect meal for his mate, then would return to the nest to bring it to her. The female eagle spent the majority of her days sitting patiently on the nest, which held the most precious gifts of all.

On one particular day, the male returned to the nest and was overly excited. Behaving like an impatient chick, he motioned for his mate to reveal the surprise she had for him. He presented her with a large fish, and as she stood to consume her meal, she revealed that which she protected from the elements: four perfect eggs. The male viewed the eggs in awe, counting them multiple times and inspecting their curves and textures, unable to hide the excitement of knowing he would soon be a father.

The days were long and the nights were cold, but the eagles knew that they had to endure the challenges of nature and the environment to provide the necessities for their unborn chicks. As is common on spring days, storms came to the area, which forced the eagles to huddle together and protect one another, as well as to guard the precious eggs in their nest. They loved to do so, despite the cold, the wind, and the rain, because it brought them closer together.

On one particular day, however, a downpour came that was far stronger than previous storms that spring. The eagles huddled together and protected themselves from the wind and rain, but despite their strength and natural abilities, they were no match for nature's fury. The wind was cold and piercing, which caused a great amount of pain for the two birds. They held on as tight as they could, embracing one another with desperation and wishing for the storm to calm and pass as soon as possible.

A bolt of lightning struck dangerously close to their perched nest, which created a crack on the cliffside. If this were not enough, the thunder that accompanied the bolt of lightning startled them and caused them to shift their bodies, which opened a tiny crack at the base of the nest. As if by fate, the smallest egg, jostled by the movement, slid ever so carefully into the tiny divot, and soon found its way outside of the nest.

The egg fell from the perch, pushed by the forces of both wind and gravity as it hurled toward the rock-covered ground. The egg dropped hundreds of meters from the nest. The wind and rain drove it toward the trees, almost as if nature knew that this egg was precious and deserved to be protected by the same elements which caused it to fall.

The egg narrowly avoided disaster, shifting from tree branch to tree branch, each carrying it in a similar manner in which a mother would cradle a newborn child. The egg rolled, but did not break, as it was pushed closer and closer to the ground. The egg made its way to a large pine tree, where the branches and needles slowed its momentum and delicately guided it to a place where the tree knew the egg would be safe.

At the base of the large pine tree was a young couple, a man and a woman, who tried desperately to keep a small fire from extinguishing. It was their only source of heat, and so they used their bodies to shield the fire from the surrounding elements. The light from the fire flickered, creating a dance of shadows that distracted the young man and woman to the point where they failed to notice the egg which fell from two nearby branches. Like a pair of arms, the branches carefully guided the egg to the ground, where it rolled towards the young couple and stopped at the base of the dying fire.

The woman was the first to see it. Confused as to how the egg made its way to them, the man and woman looked at one another briefly before the man sprung to action. He put his arms over his head and ran to a place just outside of the shadows of the trees, where a small, poorly made tent was pitched. The man quickly went into the wind-stricken tent, grabbed a small bag, then ran back to the fire, ignoring the cold droplets of water that hit him from every direction. He gently grabbed the small egg and placed it in the bag to protect it from the cold. The man and the woman glanced at each other, shrugged their shoulders, then peaked inside the bag.

The storm passed through the night, which then revealed the perfect morning of a beautiful spring day. The egg bounced slightly as it rested in a bag inside of a car that travelled even further away from the nest. The roads were clear, and the man held the small bag as the woman drove down a long and winding road. The car then pulled away from the main road and travelled along a paved path, which led to a large farm. In the distance, the car came to a stop. The woman was the first to exit the car, followed by the man, who held the small bag as one would hold a valuable heirloom.

As they walked with utmost delicacy, the man and the woman slowly made their way to a small area between their home and the side of a barn. They entered a chicken coop, where dozens of hens waited for their meal of the day. Instead of spreading food, the man walked to the largest hen in the coop. As she sat on her nest, the man placed the egg beneath her. The egg he placed was larger than what the hen recognized, but she knew that it contained a precious life and thus made no objection to care for the egg as if it were one of her own.

A few weeks passed. The eagle egg was accompanied by other eggs. It looked different than the rest, but the hen gladly treated it as she treated her own. Every day, the man came in and inspected the eggs, wondering just what would become of the one egg that was unlike the others.

Soon, the day that the man, the woman, the large hen, and every bird in the coop had patiently awaited, finally arrived. One by one, the young chicks cracked through their protective barriers and saw the light of day for the very first time. With each new hatchling, the coop celebrated, though all were intent on seeing what would emerge from the slightly larger egg within the nest.

At last, after much anticipation from every bird in the coop and every animal on the farm, the larger egg hatched. Gradually, as the hatchling made its way to the light, every being on the farm stood in complete awe. There were no howls, no clucks, no noise of any kind, as everyone saw that which was now among them: a baby golden eagle – a child of the skies that somehow made its way to the farm.

Time passed. The young eagle, having no other family, was protected and loved by every hen in the coop. Knowing no other manner of raising their offspring, the young eagle was treated like all the others, and soon, no one noticed the differences between any of the birds in the coop. The young eagle regarded all the birds as his family, and all the other animals as his friends. He ate with his brothers and sisters, played with them in the yards, mimicked their every move, and in the summer, went with them to school – a small corner of the large barn where other birds came and went as they pleased.

On the day when the lesson was taught by one of the elder roosters,

4

the chicks gathered to learn about other birds of the world. They learned of birds in the arctic, who are flightless but swim gracefully in the coldest waters on Earth. The chicks learned of birds of all sizes and colors, from blackbirds and vultures to the colorful birds of the tropics. More importantly, they learned about the elusive eagle, who is the king of the skies and is thus the ruler of all birds.

Every so often, a single crow would appear on the farm. The crow kept its distance, almost as if to observe the eagle who lived amongst the chickens. The crow would only stay for a few minutes, and no other bird or livestock on the farm ever knew that the crow had visited.

Years passed. The once young eagle was fully grown. He was a gorgeous bird, clearly a relative of royal lineage, but lived a life according to what he saw and knew. The eagle was out of his natural element, though it was the only reality that he understood. As more time passed, and the seasons changed from warm, to cold, to freezing and then back to warm, the eagle noticed that many of his brothers and sisters – the young hatchlings who were born on the same day – were no longer on the farm.

More time went by, and no other chicken who lived in the coop knew of the day when the eagle hatched among them. The formerly elusive, once-beautiful golden eagle was now old, and his immaculate feathers slowly molted from his frail body. He came to be respected as an elder among the farm birds and the farm animals. Though little joy remained in his later years, the eagle liked to see the new chicks in the spring.

On an oddly warm spring day, the youngest hatchlings were permitted to go into the yard and enjoy the light of the sun. They loved to be free; they ran about the small plot of land and delighted in the breeze. As the young chicks played, a crow made its way from the sky and landed on a nearby fence, taking a moment to rest and to observe the scene. The crow was neither seen nor heard by the other birds.

The young chicks ran, jumped and moved about the yard, laughing and experiencing the day in the same manner enjoyed by the youth of all species on Earth. One of the chicks looked up and was intrigued by a strange object he saw in the sky.

"What is that?" the young chick asked. He pointed his wing at the object far above the ground and looked at his brothers and sisters for help to identify it. The elder eagle looked up.

"That?" the elder eagle asked, his voice as old and coarse as his body. "It's an eagle. That bird rules the skies. No other bird like him exists."

The young chicks squirmed with excitement. "I want to be an eagle! I want to be an eagle!" they all exclaimed as they ran about the yard with their small wings spread, mimicking the bird in the sky.

"Not us," the elder eagle said. "We are chickens. We belong on the ground, where it's safe. We will never be eagles."

The chicks verbally displayed their disappointment but continued to playfully pretend to be birds of flight. The elder eagle momentarily looked up to observe the magnificent bird in the sky. He then limped away and pecked at the ground for food.

The crow briefly observed the actions of the eagle, then flew away and disappeared into the distance.

Chapter Two

"Buried in the tropical forest of northern Guatemala, as though it has no business being where it is, are the remains of what was once a grand, ancient city. The people of this city were rulers of their kingdom, and made incredible progress in terms of civilizational infrastructure, technology, and engineering. Their accomplishments were unlike any other native population, and their ideas are still relevant to this day."

A young man, no older than 15 and who had a slight, noticeable Spanish accent when he spoke in English, smiled as he walked about the interior of a small tour bus in motion. His hair was dark in color, with streaks of a lighter brown tone which were the result of heavy exposure to sunlight. His tanned skin matched the hazel of his eyes, which emanated an innocent glow that captured the attention of even the smallest of spotlights.

"The Mayan people ruled their world unlike any other civilization, and evidence tells us that the metropolis of *Tikal* once had over 1 million people living in it. The Mayans were the best architects, builders, astronomers, mathematicians and engineers of their time. And for those of you who like sweets, they were also the makers of the best chocolate in the world, a proud tradition of all people of Guatemala."

"The best chocolate in the world is in Belgium, not in Guatemala," said an older gentleman.

"I see we have *un europeo* on our tour today," responded the young man.

"Yes, sir, the finest chocolate in the world may be in Belgium, or even in Switzerland, but the absolute best chocolate in the universe was made by the Mayan people, using cacao beans that were given to them directly by the gods."

The young man paused to read his audience. With the exception of one much younger passenger, their interest in chocolate came second to the history of the ancient society.

"Unfortunately," the young man continued, "all that remains of their once magnificent city are the structures that were left behind, which is why you are all here today." He walked to the front of the bus then turned to face his audience.

"Welcome to *ToursTikal*, and thank you for choosing us as your tour guides to *el mundo Maya*," he said to the group. "Once again, my name is Dionisio, and since you are all now my friends, you may call me Dioni. I know, it sounds like I am saying 'the only', but it is Di Oh Nee. Does anyone have any questions before we go to the park?"

The passengers looked at one another, excited to visit one of the most majestic sites in the world. For some, this was a chance to live a lifelong dream; for others, it was an opportunity to witness an unforgettable experience. For the rest, it was business as usual.

Aside from the employees of *ToursTikal* – the young guide and the bus driver – none of those among the tour group were familiar with their surroundings. They were tourists, 14 of them in total. Three of them were a small family – a mom, a dad, and a son who was approximately 8 years old – who visited from Spain. A man and a woman, who sat near one another though they did not travel together, shared a common continent of origin: Europe. The man travelled to Guatemala, along with his son, from the United Kingdom (he mentioned Liverpool more than once during his introduction), while the woman passed through the UK as she made her way to Guatemala from her home just outside of Berlin. The elders of the group were American: 4 were from New York City and made it known that they were proud of their New Yorker heritage; a more reserved couple came from Chicago; and the remaining two passengers were from California and Arizona. It was their first visit to this part of the world, yet none was more excited to be there than Dioni.

"If you don't have any questions," said Dioni, "I want you to remember that the walk from the entrance of the park to the Mayan city is about 4 hours, so please rest your legs now because we will be walking for the rest of the day."

The bus driver made a quick stop at a small shop within a tiny village, to allow each of the passengers to get out, stretch, and buy any supplies that were needed. While the couple from Chicago stocked up on sunblock and mosquito repellent, others filled their plastic water bottles, took photos of themselves on their mobile devices, or browsed the many intricate items found inside the small store. After a few minutes, Dioni asked the passengers to return to the bus, where the final destination was the entrance of Tikal National Park.

As the bus entered the gates to the Mayan kingdom, Dioni's eyes opened just as widely as they did when he first gave this tour. He lost count of the number of times he had come through the entrance gates, and how he waited with great anticipation to see what was once, to him, just a myth. He remembered how Alma – his best friend – would tell him stories of the Mayan world, and how he would rarely believe her until he visited Tikal and saw it with his own eyes.

The group exited the bus. They began their walk toward the great plaza, which was the main attraction for all who visited Tikal. The tourists were asked to gather in front of the elusive *ceiba* tree, located a few meters along the trail.

"*La ceiba*," Dioni addressed the group, "is unlike any other tree in the jungle. It is the national tree of Guatemala, and it is unique to us because of its form, its age, its height, and the size of its branches." He paused briefly to allow the tourists to capture the moment.

"I do not know how old this tree is," Dioni continued, "but the oldest *ceiba* in Guatemala is more than 400 years old. This tree, and all other *ceibas*, are protected by the national government, as is the national bir—"

"—Is it safe to climb?" interrupted the man from Chicago.

"It might be," Dioni responded. "But I would not try to climb it if I were you. This tree is protected by more than just the national government."

"What do you mean?" asked the gentleman from England. Dioni smiled.

"The legendary myth states that *la ceiba* acts as a gateway to another world. Some say that it is to a hidden Mayan kingdom – one that we cannot see because the entrance is heavily guarded and protected. Others say that *ceibas* are so big because they are hiding something even bigger… something we are not wise enough to understand."

"And what does science tell us?" asked the man from New York.

"That it is a big tree with big roots," Dioni responded. "That explanation is not very exciting, so we like to change the story for tourists. Another story we like to tell is about the resplendent *quetzal* – the most beautiful bird in all of nature."

"Oh oh oh!" the young Spaniard boy shouted excitedly. "Will we see any *quetzales* while we are here?"

"Oh, no, my friend," responded Dioni. "When the Mayan people abandoned the city, the *quetzales* left as well. They now live in the mountains, and they prefer to be in places where they are not bothered by humans or other birds. You will see other tropical birds here in the jungle, like *tucanes* and maybe *un alcon*."

Dioni turned to address the tour group. "My friends, I can talk about birds and trees for the rest of our time, or I can guide you through this forest and take you to the great ancient city. Please follow me."

The group followed closely behind their guide, and before long they were well into the path that led through aisles upon aisles of trees. The path was not a simple one to hike, and it required the members of the group to stay together and oftentimes help one another as their fatigue grew stronger in the heat of the Guatemalan forest. However, the tour was more than just walking through endless rows of trees. Knowing that their stamina for considerable pacing on rough terrain was not level to his own, Dioni stopped every so often to teach the tourists about some of the ancient artifacts that were conveniently placed at key points along the trail. Sporadically, the sounds of local wildlife echoed through the forest, though the birds knew better than to be in full view of visitors from afar.

The first pyramid encountered by the visitors was indeed large, but not nearly as grand as what the tourists expected. Dioni explained that these outside pyramids were just a few that were recently uncovered by archeological diggers, and he made mention of the team of foreign researchers who visited the area in hopes of uncovering more of the ancient city. Dioni led the way and almost sprinted to the peak of the flat-topped, short pyramid. The direct heat from the sun caused the roof of the stone structure to be incredibly hot, and just as a few of the brave tourists made their way to the summit, Dioni easily made his way back to the ground level, where he patiently waited for the others to return.

By noon, despite the heat and the punishing landscape of the region, Dioni led the group to a large wall that was conveniently located near a shaded rest area.

"This is the base of the largest temple in Tikal," he stated, proudly describing the ancient structure behind him. "You will not forget the first time you see this, so please prepare yourselves for this experience." Though exhausted, the tourists became excited to have finally reached their intended destination.

"Behind me is the ground entrance to the "Star Wars" temple," Dioni continued.

"That can't be its name, can it?" asked the woman from Germany.

"No," Dioni responded. "It is actually Temple four. We call it 'the Star Wars temple' because it was in the movie Star Wars. I do not know this movie, but from what I understand it is about a war in space, with robots."

"It's about so much more than that, guv," responded the Englishman.

"My friend, Oscar, said the same," Dioni continued. "Perhaps one day I will learn about this war-in-space movie and finally understand why so many people love this temple. I love it because, from the very top, you can see the entire forest. Would everyone like to see it?"

The visitors looked up to see the sheer scale of the large stone structure. Though drained of their energy, they were not deterred to make the climb, and not a single one of them objected as they followed Dioni to the top of Temple IV.

Their view from the peak of the structure was unforgettable. In the distance, they saw the tops of the temples of the main plaza and the surrounding greenery that was once undoubtedly enjoyed by the ancient Mayan civilization. The trees, many of which had been there for centuries, held stories and secrets that no living man or woman would ever hear nor comprehend. The only beings who understood where they dwelled – of the history of the people who inhabited the land prior to the many visiting scientists and tourists – were the thousands of birds and animals who never left the only home they had ever known.

Dioni loved this portion of the tour. He imagined what it would be like to live without limits and to be unbound to the ground. Each time he returned to the site and made his way to the very top of the temple, he took a few moments to recollect something he once saw, in hopes that he would repeat the moment he experienced when he first visited the exact place where he presently stood.

. . .

As the youngest of the tour guides for *ToursTikal*, Dioni learned to work at an unusually young age. He did not possess a single memory of either a mother or a father to call his own. His family, from his earliest recollection, was the group of children who were brought to the orphanage. Some, like Dionisio, remained residents for years and departed after they had grown too old to stay. Others stayed for some time, only to be adopted and then taken away by people from other countries, who had it in their hearts to help these poor, parentless children.

The orphanage itself was located along the outskirts of the Guatemalan city of Flores, by the edge of Lake Peten Itza, where the local residents went about their concerns. As time passed, Dionisio learned to call Flores his home, and he took it upon himself to be the ambassador of the orphanage. When a new child arrived, usually frightened and unsure of what to do or on whom they could depend, Dionisio quickly made them feel like a part of the family. Because of his behavior, he was the most popular student in the home; he easily made friends with children and adults alike, and in his 15 years of life, he never met anyone with whom he could not get along.

Alma, however, was special. She and Dionisio were so young when they first met that she was unable to say his name, uttering "Dioni" as best a toddler could. The name stuck. Alma was the one person who had known Dioni the longest, and every other child in the orphanage envied the closeness between them. She was his best friend, and she was far more than just the person he relied on the most; she was his greatest source of motivation and inspiration. Even at a young age, they always sat together, talked to one another, and spent as much time together as possible. Dioni taught her to run fast and jump high, and Alma taught him to read and write. Dioni helped her clean around the home and cook for the other orphans, and Alma taught him mathematics and literature. They were as close as two friends could be, and while he spent much of his days away from her, she always waited for him with utmost anticipation.

It was Alma who encouraged Dioni to try to communicate with the many foreign visitors, and he never forgot the first time he learned the word *gringo*.

"What does that word mean? *Gringo?*" Dioni asked her, the question posed by an innocent child who was clearly unaware of the ways of the world.

"It's the word we use for them," Alma responded as she pointed at the visiting Americans. "Do you see their green eyes?"

"Yes," responded Dioni.

"Well, *verde* in Spanish is 'green' in English."

"Oh, I get it. And the *go?*"

"'Go' means *ándale*. Like, 'get out, leave!' Our people wanted the greens to go, so that is why they called them *gringos*. The name just stuck."

Dioni had never laughed so enthusiastically in all his years. The story may or may not have been accurate, but the fact that it was the story told by Alma meant that he cherished it long after he learned the language most commonly spoken by the *gringos*.

13

When the foreigners visited – some from churches or religious groups and others who just hoped to be of service and help around the orphanage – Dioni maintained his status as ambassador and was the first to make the guests feel welcome. He used his youth to his advantage and learned to speak English by listening as the visitors spoke to one another, where he occasionally joined their conversations. In time, Dioni was not only able to communicate with his newfound friends, but he was also chosen as the unofficial translator for both the orphanage and the nearby church.

The best part of learning this new language was that it opened Dioni to the study of other cultures, and to hear new stories from strange lands. He learned that there were places with buildings so tall that they soared above the clouds. He learned that there existed places that were so cold that the ground changed from green to white, and that the lakes and rivers turned from water to ice. He tried to remember as many stories as possible, then would return to Alma and tell her of what he would one day take her to see.

As the younger children left the orphanage, year after year, to depart from Guatemala and never return, it was Dionisio who talked to the new parents of the adopted children; he was the last person whom the children saw as they entered a car and went away to their new home in a new land.

By a large margin, the majority of those from other countries who visited the orphanage were older in age or were established enough in their lives that their visit was temporary and strictly for a cause or for a business transaction. On a day no different than any other, a young newlywed couple visited the orphanage on their way to the Mayan city of Tikal, much to the surprise of the children and adults alike. Despite living nearby, Dioni had only heard stories and legends of the city but had never actually visited. As was his custom, Dioni introduced himself and spoke to the newlyweds in English, to their amazement. Having no knowledge of the area or any way to communicate with the locals, they asked Dioni if he would be willing to go with them and serve as their translator while they visited the ancient temples. Dioni agreed before they finished their question.

Though Dioni knew not of what to expect aside from a serious amount

14

of bugs and trees, he was nevertheless excited to visit someplace new. The trails were long, and the heat of the sun was as punishing in the forest as it was in Flores, but nothing stopped Dioni from wanting to see it all. He stayed with the newlyweds and acted as their translator, dictating the words said by the official tour guide of the Mayan city. If he did not know the correct word to translate, Dioni would create one of his own and change the tour guide's story, which kept the newlyweds ignorantly happy.

Every step forward was more awe inspiring than the many he had taken to get to where he stood, though no step had rendered Dioni speechless until the moment he reached the top of the highest temple in the land. It was known as *Templo Cuatro*, Temple 4, and it gave Dioni a view unlike any other. For a brief moment, Dioni stood at the very peak of the world, high above the trees and taller than any being on the planet. He was astonished, and he failed to notice that the tour guide had led the group back to the base of the temple.

"Dioni!" the newlywed man shouted, which snapped Dioni out of his trance-like state of wonder. "Are you coming down?"

Dioni looked down and saw as his group walked away. "Yes! I am sorry! I did not know you leave from here," he responded, in a broken accent.

"Well come on down. I think we're going to the plaza next," shouted the young newlywed bride.

Dioni turned one last time to see the magnificent splendor of what was once the homeland of his people. One last look, for just a second, as the moment could very well be the last time he would witness something so beautiful.

In the distance, Dioni noticed an odd creature in the sky. It was a bird, and its flight pattern was unlike any other he had ever seen. It glided in the air like waves that streamed from the sea, and it appeared as if it carried two long and slender objects which flowed in the same aerial pattern. Dioni saw only the silhouette of the bird as it passed directly in front of the sunlight; he noticed that the bird was entirely blue in color, and that its wings absorbed the light.

"Dioni! You comin'?" shouted the man.

The other tourists were further away.

Dioni turned his head to respond. "Yes, I am coming down to you now."

He quickly glanced for one final look at the resplendent bird, which disappeared without a trace. Dioni had no choice but to get back to work, though he knew the perfect person to ask of the mysterious object he saw over the Mayan sky.

By the end of the tour, the members of the group were exhausted after a long hike on a very hot day. Dioni wanted nothing more than to return to the orphanage and tell Alma everything he saw that afternoon, including the sighting of a mysterious bird. The visitors were guided onto a bus, where they were taken back to the start of the tour near the city limits of Flores. Dioni sat impatiently the entire trip.

After the bus unloaded the passengers and as the visitors said their goodbyes to each other, the tour guide – an elder man from Belize – asked Dioni if he would be willing to return the next day to help translate for other visiting tourists from English-speaking countries. Dioni did not hesitate to accept. To him, nothing could be more magnificent than Tikal, and the chance to return was an offer he simply could not decline.

Dioni did not wait for the newlyweds' vehicle to come to a complete stop before he opened the door, jumped out of the car, and shouted for Alma. It was much later in the day, which meant that Alma was doing one of two things: either helping the adults to cook dinner for all the pupils, or reciting her prayers at the nearby church. Dioni sprinted towards the kitchen of the orphanage.

"Alma!" he shouted, which startled some of the younger children.

"Shhhhh!" responded a young nun. "She's at the church, where *you* should be!"

"Sorry sister!" he said to her, then ran to the door.

Dioni sprinted towards the church, jumping over any child or obstacle in his path like a skilled hurdler. He opened the large doors of the church entrance then ran inside. Almost immediately, he was stopped by two of the other children from the orphanage, who were clothed in oversized robes and who each held a large, white candle.

"Hey Dioni," said Oscar, a boy of Dioni's same age though a few inches shorter. "You're late…again."

"I know," Dioni responded. "Where's Alma?"

"You mean your girlfriend?" said the other boy, mockingly.

"She's not my girlfriend!"

"Whatever," the two boys responded simultaneously.

Oscar smiled. "She's at the front, by the prayer candles. Don't ru—" was all he was able to say before Dioni rushed to the front of the church. He saw Alma, who knelt before a large display of candles.

"Alma! Alma!" he whisper-shouted to her.

"Not now, Dioni," she whispered back forcefully, her head bowed, her eyes closed, and her hands clasped. "I'm in the middle of something."

"You're never going to believe what I saw today," Dioni responded. He paused to catch his breath.

"SHHH!" exclaimed an elder nun, who prayed a few feet away and was visibly upset at the two youths for the noise they made instead of reciting their prayers.

"She's going to throw her *chancla* at you if you don't be quiet," whispered Alma.

"She can't see me. It's too dark in here," Dioni responded.

"She can hear you, Dioni…her hearing is like a wolf now. It doesn't matter. I'm in the middle of something. Can you just wait a few min—"

"—The Mayan temples are so big!" Dioni interrupted, unable to contain his excitement. "There were trees everywhere and there was this path that we had to follow and the tour guide was talking and talking about the ancient people who used to live their but had to leave because there was a big drought a long time ago but most people think that the people just suddenly abandoned the city but that's not true because there are more temples that they haven't uncovered and one of the temples was so tall that it went over the trees and I got to see the entire forest and it was—"

"—Dioni!" Alma interjected. She stopped him before he completely ran

17

out of breath. "Slow down."

"I can't slow down! It was just so....so—"

WHAM!

As if tossed by a skilled samurai, a *chancla* nailed Dioni in the forehead, which immediately threw him back and onto the hard floor. Alma looked in the direction from which it came, shocked by the speed, stealth, and precision of the throw. The elder nun, still on her knees, held and shook another *chancla* in her throwing hand, as if to be dared to try again.

"Keep talking and you'll see what happens to you next," said the nun, in a raspy voice.

"Okay, you win," Alma responded, her hands up in surrender.

Alma stood and walked toward the large doors at the back of the church. Dioni, in a semi-daze from the unexpected blunt-force head trauma, followed behind her. He walked slowly at first and was able to regain his composure after a few steps. Alma had not taken a single step outside of the church when Dioni continued.

"So the Mayans built these temples and there are two big ones that are looking at each other. The tour guide said I couldn't climb those because they are too old, but there were some other ones on the side that I was able to climb so I did. Oh! And one of the temples, the four temple, was in a movie about wars in space. OH! And at the top of that temple I saw the strangest bird."

"A bird, Dioni?" Alma asked. They walked together toward the orphanage.

"Yeah, a blue bird," Dioni responded. "I think it was blue. It flew like this." Dioni made wave motions with his arm to mimic the flight pattern of the elusive bird. "And it was carrying something long on its back or was holding something long in his feet because in the air it looked like it had a huge tail. Birds don't have super long tails, do they?"

Alma stopped and looked at Dioni, suspiciously. "Wait, how did it fly?" she asked.

"Like this," he responded. He repeated the same wave motion.

"And it had a long tail?"

"It looked like one long tail that was split in two."

Alma smiled. "Those were its tailfeathers, dummy," she said to him, then continued toward the orphanage. "And you said the bird was blue?"

"It looked blue. I didn't see it clearly because it flew in front of the sunlight, but it looked blue. You know, like how the mountains look blue in the morning."

"So, like a shadow?"

"Yes, a blue bird's shadow," Dioni responded.

"No, that wasn't the bird's shadow," Alma said. She looked at him as she walked. "It looked blue to you because of the angle of the light. The bird is actually green."

"What...green? How do you know? Did you see it too?" Dioni asked, shocked but not surprised that she would know such a thing.

"Dioni, do you know what you saw?" Alma asked. "Do you know what kind of bird that was?"

"A Mayan jungle bird?"

Alma stopped, turned her head to the night sky, then sighed. She looked at him and smiled, the way only young love can smile at another's innocence.

"It was a quetzal!"

. . .

"Earth to Dioni...hello! Come in, Dioni," said the man from Chicago, in an attempt to regain Dioni's attention. Dioni quickly realized his mind was elsewhere, and he was slightly embarrassed by it.

"Yes! Sorry about that," Dioni responded. He focused his attention back to the present. "I was just looking for something."

"Looking for Waldo, were you?" said the Englishman, mockingly.

"Uhh, no," he responded, ignoring the insult. He turned his attention to address the group. "Would you like to visit the plaza of the Mayan city?"

The tiredness of the tourists transitioned to excitement as they made their way down a series of steps which led back to the path they had travelled all day. As they walked, one of the guests became curious.

"Dioni?" she asked. "We are going to the plaza, correct? Where the Jaguar Temple is located?"

"Yes, that is correct." Dioni responded.

"Well, I have a question," the woman continued. "I read that there is a whole other city beneath the plaza, that is buried and cannot be accessed because it's a system of tunnels that the Mayans built to protect themselves from attacks. Is that true?"

Dioni chuckled. His head dropped playfully as he led the group along the trail.

"This is a myth, my friend," Dioni responded. "Scientists and researchers have uncovered as much of the plaza as exists, and all that is underneath the temples is more Earth. The Mayan people were brave and fearless, and they preferred to build to the sky instead of to the dirt. But that is a great question."

The group continued, and before long they walked onto the plaza that was once the heart of a prosperous city. It was smaller than it appeared in photographs, though much larger than most visitors imagined. The plaza was a place of wonder and mystery, and Dioni loved it more and more upon each return to the site.

"Ladies and gentlemen, *damas y caballeros*, this is *el Mundo Maya*," Dioni said as he gathered and addressed the members of the group, who stood on the grounds of the Great Plaza. "Behind me is the great Temple one, which is known as *el Templo del Gran Jaguar*. It was built more than 1,500 years ago. Temple two is behind you. Temple two is 125 feet high and is also more than 1,500 years old. I will give you some time so you can explore this area on your own. Feel free to take as many photos as you wish, but please do not go far from *la plaza*. You are able to climb and explore the smaller structures around *la plaza*, but please do not go up the steps of either of the large temples."

"What happens if we do?" asked the Englishman.

"The grounds are protected by the national government of Guatemala," Dioni responded. "The temples, however, are protected by the spirits of those who lived here thousands of years ago. I strongly advise you to not anger either of them."

"But why can't we go up the steps?" asked a New Yorker.

"These temples are very old and fragile," said Dioni, "and the Guatemalan government would like to preserve them as much as possible so that more people can see the beauty of what our people created such a long time ago."

For over an hour, the tourists climbed the ancient structures, took hundreds of photos of themselves and of the plaza, marveled at the architectural magnificence of the main temples, and enjoyed the splendor of the ancient city. The sun, though far in the sky and relentless on most days, was relatively calm, which was a pleasant surprise. For Dioni, this was the time he was able to rest. He was accustomed to working on the tours almost every day of the week, oftentimes without a break between each group, and he absolutely loved to do so. He was surrounded by nature and culture, yet there existed a mystery to the city which he sensed but was unable to describe to others.

Dioni found an empty location beneath a nearby tree, where he sat and observed as the many tourist groups rotated in and out of the plaza. What he loved most about his rest period, where he sat in the shade and surveyed the sky while he snacked on various fruits or treats, was the opportunity to once again see the elusive bird that he noticed years prior. Dioni knew that quetzals migrated away from Tikal hundreds of years ago, but he always secretly wished to once again catch a view of the bird that made such an impression on him, in the hopes that he could tell Alma and cease her relentless teasing once and for all.

"What are you eating?" asked the Spaniard child as he observed Dioni seated all alone and snacking on what appeared to be small beans.

"*Cacao.* Chocolate," responded Dioni. He offered a piece to the boy, who took a single bean and placed it in his mouth. The child immediately spat it out.

21

"This is not chocolate!" the child shouted, who desperately attempted to clear the taste from his tongue.

Dioni laughed. "It is *cacao*, raw chocolate. It is bitter, but here, let me show you something." He reached into his backpack and removed a small, stone bowl. "This is something I wanted to show you earlier. This is the stone that the Mayan people used to make their favorite drink. Would you like to see how they did it?"

The boy nodded. Dioni quickly stood and searched for a plant nearby, just beyond the safety of the marked path. The boy followed but was cut-off after Dioni found what he wanted then returned to his place of rest. In his hand, Dioni held two large rocks.

"This is a *criollo*," Dioni continued. "It is the rarest cacao seed in all of Guatemala. We must break it open and remove the seeds. Can you help me?

The child was thrilled to be of service. Though he was evidently uninterested moments ago, the task of breaking large seeds garnered his attention. Dioni gave one of the rock-like shells to the boy, who immediately pitched it against a tree and lost it to the Mayan forest.

"Well, that's one way to do it," Dioni said. "How about this? I will open it, and you can help grind the seeds."

The child complied, knowing that at one point he would get a chocolaty treat for all his work. Dioni reached into his backpack and pulled a small knife, which he used to open the incredibly solid shell. He pulled two of the pieces apart and revealed a small treasure of cacao beans.

"Now we have to take these and cook them," Dioni instructed. "Then we have to use a grinding stone to make them into a paste."

"When do we get to eat it?" the child asked, who craved chocolate more than he did at any previous point in his young life.

"I will take these back to the bus with me, and before you go to your hotel, I will show you how my friends make these beans into a powder, and then use that powder to make the most delicious cocoa you have ever tasted."

Under normal circumstances, the child would not have had the patience for such a ludicrous proposal. However, he was intrigued, and was more than willing to wait for the chance to taste the extraordinarily delicious chocolate.

Dioni's tour group was given ample time to discover the ancient plaza, and they took advantage of every second of the experience. After sufficient time had passed, Dioni gathered the group and guided them back along the long trail to the entrance of the National Park, where their tour bus and its driver happily awaited their triumphant return.

Exhausted by the events of the day, the group wanted nothing more than to return to their hotels, then find the nearest restaurant and eat as much food as it had to offer. The boy, however, desired the much-anticipated chocolate, to which Dioni happily obliged.

At a town along the return route, Dioni escorted the group to a small *tienda*, where an elder native woman heated the beans which Dioni carried from the Mayan plaza. She showed the tourists the entire cocoa-making process; from heating the beans, to grinding them, to making a paste, and finally, to enjoying them in the same manner as did the ancient people who once ruled the land – as the finest chocolate drink ever made, the beverage of the gods.

With the child's craving more than sufficiently satisfied, the tour continued to *Tikal Libre*, a local restaurant which served the best native food in Flores. The tourists were seated and served, then given more food than they thought their large table could hold. As they enjoyed their feast, Dioni tapped on a glass to gather everyone's attention.

"My friends," Dioni addressed the group. "Thank you for a beautiful day. I must go home for now, but Mario – *TourTikal*'s best driver – will take you back to your hotel. Tomorrow we will all get together again and travel to the town of Ipala, where I will show you a lake that is at the very top of an inactive volcano."

"Sounds great, mate," said the Englishman. "Can't wait to see it."

"You are going to love it," responded Dioni. "Please remember to bring clothes in case it rains because the weather in Ipala can change very quickly and without warning. Okay? Sound good? *Muy bien, amigos. Buenas noches.*"

"*Buenas noches,*" the group collectively responded.

The walk from the restaurant to the orphanage was the most peaceful moment of Dioni's day. He often used the time to create stories to tell Alma upon his return, or he would just play a melody in his head and playfully dance his way home. What Dioni did not do on his short walk, however, was utter a single word to anyone in his town. The energy to speak was reserved for the person he longed to see most in the world, who usually sat on a stoop near the front entrance of the orphanage.

This was Alma's favorite time of the day. She loved Dioni, the only way a young lady of her age was able to innocently love another. She and Dioni had known each other their entire lives, and she dreamt of the day in which he would be able to live the life he always wanted. She enjoyed helping the kids of the orphanage, and as one of the elder residents, her work was greatly appreciated by the aging nuns who had invested a lifetime in raising dozens of parentless children. She loved to take a moment to look toward the evening sky; she hoped to discover the infinite wonder of the stars, though a part of her never agreed with the adventurer within.

"How many tourists did you have today?" Alma asked. She smiled as Dioni approached from the distance.

"Fourteen," he replied, then sat beside her. "One of them was a boy who really liked chocolate. Like, he could not get enough of it. I tried giving him raw *cacao* and he ate that too."

Alma smiled. She had heard all types of stories about all kinds of tourists, and she loved how Dioni had the unique ability to bring joy to everyone with whom he would come in contact.

"Oh…and did you finally see it again?" she asked, mocking him.

"You're never going to drop that, are you?" Dioni asked, playfully upset. "I'm telling you, it was a blue bird with a tail!"

"I believe you, Dioni," she replied. She tried desperately to withhold a fit of laughter. "The legend of the blue quetzal."

He sighed, knowing what was to come. Unable to hold it in any longer,

Alma burst into laughter. Dioni was visibly annoyed by her reaction, as her performance occurred more often than he cared to admit. He sat and waited for it to pass…again.

"*Ay, Dioni,*" she continued. Her laughter slowly subsided. "Okay…okay… it's not that funny."

"Yes it is."

"YES IT IS!" she responded, then once again burst into laughter.

"One day I'm going to find that bird and show it to you, and then you'll finally believe me." Her laughter overshadowed Dioni's words.

"Okay…okay. *Ya…ya….calmada, calmada. Ay,* my stomach hurts," Alma said. She looked at Dioni, calming herself and clutching her abdomen. He loved to see and hear her laughter, and would gladly restart the conversation if it meant hearing her laugh uncontrollably.

"Well, it looked blue to me," Dioni said.

Again, Alma burst with amusement, even harder than before. The moment – unlike the sight of the greatest temples, the brightest stars, or the bluest mountains – was Dioni's favorite. He came to his feet and stood before her.

"And it's wings were made of *chorizo,*" Dioni said. Each sentence increased the strength of her glee. "It also flew upside down and sounded like this: '*Packau! Packau! Yyyyyyyy-po!*'"

Dioni raised his arms and jogged in a small infinity pattern, which poorly mimicked the flight of a bird though it raised the concerns of nearby onlookers.

"*Cállate,* Dioni! No more!" were the only words Alma was able to say. Her body shook uncontrollably from so much laughter.

All that existed in the innocent moment were the two of them – her in tears of joy, and him in his ridiculous rendition of a resplendent bird.

Chapter Three

The greatest benefit of being early to rise was for the opportunity to see the morning light cascade over the Guatemalan landscape. Dioni had seen it countless times, yet he never ceased to be in complete awe of the splendor of its natural beauty. The mountains really did look blue, as they did during every dawn of every day, until the sun reached a high enough point to expose the highlands to their natural color.

The tourists, who booked a two-day trip to see the place which Dioni so much admired, were not nearly as enthusiastic to witness the break of day. Previous experience had taught Dioni that the early morning was the worst time to get to know any of the visitors or to make intelligent conversation, and asking the group to take a photo was certainly out of the question. Even Mario, *TourTikal*'s most enigmatic bus driver, looked as if he needed a few more hours of sleep.

"*Buenos dias, amigos,*" Dioni greeted each passenger as they boarded the small tour bus. Once every passenger was onboard and accounted for, Dioni made a final announcement to inform everyone that the drive would take approximately 2 hours, and any stops along the way would only be made by request.

The second day of the tour was traditionally less exciting, which also meant a lesser likelihood of something gone wrong. For the most part, day two was very predictable. Most of the passengers would undoubtedly fall asleep along the way, which meant that the first stop would require a restroom. The bus would make a stop at a local coffee shop just outside of the town of Ipala, where Dioni would inform the tourists that Guatemala has the best coffee in the world – a topic which was oftentimes controversial and hotly debated. After coffee and a light breakfast, the tourists would trek to the base of *Volcan Ipala,* where they would meet a new tour guide and follow him or her to the crater lake at the very top of the volcano. Although not required, Dioni would oftentimes follow the tour group to the summit and then take a nap on a tree, away from the others. This allowed him about an hour of rest, which would help him re-energize for the remainder of the day. After they had a chance to enjoy the location, the tourists would take a secondary path back to the base of the volcano, return to the *ToursTikal* bus, then drive out to Antigua, where they would visit the traditional gift shops as well as the famous *Choco Museo* – a favored stop among chocolate lovers. The plan was both simple and easy to remember.

As the re-energized group members made their way to the entrance of Ipala's only natural tourist attraction, they were greeted by Gabriella – the most popular of Ipala's trekkers. Gabriella, or Gabi as she preferred to be called, was just over ten years older than Dioni. Her long, blonde hair helped accentuate the fairness of her tanned skin and light-colored eyes, which attracted the views of almost every male visitor to Ipala. Her excitable personality was just as beautiful as her external features, and she was well aware of the effect she had on others. To Dioni, Gabi was more of an elder sister than a co-worker. They had worked together for years, which enabled them to develop a great friendship and admiration for one another. Gabi boarded the bus to greet the guests.

"Welcome to *Volcan Ipala,*" she opened. "My name is Gabriella, but you can call me Gabi. I will be your lead climber for your tour of our volcano. *¡Buenos días, amigos!*"

"*Buenos días, ¡Gabi!*" responded the Spaniard man, excitedly. He hoped against all odds that another member of the group would greet her with such enthusiasm. His motivated greeting did not please his wife. Gabi smiled at the compliment.

"The climb to the top of the volcano will take approximately 40 minutes," continued Gabi, "and it can get very warm because we are going to be in the sunlight the entire time. If you need sunscreen or insect repellent, please get it now or feel free to buy it from *la tienda* before we start on the path."

The tourists proceeded to *la tienda* to purchase supplies while Mario moved the tour bus to a small parking area. His next few hours would be spent in the shade, where he would read the daily newspaper, talk to other drivers, or would just enjoy the tranquility of the natural surroundings. On this day, however, Mario would take delight in doing what he enjoyed most: take a nap.

Dioni approached Gabi. He enjoyed working with her more than any of the other tour guides, but not for the same reason the other, older male tour guides chose to work their shifts according to her schedule. She and Dioni were trustworthy confidants to one another and were two of *TourTikal's* most regarded employees. Outside of work, they were close friends who lived near one another. Dioni met Gabi's parents, her grandmother, two of her aunts and one uncle. She, in turn, developed a friendship among the children and the nuns who lived at the orphanage; while the nuns kindly disagreed with Gabi's sense of fashion, Alma wanted to grow to be just like her one day. Moreover, she was Dioni's mentor, whether he knew it or not.

"*Hola*, Dioni," said Gabi.

"*Buenos dias*, Gabi," he responded.

"Are you joining the group today?"

"I am. I feel a little tired so I'll be by my usual tree. Can you come find me and make sure I'm awake before you bring the group back down?"

"*Si, claro*," responded Gabi. "If you're that tired, why not stay here and sleep on the bus? You can get more sleep and stay out of the sun."

"Have you heard Mario snore?" Dioni said. "It's like *un motor de lancha*. He shakes the entire bus!"

Gabi laughed. "Fine, feel free to join us. But can you stay at the end, behind the group? We have *un niño* in the group today and I don't want anyone to get left behind."

"That's fine."

A few minutes later, the tourists regrouped and were ready to go. Not sure of what to expect of their journey, a few of the guests doused themselves with enough sunscreen to produce a wax-like reflection on their skin.

"Shiny group," said Gabi. She smiled at Dioni. "*Vamonos!*"

The climb to the summit of *Volcan Ipala* was not as difficult as what the group experienced the day prior. It was a simple path that slowly elevated to direct visitors from a ground-level full of trees and greenery to a series of open areas where the sun shone relentlessly. The problem was not so much the sunlight, but rather the long walk of an unpaved trail. Once further along, the heat which radiated from above made the walk increasingly difficult for novices and experienced hikers alike.

Luckily for Gabi, no one in the group had a desire to miss the sight of the crater lake at the top of the inactive volcano. Dioni stayed behind the group, as requested, and hiked the trail along with the tourists. He kept his distance and ensured that everyone stayed on the path. Still tired from the previous day, Dioni's feet dragged with every step; he looked forward to finding his tree, resting his eyes, and enjoying the tranquility of nature. More than 60 minutes later, his wish came true.

Gabi was the first to see the top of the volcano, whose summit held a natural lagoon which seemingly had no Earthly business in that location. Dioni trekked at the tail end of the troop as Gabi began her, "…at the top of the volcano…" speech, one which he heard too many times to count. With hand gestures, Dioni signaled his separation from the group to go to his usual rest area. Gabi nodded, which meant she knew where to find him.

Dioni walked to a nearby tree conveniently located away from the water. The sound of Gabi's voice was clear and audible at first, but within a few seconds after he placed his backpack on the ground and got into a comfortable position, Dioni was fast asleep.

Tour groups came to *Volcan Ipala* to see a completely new side of the Guatemalan landscape. This land did not belong to anyone, but was rather a creation of the Earth, and one which had to be protected and preserved. The water in the crater lake was warm and void of waves or currents, though it held secrets far greater than its peaceful demeanor displayed.

In the short time in which *ToursTikal* was in business, few accidents or complaints were ever reported, especially for Gabi's groups. To the tourists, swimming in the lagoon was akin to swimming in the waters of ancient Mayan gods. Many felt cleansed and refreshed, almost as if they transcended into a space void of time, only to emerge anew. The crater lake represented far more than just a natural phenomenon; it was a channel by which people, animals and birds alike found a place of peace hidden among the clouds.

Gabi's current group of tourists were surprisingly inactive during their visit to the summit. Most of the women lounged near the shoreline, where they remained on dry ground as they soaked the rays of the mighty sun. The men mostly huddled in the water, where the Americans did their best to teach their fellow foreigners their own version of football. As the day progressed, however, the winds shifted from warm and calm to cold and increasingly fierce. One particular breeze was not very strong, but it brought forth a sudden drop in temperature. Most of the tourists were from colder climates and did not mind the slight difference, though Gabi was well aware of how fast the winds of Ipala could change.

Dioni felt a chill. He reached into his backpack and grabbed his sweater, then covered himself from the colder wind. He saw that the sun continued to shine ever-so-brightly over the mountainside, and so there was no cause for alarm. Within seconds he returned to his state of slumber.

What began as a sudden change in the wind quickly became a coverage of dark clouds that completely obscured the sun. They did not appear as normal storm clouds, though they brought forth a forceful wind which Gabi knew better than to ignore. However, also too strong to ignore, was the unmarried Englishman who affectionately charmed and maintained her attention. The flirtatious banter distracted Gabi from her responsibilities.

Within minutes the winds grew stronger. The tourists changed their attitudes from relaxed and overjoyed to slightly worried; they were aware that the return trip to the base was long and exhaustive. The youngest of the group was barely out of the water when rain began to fall, which forced everyone to run towards the small area where they placed their belongings.

"I am sorry, *amigos!*" Gabi said to the group. "We must cut this part of the tour short today. There is a faster way to get to the base of the volcano, but it is much steeper and more dangerous. The storms in Ipala come fast and without warning, so we must move quickly. I will be at the front and will guide you, but please do not rush to get to the bottom. Stay together."

Gabi hardly finished her sentence before her prediction came true. The winds swayed the leaves of the trees, though not a single drop of rain fell on Dioni as his chosen tree protected him from the elements. Gabi and the group of tourists, however, were not so well shielded from the rain. With each passing minute, the waters poured more heavily, and the once bright and sunny sky grew darker and darker. It was more than just a passing rainstorm, and Gabi knew she had little time to safely return to the base of the volcano.

Gabi led the group down a secondary path. The route further exposed the group to the rain, though it cut the time to a fraction of what it took to get to the top. As they came closer to the ground level, the storm grew more severe and drenched the unsuspecting tourists to their core. They were approximately halfway down the path when in the distance they saw a flash of lightning. The group froze, as they expected that their proximity to the source of the lightning would produce a merciless crash which would undoubtedly distress the land; alas, the thunder did not come.

"We are almost there!" Gabi shouted; her voice less audible through the howling wind. "Everyone stay together and get to the bus!"

Mario was clueless of an existence outside of his state of deep sleep. Had he not been startled by a hard knock on the door of the bus, he surely would have never noticed that the perfectly beautiful day which existed prior to his nap was now the complete opposite. He awoke in a panic and almost fell from his seat. He opened the door to the bus and allowed a man to board.

"There's a bad storm coming," said the man, a driver from another tour company. "We have to move. It's getting bad here."

"Is everyone back?" Mario asked as he collected himself.

"My group is in *la tienda*, and I think that is your group coming down the secondary path," responded the man as he pointed at the group of tourists near the base of the volcano. A sense of relief came over Mario when he saw Gabi.

"That's them," Mario said. "*Gracias, hermano.*"

The man exited Mario's bus and returned to his own.

Mario peeked out of the door and saw his group 50 meters or so away from the base of the volcano. Each of them was soaked from head to toe, and Mario knew he had to warm the bus in order to prevent them from getting too cold. He immediately started the engine and moved to be as close to the base as possible.

The storm shifted from thousands of droplets of rain which fell from the sky to that on a much grander scale, as if the clouds released years of stored water in a single instance. Gabi led the way as the tourists sprinted to the bus, where Mario intercepted them, opened the door, and let everyone inside.

"I can't stay here," Mario told Gabi. "It's too much rain. I have to move the bus, otherwise we'll all be stranded."

"Let's go to the village," responded Gabi. "We have to get towels for everyone or they'll freeze."

Gabi turned and looked at her group, many of which shivered while seated, though grateful to be out of the rain. Mario placed the bus in gear and quickly left the scene. The storm transitioned from bad to worse.

"Is everyone on the bus?" asked Mario. He struggled to see through the windshield as it was pounded by the rain.

Gabi turned and saw the passengers huddled near one another for warmth.

"Yes, all here. Can you make it warmer on the bus? They're freezing."

Mario turned a knob to increase the warm air which flowed through the bus. He drove onto the main road and away from the park entrance.

Dioni's tree protected him for as long as it was able to do so but was ultimately forced to surrender to the storm. What began as small, annoying droplets of water quickly became an increased series of drips which poked at his body. Dioni was more exhausted than worried. He repositioned himself to move away from the water in an effort to get just a few more precious moments of sleep. He was awakened, without warning of any kind, by perhaps the loudest crash of thunder he had ever heard; it was so loud and so relentless that it shook the ground, which frightened Dioni and immediately forced him to get to his feet.

He made a bold attempt to rise from beneath the tree's protection, yet the strength of the wind pushed him back and held him in place. It was cold, and the storm was ruthless, but he knew he could not stay at the top of the volcano and wait for the storm to pass. Dioni reached into his backpack and pulled a flashlight, hoping that the beam of light would pierce both the darkness and the falling rain. He waited for a brief moment in which the wind gusted in his favor, then bravely ran from beneath the tree. He used his backpack as his umbrella, his free arm held the backpack in place above his head as a shield from the enraged downpour.

"Gabi!" he shouted.

Dioni waved the flashlight in every direction. The only response he received was another crash of thunder, which knocked him down to one knee and caused him to lose grip of his only form of head protection. The backpack fell to the ground, claimed by the storm. Dioni did not need it, and thus left it behind as he pushed through the sheets of rain to find the fastest path toward the base, where the group was undoubtedly worried for him.

The storm grew stronger, almost as if it knew that no living being would come to Dioni's aid. The winds pushed the rain in every direction. He could barely keep his eyes open. The beam of light brushed by an image of an object in the sky, which Dioni failed to notice. Though he had years of experience in navigation and was superbly familiar with the many trails and paths of the volcano, the sheer strength of the storm disoriented him and led him down a path with a sudden stop and a steep drop. Dioni attempted to move faster and failed to realize that his impending doom was just a few steps ahead.

A bolt of lightning illuminated the sky for an instant. The light stood just long enough for Dioni to look down and see that there was no ground beneath his next step. He made a desperate attempt to pull back but was too late to do so. The strong wind pushed Dioni forward to a steep cliff, where at the bottom awaited a bed of sharp rocks, eager to meet their next victim. The storm claimed victory.

Dioni's descent toward the rocks below felt as if it lasted an eternity. He shouted and lifted his arms to cover his face, a final attempt to brace for sudden impact. Dioni felt a strong and swift force take hold of each of his shoulders, then felt an abrupt jolt which pulled and lifted him away from the fast-approaching ground. He yelled in pure shock and terror as he was suddenly airborne; he aimlessly waved his flashlight and struggled to free himself from the grasp of a mysterious being.

The wind and rain grew more severe as he soared through the sky. Dioni was unable to see where he was taken, nor was he able to determine that which caught and rescued him, mid-fall. His flashlight provided a sense of direction but nothing more. Had it not been for another bolt of lightning which lit the stormy landscape, Dioni would have failed to notice a small opening underneath a set of carefully placed rocks on the side of the volcano. The mysterious being darted toward the rocks and forcibly pushed him toward the opening. He closed his eyes and braced for impact.

The object released its grip on Dioni, which caused him to land hastily into what appeared to be a small cave. Despite his vast knowledge of the volcano, Dioni never knew of the existence of a cave in Ipala. The flashlight managed to survive the entire experience, though it found refuge at a further distance from where he was able to reach.

Dioni heard the crashing sounds of the storm, though at a much lesser extent. He was unable to see beyond what was revealed by his only source of light near the opening of the cave. He crawled to his flashlight and reached for it, the raindrops on his face blurred his vision. He quickly pulled his hand back when a shadow pierced the light.

Dioni fell back in fear. What was that?

He reached for his flashlight, grabbed it and aimed the beam of light in every direction. The light only revealed more rocks and the inside of the cave, which was hardly large enough to allow him to stand. He calmed himself, though he breathed heavily, and attempted to make sense of what occurred.

Near the entrance of the small cave he saw a silhouette of an object, as if camouflaged by the cave and illuminated by the storm in the background. Dioni aimed the light towards the object and saw a mysterious…bird?

Dioni was uncertain of what it was, though the creature was unlike any he had ever seen – completely void of color and with severely damaged feathers. Whatever it was, the creature was definitely in pain.

Dioni became curious. He gathered the courage to inch closer to the creature, as quietly as possible. His light flickered, strobing on and off. He hit it against his free hand, which forced the light to shine once more. He aimed the light in the same direction as before, but the creature was gone.

Dioni froze. Where did it go?

A loud crash of thunder forced the cave to tremble. Dioni's courage faded, as did his curiosity. He stepped back and away from the entrance to the cave. He positioned his back against the solid cave wall, which meant that an attack by the mysterious creature would have to come from his front.

The flashlight flickered and turned off. He hit it once again, but it refused to come back to life. Dioni forcefully hit the light against the stone wall behind him, which miraculously revived the faded light once more.

A strong force pulled Dioni's legs. He immediately fell onto his back. He shouted and pointed the flashlight towards his feet. He saw it!

The eyes of the creature were locked onto him in the manner a fierce predator vehemently observed its prey. The sighting lasted a fraction of a second before the creature bolted toward Dioni's face and made a screeching sound that penetrated through Dioni's body. In a final effort, Dioni threw his arms up for cover and desperately attempted to protect himself from the oncoming attack.

The flashlight slipped from his grasp as he lifted his arms. The light crashed against the stone wall and immediately turned off as it bounced and came to rest on the ground.

The shrieking scream made by the creature echoed through the cave, which was lessened by the sound of the unyielding storm.

Chapter Four

Mornings after major storms usually dawned with cloudless skies, with the start of this day being no different. Dioni heard birds nearby, who chirped and sang as usual. To him, it almost sounded like an exchange of dialogue; instead of calls, whistles and random sounds, each bird spoke. He heard more than one voice, but the discussion was not clearly audible.

The majority of the cave was dark, except for a single beam of sunlight that funneled through a small opening and landed directly on Dioni's face. He was unable to see much; even the little he saw was cloudy and out of focus. He looked at his surroundings to try to make sense of where he was and what had occurred the night prior. He was unable to distinguish anything, except for the light which led to the opening of the small cave. He stood up, painstakingly so as every bone in his body cracked into position. Dioni wobbled as he navigated toward the light. His entire body felt odd — not sore, but more like it was completely disproportioned — which caused his walk to be unbalanced and oddly difficult.

As he wobbled to the exit of the cave, Dioni was relieved to find himself in a familiar location. He recognized the surrounding landscape of Ipala, and based on years of navigating the area, he knew that the lagoon was just a few short meters behind where he stood. He walked further outward then turned to inspect the entrance of the cave from its exterior. Dioni had hiked by the location countless times over the years, and not once did he notice an entrance to a cave of any kind. Under different circumstances he would have made more of an effort to revisit the cave and perhaps taken the time to create a small hideout for himself. All he could think to do was to walk to the lagoon.

The short and uncovered path to the water was significantly longer than usual. Still groggy and processing his lack of clear eyesight, Dioni hung his head as he walked the trail. The sunlight hit his back and helped him draw warmth. It was far too early in the day for tourists or trekkers to be in the area, so there would be no assistance to descend from the crater lake. If he could manage to make it to the water, he would surely be able to muster the energy required to walk toward the base.

From the same direction as the sunlight, Dioni noticed the shadows of two birds which flew at a high altitude. He looked up and squinted to protect his eyes from the brightness.

"Huh," Dioni said. "Bat falcons. Nice. Flying higher than usual today."

Dioni continued along his path. The pair of birds in the sky made calls and sounds, which struck Dioni as odd; even from a long distance, he wondered why the falcons sounded as if they spoke to one another instead of making random bird sounds. His sense of wonder was not strong enough to evolve into curiosity and was thus not enough to attract Dioni's attention.

In the distance, Dioni was able to see the reflection of the sunlight as it rebounded off the surface of the water. Never in his life had Dioni felt such thirst, and by that same notion, never did the extraordinarily large lagoon ever appear so beautiful. Dioni ran to the shore as fast as his small feet could carry him, his recovering eyes focused on the water. He was far too thirsty to care for anything or anyone at that moment, and when he sensed he was close enough to do so, he carelessly dunked his entire upper body into the lagoon. The water tasted better than any form of hydration on Earth, and the cleansing of his face allowed him to regain more of his sense of sight; Dioni instantly became better aware of his location and of his surroundings.

In the sky, the two bat falcons hovered in a circular pattern, which they seemed to do at a lower altitude. Dioni noticed the two falcons because he heard them speak to one another – not in the manner in which one overhears an object in the distance, but as if he overheard a secret conversation spoken in a strange language.

Dioni once again dunked his head in the water. He opened his mouth and took in a huge gulp before he came up for air. The gentle stream of water which flowed from his head and down his spine felt incredible. A few droplets of water fell from his body, which created a series of tiny ripple-waves that slowly worked their way out from the point where they splashed on the lagoon's surface. As the waves cleared, Dioni noticed a strange reflection on the water. His vision improved though it remained less focused than what he was accustomed. The sounds of the bat falcons drew closer, which seemed more like voices than random noises, though he could not comprehend what they spoke to one another. Dioni looked up to see them once more. He noticed that their circled flightpaths were in shorter distances and were lower to the ground.

Dioni lowered his head into the water once more. His nose barely made contact with the surface when he looked down and noticed a strange object reflected by the water. He immediately lifted his entire body and backed away.

What in the world was that?

Dioni lifted his head and looked in every direction, hoping against all odds to find a credible witness to confirm what he saw. He was alone. He looked at the lagoon, then inhaled and exhaled, deeply and slowly. He placed one foot forward and inched toward the shore. He felt the warm water on his foot, then closed his eyes and bent at his waist to lean his body forward. He opened his eyes and saw a mirrored image; the water reflected not the face and body of a fifteen year old boy, but rather that of a mystic being.

"AH!" Dioni shouted.

He jumped back, unsure of what the lagoon had exposed. He turned his head to look at his extremities; his arms and hands were gone, replaced by a perfect assortment of blue-colored feathers.

"AHH!" Dioni shouted once more.

He turned to the water to see the full, clear reflection of what could not possibly be true. He looked down and confirmed his fear: the water reflected his every movement. Where he had arms, he now had wings. His hands were gone, replaced by feathers which covered his entire body. Dioni inspected himself. He searched for any remaining signs of humanity and wondered where it had all gone. He looked to the left and to the right, his breaths faster and more severe. He tried desperately to find anyone who would be able to help, but only the sun, the trees, and the water of the lagoon were witnesses to his current state of being.

Dioni breathed heavily. He had not the faintest idea of what to do. He dunked his entire body into the lagoon, hoping to somehow magically wash away his new self. He stood up then looked down and impatiently waited for the ripple waves to clear. The waves grew larger and further apart, and the same reflection returned to him. With his face down, Dioni spread his arms and displayed a perfect wing formation. He quickly constrained them. He repeated the same action, though slowly, to confirm whether his movements were mimicked by the reflected image on the surface of the water. His actions and his appearance were mirrored immaculately.

"What is happening to me?" Dioni cried aloud.

He lifted his wings above his shoulders. The water mirrored his every move. He felt sick; perhaps drinking so much water was not such a good idea.

Dioni placed his wings at his side. He looked beyond his own reflection and noticed another object beneath the surface, which approached him. It appeared as if it were a strange, tiny fish, but its body was not in the water. Dioni lowered his head to be closer to the surface and to better identify what he saw. He pulled himself back, just enough to notice that the small spec in the water slowly became larger. It looked like a shadow, but as it grew, the water reflected more details of its body. It was an oblong shape, an odd object which Dioni had never seen. It approached quickly and swiftly, and made absolutely no sound.

Almost instantly, the water reflected precisely what it saw – the stretched talons of a bat falcon which dove in a direct path toward Dioni. He had absolutely no time to think. Dioni squatted and lowered his head into the

40

water; he narrowly escaped the razor-sharp talons of the predator who craved him for breakfast.

The bat falcon missed the target. As quickly as it attacked, the falcon lifted itself to return to the sky. It cried in protest for having missed its intended prey. Dioni slowly regained his stance and looked in every possible direction before he made any sudden movements. If the falcon were to return, Dioni realized he was an easy target, with no shelter from the predator's perfect eyesight.

Dioni carefully stepped away from the edge of the water and made his way onto the grass, which led back to the path toward the base. The skies were clear; Dioni neither saw nor heard any immediate threats. He took long, odd strides. He desperately attempted to remain discreet with each step forward. One step. Two steps. Three steps. Nothing… no danger of any kind.

As he felt slightly more confident, Dioni stood and walked upright, the way he had done every day prior. With each step he looked up and turned his head in every direction, but he failed to notice a crucial piece of evidence. Though the sky was indeed above, his current elevation was far above ground-level; a predator could remain airborne, even if out of sight. In the same manner a fighter jet would appear over a range of mountains, the bat falcon emerged in the distance, behind Dioni. The hunter was on a mission, and it had its prey clearly locked on target.

A strange sensation overcame Dioni. He hesitated for only an instant, which was long enough for him to be pushed forward and onto the ground by an unseen energy that forced him to dive just beyond the merciless grasp of the swooping bat falcon. A second attempt to capture its meal resulted in failure, which eliminated what remained of the predator's patience. Dioni raised his head and saw the entire panorama of the Ipalan landscape, which included a furious falcon who made a large loop in the sky and reengaged its attack.

Dioni jumped to his feet and ran as fast as his small, avian legs could carry him. He sprinted in the same manner as would any teenager – he used his arms for balance and moved his legs as fast as his body allowed. Dioni turned his head to look over his shoulder; the unrelenting talons of the falcon approached at incredible speed. Dioni shouted.

Unable to fully balance himself, Dioni tripped over an object that he failed to notice as he faced the opposite direction his body ran. He tumbled forward, which caused him to once again escape the grasp of the bat falcon. The predator continued its forward momentum as Dioni, unable to stop, continued and tumbled down the volcano. His body bounced as it fell further downhill, down a steep section of the volcano, which settled onto flattened land as he stumbled closer to the base. The object which caused Dioni's stumble was in the absolute perfect location at an impeccably perfect time.

The two bat falcons – one who attacked and the other who only observed – watched as their meal tumbled down the side of the volcano. They slowed their airspeed and momentarily hovered above the ground. They found no reason to waste excess energy when they could just as easily wait for gravity to serve their breakfast for them.

Dioni's momentum was stopped by the thicker grass along the side of the volcano. His adrenaline was far too active to allow him to feel the full extent of his injuries, though he did not have a single scratch on his body. He did not pause for even an instant before he got to his feet and once again ran towards safety. The falcons noticed Dioni's movements. They observed how he ran at a slower pace and in a predictable pattern. They looked at one another, smiled, then spread their wings and lowered their heads to reengage their attack.

Dioni sprinted faster than he ever knew his short legs could allow; he knew full well that failure to find safety within the next few seconds would cost him his life. In a state of panic, Dioni saw a ceiba tree within a short distance. He never noticed that particular tree prior to that day, but in that moment, Dioni had no time to think of why this ceiba appeared from nowhere. The bat falcons set their sights on their target. They raced one another to be the first to claim victory and thus take a greater share of the reward.

As he ran downhill and the trees near the base came closer to eye-level, Dioni saw a gap in the land directly in front of him. Instinctually, he knew to jump, which allowed him to continue his speed and motion. His small feet were millimeters away from the dirt when he felt a strong force pull him back by his shoulders, which caused him to immediately spread his arms. Dioni discovered a way to lift himself from the ground.

The bat falcons looked to one another then turned their attention to what occurred before them. The bird they chased was airborne, just a few inches off the ground, though its legs continued in motion as if it struggled to run while in flight. The falcons had witnessed many peculiar events in their lifetimes, but this was new.

Dioni glided towards the ceiba. His small legs ran as fast as they could while he kept his arms as open as possible. He drifted closer to the tree and noticed a small opening between three mighty branches. Dioni felt a strong gust of wind that pushed him closer to the ancient tree, and which shoved the bat falcons back. To the skilled, lifelong aviators, a gust of wind was nothing more than an insignificant setback that gave their prey a few precious seconds of time.

The two predators screeched, a sound which was deafening to Dioni. The small opening on the ceiba was just a few meters away. He could make it, if he could just get there before the bat falcons caught him. Dioni glided and moved his wings in every possible direction, in a wild effort to navigate himself to the tree. His airspeed increased, as if pushed by the wind itself. Should he miss his target, a hard crash into the ceiba could be fatal.

The bat falcons remained moments behind. In their minds, they could already taste their breakfast. Dioni felt the talons of the falcons on his long tailfeathers. At just a few centimeters away from the entrance to the ceiba, Dioni closed his eyes, shouted, covered his face with his wings to brace for impact, and hoped against all odds that the ancient tree would provide refuge.

In the same speed in which he flew, Dioni completely disappeared into the tree. He instantly vanished, as did the perfectly sized entryway into the ceiba. The entire ordeal happened so rapidly that the bat falcons were completely mystified by where the bird had gone. The two predators narrowly escaped from a violent crash into the tree. The exact location where their meal had fled instantly became solid bark; their breakfast completely vanished.

"*Pharomacrus* identified, *mocinno*. Approved for entry," said a strange, feminine voice.

Dioni lifted his head and slowly opened his eyes. He was not aware of any point in which he had reopened his wings, yet he was airborne and in perfect formation – not like a human attempting to recreate a foreign ability with the use of false wings, but rather in the method that mythic birds were meant to fly. A force unknown to Dioni overtook his avian frame and guided him as if by automatic technology. He flew effortlessly, suspended by a system which gently guided him along a tunnel.

The tunnel in which Dioni hovered was far bigger than what it appeared from the exterior. The ceiba acted as a portal, which explained why Dioni was not familiar with that tree in that location. The tunnel itself was evenly illuminated, though by an organic source of light. Along the walls were a series of round, interconnected spheres which radiated; there were no bulbs or lanterns, but rather a series of streams of sunlight. The illumination from each sphere followed Dioni's every move, which lit the path before him and dimmed as he went by.

The walls of the tunnel were decorated with drawings made by beings from an ancient time. They were Mayan hieroglyphics that moved along with Dioni, like a live zoetrope, as the system directed him through the tunnel. There was no wind, but rather an energy which carried and held Dioni while it simultaneously navigated him and illuminated his path.

Dioni looked up to see a translucent, low angle view of the Earth. He travelled in a completely sealed area, yet the semi-transparent view above him reflected an image of a life on the ground. He moved within the Earth yet below the surface, while the surface-level outside of the tunnel was clearly visible to him. Though Dioni was able to see the outside – the landscape of Ipala which he knew so well – no creature in the exterior was able to see him.

Dioni glided over a series of moving lights, all organized by color: green, red, and blue. The lights marked a path which provided a direction of travel. Without moving any more than his eyes and his head, Dioni was gently guided to a landing. The landing area was neither ground nor gravel, but rather a translucent, protective shield which created an illuminated, blue-colored aura around Dioni.

Once firmly on his feet, Dioni walked in the direction guided by the series of lights he saw as he glided. With each step, a circle beneath him moved at his pace and created a glow with his every movement. Dioni followed the colored lights until they reached an end, near what appeared to be a large entryway. He saw that there was a small, engraved circle on the ground directly in front of the entryway, which was in exact size as the blue circled that followed him. He stepped into the engraved ring, which illuminated a series of larger circles beneath it.

Dioni was quickly surrounded by a transparent, cylindrical cover which rose from beneath him like a translucent forcefield. The circles that surrounded Dioni flickered slowly, then faster and faster, until they flashed so quickly and brightly that every visible element vanished in an energy of blinding light.

...

Gabi knew more of *Volcan Ipala* than any of the tour guides, visitors, and residents combined. She had explored the land and its surroundings hundreds of times. She knew every path, every trail, and every entrance by memory, and she loved the unbelievable sight of the Guatemalan landscape. She was also aware of the potential severity of the storms, of the sheer darkness that fell upon Ipala each night, and of the penalties of being left behind with no form of navigation.

As was her job over the course of many years, Gabi had taken countless numbers of tourists from the base to the lagoon, and not once had she ever left anyone behind. In her mind she repeated the actions of the prior day, over and over; she desperately searched for justification to uncover any possible trace of what may have caused her to forget her dear friend.

Mario drove the bus toward the base of the volcano, with Gabi as his only passenger. Neither of them uttered a single word. They were anxious to get to their friend, and they hoped against all odds that they would find him shaken yet unharmed. The bus failed to come to a complete stop before Gabi opened the door and sprinted to the visitor's center. Every door was locked. She pounded her fists on the surrounding windows and shouted for Dioni, as if by any chance he found a way inside. There was no response. Not a sound. Nothing but silence.

Mario parked the bus nearby and made his way to stand by Gabi. He was well aware of Gabi's feelings, for he also felt the same guilt, shame, and pain associated with the uncertainty of searching for a lost person. He did not speak a word but instead proceeded to search around the area. Though the storm of the previous night was fierce, both Gabi and Mario knew that Dioni was intelligent enough to save himself in case of an emergency. All they had to do was find him.

The municipal police of Ipala arrived at the scene. Mario saw the first pair of officers on site, then proceeded toward their vehicle. Gabi ran to the primary entrance of the park near the main trail, which serves as the final stopping point before tourists are taken through the path that leads to the lagoon. It was locked, and there was no sign of Dioni anywhere. If he was still alive, there was only one other place Dioni could be.

Not caring to wait for Mario or the police officers, Gabi ran onto the trail. She had years of experience going up and down the same path, often multiple times a day, but never had she attempted to sprint from the base all the way to the lagoon. She did not care how tired her body felt, the result of a restless night. She did not care whether or not her worn shoes had enough traction to get to her destination safely. All that was on her mind was to find Dioni. What if he was hurt? What if the wind pushed him down the other side? What if she found him and he was too weak to walk? What if...?

...

Dioni had a terrible habit of repeating actions which made Alma nervous. She hated heights, so he would purposely climb trees or walk along the ledge of a tall building, just to get a reaction from her. She did not like for him to carelessly ride his bicycle through the village, so he would show extravagant displays of how well he controlled his bike without the use of his hands. She hated the days when he would return home late at night, caused by a flat tire on the bus, a tourist who drank more than necessary, Mario's necessity to talk to someone about a myriad of problems, or a series of other scenarios. No matter what, Dioni always returned to the orphanage. He always came home.

Last night, however, was different. She felt something, like a mysterious vibe which aroused the sensation that something was out of place. She rested on her bed and stared at the ceiling, and occasionally glanced at a nearby clock. Tick…tock…tick…tock. Her heart raced at the sound of every car which she heard pass by, then she became even more worried as each vehicle drove away. Tick…tock…tick…tock.

The sun arose, and it seemed as though only she recognized Dioni's absence. The elder children had the knowledge of previously witnessing this behavior; it was the act of those who reached a point where they found it unnecessary to return, and would vanish from one day to the next, never to be seen again. They knew better than to form too strong of a bond among one another, as situations such as these were all too common at the orphanage.

For Alma, this was an entirely new experience. She knew, beyond a shadow of a doubt, that Dioni would never abandon her. Even if he ever intended to leave the orphanage, no force on Earth would prevent Dioni from saying goodbye.

…

Gabi raced from the trail to the furthest edge of the volcano, a point which gave her the best view of the entire landscape. She looked in every direction, multiple times, and shouted his name. There was no response, no movement of any kind. She recalled the last place she saw him – at the end of the trail as he headed towards his favorite place to nap. Gabi immediately ran to it and searched for any clues along the way.

She found nothing…no clues of any kind. He had to be nearby. There was no way he could have made it very far.

Gabi walked closer to the water. She silently prayed to not find Dioni beneath the surface. She heard something nearby and froze in place. She turned her head to face the sky and saw two bat falcons, one of which hastily swooped from above and attacked something on the ground. Bat falcons do not attack humans, nor was the target of its attack large enough to be confused with an actual person. Whatever it was, the falcons would surely capture it.

She reached the edge of the water and saw only her own reflection. Gabi shouted his name once more. No response. Not pausing to think prior to her action, she walked into the lagoon. The water was colder during the morning hours, which was of no concern to her. Gabi walked in deeper, the water almost to her chin, yet there was no sign of Dioni anywhere.

Gabi swam further from the shore and towards the center of the lagoon. She shouted for Dioni while she searched in every direction for any signs of life. In the distance she saw a familiar object gleaming in the sun, its surface reflected the light. It was on the grass just outside of the water, and it appeared as though it was made of glass or metal. Though she was not a fast swimmer, Gabi swam from the center of the lagoon to the shore in record time. Her swim became a sprint on foot as she exited the water and ran to the object.

Her fears were confirmed. It was Dioni's backpack, still wet from the rain of the previous night. He never went anywhere without it, so she just knew that he would not be all too far away. She shouted his name. No response. Gabi searched the backpack, which contained random objects, a few candies, and a photo of Alma.

The day progressed. Mario, accompanied by a team of police officers and employees of the park, joined the search. They shouted Dioni's name, inspected every tree, every blade of grass, every possible inch of the volcano, and even searched beneath the surface of the lagoon. There was no sign of Dioni whatsoever, except for a backpack which contained random objects and a single photograph.

...

The day continued as normal at the orphanage. Breakfast was made, the children were escorted to the nearby school, and it was Alma's responsibility to care for the youngest of the inhabitants. There was a daily routine to follow, and no one broke protocol. However, Alma was evidently distracted, as in her mind raced a million thoughts. Maybe Dioni met someone while giving a tour. No, he would never do that! Maybe he was there the entire time and she failed to notice. Not likely.

Alma walked through the main hallway multiple times. She inspected every room and every space large enough for Dioni to somehow hide himself; if this were an elaborate prank, Dioni would surely go well out of his way to find the most complex place to hide. Every cabinet she opened, closet she inspected, or closed space she checked gave the same result: nothing.

"The roof!" Alma said aloud. She remembered how Dioni liked to occasionally climb onto the roof just for a chance to be by himself. "Yes, he must be on the roof!"

Alma ran outside. She found a tall ladder and placed it against the exterior wall. She hated to climb it, but if it meant she would see Dioni and ease her worries then it was well worth the risk. With each step up, Alma felt the weight of the world pushing her down. It grew heavier until she made it to the top, where her fear became second to her worry. She searched every corner of the flat rooftop and shouted his name as she did so. Her fear had won the argument over her suspicion: there was absolutely no sign of Dioni.

...

Gabi could not be comforted, nor could any force on Earth pry the backpack from her grasp. The police overtook the investigation and forced her off the volcano as they escorted her and Mario back to the base. She felt powerless, as did he, for it was their carelessness which resulted in Dioni's fate. Their guilt outweighed their sadness, though they both knew a disheartening task remained to be completed.

Gabi's conscience ate at her. As Mario drove the bus into town, she rocked herself back and forth. Her body searched for a sense of comfort as she embraced the only evidence of her dear friend. Mario needed not be told where to go; he knew very well that there remained one person who had yet to hear the news. Neither he nor Gabi spoke a word; all that was heard were the subtle sounds of Gabi's sobs. How could they let this happen?

The rattle of the ToursTikal bus was unmistakable to Alma. She heard it as she swept the hallway. She immediately dropped the broom and rushed to the front entrance of the orphanage as the bus came to a halt.

"He's home!" her mind exclaimed. "He's home! Oh please let him be home!"

Mario stopped the bus a few meters away. He knew that this could very well be the longest walk he would ever make. He opened the passenger door and looked to the back of the bus, at Gabi. She attempted to compose herself, but it was of no use. Mario exited through the passenger door, an emotionless look painted on his face which Alma noticed the instant she saw him. She paused in her tracks. Her mind went entirely blank to brace for what was about to occur.

Gabi found the strength to get up, the backpack clutched firmly in her arms. She stepped out of the bus and ignored the blinding light of the Guatemalan sun. She slowly lifted her head and saw the image which would be engrained in her mind for the rest of her life. It was Alma, petrified in despair.

Tears flowed from Gabi's eyes as she walked slowly towards Alma, every step an eternity away from the one prior. Alma placed her hands over her mouth; she tried desperately to withhold her emotions. Her eyes swelled and her legs lost their strength. Alma dropped to her knees. She moved her hands from her mouth to her eyes.

Gabi approached Alma and immediately became overwhelmed. Without saying a single word, Gabi offered the backpack to Alma, who was unable to hold it as she touched it with her own hands. Gabi dropped to the ground and knelt before Alma; she hugged her, to provide any possible comfort and to share her loss.

Mario returned to the bus and closed the door. He sat in the driver's chair and closed his eyes. He paused, sighed, looked blankly to the sky, then released the tears he withheld from the moment he realized he would never again see his young friend.

Chapter Five

The sound created by wings as they flapped and glided at high speeds; the chirps and whistles made by unfamiliar creatures of a distant yet recognizable nature; the noise of a massive workspace, along with the seemingly endless number of small feet which stepped on solid ground; and the soothing sound of a marimba played in the distance were what Dioni absorbed as visible light slowly returned from a bright blur.

Dioni had not lost his sense of sight, yet his visibility was limited by a high wall of solid stone. A glass-like shield dissolved before him, which dropped a translucent, electric curtain that began above his head and extended beneath his feet. His eyes followed the shield as it fell. The same blue circle radiated its light around him and throughout the enclosed space.

Dioni slowly lifted his wings and pushed them forward as if to shove away an invisible barrier. He felt a light, slightly chilled breeze as his feathers made contact with the cooled air outside of the pod in which he stood. Like a child carefully stretching to gain a better perspective of a swimming pool's water temperature, he pulled his wings back, adjusted his posture and stretched his leg outside of the pod, as far as it could go. The circle beneath Dioni followed his movements, which provided the added benefit of an increased amount of available light.

The tip of Dioni's foot safely tapped the solid ground. As he felt no pain nor did he have cause for a reaction of any kind, he immediately felt relieved. Continuing his momentum, he moved his foot and stretched it as far as it could go until he felt his entire foot safely on the ground. With half of his body out of the pod, the sounds made by the creatures who were on the other side of the stone wall grew more intense. He became intrigued; with slightly more confidence, Dioni slowly moved his hind leg from the pod and placed it onto the ground. He stood with both feet securely on the solid surface, removed from the pod which closed behind him as quickly as it had opened. He turned and panicked.

"Wait wait wait!" Dioni pleaded with the automated system that was designed to shut down after it served its designated purpose.

His request was ignored.

The pod went dark, which left only the glowing blue circle beneath him as his sole source of light. He was no longer confined to a pod, but rather to a custom-designed enclosure. He stood in fear and silence. Dioni turned himself in every direction, hoping to see signage to guide him toward an exit. He found no signs of any kind, except for a reflection of blue light which emanated from the ground. A nearly invisible triangle of reflective material returned the light which glowed beneath Dioni, each step forward more illuminated than the one prior. A few paces away was another triangle of reflected light, followed by another and another, which created a semi-illuminated path for him to follow.

Dioni looked at the ground and saw that the light from the blue circle became less intense as he followed the reflective triangles. He paused. He took two steps back, to which the circle responded by increasing its glow. The same reaction occurred when Dioni shifted half a step to each side – the circle shifted with his movements, though its luminescence did not change until he walked forward.

Dioni followed the path created by the reflective triangles. The light beneath him became faint as he walked down a narrow passageway – one that was made to his exact size and shape. With each step, the solid walls shifted and the source of the sounds grew louder; he heard the voices of individuals engaged in conversation, though not in a language he understood.

The solid structure of rock shifted to allow Dioni to catch a glimpse of what appeared to be natural light. The reflective triangles became more distant from one another; their effect lessoned as the light beneath Dioni became more faint with each step while the natural light increased in intensity. He continued to walk toward the daylight, though he was weary of what was on the other side of the wall. With each pace forward, the light from the wall became brighter as the opening to the other side became larger. The light revealed that he walked along a path within a cave whose walls shifted according to his movement. With the cave entrance fully open, the natural light was blinding while the sound was nearly deafening. He could no longer wait; Dioni had to know what awaited just beyond the enclosure.

Dioni stepped to the end of the cave and saw the magnificence of a fully developed city, the likes of which every man, woman and child on Earth would envy in comparison to even the greatest cities on the surface level. Though it took a moment for him to absorb it all, he became fully aware of what caused the sound he previously heard. The colors he saw were beyond the spectrum of what was granted to him in his previous form, which made the massive metropolis of light an avian sanctuary unlike any other. This far exceeded the limits of what Dioni understood to be real; he stood in awe as his mind absorbed the vastness of a discovery so divine.

There were no skyscrapers but rather a system of trees, vines, and roots that acted as both housing as well as channels of transportation. In the epicenter of the mega metropolis stood a massive tree – one which resembled the mighty *ceiba*, though different in its exterior. Instead of a tall bark with long, stretched branches and a series of interconnected leaves, the tree more-so resembled a hybrid creation, one comprised of the world's most magnificent redwoods, willows, maples, and cherry blossoms. The tree had no Earthly business to exist in such an environment, with the exception that it was the source of light which showered the city with an elegant glow.

With his feet planted firmly on the ground, Dioni looked up. His mind could not fathom the story his eyes attempted to tell. He knew for certain that he was beneath the ground level, yet the sky above the city allowed for natural light; it was not a ceiling made of glass nor of artificial light, but rather a transparent surface that was somehow hundreds of feet below the land, yet as naturally lit as a cloudless day.

Dioni looked to each side. He saw a ledge along a mighty wall, a path which was put in place to save him from the experience of a substantial fall. He shifted his entire weight onto one side as he carefully placed one foot in front of the other and walked along the ledge. He went entirely unnoticed or unseen by any other bird in the city.

As his feathers brushed along the side of it, Dioni felt an odd pattern carved into the wall. He carefully shifted his weight to stand upright then turned his body to face the wall, which left his back entirely exposed. There he saw a series of meticulously crafted carvings and hieroglyphics that spread as far as his eyes could capture, in either direction. Dioni's gaze followed thousands upon thousands of centuries-old markings, each of which was perfectly created to represent the life of a civilization long since removed.

Dioni looked up and followed the designs on the wall, which allowed him to see what appeared to be the base of the *Gran Jaguar* Temple of Tikal. The crown of the temple stood at a height and distance so great that it was inconceivable for the structure to have been built by the previous residents of the ancient city. Despite his lack of understanding of civil engineering or of architecture, Dioni acknowledged that the wall on which he stood was far more than just a canvass of epic proportions, but was also the base of a creation far larger than could ever be conceived or created by man or machine. It was a glorious sight.

Dioni turned and directly faced the majestic underground city. Beyond the tree at the epicenter stood a second, inconceivably enormous wall. He followed the light which reflected off the wall's golden surface. Across the way was the base of Tikal's *Templo de las Mascaras*, which was as magnificent below the land as it was above. The entire structure – which was an interconnected mega-metropolitan utopia for birds – was directly beneath the Grand Plaza of Tikal National Park.

In what was likely hundreds of visits to the park, not once did Dioni ever notice even the slightest clue that something of such splendor existed underneath the sacred ground of the Mayan people. The light of day was clearly visible – which meant tourists were in the park – yet no shadow was cast from the surface level and onto the city. The sun penetrated through trees, through people, plants and animals, and through any machine that was normally used to maintain the grounds. It was as if the light naturally moved to the sounds of this metropolis, synced to the rhythm of the marimba. This was a city of futuristic light, engulfed in a technology more advanced than any form the human mind could fathom, yet placed within the confines of an ancient civilization.

With his sight once again fully restored, Dioni's mind absorbed the greatness of what was before him. This extraordinary city served as a capital for thousands of quetzals, all of whom glided effortlessly through the windless skies. The birds in the air did not flap their wings; instead, they were guided from one location to another by a light source that carried and trailed closely behind each airborne quetzal, which slowly dissolved as they passed by. Their flight was flawless.

Dioni continued to walk along the path until he came to a bridge made entirely of the roots of a large plant. Beneath the bridge was a river which consisted of an aquamarine-colored liquid, resembling the water seen only in the world's most pristine beaches. The liquid flowed smoothly from the center of the metropolis, the source of which appeared to be beneath the mystic tree at the center of the city.

Dioni paused to better observe the flowing liquid. Upon closer inspection he saw a stream of dozens of tiny, semi-transparent globes. They reminded him of glass marbles, though the globes were far more sophisticated. They floated on the surface of the liquid, and each globe emitted a miniscule flash of light – a reflection of sunlight captured at the perfect angle.

Dioni reached down to grab a globe, only to stop once he recalled he no longer had hands or opposable thumbs. He saw only the tips of his wings, which he noticed with even greater detail as he shifted his focus from the surface of the aquamarine liquid to its reflection. He once again noticed himself – a boy somehow trapped in the body of a bird. He stood and continued to walk to the center of the city as he observed the spectacle of light and sound created by the aerial quetzals. He was among his own kind, in a strange way, yet went completely unnoticed by any bird in the entire city. Perhaps they, too, were all humans trapped in the bodies of birds, and that this was as normal to them as the tides caused by the moon.

With solid ground beneath his feet, Dioni more closely observed the traffic in motion. The quetzals in the air travelled to different points along the perimeter of the grand plaza. They knew to stop just before they crashed into one of the mighty walls and were then guided towards a perfectly carved portal from where they then disappeared. Thousands of similar portals aligned the walls of the city, which opened and closed like mystic doors of wonderous caves.

Dioni continued. He captured each moment with the same sense of awe he experienced the very first time he visited the temples located above the surface. In his state of wonder, Dioni failed to pay attention to his immediate surroundings; he was startled by a male quetzal who landed a few paces in front of him. With its back to Dioni, the quetzal stood as though an unseen force of energy had intentionally placed it at that exact location, along the edge of the flowing liquid. The quetzal took a few steps forward to place its feet in the shallow river, then lowered its head, spread its wings, and bowed.

Dioni froze. He was a stranger within a strange land, and he felt no need to make a negative impression on the first bird which came nearby where he stood. However, the mighty bird before him was a quetzal, and the opportunity to see such a bird – in its supernatural habitat, with no sense of fear, and at such close proximity – was an opportunity which he simply could not let pass. Dioni slowly stepped back, carefully doing so to prevent making any sound, then moved further away from the edge of the river. He observed the resplendent bird in all its splendor, a sight which he thought he would never live to see.

With its torso bowed, the quetzal spread its wings – a flawless sight of perhaps the most beautiful bird in the natural world. Slowly and carefully, the bird lifted its upper body and shifted its wings from side to front. From the water, just below the quetzal's outstretched wings, arose a globe. The quetzal somehow controlled the globe telepathically, in a method which made the globe respond with the bird's every movement. The quetzal stood at full height, its wings placed directly in front of its body and separated from one another by a small globe of sparkling energy.

The quetzal gently moved its wings to cover the globe, similar to how Dioni would use his arms and hands to house and embrace a delicate object. Dioni noticed the bird's every movement and paid particular attention to how the quetzal inspected and studied every detail of the suspended sphere.

The quetzal retracted its wings. The globe did not respond to this action by returning to the water, but instead adjusted itself to be centimeters in front of the quetzal's face. The quetzal leaned forward and took the globe in its beak, which created an aura of green light around the bird. It once again fully extended its wings to its side, then shifted its head to look towards the surface level; it stood at full attention in what was the most perfect posture an avian creature could maintain. With the globe secured, the quetzal lifted from where it stood within the aquamarine liquid. As if carried from the river by a force which raised it to the sky, the quetzal's flight was trailed by the same green light which Dioni previously saw.

The quetzal glided vertically momentarily, then was gracefully directed to the center of the furthest wall – the base of the *Templo de Mascaras*. It then drifted into an open portal, perfectly designed for the quetzal's exact size, where it quickly passed through and disappeared.

In a state of astonishment, Dioni observed the paths of the hundreds of other quetzals which flew through the windless, internal sky. He observed how many of the birds copied the same behavior: the quetzals carefully positioned themselves along the river, where they walked into the liquid and bowed, then lifted a globe from the surface, inspected it, placed the globe in their beak, then were guided up, only to disappear into a portal along key points on the massive stone walls.

The entire system was neither orchestrated nor synchronized in any way. This gave Dioni the impression that the quetzals instinctively knew what to do and how to do it, and that their behavior was done for a reason he was yet to understand. Still, somehow it all seemed familiar, as if he had previously visited the location and had observed the resplendent birds in all their glory.

Dioni continued to walk in a directionless daze. He wondered how the entire habitat existed, and how the countless male and female quetzals flew, paced, or were otherwise transported in what was the world's best kept secret. It was a place where they were neither endangered nor envied, nor were they hunted. This was their utopia, and Dioni somehow stumbled upon it.

"I have to tell Alma about this," Dioni thought. He momentarily forgot his place among the true inhabitants of the city.

In his continued state of inattentiveness, Dioni accidently tipped the wing of a female quetzal just as she was to lift from the river. Dioni stopped, not a single feather on his body made a single movement. With a globe in her beak, the female quetzal turned to him and scoffed at Dioni's rude interruption. Her face did not express anger as much as it expressed confusion; she looked at Dioni as if she questioned his purpose for being alive. He opened his beak as if to speak but failed to make a sound.

The female quetzal briefly paused. She visually inspected him from toes to beak, then shifted her head back to its upright position before she lifted from the surface of the aquamarine river. Though confused as to what had just occurred, Dioni's eyes followed her until he was distracted by something elevated in the distance. It was a series of electronic screens – similar to a horizontal wall of televisions – which projected images and words with legible lettering.

Dioni quietly walked closer to the area where he saw the screens, which was higher than the ground level where he stood. The screens were protected by a natural awning, encased as if purposely carved into one of the massive interior walls. The area was recently constructed and not made according to ancient Mayan architecture, as was every other part of the city.

As was his behavior in human form, Dioni became curious. He felt the urge to know what was broadcast on the television screens. He paced close enough to see the emitted light, but his line of sight was blocked by a small wall which he would have to climb should his curiosity get the best of him. With a lack of hands and the inability to lift himself from the ground, climbing a wall would be far easier said than done.

Dioni fought to find his grip. He used the small claws on his feet to locate divots within the wall while utilizing his beak as a way to balance himself. None among the thousands of quetzals noticed Dioni's actions, though it was the most abnormal behavior in the entire city. He discovered an impractical method to climb the wall, and centimeter by centimeter, he pulled closer toward the bright displays.

As a young man, Dioni was not particularly strong, which was much the same in his current state of being. This proved to be a struggle for Dioni; though he consistently lost his grip and slipped back, he was determined to continue his climb. Each step was more exhausting than the step before. Every so often he peaked his head away from the wall to check if the images on the screens were visible. Despite the progress of his climb only a few inches from where he began, Dioni accepted the fact that he would not make it much further. He secured one foot onto the wall, followed by the other, then clamped his jaw into a small opening.

The television screens changed from white displays to green-colored light, which became brighter by the second. Dioni carefully spread his wings and used them to push his head upward, where he saw five male quetzals who glided in perfect formation. None of them noticed how one among their kind was spread on the wall, like a bird who came into unexpected contact with a large piece of clean glass.

Dioni did not see the quetzals land, though he noticed that they did so on a platform that was at the same level as the large screens. The five quetzals made sounds not typical of bird noises; they spoke to one another in a foreign language which sounded familiar yet was completely indistinguishable. Dioni's curiosity fueled the strength he needed to continue his climb. Unable to coordinate the use of his wings, he was only able to raise himself high enough to peak his eyes over the summit of the unexpectedly tall wall. Though not ideal, this provided him with a clear view of the screens, as well as an uncomfortable angle of the five quetzals.

The five green birds – in perfect synchronization – spread their wings with absolute ease, allowing only millimeters of empty space between each of their flight feathers. The images on the large screen did not change. At closer inspection, Dioni noticed that it was not one long television, but rather a series of interconnected projections. The five quetzals bowed before the screens, which allowed Dioni to see what was written across the long, projected image: *Departamento de Control del Clima Global.* Dioni knew to read, write, and speak Spanish, yet despite his knowledge and understanding of the language, he could not comprehend what was projected on the screens.

The five birds lifted their heads to stand in perfect posture. In unison, they slowly began to perform an intricate dance. The bird in the center led the dance, and the pair of quetzals to each of its sides moved perfectly in accordance with the central bird's motions. With their performance underway, the five quetzals furthered the mystery of their behavior; their voices echoed throughout the entire city as they rotated their bodies and shifted from side to side.

Dioni saw as the central quetzal stepped back, away from the screen, then turned itself to face the opposite direction. Following the leader, the remaining quetzals did the same, which provided them a clear view of the entire mega-metropolis. As if they performed a perfectly rehearsed and choreographed dance for an audience of millions, the five birds looked up, extended their wings, then looked down, all while they moved their hips and maintained perfect harmony. Upon looking down, the central quetzal noticed a pair of eyes that peaked over the edge of the lower wall.

The dance came to an immediate halt, ending the birds' trance-like state of focus. The center bird looked down with disparity and vigor. The four supportive birds followed the central quetzal's eyes and sighted the stranger who observed them from below – a bird who had absolutely no reason to be among them.

The five quetzals looked at one another, spoke among themselves, then walked closer to the ledge of the wall. As they stood above him, Dioni was only able to smile at them. He hoped that their look of anger was more of a natural gaze and not a stance of attack. In a state of panic, Dioni lost his grip, which caused him to fall even further than what he had climbed. He plunged into the aquamarine river below.

Dioni became temporarily blinded by the liquid, which was as transparent as water. In his state of shock and fear, he could not calm himself enough to get back onto his feet. He struggled and brought unwanted attention to himself as he waved his wings back and forth, causing a commotion that could have easily been prevented had he simply lifted his head. The noise caught the attention of the many residents of the city, who turned their attention to the bird in the river.

Dioni shifted his head in every direction, in a state of panic, as he searched for air. He hoped against all odds that his sight would soon return. It was of no use. The aquamarine liquid had him trapped and surrounded, and within moments, it would claim the soul of the intruder who dared enter the ancient kingdom.

Dioni felt the grasp of a strong force from an unknown being, which grabbed him by the shoulders and lifted his body from the river. He coughed forcefully, spreading droplets of liquid in every direction, from which the gathered quetzals maintained their distance. With his feet planted firmly on solid ground, he was finally able to inhale fresh air.

Dioni breathed heavily. Instinctively, he shook his body, which allowed the drops of liquid that covered his eyes to clear away and which eliminated the barrier between blurred vision and perfect sight. As he regained his sense of sight, he noticed the thousands of resplendent quetzals who stared at him. Their glares confirmed his suspicion: every one of them knew that he did not belong within their mythic city. Dioni stood upright and slowly paced in reverse until his back was against a solid surface.

The dominant quetzal broke formation from the other four and approached Dioni. The quetzal spoke to him in a dialect he failed to understand. The bird's stance and body language gave the impression of an attempt to communicate, as if asking a question. Unable to respond, Dioni searched for assistance.

The intrigued community of quetzals spoke amongst themselves, a few of which slowly approached Dioni. He was unable to comprehend what they said, yet he was able to identify that the language the quetzals spoke was similar to that of the native Guatemalans. It was a foreign dialect which sounded strangely familiar.

"Bloo," said a quetzal, in response to the question of another. "*Ne che le ma te pe-que,* 'bloo'."

The quetzal closest to Dioni walked around him, slowly.

"Bloo-go," said the quetzal. The bird raised its chest, which solidified its position of dominance over Dioni.

"What?" Dioni responded, clueless on how to decipher the instruction he was given.

"Bloo-go," repeated the quetzal. It then signaled the others to follow along.

"Bloo-go, bloo-go, bloo-go," the birds said to Dioni. They chanted words he was unable to comprehend.

The quetzals moved closer and their chants grew louder. They created a circle around Dioni and raised their voices with every stride. Dioni lowered his body and covered his face with his wings; he anticipated their next step to be both painful and terminal.

Before a final, striking step was taken by any one of the hundreds of quetzals who were ready and anxious to eliminate him from existence, a large bird suddenly landed in front of Dioni. The chants and forward motion of the quetzals stopped immediately, as the large bird protected him from oncoming doom.

The bird was physically larger than any of the quetzals in the kingdom – excluding their tailfeathers – and was clearly powerful enough to overtake an attack by any number of them. Dioni peeked through his wings and saw the back of the large bird, which was entirely void of color. The large bird turned its head and made visual contact; Dioni saw that its beak was pointed and that its eyes were as dark as the feathers which outlined its entire body.

"*Che me-que ple mo deple,*" said the large bird, a crow. Its voice was evidently strong and commanding, yet soothingly feminine. She stood on-guard before Dioni, as if to protect the most precious bird on the planet.

"*Te mete dela-pe que se me-que,*" replied a nearby quetzal, visibly upset by the intruder among them.

The crow once again turned her head and looked at Dioni, who was as intrigued as he was mystified. This was too much for any person to

63

accept, nonetheless a person trapped in the body of a bird. Dioni noticed the darkness of the crow's feathers. He simply could not fathom how a bird of such caliber was able to exist in the Guatemalan forest, yet he was grateful for her current position between himself and the angry quetzals. Her attention returned to the gathered crowd.

"*Este ele epe neve,* Omega," the crow said. In that moment, the demeanor of the quetzals changed entirely; they shifted their bodies and backed away from Dioni, in fear of his retaliation.

"*Nope pede sepe,*" replied the quetzal. "*Ele epe azel.* Bloo."

The crow looked at Dioni, who remained guarded.

"Any one of a million different types of birds and you choose a quetzal," the crow said. "And a blue one, at that."

Dioni froze in place. He understood every word the crow spoke. He looked up at her and opened his beak but was unable to produce a single sound.

"Is this how you talk to every girl who speaks to you?" she asked. "Because if it is then those tailfeathers are useless."

Dioni's eyes scanned the room, the rest of his body failed to move. Perhaps she spoke to someone else.

"Yeah, I'm talking to you, blue," continued the crow. "Get up and act like you belong here."

Dioni slowly lowered his guard. He placed his wings at his sides and stood with a slightly better posture.

"*Epe este ele,* Omega," said the crow to the quetzals. She pointed at Dioni as she addressed the group.

Every bird in the mighty metropolis was immediately intrigued; their faces changed from fierce to puzzled as they looked at Dioni with wonderous gazes. In their minds, there was absolutely no possibility that it was real. The quetzals turned their attention away from Dioni and onto the rest of their kind. They quietly conversed amongst themselves and began to spread rumors of an oddity they simply did not understand.

"Who are you?" Dioni nervously asked the crow. "What's happening?"

"Nothing yet, blue," the crow responded. She maintained her attention on the surrounding birds. "They don't believe you are who you claim to be."

"What? I didn't claim to be anything!"

"Well, one of us had to tell them. You're an intruder in their sacred land, kid. These birds don't care for strangers."

"What are they going to do?" Dioni asked. The tone of his voice shifted to a slightly higher pitch. The crow turned her body to face Dioni directly.

"Look, blue, you're gonna have to do whatever I say if you don't want these birds to use you as a sacrifice."

The quetzals were too intelligent to fall for a trap. They were descendants of warriors, derived from thousands of years of tradition – who helped build the most advanced civilization of ancient times – and the claim made by the crow was not substantial enough to have them think otherwise.

"*Este epe no-pe pede sepe du* Omega," said a quetzal, who stood at a distance. "*Epe bloo.*"

The eyes of every bird shifted to Dioni.

"What are they saying?" Dioni asked, in a deep state of worry.

"They're upset that you chose to be one of them and that your feathers are blue," the crow responded.

"I didn't choose this! I'm not one of them! I'm… I'm…w..wait…I'm blue?"

"Well, mostly blue," said the crow. She looked at Dioni's feet and lifted her head until her eyes were at level with his. "And you look ridiculous."

The quetzals lost their patience. Their whispered gossips once again returned to a synchronized chant.

"*Bloo-go, bloo-go, bloo-go,*" they sang in unison.

The crow looked in every direction at the thousands of quetzals who were determined to rid their city of the intruder and of she who dared to protect him. The crow turned to Dioni. "We have to go."

"What are they saying?" Dioni asked.

65

"You're blue, and we have to go!" she exclaimed.

The chants grew louder. The males of the tribe lifted their bodies and pushed out their chests, while the females lowered their heads and spread their wings. Every set of eyes was squarely on Dioni.

"How do we get out?" asked Dioni, near a state of panic.

"Bow," said the crow.

"What?"

"You need to bow down to them. It's a sign of respect. Just do what I do."

The crow spread her wings and dropped her head to be lower than that of the mass of birds which slowly and angrily approached. Dioni mirrored her every move. The chants became louder.

The crow lifted her head and looked directly up, which aligned her body to perfect posture. With her wings spread, the crow pushed herself from the ground. Her body lifted vertically, and the same effect of light and shadows trailed closely behind.

As he was instructed, Dioni mimicked her movements. He lifted his head, though slightly tilted as he feared a sudden attack by the quetzals. He raised his wings and silently prayed that he could duplicate the actions of the crow.

Dioni pushed the ground beneath his feet, only to lift a few centimeters before he returned to the exact spot from where he began. He tried again and again, and repeated the same results with each attempt.

"Hey!" Dioni shouted to the crow. "It's not working! I think I'm broken!"

The light of hope in Dioni's eyes faded as he saw the trails of the crow move further away from where he stood. The quetzals immediately noticed Dioni's inability to lift himself from the ground. They moved closer to him and used their voices to strike fear.

"*Bloo-go, bloo-go, bloo-go…*"

The quetzals closest to Dioni raised and spread their wings; it was a sign of intimidation which clearly worked. Dioni looked at them as they drew closer and became larger. His eyes filled with fear. In desperation, he closed his eyes and shouted. He jumped and flapped his arms repeatedly, begging for his liftoff mechanism to miraculously work before the birds could take hold of him.

In an instant, Dioni felt a powerful pull from his shoulders. He sensed as his feet lifted from the ground. He opened his eyes and noticed a sea of green birds beneath him, who became smaller and more distant with each moment. Dioni looked up.

The crow glided smoothly in the internal sky. She used her body to direct her positioning while in flight, but otherwise made no other motion. In her talons she held the elusive blue quetzal, who was seconds away from becoming a sacrifice to the Mayan gods.

Dioni did not struggle or make motions of any kind. Though his body was held tightly in position, his eyes were free to roam and wander. From the vantagepoint of the air, Dioni saw the magnificence of what was undiscovered by those above the surface; he was better able to see more of the metropolis, which was far larger from the air than it was from the ground. The dominant tree – which stood as the massive centerpiece of the city – was larger in size than the world's greatest sequoia, though with the bark and structure of a ceiba tree. Dioni saw how the aquamarine liquid that streamed from beneath the mighty tree flowed outward in every direction. Within the river's flow were an endless amount of miniature globes which, from such an elevated position, resembled glimmers of illumination that reflected the light of the sun.

Within the stone structure of its perimeter, the city walls were decorated in turquoise, jade, and gold – remnants of a once proud and prominent civilization. As the two birds gracefully glided in the underground sky, Dioni looked up and saw the sunlight that beamed through the transparent ceiling, almost blindingly so. The light nourished the city, which was far larger than he initially understood. No matter the direction he turned and looked, the interconnected system of tunnels, trails, and open sky went on for what appeared to be hundreds of kilometers. Dioni's anxiety transformed into wonder and awe; in his mind there was no logical explanation for how any of it existed.

"Alma would absolutely love this," he said in thought.

The crow held firmly to Dioni's shoulders as she climbed higher above the surface of the city. She glided towards a blinking red light in the distance, clearly placed away from incoming flight traffic.

"Hold on," the crow said to Dioni. "This is going to get fast."

The flight pattern held by the crow remained intact in that she did not use more than her momentum to stay adrift, though she mysteriously gained speed and altitude. With a lack of hands, or anything on which to hold, Dioni pulled his legs to his chest. His long tailfeathers flapped in every direction. The blinking light provided guidance for the crow, who pushed her wings downward with all her might while she towed Dioni along. She flew towards a vortex constructed into a wall, which slowly opened like a camera shutter to reveal their exit. The tunnel became illuminated with every stroke of her wings, as if powered by her motion. Dioni's eyes remained widely opened the entire time.

In the adjacent wall, Dioni noticed how the hieroglyphics moved as the crow's momentum increased. It was an actual zoetrope of prehistoric carvings and paintings, which gave the illusion of movement. The wall depicted a frame-by-frame fable of a man planting seeds; in the moving images, Dioni saw a man who stood in a field and threw seeds into the distance. The seeds grew to become plants, and the plants created more seeds. The crow increased her airspeed.

Other human-like images appeared on the animated walls. The beings extracted seeds from the plants. They then rolled the seeds and used a stone to crush them into a fine powder, which was then placed in a fire. Once in the fire, the seeds liquified and dripped into a golden cup, where other human figures took the cup and drank its contents. The moving images came to a sudden end after that scene, which made little sense to Dioni.

The crow spread her wings in absolute perfection. The weaved pattern of their momentum stopped. Dioni felt the thrust of a sudden burst of energy in a forward motion, which immediately forced the two birds toward a solid, stone wall. Dioni's eyes became watery from the rapid wind that hit his face. He shook his head to wipe the tears then noticed the oncoming solid structure in which his fate would undoubtedly conclude. For just a fraction of a second, Dioni wished to be back with the 'bloo-go' quetzals.

The crow, with Dioni in her grasp, soared at unimaginable speed. Almost instantly, the tunnel system – which resembled the passage from where Dioni entered the quetzal kingdom – shifted from horizontal to vertical. The two birds were forced upward, toward the ground surface, where natural sunlight beamed across the cloudless sky.

Dioni looked up. The sunlight never looked so beautiful as it did in that moment. The two birds crossed through a series of colored lights, the source of which was somehow buried within the walls of the vertical tunnel. As the light at the end of the tunnel grew bigger and brighter, Dioni heard the same voice from when he first entered the underground city.

"Pharomacrus identified, mocinno. Approved for exit," said the voice. "Goodbye."

The sound created by the automated voice was all Dioni heard before he and the crow exited the tunnel system and left it far behind. They ascended to an elevation no bird alive had any business to attain. In what was several kilometers above the surface, Dioni looked down and saw the ancient ruins of Tikal National Park – a city he once thought he knew so well. He looked in every direction and saw clouds beneath him, and in the distance were the soothing waves of both the Atlantic and Pacific oceans. No other creature was worthy enough to see such natural magnificence, to sense the atmospheric air far above the land, and to feel the breeze of winds exclusive to the world's most precious beings.

Chapter Six

"For the first time since opening to the general publc as a national park, Tikal, along with the Ipala volcanic tourist site, will be closed for the next 24 hours."

"Local authorities are coordinating a large effort to find an adolescent teenager who went missing from last night's major storm."

"Authorities are saying that the likelihood of finding the young man alive are miniscule at best, but they do believe in miracles and they just want to find him safely."

"As you can see on your screen, this is a recent phot of Dionisio Sedano, the 15-year-old boy who mysteriously vanished without a trace during the big storm last night. He was last seen here in Ipala, taking tours to the top to enjoy the crater lake. Sadly, while the tour group he was guiding at the time came down, he did not."

"We are asking all local residents to be on the lookout for a young man, 15 years old, approximately 5 feet and 3 inches in height, with a meduim-light complexion, and to notify the authorities if they spot him in the area."

"With a search area of over 200 square miles, the hope of finding Dionisio is fading with every hour."

Alma had enough from the sea of news reporters who somehow

70

managed to simultaneously arrive at the base of the volcano. Their cameras were setup, along with small lights and microphones, within a matter of minutes. There were cars and vans spread throughout the park entrance, which was normally reserved for tour buses and local visitors.

She was angry. Alma knew that the chance to find Dioni was marginal, but her anger stemmed from the knowledge that the entire spectacle was put on for entertainment. Other than a handful of volunteers – including some of the elder children of the orphanage – no one really cared whether or not Dioni was found. They did not care about him before, so why would they suddenly care now? Some of them probably hoped that Dioni was either found dead or not at all. It would certainly provide more sustenance to fill an endless news cycle.

Every camera and its corresponding news reporter was more repugnant than the last. Alma walked amongst them. She listened intently to each of their words as she searched for any opportunity in which she could provide her opinion on the matter.

"Alma!" Oscar shouted from a distance, away from the chaos of the impromptu media center. "Another group is forming. If you want to go with this one, we have to go now."

She paused momentarily to consider her options. She wanted nothing more than to see Dioni, to hug him and to never let him out of her sight ever again. She dreaded the thought of what she would find at the summit, to see clues of his faded existence, and to have an imprinted memory of seeing the love of her young life face-down, floating in the water. The image repeated itself over and over in her mind.

"No!," she exclaimed to herself. "He's fine! He's not gone! Stop thinking that!"

"Alma, vamonos! They're going now!" yelled Oscar. His voice expressed urgency.

Alma gathered the courage to join Oscar, along with a small group of locals, at the entrance of the trail which led to the crater lake at the top of the volcano.

"Ladies and gentlemen, my name is patrolman Francisco Herida," said a man in a service uniform. He stood at attention near the start of the trail and held a photograph of Dioni, which he displayed to the group.

"This is the child we are searching for," he continued, "and we have every reason to believe he is alive and near this area. We do not want to lose more people in search of one person, so it is very important that this group stay together. I am the group leader for Group 2, one of only two groups that will actively search along designated areas near the top of the volcano. It is very important that we always stay as a group and remain accountable for one another at all times. We have approximately 8 hours of daylight remaining, and we will use every second of that light to find this young man."

Alma paid little attention to the man in uniform. She wanted to get on the trail and begin the search for Dioni without further delay. A million scenarios came to mind; her thoughts raced in every possible direction, in search of clues of how it came to be. A part of her blamed Gabi; had she not been in such a rush, Gabi would have remembered Dioni before she and her group fled the storm. A part of her blamed Mario; had he not been asleep, he may have noticed someone missing from the group. She blamed the tourists, who should have been held accountable. In her mind, all were guilty for their part in the loss of an innocent young life on the verge of adulthood.

She looked in every direction as she walked, ignoring the other searchers as they cried out for Dioni. Oscar felt her anger. He held her by the arm as they walked together along the trail. His doing so was not an ill-intended act, but rather a way to provide comfort for his sister who was a single spark short of a massive flame.

The sun showered its heat onto Ipala, similar to how the rain had done the night prior. As beads of sweat dripped from her brow, Alma's unchanged expression showed everyone in the group that no priority on the planet was greater than to find Dioni. She loved him yet hated him for doing this to her. Every pace was done so with both fear and agony.

She wore Dioni's backpack, the same which accompanied him along the same path just a few hours prior. Her legs began to ache, though she refused to show it. Her hands grasped the straps of the backpack on each side. After some time on the trail, her overwhelmed emotions could no longer remain hidden and made their way to the surface.

"He's fine!" she once again exclaimed to herself. "I will see him again!"

Near the peak of the volcano, on a small, man-made wooden dock, stood a taller man in uniform. He looked as if on-guard and kept his eyes on every person in the vicinity. Patrolman Herida walked ahead of his group and toward the taller man.

"We are the second group," Herida said to the taller man. "Where do you want us?"

"We have 5 people spread from here to the bank along the other side," replied the taller man, "and the water rescuers arrived a few minutes ago. Your team can search along the base on the sunny side of the volcano."

Herida returned to the group. He shared instructions on where their search was to be conducted, and he reminded the team to stay together. Most importantly, he instructed them to call out if they found any item that could be identified as Dioni's. The members of the group went along as instructed, with the exception of Alma who looked intently at the water. She lost her ability to pay attention to Herida and was solely focused on the two men who equipped themselves with underwater search gear.

"Why are they here?" Alma asked Herida.

"We have to exhaust all possibilities, señorita," he replied. She understood what that meant.

"Come on," Oscar said as he pulled at Alma's arm. "Let's start looking over there. Those divers aren't going to find anything."

Oscar guided Alma along the outer bank of the lagoon, near a set of trees which faced the sun. On any other day, Alma would have been happy to see such an extraordinary view. Much of Guatemala was visible from such height, and it was just as beautiful as Dioni loved to describe it to her.

She had stood there only a few times prior – mostly at Dioni's insistence – though it was the first time she finally recognized why he loved it so much. Dioni was her dreamer – the orphan boy who taught himself everything, who wanted to see the entire world and take her along to witness it all. He

73

did not need much to be happy; all he ever wanted was to soar. He did not care for money or fame or luxuries. He wanted the experiences of a life lived to its fullest. More than any desire or dream he may have had, nothing brought Dioni more joy than when he made Alma laugh or smile.

As time progressed, two other groups made it to the summit, each of which carried different supplies, food, and equipment. One of the groups brought a large dog who was trained to detect the whereabouts of targeted individuals.

After hours of search along the grounds, the second group was forced to take a break. Each team member momentarily stepped away from the heat to nourish themselves before they continued their search. Alma was neither thirsty nor hungry; her eyes expressed the emotions her voice dared not say. Nearby was Gabi, who summoned the courage to approach Alma.

"The heat can make you ill," Gabi said to Alma. She held a bottle of water to her ailing friend, which was more of a peace offering. "Please take it." Gabi sensed Alma's anger through her cold expression.

"Thank you, Gabi," replied Oscar. He took the bottle from her hand. "Can we have another one, please?"

"Yes, of course. Here," Gabi responded. She placed a second bottle in his free hand.

Alma stood her ground. Gabi politely forced herself to smile, nodded her head, then turned and walked away from the scene. She then paused and turned to face Alma directly.

"I know you don't want to speak to me," Gabi began, "and that's fine. I understand why you're so angry with me, and I'm sorry." Her voice trembled lightly. "It happened so fast that I completely lost track of him. There was no way I could've known that the storm would be so strong."

Aside from blinking her eyes, Alma did not move. Her mind was somewhere else entirely. The woman in front of her was merely a mirage, almost a silhouette of a human being that was neither seen nor heard. Gabi's eyes filled with tears, the result of strong feelings of sorrow and regret, to which Alma responded in the complete opposite manner: cold, stoic, and emotionless.

"Hey!" sounded a man's voice in the distance. "I think I found something!"

Everyone in the group turned to look in the direction of the man's voice. He was one of the rescuers in the water.

"Ay, Dios mío. This is it," Gabi said. Her hands covered her mouth. She inhaled deeply.

Everyone rushed to the edge of the water. Alma walked far behind the others. Every step seemed like an eternity; what occurred next would become an everlasting memory, a sight that would never be unseen, and an agony the likes of which she would never again allow herself to feel.

The search groups came together and formed a small crowd along the bank of the lagoon. They patiently waited for the rescue diver to return from deeper water. It was not clearly visible as to what the diver carried as he moved slowly toward the shore. The gathered crowd was tall enough to cover Alma's view. She did not see when the diver emerged from the water, nor did she see what he held in his arms upon his rise to the surface.

"Alma!" shouted Oscar. He turned to look for his sister. "Alma!"

The crowd parted. Alma saw the diver's rescue suit as the water covered only his ankles. In his hand the man held a heavily worn shoe.

"Is that Dioni's?" Oscar asked.

Alma knew the answer immediately. Oscar seized the shoe from the diver then ran to show it to her. The first detail she noticed was a pen mark, the sight of which returned her to the day when Dioni took a blue pen and created an outline along the edges of his shoe. She remembered.

Dioni was happy as he carefully guided his pen the way an artist meticulously aligned brushstrokes on a canvass. Alma asked him what he was doing, and he responded by saying that he wanted to try something. She told him that he was ruining his new shoes, a comment Dioni chose to ignore. Oscar came into the room and saw Dioni so intensely focused on outlining his shoe with a pen. He decided to interrupt the progress by bumping into Dioni's arm, which caused Dioni to make a squiggle mark on the otherwise perfectly white shoe. Dioni looked up, a fury in his eyes aimed squarely at Oscar. Sensing what was to follow, Oscar ran. Dioni dropped the shoe and chased after; he was going to teach Oscar a lesson. Alma lifted the shoe from the ground and inspected the odd pen mark created by Dioni. Only he would want to do something so…so…

The same mark was distinctly visible on the shoe Oscar presented to her, though in its present state was highly worn from miles and miles of walking through the Mayan forest. She took the time to inspect it; other than normal wear, the shoe showed no signs of stains. The bottom was still intact, as were its worn laces. It looked almost as if the shoe was purposely thrown into the water, hidden from view yet intentionally placed to be found.

Alma held the shoe then looked at Oscar. Her breath took a moment to travel from her lungs to her larynx, which was just long enough to be interrupted by the howl of the dog. This drew the immediate attention of the people who crowded around Alma, including the rescuer in the water.

The dog was a short distance away, near the edge of the peak of the volcano. A step behind the dog was its handler, who waived his arm in the air – the universal signal which indicated he had found something. Oscar reached for the shoe in Alma's hand. He released his grasp of it when he realized he would have to pry it from Alma's hands with more force than he could possibly produce.

The crowd of searchers walked toward the dog, curious as to what was discovered just a few meters away. The dog, having successfully completed his intended task, returned to the source of his discovery. Alma and Oscar tailed the group. If the shoe was a clue as to Dioni's fate or whereabouts, then what had the dog found just beyond the peak of the volcano? Did Dioni fall? Did he hurt himself? Was he there? Maybe the dog found him! Please let it be him!

The crowd moved closer to the edge of the volcano, a location along the perimeter with an angled drop that only the most skilled hikers could climb or descend. A few yards down, just far enough to be in a safe location but further down than what most people found comfortable, was the evidence the dog discovered.

With the shoe in her hand, Alma made her way to the front of the group; if there was something to see, she was going to see it for herself and not wait for her brother to retrieve it for her.

The dog sat beside a dark object, what appeared to be a piece of cloth. The dog's handler walked to the cloth, bent down and pulled it from the ground, then extended it as to present his discovery to the gathered crowd. In his hands he held a shirt – dark in color, a ToursTikal logo embroidered on one side, the name 'Dioni' sown on the other – with its shoulders and sleeves shredded, though with no visible stains.

Alma and Oscar froze. There it was…Dioni's work shirt.

Oscar found the strength to move. He cautiously paced forward, slightly down the side of the volcano, then carefully took the shirt from the handler. The dog became quiet; it sensed the sorrow which emanated from the young man.

Aside from the bristling of the wind against the grass and trees of Ipala's landscape, no sound was heard. The water was tranquil, as were the many birds and animals who lived among the flora of the naturally stunning locale. At any other time, on any other day, the moment would have been the envy of every artist, living or deceased. It was the euphoric sensation of being connected with nature – as though living as one, where the emotions of both incredible joy and incredible sadness could be felt yet were indescribable by written or spoken words.

Oscar approached his sister, who stood before the gathered crowd. He was far too young to understand the magnitude of what had occurred, though was old enough to know the agonizing feeling of tragic loss. Tears flowed from Oscar's eyes, which extended from his face and onto his clothing. Alma gripped the worn shoe in her hand, tighter and tighter with every step her brother made to her. He needed not articulate a single word; his actions were far more courageous than anything he could have possibly said.

Oscar stood before Alma and raised the shirt, to display the remains of that which belonged to the person she loved most. He placed the shirt in her empty hand, and she inspected the damage. The tattered cloth circled around her fingers, guided by a volcanic breeze.

Alma made a fist, as if she intended to choke any remaining signs of life from the shirt. She lifted her hand to her face, closed her eyes, and inhaled the last remaining essence of Dioni which remained in the tattered cloth. With her lower face covered by the shirt, Alma opened her eyes and looked at the horizon. In that moment even the sun grew calmer; it too felt the loss that no young love should endure.

Tears flowed from Alma's eyes. She grasped the shirt even tighter. She inhaled deeply. She felt as if Dioni was beside her. She released the shirt, which gently glided in the breeze before it settled on the volcanic grass.

Alma fell to her knees; her tears flowed as she grasped the sole remains of all she held dear. She leaned forward. Her head fell toward the ground and her face rested on Dioni's shirt. Her shouts of sorrow were muffled by the tattered cloth.

Dioni had never seen any part of the landscape from an elevation higher than the peak of the Ipala volcano, which, after such an experience, seemed minuscule by comparison. He also never understood the vastness of the ocean, as if though it were a portrait of the Earth created by the finest artist in the galaxy. He was awestruck as he floated among the clouds. The large black bird grasped Dioni by his shoulders.

The flight lasted only a few seconds before the crow descended toward the ground level of Tikal National Park. She always enjoyed the visit to this part of the world, and the unique experience of the recently completed adventure marked yet another unforgettable instance of why the Mayan kingdom was unlike any other on Earth. The crow slowly drifted downward, which allowed Dioni to touch down first and comfortably place his small talons on the top of a flat temple, away from the normal path and restricted from tourist visitation.

"Who are you?" Dioni asked the black bird, who took a moment to expel her remaining energy.

"I'm the bird that saved your life. Twice," responded the crow. "Quetzals are very territorial. You being blue did not help at all."

"Okay, wait. What is going on?" Dioni asked impatiently. "Do you have

78

any idea of why I am a bird, because I wasn't a bird yesterday and today I have these feathers and this beak and everyone seems to want to eat me and—"

"—One question at a time, kid. Slow dow—"

"—Why am I a blue bird?" Dioni interrupted. "All I remember is a big storm and somehow I was in a cave and that something attacked me!" Dioni's demeanor changed entirely in that moment. "Oh my god, am I dead?" his cracked voice asked.

"First of all, let's get our story straight, shall we?" the crow responded, less enthused for having to remind Dioni of what actually occurred. "You fell asleep on a volcano, one with its own crater lake at its summit, on the day of the worst storm of the season. Instead of doing the sensible thing and going back to the base, you decided to walk around like a… a…uhh."

"A tourist?"

"Yes, like a lost tourist. One with a terrible sense of direction, and who was – for some unknown reason – only wearing one shoe. Why were you wearing only one shoe?"

"I couldn't find the other one when I woke u…Wait…stop. You saw me in Ipala?"

"You mean, I saved you in Ipala," the black bird responded.

"Huh?"

"Look, kid. There's no easy way to say this. You were going to drown. It was either the rain or the wind, but one way or another, you were going to fall into that lagoon."

"So you saved me? How?" Dioni asked, a puzzled look etched on his quetzal face.

"How about we change the order of questions?" said the crow as she walked toward Dioni. "Answer me this: what's your name, kid?"

"Dioni."

"The… only, what?"

"No, not 'the only'. Dee Oh Nee."

79

"Ohhhhh-kay. Different," the black bird responded, thinking aloud. "Not the most original name I've heard but certainly acceptable for an Omega bird."

"Why am I a bird?" Dioni questioned.

"I'm thinking of a simple way to explain it to you, the only."

"Dee oh nee!"

"Dee-oh-nee. I wasn't finished," responded the crow.

She turned away to ponder her next move. She looked at Dioni, opened her beak momentarily then turned away once again, unable to think of a way to explain it all to him. She took a few more steps away, then once again looked at Dioni. She proceeded slowly.

"I don't know why you're blue."

"Oh, I'm glad you mention that," Dioni responded, sarcastically. "I don't know why I'm a bird!"

"Dioni, listen to me for a second. I…I don't know how to say this to you."

"Say what? Why I am a blue bird? Because a lot has happened since last night and you haven't told me anything that makes any sense!"

"I know, I know," the crow responded, nervously. "It's just…I think this is the first time this has happened."

"That a person turns into a bird? I hope so!" Dioni exclaimed.

"No, not that. It's just…forget for a second that you're blue."

"That still leaves the fact that I am not the same person I was yesterday."

"Dioni, it's not so simple to explain," said the black bird. She took a few short paces closer to him. "I want you to understand that this happened to you, specifically you, for a reason."

"And what reason would that be?" Dioni asked.

"I'm not entirely sure how to explain it," responded the crow. She once again looked away. Something was evidently not how it was supposed to be. "What do you know about birds?"

"They fly, and eat seeds, and the boy birds are colorful and the girl birds are not," Dioni said, irritated by the inconclusive responses from the crow.

"Okay, let's start there," the black bird said. "Birds are not just things that fly, Dioni. They do a lot of work."

"So does everything else on this planet."

"Yes, true, but birds are special. Birds have responsibilities that other animals and species do not."

"Well that's great. How wonderful to know that birds are both colorful and responsible." Dioni responded. "How does that explain anything?"

"I had a certain responsibility, okay? And during the storm, I passed that responsibility on…to…you…"

"What are you saying?"

Dioni was taken aback. Her words made absolutely no sense to him. The crow looked at him. She breathed a heavy sigh.

"You could've died in the storm," said the crow. "I made a decision because it was the only way to save you. I had to pass it on."

"So you made a decision and now I'm a bird?" asked Dioni.

"No, that's not…" the blackbird looked toward the sky to search for answers. "I know nothing makes sense to you right now, but the only thing I can tell you is that I felt the exact same way when it happened to me."

"Thennnn….you weren't always a bird?" Dioni tilted his head.

"No, I wasn't always a bird," the crow responded. "It was a responsibility that was given to me, and I gave it to you. Does that make sense?"

"Not really, no," Dioni said.

The black bird became frustrated, unable to communicate her thoughts to the young quetzal. She turned away from him and walked to the edge of the temple. Dioni followed closely behind, desperate to understand what happened to him.

"You didn't die last night, Dioni," the black bird opened, "but your human body is not really alive. It's somewhere else."

81

"Where? Where is it?"

"Somewhere you and I can't go."

"Why not? Is it too far away?" Dioni asked. "What if we get a camioneta or something? If we can get a message to Mario he can take us anywhere we wan—"

"—It's not really a place. It's more like a thought. Like an idea."

"So can I think myself back to being me?" Dioni asked, naively. The black bird cautiously smiled. She sat and rested her tired legs.

"No," the crow responded. "You're a part of something bigger now, Dioni."

Dioni sat beside her. "I don't want to be a part of anything," he said. "I just want to go back to being me and then go home."

"To see Alma?" asked the crow. She looked directly at him.

"Yes, to see Alm—" Dioni paused. "How...how do you know Alma?"

"I wish I could explain it in a way you would understand."

Dioni jumped to his feet. None of what she said made any sense.

"When I was about your age," the black bird continued, "I lived near a big field where I saw and heard the local birds every day. I remember hearing the song of this one particular bird, over and over again, but I couldn't see the actual bird that was making the sound. And every time I turned in the direction of the sound, it would immediately stop, and I couldn't find its source. Then one day, I was walking near the ocean, by a few trees that I liked to visit, when I suddenly heard that sound. I looked in every direction, and it was like that bird was invisible, but...but taunting me in a way, you know?"

Dioni sat. He had no clue to where her story headed.

"And I looked and looked, everywhere, and nothing," the crow continued. "I knew I wasn't just hearing things. And then, it seemed as though the wind just stopped. I was right on the beach, I heard the waves crashing, but it was the first time I had ever been by the water when there was absolutely no wind. That was probably the weirdest sensation I had ever experienced up to that point…the wind was entirely gone. So I start walking toward the water, when suddenly a mysterious bird just lands a few steps ahead of me."

"What kind of bird was it?" asked Dioni.

"That's just it. It wasn't just any bird. It was every bird. It was completely colorless, can you believe that? Not black, not white…no color of any kind, but I knew it was a bird. Does that make sense?"

"It's hard to follow. How would you know it was a bird if you didn't see any color on it?"

"I just knew,' responded the crow. "So I'm looking at this bird when it turns away from me. We both faced the water, and I stop because I don't want to scare it away or step on it or something. Then it rotated its body and looked at me. There was no color anywhere on this bird, except that it had these eyes that felt like they looked directly through me. It gave me this odd look, like if it had somehow made a mistake then realized I was there. Have you ever felt something like that?"

"It's hard to say," Dioni responded. "This one time I took a nap during a storm and when I woke up, I was a bird."

"So this colorless bird turned and looked at the water, and it spread its wings. A few seconds later, the Earth started to shake, to tremble uncontrollably, and then the water from the shore quickly moved further and further away into the ocean."

"The bird made the beach tremble? Like an earthquake?"

"Yes, exactly!" the black bird responded, excitedly. "The earthquake stopped and the bird is nowhere in sight. I look everywhere and there is no trace of it. Suddenly, from out of nowhere, that same bird attacked me! I try everything to defend myself, to swat at it or punch it or kick it, to try to protect myself from this crazy thing. And then I think I hit it or something, because it flew away to the trees by the beach. I watch it completely disappear into the woods. Then, like if every bird in the woods simultaneously heard some kind of noise that caused a mass panic, every bird flew away. Every one of them, at the exact same time. There must have been thousands of birds in the sky at that moment. It was beautiful."

"Seems more scary than beautiful," Dioni commented. "Why didn't you turn and run?"

"I don't know," the crow responded. "I was paralyzed from this swarm of birds. Then I felt something pull me; pulling me as if to lift me off the ground. I fight it, but there was nothing there. I struggled and I suddenly feel myself lifting off the sand, so then I start screaming and waiving my arms and legs in every direction…I'm freaking out! Then, whatever it was that lifted me, turned me in the direction to see the ocean. I stopped panicking and my body went completely numb. All I remember is seeing a massive wall of water rushing toward me. It was so big that it blocked the sun. Everything suddenly went dark. When I woke up, I was what you see now."

"Which is…what, exactly?"

"A bird, Dioni. A Hawaiian crow. It's a mythic bird where I come from."

"What color is it?" Dioni asked.

The black bird smiled.

"All black, from beak to feet to cheeks."

Dioni looked at the vista ahead of him. The sun slowly descended, and soon the jungle would have only the moon as its source of light.

"I'm sorry that happened to you," Dioni said. "But I have to be me again and get home. I can't stay like this. Alma is probably so worried about me."

"Everyone you know is worried about you," responded the Hawaiian crow. "They're probably out looking for you now, wondering where you disappeared. They don't know it now, but they are never going to find you."

"Why not? I'm right here!"

"A part of you is here. The rest of you is gone."

"So I did die during that storm," said Dioni.

"No, Dioni. You were saved, but you had to lose your former self in order to stay alive. Someone else made that decision for you. That's how we're both here now."

Dioni looked away though he remained seated beside the black bird. All he received were a series of vague responses.

"Can you take me to see her?" asked Dioni, slightly optimistically.

"It's too late," the crow responded. "The sun will be down in a few minutes. It's best if you're not out when there's no light."

"Tomorrow, then. Can you take me to her tomorrow?"

The black bird shook her head. She looked at Dioni, who was desperate to get an honest response. She sighed.

"Yes, Dioni, I can take you," she said to him.

"Great! Thank you! As soon as the light comes up we'll go to Flores! I know exactly how to get there from here, I think."

"Sounds good, kid," responded the blackbird, an obvious sadness in her voice.

She lowered her head. She knew all too well that the visit to the town would be a terrible mistake. Dioni, having heard his desired response, stood and walked away.

Dioni's voice echoed further beyond the temple as he walked and provided step-by-step detail of what he would say to Alma upon meeting her the next day. He stopped himself when he read the black bird's body language. She was quiet, as if withholding something she wanted desperately to say but was unable to do so. Dioni moved to stand beside her.

"What's your name?" Dioni asked, in a much gentler tone.

The Hawaiian crow turned to face Dioni. He truly was a resplendent bird, even if he failed to recognize it.

"Alalā," the black bird responded. "My mother gave me that name. It was her favorite bird." She forced a smile which seemed painted on her face. "You can call me Ally."

Chapter Seven

Sleepless nights were not a new phenomenon for Alma. There was the one Christmas where she, Oscar and Dioni stayed up all night and waited for Santa Clause to make it to the orphanage to distribute presents. Santa never came. Instead it was the elder lady from the church, who, on that special night of the year, was the helper who worked on Santa's behalf. There was also the time when Oscar was ill and was rushed to the hospital. Alma thought only of him the entire night. She prayed in the same manner that any child would, and she hoped against all odds that her brother would survive.

She lay in bed, motionless, as the dark night sky became a deep blue. The rising sun brought with it the sounds of the resident songbirds, none of which she heard. She was in pain; a pain so deep that it could not manifest itself in physical form. With one hand she made a fist, which was pale from hours of being held in the same position. Beside her face was her other arm, covered by Dioni's tattered shirt. Alma held it the entire night, grasping whatever scent of Dioni remained on the cloth.

The shirt was soaked, drenched with her tears. Dioni loved this shirt. He wore it proudly as he guided tourists through his favorite place on Earth. The ragged piece of cloth was there during Dioni's final moments, and by having it near her she could almost feel Dioni's fear as he grasped for dear life during the storm.

Her mind raced in a million different directions, which prevented her from getting any rest. For Alma, it was a curse. In her mind she declared her hatred for those who allowed this to happen. Dioni deserved a better life, or at the very least a much better death, and it infuriated her to repeatedly come to the realization that life would continue without him. Never again would she see his smile, and never again would he hear her laugh. Never again would she hold his hand, and never again would he make her feel like the most precious girl in the entire world.

Alma heard a truck stop just outside of the front entrance of the orphanage. A door opened and someone came out of the vehicle. Alma heard as a man took a few steps then opened the rear gate of the truck. Something was pulled, a large and heavy object, possibly made of wood. The man moved to position the object from the truck to the front entrance. He made a hard sound on the ground as the object was lowered, and then he dragged the object to lean against the wall near the front door. The man returned to the truck and departed as quickly as he arrived.

The birds seemed busier than normal. They sounded different, louder and more intense than usual. Did they know Dioni was gone? Did this make them happy? Maybe they were sad. Maybe the birds knew something she did not. Maybe she never really cared or paid much attention to birds anyway.

More time passed. Every hour seemed like only a few minutes had gone by. Alma heard the cries of an infant. A few seconds later she heard an adult move in another bedroom. It must be Martita. She always got up when Penelope cried. A door opened. A woman paced quickly toward the cries of the young child. Another door opened, the cries momentarily grew louder, then the door was closed. The child was lifted from her crib.

"Sh sh sh sh sh…" Alma heard.

It was Martita, who gently rocked Penelope with the hope that she would go back to sleep. It almost never worked; there was no sense for Martita to even try. Penelope's sobs slowly came to an end.

Martita stepped out of the room with Penelope in her arms. She walked across Alma's open door. Her *chanclas* made the all-too-familiar sound of being lazily dragged on the cement floor. The footsteps stopped. The dragging sound returned. Martita came and stood at the doorway. She held Penelope and noticed Alma was wide awake.

"She woke up," Martita whispered.

"I heard," Alma responded, annoyed.

"I didn't want you to get her today, so I got up."

"Thank you."

"I was hoping you would be asleep. I'm sorry if I woke you."

"I wasn't. You didn't."

"Okay." Martita rocked the child in her arms as she stood at the doorway.

"Do you need something else?" asked Alma, her frustration evident in her tone.

"N…no. I don't want to disturb you. I…I know with Dioni…that you must be…"

Alma turned her head. She gave Martita the coldest look Martita had ever seen, then returned her head to the exact placement as before.

"I lost my husband a few years ago," Martita whispered. "It was a car accident. I asked him to go to the store to buy something for me and I never saw him again after that."

"I know," replied Alma. "I've been here longer than you."

"Right…right. I just…I still miss him, and I think about him all the time. It doesn't go away, but it does get better."

Alma exhaled, slowly and deeply. She did not care about the widow or her story, nor of the child she held in her arms. The world was much darker today, despite the sun blanketing its light across all of Flores. Alma repositioned herself to face the outdoors. The mountains in the distance were blue, a panoramic view that was as familiar as the voice she missed so dearly.

"Why are the mountains blue here?" she wondered as she absorbed the vivid detail of the start of a new day.

...

Ally had a fondness for Guatemala's blue mountains. She had witnessed the sunrise from almost every vista around the world. So many great memories. She learned the sport of free falling while visiting Victoria Falls, where she and a pair of curious schalows practiced the fine art of graceful flight between the splashes of falling water. She visited the habitat of the chinstrap penguins, who taught her to glide as gracefully in the water as she did in the sky. She witnessed both the sunrise and the sunset while standing at the peak of Mount Everest, where she and a small group of alpine chough's spent hours watching and laughing at the many tourists who attempted to trek the world's highest mountain.

Guatemala was special. Not only did it house the mystic Mayan city – established by birds whose technology was far superior to even the most advanced human societies – it also gave her a sense of belonging. The birds of Guatemala were unquestionably territorial, especially the quetzals, yet they rarely treated her with anything other than utmost respect, like a guest who belonged among them.

Perched high above the ground, on a branch of a mighty ceiba tree, Ally observed the rise of the sun. She thought not of its splendor as it splashed its light over the ancient Mayan jungle, but rather of what she would tell Dioni once he awoke. Dioni was in deep sleep, cradled within a hollow opening on the bark of the ceiba and protected from any potential predators who were anxious to get an early start on breakfast.

Ally wondered if she had chosen correctly and if Dioni would be able to continue a tradition that began prior to the advent of recorded time. It was a legacy as much as it was a responsibility, and it was time to pass it on to the next suitable bird. There was no application process, no way to know whether or not she made the right choice. It was a risk she had to take.

The sun was high above the mountains by the time Dioni awoke. The transition and the distress from the previous day had made him weary; if this was indeed the nightmare he thought it was, then perhaps a few hours of rest would bring him back to his former self. Fifteen hours, even for a teenager, was too much.

Dioni barely made a sound as he stumbled from his perched tree hole. Ally noticed Dioni's waddle as he walked to one of the branches in plain sight of every living being in Tikal. The feathers on his head were tousled and he looked a complete mess; it was an odd sight for one of the world's most beautiful birds.

"Good morning," said Ally. She wondered whether Dioni remembered what occurred the day prior.

Dioni grunted. It was not a bad dream after all.

"Are you hungry?" asked Ally.

Dioni moved only his eyes. He did not care whether breakfast was served that morning.

"I have to tell you something," Ally continued. "Something important."

Dioni did not move. His eyes froze and remained locked in the same position.

"Birds are special, Dioni," she began. Ally turned away from him and paced slowly toward the far end of the large branch on which she and Dioni stood. "We have a certain responsibility on this planet that was given to us millions of years ago. But not all birds are the same. Some have specific responsibilities, like to help clean cities or to protect certain plants, and then we all have a shared responsibility with all other birds. Think of it like being a part of a big boat – some crew members are responsible for the deck, others are responsible for the sails, and so forth, but no matter who does what, the boat has to stay afloat. Does that make any sense to you?"

She looked at Dioni. He blinked. Absolutely no other part of his body moved.

"Okay," she continued, once again pacing. "Every so often, though, you find that a bird has missed its purpose. Like it was meant for so much more but it never had the chance to live up to its potential."

She looked at Dioni, whose expression transitioned to a deep frown.

"Right. We're not there yet," she said.

Dioni was not interested in anything she had to say, evident in his body language.

"I once visited a farm where an eagle thought it was a chicken," continued Ally. "Not like…not like an eagle who was scared or anything like that. No, I mean it was a huge, male eagle who was completely convinced that it was a full-fledged, seed-eating, farmer-raised chicken. I learned that the eagle was raised as a chicken from the moment he hatched. Being a chicken is all he ever knew. He clucked like them, moved like them, and only jumped a few inches off the ground, just like any other chicken on the farm. I didn't make anything of it, other than thinking it was odd for an eagle to behave that way, so I let it be and went on my way."

"Then some time passed and I get a chance to visit this farm again. So I go back and I see this eagle-chicken – who I remembered from my last visit and was curious to see how he was doing – and he seemed sick, like really old. He was outside and just kept to himself as he watched a small group of young chicks playing in the yard. Everyone is minding their business, when in the sky flies the fiercest eagle I have ever seen. I mean, he was just the perfect looking bird, truly a king in the sky."

Dioni's face maintained its original, expressionless demeanor. Ally saw him and continued.

"One of the chicks looks to the sky and sees the eagle, and then asks, 'what's that?' Every chick in the coop looked up and they see this eagle flying way up in the air. The eagle-chicken is the oldest one there, so he looks up too and he says, 'that's an eagle'."

"So the little chicks are all excited because they had never seen an eagle, and one of them raises his little featherless wings and says, 'I want to be an eagle,' and starts pretending to fly like an eagle. Not literally flying, but running around with his arms spread. Then the rest of the little chicks start pretending to be eagles too, and then all of them say they want to be eagles."

Dioni rolled his eyes. The story was already far too long for that time of day. Ally continued.

"Then the elder eagle-chicken gets up and stops them, and says, 'We are chickens. We belong on the ground. We'll never be eagles.'"

She paused and turned to face Dioni. She wondered if any of what she said had made an impression on him. A gentle breeze flowed, the ambient sound of whispering leaves was heard throughout the jungle.

"That's a pretty stupid eagle," Dioni said, the only notion of movement which proved he was indeed not entirely in a fossilized state of being.

"Alright, never mind," Ally responded. "That was a bad way to start the day."

"Chickens are stupid," Dioni said. He more closely resembled a recently woken child than a mature, well-mannered teenager.

"Okay," responded Ally. "We've had enough of that. All done. You're probably hungry."

"I'm tired."

"I know you are."

"I'm hungry," Dioni said. He straightened his posture and stretched his neck; both actions proved more signs of brain activity.

"That's good! Yes, let's get you something to eat," responded Ally. She looked in every direction to search for any nearby food which she could pick for him.

"Bananas."

"We don't have bananas here, buddy," Ally responded, speaking to his current mindset as opposed to his actual level of intellect.

"Ba-na-nas!"

"How about berries? Would you like some berries, big guy?"

Dioni looked down. "I'm tired."

"I know you are."

"I want berries," Dioni responded, in a somber tone.

"Great! Let me get you some berries, okay? You wait in your room and I'll come back with some berries."

"And a banana!"

Ally sighed. "I'll try to find you a banana."

Dioni gave Ally the meanest look he could muster. He exhaled profusely then waddled back to his perched hole. His level of maturity was evident, and Ally had to remind herself and respect that it was only his second morning as a bird.

Dioni peaked his head out of the tree hole. He looked at Ally, whose eyes locked on him as she worried for his every move. Annoyed, Dioni mouthed the word "ba-na-na". He used his wings to emphasize the importance of what he demanded.

Ally immediately turned away and scanned the grounds to search for the nearest source of food.

...

At the very front of the church, by the alter, was a small wooden box which rested on a wooden table and was surrounded by a series of small, white candles. To the side of the wooden box and on the table were photos of Dioni, ones that depicted him at various times in his short life.

Alma liked the photo where she and Dioni smiled. The captured image showed them eating far more ice cream than any 7-year-olds should. They sat on a curb, Alma laughing while holding a spoon, and Dioni – covered in what everyone hoped was melted chocolate ice cream – happy as a child could be. He loved chocolate. He even loved it in its purest form, as cacao beans. He was able to eat them without being baked or anything. What an odd boy.

On the other side of the table was a group photo of all the children of the orphanage, taken just a few years prior. Oscar was in that photo, along with Pedro, Cesar, Elba, Noel, Rafael, the twins Corina and Cindy, Diego, Maria, Ximena, a very young Luis, and Alma and Dioni. Most of the children in that photo had long left the orphanage behind. Alma smiled when she noticed the soccer ball and the oblong-shaped ball in the photograph. The oblong ball was brought by an American visitor, who tried his best and ultimately failed to teach the children the American version of football. He was the one who took the photo of the kids and mailed it to them a few weeks later. It was still in its original frame. Dioni looked so happy.

Alma had seen enough. The box was at a high enough level where everyone could see it, and everyone present at the church knew what was inside. Alma reached into the backpack she carried with her, Dioni's backpack, and pulled from it the two items found in Ipala: a tattered shirt and a worn shoe. She opened the wooden box, which revealed numerous small items that were carefully placed in loving memory by those who had fond recollections of the child who was taken much too soon.

Inside the box were other photos, a few paintings created by the younger children, Dioni's favorite soccer jersey, a very old stuffed animal, a crucifix, a pin from ToursTikal, a neatly placed Guatemalan flag, and a miniature stone carving of the Jaguar temple. He loved Tikal, especially the Jaguar temple…it was only right that a small part of it be buried with him.

Oscar approached the box and stood next to his sister. He reached into his pocket and pulled a small, glass figurine. The object was sculpted to depict the national symbol of the Guatemalan people, the mighty quetzal. The figurine may have boasted a marvel of green, red, and white when it was produced in its original form, but in its current state it was a nearly transparent, sun-bleached rendition of a resplendent jungle bird. Alma looked at her brother, puzzled as to why he would include that particular object along with the other items in the wooden box.

"He liked it," Oscar said to her. "He liked how the colors could change if you hold it up to something."

Oscar placed the glass figurine in Alma's hand. She lifted it and immediately understood what her brother meant. The quetzal was entirely white when held directly towards the ceiling; it was entirely yellow when held in contrast to the surrounding walls; and was mysteriously blue in color when held before the light which penetrated the large stained-glass window. She held it there for just a moment longer.

Oscar interrupted her train of thought. He gently retrieved the figurine from her hand and placed it in the box, then took a few steps back as to not block his sister. Alma followed her brother and placed her selected items in the wooden coffin. She refused to allow the other children to witness her sadness. She paced back. She could not bring herself to leave. As the items came to rest within the coffin, Alma stared at what was left inside. She showed no expression aside from a look of deep sadness.

Oscar noticed Alma's resistance to leave her belongings. He approached the table, stood beside his sister, then slowly closed the lid to the coffin. He did not know what to do nor what to say to her, but he knew that she could not remain standing. He guided her away from the wooden box and toward the nearby pews, where they sat together and observed as more people approached the alter.

. . .

Dioni displayed more signs of life than he had prior to eating a few of the berries. Maternal instincts were not among the strongest of Ally's personality traits, but she understood what it was like to be fifteen years old and forced to undergo a very traumatic experience. If all it took to make Dioni happy was for her to gather a few nearby pieces of fruit, it was the least she could do for him.

There were more berries on Dioni's face and body than anywhere else. He ate and regained his strength, and did so in a more bird-like manner, which was proof of progress.

"What is the fastest way to get to Flores?" asked Dioni, his mouth stuffed with more berries than it should safely contain.

"I can carry you again, unless you want to walk," replied Ally. "With those tiny legs of yours it will take us a very long time."

"Can you fly fast like you did in the cave?"

"No. Not like that. Not here."

"Why not?" Dioni asked. He swallowed the mouthful of berries at once. Ally deeply inhaled and slowly exhaled.

"It's part of something we do, something you have to learn. I can't teach it to you. It's something you have to figure out on your own."

"That's fine," responded Dioni. "I'm not going to be a bird for very long anyway. I just need to let Alma know that I'm okay and then I can change back to being me."

Ally sighed. She wanted to tell him more, but she knew he was too young to understand.

"Dioni…listen, I don't know how to tell you this," began Ally.

"Tell me what?"

"The thing is—"

Whoosh!

Ally was interrupted by a male toucan, who rudely landed between Ally and Dioni. The bird was mostly black in color with an exceptionally large and colorful beak. The toucan made random, wild sounds at Dioni for reasons he was unable to identify.

"Ahh!", Dioni yelled. The toucan used its large beak to push Dioni. "Go away, bird! Go away!"

Dioni fell onto his back. The toucan drew closer to Dioni and displayed clear signs of intimidation. The bird, for its size, was unbelievably territorial.

"*Oye!*" yelled Ally. The toucan immediately stopped. "*No tome ni un solo paso más para adelante ¿Me entiende?*"

The toucan moved its head in every direction to search for the source of the voice that spoke to him.

"*¿Quién habla?*" asked the toucan, nervously.

"*¿No sabe usted quien es ese pájaro?*" Ally asked. The toucan looked at Dioni, who was confused by what was happening.

"You speak toucan?" Dioni asked Ally.

The toucan looked at Dioni with anger in its eyes.

"*Un pájaro extraño que se está comiendo mis bayas,*" said the toucan. He raised his chest and marched forward. He used his size to intimidate Dioni.

"*Un paso más y se arrepentirá por el resto de su vida,*" Ally threatened. The bird stopped once more and looked in every direction. "*Solo un pasito más y caminara el resto de su vida reconocido por toda la selva como el pájaro que le falto el respeto al nuevo* Omega."

Upon hearing the word, "Omega," the toucan lifted his head and changed his demeanor entirely. The toucan appeared worried, as if he did not fully realize the extent of his actions.

"*Disculpe, señor. Discúlpeme, no…n…no sabia,*" said the toucan. His mannerisms became stranger as he spoke in a toucan language Dioni failed to understand.

Dioni became puzzled. What did Ally say to him? Do all alalā's speak toucan?

"*Disculpe, señor* Omega. *Lo que es mío es suyo,*" continued the toucan. He slowly walked away from Dioni, his head slightly bowed. "*Perdone mi insolencia.*"

The toucan paced further back, leapt from the high branch and flew away as fast as his wings could carry him. Dioni and Ally observed as it disappeared into the jungle.

"What happened?" asked Dioni.

"He was lost," responded Ally. "He thought you were someone else."

"You speak toucan? Or do all birds have a special language?"

"Did you understand anything the toucan said?" asked Ally.

"He opened his huge beak and talked," Dioni responded. "Not like making bird noises, but actually saying words."

"Yes! Yes! Great, Dioni! What else? Did you understand any words he said?"

"I don't know…no, I don't think so. And why did he fly away so fast? And why did he suddenly look so scared?"

Ally sighed. "Well, at least you heard him speak and it wasn't random bird noises to you. That's a start."

"A start for what?" Dioni asked as he attempted to wipe away the excess berry juice from his beak.

"If you want to go to Flores, we should probably go soon," said Ally.

She turned her attention to the fully awakened jungle beneath her. She knew he would be relentless in his desire to return home.

"Oh, right!" said Dioni. "Yeah! Flores! Let's go!"

"Okay," responded Ally.

She closed her eyes, lifted her wings and tilted herself forward. Ally dropped from the branch then immediately lifted skyward. She made a wide turn to position herself to grab Dioni by the shoulders. As she approached from above, Dioni moved away and dodged her grasp.

"Wait!" Dioni shouted. Annoyed, Ally circled and returned to the branch. "How do I look?"

"Like an odd-looking blue bird who tried to wrestle but lost against a berry tree," Ally responded.

Dioni immediately lifted his wings to his beak to cleanse himself. In doing so, he noticed other areas of his body with clearly marked berry stains. Dioni panicked and spun in circles as he attempted to locate every stain on his feathered body.

Ally rolled her eyes. He clearly was not the brightest blue bird in the jungle, on multiple levels, but he had the capacity to learn. She lifted from the branch once more, circled around and successfully grasped Dioni by the shoulders. She pulled him away from the branch and flew upward toward the Guatemalan sky.

"Wait! Wait! I'm not done!" Dioni exclaimed. "It's so sticky!"

...

Funeral processions in Flores were traditionally small events. The priest from the local church would say a few words, and a group of people would march behind a casket which was carried by some of the stronger men in the village, usually friends or family of the person who passed, and were then typically followed by a small group of mourners. The entire event resembled a sad parade, where some people sobbed, others just walked and stared emotionless at the gravel-stone ground, and some recited prayers as they followed the procession.

This funeral was different. First, there was no casket but rather a small wooden box which represented the same as the passing of a loved one. It was small enough for four people to carry it with ease. Oscar volunteered among the four; at his age he was strong enough to march alongside the others.

Alma wanted no part of the procession; she went along out of sheer obligation and peer pressure from the other orphans. Given the choice, she would have preferred to personally search every inch of Tikal to find Dioni alive. In her opinion, the search was suspended far too quickly. She knew there was a chance he might still be out there. He would be frightened, but still alive. He would never run away without her nor would he leave her behind without saying goodbye. He could not have just disappeared.

The procession continued along the main street which led to the central plaza. Alma kept her distance from the others; as she marched with the rest of the mourners, she looked at those who just stood to the side and cared not of who or what was in the wooden box. It was not someone they knew, so why would they care? They never knew Dioni. They never knew how good of a person he was, and how he was going to grow up and be the best that ever came from Flores. He was going to be a leader one day and would build a school for the town. He was going to have every street in Flores paved and not just the ones near the village square. He wanted the town to have a restaurant, and the restaurant would be named *Almita's*. It would serve the best food in all of Guatemala and would always have fresh cacao. Dioni and his cacao beans…

All that remained of Dioni was in a large wooden crate. Some items were his, some were just memories of him, and some were random items placed by the children for the sake of saying they did so. The entire event was a sham to Alma, who used all her strength to fight her tears and anger.

Dioni had never seen Flores from the sky, from a literal birds-eye view. He could not wait to see Alma and let her know that he was perfectly safe, albeit in different form. In his mind, she would not care whether or not he looked different.

99

Ally knew what to expect. She saw how Dioni was innocently optimistic. She flapped her wings and towed him through the sky. She thought of how he would react to what he was about to experience. Dioni pointed at the small building a few yards away from the church.

"There!" he said. "Everyone is probably back home by now. Put me down over there."

Ally proceeded as instructed and landed in the small courtyard of the orphanage. The moment he felt the ground beneath his feet, Dioni ran towards Alma's room. He was so excited to see her. His legs and feet where small, which, along with his long tailfeathers, made it far more difficult to run at his usual speed. Nevertheless, Dioni was on a mission. He entered through the open kitchen, which was surprisingly empty. There was no time to wonder why no one was in the kitchen. He turned the corner and saw the common area, which was also strangely empty. He turned back and to the left and ran by the eerily clean and quiet dining room. He passed the bathroom, the main closet and the nun's room, then sprinted towards Alma's open door. If she was anywhere to be found, it was more than likely in her room.

Ally, perched on the branch of a small tree in the courtyard, observed from afar as Dioni ran from room to room. She knew where Dioni headed, and she decided to let him discover it by himself. She flew to the window of Alma's room and waited momentarily for Dioni to arrive.

"Alma! Alma!" Dioni yelled as he ran into her room.

Everything was where he remembered. He was too low to the ground to see the top of Alma's bed, and so he did the next best thing.

He jumped. "Alma!" He jumped again. "Alma!"

There was no response. He repeated the gesture, his arms flailed as he tried desperately to hold himself up longer. No response; no one was in the room except for Ally, who witnessed Dioni's actions from the windowsill. Exhausted, Dioni ceased his actions. He looked to Ally.

"Where is everybody?" he asked. Ally glided down to be at his level.

"They're in the garden, Dioni," she said. "I can take you to them if you would like."

"Yes! Let's go, go, go!" Dioni responded, excitedly.

Ally lifted herself off the cold floor and circled around the small bedroom. Dioni lifted his wings. She once again grabbed him by his shoulders, then together they flew to the open window.

The procession entered the nearby public garden, which was as close to an actual cemetery as the town of Flores was able to attain. There were bushes and trees, and despite it not kept very well, there was a sense of peace in the small patch of land off the unpaved road.

In the center of the garden was a hole in the ground, undoubtedly made by the man who stood off to the side and who held a shovel and perspired profusely. The priest led the procession into the garden and positioned himself in front of the hole. A few steps behind him were the four persons who carried the wooden box. Those who followed the procession gathered around the priest and created a circle, with the wooden box in the middle.

Alma was the last to enter the garden. She looked at the wooden box and stayed toward the back, almost as if to remain unseen and ignored. The priest spoke; he made a series of gestures and recited prayers he read from his book. None of it captured Alma's attention as she was more interested in the odd silence of the garden. For once, there was no wind, no breeze, and no birds making noises of any kind.

From the sky, Dioni was able to see everyone he knew: all of the kids, the nuns, some of the people from the town, and the priest. Dioni found it odd to see the priest in the garden, especially because it was not Sunday.

Ally touched down on a nearby tree which was tall enough to keep herself and Dioni from the view of those in the garden. She hoped for the best but expected the worst.

"Why are we up here?" asked Dioni. "Take me down there so I can—"

"—You can't go down there yet, Dioni," interrupted Ally, in a whisper. "They are in the middle of a ceremony."

"Oh. Okay." Dioni paused. He looked briefly in every direction.

"ALMA! ALMA! ALM—" Dioni yelled. In his mind he was a child who wanted to get the attention of his best friend.

Ally immediately covered his beak and raced the both of them toward the bark of the tree, in desperate hope that they would remain unseen. A blue feather fell from Dioni's wing.

Alma heard the call of a bird; strangely, it was the only audible sound aside from the voice of the priest. She turned in the direction from which the sound was made yet saw nothing. It was as if the bird was suddenly silenced.

"What are you doing?" Ally whisper-yelled at Dioni. "You're a bird, remember? Act like one!"

"Waa woo wirr waa whhy?" responded Dioni, his voice muffled by Ally's wing.

"What?" she asked.

She removed her feathers from his mouth.

"What do birds act like?" Dioni asked.

"Quiet and scared, especially around people! We can't let them see us."

"Why not? Alma's right there!"

"Dioni, you're just going to have to wait, okay?"

"Okay…fine. So angry…" Dioni said in a bitter tone.

Alma looked in every direction above her but was unable to locate the source of the sound. She definitely heard something, but where did it come from?

A small feather fell ever so slowly. It was blue in color, and it belonged to a nearby bird. She failed to notice as the feather landed on her shoulder.

The priest completed the prayers and motioned for the four pallbearers to place the box in the ground, slowly and carefully. Oscar tried desperately to withhold his emotions, which was of little use. A tear of his landed on the wooden box as he assisted to place it into the ground. It was now Dioni's final resting place. The pallbearers released the box and let it be, then turned and walked away.

The priest motioned for the man with the shovel to return to the hole in the middle of the garden. The man wiped the sweat from his brow, lifted the shovel, then walked a few paces toward the hole. He buried the head of the shovel into a pile of dirt beside the hole, and everyone watched as he poured the dirt onto the wooden box.

The emotion of the moment hit Alma like a strike to the chest. The sound of the dirt hitting the wooden box rendered her powerless, as if though every sentiment and every memory of herself and Dioni came to her instantaneously.

"What are they burying?" asked Dioni.

He peaked his head over the edge of the branch to see below. Ally turned her back to him; he must be strong enough to discover this on his own.

A second shovel of dirt was dropped onto the box, which was too much for Alma to tolerate. Each drop of dirt was worse than the last. Seconds felt like hours, and soon the box was almost entirely underground.

Alma ran from where she stood and dove to the ground above Dioni's grave. Dirt from the man's shovel landed on her arms, which she ignored entirely. She frantically removed soil from the top of the box.

"What is she doing?" asked Dioni. He witnessed the entire scene from a perched location. Ally closed her eyes and hunched her back.

Alma opened the top of the box, as if she needed final proof that it would forever house the remains of the love of her life. She removed the lid, which allowed the contents of the box to be revealed to all who were in the garden.

"That's my stuff," said Dioni. "Those are all my things. Why are they...?"

Silence.

Alma rummaged through the items. She wanted one last chance to see it all, to engrave it in her mind and to never forget him. Everyone looked at her in shock as she pushed aside the many artifacts of Dioni's history. She found and pulled his backpack from the bottom of the wooden box.

"Not this!" Alma said. "Not this..." she repeated, her voice slightly higher the second time. She held the backpack tightly. Tears formed in her eyes.

Oscar assisted her from the ground and led her away. She held the bag closely as she and her brother walked to the edge of the small garden. Dioni heard her agony and despair. To him, that was the worst sound ever created.

The priest reached down and resealed the box, then motioned for the man to continue to pour the dirt. Within seconds the hole was filled, the wooden box claimed by the Earth.

Alma and Oscar stood together. He tried to comfort his sister as best he could, but to no avail. She held the backpack in the same manner as when Gabi presented it to her, close to her heart.

The priest and those in the procession walked away from the garden, with Oscar and Alma left by themselves. She refused to leave, despite the pain it brought her to be there. With Dioni gone, Oscar was the next best person to be with her in that moment.

Dioni turned to look at Ally, who had his back to him. He became enraged. Not only was his life stripped from him, he was also forced to witness his own burial. This was cruel, even by supernatural standards. No living being should ever have to endure such pain.

Dioni's eyes filled with tears. Ally sensed she was in danger. She turned her head to look him in the eyes as he approached. To her, this was predictable; she envisioned this from the moment she agreed to bring him back to Flores.

Unable to speak, Dioni breathed heavily as tears streamed down his resplendent face. He stopped and stood beside her. Unable to convey any other sentiment, he lifted his wing as if to strike Ally with all the force and rage his small arm could produce. He yelled the cry of a thousand birds, a pain no other bird could understand. Before he was able to deliver his strike, his mind became too overwhelmed by emotion.

Dioni collapsed onto the long branch. His body rolled to the side, onto the edge of the branch and an instant away from plummeting to the ground. Ally sprang into action; she grabbed him and pinned him against the branch. Dioni was completely unconscious.

Oscar held his sister as she trembled with sorrow. She was weak, though strong enough to stand. Oscar placed his arm around her shoulders then guided her away from the garden. Though he was older and bigger than her, he was only strong enough to partially support her. Alma walked away slowly, with her eyes closed.

Ally pulled Dioni to lift his body away from the edge of the branch. He was a heavy bird, even by Alalā standards. She took a moment to gather her strength, then grabbed Dioni by his shoulders and lifted him away from the garden and toward the mountains. With Dioni unable to provide any balance or assistance, she struggled to maintain her altitude and airspeed.

Alma opened her eyes ever so briefly. In the blur created by her tears and the morning sunlight, Alma saw two long tailfeathers of a bird which hovered gracefully in the distance. With her swollen eyes – filled with sorrow and deep resentment – the long tailfeathers of the bird looked as blue as a cloudless sky.

Chapter Eight

Hidden deep within a space of the Earth which had no business to host life of any kind, buried under centuries of human structures and of civilizations that had come and gone, was the mythic lost city so often sought after by the world's greatest archeological minds. Its magnitude was the definition of vast, and within its structure was the most sophisticated form of technology ever conceived by all living beings.

The walls of the mighty, unequivocally-advanced design of the structure allowed the sun to penetrate and provide natural light, while a series of carefully constructed tunnels and aqueducts provided a constant source of fresh water and oxygen. The construction itself housed two distinct sections under one massive roof. Though there was no one entrance nor exit, the atrium housed metallic structures created by a series of colorful lights, almost as representations of artificial trees.

The existence of this hidden fortress was far beyond the understanding of what was physically possible on any life-sustaining planet. It had stood, strong and steadfast, long before the concepts of both history and time were invented by people. It was both visible and invisible, hidden in plain sight but accessible only to those who knew how to find it. To the untrained eye, it was the largest bird sanctuary on Earth – which was neither a sanctuary nor a place strictly located within the boundaries of the blue planet. In its infinite capability of adequately housing life in all its forms, only one species was allowed access to and from this place of wonder: those who ruled the skies.

Every species of bird that ever lived, whether gifted with flight or talented in a number of ways, had at one point in time found adequate representation by the countless generations of birds who had come and gone over billions of years. This structure was not intended to provide refuge or housing, but rather to enable hundreds of thousands of birds to work in an environment which was most conducive to ensuring the highest quality of productivity.

In this space, all birds were at peace with one another. There existed no predators, prey, nor scavengers among them. Size, age, abilities, color, or gender made no difference to their ability to coexist; so long as they were within this compound, their physical dissimilarities were of little to no importance. The most important characteristic of any bird who worked in the avian kingdom was the ability to negotiate well, and to work quickly and efficiently against an endless cycle of competitors who fought tirelessly for every remaining resource. Second chances were few and far between.

As would an impeccably timed orchestra of rapid movement, hundreds of birds flew, glided, whisked, jumped, walked, zoomed, ran, or waddled in an endless cycle, in every direction. They travelled back and forth, many flew from one area to another, with absolutely no need for navigation. There were no logical flight patterns, no cages, and no restrictions to limit their movements. While hundreds of birds moved independently or in small teams, others huddled in groups and spoke loudly to one another in tones, voices, and noises which only they understood.

The sound created by the innumerable amount of birds was as mythical as it was deafening, as their voices and movements emanated a resonance far beyond what was tolerable for human ears. Yet within the chaos there was control; these birds were present to work, and it was by far the most efficient workspace ever conceived. It was not a preserve or place of refuge for birds, but rather a place where the Earth's most important business was conducted. The entire habitat was constructed for the sole purpose of providing a technologically sophisticated environment for countless generations of birds; it was a global headquarters the likes of which any and every major corporation would envy.

A series of private conference rooms floated among the atrium, where workers had access to conduct meetings while away from the view of others. Every few seconds, one of an endless score of hummingbirds zipped from one place to the next, like tiny couriers who delivered important messages from one location to another.

Along the great wall was a massive screen which projected a multi-dimensional, holographic map of any point of the entire world. No detail was too great for this map to capture, which it did so in actual time or as programmed to simulate a series of pre-calculated conditions. In front of this screen and on the ground level were hundreds of small workstations, open for all to see. Each workstation was custom-designed and built for the bird assigned to that particular space, which corresponded to a specified designation on the large map. Most of the birds assigned to a workstation added personal touches to their spaces, which allowed newcomers the added benefit to easily identify the species of bird, its local field office, its primary objective, as well as its area of responsibility on the colossal screen.

There were no computers, keyboards or wing-controlled devices of any kind. Instead, the birds in their respected workstations were a part of a connected network of glass-like monitors, each of which replied to the commands instructed by the eye and body movements of each bird's workstation. The system was so impeccably programmed that it recognized even the most subtle of motions, which it automatically translated into various commands. The entire system, at a scope and scale beyond the understanding of modern science, was entirely controlled via a series of carefully calculated movements recorded by voice and motion sensors on each monitor.

Every bird who worked on this side of the great wall wore a unique identifier on one side of their heads. The units themselves were clearly visible, not only by their shape and position on the head of each bird, but also by the small row of lights which flashed according to movement or speech. While they all varied in size, the small, crystal-like identifiers provided the added benefit of motion tracking as well as instantaneous language translation. The small device served as a powerful communications tool as well as a global positioning system for the thousands of birds who had access to this domain.

Every so often, a series of seemingly random images displayed on the massive screen. This indicated when a transaction took place or where a particular action was witnessed on Earth. Trillions of mathematical calculations were made in nanoseconds by a system which controlled the most powerful force on the entire planet.

In its magnitude and entirety, the avian wonderland served as the primary location for the trading, negotiating, and exchanging of stock. However, this stock had absolutely no monetary value; with each successful transaction, an action would occur on the screen, which provided the credit to the bird who successfully produced it. At no point was any bird misinformed, confused, or otherwise not told every detail of every transaction. As it was, the birds had perfected the notion of internal communications.

Engraved along the buttresses of what appeared to be a precious, unearthly glass-metallic structure which housed the entire ecosystem under a single roof, was the branding and logo of this inconceivably advanced society: Department of Global Climate Control.

At the very top of the dome-shaped structure was an ultra-luxurious, triangular-shaped executive suite. It contained smaller versions of the large screen seen in the main atrium and was connected to the same network as those who worked within the open workstations. The luxurious suite contained a desk that was made of the most precious wood on Earth – the only lingering remains of a long since extinct tree – which was beak-carved by ancient woodpeckers, the most skilled woodworkers of all time. A single decorative element was visible on the desk, a placard on the front edge.

The only wall which was not open facing, nor which provided a source of light, was the wall behind the desk. On it was a painted portrait of a proud and fearless hooded vulture, a bird whose physical beauty could be summarized as nonexistent. Along the bottom of the frame read a single name, which matched the placard on the desk: ALPHA.

The suite itself was dull and colorless, as though designed to purposely remove a visitor's sense of hope. Color and decorative elements were added by the natural sunlight which glimmered along the perimeters of the suite. Sophisticated artwork hovered near glass-like pedestals; the works of art were not paintings or sculptures of any kind, but rather a collection of holographic images which encapsulated a frozen moment in time. Each moment repeated on an endless cycle. The open walls allowed open access to all birds – all of whom knew better than to arrive without previous approval – but more importantly, allowed the main resident of the suite to have unrestricted access to every inch of his empire.

In a sudden haste, a mockingbird flew through the large, atrium-facing opening. In its beak it held small leaves of various colors, each of which displayed its own aura and cast multi-colored illuminations around the mockingbird. The bird frantically placed each of the leaves on the desk of the executive suite, organizing them perfectly. The light that emanated from the leaves created a series of moving images which contained a specified message understandable only to the intended recipient; they contained no legible writing, but rather a series of animated icons that contained an invisible code.

The mockingbird zoomed toward another opening, which led to a corridor. The bird stopped and stood near a large piece of glowing glass. She then lifted her wings and began a series of motions, which caused the glass to activate. The words "Department of Global Climate Control" projected from the center of the glowing glass.

"Good morning, Mimidae," said a strange voice. The sound came from an unseen audio system within the suite. "Please specify operating instruction."

"Setup opening protocol and startup procedures," responded the mockingbird.

Mimidae moved around the room, going about her daily opening procedures as would any bird with her level of experience. Given that mockingbirds were known and recognized to be the world's finest multitaskers, Mimidae proved to set the standard on this specific stereotype.

"Command confirmed. Meal choice preference, please," responded the voice.

"Beta 4-7-8-7, carrion. I don't know how he is going to take today's briefing, so it's best we not start on the wrong wing today."

"Confirmed."

The sound of the executive food dispenser began as Mimidae heard an unusual noise in the near distance.

"Locate Alpha," Mimidae said aloud. She did not pause from her daily routine.

The resident bird of the executive suite enjoyed the occasional surprise, though it was unlike him to do so on a day when big news was on the horizon. Before the system was able to respond, a large, hooded vulture entered the executive suite. Beside it was a floating tray of food, which held fresh roadkill. The meal itself was as appalling in sight as was the vulture.

The vulture stood proudly, with a build similar to that of an eagle, though the white-and-pink face of the bird gave it a menacing appearance. His back was hunched, as if centuries of being perched to oversee all beneath him had automatically adjusted his spine. The vulture's eyes were deep in color, which gave soulless glances no matter which facial expression the large bird made. His feathers resembled the colors and patterns of rusted iron that likely mimicked what it pushed outward from within.

"Alright! Just in time, Mim!", said the vulture, who did not pay the slightest attention to the mockingbird. "Birds are working, negotiations are happening, I'm on track for another high season, and breakfast comes in right when I get in the office. What am I eating this morning?"

"Carrion, sir," responded Mimidae. "Imported fresh from the Kalahari." She paused her motions and gave her full attention to the vulture.

"Excellent! I love carrion!" said the vulture. "Mim, it's like you know everything about m...wait. It's not meerkat is it? I got sick from meerkat last time. I think I have some kind of mongoose sensitivity."

"No, sir," Mimidae responded. "This specimen has undergone strict inspection to avoid that from happening again."

"Good," said the vulture.

He shuffled his body to his executive desk as if trained by penguins on how to best carry his body weight. The tray of fresh food followed alongside and placed itself directly in front of him, on the desk.

"So what's the status for today, Mim? What's happening on my planet?" the vulture asked as he bent his body and scooped food into his ancient beak.

"All systems are checking-in as normal, sir," began Mimidae. She stood at the front of the desk, only the top of her head visible to the vulture. She spoke as he ate his disgusting meal. "Air quality is checking-in normal across the sectors, pollution is higher in some areas than in others. The skyway system is free of any delays and orders are moving as scheduled. There are no major disasters scheduled for this week."

"That's a shame," responded the vulture, his mouth full of freshly torn, decomposed flesh.

"We do have a minor anomaly in the western jetstream which may cause a few problems."

"Anything we can't handle?"

"No, sir. This is only minor and temporary."

"Good. What else?"

"The roadrunners are pushing heavily for a sandstorm in Arizona. They want to schedule it for some time next week, pending your approval."

"Ah-rooved," responded the vulture.

"I'm sorry, sir?" asked Mimidae. The vulture coughed then swallowed what he held in his beak.

"Approved."

"Got it. The Tibetan pheasants are asking for relief again, sir. They look serious."

"Declined. They'll be fine."

"Okay," responded Mimidae. "We expect negotiations to be successful for rain next week, especially across the highlands."

"Gotcha," said the vulture, rudely.

"A new Omega bird was chosen."

"Good to know."

"Donna requested some time off to watch the college basketball tournament later this month."

"That's fine." The vulture paused mid-scoop and looked up. "Wait, did you say there's a new Omega bird?"

Mimidae slightly lowered her head into her shoulders.

"Yes…sir," she responded, in a slightly higher pitch.

"Well why didn't you say so, Mim?" asked the vulture, joyously. "A new Omega, huh? Ally's out? That's perfect! That's the best way to start my day! Such a useless crow… I guess that's what happens when you get chosen by an owl."

The vulture corrected his posture and became strangely optimistic.

"So what is it now? Something tells me it's a big one. Oh, I hope it's a condor! We can use an Omega with some pizazz."

"Pizzazz, sir?" asked Mimidae.

"Pizzazz, moxie, character, attitude…whatever you want to call it," said the vulture. "As long as it's not like her…all idealistic and whatnot. These new-age birds are gonna be the death of me."

"It's a blue bird, sir."

"A blue jay? That's North American! Oh-hoh, yes…that's perfect! Those birds are easy to negotiate with. We can finally start on phase two!"

The vulture looked at the tray of food before him. He was too excited to continue his meal.

"I'm done," he said, to which the tray responded by immediately dispensing itself into the executive desk.

"It's a blue bird, sir, but it's not a blue jay," said Mimidae.

"What? *Not* a blue jay? Huh. I assumed a Hawaiian bird would choose a successor from North America, especially after…the umm." The vulture paused to think. He looked at Mimidae, who took notes. "Oh please don't

113

tell me it's another tropical bird. It's not a parrot, is it? Ugh, they talk so much. It's like trying to negotiate with Alexander Hamilton."

"No, sir. Not exactly."

"Well that's good," responded the vulture. "If it's not a blue jay, then... what are we dealing with here, Mim?"

Mimidae paused and took a deep breath.

"A quetzal, sir," she said, timidly.

"I'm sorry?" the vulture asked. "I thought I heard you say something crazy. Speak up, Mim."

"A quetzal, sir," she said, louder.

"A quetzal?"

"Yes, sir."

"A blue...quetzal?"

"Yes, sir."

Mimidae took a short step back. She expected the worst. The vulture lifted his prehistoric torso and sighed heavily.

"Now *that's* comedy!" the vulture responded before he burst into hysterical laughter.

"Sir?"

"That has to be one of the weirdest looking birds ever!" he continued between fits of laughter. "And I was once in a comedy troop with a group of shoebills!"

The vulture's laughter grew stronger. Mimidae took a cautious step forward, ever so carefully.

"Did we get sighting confirmation?" the vulture asked.

"Yes, sir," responded Mimidae. "It was first spotted by two bat falcons, then confirmed as the Omega by a toucan. We received word from the Mayan kingdom that a blue bird was trespassing, although they did not know it was the Omega, sir. They refused to say whether or not it was a quetzal."

The vulture's laughter slowly subsided. It was a perfect start to his day, which came as a shock to Mimidae.

"Well, Mim," the vulture said, "I guess there's only one way to find out." He turned his head as if to address a bird from afar. "Donna!" he shouted.

Four hummingbirds instantly appeared from the atrium opening. They stopped short of striking the executive desk.

"I only need one," said the vulture.

Three of the four hummingbirds turned and departed as fast as they had arrived; the remaining hummingbird hovered to be at eye-level with the vulture, though at a respectful distance.

"Donna," the vulture began, "send a directive to the puffins to draft a global memo for a new Omega."

The hummingbird nodded then zoomed back in the direction from where it entered.

"Mim," the vulture continued, "we need to make a good impression this time."

'Sir?"

"A positive one. I never really cared for Ally. We butted heads from day one, and I don't need that this time around. No need to delay the inevitable, right?"

"As you wish, sir," she responded.

Mimidae exited the room and walked toward the long hallway at the far entrance near her perch station.

The vulture lifted his rusted wings and stretched his body as he inhaled deeply. He moved from behind his executive desk and walked to the large opening which overlooked the atrium. From his vantage point he was able to see the enormity of his empire.

His eyes opened wide as his repulsive cheeks filled with the air that came from his lungs. He once again burst into laughter.

"A blue quetzal!"

Chapter Nine

Dioni paced back and forth along the edge of a large body of water. In the distance was the immaculate landscape of the Guatemalan highlands. Though still in his home country, the location was entirely unfamiliar to him. The volcanos looked pristine, their reflection glistened in the water. From his location there was little evidence of people nearby, with the exception of small plastic objects washed onto the shore.

The two birds were in plain sight, with no trees to provide shade or protection from potential predators. It made absolutely no difference to Dioni; he was furious, and his demeanor clearly showed it. Every so often he stopped and looked up, as if he attempted to express that which was on his mind, only for him to return his gaze downward and continue to pace back and forth. In doing so, Dioni made a small trail for himself to follow.

"Explain it to me again," said Dioni, an anger evident in his tone of voice as he looked at the ground beneath his steps.

"Dioni, I already told you like 12 times," responded Ally.

She was ankle-deep in the water. She looked out to the mountains; it was a sunny day. She enjoyed the splendor of nature's beauty.

"Then explain it again," said Dioni.

Ally shook her head and looked down at the water. She saw her talons. In her current state her eyes had the ability to pierce through the water.

The lack of reflection made no difference to her.

"It was not entirely about you being at the wrong place at the wrong time," she began. "There is something about you that—"

"—That chose this," Dioni interrupted. "Yes, I got that. So I'm some kind of 'chosen one' to be a mega bird."

"No, Dioni. That's not how it works."

"How *what* works?" Dioni asked, angrily. "I was a 15-year old person two days ago, and now I'm a bird."

"By *it*, I mean that you weren't chosen." Ally paused. She looked up and turned her body to see Dioni's face. "Wait, you're 15?"

"Yeah. Why?" asked Dioni.

"Well that explains the tailfeathers. Someday you're going to thank me for having those."

"What?"

"Dioni," Ally continued. "It's difficult to explain, and even more difficult to understand – I know – but this is something that *you* chose."

"How could I have chosen this?" Dioni replied, his emotions evident in his response.

"Somewhere deep inside that 15-year-old brain of yours is a desire to do something special. Whether you know it or not."

"I just wanted to visit all the places that Alma kept talking about in the books she read," Dioni said, in obvious frustration. "And now I'm a bird, and she thinks I'm dead. How is *this* something I *wanted* to happen?"

"I don't know, Dioni. Every Omega bird is different. It's just something that you're going to have to lear—"

"—Have to learn. I get it."

Dioni sighed. Even after repeated telling, he was far from understanding how and why this had occurred. He turned his back to Ally and continued to pace along his trail. Ally stepped out of the water.

"This world has a delicate ecosystem, which requires a strict balance."

"And how is that my problem?" responded Dioni, rudely.

"If there is no balance, then the entire ecosystem will collapse."

"And birds are responsible for maintaining the balance."

"No, Dioni,' Ally responded. "Birds control only one portion of the ecosystem. Each type of bird has certain responsibilities, but every bird has a shared responsibility."

"Arrggh!" Dioni groaned. "You're not making any sense!"

"The quetzals!" responded Ally. She raised her tone to match Dioni's. "Do you remember what they were doing?"

"Yeah. Some kind of weird dance in front of a big TV."

"Yes, right. But what else?" Ally asked. "Did you see them pull tiny globes out of the water? They look like glowing marbles."

Dioni turned his attention to her.

"They weren't pulling them out," he responded. "They lifted them with their mind or something. It was so strange."

"Yes! That's their primary responsibility as a society."

"To pull glowing marbles from water?"

"No, not that," Ally responded, optimistically. "Those tiny globes are mystic seeds. They have been cultivated by the quetzals for hundreds of thousands of years."

"So quetzals are farmers?" Dioni asked.

He slowly walked toward Ally.

"Not exactly…more like protectors," she replied. "They're a native culture. Their responsibility is to protect and supply life-energy to criollo seeds."

Dioni's confusion was beyond measure.

"Criollo seeds?" He paused. "So it's a chocolate factory down there?"

Ally rolled her eyes. The kid was just not going to get it.

"No, they don't make chocolate," she said to him. "It's like…how can

I explain it?"

Ally looked to the water. She saw a small force of energy formed by the stream, which created a pattern that circled around her legs. It was invisible to all but her.

"How about this?" Ally continued. "You know about the Mayan people who built Tikal, right?"

"Yes," Dioni responded.

"Okay good. To the people, according to legend, cacao was provided by the gods."

"I know that."

"But it had to come from somewhere, right? As cacao developed, and after determining how important cacao was to the balance of the ecosystem, the quetzals were assigned with that responsibility and they've been doing it ever since, for thousands of yea—"

"—Who assigned it to them?" Dioni interrupted.

Ally momentarily froze; he might finally understand.

"The Alpha bird," she said.

It was too much for Dioni to comprehend. He placed his left wing over his face and shook his head.

"And who or what is an Alpha bird?" he asked, annoyed by her vague responses.

"The Alpha bird is in charge of assigning responsibilities to every bird on Earth."

"That's a lot of birds."

"Right! It is! So instead of assigning a job to every single bird, the system is separated by bird types. Quetzals are responsible for criollo seeds and ceiba trees, and they govern themselves. But there has to be someone to make sure they do it properly, and that they are not taking resources away from other birds. Someone has to control the balance. Does that make sense?"

"Yes," Dioni responded. "In other words, the quetzals can't take what the toucans might need in order for them to do their jobs."

"Yes! Right! Excellent!" Ally shouted, victoriously.

"So what do the toucans do?" Dioni asked.

"We'll get to that, but let's make sure you understand it first. So if the Alpha bird creates the responsibilities to establish the balance, there must be another bird who ensures that all birds are doing what they were assigned to do."

"And that's the mega bird."

"The *O*-mega bird."

"Fine, the *O*-mega bird," Dioni said in a taunting manner.

Dioni turned and once again walked away from Ally. He wanted nothing to do with any of what she explained.

"Dioni," she continued. "It's part of a delicate balance. That's all I can tell you."

"So what do I do now?" Dioni asked. "Do I talk to someone, or how do I tell the person in charge that I don't want to do this? How does it work?"

"It's not like that, Dioni," Ally said. She looked up and closed her eyes. "There is a way to get you back."

"Back to being me?" Dioni changed his tone. He suddenly became interested in what Ally had to say. "How? What do I have to do? Can we do it now?"

"It's part of a choice you have to make, if you just list—"

"AHHH! There you go with that again!" Dioni marched directly to her, his patience long worn thin. "If I can be me again, and not this...this... bird, then do it!"

"I can't."

"Why not?"

"Only the Alpha bird can do that. It's something you're going to have to negotiate with him."

"Negotiate? With a bird?" Dioni asked.

The thought of it alone seemed ridiculous.

"That's how the system works, Dioni," she responded, maintaining her composure. "There must always be an Alpha and an Omega. Everything is a negotiation with the Alpha bird. If you absolutely must be your old self again, that's the only way."

Dioni turned away from her.

"Fine…how hard can it be to negotiate with a bird?" he asked. "What do I have to do or where do I have to go?"

"You have to get through the portal," responded Ally.

Dioni shot her a puzzled look.

"Portal? Can't we just send a message or something?"

"Birds stopped using messaging systems decades ago." Ally responded. "Portals are hidden but can be anywhere. Only certain birds are allowed access."

Dioni tossed up his wings.

"Do I need a few falcons to chase me? Because that seemed to work last time," he said, briefly recalling the encounter that led him to the Mayan kingdom.

"No, you don't. You have the permission you need. But there's a catch."

"And what is *that*, exactly?" Dioni asked.

"You don't know how to fly," Ally responded.

"So? Birds that don't fly can't get in?"

"All birds fly, Dioni. They might not lift, but they can all fly. Some just have to fall."

"Fall? That's it?" Dioni questioned. "I can do that! We could've been there hours ago."

He jumped and landed on his side, enacting the advent of a short fall. Nothing happened, nothing changed. He made more attempts at the same, with no success. Ally watched in partial amusement. Dioni then changed his strategy; he walked away and tripped on his own two feet, nearly collapsing on his face.

"It's not working, this falling idea of yours," Dioni said angrily, with his beak on the soiled ground.

Ally reached her limit with Dioni. He was just a child, and he was never going to understand unless he was forced to do so. With his back to her and his face on the ground, Ally lifted up and flew slightly above the surface. Dioni failed to notice her actions, and with the same silence and swiftness that she used to lift from the ground, she grabbed Dioni by his legs and raised him skyward.

Dioni was unable to say a single word. Instantly he was upside-down, hundreds of meters above the ground. From a distance the scene looked surreal: a crow flew skyward, holding a blue quetzal by its legs and lifting it to majestic heights.

"What are you doing?" Dioni shouted.

He used his wings to fight the tailfeathers that flapped on his face.

"You have to fall, Dioni!" she responded.

She spoke loudly and clearly, over the sound of the rushed wind.

"ARE YOU CRAZY?"

Ally flew further and further above the surface. The two birds were far higher than any altitude a natural being could survive. There was peace among the solidarity; it was the advantage the Omega bird had over all the others.

This was the true-to-life reenactment of Dioni's worst nightmare. Motivated by intense fear and more adrenaline than his young body had ever produced, he struggled and attempted to find refuge in any direction. He freed his eyes and looked up and saw a surface where colossal trees appeared as small as blades of grass.

Having gained the necessary altitude, Ally's climb came to a sudden halt. No sound was heard. She flapped her wings to maintain her distance in the air above the clouds.

"Ally, what are you doing?" Dioni asked. He realized what was to occur next.

"Just keep your eyes open and look towards the ground, okay?" she responded. "If the ground gets too close just open your wings and pull your head back."

"Pull my whaaa—" were the only words he was able to utter as Ally released her grasp, which instantly forced gravity to pull him back toward the ground.

Alas, for one precious moment, there was relaxing silence. Ally flapped her wings and looked down. She saw as the blue bird fell faster and faster towards the Earth.

"That'll shut him up."

The sound a quetzal makes as it screams in pure terror while falling from an unfathomable altitude is far different than the songs it sings on a regular basis. Dioni learned this lesson the hard way. As he fell at an airspeed far greater than what was naturally possible, Dioni dove heard-first toward the ground below.

He became desperate. He struggled and fought the elements that worked against him and did all he knew to slow his pace. Gravity and the wind worked together, pulling his body down while pushing his feathers in every direction. He discovered that he was able to stop twirling in the air by keeping his beak pointed in the same direction in which he travelled. This made him fall even faster, like a tiny, blue-feathered missile in the sky. Dioni headed beak-first in the direction of his oncoming doom.

The fierce wind brushed his eyes and made them water. As tears streamed from his face, Dioni saw what appeared as another quetzal, which flew directly at him from below. The odd quetzal's airspeed matched his own, and though it physically resembled a bird, it was unlike any in the universe. To Dioni – whose natural inclination was both panic and survival – the strange quetzal looked as though it was made entirely of light. It was a pristine image of a quetzal, an exact replica of himself, only void of visible color.

For the briefest of moments, Dioni saw the other quetzal and temporarily forgot his fast-approaching demise. He failed to notice his distance to the ground as his eyes fixated on every movement of the mysterious bird. It copied Dioni's every motion and flew directly at him at the same speed in which he fell; neither bird had a mechanism to stop one another.

Dioni quickly concluded that he had only a few moments left to live. He would either die on impact with the ground, or upon crashing into the mysterious quetzal. With certain death only a few seconds away, Dioni opened his wings. The bird of light copied Dioni's actions then gained both speed and altitude; a midair collision was inevitable. An instant before impact, Dioni widened his wingspan, turned his head and closed his eyes – the exact behavior of a bird who braced for sudden trauma.

The two birds collided in dramatic fashion. Dioni absorbed the light from the mysterious quetzal, which, at the exact moment of impact, created a sonic boom that resonated for miles. A blue wave of light and sound was emitted by the collusion, which was absorbed by the light of the sun. Dioni instantly disappeared from the sky and was transported to an alternate dimension.

There was no sound – no wind howling, no flapping of feathers, no screams of a blue quetzal. Dioni was both here and there, anywhere and everywhere, surrounded by a nothingness which was hidden within view of the natural Earth.

Dioni opened his eyes. He glided through a transparent tunnel where he was able to see a view of nature unlike any other. The tunnel was not governed by physical laws, but rather by streams of energy in the form of light. As if looking at a star-soaked sky of a cloudless night, Dioni saw the visual representation of nature's overwhelming force. Every seed buried in the ground; every root, branch, and leaf of every tree; every plant, every animal, every fish, every bird, and every source of natural life from every living being on Earth, provided a source of energy. The array of space transcended color, time, and any logic by which life itself was possible.

Dioni made no effort in his movement. With his wings spread, he glided through the portal and looked in every direction. The light embraced his every move, which created an aura around his body. In this space he was neither dead nor alive, neither awake nor in a dream, but rather in a state of living energy. As rapidly as Dioni transcended to this form of existence, the particles of his aura swiftly drifted away, which left a trail of blue-colored globes as proof of his movement. He did not fly, nor float, nor glide, nor was he carried. He was the energy that always existed, and it was through the same energy that he transcended from one dimension to the next.

From the vastness of the portal appeared another bird. The bird's aura was made entirely of a golden-yellow beam of light, accented in the color red. It was clearly a bird, though unlike any Dioni had ever seen. The bird's eyes were completely invisible, and it had a small, pointed beak. The bird transcended effortlessly as it glided to match Dioni's speed and location. Dioni's nervousness intensified as the bird approached.

"Welcome to the Department of Global Climate Control," said the strange bird.

"The *what?*" asked Dioni.

"Please standby as we prepare for your initial arrival," responded the bird.

"What are you saying to me?"

The strange bird increased its speed. It placed itself in front of Dioni, then disappeared as it burst into a series of lights and particles which flowed around Dioni but failed to touch him. Dioni covered his eyes as he glided through the dust. With his wing blocking his frontal view, he looked to his side and noticed other beams of light. Each ray was another bird, and thousands of them travelled in every direction. Together, the flock of transcending birds created a visual display the likes of which no spectrum of color could contain.

Each bird, in the form of a beam of light, slowly descended onto an invisible platform, where they stopped and walked or hopped for the remainder of the distance to their destination. The energy emitted by each bird slowly dissipated as they moved forward, as if they passed through a set of invisible automated doors. To Dioni, it appeared as if every bird walked through a forcefield then completely removed itself from existence.

The red bird, which moments ago became a series of particles, returned as a physical being. This startled Dioni, who understood nothing of what took place. The red bird reduced its speed and glided to be beside Dioni. The two birds looked at one another.

"Your landing coordinates are clear," said the red bird.

"What does that mean?" Dioni asked.

"Caution," responded the red bird. "Your velocity is greater than required for successful entry."

"My what?"

"Caution. Your velocity is greater than required for successful entry."

"What are you telling me?"

The dimension in which Dioni glided, along with the red bird that travelled beside him, instantaneously disappeared the moment he passed through an automated barrier. Before he was able to understand what occurred, Dioni once again found himself at a great height in the sky. Beneath him, however, was a rotunda – a massive complex where thousands of birds glided in every possible direction. Dioni drifted aimlessly in the artificial sky, in a state of amazement by what he saw.

If this was some type of avian zoo, it was by far the most sophisticated and technologically advanced bird refuge ever conceived. Dioni saw walls upon walls of images projected onto sophisticated screens; some displayed charts, numbers and figures, while others served as communications mechanisms. Between the screens were a series of open spaces and private rooms in various sizes, each with differentiating décor.

The avian kingdom was entirely occupied by birds, hundreds upon thousands of them in every possible size and shade of color, each of whom wore a sophisticated headset. The headpieces were circular in shape, were worn on either side of the head, and contained a small light which blinked with every spoken word or motion of the bird on which it was placed. They were more than communications tools, but rather a combination of body-scanning technology that understood vocal commands, which enabled all birds to communicate by voice as well as through body language. Only one type of bird did not wear the headgear: the scores of hummingbirds who zipped in every direction – most in small groups, few by themselves.

Every conceivable class of bird existed in this habitat. Though impossible to comprehend by the standard limitations of human science, it was far more than an ultra-sophisticated communications center. It, too, was a place of business. At the highest peak of the massive dome – and scattered about at key points along many walls, on every screen, and spelled out in incredibly large print on the domain floor – were the words which defined the supernatural ecosystem: Department of Global Climate Control.

With no knowledge of how to navigate himself or reduce his speed, Dioni glided toward oncoming aerial traffic. He nearly crashed with multiple birds, each of which warned him to stop or slow down, or yelled at him for flying in the wrong direction. The same laws of flight and physics which governed the Earth were also prevalent in this space, which left Dioni with no automated system to guide his path. He kept his wings open as wide as he could, and navigated direction by shifting himself from one side to another. Unfortunately, shifting his weight was only a temporary solution; gravity had perfected what was to happen to him next. He shifted the front tips of his wings downward, which forced him to dive. Dioni closed his eyes and braced for impact.

A tall, pink-colored bird, with long and skinny legs, minded her own business and watched as a series of numbers displayed on a large video screen. She was calm, and she stood patiently as she waited to record and report data that was important for her particular region. She was one of perhaps four dozen different birds who did much of the same, though spread across a much larger area. As the numbers she awaited displayed on the screen, she was unexpectedly surprised by an object which struck her backside.

"*Ay!*" exclaimed the pink bird.

A small puff of pink feathers drifted aimlessly behind her. She turned around and saw nothing out of place; not a single bird noticed nor cared for what had occurred. She then looked down and saw a blue ball of feathers on the surface. She bent down for a closer look, then noticed Dioni, who shifted onto his back and who seemed as though he had flown into a wall.

"Pues chico, hay que tener cuidado a la entrada, ¿no crees?" said the pink bird, in a strong Puerto Rican Spanish. Her tone was polite and friendly, almost as if she felt bad for the blue quetzal.

The focus in Dioni's eyes slowly returned. Still on his back, he looked straight ahead and froze as he noticed the enormity of the bird. She was almost entirely pink in color, with two long, slender, flesh-colored legs and a very long neck which allowed her to tower over most other birds. Her beak pointed downward, and her eyes were a soft yellow with a distant expression. She was as graceful as could be expected of all Caribbean flamingos.

"Alpha?" mustered Dioni as his lungs slowly regained air.

"¿Tu buscas el Alfa?" the flamingo responded. *"A ver."*

Dioni was unable to understand what she said.

"¡Ah! Ya sé." She stood up and looked toward the open dome. *"¡Donna!"*

Three hummingbirds appeared almost instantly.

"Solamente uno," the flamingo told the hummingbirds, two of which departed as fast as they had arrived. *"Este hombre busca el alfa. ¿Lo puede llevar a la oficina ejecutiva?"*

The hummingbird responded by a series of gestures made with its small body. Both she and the flamingo turned their heads downward and looked at Dioni. He failed to move.

The hummingbird nodded then zoomed to be at eye-level with Dioni. The hummingbird motioned for Dioni to follow, then zoomed to the open airspace. He remained motionless on the surface. The hummingbird returned, repeated the same gestures, then zoomed away once more. He failed to move.

The hummingbird returned once again, repeated the same motions, then waited momentarily for Dioni to follow. He did not understand the body language of the small bird. Annoyed, the hummingbird zoomed to be at eye-level with the flamingo. As the small bird made a series of quick gestures to its taller counterpart, Dioni noticed how the light on the flamingo's headgear changed color and blinked with each of the hummingbird's movements.

"*Ey, azulín,*" the flamingo said as she looked down to Dioni. "*Donna quiere que la sigas.*"

The look in Dioni's eyes proved he was far more confused than frightened.

"*Míralo,*" the tall bird said to the hummingbird. "*Pobrecito azulín no sabe ni donde está, ni que le está pasando.*"

The tall bird bent down to be at a closer level to Dioni. She used her head and beak to direct Dioni via non-verbal commands. As she motioned, she spoke very slowly to him.

"*Siga a ella para ver el Alfa. El…Alfa…Alfa.*"

The flamingo lifted her head upright as Dioni came to his feet. The hummingbird motioned for him to follow, then quickly zoomed away. Dioni's eyes followed the small bird as it momentarily disappeared into a sea of avian chaos, then returned, more annoyed than it had been previously. It hovered in place with its eyes open wide. Dioni looked at both birds.

"I don't know how to fly," said Dioni.

The light on the flamingo's headgear once again blinked and changed colors. The hummingbird and the flamingo looked at one another. They fully understood what he said, though were puzzled as to why a mature quetzal was unable to fly.

"*El elevador entonces. ¿Pues qué otra, chica?*" the tall bird said to the hummingbird.

They both shrugged their shoulders, and the hummingbird once again motioned for Dioni to follow. This time, however, the hummingbird stayed near and waited for Dioni to walk in the same direction. The flamingo pointed her mighty wing in the direction both she and the hummingbird wished for him to go. Reluctantly, he did as instructed, like a nervous child unsure whether or not it was all an elaborate prank.

Dioni followed the hummingbird who hovered nearby. He was in awe as he walked and looked in every direction, distracted by the countless number of birds who filled the space. Ahead of him, the hummingbird paused and hovered in place as she waited for Dioni to catch up. The same process was repeated more than once.

It took more time than what the hummingbird would have preferred, but at long last she and Dioni made their way to the elevator bay. The elevators were designed for both small and tall flightless birds, and though there were entrance and exit doors, the entire elevator system was completely hallow. The hummingbird used her long beak to press a button which activated one of the smaller elevators. As she waited for the doors to open, the hummingbird positioned herself to be at eye-level with Dioni. She avoided eye-contact, which was well known behavior for all hummingbirds who dreaded the idea of forced conversation with other birds.

A sound was heard behind them, followed by the sliding of a glass door. Dioni turned in the direction of the sound. He saw two enormous ostriches step out from the elevator, followed closely behind by an emu. They laughed and spoke amongst themselves in what sounded like two different languages. The ostriches spoke in English, though with a South African accent, while the emu spoke in a native Australian dialect. The three birds understood one another perfectly.

A second sound was heard, and the smaller elevator door opened. Inside the elevator were three emperor penguins and four gentoo penguins, none of whom said a word but who all gave Dioni a look of judgement as they exited the elevator and walked away from him and the hovering hummingbird. The hummingbird flew in, followed closely behind by Dioni, then used her beak to press a button at the very top of the floor selection panel, which immediately launched both birds to a higher floor.

The hummingbird floated at eye-level with Dioni; her wings flapped at an incredibly fast rate. Both of the birds looked straight ahead as they waited for the elevator door to open. The hummingbird turned its head and looked at Dioni. She visually scanned his entire body, from bottom to top, and absorbed how strange it was to see such an odd bird. In the reflection of the glass door, Dioni noticed how the small bird inspected him. He turned his head to look at the hovering bird, who then immediately shifted her body and faced forward in fear of being caught.

The elevator came to a stop. The glass doors opened and revealed the executive lobby of the Department of Global Climate Control. A few paces ahead of the elevator entrance was a desk made entirely of crystal, which changed color when viewed from various angles.

Mimidae was perched behind the desk; she made intricate motions with her wings, directed at a projected screen. Aside from a few decorative items placed carefully at arm's length, the only noticeable objects in her workspace were an autographed portrait of a bird, and a glass containing a ruby-colored liquid. Beyond Mimidae's workstation were two large, iridescent doors, which served as a barrier between the lobby and the executive suite.

Dioni followed as the hummingbird exited the elevator. The hummingbird zoomed to the desk and made a series of motions directly in front of Mimidae. She then stopped her rapid movement and hovered; both she and Mimidae turned to look at Dioni. The hummingbird noticeably chuckled, then immediately zoomed away.

"Hello! Welcome to the Department of Global Climate Control," Mimidae said to Dioni, who stood at attention directly in front of her desk. "I was informed that you would like to see the Alpha?"

"Uhh…," Dioni reluctantly responded. "Ye…yes…pul…please."

"Just a moment."

Mimidae made a motion which caused the projected image on her screen to close. She then hopped away from her perch and paced to the executive suite.

Dioni heard a mumble. It was Mimidae. She spoke at an inaudible tone, almost at a whisper.

"Sir, there is a blue bird here to see you," Dioni heard, just barely.

"What blue bird?" responded the not-so-subtle voice of a larger, more prominent bird. "I know lots of blue birds, Mim. You're gonna have to be more specific."

A pause. Dioni was unable to hear her response. A loud thump was heard.

"He's here? As in *here*, here?"

A pause. Dioni leaned forward in an attempt to overhear the conversation.

"Uh…yeah, sure," they elder voice continued. "Let…um…let him in. Let him in."

Dioni heard Mimidae pace back to her workstation. She came into Dioni's field of view when the elder voice forcefully whispered, "Wait! What's his na—?"

"—Right this way," Mimidae said to Dioni.

She completely ignored the question asked by the vulture and pointed her wing in the direction of the executive suite. Dioni cautiously walked further into the lobby, through the iridescent doorway, and into the lavish room. Mimidae stayed at a respectable distance.

The executive suite was unusually cold. Though natural light entered the room from nearly every direction, it was the shadows which seemed more prominent to Dioni. There was a severe lack of color, which was not immediately understood until the moment Dioni gazed upon the proprietor of the luxurious establishment. It was a bird of nightmares, who stood prominently and with a smile which matched the cold and emptiness of its domain.

"So you're the new Omega, huh?" said the Alpha bird.

Though he made no motion towards the sentiment, it was the ugliest bird Dioni had ever seen.

"Ye—Yes, sir," responded Dioni, nervously.

Prior to that moment, Dioni had only ever heard of vultures, and had at one point possibly seen one in a photograph or on television. What he saw before him was not the bird he envisioned.

"Sir?" said the vulture. "You hear that, Mim? He's respectful."

Mimidae sighed, rolled her eyes, then paced back to her desk.

"Please," the vulture continued, "I am the Alpha. 'Sir' is an unnecessary formality."

"Hello, Mr. The Alpha," responded Dioni.

He reached out his wing to formally greet the Alpha, as if they were both human.

"Oh, that's also not necessary," the vulture responded. "No hands. You're good."

Dioni lowered his wing.

"So…what did you say your name was?" asked the Alpha.

"Dioni, sir."

"The only *what?*"

"No no, not *the only*. Dee-oh-nee. Dioni."

"Dioni? Huh…that's a unique name for a unique bird," said the Alpha. "Okay, I get it. I'm liking it. So, Dee-oh-nee, are you hungry?" He paced toward a pile of vile meat stacked near a large window which faced the atrium. "I had this brought in from Madagascar. It's yours if you want it."

Dioni glanced at the Alpha's disgusting offer. It took almost everything within him to not vomit on the spot.

"No…no, I'm not very hungry, sir," Dioni responded, respectfully.

"Please, not 'sir'."

"But thank you for your offer."

"You sure?" asked the Alpha. "Okay, more for me later then."

The vulture made a motion, at which point the stack of vile meat disappeared into the floor, behind a piece of colored glass. He used his wing to point to two perched pieces of elegant wood, slightly elevated off the floor.

"Have a seat, Dioni. Stay a while."

"Thank you," Dioni responded. The two birds paced toward the wooden perches.

"So what brings you to the main office today?" asked the vulture.

Though he sat, the Alpha's perch was strategically placed to be much taller than Dioni, in a menacing way. Dioni was forced to look up to him.

"You are the Alpha bird, right?" Dioni asked.

"He is I and I am him."

"I was told you can change me back to being me. To not be a bird."

"Oh yeah? Who told you that?"

"Ally…the black bird?"

The vulture sighed.

"Ah. Yes. Ally. The black bird. I am familiar with her. She's a Hawaiian crow. Have you ever been to Hawaii, Dioni?"

"No."

"That's a shame. You should visit there if you can. It's a beautiful place. Nice people. There's so much to see and do."

"Maybe someday when I'm old—"

"—So you want to change back to being you, huh?" asked the Alpha. "Why the rush?"

"I'm a bird."

"I see that."

"And I shouldn't be," said Dioni. "Or…I don't want to be a bird. I want to be me."

The Alpha stood and turned his back to Dioni. He inhaled deeply, pretending to be in deep thought.

"Well, have you ever tried being a bird?" the Alpha asked.

"N…no, this is new to me," Dioni responded, confused by the question.

"Well then how do you know you *don't* want to be a bird if you have never *been* a bird?"

Dioni had no response. The vulture turned its decrepit body to once again face him.

"Kid," he continued, "you can't just rule out the chance for something different in your life. Otherwise you're going to miss out on so many great things."

"Does that mean you can't change me back?" Dioni asked.

"What? No, of course I can. I'm the Alpha, I can do practically anything. What I'm saying is why not try being a bird for a few days and…see if you like it."

"But…" Dioni contemplated. "I don't know anything about being a bird."

"So? Neither did I when I was your age and look at me now. This could be your office in a few years if you play your cards right."

Dioni looked around the room. Absolutely nothing of the setting impressed him.

"I'm not supposed to be a bird," Dioni said.

"Why not?"

"I don't know. The birds look at me in a strange way. Some of them attacked me."

"That's all a misunderstanding," the Alpha responded. "No bird is going to try to eat you. But I agree, you are a strange looking fellow…even for a tropical bird."

Dioni was unhappy with the Alpha's response. He did not choose to be a bird, he had no desire to be a bird, and the burden of being ridiculed for something not of his own accord was not a method to encourage him to think otherwise.

"Alright, kid," the Alpha continued. "You're not convinced, I get it. But before you go back to being you, let me show you what you are going to miss out on. The least we can do is educate you about avian culture."

The Alpha walked toward the executive lobby and motioned for Dioni to follow. Dioni was hesitant but chose to follow along as the vulture exited the suite through the translucent doors.

"I'm going to give our Omega here a quick tour," the Alpha said to Mimidae, who sat behind her desk and ate seeds. "Hold all my calls 'till I get back."

With a full beak, Mimidae nodded her head to acknowledge the Alpha's request. She waived her wing in front of a sensor, which displayed a digital layout of the executive suite. She then touched a button on a projected screen, which turned a small icon of a vulture from green to red.

"Thanks, Mim," said the Alpha.

Dioni followed closely behind as the vulture turned the corner and walked out of the lobby.

Mimidae waited momentarily for the Alpha to be out of sight. Once clear, she lifted her head in the same direction in which Dioni and the Alpha exited. Assured that they were gone, she returned her attention to the projected screen on her workstation and waived her wing, which instantly changed the image on her screen. Mimidae ate from her bowl of seeds while she watched her favorite movie.

Chapter Ten

"The most important thing you need to know about birds is that we're a lot more than just pretty feathers and noisemakers," said the Alpha. "Well most birds, I should say, are more than just songs and feathers."

The elder bird walked beside the blue quetzal as they passed through an elaborate corridor which displayed a series of incredibly realistic works of art. On the walls were massive, extravagant portraits of various scenes of nature from different parts of the world. As if painted and crafted by the finest artists in history, the abundantly sized rectangles displayed moving images which were so realistic that Dioni could not tell whether or not they were made by hand.

"What's so great about being a bird?" Dioni asked, rudely.

"Are you kidding me?" responded the Alpha. "Birds see everything. Just ask any bird, 'what's the craziest thing you've ever seen?' They'll gladly tell you."

The Alpha paused before one of the large portraits. He lifted his wings to it, then made a rectangular shape with just the tips of his feathers. His movement created a white screen within the portrait, which he stopped after the shape reached the size of his choice.

"Here, take a look at this," continued the Alpha. He leaned his upper body toward the small, rectangular shape he created. "Roll story reel...

umm…one one zero eight."

The white screen flashed the numbers 1-1-0-8. Dioni watched diligently at the smaller screen as the radiated light from the massive portraits dimmed for this purpose. The screen flickered, and a bird appeared within the rectangle.

> A female Eurasian magpie rested on the ledge of a tall building. She was recorded via a camera feed, and she spoke directly into an invisible lens. In her background was the city of Paris in all its splendor.

> "We usually visit so many restaurants, we forget them. After all, this is Paris!" the magpie said. She spoke in English though with a strong French accent. "But this one was much different. The chef was a rat! Can you imagine? I don't have to imagine, I saw it for myself! A rat cooked the meals for the entire restaurant! And the food…" The magpie brought the tip of her wing to her beak and made a kissing sound. "*Tres magnifique!*"

The image on the rectangle once again changed to a bright, white screen. The numbers 1-1-0-9 appeared. The screen flickered, then another bird appeared within the rectangle.

> A male black-capped chickadee stood on the edge of a bench, a few paces away from a willow tree near a small body of water. It was a perfect summer day. Behind the chickadee, slightly out of focus, was Boston Common. He spoke directly into the lens which recorded him.

> "No no no, you're not listening," said the chickadee, argumentative and in a strong accent which proved it was from Boston. "It was a trumpeter swan, right? A trumpeter swan that didn't have a voice. So instead, he's playing the trumpet in front of those swan boats right here in the Common. And there were these huge lines of people waiting to watch him play. I'll never forget it – a voiceless trumpeter swan playing the trumpet in front of a boat shaped like a swan."

The image on the rectangle once again changed to a bright, white screen. The numbers 1-1-1-0 appeared. The screen flickered. Ally – much younger and physically stronger – appeared within the rectangle. Dioni slightly tilted his head; he immediately recognized the crow shown on the screen.

Ally was in the Alpha's executive office. She looked out from a large window which oversaw the Department of Global Climate Control. She sighed, then turned her attention to directly face the Alpha.

"I was in Rishikesh, in India, on my way to talk to Deepa and Lakshmi," Ally began, in deep thought. "I had some time, so I rested on a tree, a few paces away from the Ganges, just off of a small path near an ashram. I wanted to inform the birds of that region that I was in their field area, so I spoke as loud as I could to make an announcement call. As I was speaking, I looked down from the tree and there stood a man, looking directly at me. He had a dark head of hair, and he was wearing the most colorful shirt I had ever seen. In his left hand he held a guitar. I looked at him, and I remember how sad his eyes were. It was so deep, you know? We stared at each other for just a few seconds…he didn't take his eyes off of me. Then he started to whistle…he mimicked the sounds he heard from my announcement call. That's never happened to me before. So I…I just left. I flew away, and he followed me with his eyes until I was far from sight. But do you know what the craziest part is? Not too much longer after that, maybe a few weeks or months later – I can't remember – I was in the crossbill field area in Scotland, and I'm resting on a shorter tree, and I see the same man, with the same guitar, but now wearing a much better shirt. He noticed me noticing him, and we both froze. He looked at me for only a few seconds, then he started whistling the same sound he heard from my announcement call in India, like if he knew I was that same bird! I didn't…I didn't know what to do, so I flew away from there as fast as I could. I don't know what ever happened to that man, but it was so strange."

The image on the rectangle once again changed to a bright, white screen. The numbers 1-1-1-1 appeared.

"The lesson here is that we birds have seen it all, Dioni," said the vulture. "That's something important you need to remember."

The vulture waived his wing over the rectangle he created, which erased it from existence. The brightness in the space lifted as the large portraits returned to their original state. Dioni paid more attention to the images on the projected screens than to the words of wisdom shared by the Alpha.

"Are all of these paintings?" Dioni asked, admiring the artwork on the walls.

The Alpha sighed. Clearly, Dioni's attention was elsewhere.

"No, these are actually live feeds."

"Live feeds?" asked Dioni.

"The perspective view of any bird. Of every bird," said the Alpha.

"Of what? Every bird is a camera?"

"Of nature. Of the Earth. At any given moment we have an instantaneous feed of anywhere on the planet."

"So this is video? Is it recorded?" Dioni asked.

"Video? What? No, that's an archaic technology, kid. We stopped using video around the time of the Roman emp…wait." The mighty vulture brought the tip of his wing to his beak. He momentarily entered in semi-deep thought. "You know, I can't remember when we last used video. I'll have to ask Mim to look that up for me."

Dioni paused to inspect a screen which displayed a view of the entire Earth as seen from space.

"How could this be live?" Dioni asked. "Birds don't exist in space."

"You wanna see how it works?" asked the Alpha. "Here, let me show you." The Alpha turned to address the screen. "Show me Chicago, United States, feed 21579 from Navy Pier."

The image on the screen flickered.

"How many live feeds exist?" Dioni asked.

"I don't know…billions, I think. Maybe more. It's hard to get an exact count."

"And you know them all by memory?"

"Ha! I wish, kid. I'm not the best at what I do because I'm the Alpha. It's because I've been here long enough to have seen it all. It's the experience."

The image on the screen instantly changed to display a live feed of Chicago, as seen from Lake Michigan. For the first time in his young life, Dioni saw the Windy City as clearly and as brilliantly as if he were resting on a perch which looked upon the mighty city from a distance. It was a beautiful spring day, with not a hint of a cloud in the sky. The trees were bare, the lake water reflected the color of the sky, and the magnificent skyline of the city beamed in all its architectural glory.

The feed displayed the current date, local time, and a series of other climate and weather-related statistics of what was scheduled for Chicago: air temperature, humidity, wind speed, dew point, barometric pressure, sunrise and sunset times, and much more. A small circle at the bottom contained the number 21579, along with an icon of a small bird.

"Huh," the Alpha continued, "looks like a nice day in the Windy City. Let's look at somewhere else. Show London, England, feed 014912."

The image flickered briefly then immediately changed to show London at night. Dioni saw the light of a tall lamp which stood on the edge between a path made of large stones and a great river. Across the river was a mighty structure; to the far right of the structure he saw a clocktower. A flash of lightning temporarily illuminated the sky. Dioni noticed the same series of statistics displayed, though customized for the new location, including an icon of a different bird.

"It's a little after midnight over there, so that makes sense," said the Alpha. He turned to Dioni. "You ever been to London? This is one of my favorite spots, the south bank by the Westminster bridge. The Florence Nightingale museum is just around the corner there. You should check that out sometime."

The Alpha leaned to look closer at the screen. He searched for detailed statistics.

"Looks like they're gonna have a nice day tomorrow. That'll make the morning rush a little easier on everyone."

"Why do you have this?" Dioni asked.

He was intrigued by such outstanding technology.

"I don't own London, Dioni. It's a major city in England, part of the United Kingd—"

"—No, not the city. All of this," Dioni said. He lifted his wings. The Alpha smiled.

"It's part of being a bird, kid," replied the Alpha. "It comes with the territory...amongst other things."

Dioni lowered his wings. He looked in awe at the vastness and detail of the mysterious corridor in which he stood. The Alpha nodded, and together they continued their walk. The Alpha mysteriously paced a few steps behind.

"Ally said that all birds have responsibilities," opened Dioni. "Is that true?"

"Yes, of course!" responded the Alpha. "All birds have their own jobs, plus they all have a shared responsibility."

"Like the quetzals are responsible for criollo seeds."

"Oh good, you know that already. Nice. Then we can skip the orientation presentation," responded the Alpha. He faced Dioni. "Exactly. Quetzals are chocolatiers, woodpeckers are loggers, flamingos are dancers..." He turned his head slightly away. "...blue jays are conceited," he mumbled.

Dioni continued. Every aspect of the environment was unreal – from the massive space which housed all birds, to the pristine executive suite, to the technological marvel of instantaneous feeds of every inch of the Earth – and with every step, he desired to learn more. The Alpha was well aware of the impression the room made on the younger bird.

The two birds walked until they reached the end of the immense corridor. Before them, as if created by the most intricately detailed craftsman of all time, stood a colossal door. It was made from the same exotic wood as the desk which stood in the Alpha's suite, though the door was far more sophisticated. The carvings on the structure told a story of hundreds upon thousands of centuries, depicting the origin of avian kind, from the inception of the species to the birds of unknown origin. The carvings were so lifelike, the images so real, that it was impossible to believe it was made by beings of the natural world.

A wing-crafted sign stood near the door, which read: Command Center Bridge.

"What is the shared responsibility for all birds?" Dioni asked.

The vulture placed himself to be directly in front of Dioni.

"Dioni," began the Alpha. "Behind this door is the answer to that question and a thousand other questions you have about birds. Before we go in there, though, you have to do something for me."

"What?"

"Erase everything you know about being anything, but a bird. You have to know that you have always existed as a bird, even if you didn't become a bird until recently."

"I don't *know* anything about being a bird. I don't know how to fly, or… or—"

"—Oh, that's right," the Alpha responded. "Thanks for the reminder, kid." The vulture turned his head in the direction from which he and Dioni walked. "Donna!"

Four hummingbirds appeared almost instantly – two from the corridor and two from a tiny opening purposely built within the marvelous wooden door. They hovered in place as they awaited the Alpha's command.

"I only need one," responded the Alpha.

All but one of the hummingbirds flew away in the direction from where they entered the room.

"Donna," the Alpha continued, "find an open class in the Flight Academy for my Omega friend here. Just find the earliest slot that's available and sign him up for that one."

The hummingbird acknowledged the request, then zoomed away as quickly as it arrived.

The Alpha returned his attention to Dioni. "Where was I?"

"Erase everything I know about—"

"—Know about anything but being a bird. Yeah, right. Because once you see what's on the other side of this door, there's no going back. Do you understand?"

"This is a door?" Dioni asked, mystified.

"Dioni?"

"Uh, right. Sorry."

"It's either a yes or a no, kid," the Alpha said. He lifted his wing to lean against the tall structure. "You're either ready to do this or you're not. One or the other. What's it gonna be?"

Dioni paused. Less than one hour had passed since he paced along the edge of Lake Atitlan, where he ensured himself that he did not care to be anything other than a young orphan. As he looked at the elements of all which surrounded him – the massive work of art, the screens of live technology of which no being on Earth had access, an unnatural environment which housed more life than he had ever seen – he completely forgot of all that was taken from him.

"Yes," Dioni nervously responded.

"Very well," said the Alpha, a sinister smile flashed across his face.

The Alpha pulled himself away from the door, took a step back, then lifted his wings forward. He slowly spread his wings apart to be at full length. As he did so, the massive door parted, obeying the Alpha's command.

Dioni moved to stand behind the Alpha. As the doors parted, he heard the almighty roar of an ecosystem so beyond the understanding of mankind that its very existence could not be explained by written or spoken word.

Chapter Eleven

Alma parted the closet curtains in Dioni's room. She cleared the remaining items which belonged to her best friend; a few used shirts, candy wrappers, and a few coins he must have found, stored, and completely forgot he had. Alma gathered all the items and placed them in a black bag, which she then took to a much larger storage place away from any of the common areas.

The orphanage was a little quieter, especially at dusk. It was the time of day when Alma went to the burial site; she spent hours in conversation without speaking a single word. She contemplated a number of scenarios, all of which arrived at the same ultimate conclusion: her dear friend – who was perhaps the greatest love of her young life – would never return. This was a cold, cruel reality for Alma. All that remained of Dioni was an empty burial site, old photographs, and memories which were surely to fade in time.

Alma's time passed at a slower pace than it had previously done so. She still completed all her chores – she helped with the younger students, was a mentor to the slightly older ones, and still assisted with cooking – but her motivation for doing so was far different. She did not look forward to the night, where it was anyone's guess as to whether or not she actually slept. She visited the local church as usual, yet her prayers were empty, like a series of memorized motions with no sentiment placed behind them.

In the morning, Alma awoke before all the others. She got up and looked out of the nearby window. She was not entirely sure of what she looked for, nor was she certain of what she would see, yet the advent of the unknown expectation of the day somehow soothed her.

Alma paid particularly close attention to the sounds made by the birds of the neighborhood. It seemed as if they maintained the same routine every day. She hoped that for just one day she would hear something different, something new; perhaps a different call or anything that sounded out of the ordinary. This hope in new discoveries gave her faith that perhaps there was a chance that life could change for the better, even if it took time for it to happen. Perhaps a life without Dioni was possible. Perhaps it all happened for a reason, even if she failed to understand why.

She stared blankly into her abyss. The birds made their sounds, nature once again awoke, and for a spontaneous instant in time, Alma felt a sense of peace as the sunlight colored the Guatemalan mountains a unique shade of blue.

...

The highest floor of the Department of Global Climate Control contained little more than a unique bridge, the likes of which even the greatest civil engineer of all time would not be able to replicate. It was constructed entirely of light and color, and it had a personality all its own. The bridge moved, not from its physical location, but to adapt to whatever bird walked on its surface; it knew the size, shape, weight and stride of each of its visitors, and it modified itself accordingly.

Perched high above all else, the bridge did not connect two points, nor did it allow easy transfer between one side and another. Instead, it served as a barrier between two sides of the massive space. On one side was the Trading Floor, where hundreds of birds rushed back and forth, endlessly taking service requests and work orders from one location to another. On this side was where the trades took place, and every bird kept in constant motion or adhered to the consequences of failing to do so.

Dioni looked over the edge of the bridge to see the motion of the

Trading Floor. He was in complete disbelief of what he witnessed.

"What are they doing?" asked Dioni.

"Trading, negotiating, making deals…whatever you want to call it," responded the Alpha. "It's business, live and in living color."

Dioni was unable to hold his attention in just one particular spot. So much action happened that it proved impossible for him to track it all.

"What are they trading?" Dioni asked. His head moved rapidly as he attempted to visually organize the chaos.

"Climate…weather patterns…today's rain, tomorrow's snow, and probably more rain in London."

"What do you mean? How could they negotiate that?" asked Dioni. The question made the Alpha smile.

"It's a very intricate system, kid. Each bird communicates with their home base and they determine what is essential to their respective field areas. In other words, they have to negotiate for what they need in their part of the world. The resources needed for one are not always the resources that are best for all, so they have to trade based on their necessities."

Dioni was completely lost by the Alpha's statement. It made absolutely no sense that the birds invested so much time and effort to control the far superior force of global climate. It was an uncontrollable event which occurred naturally, and as such it was impossible to predict its patterns with absolute accuracy.

"Come on, check this out," said the Alpha. He directed Dioni's attention to the opposite side of the bridge.

The second side of the bridge was as indescribable as the first. What Dioni saw from his high vantage point was the largest projected map he had ever seen. The map was created by billions of lights and crystals which projected an image onto a screen; the same image was also displayed on various smaller screens scattered sporadically throughout the entire ecospace. The massive screen on the second side of the divisional bridge was easily the largest piece of visual technology ever created.

The screen intricately displayed information of global weather patterns.

With absolute precision, it accurately measured billions of statistical data points that occurred simultaneously. In front of the massive screen was a sophisticated amphitheater, where scores of workstations were constructed for the thousands of birds who worked in the area.

"What are they doing?" Dioni asked, arguably more in shock than he was previously.

"This is how we control the Earth's climate," the Alpha responded, almost as if read from a script. "All of the negotiations on what certain regions want or need is done on one side, and once they come to an agreement, the orders are passed down to this side."

Dioni stood motionless, momentarily dumbfounded. He recognized that this was not a dream, and he quickly came to his senses.

"How do birds control the weather of the Earth?" Dioni asked.

"Oh, no…no no, we don't control the weather," the Alpha responded. "We are responsible for the balance of the Earth. We like to say we control global climate, not just the weather."

Dioni's attention remained on the large screen.

"But…it's impossible!" he said to the Alpha. "No one can control the weather."

"Ha!" the Alpha chuckled. "No *person* can control the weather. That's right. But we are not people, are we, kid? We're more than that, Dioni, and now *you* are a part of it."

Dioni slowly turned his head to make eye contact with the vulture. "This can't be real. How can birds possibly control this?"

"Okay, easy there, kid," the Alpha responded. "We're a lot more intelligent than you give us credit for…except the dodos…those ugly birds got what they deserved."

Dioni looked confused. The explanation did not make the least bit of sense.

"Look," the Alpha continued. "We are responsible for maintaining the balance of the world, and we do it by controlling the climate. We don't start wars, we can't control time, we abide by the same laws of physics, and we live, breathe, and die just like all living creatures. We are not here to interfere with life, but to adjust it accordingly. So if we have too much rain in one part of the Earth while there is drought in another, we have to determine how to share the resources. The planet can only sustain so much, and we control those limitations."

"And how do you do that?" Dioni asked.

"Communication. It's really not that difficult of a concept. There are millions of stations setup around the Earth, and they each have access to give continuous feedback to their respective representatives here. So – hypothetically speaking – when you…let's say…have an intruder in the Mayan kingdom who interrupts the quetzals on their daily check-in, we are notified of that right away."

"I just wanted to know what they were doing," Dioni responded.

Dioni searched the Control Room floor. He looked for a familiar bird among the thousands in the amphitheater. In the distance he saw a green quetzal which stood beside a mallard duck, and he paid close attention to what took place between them. A hummingbird flew to the quetzal and presented it with a small leaflet. The hummingbird then zoomed away, and the quetzal read the note; it then opened its wings and created a projected image in front of itself. On the quetzal's screen was an aerial map of a region of the Earth. The screen was too far for Dioni to notice any significant detail, though he noticed how the image on the screen was controlled by the quetzal's movements and not by keyboard or touch.

"I can sit here and try to explain it to you all day," said the Alpha, "but you're not going to get a full grasp of it unless you're on the floor. What say you and I go down there and we give you a proper tour of the place?"

"Absolutely!" responded Dioni, absorbing the magnificence of what he saw.

The vulture lifted from the bridge with its wings spread widely in an obnoxious attempt to show its immense size over Dioni. He glided downward and reached the ground-level within seconds. He landed harshly on the cold surface of the Trading Floor, and rudely disregarded the nearby birds who knew better than to complain of the vulture's interruption.

149

"So what we have here is the Trading Floor," continued the Alpha, as if Dioni were beside him. "Most of the negosh...kid? Where'd he go?" He looked around and failed to see Dioni; he looked up and saw as Dioni waved his wing. "Oh...that's right. Flight school."

Dioni and the Alpha exited from the massive elevator; Dioni's face displayed a smile too large to be overcast by the Alpha's annoyance of the matter. If being a blue quetzal was not disrespectable enough, existing as one that did not know how to fly was beyond comprehension. It was yet another strike against Ally, but the Alpha knew better than to worry about that for now.

From the ground level, the Trading Floor was the resounding definition of efficiency. Like a metropolis of symphonic chaos in constant motion, the scores of birds who worked in this department either ran, hopped, flew, glided, or slid in almost every direction. Not a single bird cared about size, color, shape, or the abilities – or lack thereof – of their adversaries. All that mattered was their intelligence, nothing more.

"The purpose of the Trading Floor is for each region to negotiate what they want or need," said the Alpha, assured that Dioni stood beside him.

Dioni walked as if in a trance. The entire ecospace was unreal, and deafeningly loud. Every bird made a unique sound, yet they all communicated with ease.

"How do they all understand one another?" asked Dioni.

The vulture pointed to a chip-like device which rested on the side of his head.

"We don't all speak a single common language, so we have these translators installed to allow us to communicate."

"Can I have one?"

"Oh...I'm sorry, kid," the Alpha responded as he stopped in his tracks. "Donna!"

Four hummingbirds appeared almost immediately.

"I just need one," the Alpha said to them. All but one of the hummingbirds zoomed away.

"Donna, let's get a universal translator for our cerulean friend here."

The hummingbird looked down at Dioni. It made a series of gestures with one of its wings.

"Yeah, yeah, I know," responded the Alpha, "even for a Central American bird. I get it. He still needs to communicate, though."

The hummingbird departed as fast as it arrived.

"Wait," Dioni said. "I don't have one of those. Why do I understand what *you're* saying?"

"Once you've done the job for as long as I have, you learn the older languages," responded the Alpha. "I don't need this to speak to you; I mostly need it for the younger birds. I honestly have no idea what they are saying half the time."

"So every bird can communicate with each other?" asked Dioni.

"All birds are connected, kid. Even the birds that eat other birds. There's a mutual respect among us. We can communicate in lots of ways, with or without translator units."

The hummingbird returned with a gold and blue macaw, a large Caribbean bird who may have spent far too much time in the sun. It moved oddly, even while it stood in place.

"Be you the Omega bird?" asked the macaw, with one eye slightly more widely opened than his other. His accent was crudely English with Caribbean influence.

"Ye...yes," responded Dioni, intimidated by the large-and-socially-awkward macaw.

"Donna, my effects," the macaw said to the hummingbird.

Donna zoomed off then returned momentarily, followed by three other hummingbirds who carried a toolbelt. The main hummingbird instructed the others to drop the toolbelt, to which they complied and then zoomed away. The macaw rustled through a few items within the belt and located a black sensor.

"Right then, mon," said the macaw. "A universal pathfinder for the new Omega bird, savvy?" He looked at Dioni. "Hold still."

The macaw took the sensor and carefully placed it on the right side of Dioni's head, above his ear. He applied a small amount of pressure as he attempted to press it on, to which Dioni displayed his discomfort. The device did not stay on Dioni's head, even after multiple attempts.

"Where did you get your head, mon?" asked the macaw.

"Is there a problem?" asked the Alpha.

The macaw turned to the vulture.

"What we have here is an Omega with an unusually shaped cranium," the macaw responded. "Seems fitting, really. There exists a probability of non-compliance with this one. It's not every day one sees a blue Q, ey?"

"Make it work, Jack," the Alpha said to the macaw. "He needs to communicate."

"Fear not, mon," responded Jack. "By my word, the blue Q shall be given the gift of universal communication."

"Proceed." The Alpha sighed.

Jack turned to Dioni. "You look funny."

The macaw reached to the same spot on Dioni's head and attempted to place the device. It stayed on momentarily before it fell once again. Jack took a step back to better observe the shape of Dioni's head; there was nothing unusual about it. He repeated the action, though on this attempt, he held the device with both wings and then signaled to Donna for assistance. The macaw held the unit in place as the hummingbird flew to the device. Donna extended one of her rapidly moving wings and then used all her strength to whack Dioni on the side of the head.

"Ow!" exclaimed Dioni, surprised by the incredible power of such a small bird.

The device stayed on as a result of the corrected action.

"Did it work?" asked the Alpha.

"Did what work, mon?" asked Jack. The Alpha rolled his eyes and lifted his wings. "Yes, the installation was a success." Jack turned to Dioni, "Give us a test, will ya?"

Dioni turned to the Alpha. "Can you understand me?"

The Alpha opened his eyes widely.

"I did before you put it on, kid. Try another bird."

Dioni looked around the room and spotted a nearby sparrow who read from a glass tablet. He walked to the sparrow, nervously.

"Eh…excuse me," said Dioni. "Can you understand me?"

The sparrow turned to Dioni, opened its mouth, then stopped itself before it made a sound.

"What a strange looking bird," responded the sparrow, who then returned its attention to the tablet.

"Did ya understand what he said, mon?" asked Jack.

"He called me 'strange looking'," responded Dioni.

"Perfect! Me job is done," said the macaw. He turned to face the Alpha. "He really be a strange looking fella, that one. Reminds me of my cousin."

"Thanks, Jack," responded the Alpha.

The macaw grabbed his toolbelt then flew away. Donna followed behind him.

Dioni was in disbelief of all he heard. As a human, the only bird sounds he understood were a series of chirps and whistles, with the occasional loud – and annoying – call of a rooster. Throughout his entire life, he only thought of their sounds as noises made by all birds; he never fathomed the concept of their speech in various languages.

As a bird himself, Dioni learned that various calls, sounds, and even movements were all manners of communication. Those that spoke did so under the native language of their respected field area. To him, the sound of a conglomeration of languages was beyond understanding. He had the ability to communicate with every bird, of every location, of every color, and of every type, with the help of a small device; all it cost him was a whack on the side of his head.

The Trading Floor instantly transformed from a chorus of movement and random bird calls to a full-fledged reprise of thousands of birds who spoke simultaneously. It reminded Dioni of the sounds made when thousands of people gathered inside *Mazatenango* stadium for a soccer game.

"What is the purpose of all of this?" asked Dioni, mystified by the transactions which occurred around him.

The Alpha stepped away and motioned for Dioni to follow as he walked through the Trading Floor.

"Have you ever seen a bird that seemed like it had no business being where it was?" began the Alpha. "I'm not saying like a parrot in Antarctica or a penguin in the Sahara. I mean, like the brightest canary you have ever seen in your life – the only canary you have ever seen, actually – just sitting on a branch of a random tree on a path that you walk every day. You must've walked that exact spot thousands of times and never once seen such a brightly colored bird. Like it was completely out of its element."

Dioni paused to think.

"It wasn't a canary. It wasn't yellow, it was orange. It stood on the roof of the church, looked around, and then flew away. I never saw it again."

"That bird was special," the Alpha said. "It was there for a reason."

"And what reason is that?" Dioni asked.

"To serve a common purpose. That orange bird you saw gathered information and sent it back here."

"Why?"

"Because we use that information to determine climate patterns around the Earth."

As he and the Alpha walked deeper within the Trading Floor, Dioni marveled at all which occurred around him. The chaos was controlled, like a symphony of both movement and sound. The structure of this side of the Department of Global Climate Control was absolutely massive. Birds of all types moved back and forth from conference rooms, the Trading Floor, a cafeteria, restrooms, and even from a system of interconnected tubes created for easy transport.

"How is all of this possible?" Dioni asked.

He looked toward the ceiling and followed the patterns of movement he saw above.

"Here's a bit of wisdom for you, kid," said the Alpha. He stopped and looked down to Dioni. "If there is nothing else you take away from what you learn today, always remember this: Birds. See. Everything. We scream in the streets and beg the people to clean-up after themselves, yet they throw bottles or rocks at us, or ignore us or chase us away. We offer humanity everything they could possibly need: food, great harvests, air transportation, open waters…you name it, we help provide it. Instead of hearing us, they cage us. Some of us are hunted for sport. They clip our wings or make trophies of us. And worse yet, they destroy the very nature that is designed to keep them – and us – alive. We can't possibly compete against them, so we find a way to restore the balance."

Dioni reflected on what he heard. It proved impossible for him to absorb the wisdom shared by the eldest of all birds. He knew first-hand of the consequences of human action on the Earth. The air was clouded with smoke, garbage and plastics roamed freely on the land and water, and much of what had taken centuries to create was either logged, burned or destroyed in a matter of days. He thought of Tikal.

"What do you mean?" asked Dioni. "Are you saying that birds fight back to punish the people? Is all of this revenge for what people are doing to the Earth?"

"What? No!" responded the Alpha. "We don't control that! We're responsible for the natural balance of the planet, Dioni. We're not evil creatures. That's what lizards are for."

"What?" asked Dioni, unable to grasp the vulture's last comment.

The Alpha continued to walk toward an exit on the far wall. Dioni trailed closely behind.

"Our biggest responsibility is to maintain the natural balance," continued the Alpha. "We have to do what is best for us *as well* as what is best for them. And not just humans, we're talking all living things."

155

"And you do that by controlling the climate?" asked Dioni.

"That's a part of it."

The two birds reached the exit along the wall. The Alpha opened and held the door for Dioni, then both of them proceeded into a much quieter corridor. The space was designed as a connection point between both sides of the Department of Global Climate Control. On the walls were multiple screens that displayed a series of numbers, as well as other screens which displayed global weather patterns. On the far side of the wall were a series of glass panels, each of which exposed an array of intricately decorated conference rooms, many with meetings in progress.

"Think of it as the birds protecting those who are unable to protect themselves," continued the Alpha. "A dolphin is just as important as a kangaroo, and a human is just as important as a bird. All life is precious, Dioni, so we have to keep a balance in order to preserve it."

The two birds walked slowly toward the glass panels. The more he learned, the more difficult it became for Dioni to understand it all.

"So…all birds have a common responsibility, right?" asked Dioni.

"That's right," responded the Alpha.

"And they all have their own jobs and responsibilities where they live, but they also control the weather?"

"Ah! You were doing great then you lost it at the end. The birds of every region have a few representatives who report to the DGCC."

"The *what?*"

"The DGCC – Department of Global Climate Control. You gotta keep up, kid."

"Sorry."

"Once the orders from the field are given to the DGCC, the birds stationed here work with each other to negotiate what each of them needs. Remember, it's what is best for them *as well* as what's best for other regions."

"And *all* birds do this?" asked Dioni.

"Yes," the Alpha responded after a short pause. "All birds do this. We balance the world."

The two birds continued their walk down the corridor.

"The birds in the field record what's happening in their respected regions, and they report back to us," the Alpha continued. "We then have raw data for hundreds of thousands of regional checkpoints around the Earth, then we use that information to determine climate for the entire planet."

"But," Dioni began as he sped his pace to walk beside the Alpha. "It doesn't make any sense. The Earth's climate is natural. It can't be controlled."

The Alpha smiled. He had heard the same phrase said multiple times, so there was no need to get upset over another Omega's ignorance. He looked through the glass panels of a conference room and spotted a meeting already in progress.

"Here, kid. Check this out," he said to Dioni as they walked to a large window.

Inside the conference room were two groups of pigeons, three from each group, who sat on opposite sides of an egg-shaped table. They were in the middle of a heated debate, which was evident when one of the pigeons stood and paced about the room, noticeably frustrated.

"No. No. No!" said the standing, frustrated pigeon. He spoke with a strong accent from New York City. "We simply don't have the infrastructure in place for a snowstorm of that magnitude."

"I'm sorry, Frank," responded a pigeon from the opposite side of the table. He spoke with a strong Bostonian accent. "I don't know what else to tell ya."

"Well think of somethin', 'cuz there's no way I'm signing-off on an order that's gonna affect over 8 million people. We're not gonna shut down the whole of Manhattan just because your team can't handle it."

"Look, I get it," responded the Bostonian pigeon, "but Boston's gettin' hammered with another season of 'unusually high snow accumulation', alright? And it's causin' all kinds of problems."

"Have you tried other field areas?" asked the New Yorker pigeon.

"Minneapolis laughed in our faces and Chicago's no longer speaking to us," responded a second pigeon on the Bostonian side.

"No surprise yous can't sell a draft of air to the Windy City," said a pigeon who sat on the New Yorker side.

"I got your draft of air right here, you poor excuse for a homing device," said a Bostonian bird.

The six pigeons immediately launched into a heated argument.

"Alright alright alright!" shouted the standing pigeon, who slowly calmed the others. "Hold on." He pressed a button on the center of the table which opened a small screen. "Hey Donna!"

Almost immediately, three hummingbirds flew into the room through small, tube-shaped openings near the ceiling.

"I just need one," said the pigeon. Two of the hummingbirds left the room. "Donna, can you page the rep from St. Louis and get him in here?"

The hummingbird acknowledged the request then immediately exited the room through one of the high tubes.

"I know dis guy. He's a good guy," said the New Yorker pigeon.

Within seconds, the hummingbird returned to the conference room through the main door, accompanied by a male cardinal who wore a baseball-themed tie.

"Jimmyyyy!" said the New Yorker pigeon as the cardinal walked into the conference room. "Thanks for flyin' in. Hey listen, I got a couple of pigeons I want you to meet."

The pigeons on both sides of the table stood and greeted Jimmy, which was Donna's cue to exit. Dioni visually followed the hummingbird as it left the room through the tube from where it first entered.

"You see?" the Alpha said to Dioni as they stood on the opposite side of the glass. "It's a negotiation. We're all friends here, Dioni. We're just trying to work together for the common good. Come on."

The vulture motioned for Dioni to follow as he continued down the corridor.

Dioni became awestruck by the power of it all. Never did he imagine that birds were anything more than flying creatures. He respected them for eating worms and for being so colorful, but he was also guilty of frightening seagulls and throwing rocks at some of the doves every now and then. In that moment, he finally understood why it always rained on his birthday.

The two birds reached another set of transparent double-doors, where a sign above read: Control Center. Dioni looked through the doors and saw a hint of the ultra-sophisticated workspace housed on the other side.

"Are you responsible for all of this?" asked Dioni. He slowly began to understand the sheer power of the DGCC.

"Me? No way! But I appreciate you thinking that highly of me," responded the Alpha. "No…no one bird should ever be responsible for this much power."

The Alpha opened the door and allowed Dioni to walk in first. The vulture was a showman as much as he was chivalrous – or as chivalrous as a vulture could be – and this was his favorite part of the tour. This is where he made his pitch, where he sold his angle, and where centuries of negotiation experience came to fruition.

"That's why we split it in two," said the Alpha.

The spectacle of what Dioni witnessed the moment he walked onto the floor of the Control Center marked yet another instance of his life which he was surely to never forget. If the Trading Floor was an avian empire designed for the purpose of business and negotiations, then the Control Center of the DGCC was both the brain and central nervous system of the entire ecospace.

The principal wall, which acted as a divider between the two distinct areas, took a secondary role on the Control Center side. As if carved, erected, and assembled by forces far beyond the understanding of physical possibility, the structure itself was a colossal, digitized culmination of aesthetics, natural wonder, and technological advancement. The wall held billions upon billions of exotic flowers which were intricately placed in a precise formation to allow the reproduction of every color found on Earth. However, the flowers served a secondary purpose; in addition to providing clean air for the entire DGCC, each flower glowed, expanded, retracted, and beamed a source of light, which – when interconnected with trillions of others – created a living screen along the surface of the gargantuan structure. The wall was literally alive, with each flower automated to react like a flawlessly synchronized orchesis of energy.

As he walked further into the Control Center, Dioni saw the majesty of how the birds charted and recorded every segment of the entire planet. He stood in disbelief of what was in front of him. The Alpha remained a few paces behind.

On the screen was a detailed map of the Earth, which displayed areas under daylight, nightfall and lunar position, and even provided comprehensive planetary information: thousands of numbers and statistics that showed relevant weather and climate calculations for major cities and areas with unusual weather patterns. The bottom of the screen held a long marquee, which continuously scrolled information about trades and negotiations made on the opposite side of the wall. Every few seconds, different messages appeared at random points on the map, which were check-in confirmations from birds in the field.

The massive screen was operated by hundreds of birds who stood or sat at a series of multi-level perches, each designed as workstations. In each workspace was a different bird, who served as the liaison between its home base, the Control Center, and the Trading Floor. While these birds were far less active than their counterparts on the other side, they were equally as loud.

In terms of degree of difficulty, the birds of the Control Center had the most demanding responsibilities. They oversaw the administration of what was negotiated and acted as communicators and auditors to ensure that the negotiations were, in fact, completed. They were responsible for the implementation of what was agreed upon, yet they had absolutely no power to overturn any decisions made by the birds on the Trading Floor.

Each workstation was decorated according to the desire of its corresponding bird; some were more sophisticated than others. Small, projected-image screens were present near each perch, and every screen contained a sensor which read the movements of the bird in each station.

The primary flyers in the Control Center were the hummingbirds, who entered and exited the area at great speeds, to and from every direction. Their job was to deliver the negotiated terms and work order confirmations – written on small leaflets – from the Trading Floor to the Control Center, and to assist with a number of other tasks as requested by the birds on either side of the wall.

Dioni stood in shock. A million questions ran through his mind, none of which he was able to ask aloud. The Alpha stood expressionless with his wings at his sides. He stood proudly, fully aware of his greatest accomplishment. He knew the affect the Control Center had on all new Omega birds, so Dioni's reaction was of no surprise.

"Come on, kid," said the vulture. "Let's go take a look around."

The Alpha led the way as he guided Dioni through the workspace; he paid little attention to what was displayed on the mighty screen. Other birds noticed as Dioni and the Alpha walked by, but they were too busy with their work to make any kind of introduction.

"This is where the negotiations are put to use," said the Alpha as he made his way through the aisles of workstations. "These birds communicate with their home base to ensure the correct work order made it through to the other side."

"How do they do that?" asked Dioni. He gawked as he looked in every direction.

"They have check-ins with their regions. Control Center birds are assigned a region which corresponds to their home base. Each region – and there are thousands of them – is required to communicate with the Control Center at least once a day. The birds at each regional center work with both the Trading Floor and the Control Center, and no one division is more powerful than the other. It's a triangular system."

Dioni paid close attention to a stork who moved rapidly in front of a workstation screen. It appeared as though the stork gestured to the monitor by using its wings and body to communicate. Its movements were strange, like a robotic dance.

"Why is he moving like that?" Dioni asked. He and the Alpha paused at a near distance from the stork.

"It's part of the communications system," the Alpha responded. "Email and texts became more annoying than useful, so we eliminated them decades ago and we created a system in which body language is the primary form of communication. Each type of bird has their own form of body language, so this system prevents fraud or hacking."

"And by using this…they control the weather around the world?"

"We…" the Alpha responded. "*We* control global climate and weather patterns."

"But…how? How does a computer control the weather?" Dioni asked.

"Dioni, it's not as simple as a computer. It's such a highly complex infrastructure that it will make your head explode."

Dioni immediately reached for his head; even if it was a manner of speech, it was not worth the risk.

"Not literally, kid. Relax," said the Alpha. Dioni slowly lowered his wings. "The best way I can explain it to you is by saying this: the birds are always watching. We control the skies, we see everything, and at no time are we not doing our jobs."

Dioni turned away from the stork and looked at the massive screen. A particular circular pattern caught his attention. At the southeast corner of the United States, north of Florida, was a large whirlwind formation which slowly trailed toward the west from the Atlantic Ocean. The weather pattern displayed in red on the screen.

"What's happening there?" Dioni asked.

He used his wing to point at the whirlwind. The Alpha turned his attention to the screen.

"Looks like a big storm off the coast of Georgia," the Alpha responded.

"The falcons usually transmit while indoors, so they'll be fine."

The Alpha looked around the massive room. He lifted his head in search of a specific workstation. A few meters away he spotted a merlin who moved anxiously on her perch, almost as if dancing to a fast rhythm. The Alpha motioned for Dioni to follow.

The merlin's workspace was decorated entirely with American football gear; every item was either red or black. Near the perch where the merlin danced was a large shirt with the name 'Henrietta' written on it, above a large number 35.

"Henrietta!" said the Alpha to the merlin.

She immediately stood at attention and looked at the Alpha.

"Hey boss!" responded Henrietta, in a strong, Georgian accent. She was excited to see the vulture out of his suite and by her workstation. "What brings ya out of your cage?" she asked, jokingly.

"Giving a tour to a new guy," responded the Alpha, who pointed at Dioni.

Henrietta looked at where the Alpha pointed.

"What an odd-looking fella," she said to Dioni, then extended her right wing to greet him. "What's your name?"

"Dioni."

"The only *what*?" asked Henrietta.

"No no, not *the only*. Dee Oh Nee. Dioni."

"Oh," responded Henrietta. "Dee Oh Nee. Got it. Well welcome to the DGCC, Dee Oh Nee. You like American footba—"

"—Yeah he loves it," the Alpha rudely interrupted. "Listen, Henrietta, what's happening off the coast of Georgia?"

Henrietta turned to her screen.

"Them a storm, boss. Looks like we got us a 2-pointer, which is fine 'cause it's about five weeks 'til the draft," Henrietta said as she returned her attention to the Alpha. "We can't have no big storm distract us. Our boys 've got a chance at the playoffs if we pickup that quarterback from

Oregon. Whoo doggie! Momma's gettin' a Super Bowl ring!"

"What is she talking about?" asked Dioni.

"American football, kid," responded the Alpha. "Seriously, try to keep up." He looked at Henrietta, who continued her dance. "Did I sign off on this? I don't remember signing off on this."

"I assume so, boss," said Henrietta. "Otherwise we couldn't've put it through."

"Huh…I really don't remem… Donna!" shouted the Alpha.

Eight hummingbirds appeared almost immediately. A ninth appeared shortly after, holding a leaflet in its beak. The hummingbirds hovered in place and stared coldly at the latecomer.

"I only need one," said the Alpha. The eight original hummingbirds zoomed away.

"Donna, can you che—"

"—Wait," interjected Dioni. "Are they all named Donna?"

"Dio—"

The Alpha paused. Both he and the airborne hummingbird looked at Dioni, then at one another. They shrugged their shoulders.

"It's always been that way," said the Alpha. "You…you're actually the first one to ask that. What an odd question." The Alpha returned his attention to the hummingbird. "Donna, did I sign off on a level 2 storm on the Atlantic coast of the United States? Georgia, specifically. For some time this week."

The hummingbird zipped to Henrietta's screen. With the leaflet still in its beak, it hovered in front of the motion sensor and made a series of rapid movements with its wings and body. The tiny bird then used its head to point to the main display.

Dioni and the vulture turned to the mega screen, which displayed an image of a processed work order. In great detail, the work order indicated the weather pattern that was negotiated, the terms of the negotiation, and each bird involved in the transaction.

"Scroll to the bottom," the Alpha instructed Donna.

The screen moved down, and in plain sight they saw a written scribble above a small line designated for the Alpha's signature.

"Huh, I guess I did," said the Alpha. "I don't remember doing that." He turned to Dioni. "I'm getting old, Dioni. Maybe I've done this job for too long."

"How long have you been here?" asked Dioni.

"It's not the years, kid. It's the miles. Right, Donna?"

The Alpha looked at the hummingbird, who refused to acknowledge the question.

"Thank you, Donna," said the Alpha.

The hummingbird made a small gesture then zoomed away.

"A long time, Dioni," the Alpha continued. "A very long time."

The Alpha walked away from Henrietta's workstation. Dioni followed closely behind. They continued down a main path of the floor of the Control Center.

"Can't you retire?" asked Dioni.

"And go back to being human? Oh, no. I can't do that."

"Why not?"

"I like my job, for one," responded the Alpha. "More importantly, it's because we still have a lot of work to do. Remember how I said we're responsible for maintaining the balance of the world?"

"Yeah," responded Dioni.

"Well, the world is still not balanced. How can I retire when my job's not done? Maybe one day when everything is running smoothly and my job is practically done by itself, maybe then I can retire. Maybe I can go into business or something. Sell yogurt, part-time."

"How will you know when the world is balanced?"

"When we all coexist. When everything is so well balanced that our jobs become simple and all we have to worry about is global surveillance. Put this whole system on auto-pilot and the regional birds can just monitor each area. Will that ever happen? Who knows. So until then I'll stay where I am. I like being the boss around here."

The two birds reached another set of glass doors which led down another long, intricate hallway. The Alpha guided Dioni down a corridor, toward an elevator bank.

"So what is the Omega bird?" asked Dioni.

"Didn't Ally tell you?" responded the Alpha, sarcastically. "Wow…it really is hard to find good help these days."

"She said the Omega bird ensures that the other birds do their jobs."

"That's actually only half accurate."

"Okay…"

"You know how I keep talking about the balance?" the Alpha asked.

"Yes."

"For every up there's a down, for every left there's a right, and so on. You follow?"

"Yes."

"So for every Alpha, there has to exist an Omega. They can exist without each other, but then we lose the balance."

"And who gives them their jobs?" asked Dioni.

"Only an Alpha can assign another Alpha. Just like only an Omega can assign another Omega."

The two birds reached the elevator bank. The vulture pressed a button to call for a lift back to his executive suite.

"I'll explain it to you in a way that's simple to understand," continued the vulture. "As the Alpha, I am responsible for managing the entire DGCC. All of these birds report to me, and I have to sign-off on all major negotiations and work orders. If something out of the ordinary happens, it has to come to my attention first."

"That makes sense," responded Dioni.

The elevator bell dinged, and two large doors opened before them.

"The job of the Omega bird is to ensure that what was negotiated, submitted and approved as a work order here, actually happens on Earth," continued the Alpha as he and Dioni entered the elevator. The doors closed behind them and the elevator began to move. "So if there's an order for a snowstorm in Paris, and it happens in Brussels, we know something went wrong. It's your responsibility to report that back to the main office. I'm sorry, *the Omega's* responsibility."

"So all I do is check to make sure the work orders are correct?"

"Oh, no kid, that's only a small part of it. I oversee all administrative and executive operations, and you...sorry, I did it again...*the Omega* oversees field operations and audits. If one of us isn't doing our jobs, the world will start to feel it. If I have to keep the balance here, it's your...the Omega's job to keep the balance out there."

"And how do I do that?"

"You have to start by getting to know your people first."

"*My* people?" Dioni asked.

"Seriously, kid, you gotta keep up with me," the Alpha responded, evidently annoyed.

The elevator came to a stop and the large doors opened. The two birds walked down the same path that led to the Alpha's executive suite.

"I don't expect you to meet with every bird on Earth, but at least get to know a few of them," the Alpha continued. "Go to India and meet a peacock or talk to a crane in Japan or something. Is there anywhere you've always wanted to visit?"

"The United States," said Dioni.

"The US?" the Alpha asked as he stopped and looked down at Dioni. "It wouldn't be my first choice, but who am I to judge?" He continued along. "I'd talk to a bald eagle if you get a chance. They're a bit much to handle, kinda prideful, but they are open minded if you talk to them respectfully."

Mimidae, two hummingbirds and a white dove intently watch the action

167

on Mimidae's screen. From a distance and outside of the executive lobby, Mimidae heard the voice of her boss as he approached. She immediately motioned for the visiting birds to move into the executive suite. She shut down the film which played on her screen, then pretended to be busy at work.

"Who else?" the Alpha asked himself. The conversation continued as he and Dioni walked into the executive lobby. "Penguins are always a fun time, if you don't mind the cold. Ostriches will try to race you. You'll never get the last word if you have a conversation with a duck. The snowy owls in the Netherlands will introduce you to something called a stroopwafel; I'm not going to spoil that one for you." He looked at Mimidae. "Hey, Mim."

"Welcome back, sir's," responded Mimidae in her most eager-to-please voice.

"The choice is yours, Dioni," declared the Alpha. He stopped at Mimidae's workstation and leaned on her desk as he continued the conversation. "It's your department, so run it as you see fit."

Dioni looked at the floor. He saw his small talons.

"What about going back to being me?" asked Dioni. "Ally said that you—"

"—Dioni, let me stop you right there," the Alpha interrupted. "Yes, it's possible to change you back. You just have to find someone else to take your place. Only an Omega can assign another Omega. We have to keep the balance, remember?"

Dioni paused. He took a moment to absorb what he was told.

"So if I can find another bird to take my place, I can be me again?" Dioni asked.

"Oh yeah, sure! Absolutely!" responded the Alpha. "I tell you what; give me ten days. You go out there, be the Omega, talk to other birds, and find one to replace you. If you come back in ten days with another bird who wants your job, then you're off the hook."

"Ten days…"

"That's not asking too much, is it?" asked the Alpha. Dioni paused once more. "Think about it like this: you go back to being you, and you'll be the most famous kid in the world. Everyone will want to know how you disappeared and came back completely unharmed ten days later. I can see the news reports already."

"Just ten days, and I go back—"

"—to your old, boring life. Yes. Ten days."

Dioni looked at Mimidae, who gawked at him as if he were a completely foreign object. She noticed him looking at her, then quickly turned her attention to her screen. She pressed a button which called the birds who waited in the executive suite.

"Okay," said Dioni. "Ten days."

"But only if you find a replacement for yourself," responded the Alpha. The vulture reached out his right wing, the universal gesture to seal the terms of their agreement.

"Right. Okay. Ten days. Find a replacement," Dioni responded. He shook the vulture's wing with his own.

"Great! I think you're gonna love it, kid!" said the Alpha, excitedly. "If I were you, I'd start thinking of the stories you'll tell when you go back home."

Two hummingbirds entered the room, followed by a white dove who wore a small, dark blue helmet. Mimidae directed the Alpha's attention to the guests in the room.

"Ah, flight school," said the Alpha. He looked at the dove. "Airman. Always a pleasure."

The dove brought its right wing to its brow to salute the Alpha.

"Sir," said the dove.

The vulture turned to Dioni. "Where was I?"

"Ten days," said Mimidae.

"Right, ten days. It'll go by faster than you think. Just enjoy it. When you come back, I'll be right here waiting for you." The Alpha looked to the

169

dove. "Airman, escort the new Omega bird to the Flight Academy. He is to receive V.I.B. treatment."

"Yes, sir," said the dove. He once again saluted the Alpha, who responded accordingly. "Mr. Omega, sir, if you would follow me," the dove said to Dioni.

Dioni followed behind as the dove and the two hummingbirds escorted him away from the executive lobby. He was reluctant at first, though he acknowledged the deal he made with the Alpha. As he walked out of the room, he thought about his task. The assignment was a simple one: find a replacement in ten days or less – preferably less. Dioni looked back at the vulture.

"Safe flying, kid," said the Alpha as he waved his wing.

"There must be over a billion birds on Earth," Dioni thought. "How hard can it be to convince just one of them?"

The Alpha and Mimidae waited to hear the sound of the elevator depart. Once they heard it, they carried on with business as usual. Mimidae returned to her screen, which was filled with work orders.

"Mim, hold my calls for the rest of the day," said the Alpha as he walked into his executive suite.

"Yes, sir."

The Alpha closed the door behind him. He walked to the large window where he oversaw his entire kingdom. He smiled, and momentarily absorbed the power he had over all birds.

He walked to his perch, behind his desk, and rested. Immediately, the perch transformed into an executive lounge chair. The Alpha placed his talons on his desk and his wings behind his head. He sighed, happily.

"A blue quetzal," he said. "What a ridiculous bird."

Chapter Twelve

Ally rested on the branch of a tree above the unmarked grave that contained Dioni's remains. Flores was not a large town, and from where she stood she saw almost all of it.

Every so often a young lady walked from the orphanage to the church. She remained at the church for some time, then walked back to the orphanage. In almost every instance, the young lady looked down as she walked. Ally observed the young lady and did not move nor make a sound as she paced between one location and the other. She was sad, in mourning, and unable to feel happiness.

It reminded Ally of her mother. She loved her parents, and it was unthinkable to believe she made the wrong choice. She would give anything to go back and have one last conversation. One last chance for a hug, to feel loved, and to once again see her mother's beautiful smile.

She made a deal – one that she thought would be simple to achieve. Ten days…all she needed to do was to find a replacement within ten days, and it would have saved her mother decades of lost time as she searched for her missing daughter.

Ally was young, and she wanted to see the world. Though she was heartbroken to leave her home, she wanted to experience more. The offer was too good to pass, until she realized what she left behind. By then it was too late…the deal was done, and she had agreed to years of loyal service.

171

Time literally flew by.

He trapped her by threatening to destroy those whom she loved. After the members of her family passed and their memories were gone, there was no reason to go back to her Earthly form. She would not, however, repeat her own mistake. If it was in her power to find her own replacement, then she would be more careful than the bird who bestowed the same fate upon her. When the time was right, she would find the perfect person to be the next Omega bird. For decades, Ally searched tirelessly for her successor.

"Someone who doesn't have a family or anyone who would miss them… that would be the perfect Omega," Ally thought. "He can't make a deal with someone who has nothing to lose."

Perhaps it was destiny – albeit one which took decades to fulfill – that she was near Ipala on the day of the fateful storm. Perhaps it was fate that at the peak of the crater lake was a young man who would have perished had she not taken action. Perhaps it was fate that the young man was alone, in more ways than one.

Ally failed to take into account the one person who loved Dionisio. They were both so young, and though they failed to understand the magnitude of their feelings, they certainly felt it for one another. It was love – a deep connection which transcended both time and distance. Ally misjudged her choice; she thought an orphan would not be missed. Her own guilt showed her how simple it was for history to repeat itself. Dioni had something to lose, and the Alpha had likely discovered Dioni's greatest weakness. She hoped against all odds that Alma would forget about Dionisio and learn to live without him.

As Alma emerged from the church during the sunset hour of a calm afternoon, Ally maintained her distance. Alma abruptly stopped and looked up. Her face welcomed the warmth of the setting sun. Her eyes were dark and fierce, and her gaze towards the sunlight reminded Ally of her own mother who did the same.

Alma stood momentarily then turned her head. She looked directly at Ally.

"Impossible," Ally thought. "How could she know I'm here?"

Ally made absolutely no movements; she refused to risk being seen by a young lady who may be suspicious as to why a crow would be at that specific location at that specific time.

Alma looked for a few moments then returned to her normal stance. She sighed, then continued her walk to the orphanage, her head once again bowed.

Ally waited for Alma to enter the building before she moved. Ally knew she could no longer stay in Flores, as it would not be productive for her to do so. She looked around, lowered her head, raised her wings, then lifted off the tree. She was in the air, where she felt most at ease. As the sun set on another day in Flores, Ally understood why Alma had looked toward the tree.

The blue mountains surrounded the village. All the business of the day had concluded, and preparations were underway for the next. The night shift awoke while the day shift returned to their nests.

The village was tranquil that night. There was peace in the sky and the birds were at ease. Only a piece of blue ribbon, trapped on a tree branch, made any movement.

...

The Avian Flight Academy's reputation for success and excellence was unmatched by even the most advanced, immaculately disciplined military force of the past, present, or future. Aviators who came from around the globe were at peace, as there existed no predators or prey among those who shared the sky. Every flyer who trained at the Academy was there for one reason and one reason only: to master the art and skill of flight, with the most effective methods by which nature allowed them to do so.

The Academy itself was a vast, treeless cave, assigned to a part of the Earth where no man or woman ever set foot. The location ensured security and provided the Academy the unique ability to recreate every possible climate scenario in which to train all aviators. One section of the cave was purposely kept dark – where the river ran, which flowed into a large lake. While indoors and under hundreds of meters of solid stone, the Academy had ample sunlight and vegetation, though nothing taller than small bushes scattered throughout.

Of the hundreds of birds who were assigned simultaneous training, only a select few were chosen as champion aviators worthy enough to be assigned to simulators. Newer aviators were lifted on sophisticated crane-like machines, which transported cadets from the ground to a distance so high that they could not be seen through the artificial clouds.

Dioni stood in formation as part of a straight line of cadets. He scanned the enormous cave and noticed the unusual collection of students assigned to flight school. Much to his surprise, even flightless birds and other creatures trained at the Avian Flight Academy. Class D-513 had colugos. Class F-606 had flying fish. Each cadet was more-or-less unique in their physicality, but not in their necessity to master flight. The Academy was not meant for competition, for all aviators were well aware of why they were selected to undergo such intense training.

Dioni was assigned to Class B-112, designated for 26 of the most gifted, natural aviators on Earth. Along with Dioni – the only resplendent quetzal in the group – were 2 flying squirrels, 3 sparrows, a snowy owl, an ostrich, an emu, 2 hawks, 5 small robins, 2 blue jays, 3 roadrunners, 2 wrens, 2 orioles, and a flying fox. While the birds of Class B-112 were younger in age, the cadets from the other units were more mature.

All of the students of the Avian Flight Academy were assigned flight uniforms and special detection eyewear, known as pathfinders, which served as both a tracking mechanism as well as a visual communication tool between the various species. Dioni was fortunate in that he was not required to repeat the process of pathfinder installation.

Commander Ballo was the most respected trainer of the Avian Flight Academy. Though he was a smaller bird, Ballo's presence commanded respect. He was an arctic tern – the only such instructor at the Academy – and was one of the most decorated aviators in the school's history with over 3 million logged air miles in all his years of service. He graduated among the elite of the elite, and the other trainers recognized him for it. His method of leadership was to lead by example and to establish bonds with his cadets. At the end of their training, each and every one of Ballo's graduates understood that the ability to fly was more than a right, but rather a privilege which nature granted to those deemed worthy.

Commander Ballo was followed closely behind by a young red knot. Though he did not have any noticeable credentials or a special uniform, every step of the red knot's carefully mirrored the paces taken by Commander Ballo. The young bird held a device which was wired to his left wing and floated alongside him, like a sophisticated tablet that contained no power source yet was synced with its connected bird.

"Class B-112," opened the arctic tern, his small chest raised and his head held high. "My name is Commander Ballo. For those of you who were assigned to this special group, I would like to personally welcome you to the most elite flight class of our academy."

The two hawks looked at one another with excitement; they knew they were the best, they just wanted him to say so.

"If for any reason you feel that you were chosen for this special class because of anything you may or may not have accomplished prior to arriving at this school, let me be the first to inform you: you were not," continued Ballo.

The hawks were not thrilled by his statement. Ballo paced slowly from the start of the lined cadets to the end.

"You are all here because you survived your first major fall. Some of you fell from a tree, others from a mountain, and others…" Ballo paused in front of Dioni. "Others among you just recently earned your wings." He continued. "If you think that I am here to congratulate you or make you feel better for having survived this far, let me correct your perceptions now: I am not."

The red knot distanced himself from Commander Ballo and began his audit. He used the device attached to his wing to scan each of the cadets in Class B-112, which instantly presented him with every detail of each aviator in the group: species, classification, location of origin, known flight abilities and limitations, plus more.

"I am here to teach you skills that you will not be able to learn on your own," the arctic tern continued. "And I only have two days in which to do it."

As Commander Ballo spoke, the red knot continued his audit, one cadet at a time.

"Now, before you get the impression that you have any type of superior knowledge of flight over me – whether it's because of your size, because of your wingspan, or for any known or unknown biological reason – let's just clear the air now: you do not. I can out-maneuver you. I can fly faster at lower altitudes and will be invisible to you at higher ones. On my worst day I am twice the pilot you will ever be on your best, so please do not take it upon yourself to challenge me or question my methods."

As the Commander's monologue continued, the red knot scanned and verify each cadet in the unit. When he reached Dioni, a mysterious classification error appeared on his screen.

"My second in command is Airman Crownhauer," Ballo continued. "Though 'crow' is in his name, please do not confuse Airman Crownhauer for anything less than a superior flyer. The Airman and I have worked together for years, and not a single one of our cadets has ever—"

"—Sir?" Crownhauer interrupted. "We have an anomaly with this cadet."

Ballo walked to Crownhauer and took hold of the device. He looked at the screen.

"What's the problem?" asked Ballo.

"This one's not classified," Crownhauer responded. "There is no location of origin, no base unit, no assigned field area, no detail of any kind…yet it says he has infinity clearance."

"Yep, I know what this is," Ballo responded softly.

He returned the device to Crownhauer, who was more confused than when he first read the error message on his screen. Ballo looked directly at Dioni.

"You've never trained an Omega before, have you, Crownhauer?" Ballo asked.

"An *Omega*? No sir!" Crownhauer responded, excitedly. In disbelief, the other recruits fell out of formation and looked at Dioni.

"Well, this will be your first and likely your last, Airman," Ballo said. He addressed Dioni. "What's your name, cadet?"

"Dioni, sir."

"The only what?" Ballo and Crownhauer responded simultaneously.

"No, not 'the only'. Dee Oh Nee. Dioni."

"Ah, Dee-oh-nee," responded Ballo. "Welcome to flight school, Mr. Omega."

"Sir," interrupted Crownhauer. "There's something else. My scanner is indicating he's a quetzal, but he's clearly not."

"What are you talking about? Look at him, of course he is," responded Ballo. "Dee-oh-nee, do you have your tailfeathers?"

With no knowledge of how to prove he had long tailfeathers, Dioni did the only action that came logically to him: he turned over and shook his butt at the two birds. The other cadets chuckled at the strange occurrence.

"See there, Crownhauer," responded Ballo. "He's a quetzal."

Dioni turned himself to face forward, his point proven.

"But he's blue, sir," said Crownhauer. "There's no classification for him."

"Then make one up." Ballo looked carefully at Dioni. "You're an odd-looking Omega, but an Omega nonetheless."

Crownhauer elevated his screen.

"What should I add under classification status?"

"Keep it simple, Airman," Ballo responded. "Just put down, 'The Blue Q'."

"The Blue Q, sir?"

"Yep, short and simple," Ballo said to Crownhauer. "That way we all know who it is we're talking about."

Ballo stepped closer to Dioni, almost beak-to-beak.

177

"If you are here at the Academy, that means two things. One: that this is not your first stop. And two: you already experienced flight, you just have no idea how you did it."

"I...I...ye...yes..." Dioni nervously responded.

"The Hawaiian crow, Ally...she was also class B-112," Ballo continued. "When I accepted the job I was told that it would be extremely rare for me to train an Omega. So imagine my surprise when I'm assigned two."

"Sir?" Crownhauer said. He lowered his device and looked at Ballo.

Ballo stepped back and slightly lowered his head. He stood proudly, though he felt unsettled over Dioni's presence in his training unit. For a brief moment, Ballo stared blankly at the blue quetzal, to see beyond Dioni's physical being.

"Sir?" said Crownhauer.

Ballo stepped further back and noticed the other trainees out of line.

"Back in formation, cadets!" instructed Ballo. "Just because we have an Omega doesn't mean we're going to do things any differently."

The trainees immediately fell back into position.

"Sir, should I continue?" asked Crownhauer.

"Let's come back to it," responded Ballo. "Pair them off while I contact headquarters."

"Yes, sir," responded Crownhauer.

The arctic tern walked to a distant screen, located away from the view of the other birds. Crownhauer, uneasy about the entire situation, nervously looked at his device while distracted by the Commander's actions. Ballo looked startled, almost worried, which was extremely unusual behavior for an instructor of his caliber.

"Umm," Crownhauer said aloud. "Let's...uh...go ahead and pair you off. There's uhh – twentyyy ssss.... Um, twen....an even number of you...okay." He paused and shook his head. "I'm going to read out your identification numbers in pairs, so step up when you hear yours. That'll be your training partner."

Crownhauer saw as Ballo made gestures toward a screen. He was unable to determine what Ballo communicated, or to whom.

"708 you are with 630," Crownhauer continued. He paid little attention to his task. "847 with 773. 224 with 815. 518 with…." He looked away. "Uhh, 401."

Ballo read a long series of notes from the screen. With his movement, the Commander responded to what was displayed. He stopped when he saw what appeared to him as a smaller version of the same gigantic map from the Control Center. He motioned his wing to the left, in desperate search of weather patterns of the past. With each movement he saw decades of climate information for the entire planet.

"Come on, come on…this can't be it," Ballo said aloud.

He motioned his wing to the right to look at the same weather data in progressive time. He came to the present then paused once more.

"It's too late," Ballo said to the screen. "Another ten years and we won't be able to stop it."

Ballo shutdown the screen. He inhaled deeply, composed himself, then paced to the cadets. Crownhauer quickly returned his attention to his device.

"How're we looking, Airman?" asked Ballo as he walked to his second in command.

"Good, sir," responded Crownhauer. "They're paired accordingly."

"Great! Let's get started."

"Sir?" a nervous voice said from a distance. Both Ballo and Crownhauer turned in the direction from where it came.

"Is there a problem?" asked Ballo. He paced and stopped to stand before the flying fox.

"Would it be possible to switch partners?" asked the flying fox. He looked at a small robin which stood at his side. "No offense, little guy."

"None taken!" responded the robin.

"What's the problem?" asked Crownhauer, a few paces behind.

Ballo took the scanner from Crownhauer.

"Check your pairings, Airman."

"I don't see the problem, sir," responded Crownhauer.

He looked at the two cadets. The flying fox gave the red knot an annoyed glance.

"Got it!" Crownhauer said after a moment of clarity. "I'm so sorry about that, sir!"

"It's a bat, Airman," said Ballo. "We all know they prefer to work alone."

Chapter Thirteen

Day one of aviator training began at the break of dawn. A small group of cadets stood across a long beam which was lifted by a crane at a slow and steady pace. To Dioni, it felt as if he was taught to jump out of an elevator with no doors, and which was raised to a higher level after each leap. The purpose of this style of training was to introduce students to the sensation of falling from reasonable heights before placing them in a situation in which they had no choice. The process was repeated over and again. With each jump, the cadets learned proper flight posture, use of tailfeathers, and principles of gliding.

Though each lesson took time to learn, Dioni found that the knowledge he acquired was simple to replicate once he observed his peers perform the same task. From lesser heights, he learned to use his wings to gently glide down and to use the wind he created to soften his landing. He also discovered that his wing strength was far less than that of the other cadets in his unit.

The ostrich and the emu, though not birds of aerial flight, used their acquired knowledge to understand how aviators navigated and communicated in the sky; they also discovered how they could use their bodies to their advantage while on the ground.

The flying fox – who preferred to work away from his classmates – was given special goggles which simulated different lighting conditions.

181

Because he lacked tailfeathers, the flying fox was taught to use wind force, speed, and agility to create lift and balance drag. His advantage over the other aviators was the small yet useful digits he had on his hands and feet, which allowed him to have superior control of each of his wings. Though one of the most naturally gifted flyers of the class, the flying fox felt most at ease when he found a branch on which he could hang upside down.

The flying squirrels were placed into special simulation tanks where they were launched into the air. Their primary learning modules were not intended to teach flight, but rather to understand the best techniques for aerial navigation and coordination. They had no wings and were thus not considered aviators, yet they were required to master the use of their bodies while airborne. It was especially important for them to learn the physical attributes of fast departures and quick and painless landings.

Dioni's favorite aspect of flight school was the educational component of how his wings actually worked. From lower heights, he taught himself how slight movements had distinct variations on his ability to glide. While his first jumps were low and from a vertical stance, he quickly gained the knowledge to glide with his wings spread widely. He then learned how to shift his wings and lower his legs to land on a specific target.

Aside from Dioni's obvious uniqueness, he also possessed a physical trait which separated him from his peers: his long tailfeathers. As the jumps from the beam were raised to higher elevations, Dioni did his best to mimic the actions and motions he saw of the others. The robins were excellent aviators; they made it look so easy. The hawks were undoubtedly the best pilots in the class, if not the entire school. Dioni learned why the hawks were in a class all to themselves.

As Dioni learned proper flight technique and was able to hold himself in the air for longer distances, he found that his flight pattern was naturally unique. This was not a disadvantage, but rather a distinct ability which all quetzals possessed. Instead of flying in a continuous forward direction, Dioni was able to alter his upward and downward movements, in a wave-like pattern, which enabled him to gain airspeed without the use of additional wing force. Though the quetzal was not physically built for speed – Dioni was nowhere near as fast as the hawks – he had the ability to make incredibly sharp turns, deep dives and fast climbs, all without a reduction in airspeed.

Commander Ballo worked more closely with Dioni than any of the cadets. He took the time to explain every intricate detail of perfect flight, including the art of barrel rolls and of dive-bombing. Dioni's classmates were neither envious nor jealous of the individual instruction he received. Instead, they cheered for him and hoped that the added attention allowed him to learn more in less time.

To further assess their aerial abilities, the cadets were taken to a wind simulation chamber where they learned to use the power of the wind to their advantage. Surprisingly, no cadet enjoyed this training more than the ostrich, who felt as if he lifted from the ground as the strong wind pushed him to new running speeds.

While in the wind chamber, Dioni showed complete control over his ability to fly. Regardless of the direction or speed in which it flowed, Dioni was able to outmaneuver the wind and continue his wave-patterned flight path, even in dangerous scenarios.

"How are you able to lift and move like that?" the younger of the blue jays asked Dioni, in awe of how another blue bird navigated with such unique patterns.

"I don't know," Dioni responded. "I just...can."

"It's his tailfeathers," said Commander Ballo, who overheard their conversation from a distance. "Those long tailfeathers give him an advantage in the air."

"Really?" Dioni asked with excitement.

"Don't fool yourself into thinking you're better than any other pilot, Dioni," said the Commander. "You inherited the tailfeathers, but there are other important characteristics of the quetzal that you still need to learn."

"Oh yeah?" responded Dioni. He smiled as Ballo walked to him and the young blue jay. "Like what?"

"This is flight school, Mr. Omega," said Ballo. "My sole responsibility is to teach you how to be in the air. Everything else is on you."

Night flight was the final training challenge for the first day of flight school. Under this training module, the cadets were taught to use their communication skills, along with their sense of sound, to calculate speed and learn to identify and dodge objects which were randomly placed before them. The flying fox had the clear advantage in this scenario, mostly because of his natural talent in dark environments.

Under the cover of complete darkness, all birds were invisible. Their assigned pathfinders – which combined sonar, radar, and motion detection technology – were finally put to use as the devices enabled the cadets to see and detect items that moved. They saw full color under total darkness, and easily noticed the distances between themselves and other objects. The cadets instantly detected air traffic patterns and weather conditions by doing nothing more than maintaining their eyes open while in flight.

Dioni particularly enjoyed the night flight class. For the first time since he arrived at the Flight Academy, he thought of his home…and of Alma.

Although she was not afraid of darkness – nor would she ever admit if she was – Alma was not a friend of bats. "*Ingratos murciélagos,*" she said every time she heard a pair of wings flap in the dark. As her best friend, Dioni did his best to convince her of two things: first, that the sound was probably a bird and not a bat; and second, that if the sound was from a bat, it was unlikely to attack her. Dioni's intention had no effect. To Alma, bats were the equivalent of flying mice. As such, she likely would have found the flying fox to be the most disturbing, oversized flying rat ever created by nature. In his mind, Dioni knew that this would be a part of the experience he would skip when telling Alma about flight school.

"How does your echo-sound work?" Dioni asked the flying fox as the two cadets performed a series of swooping tasks.

"Echolocation?" responded the flying fox. "It's simple, but I have to use my pathfinder. I can't echolocate without it. You have to think about how the sound travels and not how loud you are. I don't have to see things to know they're there. I listen for the sound to come back to me and I calculate its distance, and then do it over and over again."

184

"Can all bats do that?"

"Little bats can. Mega bats don't need it."

Dioni felt the need to challenge himself. He decided to ignore instruction and his own better judgement in an attempt to test whether or not he was biologically capable of outperforming the flying fox. Dioni disabled his pathfinder, closed his eyes in mid-flight, and emitted a high-pitched sound which was heard by the entire unit. He listened for the sound to return to him, then immediately opened his eyes and placed his pathfinder back into position.

"Nice!" said the flying fox. "That was really good!"

"Now what do I do?" Dioni asked.

"Pay attention to the details of how the sound travels back. The faster and louder the sound comes back to you, the closer and larger an object is to you. It's like trying to hear the distance of an echo."

"Okay."

Dioni once again disabled his pathfinder, closed his eyes and repeated the process. The other cadets noticed his actions and slowly fell back to observe. He was the Omega bird, so perhaps he possessed and ability they did not. The suspense and curiosity were too great to ignore.

As the random pattern of objects changed in the dark, Dioni failed to notice a simulated wind turbine, which was difficult to see even with special eyewear. The large blades of the turbine moved and hardly made a sound. Though perfectly safe when instructions were followed, this particular portion of night flight training startled all of the cadets, including the hawks.

At such altitude and airspeed, a strong hit from a simulated turbine blade could cause permanent damage to any aviator. Even if being the Omega bird enabled him to survive the blow, Dioni would be useless to the world if he were to lose his ability to fly as a result of an accident at the Flight Academy.

The flying fox heard the subtle variations in the echoed sound that returned to him. He saw the mighty blades. He slowed his air speed and drifted to his right, which placed him at a safe distance from potential injury. The flying fox expected Dioni to follow him and perform the same maneuver; he failed to notice as the blue quetzal headed for impending doom. For a brief moment, every bird in the class, including the flightless birds who followed from the ground, took a deep breath and braced for the worst.

A beam of light in the shape of an artic tern instantly flashed in the sky. It was Commander Ballo. He neither flapped his wings nor made a sound, yet he flew faster than anything the cadets had ever seen. The beam of light created by the Commander trailed behind him and slowly faded as he moved through the darkness at incredible speed. He glided through the sky with grace; his light emanated a bright glow which altered his appearance.

An instant before he was struck from the sky, Dioni saw the reflection of a light in the massive blade of the wind turbine. In a flash, Commander Ballo pushed Dioni back, then grabbed Dioni by the shoulders and lifted him away from the turbine. Had any of the cadets blinked, or had Ballo hesitated just a fraction of a second longer, they all would have witnessed a tragedy.

At a safe height and distance, Commander Ballo released Dioni, who knew to use his own wings to glide himself back to the ground. The cadets formed a circle around Dioni to ensure that he was safe; they looked to the sky and witnessed as the light from Commander Ballo slowly faded away.

"What did you do?" asked an oriole.

"I was just trying something," responded Dioni. "I disabled my pathfinder and I was—"

"—Two flaps away from getting yourself killed," interrupted Commander Ballo. He landed just outside of the circle. "What would possess you to do that?"

"I wanted to use sound to see, just like—"

"—You are not a bat!" exclaimed Ballo. The cadets moved away from his path as he broke their circle and marched directly to Dioni. "You do not have the ability to do what bats can do, so the pathfinders do it for you! This was all explained to you!"

186

Dioni became frightened by Ballo's response. Ballo had explained that the entire training exercise was simulated, so what was the worst that could have happened?

"I thought it was all fake," Dioni responded. His voice cracked and his body trembled. "I would've just gone right through it, right? That big fan thing?"

"No, you wouldn't!" Ballo responded with intimidation. "It's a wind turbine. Simulated or not, it would've hit you harder than anything you've ever felt in your life. You nearly died right then, do you understand me? Tell me you understand me!"

"Sir?" a young robin asked, timidly. "How did you do that?"

"How did I do what?" responded Ballo. He kept his eyes on Dioni.

"You were a beam of light, sir. You were in the air without flapping your wings, and the light followed you."

Commander Ballo paused. He did not blink or change his gaze at Dioni.

"That's none of your concern," Ballo responded.

"Sir?"

"It's not something I can teach you nor anything you can learn," Ballo said. He turned his attention to the other cadets. "We're done for the day. You all have two seconds to head to the aviary barracks or I swear that you will never again feel the draft of a cool breeze beneath your wings."

Every member of class B-112 immediately left the premises, only Commander Ballo and Airman Crownhauer stayed behind. Ballo kept his eyes on Dioni as he joined the rest of his classmates. Crownhauer opened his tablet.

"Commander," said Crownhauer. "Sir, can you explain what happened?" Ballo turned away. "I have to fill out an incident report."

"He's the Omega, Crownhauer," responded Ballo. "That wouldn't have been another bird sent to the infirmary. It would've killed him."

Crownhauer moved to get in Commander Ballo's line of sight.

"We have accidents all the time, sir. The simulator is not strong enough to—"

"—I know that!" interrupted Ballo. "I am well aware of the simulations. But he still would've gotten hurt, badly. Accidents like that can make a bird like him afraid to fly."

Crownhauer inhaled deeply then exhaled slowly.

"Not all birds are meant to fly, sir."

Ballo looked directly at Crownhauer.

"This one is, Airman. If that bird is not in the air, then the rest of us don't stand a chance to…to…"

Crownhauer lowered his device.

"There's nothing to report, is there, sir?"

"No…nothing."

The aviary barracks were little more than a series of small housing structures designed for only two-night usage for each of the cadets; all cadets were assigned to the same barrack as the rest of their class. That night, B-112 was the quietest among the dozens of barracks of the Academy.

The cadets rested in formation. They stood with their heads lowered and with their talons either on the ground or on a lifted perch.

"Why would you disconnect your pathfinder?" asked a hawk, the first to break the silence. He asked the question every cadet wanted answered.

"I was…" responded Dioni, angrily. "Leave me alone."

"I mean, I get what you were trying to do," the hawk continued, "but even mythic birds can't echolocate."

Dioni turned his back to the hawk.

"He's right, you know," said the emu, who Dioni saw at eye-level. "That was really dangerous. You're lucky Commander Ballo stopped you."

Dioni leapt from the perch and onto the floor.

"Are you sure you're the Omega bird?" asked a flying squirrel.

The question was out of line, though she had a right to ask.

"I don't know!" responded Dioni. "I was me one day, and this the next! I didn't ask to be a bird! I just want to go home and be me again, but I have to wait 10 days and go through this stupid school before I can go back."

"So you *don't* want to be the Omega bird?" asked the flying squirrel.

"No! I don't even know what that means!" Dioni's eyes began to water. "I just want to go home."

The cadets hung their heads and faced down.

"Ey…mate," the hawk whispered. "Did you see how upset he was? The Commander?" A few of the classmates smiled. "He looked like one of those red-faced buzzards."

The bigger birds looked up. Some of the smaller birds held their laughter.

"His head was all inflated and his chest looked like he swallowed a balloon," said the other flying squirrel.

Dioni chuckled yet kept his head down.

"It would've knocked you colder and harder than anything you felt in your life," said a roadrunner, mocking the Commander.

Every cadet found it to be hilarious. Another of the roadrunners joined the performance; she mocked the Commander's speech and exaggerated his movements.

"You all have two seconds to head to the aviary barracks, or I swear that you will never feel a draft of wind again! I am Commander Ballo, and no one in this Academy breaks wind harder, louder, or with more force than me!"

Barrack B-112 roared with laughter. The second, more comedic of the roadrunners continued her performance, though none of her classmates heard her from the sound of so much hilarity. Dioni looked up. He wiped the tears from his eyes and sniffled as he released a small chuckle. He made friends among the group, which was the first unexpected benefit of his 10-day agreement. The cadets noticed Dioni's change in attitude and turned their attention to him.

"Hey, '*the only*'," began the flying fox. He smiled as he faced Dioni. "If you need to fly at night without a pathfinder, you come find me, okay?"

Dioni laughed as a single tear streamed down his small face.

"I will," he said with a smile.

"Hi, my name is *'The Only'*," began the third roadrunner. He mocked Dioni to complete the performance from the comedic trio. "And I am the Omega bird. I wasn't a bird yesterday, but I am today, so now that I know how to fly, I'm going to go full speed into the blade of a wind turbine. Can someone hold my pathfinder?"

The roadrunner ran toward the ostrich, who quickly improvised and used its head to playfully knock him into the air. The roadrunner's successful airlift pushed him between the two squirrels, who immediately raised their little arms to indicate a perfect field goal.

All the birds paused as the roadrunner landed roughly and tumbled to a stop. He slowly got to his feet and dusted himself off.

"Well, I guess I'm an *alebrije* now," said the roadrunner.

The roar of laughter from barrack B-112 was heard throughout the entire Flight Academy. Dioni laughed along with his classmates. He regained his confidence and joined the rest of the birds on the perch.

"You guys are morons."

Chapter Fourteen

The second day of flight school was less intense than the first. The cadets of class B-112 remained on edge over what occurred the previous night. As a result of the experience, however, the cadets formed a tight bond. They stood just outside of a simulation room.

With his pathfinder firmly in place — and with absolutely no desire to remove it or disable it in any way — Dioni was assigned a special course that was not required for any other cadet in the group.

"Dioni," began Commander Ballo, "you may or may not use this knowledge, but it's important that you learn it. It could save your life."

"Yes, sir," responded Dioni.

"Your pathfinder is going to have to stay on. Got it?"

"Yes, sir! Absolutely, sir!"

"Good. Now, do you know what a bird murmuration is?"

"No…is that something painful?"

"What? No, no, no. It's a formation we use to escape predators. Sometimes we use it as a distraction."

"A distraction from what?"

"You won't really know until you need it."

"Okay."

"Basically, what you're doing is learning to fly as part of a large swarm, without a leader. Everyone is looking out for one another. You have to navigate your flight pattern by calculating even the smallest movements made by the birds surrounding you."

"Got it," Dioni responded. "How do I do that?"

"First of all, by not disconnecting your pathfinder," said Ballo. "It will help you see exactly which birds around you are moving, and how they're moving. All you have to do is match their flight pattern, and they match yours."

"So it's a game of follow-the-leader?"

"N....yes and no. It's a lot more sophisticated than that. If any single bird is out of formation, the whole murmuration fails. It's more like a game of follow-the-flight-pattern with about a hundred birds.

"Huh...okay. Got it," responded Dioni, nervous yet excited over the new training.

"Some of the best aviators to perform murmurations are starlings, so we're going to simulate a starling environment. Don't take off your pathfinder, you hear me?"

"I won't!"

"Good. Get inside and we'll start the program."

The murmuration flight simulator was designed similar to the air tunnel where cadets learned to navigate and use wind power in their favor. The simulator was roughly the size of Dioni's former bedroom, by comparison. It had no corners, and the lining of the interior surface had a mesh-like screen which contained thousands of tiny holes. As the door to the simulator closed behind him, Dioni stood in a circular room that was illuminated by the streams of light which passed through the tiny gaps in the mesh.

"Stand in the center, Dioni," said a voice from a loudspeaker system. Dioni immediately complied. "Flight formation."

Dioni lowered his head, looked forward and extended his wings. He felt a breeze push from below, which lifted him off of the surface. At first, the sensation was odd, which caused him to lose his balance. Regardless of his actions, the breeze automatically shifted to keep him airlifted and in the center of the room. The simulator detected the slightest of movements from the aviator-in-training, which made it one of the safest programs in the Flight Academy.

As he stabilized his flight, Dioni saw a small dot of light directly in front of him.

"Look straight ahead," instructed the voice. "The simulation starts like a tunnel. The light in front of you will get brighter and larger as you get closer to the end."

"Got it!" Dioni responded.

"Don't disable your pathfinder, Dioni."

"I got it."

Dioni focused his attention on the growing light.

"And watch out for those wind turbines," said the voice.

Had he not focused solely on the task at hand, Dioni would have realized that the voice which provided instruction received notes from one of Dioni's classmates. Ballo wanted Dioni to learn his lesson.

Dioni concentrated on his objective. In the near distance he heard the chirps of a large group of birds. He did not see them, but they grew louder as the light became more intense.

The simulator displayed a beautiful blue sky from the moment he exited the virtual tunnel. The entire mesh-covered room displayed his new surroundings; Dioni saw the replicated simulation of a real location.

As he drifted through the simulated sky, he noticed a group of starlings behind him. The starlings were not real, though had he not been informed that this was a simulation, Dioni would have never known the difference. As he turned his body, the simulator calculated his movements and displayed a change in scenery. No matter the direction in which he moved, the air blown from the gaps in the simulator held Dioni securely in the center.

The group of birds behind him was a swarm of approximately 50 starlings. As they flew in formation, half of the starlings positioned themselves in front of Dioni while the others surrounded him on both sides; only a select few remained behind. His pathfinder easily identified each starling, just as Ballo said it would.

By looking through his pathfinder, Dioni saw the instantaneous movements of every bird near him. All he had to do was remain in formation with those closest to him and pay particular attention to sudden movements made by the surrounding starlings. At the start, every bird flew forward, with no variation or shift in direction.

"Alright, Dioni," said Commander Ballo through the speaker system. "Stay on course with each bird immediately surrounding you. Your pathfinder will detect their movements, so just follow the pathfinder's guidance. Is that understood?"

"Understood," Dioni responded.

"Okay…here we go."

The simulated starlings beside Dioni slowly shifted their bodies and their flight pattern to the right. As Ballo said, the pathfinder successfully determined the distance and movement of every surrounding bird, which provided simple guidance for Dioni to follow. The starlings repeated the same movement to the left. Again, Dioni easily stayed in formation.

From within the control room, Commander Ballo directed the simulation. Ballo stood behind three actual starlings, who operated the simulation program. The bodies of the three starlings were suspended by a system of magnetic levitation, which kept them in perfect flight formation while instructing their screens; their movements translated to commands for the simulator.

"We're keeping the movements simple, sir," said one of the starlings. "Standing by for jolt."

"On my command," responded Ballo, who paid close attention to Dioni's movements.

The cadets of class B-112 were allowed to observe from a distance, and only within the observatory. Though Dioni could neither see nor hear them, his classmates observed his every move and cheered for his success.

"Jolt," Ballo instructed.

"Jolting," the starlings simultaneously responded.

In the simulator, Dioni's simple maneuvers were interrupted when the starlings lifted to gain altitude. As it was unexpected movement, Dioni failed to notice the warning from his pathfinder. The birds beneath him lifted and collided with Dioni and with one another, to which the simulator produced the scene of a crashed murmuration. Dozens of birds fell from the sky as Dioni struggled to maintain his balance. The internal breeze slowly lowered him onto the floor until he was able to place his feet on solid ground. The room went dark.

"What happened, Dioni?" asked Ballo, through the loudspeaker.

"I didn't expect them to lift," Dioni responded. "I got hit from below."

"If you're in the center, you have to be mindful of birds from every direction. A single bird out of alignment is enough to crash the whole thing."

"Yes, sir."

"Let's try it again."

Dioni re-composed himself and shook his entire body. He mentally prepared himself for another attempt.

"Flight formation," said the voice of a starling.

Dioni once again spread his wings and lifted from the floor. Within moments he was back in the sky; the simulator recreated the exact scenario as before.

Dioni's classmates watched intensely from the observatory. Neither of them were required to undergo the training, yet they followed along and observed Dioni's simulation on a projected screen. They moved their bodies in coordination with Dioni, almost as if to telepathically coach Dioni on the proper movements to make. Even the flightless birds contributed.

"Let's try this again, Sergeant," directed Ballo. "In three...two...one... jolt."

As before, the birds beneath Dioni lifted. Dioni's pathfinder created the same alarm. On this attempt, Dioni pulled up and stayed in formation. The cadets cheered.

Dioni's pathfinder worked flawlessly; it knew that Dioni was in a murmuration formation, and by means of math and physics, made millions of instant calculations to a fraction of a centimeter. To Dioni, it appeared as though his pathfinder was connected and synced to the pathfinder of every simulated starling.

"Good, Dioni…good," Ballo said to himself as he watched Dioni maintain formation. "Let's go ahead and change the pattern," he directed.

"On your cue, sir," responded one of the starlings.

"Dive," instructed Ballo.

The starlings moved in perfect unison. They pitched their heads and lowered their bodies; the simulator instantly responded to their choreographed movements.

In the simulator, Dioni noticed a sudden shift in the brightness of the room. The pathfinder immediately detected the change. Dioni saw dozens of simulated starlings dive toward the ground. He failed to copy the pattern in time, which resulted in a collusion from above. Once again, Dioni caused the failure of the murmuration. The simulator came to a stop as Dioni regained his composure.

"What happened, Dioni?" asked Ballo.

"I was too busy looking at the birds beneath me," Dioni responded. "I didn't pay attention to the ones above."

"Use the pathfinder, Dioni. That's what it's there for."

"Okay."

"Again."

On the third attempt, Dioni successfully passed the jolt and the dive but failed to notice his physical space and slammed into a seaside cliff, which destroyed the murmuration. In a real-life scenario, many birds would have lost their lives at that moment.

On the fourth attempt, Dioni was more mindful of his surroundings but carelessly broke formation when the sunlight temporarily blinded him. He failed to see the warning produced by his pathfinder, and he once again crashed into the birds above.

On the fifth attempt, Dioni learned a new skill – placement within formation – which meant he was able to determine where to position himself within the group. Unfortunately, he did not take into account his elevation from the ground.

On the sixth attempt, Dioni heavily miscalculated wind speed and caused a tremendous collusion in the sky.

On the seventh attempt, Dioni learned why murmurations do not occur in circular patterns.

On the eighth attempt, Dioni confused the sky with a large body of water and was responsible for the drowning of hundreds of simulated starlings.

Twenty attempts and twenty failures later, Dioni's classmates wondered if he would ever complete the training. They cheered when he performed correctly, they silently coached him by providing instruction to a projected screen, and they felt dismayed when he failed again and again. Nevertheless, they stood with their teammate.

By the thirty-second attempt, Dioni successfully analyzed every change in movement. He gracefully airlifted and calculated every action of the flock, using his pathfinder for guidance.

"Roll predator," Ballo instructed the starlings in the control room.

"What's your target, sir?" asked a starling.

"Let's challenge the kid. Brown eagle. Target on the Omega."

"Confirmed, sir."

The observation room became quiet. The cadets looked at one another, worried over what was to happen next. They turned their attention to the screen.

Dioni easily maneuvered through the flock of hundreds of simulated starlings. With each attempt and each failure, he gained more knowledge and experience, which meant the challenge had to be more severe.

From the horizon, Dioni saw a large object fly toward the flock. The pathfinder registered the object as an unclassified bird, though he immediately noticed it was not a starling. He continued with the murmuration and flew in and out of the center of the formation, careful to remain coordinated with the movements of the starlings. Dioni turned toward the horizon and saw that the large bird disappeared.

With absolutely no prior notice or warning from his pathfinder, the mighty talon of an angry brown eagle appeared above Dioni. In fear for his life, Dioni fled the formation and was momentarily chased until he was easily captured by the eagle. The entire simulator went dark. Dioni landed harshly on the floor.

"What happened, Dioni?" asked Ballo.

"An eagle came out of nowhere and attacked me!" responded Dioni. He breathed heavily.

"You were his target."

"What does that mean?" asked Dioni

"You don't look like a starling, so predators are going to see you first."

"Even though it's also a bird?"

"You have to be mindful, Dioni," Ballo said. "You know how the world works."

"So what do I do? I tried to fly in another direction but he caught me."

"You have to use the murmuration to your advantage," said Ballo. Split the formation."

"That doesn't make any sense, sir," Dioni responded, annoyed by the lack of clarification.

"The eagle can easily catch one bird, but the formation of every starling's movement confuses it. Change the formation and it won't be able to catch you or any of the starlings."

"I'm just one of a hundred birds up there!" responded Dioni. "How can I change the entire murmuration if I can't control the flight pattern of every bird?"

198

"Intuition, Dioni. Act like a starling, think like an eagle," responded Ballo.

"What?"

"Again."

Twenty-seven attempts later, Dioni remained unable to either split the murmuration or outfly the eagle. The task was impossible. With each failed attempt, Dioni became increasingly frustrated.

The cadets saw it all. They wanted their teammate to succeed, and his failures were just as frustrating to them as they were to Dioni. The flying fox opened the communication screen to the control room.

"Sir?" asked the flying fox, prior to Dioni's seventy-eighth simulation. "How much more is he going to have to do, sir?"

Ballo looked at the large bat. He saw how worried he and the rest of the cadets were for their fellow classmate.

"He has to pass. He doesn't have a choice." Ballo turned his attention to the starlings. "Again."

"Sir...can I talk to him?" asked the flying fox.

If granted permission, he knew how he could help Dioni. If denied, then at least he bought a few precious seconds of time before the start of Dioni's next simulation. Ballo turned to the flying fox.

"That's why we have the intercom system, cadet. I talk to him here, you stay in the observatory."

"Sir, just one minute. That's all I ask."

Ballo noticed how the cadets looked at him. They hoped he would show even the slightest compassion. Ballo sighed.

"Sixty seconds," he said to the flying fox. "That's it."

"Yes, sir! Thank you, sir!"

The flying fox quickly ran out of the control room and to the door of the simulator. The simulator opened and there stood an exhausted bird. Dioni turned to look at his friend.

"What are you doing here?" asked Dioni. "I thought you were Ballo coming in to yell at me."

"Are you okay?"

"I will be once I convince this eagle that starlings taste better."

"Listen," said the flying fox. "You're trying to out-fly the eagle, and it's just not going to happen."

"You think?" Dioni responded with evident sarcasm.

"Hear me out, Dioni. You have to use your other abilities to outsmart him."

"How the heck do I do that?" asked Dioni. He silently wished his fellow cadet had entered with a glass of water.

"Use your senses. He's faster and stronger than you, but not smarter. Remember the echo trick I taught you?"

"The same one that almost got me killed by a fake turbine?" Dioni responded.

The door of the simulator began to close, which indicated the end of Ballo's patience.

"Forget about that," said the flying fox. He quickly exited the simulator as the door slowly closed. "Use your body and your abilities to your advantage. What do you have that it doesn't?"

The simulator door shut. He was once again on his own.

"Think Dioni, think…" he said to himself. "What do you have that the eagle doesn't? These tailfeathers for one. That won't help. What else? Think think think…"

The simulator began just as before. This had become familiar to Dioni – by means of trial and failure – and he knew what to expect.

"Brown eagle target on Omega, roll predator," Ballo instructed from the control room.

The starlings followed the command and simulated the brown eagle to once again attack Dioni. As expected, Dioni broke away from the murmuration. He was the intended target, and despite his best efforts, he would never out-perform the eagle – simulated or not.

For this attempt, however, Dioni tried a different tactic. He saw the eagle close behind, a short distance from his tailfeathers, when he remembered his unique flight pattern. Dioni barrel-rolled and dove directly toward the ground. The eagle immediately copied his strategy and followed closely behind. Dioni's plan did not work as well as he had hoped.

The cadets in the observation room knew what occurred.

"Come on, Dioni," said the flying fox. "Be smarter."

Just as he was to hit the ground, Dioni lifted his head and pulled up, which forced him into a scoop. At the closest point to crash-landing in a grass field, he turned his head and shouted in the opposite direction in which he moved his body.

The eagle, immediately confused, dove to momentarily follow Dioni's sound. The predator's reaction allowed Dioni enough time to escape. He did not flee from the eagle but was instead able to outsmart it. With his mission accomplished, Dioni returned to the starling murmuration.

"Well I'll be damned," said Ballo, from the control center.

Once again, the eagle reengaged his attack with Dioni as his target. Just as before, Dioni escaped, outsmarted the eagle, then returned to the murmuration. This sequence was repeated twice more before the eagle became exhausted and flew away. The simulation ended when every starling landed safely on the ground.

The entire cadet class cheered for their teammate. They wanted nothing more than to run out of the observation room and personally congratulate Dioni, but they froze when they heard the word—

"Again," directed Commander Ballo.

The cadets felt defeated. There was no way to further help their friend.

On the seventy-ninth attempt, Dioni repeated his maneuver and completed the task successfully.

On the eightieth attempt, Dioni stayed with the murmuration the entire time and learned to use the starlings as decoys, none of which the eagle captured.

By the ninety-fifth attempt, with simulated rain and wind, Dioni used his unique flight style to outsmart the eagle. Once again, he prevented capture.

A second eagle was introduced on the hundred-and-first attempt, which Dioni particularly enjoyed; he learned the result of what would happen if two of the most ferocious and talented aviators collided midair.

No attempt after that was a failure. Dioni, as did the rest of the cadets, lost track of the total attempts made before he was able to perfect the exercise.

When he finally exited the simulator, Dioni was thrilled as his classmates cheered. In that moment, Dioni failed to think of himself as anything other than a bird. He was not Dionisio from Flores, nor was he an orphan boy who gave scenic tours to tourists. He did not think of Alma, nor did he think of the deal he negotiated with the Alpha. He believed in himself as the Omega bird.

Commander Ballo was a few paces behind the rest of the cheerful group. He clapped slowly, though proudly, for Dioni.

"Not bad, cadet," Ballo said to his exhausted student. "Not too shabby."

"Thank you, sir," responded Dioni.

"Sir?" began a blue jay. "Do the rest of us have to complete this training?"

The cheers of the group came to a sudden stop. Commander Ballo smiled.

"No," responded Ballo. "You're not required to complete this exercise. This was for him."

The cadets breathed a collective sigh of relief.

"Dioni, how are you feeling?" asked Ballo.

"Tired, sir. And hungry."

Ballo inflated his chest.

"I'm a bit peckish myself," said Ballo. The stars on his uniform reflected his pride. "Class B-112 cadets, report to the mess for chow. After which,

Crownhauer will provide you with directives for graduation as well as portal instructions to get you home."

Chapter Fifteen

The Department of Global Climate Control was busier than ever. News quickly spread that a new Omega bird was selected – a quetzal – and that he was training in flight school. Business was livelier than it had been in some time.

The Trading Floor was chaotic, as usual. Birds from around the world communicated and negotiated, then reported their results to their designated home base. Rarely were there physical altercations, though every so often there would be an impasse between two or more parties: too much rain in one part of the world, not enough in another; orders for winter to end and trees and flowers to blossom commonly contradicted other negotiated orders for late-season snowstorms; hard-headed negotiators such as the woodpeckers of the Californian redwood forest refused to accept any offers which did not benefit them directly, even if it stalled weather patterns and created season-lasting droughts in their territory.

Spring was the best time for a new Omega bird to enter the scene. It was an exciting time of the year for all birds assigned to stations on the Trading Floor. Not only had negotiations begun for the mid-summer months in the northern hemisphere, some birds also started their climate plans for the fall and winter.

The current season, however, included the addition of two new work order instructions which were directed by the Alpha. First, every negotiation required double confirmation of approval. Instead of submitting completed work orders directly to the Control Center, all unusual climate activity required the Alpha's signature and approval. Major events – such as hurricanes, tsunamis, and any damage-causing storms over a city with a population greater than 1 million inhabitants – required justification and proof of necessity. The new directives were not implemented as a way to limit falsified work orders, nor was it the malicious intent of the Alpha to create more steps for an already lengthy process. The directive was instead a way for the Alpha to have more oversight for his latest planned initiative.

The second and more important aspect of the submitted climate work orders and negotiations was the inclusion of heat. Having conducted a thorough audit of global weather patterns and of population densities, the Alpha and the former Omega came to an agreement with the trial of a new concept, which was titled the Global Climate Initiative. As part of a pilot program for only one summer season of the northern hemisphere, global climate was to adjust to increase worldwide average temperature by .005 degrees, Fahrenheit. Though likely to go unnoticed, the Alpha and the Omega agreed that the single-season test provided valuable data on how to potentially shift global weather patterns and possibly allow future planning to be much simpler for all birds across all regions. The details of the initiative were kept private. The memo distributed from the executive suite to both the Trading Floor as well as the Control Center required all negotiations to add a factor of heat; all actions from the Control Center required proof of added heat that did not exceed the temporary standard temperature.

None of the directives were questioned by any bird, although the Magellanic penguins of the Patagonia region complained of insufficient heat for their area during their cold season. The problem was successfully negotiated by use of a special circumstance petition, which forced the streamertail community of Jamaica to willingly accept one extra rainstorm for the summer.

The Global Climate Initiative was a highly anticipated negotiation between the Alpha and the Omega. Rumors swirled throughout the avian world; no one knew which of the two birds would claim victory. While the Alpha had held his post long enough to experience and be knowledgeable of repeated global climate patterns, the Omega refused to accept any changes which could not be reversed. She knew the vulture all too well to allow him to act in a manner which suited only his interests.

The Alpha and Ally rarely agreed on much, but in the end, the results of the global climate audit concluded that the initiative was necessary. It was certainly not the first time that a global climate trial was agreed upon – especially not one of such grand scale – though it was the first time heat was introduced. Prior to this, negotiations included one of two possible outcomes: slightly cooler overall global temperatures, or slight extensions of a season. This resulted in unusually warm days in October in the north, unusually cold days in May in the south, and sufficient rainfall to both regions.

Trial years were oftentimes marked by extra sunlight in particular areas of the world during the month of February; to prevent people from understanding the cycles and therefore predict them, work orders for the region of Punxsutawney, Pennsylvania, were deliberately submitted to randomly select overcast or sunny skies. Birds from the region found it hilarious how the people selected a groundhog – who was clueless as to why he was paraded before such large crowds – as a means of predicting the weather for the six weeks that followed.

Ally wanted no part in allowing birds to negotiate weather patterns based on the rise of global temperatures, but she was powerless after the results of the global climate audit. Eight birds – from different regions and who were not members of either the Trading Floor or the Control Center – were selected to conduct stress tests to determine the amount of weather differential the Earth could successfully sustain. While operations continued in both divisions of the Department of Global Climate Control during the audit process, the eight selected birds monitored climate cycles and reported findings after slight variations of heat were introduced in certain regions. Audits were recorded as one to three unusually warm days, which occurred within the same week. While their collected data provided sufficient results, the eight auditors discovered that other parts of the world experienced different weather anomalies. This was ultimately attributed to negotiations back at the DGCC. Nevertheless, the results were highlighted in the final audit report.

In the end, the report concluded that no significant change would result if the entire Earth was exposed to a global temperature increase no greater than .007 degrees Fahrenheit, for a period no longer than six months. Anything beyond that time frame or above that temperature threatened the possibility of irreversible damage. After weeks of heated debates and arguments between the Alpha and the Omega, the two birds agreed that the trial period would last three months, and that global temperature would not exceed .005 degrees.

As with all deals made by the Alpha, there was no formal contract or signed agreement. Instead, the two birds verbally agreed and shook wings to secure the settlement between both parties. A bird is only as good as his word, and the Alpha did not want to tarnish his reputation by leaving his name on signed documents.

The initiative was Ally's final completed negotiation. After multiple decades of service, she reluctantly agreed to the Alpha's demands. Once again, the Alpha was victorious. She felt that she had lost all her credibility, and that it was in her best interest to find a solid replacement. By no means was the balance of the Earth a democratic process, but rather a strict system of weights and measures, checks and balances, which provided the necessary information for birds across the continents to determine the weather patterns that were best for their regions. Or, more importantly, if it was what the Alpha desired.

Shortly after they exchanged formalities, Ally took one final look at the place she had known as home for so many years. She vowed never to return. She gave an entire lifetime of service, and a return to life in human form was of no interest to her. Ally knew that it was of utmost importance to find a suitable replacement – someone who had little to lose and no one to leave behind. As her last action before her final departure, she removed her assigned pathfinder and left the device on the floor of her former office. There was no note, and no indication of the reason behind her actions; she just disappeared and left the fate of the world to chance.

...

The Alpha stood proudly on the perch of his executive suite. He overlooked his creation in the same manner an arrogant king looked upon his empire. His wings were tucked at his side. To the Alpha, it was a reminder of his unique ability to fuel his ego. He did not care if he did not win, but he would destroy the Earth before he admitted defeat. With Ally gone, the process of doing so was far simpler. The Alpha was happy with his lifetime of accomplishments, and he spared no expense to acquire what he deserved…even if it meant the falsification of audit reports.

Mimidae had no desire to interrupt the Alpha in his state of illusion. She gently knocked on the door of the executive suite.

"Sir?" she said. She hoped to not upset the Alpha, as he was in deep thought. "Just a quick update?"

"Ah, Mimidae, my faithful executive assistant," the Alpha responded. "I was just thinking about our former Omega."

"Ally, sir? The crow?"

"An Alalā, Mim. Not just any crow; a Hawaiian one. She was unique. Yeah. She was a great Omega. She really was. But you know what? I'm glad she's gone."

"Sir? Then why were you thinking about her?"

"A fresh start, really. New blood. In this case, blue blood. It's a chance to start anew with the next Omega."

"Now that you brought that up—"

"—And the timing couldn't be better," interrupted the vulture. "We're going forward with the test this summer, negotiations are at an all-time high, and we haven't had a single catastrophe that was unaccounted for. I'm pitching a perfect game, Mim. And I have Ally to thank for it."

Mimidae stood quietly, motionless. She wanted the vulture to tire of the sound of his own voice, or at least for him to recognize that the conversation was one-sided. The Alpha turned and paced toward his executive desk. He failed to look in Mimidae's direction.

"I think…" the Alpha continued. "If I had to rank all of the Omega's in my lifetime, I would put her in the top ten. I mean, she wasn't a bright or colorful bird, but she had a lot of spunk, you know? I was really quite shocked when she left. I guess the job does that to weaker birds. One day you're at the top of your game, and a few minutes later you're scouting your own replacement. It's kinda sad, actually…if you think about it."

The Alpha rested on the perch behind his desk. A small beam of light emanated from his screen, which displayed trade results as well as global climate data.

"Lucky for you, I don't have that problem," he continued. "I have a job and a responsibility up here, Mim, which I am proud to say that no one can do as well as I can. Well, I have held this job longer than any other Alpha. Not that that's a bad thing, it's just that you don't replace greatness, you know? The job is to look after and do that which is best to restore the balance of the Earth, and I'd like to think I'm doing a fantastic job. More than fantastic…exceptional. Yeah, that's how I would describe it… exceptional. And why quit when you're ahead? No…I am the Alpha and I am going to continue to be the Alpha long after this poor excuse of an Omega quits on me. HA! A blue quetzal. What a ridiculous bird."

The Alpha looked at the screen yet paid no attention to what he saw.

"Who would do my job if I wasn't here?" he continued, aloud and mostly to himself. "Or, more importantly, what would I do if I wasn't here? I can't finish my work if I were to go back! I wouldn't know what to do or even where to start. I'd probably end up doing something absurd like being a yogurt salesman or something. Oh, yogurt sounds good."

"Would you like yogurt, sir?" asked Mimidae.

"AH!" yelled the Alpha as he fell from his perch. He failed to notice Mimidae, who stood closely beside him.

"How long have you been there?" he asked as he rolled himself over to get proper footing.

"Far longer than I should have," Mimidae responded. "Sir, would you like yogurt?"

"Not anymore! Jeez, Mim…we have to put a bell on you or something."

"We can discuss it at the next team meeting, sir," Mimidae responded, frustrated. "I'll add that to the agenda."

"Fine. Did you need something or are you just trying to give me a heart attack for no reason?"

He regained his balance and stood on his perch.

"The new Omega completed Flight Academy training," said Mimidae.

"Oh good. We'll get him out in the field right away."

"He'll be coming back here within the next few minutes."

"Fine, fine. Just give him Ally's old office and show him how to use the seed machine."

"I get an office?" asked Dioni, who stood at the entrance of the Alpha's executive suite.

Beside Dioni was Airman Crownhauer, who gave the impression of discomfort in the surroundings.

"You sure do, Mr. Pilot!" the Alpha responded, being coy.

He turned his body and lifted his right wing to cover himself for a private side-conversation.

"I thought you said, '*a few minutes*', Mim!" the Alpha said to her, quietly yet sternly.

"That was a few minutes '*ago*', *sir*," she responded. The Alpha lifted his wing. "The Omega bird is here to see you," she continued, her tone entirely shifted. Mimidae ignored the Alpha's position and his power over her.

"I see that now," the Alpha responded. He rose from his perch and changed his demeanor from cold and angry to unusually happy. "Dioni! Welcome back! And Airman Crownhauer...I haven't seen you in quite some time. Welcome back to the main office."

"I am only here momentarily, sir," responded Crownhauer. "Just to escort the Omega."

"Hey Crownhauer... Crownhauer. Can you say something funny?" the large vulture asked the Airman, who was annoyed by the request.

210

"I doubt it, sir," Crownhauer responded, which the vulture found to be hysterical.

"I doubt it, sir," the Alpha responded, mockingly.

Crownhauer rolled his eyes and looked at Dioni.

"Thank you, Crownhauer," said the Alpha as he attempted to calm his laughter. "Ugh! I needed that. You're free to go."

"Thank you, sir," Crownhauer responded.

Crownhauer turned his body, looked at Dioni, shook his head, and exited the executive suite.

"How was the Flight Academy?" the Alpha asked as he walked to Dioni.

"It was so awesome!" responded Dioni. He was excited to return and was anxious to see his office. "There were all kinds of birds there! And not just birds…squirrels, a mega bat, and…oh, and the best part was when I was in this simulator for murmuration training, and it was like—"

"—It's good to have you back, Dioni," interrupted the Alpha. "How about we check out that office of yours?"

"You were serious? I get an office?"

"You sure do! And why wouldn't you? You're the new Omega! It's part of the benefits package." The Alpha turned to Mimidae, who he thought was still near his desk. "Mim, can we open Dioni's off— "

"—It's already open, sir."

"AH!" the Alpha yelled. He failed to notice Mimidae beside him the entire time.

"A warning, Mimidae! A simple warning…that's all I ask," said the startled vulture.

"Maybe next time, sir," she responded.

"Thank you," said the vulture, unhappy for having been frightened a second time.

"Dioni," Mimidae said in a friendly tone. "Will you please follow me to your office?"

"Yes!" responded Dioni.

He followed as Mimidae led the way out of the executive suite.

"You're gonna love it, Dioni," said the Alpha as they vacated the room. "You have a great view. Plus, you're closer to the cafeteria than I am. Oh, and Mim, tell him about the seed machine. Kid, it's going to make your head explode!"

"He's just saying that," said Mim. She walked a few paces before Dioni as his guide down a long corridor. "Your head won't explode. He tends to oversell these things."

"I didn't think it would," Dioni responded.

"You can never be too careful. Head explosions do happen, you know. One minute you're you, the next you're a puff of feathers. Saw it happen once… at a baseball game. Poor dove never saw it coming."

Dioni was excited to see his executive workspace. He never even had a bedroom to himself, so an office to call his own was a luxury he never dreamed he would live to experience. Mimidae opened the door and turned on a light. Dioni slowly walked in, in awe of the only place on Earth which was exclusively his.

The Omega's office was, by comparison, significantly smaller than the Alpha's executive suite. It contained a small desk behind an even smaller perch, and a long, rectangular window which was too low for Dioni to see out of while he stood, yet too high to see out of while he sat. The only decorative element in the small room was a large, framed feather, which likely held a significance that only Dioni cared to investigate. The office was less of an executive workspace and more of a converted area which previously served as extra storage space for the Alpha. If this room was ever Ally's office, there was no evidence that she had conducted business of any kind.

"So if you want to see the seed machine, it's just a crank-style dispenser," Mimidae said. "You just turn the nob a few times and seeds come out."

"Uh-huh," responded Dioni, fascinated by his surroundings.

He inspected every corner of the room.

"Okay, then," Mimidae continued. "The seeds have likely been in there for a long time, so I wouldn't get emotionally invested if I were you."

"Uh-huh," Dioni responded. He looked out of his window at the vastness of the avian empire.

"Restrooms and fresh water are just down the hall and to the left. And the cafeteria is not so much a cafeteria as it is a place where you could store seeds. Every other Thursday a group of grackles comes in and makes popcorn."

"Listen, Mim…can I ask you something?"

"It's not as difficult as it looks, Dioni," responded Mimidae. "We don't wear pants for that reason, because it limits our movement and makes it more difficult."

"What?"

"What?"

"No no," Dioni said, unsure as to why Mimidae responded in such a manner. "I wanted to ask you, if you could visit anywhere in the world – any place at all – where would you go?"

Mimidae stood stunned. She had worked for the Alpha for countless years, and though she had taken the occasional day to rest or to be away from the DGCC, she never explicitly took time for herself. A vacation was a foreign concept.

"No…no one has ever asked me that before," Mimidae responded.

"No one? Really?"

"No…I…wow. I wouldn't know where to go."

"Come on, Mim," Dioni responded. "When was the last time you left from here?"

Mimidae paused. "I can't remember, sir."

"Really? Why?"

"It wasn't ever presented as an option," she said. Tears formed in her eyes.

"Mim? Are you okay?" Dioni asked.

"Yes, sir. I'm sorry. It's just...no one has asked me something like that and I didn't know how to respond."

Dioni walked to be closer to her. "I'm sorry, Mim. I didn't mean to make you sad."

"Sad? What? No! It's just...there's one place I have always wanted to visit, Dioni."

"Oh yeah?" Dioni responded, relieved that her tears were of joy. "Where would that be?"

"India, sir."

"India? Why India?"

Mimidae took a deep breath. "A long time ago, I had a friend...a roller—"

"—Wait," Dioni interrupted. "What's a roller?"

"A bird. A bird from that region. They are not very big, but their feathers and colors are absolutely beautiful."

"Sounds fascinating."

"They are, Dioni. They truly are. My friend would always come visit me in the office and would tell me these fascinating stories about his home."

"In India?" Dioni asked.

"Yes, in India," Mimidae responded. She lowered her guard and showed a side of herself that few other birds had ever seen. "I remember he once told me that the origin of wisdom is found in India, and that the wisest bird in the world is there."

"Really? Who is he?"

"*She...*" Mim responded. She looked up to Dioni. "A peahen."

"The smartest bird in the world is a *girl* bird?"

Mimidae smiled and lowered her head. It was a typical response from an oblivious young man.

"You have so much to learn, Dioni," Mimidae said. She collected herself then walked to the door. "If you only knew."

"What's her name?" Dioni asked as she walked by him.

Mimidae stopped and turned to face him.

"Is there anything else I can do for you, sir?" she asked.

Dioni felt guilty. He knew he crossed a line, he just did not know what he said nor how to apologize for it.

"No…no, I'm fine, Mim. Thank you."

Mimidae turned and continued to the door. She paused when she reached the doorway.

"If you look for her, Dioni, you'll find her," Mimidae said. "He used to always say that."

She smiled, slightly nodded her head, then walked away from Dioni's office and back towards the lobby.

Dioni returned to his window. He looked out and absorbed the vastness of the Department of Global Climate Control. Thousands of birds swirled about the Trading Floor, all on a mission, and each of them determined to do what was best for their regions. Greed had no place here, nor did selfishness, for if they had even the slightest presence among these birds, it would cause a complete and total collapse of the entire system. The birds of the Control Center were no different. Their work was incredibly diligent, and they understood that even the slightest mistake on their part resulted in lost lives across the globe.

The mission of the birds was not to do what was best for their kind, but rather to do that which was best for all living beings on Earth, including the Earth itself. There was no greater responsibility placed on any creature than that which was bestowed upon the beings who rule the skies.

Dioni stepped away from his window and sat at the small perch behind a very old and frail desk. The desk itself gave the impression that it was previously used by the woodpeckers at some point, and perhaps the pieces of wood they rejected were ultimately used to create the Omega's workstation. A projected image appeared before him. It displayed a multidimensional map of the entire world.

With limited knowledge or practice with advanced computerized devices, Dioni looked at the screen with awe. When he moved his head, the screen automatically mimicked his every motion and adjusted itself to provide him the best possible view. Dioni had fun with the device, almost as if he danced with a projected image. He pulled his head back and hit himself against the far wall.

"Ow!" he cried.

He lifted his left wing to rub the back of his head. The screen read his movement, and the projected image changed to show a different part of the Earth.

"Whoa," Dioni said.

He moved his wings to rotate a live map of the planet. He quickly learned how to see detailed aspects of the map: where storms were underway, the position of the sun, where there was sunlight and where there was darkness. He saw the flow of every river on Earth and saw the full extent of where waves crashed along every seashore.

"How do I see Guatemala on this thing?" he asked aloud.

The image on the screen immediately responded and rotated to show a live feed of the Central American nation.

"This is so awesome!" Dioni exclaimed, excitedly. "Show me Flores!"

As instructed, the image rotated and expanded to show his hometown, at night. He saw a few lights on the streets. A series of indicators on his screen gave him the exact temperature at that moment, wind conditions, and air quality levels. Other, smaller screens displayed the negotiated weather for the next five days. Dioni looked at the temperature.

"It's a little cold," Dioni said to the screen.

He searched for his home. He navigated the map as best he could until he found the orphanage, where no visible light was seen.

"It's late. They're probably asleep."

Dioni navigated the map until he found Alma's bedroom window.

He shifted his perspective in an effort to see inside the room, but the darkness proved to be stronger than his desire to see his friend. As the angle of the image changed, all he saw was the reflected image from Alma's window. With no light from inside the room, Dioni saw the reflection of the bird which generated the image on his screen. The video feed came from a mechanical bird which had two blue lights instead of eyes.

"It'll scare her. Better if I don't," Dioni said to himself.

Alma was nearly asleep when she turned over in her bed and saw two tiny blue lights. With foggy eyes that were not fully adjusted to the dark, she squinted and saw a strange bird on the other side of her window. To her, it appeared as though the bird was discovering its own reflection. As quickly as she saw it, the strange bird used its wings to push itself back, then disappeared. Alma shook her head as if to clear her mind. She closed her eyes, leaned back, and rested her head on her pillow.

Dioni saw an image of the Earth from a much higher elevation. He expanded his view and saw how the world appeared to the few beings who had left its orbit and had experienced the greatness of the magnificent blue planet.

He dropped his wings to his sides. The image on the screen moved slowly to match the Earth's current movement. He paused. Dioni lifted his wings, to which the image immediately shifted its perspective. He spun the projected image once again, then stopped after he circled the entire globe.

A smirk came across his face, one which seemed odd for a bird. He, however, was no ordinary bird. He had an idea and a desire to act on it. More than anything, he was curious.

"Show me India."

Chapter Sixteen

A few hours passed, which to Dioni felt like a few minutes. He was fascinated by what he learned – not as much by the technology, but rather by the level of access he had to every possible location on Earth. He saw the tallest peaks, the deepest valleys, the rarest caves, and even the depths of the greatest ocean. In a matter of hours, Dioni saw and studied what would otherwise have taken several lifetimes to accomplish.

Beside his motion-activated screen was a single sheet of paper in which Dioni wrote the names of three locations: United States, India, and Antarctica. The last entry on the list was added more out of sheer curiosity than as a location he actually had a desire to visit. In his simulated travels, Dioni discovered a part of the world which was covered entirely in snow; with no experience in such an environment, he wanted to know what it felt like to hold snow in his hand…or whatever comparison he could make to his own hand.

Dioni stepped away from the projected image. The screen immediately powered down. He looked at his note once more – United States, India, Antarctica – then grabbed the paper and walked to the doorway of his office. He paused momentarily and turned around. He walked to the window to once again see the vastness of it all.

Mimidae was at her workstation when Dioni returned to the executive suite. She was in deep thought; she concentrated so vehemently that she failed to notice anyone else in the office.

"Mim?" Dioni asked.

She ignored him, not purposely, but because she simply did not hear him. Dioni thought it best to let her be, and so he escorted himself to the executive suite.

The Alpha stepped back and forth, his wings full with multiple sheets of paper. It made little sense to have printed documents, considering all the information he desired was easily accessible through a number of ways. As he paced, he mumbled and dropped the top sheet of the pile he carried.

Dioni gently knocked on the door.

"Mr. Alpha, sir...?" He opened it further and glanced in.

"We're going by 'Sir' again, Dioni?" the Alpha responded. He did not slow his pace nor lose his place in the documents he read. "Yes, Dioni. How can I help you?"

"I think I'm ready to go."

"What are you talking about, Dioni? You just got here. We had a deal, remember? Ten days."

"Yes, I know. What I meant to say is that I would like to go find a new Omega bird."

The Alpha stopped his pacing and turned to face Dioni. He lowered the pages he carried.

"Do you, now? Well, that's good to hear. Straight out of the academy and the kid's ready to go, huh?" The Alpha slowly walked to Dioni. "I'm impressed, kid. I really am. You're more ambitious than your predecessors."

"Than my what?"

"Nothing. Let me ask you this, have you determined where you want to go first?"

"The United States of America," Dioni responded proudly.

"Really?" the Alpha asked, with an odd facial gesture. "You could go literally anywhere on Earth and your first stop is the United States? That's new. Wait, where are you from again?"

"Guatemala," said Dioni.

"Oh, that's right. A quetzal. Duh," said the Alpha. He walked by Dioni and toward Mimidae's desk. "Well, the U.S. has its nice areas. The roadrunners requested another big sandstorm in Arizona so I would stay away from that area if I were you."

"Okay."

"Other than that, I'd say you are off to an interesting start." The Alpha leaned in to look through his doorway and saw as Mimidae worked diligently. "Oh, she's busy." He turned to Dioni. "Have you used the portal?"

"The what?" Dioni asked.

"I didn't think so." The Alpha looked away. "Donna!"

Immediately, four hummingbirds entered the room – two from the open window that looked out to the Trading Floor and the Control Center, and two from the suite entrance.

"I only need one," said the Alpha. Three of the hummingbirds exited the room.

"Donna," the Alpha continued. "I need you to escort the Omega to the portal. He's never used it before."

The hummingbird nodded then zoomed to place itself in front of Dioni's face. The small bird made a series of gestures with its wings and body.

"Donna is asking you to follow her," said the Alpha.

"Yeah, I know," Dioni responded. "This pathfinder is incredible."

"I completely forgot you had that. I'm glad it's working."

The hummingbird zoomed toward the large window then waited for Dioni to follow.

"Have fun, kid," the Alpha said to Dioni. "I hope you find what you're looking for."

"Thanks," Dioni responded. He smiled. "Me too."

Dioni walked to the large window and saw that the hummingbird had made its way towards the portal. He looked at the Alpha.

"Can I ask you something?" asked Dioni.

"Yeah, sure, kid. What's on your mind?" the Alpha responded.

"You have been the Alpha bird for a long time."

"I have. Is that your question? Because you didn't phrase it like a question."

"Will you ever find another bird to take *your* place?"

The Alpha smiled. He took a few steps forward to join Dioni at the ledge of the large window.

"I've done this for a very long time, kid. Eventually, yeah, I would love to find someone else to do the job and go back to being me. But I'm not gonna leave here until I finish what I started. I have a responsibility, Dioni, to the Earth, and I'm not going anywhere until I have exhausted every resource to ensure the world is how it should be."

"To restore the balance?" asked Dioni.

"Of sorts…" the Alpha said, an element of sarcasm evident on his face. "You better get going, kid. If you fail to find a replacement Omega, you and I are gonna work together for a *really* long time."

Dioni looked out, lifted his wings, leaned forward then jumped. The hummingbird stayed a few lengths in front of him.

The Alpha looked down from where he stood. He half-hoped to see the blue quetzal suddenly lose control and crash onto the Trading Floor. With envious eyes he momentarily followed the long tailfeathers of his rival until they were lost among the commotion of the birds hard at work.

"What a ridiculous bird," he said aloud.

The vulture turned away from the window and walked into his executive suite.

The hummingbird landed a few lengths away from the border between the Trading Floor and the Control Center. Dioni followed closely behind

221

and maintained his focus on the direction of his flightpath. When he landed, the hummingbird lifted itself from the ground and motioned for Dioni to follow. He did as instructed.

The two birds entered through a wall of glass doors then proceeded to a rotunda, where the hummingbird pointed Dioni in the direction of a sign which read "Transportation Center". Dioni followed as directed. Once the hummingbird felt it was safe to allow Dioni to navigate himself, it zoomed away from the rotunda and flew back to the Trading Floor.

The tunnel that led to the Transportation Center was illuminated by a series of lights which emanated from a semi-transparent floor. Although each light beamed a different color, every light moved at various speeds. Dioni could not determine the source of the lights nor the reason for their corresponding colors, though he noticed that the faster lights had long shadows or trails that followed the source, while the shadows of the slower lights caught up to the slower sources once they came to a stop.

Though not nearly as busy as the Trading Floor or the Control Center, a heavy amount of bird traffic moved in every direction. None of the birds in the area were airborne. Every bird either walked or hopped through the tunnel. Each bird that passed noticed Dioni, who was mesmerized by the lights beneath him as he walked further into the Transportation Center. To the other birds, Dioni looked like a tourist. His attention remained on the lights that penetrated through the floor, and he failed to notice the seasoned birds who gave him a strange glance as they passed him by.

A large bird stood on guard at the entrance gate of the Transportation Center. Dioni stopped his forward progress the moment his head bumped into the leg of the large bird. He looked up and smiled as he recognized a familiar face.

"I know you," Dioni said to the tall bird, the same flamingo he met when he first arrived at the Department of Global Climate Control. "I saw you before."

"You must be the new Omega," the flamingo responded. "I am happy to see you have a working pathfinder."

To Dioni, the flamingo spoke in English, though it did so with a heavy

Puerto Rican accent.

"How did you know I was the Ome—"

"—We were all informed of your arrival, Mr. Omega, sir," interrupted the flamingo.

"Can I ask you something? Is every bird I meet going to call me 'Omega' or 'Sir'?"

"Not if you do not wish to be called Omega, sir," the flamingo responded.

"Good. I was worried about that."

"If you do not wish to be addressed as the Omega, then what shall we call you?"

"Dioni."

"The only what?"

Dioni sighed.

"No, DEE OH NEE. Not 'the only'. Dee oh nee. Dioni."

"Okay, Mr. Dioni. Got it. To where would you like to travel?"

"The United States, please," Dioni responded.

He assumed a type of ultra-sophisticated train would take him, which excited him because he had never experienced a train ride.

"America!" responded the flamingo. "*Muy bien*. Very good. Where in America? It is a big country. You have to be more specific."

"Oh," Dioni responded. "I haven't been there before."

"Hmm," responded the tall bird. "What would you like to see? If you want bright lights and a big city, Las Vegas and New York City are always illuminated. What else? There is a zoo in San Diego that you might enjoy. If you want unforgettable food, you can visit New Orleans. I strongly recommend a *beignet* from Café Du Monde."

Dioni paused. For as long as he could remember, he hoped to one day visit the United States. Now that the opportunity presented itself, he was clueless as to where to go, what to see, or what to experience. His primary objective remained on his mind.

"Well," Dioni opened. "Is there a bird in America who can help me?"

"Absolutely! Help you with what?"

"I need a bird who knows everything there is to know about being an Omega. Do you know a bird like that?"

The flamingo thought on the question momentarily. She smiled.

"Actually, there is a bird who may be able to help you."

"Excellent!" responded Dioni.

"Her name is Makawee. You will like her."

"Makawee…yes, that's perfect. I can meet her then I can ask her where I can find another Omega bird."

"Another Omega bird?" the flamingo asked. "There can only exist one. One Alpha, one Omega. Why must you seek another?"

"Not another," replied Dioni. "A replacement."

"Do you not wish to be the Omega?"

"I want to be me again. Another bird can be the Omega and will do a better job."

The flamingo leaned forward and bent down, which made Dioni nervous. Dioni took a step back to create some space between himself and the large bird. From such close proximity, the flamingo's bright feathers created a pink glow around its body.

"Each Omega is chosen for a reason," the tall bird said to Dioni. "You must discover your reason, and then you can decide whether or not to be the Omega."

These were wise words. Had Dioni not had a goal in mind, he certainly would have taken the tall bird's words to heart. Perhaps he would have pondered why he was chosen, and the meaning of his responsibilities as the Omega bird. Perhaps he would have kept an open mind.

"No…I can't do this." Dioni said to the flamingo. "I have eight days to find another bird to do the job, and when I do, I can go back to being me and I'll be a hero in Flores. I don't want to be a bird."

The flamingo smiled.

"Very well. Then you shall see America and find a new Omega."

"Yes!" Dioni responded, excited for his travel. "What do I do? Do I wait for the train to pick me up, or do I follow those lights?"

"Follow me," she said.

The flamingo raised her long neck to stand at full height, which towered over Dioni. The two birds moved through a row of turnstiles, of which scores of birds walked to and from in both directions. Some of the birds rushed in or out while others had conversations amongst themselves as they passed through. Not a single bird flew while in the area.

The flamingo led Dioni to an empty turnstile, which was made of a shiny, chrome-like material that reflected the various colors around it. Dioni saw himself and the flamingo in the reflection, albeit oddly shaped.

"When you go through this, you activate the portal. Your pathfinder will guide you if you tell it where to go," the flamingo instructed. "So long as you know where you are going, or the bird you wish to see, the portal will direct you."

"So I just tell my pathfinder that I want to see Makawee in the United States?" Dioni asked.

"Yes. You say, 'portal travel, location: United States, find Makawee'. When you see the word 'confirm' on your pathfinder, you say 'confirmed', then pass the gate.

"Then what happens?"

"Then you pass to the other side of the gate."

"Okay. Here we go," responded Dioni. "Portal travel."

Dioni saw a light glowing from the view of his pathfinder.

"It's glowing, is it supposed to do that?" Dioni asked. "Did I break it?"

"That is what it is supposed to do. It's working perfectly," said the flamingo.

"Oh, okay. Sorry. Let me try this again." Dioni collected himself. "Portal travel." The same sequence reappeared on his pathfinder. "Location, United States of America." A map of the United States appeared in Dioni's view. "Find Makawee."

The pathfinder immediately altered its coordinates. It identified the exact location of travel and displayed an image of a bald eagle.

"Makawee is an eagle?" Dioni asked, suddenly nervous over the prospect of confronting a predator.

"Not just any eagle, Mr. Dioni," the flamingo responded. "Do not be afraid. Makawee is a friend to all birds."

The entrance gates opened. The portal was activated.

"You must pass the gates," said the flamingo. "After you do, keep your wings out and walk with your head up, face forward. The rest happens automatically."

"Wings out, head forward. I can do that," Dioni said.

Dioni cautiously walked through the open gate. A series of lights led toward an exit that was further away than what he was able to see. The other birds on the same side of the gate were at ease as they walked or ran down their respected runways. They quickly disappeared into the exit tunnel which led away from the Transportation Center.

Dioni walked across a solid line. He immediately felt as the floor pushed him forward. He opened his wings and looked up, just as the flamingo instructed.

"Wait!" Dioni shouted.

He tried desperately to step back, and quickly realized that the forward progression of the portal did not allow him to go in reverse. Dioni turned his head. Upon seeing this, the flamingo became filled with anxiety.

"Face forward, Mr. Dioni! Face forward!" the flamingo shouted.

"I forgot to ask you; how do I get back?"

"The same way you came in!"

"What?" Dioni asked. The portal pushed him further from the gate.

"The same way you arrived, Mr. Dioni!" the tall bird yelled. She lifted her wings to create a funnel around her beak. "Just tell your pathfinder you want to go to the Transportation Center, or use my name!"

"Your name?" Dioni shouted in response. The ground beneath him moved faster. "I don't know your name!"

"Just say—"

BOOM!

In a flash, Dioni was immediately thrust forward. He bolted out and away from the Transportation Center at an unbelievable speed, then disappeared without a trace. The flamingo stood upright and lowered her wings to her side.

"Jelanni," she said to the empty runway.

Chapter Seventeen

Dioni immediately regretted the decision to look back. As he was not in proper flight position, his body was forcefully pushed through the portal while his head felt as though it sank into his chest. Dioni, who had never so much as ridden a rollercoaster, felt the sensation of gravitational force in spectacular fashion.

Though he struggled to lift his head from a downward position, Dioni kept his eyes open. He saw as the portal exit occurred in a series of phases. The first phase was no different than exiting a tunnel. Once beyond the initial tunnel phase, the walls of the portal became a series of lights which flowed like a river. Dioni did not transcend space or time; instead, the gravitational force and momentum of the Earth's rotation moved around him. Though he was physically motionless, the movement of the planet rotated at such an incredible speed that its very energy enabled portal travel, almost instantly, to any location in the world. The pathfinder was thus used as a navigation tool, which enabled portal transfer and allowed precise accuracy for every bird's final destination.

Had Dioni known any of this prior to stepping foot near the Transportation Center, he would have asked the flamingo for more detailed instructions. As it was, he did not have the ability or knowledge of how to navigate himself and was thus lost among a myriad of blinking lights. His pathfinder showed a continuous flash of images of his relative position, none of which was understood by a first-time traveler. Dioni had every reason to panic, and so panic he did.

The slightest motion of his wings moved Dioni in a different direction. There was no wind to push him or guide him, though he felt a hard shift up, down, to his left and his right, as the portal guided him to his destination. As he moved his body mid-transfer, Dioni's pathfinder updated his map projections. The final destination remained the same, though the live view on his pathfinder changed with each attempt he made to control his own flightpath.

The last phase of portal travel was engineered to allow all birds to exit gracefully from the transfer state and glide effortlessly into the normal rotation of the Earth. Once out, a sonic boom marked the exit from the portal. The sound not only informed all birds in the area of an incoming traveler, but it also cleared any debris or rain which could be dangerous for any flyer to come in contact with at such a high speed. Birds with sufficient knowledge and experience in portal navigation had no problems as they made their way to their respected destinations.

Dioni's inaugural experience through the portal was not a pleasant one. Though his training at the Flight Academy proved beneficial, simulated flight was of no comparison to flight in the real world. Dioni's movement during the transfer caused him to shift, which forced his body to unintentionally alter to an upside-down position upon his exit from the portal. He faced downward and saw a vast blue sky, which to him appeared as a large body of water as seen from a high altitude.

Two large birds rested and conversed as they sat beneath a bridge that carried cars and trucks from one side of a river to the other. The larger of the two birds was a female American bald eagle; the slightly smaller bird was a female Mexican golden eagle. The bald eagle spoke in English, and by its accent, it was clear that she was from Texas. The golden Eagle spoke in Spanish; to the bald eagle, her spoken words were in English though with a heavy accent.

To any onlooker, the sight of the two birds was exceptionally rare. To any living beings within the river, the sight of the two birds was terrifying.

To the uninitiated, the sight of the two magnificent birds easily caused confusion. They appeared as enemies, with their resting gaze a look of two ferocious predators. The two eagles sat beside one another and looked out to the flow of the river beneath them, their eyes were able to strike fear in even the bravest of creatures.

"Stop me if I told you this one before," said the bald eagle. "It's a good story."

"Okay," responded the golden eagle, who kept her eyes on the water.

"I heard it on a television show which I thought was about birds, but I was so wrong. The title was misleading."

"Misleading television, got it."

"So there's this guy who's walking down the street, minding his own business, when he falls in a hole."

"Wow, that's dangerous. He could've gotten seriously hurt. Was he not paying attention?"

"Maybe he walked over old wood. Who knows why these things happen?" said the bald eagle.

"He fell in a hole. Like a well?" asked the golden eagle.

"Let's call it a well. So this guy falls in and he can't get out. And he starts shouting so that someone might hear him and help him…throw him a rope or something."

"How deep is the well?"

"It's deep enough where the guy could look up and see light, but no one from the top could look down and see him. Make sense?"

"Yes. Continue."

"Suddenly, a doctor walks by and hears someone shouting from the well. The doctor looks down and doesn't see anyone, but the guy at the bottom sees that he's a doctor. 'Hey doctor,' says the guy. 'I fell down this well. Can you help me out?' The doctor writes a prescription on a piece of paper, throws the paper in the well, and keeps going."

"What good is a prescription going to do?"

"That's what I said! But wait, it keeps going. So time goes by and the guy is yelling up when he thinks he hears someone close by. After some time, a priest walks by and hears the man in the well. 'Father, I fell down this well and I can't get out, can you please help me out?'"

"He's a priest, of course he will help."

"The priest says a prayer, bows his head, and walks away."

"A prayer? That's it? And then he walked away?'"

"It wasn't even a long prayer," said the bald eagle.

"I think I know that priest."

"So a few hours go by and our guy is losing hope, right? Finally, he sees someone at the top of the well and he recognizes him as a friend. 'Hey buddy! I fell down this well and I can't get out. Can you help me out?' Without thinking it twice, the friend jumps into the well."

"*¡No lo creo!*' the golden eagle responded, in shock. "Why would he do that?"

"The guy asks the same thing! 'Why would you jump in here? Are you dumb or something? Now we're both stuck down here!' The friend just looks at him and says—"

—BOOM! SPLASH!

An object in rapid motion crashed a few meters in front of them, directly into the river, which startled both eagles. They looked in shock at the mysterious object, whose momentum carried it to the bank of the river. Whatever it was, its body floated on the surface while its head remained submerged.

The two eagles looked at one another. Instinctually, the golden eagle raised her chest and opened her mighty wings. The bald eagle stopped her just before she dove from their perch.

"Wait," the bald eagle said. "What is it?"

"It looked like a bird," the golden eagle responded. "It was out of control and it crashed."

The bald eagle took a second look. She saw feathers in the water.

231

"You're right, it is a bird!"

The two eagles leapt from their perch beneath the bridge and flew directly to the mysterious bird in the water. The golden eagle lifted the blue bird from the water, which revealed its long tailfeathers.

"Put him on the ground! Put him on the ground!" said the bald eagle.

She saw that the bird was smaller than her and noticed its peculiar blue color.

The golden eagle placed the blue bird on solid ground, face up. She and the bald eagle towered over the smaller bird, who was unconscious.

"What do we do?" asked the golden eagle.

"Stand back," responded the bald eagle.

The golden eagle stepped away as instructed. The bald eagle lifted her wings towards the sky, then forced them down just inches away from the unconscious blue bird; the action created a strong gust of wind which flew directly into its lungs. The smaller bird inhaled deeply and instantly opened its eyes.

"Did you see that?" Dioni asked, with little regard to the two predators who towered over him.

His wings were spread at his sides and his head rested firmly on the ground.

"We heard it. We didn't see it," responded the golden eagle.

"What were you trying to do?" asked the bald eagle.

"I was in the portal!" responded Dioni. "All of a sudden I was in the sky. Or I thought I was in the sky!"

Dioni quickly lifted himself to his feet and began to walk in circles. His adrenaline ran fast. Even for a small bird, there was an excessive amount of energy contained and expelled in his state of disbelief. The two eagles looked at one another.

"Pilot error," the eagles said simultaneously.

"Pilot error?" asked Dioni. "What does that mean?"

The two eagles gave Dioni more room to move as he paced faster.

"It means you failed rule number one of the portal, kid," responded the bald eagle. "You don't fly it, you let it fly you."

Dioni paused abruptly. He shook his body to remove the water trapped in his feathers.

"Well nobody told me that!" Dioni responded. "I tried asking but as soon as I did it just pulled me. And then I tried to put my head up but I don't know what happened."

"You have to be more careful, *amigo*," said the golden eagle. "You could really hurt yourself if you don't know how to use the portal."

"Well now you tell me," responded Dioni.

He brushed a few spots of mud from his body, then wiped away the water which fell onto his face. He looked up and saw the two predators who stood above him.

"Are you eagles…?" Dioni was excited when he asked the question but became nervous as he remembered the predatory reputation of the two birds.

"That depends on who's asking," responded the bald eagle.

She lowered her head and looked fiercely into Dioni's eyes.

"My name is Dioni," he said.

He saw his reflection in the eyes of the bald eagle.

"The only what?" she asked.

"*No, no es* 'the only'. *El dijo, 'Dioni'*," responded the golden eagle.

Dioni was shocked; another bird finally knew the name.

"Dioni?" questioned the bald eagle. "As in, dee-OH-knee."

"Yes, yes…dee-OH-knee," responded the golden eagle. "It is a common name. I have heard it said before in my country."

"I haven't," said the bald eagle. She faced Dioni. "Well, Dee-Oh-Knee, welcome to Progreso Lakes, Texas," she said excitedly.

"Or to *Nuevo Progreso, Tamaulipas*," said the golden eagle.

"Tha…Thank you…" responded Dioni. "Is this the United States?"

"This side is," the bald eagle said. "You flew into the Rio Grande. The other side of the river is Mexico."

"Meh-hee-co," said the golden eagle. "Pronounce it correctly."

"Fine… Meh-Hee-Coh," the bald eagle snarked at her friend. She looked at Dioni. "What brings you to Texas, blue? You fixin' to try catfish or bluegill? What's your policy on barbeque?"

Dioni understood the language and the words spoken by the bald eagle yet had no idea what she had asked.

"I came to find someone," Dioni said. "An eagle by the name of Makawee."

"*Mira*, Makawee," said the golden eagle. "Now what did you do?"

"Nothing!" the bald eagle responded. "You seriously can't be looking for me because of that story I was saying, can you? It's not plagiarism! I never said it was *my* story! I said I saw it on a TV show with a *very* misleading title—"

"—You tell stories?" Dioni asked, much to Makawee's relief.

"Oh, thank God," Makawee responded.

"That's not all she does," responded the golden eagle.

"Thank you, Atzi," Makawee said to the golden eagle, sarcastically. "Blue, you scared the bejeezus out of me, but you found me! My name is Makawee. It's a pleasure to meet you."

"Are you an American bald eagle?" Dioni asked her.

"More bald than American," responded Atzi. Dioni chuckled.

"Thank you, Atzi. That's two," Makawee said. She turned to Dioni. "What brings you to Texas?"

"Or to *Mexico*?" said Atzi.

"Or to *Me-he-coh*?"

Dioni looked to the other side of the river. One side did not look so much different than the other, yet the territories were clearly marked. On this side of the river he saw a flag that was red, white and blue in color, with stars and stripes. On the other side of the river he saw a different flag that was red, white and green in color, and had a golden eagle in the center.

"Is this river what separates the two sides?" Dioni asked.

The two eagles smiled at one another; the blue bird was young and unaware of the real world.

"No, *amigo*," said Atzi. "The river did not always divide us. The land was once one and the same. It didn't belong to one side or the other."

"What happened?" Dioni asked.

"A war," responded Makawee.

"They created a border where the Earth was naturally separated," Atzi intercepted. "And where it wasn't, they made a fence to force the two sides apart. They think it serves to protect one side from the other, but they don't understand what they're doing to themselves."

"What fence?" Dioni asked.

He looked in both directions and saw the river which served as a natural separator, with a bridge that connected each side.

"Hey blue, do you have some time?" Makawee asked.

"Time for what?" asked Dioni.

"To see something you've never seen before," Makawee responded, excitedly.

"Yes, absolutely!" said Dioni.

Her words sparked his sense of discovery in a land he always hoped to visit.

The bald eagle tilted her head, opened her wings and lifted to the sky. The golden eagle followed, with Dioni closely behind.

Despite his much smaller size and wingspan, Dioni was able to fly beside the far more experienced eagles. However, his flight pattern was different than theirs; Dioni flew in a wave-like pattern while the fast-flying eagles travelled in a forward direction. Both the bald eagle as well as the golden eagle recognized the quetzal's limited flight abilities, and that his flight pattern was as natural to him as was their superior ability to hunt.

As they gained altitude, the two larger birds flew at each of Dioni's sides as if to protect him. Dioni did not fathom the speed and ferocity in which the two eagles could tear him to pieces; he blindly trusted their guidance. Perhaps it was his youthful ignorance or lack of experience which caused this sentiment for Dioni, who would otherwise never witness such peace and restraint among rivals.

Dioni looked to his left and saw a large city in the distance.

"What is that?" he asked.

"The buildings over there?" responded Atzi. "That's Monterrey. Up ahead…do you see that city?" she asked. She used her beak to point to another metropolis in the distance. "That's Laredo, Texas."

Dioni was mesmerized. Only in his dreams had he seen such magnificence. He always knew there was far more to the world than Flores, Tikal, and Ipala. With every moment he flew above the Earth, the more he felt the urge to see it all.

On his right, far off to the northeast, a series of storm clouds gathered over a large city. It was too distant for Dioni to observe any details, though he admired the size of the buildings that reached up and touched the sky. He saw as the clouds opened and covered the ground below with waves of water.

"Check it out," Makawee said to Dioni. "Looks like the mocks ordered water in San Antonio today."

"Mocks?" Dioni asked.

"Mockingbirds," responded Atzi. "They oversee the weather for Houston, San Antonio, and Dallas."

"They're some funny birds," Makawee said. "They mimic every sound they hear. Did you know that? Mocks are great at parties!"

"Really?" Dioni asked.

Atzi flew closer to Dioni. She shook her head and looked directly at him.

"They're so annoying," Atzi said. "They always have the last word, no matter what. You'll never win an argument with a mockingbird. Ever."

Dioni smiled. The thought of an argument with a mockingbird had never crossed his mind.

…

The three birds remained in the sky for hours. Makawee made the most of the time by telling stories of herself, and of ancient myths and legends of Texas and the Rio Grande. Atzi, who had experienced many similar, long flights with Makawee, dedicated her flight time to correct Makawee's misperceptions and exaggerations:

Makawee never fought in the Mexican-American War.

Makawee never carried nor lifted a truck off the road.

Makawee never survived eight days in the desert by herself, and in not doing so, she did not find water by negotiating with a cactus.

Makawee did not invent the teepee.

Makawee never ate a rattlesnake. She was actually afraid of them, which was odd for a bald eagle.

As Makawee continued her mid-air, one-sided conversation, Dioni opened the dialogue to his other flight companion.

"Atzi," Dioni said. "Your name is familiar to me. I have heard it before."

"Atzi is a very old name," the golden eagle responded. "I was named after my mother, Atzilinda. It is a hybrid name – half Aztec, half Spanish."

"What does it mean?" Dioni asked.

"Beautiful rain. You may have heard the name Atzi in Guatemala, just like I have heard the name Dioni in Mexico."

Dioni's eyes widened. "How did she know I am from Guatemala?" he thought. "Is she another alpha bird?"

Dioni was only able to express his thoughts with facial expressions.

"*Eres un quetzal*, Dioni," she replied as she sensed Dioni's discomfort. "It would be odd if you weren't from Guatemala."

For the remainder of the flight, Dioni listened more than he spoke. It was important for him to hear their stories, and on occasion, he smiled and laughed at the unbelievable experiences shared by the large birds. He wondered if the eagles knew more of him than he knew of them. Had they desired to do so, the eagles could have easily wasted no time in making Dioni their next light snack. Instead, they guided and befriended him.

Dioni's mind raced in every direction. He became skeptical of the eagles' kindness, mostly because he could not understand their actions. Were they Omega birds in the past? Did they retire from the Department of Global Climate Control? Why did they reveal so much to a bird they hardly knew?

Dioni's excitement faded the further they flew. He became consumed by his own thoughts and worries; every scenario which caused stress was one he created for himself, which was far from reality.

"You worry so much, Dioni," Makawee said.

"Why do you say that?" asked Dioni. "I'm not worried."

"We are birds, Dioni," responded Makawee. "We see everything. There is very little that is new to us. Do you think you're the first bird to have that worried look on its face? As an Omega, you'll have to learn to better hide your feelings."

Dioni's expression changed. How did they know? Did every bird know?

"*Eres un quetzal azul*, Dioni," Atzi said. "No one had to tell us. It would be odd if you *weren't* the Omega."

"But...how did you know? Did the Alpha tell you?"

"*¿El buitre Alfa?*" asked Atzi.

"He said nothing," responded Makawee. "Birds observe and study. Eventually, everything comes back to us. A snowy owl has no business in Texas, neither does a Hawaiian crow... nor does a blue quetzal. It wasn't a guess, Dioni. It's logic."

Before Dioni asked another question, the bald eagle pointed at a location hundreds of meters below. Atzi rotated her body to the side and began a figure-eight flight pattern. Dioni and Makawee followed closely behind. Together, the three birds descended from the sky and settled on the ledge of a long and tall fence, which served as a divider between two sides of a large desert. The fence went on for miles in both directions.

Dioni felt exhausted; he performed far beyond his own expectations, considering it was his first flight after graduation from the academy. Ballo would have been proud. The three birds sat on the top edge of the fence, which they used as a perch – a place to both observe their surroundings and to rest after a long flight.

"Do you know where you are?" asked Makawee.

Dioni looked around and saw a vast space of nothingness. The land showed no signs of life, no vegetation, not even a snake slithering its legless body along the ground. All he saw was rocks and dirt, with no indication of location from his pathfinder.

"That's Arizona," said Makawee.

"And behind us *es Sonora*," said Atzi.

Atzi lifted from the fence and glided onto the dirt. She landed a few paces in front of the fence, on the Mexican side.

"What do you see, Dioni?" asked Makawee. "What can you observe from here?"

Makawee lifted her mighty wings, pushed herself away from the fence and slowly guided herself to the dirt, on the American side.

Dioni remained on the edge of the fence. The warm wind blew his long tail feathers in front of his face. He leaned forward and looked to one side. It was a vast sight of emptiness for miles, except for a long fence. He looked to his other side and saw the same desolate land with the same fence, which ran further than what he could see.

"It's the same on both sides, is it not?" asked Makawee.

"Yes. It's just a lot of dirt," responded Dioni.

"So what would happen if the fence wasn't here?" asked Atzi. "Would you know which side is Sonora and which is Arizona?"

Dioni looked around. He lifted his head as far as it could go. He did his best to find differences between one side of the fence and the other. He found none.

"It's almost the exact same," Dioni said. "The fence is the only thing that does not belong."

"Good, Dioni. Good," replied Makawee. "There was a time when the people of our land lived together, peacefully. Before there was a fence."

"There was a time when they were friends," said the golden eagle. "There were no rivalries, no divisions."

"What happened?" Dioni wondered, aloud.

"Time, Dioni," said Makawee. "Time separated us. The people found ways to distance themselves from one another. They created walls and fences and barriers to separate themselves, but they failed to understand that they divided us as well."

"That doesn't make sense," Dioni responded. "You're birds. There are no fences in the sky. You can just fly above it."

"Invisible borders do exist, Dioni," Atzi responded. "Hatred and fear start from the ground and lift to the sky. And no matter what, everything that goes up must also come back down."

"They're not our enemy," said Makawee. "This is their land as much as it is ours. But there can't be a balance so long as they continue to make bigger and stronger barriers. Does any of this make sense to you?"

"No...not really," responded Dioni. Makawee sighed.

In the distance and on the Mexican side, far from the view of any creature, was a hidden animal. It quietly and nervously observed the three birds at the fence.

"The fence is justification to separate us from one another," continued Makawee. "It was built long ago, but the land remains the same."

"So what does that mean? Should countries not have borders?" asked Dioni.

He glided down and landed on the Mexican side. He faced Makawee through the bars of the fence.

"Borders are one thing," Makawee responded. "Every country has borders, and that's fine. However, when borders become cages, we isolate ourselves and are no longer doing what is best for the Earth. We lose the balance. You of all birds should be particularly weary of cages—"

Atzi detected movement from the direction of the hidden animal. She immediately shifted her head to search for it. The animal lowered itself to hide, which caused Atzi to miss any detail of its whereabouts.

"There's nothing there, Atzi," said Makawee. "You'll have to excuse my overzealous friend here, Dioni."

"I saw it," responded Atzi.

Her eagle eyes searched for the slightest movement on the ground.

"She does this every time," Makawee said to Dioni.

They both looked at Atzi, who shifted her body to locate the animal.

"There's nothing there, Atzi. I'm telling you. Bald eagles have a sense about these things."

"It's there," Atzi responded. "It just thinks it's smarter than me. *A ver.* Show yourself, coward!" shouted Atzi.

"This is what happens when you leave a golden eagle in the sun for too long," Makawee said to Dioni. "They start seeing things that aren't there. One time she flew full speed at what she thought was the biggest squirrel ever."

"What was it?"

"A bus," both eagles responded simultaneously.

"Ouch!" said Dioni.

"It's hiding, but I know it's there," said Atzi. She observed the area with stealth.

"Five to one says it's only a rock," Makawee said to Atzi.

"Ten," Atzi responded.

"Six."

"Seven, and no rain on your side for Memorial Day weekend."

"Deal!" responded Makawee.

Makawee felt positive that her gamble secured a great holiday weekend for millions of Texans.

"*Me la vas a pagar,*" Atzi said. Her eyes focused on every subtle movement in the dirt.

A moment passed. Silence. Only the desert wind was audible. Nothing moved. Atzi lifted herself from the dirt and quickly ascended in the air. Within seconds she was out of view, hidden in the cloudless sky.

"You'll have to forgive her," Makawee said to Dioni through the bars of the fence. "It's always something with that golden eagle."

"Is she okay?" asked Dioni. "Hitting a bus at full speed could have killed her."

"She was fine. She flew sideways for six weeks after that. The mocks thought it was the funniest thing ever. She still can't go to Austin without a bird reminding her."

"What did she mean when she said, 'Memorial Day'? What is that?" Dioni asked.

"An American holiday to remember the people who fought and died in wars. It happens on a Monday, every May. It's mostly a way to sell furniture and hot dogs."

"Oh. So Atzi controls the rain for this entire area?"

Makawee smiled.

"No, not her. Not alone at least. Other birds oversee the larger cities on the Mexican side. She's just the leader of her tribe."

"Eagles live in tribes?"

"Tribes, families – whatever you want to call it – it's all the same. The people don't know that. We like them to believe that we mostly live alone."

"Why is that?" Dioni asked.

"For us, it's safety. For them, it's symbolic," Makawee responded. "Anyway, golden eagles are wind birds, so they oversee wind patterns from the Gulf of Mexico—"

"—*Meh-hee-coh*," interrupted a small quail. "Don't let her hear you say that."

The quail stood beside Makawee, almost entirely overshadowed by the mighty eagle. The quail looked in the distance to understand what the others observed.

"Hi Pelo," said Makawee. "Atzi thought she saw something. She went to catch it."

"What's the wager?" Pelo asked.

Pelo placed his wings before his face to create improvised binoculars.

"Is his name really Pelo?" Dioni asked Makawee.

"Seven to one, plus no rain on Memorial Day weekend," Makawee responded. "Yes," she said to Dioni. "Atzi gave him that name. See the single feather on his head?"

"There's nothing there, chief," said Pelo. "Even with thermal registers all I'm seeing is hot rock. Looks like we're in for a good three-day weekend in May." Pelo lowered his wings and acknowledged Dioni. "What's with blue? Friend or foe?"

"He's a friend," responded Makawee. "He's one of us. He's cool."

"Does it have a name, or should I just call it 'Bluey'?" Pelo asked, rudely.

"Dioni," responded the blue quetzal, from the opposite side of the fence.

"The only what?" asked Pelo.

"No, not 'the only'," said Dioni. "Dee-Ohh—"

WOOSH!

At a faster speed than any land animal could possibly outrun, Atzi dove from far in the sky to swoop and grasp a small animal in her mighty talons. Given her strength and speed, the small animal had absolutely no chance to escape. Her hunt was executed flawlessly. The three birds who stood at the fence turned their attention to the golden eagle.

"That's...disappointing," Makawee said. She acknowledged the stakes of the wager she lost.

"I see it now," responded Pelo, his binoculars back in position. "A *javelina*. A little one. One in a million chance Atzi could've caught it."

"What's a *javelina*?" asked Dioni.

"A peccary," Makawee responded. "It's like a small boar."

"Oh."

Pelo followed Atzi's flight with the use of his binoculars. The two other birds lifted one of their wings to block the light of the sun.

"There's going to be a lot of disappointed little-leaguers this year," said Makawee.

Atzi released the *javelina* from a high altitude. It fell fast and hit the ground vigorously, a few inches from Dioni. The three birds lowered their wings as Atzi landed beside her prey.

"*¡Viste! ¡Una javelina!*" Atzi said to Makawee, in a boastful manner. Makawee rolled her eyes. "What was it you said? 'It's just a rock'? Well here's your rock!" Atzi saw the quail. "Oh, hey, Pelo."

"Hey," Pelo responded.

"Dioni, Pelo, would either of you like some fresh *javelina*?" asked Atzi.

Dioni made a face, clearly disgusted by what he saw.

"Any bugs on that thing?" asked Pelo. "I could use the protein."

"Maybe underneath," responded Atzi. "Dioni?"

"No thank you," said Dioni.

"More for me then," said Atzi.

Pelo lifted from the American side of the fence and landed near the *javelina*. Dioni stepped back a few paces; he wanted no part of it. Atzi looked at Makawee.

"Oh, that's right. Where are my manners? Makawee, would you like a share of my hunt?" Atzi asked, with a boastful tone.

Pelo lifted the edges of the dead animal to look for insects.

"No, thank you," responded Makawee. "I'm not really hungry."

Dioni walked through a small space between two bars of the fence. He stood beside Makawee and observed with disgust as the golden eagle devoured its meal.

"No? Not hungry?" asked Atzi. She took a large piece off of her prey. "*Mírala,* Pelo…*la envidia.*"

"I'm gonna pass, Atzi," said Pelo. "There's no bugs anywhere on this thing."

"Your loss," Atzi responded.

The quail walked away from Atzi's meal and looked at Dioni on the other side of the fence.

"So, what brings you down from headquarters, The-Only?" Pelo asked Dioni. "Seed machine broken?"

"No…I don't think so," responded Dioni.

"Jelanni sent him here, from the portal," said Makawee. "He had a rough exit."

"You don't fly it, The-Only," said Pelo. "You let the portal fly you. It's easy with that pathfinder."

"You can see my pathfinder?" Dioni asked. He lifted his wing.

"Either that or you have something serious growing on the side of your head," said Pelo.

Dioni made an attempt to cover the device with his feathers.

"Actually, I asked you that same question and you never answered it," Makawee said to Dioni.

"What question?" asked Dioni.

"Why did you come here?"

"Oh, right. I'm looking for someone," responded Dioni.

"Who're you searching for?" asked Makawee

"Well, not any bird in particular. I just…I need to find a replacement so that I can go back to being me."

"A replacement what?" asked Pelo. "You need a new tail feather? You're going to be happy you have those."

"An Omega bird," said Dioni.

The three birds froze. Atzi, who had a large chunk of *javelina* in her mouth, paused mid chew.

"What?" Dioni asked the three shocked birds. "What did I say?"

"Dioni…" Makawee sighed. "It's not a job that can be replaced."

"What do you mean? Why not?" asked Dioni.

With great difficulty, Atzi swallowed the large chunk of food in her beak.

"Wait," chimed Pelo. "Bluey here is the new Omega?"

"An Omega bird can only be chosen by another Omega, Dioni," said Atzi.

"Right. That's what the Alpha said," Dioni responded, naively. "That's why I'm looking for another bird who wants the job."

"Another tropical Omega bird?" asked Pelo. "Am I missing something here?"

"Nobody *wants* that job, Dioni," said Atzi.

"Why not?" asked Dioni.

"Because it's not a job," said Makawee. "It's a responsibility. It's not something you can just swap for something else. That's not how it works."

"The Alpha bird said I can go back to being me if I can find another bird to take my place," Dioni said.

"Yeah…good luck with that," said Pelo, rudely.

"What is that supposed to mean?" asked Dioni.

Atzi pushed away her meal. She lost her appetite.

"Did he explain that there could only be one Alpha and one Omega?" asked Makawee.

"Yes, that's exactly what he said."

"Okay, good," said Atzi. "How much time did he give you to find a replacement?"

"Ten days."

"Ha!" Pelo exclaimed. "Excuse me?"

"So you have ten days to find a bird to *want* to be an Omega?" asked Atzi.

"Now it's only eight days," responded Dioni.

"Well, that answers my question," said Pelo. He looked at Dioni. "It was a pleasure meeting you, The-Only. Good luck making the impossible happen."

Pelo turned away and opened his wings.

"Wouldn't you want to do it?" Dioni asked Pelo.

"Not in a million years, Bluey. Not after what I've seen," responded Pelo. "Atzi. Makawee. Always a pleasure."

Pelo lifted and flew away. The three birds on the ground watched as the quail flew further from where they stood.

"Why did he say, 'not in a million years'?" Dioni asked.

"Ally must've chosen you for a reason," said Makawee.

"You know Ally?"

"*Knew* Ally," Atzi responded.

"Huh?" Dioni asked, in total confusion.

The two eagles paused. Atzi rubbed her face with her wings.

"Should we still show him?" Atzi asked Makawee.

"Show me what?" responded Dioni.

He looked at Makawee, who looked down at the quetzal and sighed.

"I don't think we have a choice," Makawee said to Atzi. "Dioni, there's something we need you to see."

Makawee took flight, followed closely behind by Dioni and Atzi. Dioni was undoubtedly confused. He did not fully understand his role, nor did it make sense as to why no other bird wanted to be the Omega.

On the second flight there was no chatter. Makawee did not tell jokes nor did she tell any exaggerated stories from the past. The facial expressions of the eagles spoke for them.

Dioni activated his pathfinder and saw the geographical markers of the ground, invisible to all others. He saw the exact divisional line between the two nations, as well as live weather patterns, negotiations, and other climate statistics for the region. The three birds followed the long fence, even beyond where the man-made barrier seized to exist. Makawee changed course and lowered her elevation. Dioni was exhausted but determined to follow the two eagles.

"There's a large pile of rocks on that hill in the distance," Makawee said to Dioni. "We'll land there."

Atzi, closely behind, gained speed to fly beside Dioni.

"Dioni, we have seen Omega birds come and go," Atzi said to him. "The balance has always existed, and the birds of the world have done their part to control it. Alphas and Omegas ensure that this is possible. It has always been this way...for billions of years. Until something changed... something the birds cannot control."

"What changed?" Dioni asked Atzi.

"You will be the first Omega to see it," Atzi responded. "This was not reported to headquarters."

From a high altitude, Makawee pointed to a large rock lodged atop a small hill. She guided them to the exact location of the rock, where the three birds landed and momentarily rested. Dioni's entire body was sore. If the first flight was not enough to cause him pain, the second flight put him over the edge. He was exhausted, far more than he had ever felt.

"Dioni, do you notice anything strange?" asked Makawee.

Dioni looked from the top of the hill. He failed to notice anything out of place or out of order.

"No," Dioni responded. "Just dirt on a hill, surrounded by more dirt and other hills."

"That's what we see also…from the sky. Even your pathfinder says the same, correct?" Atzi asked.

"Yes. The pathfinder is not showing anything other than dirt on a hill."

"Dioni," Makawee said. She faced him directly. "Walk to the bottom of the hill then tell me what you see."

"Okay…" Dioni responded.

As long as he did not have to fly, he was more than willing to walk down a small hill.

A quetzal in the sky had different challenges than when it walked on solid ground. For one, its wings were not in use, so there was less energy to use. However, while on the ground, all male quetzals constantly ran into the problem of having their long tailfeathers caught on various objects. Dioni was unable to bypass the same fate all males of his kind were forced to endure. His tailfeathers flowed freely with his movement while in the sky, but on land they were more cumbersome than he expected. After every few steps, he felt a slight snag as his feathers tangled with other objects. Each time, he pulled his tailfeathers to free himself then continued. Doing so was bothersome to Dioni, but not enough for him to take flight.

Makawee and Atzi stayed behind on the rock. They scanned the skies for any predator who would try to make a meal of the Omega bird. In that moment, they had no greater responsibility than to ensure Dioni's safety.

Dioni's feet were neither weary nor soar, so it was odd for him to feel a strange burning sensation rise from his toes. He looked down and saw nothing unusual. Dioni continued down the hill. A few paces along, one of his tailfeathers became stuck on an unusual object. Dioni turned to pull his tailfeather in an effort to free himself; he pulled yet remained caught on the strange object. He pulled with greater force and saw the object rise, ever so slightly.

Dioni approached the source of where his tailfeather was tangled. It was caught along with the feathers of another bird. The bird was motionless on the ground, covered in a thin layer of dirt. It appeared alive, as if resting on its side with its feathers flowing carelessly in the wind. It's body, however, was void of life.

Dioni's face became pale. He pulled his tailfeather to free himself from the grasp of the lifeless bird, yet the dead bird did not let go. The two eagles observed his actions from a distance. Dioni panicked and pulled harder. He freed his tailfeather and tripped over another object on the ground behind him. He fell on his back. He huffed in pain as a small cloud of dirt lifted when his body hit the ground. Dioni turned his head and saw his own reflection in a motionless pair of eyes. It was another lifeless bird.

Dioni crawled back to get away from it, frightened by the sight of another dead body. He placed his wings on the ground and pushed himself back, the burning sensation from his feet transferred to his wings. He scooted back as fast as he could until he was abruptly stopped by a hard object. He looked up and saw Makawee.

"Look closer," Makawee said to him.

Dioni slowly came to his feet. He looked down the hillside and saw dozens of lifeless birds. Their bodies were scattered at an equal distance from one another. It was the sight of a perfect execution. Each bird's demise was identical to the one beside it, and the exact same expression was seen on the face of each victim. From the sky, the birds were unseen as their bodies were hidden by a thin layer of dirt. Once on the hill, however, the evidence was uncanny.

"What happened here?" Dioni asked.

"We don't know." Atzi responded, a few steps behind Makawee. "This entire flock was thriving. They oversaw the land and kept a perfect balance. There is no record of anything unusual."

"Did they fall out of the sky?"

"These birds are not strong flyers, Dioni," responded Makawee. "Something must've attracted them here first, then frightened them enough for all of them to flee for their lives."

"None of them made it," said Atzi. "It doesn't make sense. These are some of the most fearless, resilient birds in the world."

"What are they?" Dioni asked.

"Roadrunners," responded both eagles.

Dioni checked the status of the land on his pathfinder. He saw no sign of unusual activity, no history of violent storms or winds or any natural phenomenon to explain what he witnessed.

"Do you feel a burning sensation…on your legs," Dioni asked the eagles.

"No," responded Atzi.

"No," responded Makawee. "Should we?"

"It feels like my feet are burning, but not so much for it to hurt." Dioni lowered his pathfinder and looked at the eagles. "Why was this not reported?"

"There are things that only the birds on Earth should know, Dioni," responded Atzi. "We cannot cause panic. Ally understood this."

"Then why are you showing this to me?" Dioni asked. "Why did you bring me here?"

Makawee lowered her body to be at eye-level with Dioni.

"If in the one-in-a-trillion chance you somehow find a replacement Omega and become you again, remember what I am about to tell you. If nothing else, Dioni, please remember this: the birds are always watching. The birds see everything. It's our responsibility to maintain the balance of the Earth, and in doing so we see it all." Makawee paused and looked at the body of a nearby victim. "This is the first time in our lives that we see something we cannot explain."

A small gust of wind moved the feathers of the lifeless birds.

"We." Dioni opened. "You said '*we* see something *we* cannot explain'. Has this happened somewhere else?"

"Yes," responded Atzi. "At least in one place we have identified."

"Where?"

"India," said the eagles.

Dioni paused. His mind searched for validation and for clues of any kind.

"What happened there?" he asked.

"An entire flock was wiped out and no one can explain why. Not even the wisest bird on Earth could understand it. They discovered something similar but were able to clear it before anything was reported to headquarters."

Dioni wondered how entire flocks of birds went missing. How could two similar occurrences happen on two different parts of the Earth without anyone's knowledge?

"How do I get there?" Dioni asked.

"Your pathfinder," said Atzi. "Use the portal and have Jelanni port you to India."

"How will I know where to go?" Dioni asked. He once again looked at the two eagles.

"The same way you found us," said Makawee. "Tell Jelanni you wish to see the wisest bird in India. She'll know where to send you."

Dioni turned to look at the dozens of roadrunners scattered about the hillside. He stretched his wings and leapt, then lifted from the ground. The two eagles followed closely behind.

"Portal travel," Dioni commanded his pathfinder.

His visual perspective changed to show different transportation icons. Dioni's viewfinder displayed the words: Submit Destination.

"Transportation center."

In a flash, Dioni burst through the sky and disappeared beyond sight. The two eagles raised their heads and shifted their wings to gain altitude. Within seconds they were far from the hill. Atzi turned to Makawee.

"Why would she choose him?" asked Atzi. Makawee did not respond. "He doesn't have a clue, does he?"

"Not in the slightest," said Makawee.

Chapter Eighteen

The sky above the Himalayas was colder than any environment Dioni had previously experienced. With a better understanding of how the portal operated, along with improved instructions from Jelanni, Dioni saw his actual flightpath. He pierced through the sky at unprecedented speeds, his flight as smooth as what he experienced in the Flight Academy simulator.

Unlike his first attempt, Dioni had a better understanding of how the slightest of movements created an effect on his transfer through the portal. Dioni faced forward, in the same direction of his travel, which allowed him to access a view of the Earth few beings ever witnessed. The portal exchange ended far above the ground. Once outside of the portal, Dioni's most difficult challenge was to locate a safe place to land.

Even far in the sky, Dioni saw the splendor of the highly populated country. The color, the heat, and the feel of the land all reminded him of Flores. All Dioni had ever known of India were the stories he read in books or those he was told by the visitors to the orphanage. It was, by all means, a land of enchantment so far away from Guatemala that surely its existence was in no way similar to the place he called home. Much to Dioni's surprise, the similarities were striking.

Though the portal provided the opportunity to travel half the distance of the Earth within a matter of minutes, the process to port from one location to another required a great amount of energy. Dioni lowered his wings and glided his body to a structure which was conveniently located at the top of a small hill. A series of colorful steps led to the top of the structure, which from a high altitude created an odd visual effect.

At the peak of the structure stood the most colorful set of stones Dioni had ever seen. As he glided closer, the building reminded him of one which was similar to what was found at his favorite place on Earth. It was no ordinary building, but rather a temple constructed at the peak of the highest hill in the area. Dioni knew better than to set foot within the temple, as doing so could be seen as a sign of disrespect by the locals. Instead, he circled above the structure and searched for a safe place to rest.

As he made his way around, Dioni saw a small bird at the peak of the temple, who made a series of aerial gestures. There were no other birds near Dioni, so clearly the gestures of the small bird were meant for him. The signaling bird was of an entirely new class of bird to Dioni. Its small body was mostly covered in white feathers, though when it opened its wings, the bird projected a bright, turquoise glow. The small bird was perfectly chosen for its job; the light reflected off of its wings masterfully to easily direct Dioni as he glided through an area almost entirely saturated in color.

Dioni landed according to the guidance of the small bird, who used the universal gestures of air traffic control that were taught at the Flight Academy. The small bird was overwhelmed with excitement at the sight of Dioni, almost as if his arrival was long anticipated. After he landed, Dioni stretched his body, closed his eyes and took a deep breath. When he reopened his eyes, Dioni saw a smile which was far larger than the small bird who expressed it.

"Welcome! Welcome! WELCOME to India!" said the small bird, its glee and excitement most evident.

"This is India?" Dioni asked the starstruck bird.

"Yes!" responded the small bird. "This is the town of Viralimalai."

"Vira-llama-what?"

"Viralimalai, Mr. Omega, sir. Welcome!"

"Wait...do you know me?" Dioni questioned the small bird.

"Oh no, sir, Mr. Omega. You are the Omega bird, are you not?"

"How did you know?"

"There is only one of you. You are either the first or the last of your kind."

"Are there no other birds here?"

"Oh, yes, sir, Mr. Omega. Billions of birds. But none like you. You are special! You are unique! And in Viralimalai, we welcome all of our special and unique guests as if they were our family!"

"Well…I…thank you," Dioni responded. "Do the other birds know that I am here?"

"Oh yes, sir, Mr. Omega, sir. News of your arrival came before you did, sir. And the new Omega bird is visiting us at the perfect time, might I add."

"Perfect time for what?"

"Holi, sir"

"What is Holi?" Dioni asked. He secretly hoped it was a type of food.

"Ahh, Mr. Omega, sir," said the small bird as he wagged his wing at Dioni. "I cannot spoil the surprise. Come, follow me. I will take you to where you want to go."

"How do you know where I want to go? Did Makawee or Jelanni tell you?"

"I am afraid I do not know Makawee or Jelanni, Mr. Omega, sir," responded the small bird. "There are only two reasons why you would visit us here, Mr. Omega, sir, and I doubt you are here to learn *kuravanji*."

"*Kava*-what-chee?" asked Dioni. "Is that some type of food?"

"*Kuravanji*. It is a dance, Mr. Omega, sir. Please, follow me."

The small bird bent its head and raised its wings.

"Wait!" Dioni said, interrupting the small bird's lift.

"Yes, Mr. Omega, sir?"

"What is your name?" Dioni asked.

The smaller bird slowly lowered its wings. He was in awe by Dioni's innocent question.

"My name is Taqhi, Mr. Omega, sir."

"Hello, Taqhi. My name is Dioni."

"The only what, sir?" asked Taqhi.

"No, not 'the only'. Dee-oh-never mind," Dioni responded. "Where are we going?"

"To the sanctuary, sir. Please, follow me," Taqhi responded.

He once again lowered his head and raised his wings, then jumped forward and lifted from the temple.

Dioni briefly scanned the small town below. He noticed the minor details of the town which resembled Flores. Dioni smiled. He wondered of other aspects of life in which he was misinformed, and of the commonalities found among people who lived half a world away from one another. He looked up and saw as Taqhi flew further out, then quickly pushed himself back and lifted to catch up to his guide.

"Welcome to the Viralimalai Sanctuary, Mr. Omega, sir," said Taqhi, a beaming smile glowed on his face.

The sanctuary was a tranquil part of the land where peace was kept and preserved among birds of the same family. The trees were large enough to cover a wide area while the grasslands provided both a place for ample sunlight as well as a location in which to view the beauty of the star-filled night sky. In addition to the ample flora of the sanctuary, there was a small body of water which was surprisingly undisturbed on the perfect afternoon of Dioni's visit.

The two birds slowly descended to a lower altitude when Dioni noticed a small group of chicks who followed his every move. The young birds were in awe of something they had not seen prior to that day, and because there was no threat in doing so, the elders of the sanctuary found no reason to prevent them from welcoming the new Omega bird.

Dioni and Taqhi landed on a large boulder nestled among the trees. The chicks had dull colored fur and only a few feathers on their small bodies.

Some of the young birds shed a few of their feathers as they raced with excitement to greet and welcome the celebrity among them.

"Are these the only birds here?" Dioni asked as he looked to the beautiful landscape.

"No, Mr. Omega, sir," Taqhi laughed in response. "There are many birds who live here. The adults are gathering wood for the ceremony tonight."

"Ceremony?"

"For Holi, Mr. Omega, sir. A celebration of the end of winter and the arrival of spring, sir. We celebrate this every year at this time, though rarely with a special guest."

The young chicks ran to the base of the boulder. They stumbled and jumped over one another to climb the rock and gain a better view of their hero.

"Who is the special guest?" asked Dioni.

Taqhi chuckled at the question. How could he not know?

"It is you, Mr. Omega The Only, sir." His laughter grew louder as he mockingly repeated Dioni's question, "Who is the special guest?"

Dioni's innocence displayed as ignorance. He was the Omega bird, and despite his limited knowledge of what he represented to other birds, they all seemingly knew everything about him. He found this confusing yet flattering.

As Taqhi amused himself by his own joke, Dioni jumped to the base of the boulder and met face-to-face with his young admirers. The gleeful chirps and squeaks which emanated from the young chicks immediately came to a halt when Dioni's feet touched the sanctuary grounds. The young chicks were starstruck, in absolute awe of the blue quetzal. One youngling could not contain her emotions; her eyes rolled to the back of her head as she lost her balance and fell to the ground.

A small, brave chick approached Dioni. He was half Dioni's height and still unable to fly. Dioni was intrigued. The young bird was harmless, yet he bravely approached Dioni and visually inspected a bird which he had never seen. The young chick studied Dioni meticulously, as if searching for flaws

257

in Dioni's design. Dioni stood at full attention. He moved only his head as he followed the chick's every motion.

The young chick circled Dioni and came to a stop directly before him. He raised his small wings to Dioni's head, then drew an invisible circle along the perimeter of Dioni's face. Dioni froze. He did not want to scare or intimidate the young bird, though he was weary of a practice which was completely foreign to him. The young chick's movement halted as he placed his wings on either side of Dioni's face.

"The Omega," said the young chick.

He smiled and looked into Dioni's eyes from a lower stance.

"Ooohh," responded the other chicks, in amazement and awe of the blue bird before them.

"Welcome to India," said the small chick as he lowered his wings.

"Thank you," said Dioni. "How do you know who I am?"

"Deepa said you would come one day," the chick responded.

Taqhi leapt from the top of the boulder and joined the younglings near the base.

"Who is Deepa?" Dioni asked. He looked to Taqhi for affirmation.

"She is the keeper of color, Mr. Omega, sir," responded Taqhi.

"Keeper of color?" asked Dioni. "What does that mean?"

"It is one of the many responsibilities of the majestic peahen, sir."

"Then this...Deepa. Is she your queen?" Dioni asked.

Taqhi and the younglings united in laughter. It was a silly question, albeit an innocent one.

"We are not ruled by a queen, Mr. The Only, sir," responded Taqhi. "Peacocks are birds of nobility and tradition. They oversee the color of life over all of the Earth."

Dioni was dumbfounded. "How do peacocks control color?"

"This is a skill known only to the sacred Indian peacock, Mr. Omega, sir," responded Taqhi. "Their ability to see and command color is far superior than that of all other living beings."

"Peacocks can see more colors than the rest of us?" Dioni asked.

The young chicks chuckled. They chirped amongst themselves and whispered of their superior intelligence over the Omega bird.

"No sir, The Only, sir. Peacocks see the same colors as you and I. To them, color is life. Color is felt, and it must be carefully balanced in order to sustain life."

Dioni was unable to respond. In his lifetime he had seen countless birds – hundreds of thousands of displays of color – though never did he consider color a state of being. Color was a natural substance, produced by the Earth without prejudice or prior planning. It was how he thought the world worked.

"How does the balance of color, balance life?" Dioni asked.

"Because it is by color that life is able to flourish," responded a feminine voice from atop the boulder, behind Dioni.

Dioni turned to look at the source of the voice; a magnificent peahen stood proudly above him. She was not as colorful as he imagined. The peahen's feathers were long and they draped to her back, like a natural gown meant to embody the essence of all birdkind. The peahen displayed a rich array of turquoise feathers that radiated with brilliance. Her body was composed of various shades of brown, white, and black. A final hint of color was seen on the feathers at the top of her head, which resembled a crown.

The native birds of the sanctuary displayed their customary greeting to the peahen; they opened their wings to present their best and brightest feathers, and slowly bowed their heads as they placed their wings directly in front of their faces.

Dioni witnessed as Taqhi and the younglings greeted the peahen. He failed miserably in his attempt to perform the actions himself.

The peahen leapt from atop the boulder and found a landing area behind the line of chicks. From a closer perspective, Dioni saw the splendor of the truly magnificent bird. More than her physical presence, her smile emanated an invisible aura of color which passed from bird to bird.

"Deepa! Deepa! Deepa!" chirped the chicks, all of whom tried desperately to get the peahen's attention.

She towered over them. She easily could have ignored their squeaks and chants and could have continued in the direction she intended. Instead, she bent her body to be at their level, and she smiled at each of the younglings.

"Deepa! Look at what I can do!" said an overexcited chick who inflated its chest and held air in its beak.

"No no, me, Deepa!" responded another. "Look at how fast I am," the chick said as it ran in circles around the other chicks.

"Wow! Look at you go!" responded Deepa.

"Deepa, Deepa!" shouted the chicks. They spoke simultaneously.

"Look at my blue feather! Wait, where did it go?

"Look at how strong my beak is!"

"I can jump almost as high as you!"

"My brother and I can climb on each other. Look!"

"I have the strongest feet of any bird in the sanctuary!"

"I can count my own feathers! 1...2...3...7...4..."

"I know how to stand so that my brightest feathers will always be in the sunlight!"

"Wow!" Deepa responded, gleefully. "Look how impressive all of you are!"

Dioni witnessed her behavior with utmost admiration. To Taqhi, this was Deepa's normal code of conduct. He smiled at the sight and sound of excitement among the younglings.

"Are they her children?" Dioni asked Taqhi.

"Deepa treats all younglings this way," Taqhi responded. "It is a gift found in special birds, sir."

"To be approachable?" Dioni asked.

"No, Mr. Omega, sir. To be one that others are drawn to, naturally."

The voices of the younglings grew louder. Despite their desire for her attention, she smiled and responded with words of kindness.

"My young friends," she said, which caused them to lower their voices. "I have to meet our guest, don't you think?"

The chicks became calm and simultaneously agreed; only one youngling protested, who was given stern looks by his peers.

"How about this?" Deepa said to them. "I need each of you to find me the biggest stick you can carry and bring it to the firepit. I'll give a special reward to the chick who brings me the biggest stick!"

The younglings chirped with excitement and quickly scattered about in search of their prize-winning sticks. Deepa momentarily watched them go before she turned her attention to Dioni.

"Welcome to India, Dioni," she said.

"Ohh!" exclaimed Taqhi. "Dee-Oh-Nee." He turned to look at Dioni. "Well you should have said so, Mr. Omega, sir."

Dioni rolled his eyes and sighed.

"Thank you, Miss Deepa," Dioni responded.

"Oh please. We don't talk like that to each other. Just call me Deepa."

"Oh…okay," responded Dioni. "He just kept saying 'mister' and 'sir'…I just assumed— "

"—He is a roller, Dioni," Deepa interrupted. "They are known to be the most polite birds in all of India."

"A roller?" Dioni asked. He turned to Taqhi. "Do you know a bird by the name of Mimidae. She works for the Alpha bird at the Department of Global Climate Control."

The color in Taqhi's face changed from a shade of white and teal to a deep red.

"Nnn..No. No, Mr. Omega, sir," stuttered Taqhi. "I do not know of this bird you call Mimidae, sir." Taqhi stepped closer to Dioni. "Did she ask about me?" he whispered.

The two birds looked at Deepa, who gave Taqhi a look of disapproval.

"I...have to go," said Taqhi.

He immediately turned his body and lifted away from the area. Dioni and Deepa stood and momentarily watched as Taqhi flew away.

"That was odd," Dioni said.

"He knows better than that," responded Deepa.

"Can I ask you something?" Dioni said to the peahen.

"How did I know you were coming?" responded Deepa.

"Well...yes. Was a messenger sent from headquarters or do you have a special power?"

"No, Dioni," Deepa smiled. "I am no more special than any other bird. News of the new Omega travels fast. We were informed that you visited the United States, and so we knew that it was only a matter of time before you came to India."

"Oh...right."

"And it was perhaps another bird who told you to come to India, was it not? An eagle...or two?"

"Yes, that's right!" responded Dioni. "So you must already know why I'm here."

"You come in search of an explanation for something you saw. Something that no other bird could explain. Something horrible, but something that must remain hidden."

Dioni lowered his stance. The memory of the field of dead birds was engraved in his mind.

"Makawee said it happened here, too," responded Dioni. "I want to know what caused so many birds to fall from the sky at the same time."

Deepa paused and looked at the younglings in the distance. Some of them astutely searched for the largest stick their young beaks could hold, while others argued whether or not a blade of dried grass constituted a stick. Another just kept his eyes on the sky, completely oblivious of the task at hand. One particularly small chick just ran around the scene and paid no attention to anything other than the wind on his face.

"Dioni, come with me," said Deepa.

She lowered her stance, looked to the sky, jumped, and spread her mighty wings to capture the wind. Dioni followed the peahen, who was surprisingly fast for a bird of her size; he struggled to maintain his speed with hers. Luckily, the flight was only a few meters away – to the peak of the tallest tree in the sanctuary.

Deepa rested on a branch which appeared as if designed to the contours of her body. It was her place of solace and tranquility, and it was an honor for another bird to share the space. Dioni did not recognize the importance of where he stood. He landed on a nearby branch and rested his wings at a respectable distance from the peahen.

Deepa looked in the direction of the falling sun. It was her favorite time of day, of her favorite time of year. The reason behind Dioni's presence put an unwelcome stain on the moment.

"Within a few moments the sun will descend on the land, and we will once again begin a tradition that is as significant for us as it is for the people of India," said Deepa. "Maybe even more so."

"What tradition?" Dioni asked.

"The start of the spring, Dioni. Or more importantly, the end of another winter. Life will begin anew, as it does every year."

Dioni looked to the setting sun. It was tranquil and peaceful. It reminded him of home.

"What do you feel when you see this, Dioni?" Deepa asked.

"Of my home," Dioni responded. "Of someone I miss."

"A girl, is it not?" Deepa asked.

She made a facial expression which was intentionally coy. Dioni smiled.

"Yes. A friend."

"Our friends are important, Dioni. A good friend can be better than a parent or sibling."

"I don't have parents or siblings. I was born in an orphanage."

"I see," Deepa responded.

She paused and returned her attention to the picturesque, Indian landscape.

"What do you seek, Dioni?" she asked, breaking the peaceful silence.

Dioni closed his eyes and looked to his feet. It was not an expression of remorse or sadness, but of wonder.

"I have to find a replacement Omega bird so I can be me again," he responded.

"And after you find another bird to take your place, and you are human again, and you return to your home and are rejoined with she whom you miss…what then?"

"I don't know," Dioni said, the volume of his voice slightly lowered. "Before this, all I ever wanted was to see the world."

"I see," Deepa responded. "Do you no longer wish to see the world?"

"I want to be me again. I don't know why I'm a bird. There must be another bird who wants to be the Omega. I can't do this."

"Perhaps," responded Deepa. "The Omega is a position of service, Dioni, not of honor. All Alphas and Omegas are selected for a reason. You undoubtedly have learned that by now. You also learned that birds do more than just fly around and eat seeds and bugs. You learned that birds have a responsibility – to their own kind, to other birds, and to the Earth – which changes almost everything you had once known to be true."

Dioni did not respond. He looked away as he fought the urge to shed tears.

"The inner conflict you feel is not sorrow," continued Deepa, "but rather the result of an imbalance. I imagine your quest to find a replacement Omega was given a time limit, was it not?"

"Ten days," Dioni responded. He faced Deepa.

"Then live those ten days better than any ten days prior to today, Dioni. Live for today, for this moment. Rediscover the balance of who you are and who you want to be. And on that tenth day, not only will you find what

264

you seek, it will also find you."

Dioni's attempt at a response was interrupted by the sound of a nearby peacock, who shouted angrily at a person near the steps of the sanctuary temple. The man held a plastic bottle in his hand and waved it above his head as a weapon in case he needed to strike the peacock.

"What is he doing?" Dioni asked. "That man could hurt that peacock."

Deepa turned to look at the commotion below.

"That is Vishal," said Deepa. "He is strong. He is not intimidated by the elder man."

"Then why is he shouting at the man? Why doesn't he just let the man go away?"

From their perch in the high tree, Deepa and Dioni witnessed as Vishal lifted his tailfeathers and cascaded them in a fascinating display of intimidation. His long tailfeathers appeared like a series of eyes which glared angrily at the elder man. Vishal knew the fear he struck in oblivious humans, as it was not his first attempt in doing so.

The elder man walked backwards, slowly. He lowered the fist which contained the plastic bottle. After a few nervous paces, he slowly turned his back to Vishal. The elder man threw the plastic bottle into an open space then quickly walked away.

"That is littering, you ignorant old man!" Vishal shouted. "This is a temple and a sanctuary, not your private garden!"

Vishal watched as the elder man walked down the steps and away from the area. He sighed angrily. He walked to the bottle, lowered his head to it, then placed it in his beak. He then carried the bottle for a few paces. Vishal's noble intention of leaving the plastic bottle neatly inside of a collection bin was shattered as he saw a large pile of overflowed garbage scattered on the sacred grounds.

Vishal lifted his head and forcibly hurled the empty bottle at the large pile. It made no difference where the bottle landed; the damage was already done. He turned his body and lifted himself away. Vishal failed to see Deepa and Dioni as they witnessed the entire ordeal from their perch within the tree. He landed in the grasslands a few meters away.

"Dioni, what did you see just now?" asked Deepa.

"A big peacock scaring a man away." Dioni responded.

"Yes. What else?"

"That same peacock throwing an empty bottle. He threw it fast, too. If he can kick as well as he can throw, that peacock could be a great soccer player."

"No no no, you're missing something. What of the interaction between the man and the bird?"

"I don't know," responded Dioni. "The peacock yelled at the old man, but the man didn't care. The only reason the man didn't throw the bottle at him was because he showed his feathers."

Deepa smiled.

"Dioni, there are millions of birds around the Earth who do this. They literally scream and yell as loud as possible, crying from the hilltops to the rooftops to the city gates, speaking truth to the people."

"What truth?" Dioni asked.

Deepa looked directly at Dioni.

"That *they* are causing the imbalance."

Dioni was taken aback.

"So you punish them? The people?"

"No, Dioni. They are only guilty of ignorance, and it is not our responsibility to punish any living creature on the planet." Deepa turned to face the sunset. "We provide balance. We work to restore to the Earth that which is taken away. We provide them with wealth and knowledge, and they prefer to ignore us."

"But…they're human. How would they know to listen to birds?" Dioni asked.

"Birds rule the skies, do they not? We have done so since long before their temples were built, long before their lights were made, and long before they forgot our greatest strength."

"Which is?"

"We have always been above them. Just like you can see the entirety of the sanctuary from this tree, so too can the birds of the world see the actions of all living beings beneath them."

Deepa jumped to a lower branch then met at eye-level with Dioni. He turned to face her.

"The birds see everything, Dioni," Deepa said. "And the birds are *always* watching."

Dioni turned to look at the nearby town. He saw cars, he saw people, he saw animals, he saw bicycles, he saw trees, he saw land, he saw lights, he saw smoke, he saw more people, he saw motion; and for the first time, he noticed the unique advantage and elevated perspective of his form of being.

It was not a bird's-eye-view, but rather a multi-dimensional outlook. It was the ability to be in awareness of what he had not previously discovered: the birds do, indeed, see everything. As a living network of billions amongst their kind, there was no single instance in which the actions on Earth went unwitnessed. The birds always observed, always studied, always persevered...and were always watching.

A few meters below, as he observed the town from an absolutely profound new perspective, Dioni looked to the base of the tree and saw as one of the young chicks jumped repeatedly. The chick grasped a long stick in its beak, which easily unbalanced the young bird's every leap.

"I gah hih! I gah hih!" shouted the young peacock as he desperately attempted to capture Deepa's attention.

Deepa looked down and smiled.

"I cannot understand you with that stick in your mouth, Manju," she said to him.

The chick dropped the stick and looked up.

"It's the biggest one, and I found it!"

"You did?" asked Deepa, in a forcefully amused tone. "Then let's take it to the firepit!"

Dioni smiled. The incredible accomplishment was the happiest moment in the chick's young life.

"What did I win? What's my prize?" asked Manju.

"Your prize, young man?" Deepa responded. "Hmmm, what can it be?"

"Can I color the fire?" Manju asked. He desperately hoped for a positive response.

"Well, that is perfect!" said Deepa. "Manju, you will color the fire for the ceremony!"

The chick chirped with uncontrollable glee; it was easily the best day of his life. Deepa turned to Dioni, who was confused by their conversation.

"Come, Dioni. This is a special tradition. I would like for you to be my guest."

Dioni nodded and smiled. He was intrigued at the opportunity to witness the tradition of an entirely different culture.

Deepa opened her wings, leapt from the tree, then glided down and landed a few inches away from the youngling. With one of her wings she made a ramp for the young chick to climb onto her, which he did without hesitation. As the chick secured itself for the flight, Dioni followed and leapt from the tree. He landed and stood beside Deepa.

"Ready to go?" Deepa asked Manju, who sat on her back.

"Ready!" Manju responded excitedly.

Deepa jumped, spread her wings, and immediately gained altitude and airspeed through the wooded area.

Dioni lowered his body, opened his wings, then felt the stick beneath his feet. He smiled and shook his head. He took it upon himself to take the stick for Manju.

"Oh wow," he said. "That little guy was able to pick this up?"

He lifted off the ground with the surprisingly large stick secured in his beak and followed behind Deepa.

Chapter Nineteen

A high pile of random sticks, twigs, branches, and logs were neatly stacked in a secluded area of the sanctuary, away from poachers and predators. The gathering which occurred on this day attracted birds and animals from near and far. It was more than a yearly celebration, but rather a sacred tribute to and from the most respected birds in all of India.

With generations of expert nest-building skills, the peahens of the village were responsible for the creation of the stack of wood which was to be burned. Ever-so-diligently, the peahens worked as skilled builders and architects as they constructed an impressive wooden tower. The tower was as aesthetically beautiful as it was effective; it served as the centerpiece to the ceremony of the sacred fire.

Manju, who sang gleefully as he rode on Deepa's back, was the envy of every chick in the sanctuary. Rumors swirled over Manju's ability to find and carry a stick of such size. Had he not witnessed as Manju carried the prize-winning stick on his own, Dioni would have likely agreed with the rumors. Though Dioni took it upon himself to carry the stick for the duration of the flight, he clearly underestimated how heavy the object felt after a short period of time.

Deepa touched ground a few meters away from the large stack of wood. Upon landing, Dioni, Deepa and Manju were immediately surrounded by a large gathering of peafowl. In his entire life, Dioni had only once seen a real peacock, and so a flock of such magnitude made a deep impression on him. The peahens – skilled artisans who worked in perfect coordination with one another – moved in unison to arrange the many intricate details of the structure to be burned. The peacocks stayed along the perimeter of the sacred grounds and created a barrier with their large tailfeathers.

Dioni was noticeably impressed by the sheer size and majestic beauty of the peacocks' tailfeathers. In their perfect alignment, the birds created an impenetrable fortress of both color and splendor. Any predator who dared breach their wall would immediately face the fury of hundreds of fearless peacocks, and would soon find itself in a failure of epic proportions. The peacocks were master workers who fulfilled the annual tradition that their kind had practiced for hundreds of thousands of years. With their experience came a profound wisdom and knowledge that enabled them to create an immense effect on all which embraces color.

"Thank you for bringing the stick," Manju said to Dioni.

Manju held his small chest high and gleefully walked from Deepa's back and onto the ground. Once he was a safe distance away, Deepa spread her wings and lowered her head to bow, which was a sign of respect for the elements before her.

"How were you able to carry this huge stick and bring it to Deepa?" Dioni asked Manju.

He slightly exaggerated his question in order to give confidence to the young chick, though he failed to admit that he was barely able to do so himself.

"I don't know," replied Manju. He bent to the ground and placed the stick in his beak, then looked to Dioni. "I wess I bone oh ny oohn stenf."

Manju walked the stick to the peahens, then bowed and almost fell over as he presented it to them. The peahens smiled at him, took the stick from his beak, and placed it in an opening within their structure. The stick fit perfectly into the gap within the arrangement, which further proved their excellence in engineering, ingenuity, and perfectionism.

Dioni stood closely behind Deepa. He observed in amazement as the peahens built the structure of wood at the center of the large circle created by the peacocks. It was a mighty fortress, the perimeter of which was heavily guarded and protected, and whose epicenter contained the object of attraction for all who lived within the sanctuary.

Deepa looked at Dioni. She saw how he was mesmerized, and she smiled.

"Dioni," she said. "What impression does this give you?"

Dioni, in a trance-like state of awe, could not respond. The coordination of what he witnessed was far more complex than even the most difficult murmuration simulation he experienced at the Flight Academy. The peacocks and peahens worked as a single entity and not as hundreds of individual birds.

Dioni checked his pathfinder. Just as it was engineered to do, the pathfinder identified each bird who walked into his line of sight.

"How are so many birds able to do this?" Dioni finally responded.

"Do what?" asked Deepa.

"Build this…so perfectly," Dioni said as he pointed to the wooden tower. "And create a wall of color like that."

He pointed at the hundreds of peacocks who secured the mighty circular fortress.

Deepa laughed. This was normal to her, as natural as the sun, the moon and the stars.

"They all know their shared responsibility, Dioni," Deepa responded. "We have done this for countless generations. It is a special tradition."

Dioni looked in awe in every direction.

"It's not like a murmuration," Dioni said. "They all know how to place themselves, without instructions. How do they do it? Do they have better pathfinders?"

"Pathfinders?" Deepa laughed with greater enthusiasm. "None of these birds use pathfinders. They work in this manner because this is how it has always been. They know by wisdom and instinct, Dioni, not by technology."

"What about the peacocks making the wall around the circle?" Dioni asked. "Are they born with the knowledge of how to do that?"

"No, not necessarily. All birds are born with certain gifts or abilities. Peahens are master engineers. They have an instinctive sense of structure that no bird on Earth can match. The peacocks can create impenetrable barriers using their bodies and tailfeathers to shield us from any predator that may try to harm us."

"Can all birds do that?" Dioni asked.

"Create a wall? Certainly. If there are enough of them and if they know how to work in unison, then they can undoubtedly create any impenetrable structure. If done properly, they can produce a force that neither wind, nor rain, nor the Earth itself will have the power to destroy."

"And all birds have these special abilities?"

"Think of them as gifts or talents, Dioni. Some are excellent hunters, others are chocolatiers, others preserve color, and then there are those who rule the skies."

"Falcons,' Dioni responded. "Falcons are the best pilots in the world. There's no way another bird is faster. They rule the skies."

"Why do you think this?" asked Deepa.

"You should see them at the Flight Academy. Even in the simulator, they were impossible to fly with. There was no other bird who could match their speed. That must be their gift."

"And this makes them the best?"

"Absolutely!"

"Then tell me, Dioni," Deepa said. She turned her body and faced Dioni directly. "Was there any type of bird that you did *not* see at the Flight Academy."

"Every type of bird was there!" Dioni responded. "Hundreds…no, thousands of them. And none were faster or stronger than the falcons."

Deepa smirked. She returned her attention to the wooden tower which was nearly complete.

"So then tell me," Deepa said to Dioni. "By your logic, the best pilots in the world not only attend flight school, they also rule the skies and live in America, correct?"

"Well…ye…yeah, I guess so," Dioni said, a lack of confidence in his response.

"Think of what you may have missed, Dioni. Of what you did *not* see, and promise that you will come back and tell me if you ever discover any other birds who are better pilots than falcons. Or eagles, for that matter."

"Okay…fine," Dioni responded, arrogantly.

He knew beyond a shadow of a doubt that there was no faster, fiercer, more intimidating nor more incredibly powerful bird than the iconic falcon. Why would an American tourist tell him this if it were simply not true?

A peahen of a younger age approached. Deepa spread her wings and lowered her head to the ground, a bow to indicate her attention was given in its entirety to the peahen. The younger bird repeated the gesture back to Deepa, which was a sign of respect for the wisest bird of the land.

"The structure is nearly complete, Deepa," said the young peahen.

"Then we are ready to begin the ceremony!" Deepa projected, which garnered thunderous shouts from every bird in the enclosed community.

The peahens sang with glee. They lowered themselves then slowly lifted their heads and their wings from the ground up, as if they swept the elements of the Earth back to the sky. A strong sound emanated from every direction of the enclosure as dozens of peahens sang and danced in absolute flawless formation. The mighty wall formed by the peacocks shivered, which created a whistling tremor that resembled both the fierceness as well as the serenity of a mighty wind brushing through a forest of the world's grandest trees.

The sun was nearly gone. The last precious moments of natural light were captured and transferred from bird to bird. Their performance was a dance of light which sprang from the wall of peacock feathers and created a countless number of colorless beams of pure illumination. As the peacocks moved their tailfeathers, they shifted their bodies and rocked softly from side to side, then directed their energy to the tower in the center. The sound of the wall of tailfeathers in motion, along with the hum created by the wind, produced a rhythm to which the other birds responded with their own actions.

Dioni stood back and observed the perfectly choreographed performance. Though visiting birds were unable to partake in the ceremony, there was no restriction from witnessing the event from a distance. Above the center of the circle yet below the peaks of the trees, a large gathering of visiting birds formed a slow-moving cyclone as they anxiously observed the wonderous tradition celebrated by the peacocks.

Dioni was in complete astonishment. His personal vision of India was far from the reality he witnessed in that moment, and he was not prepared for a surprise of such magnitude. He failed to understand how such flawless formations were created with absolutely no form of superior technology to guide their movements. He saw how the birds who were strangers to the land were welcomed, and how they respected the sanctity of the ceremony. Tears formed in Dioni's eyes; it was the most beautiful performance on Earth, and he could not fathom how he was allowed to stand amongst the fairest birds of the land.

A powerful beam of pure light flashed and ignited the wooden tower in the center of the circle. It began as a small structure fire then quickly evolved into a magnificent blaze, fueled by the oxygen produced by the mighty tailfeathers of the peacocks who formed the outer circle. Dioni looked to the base of the fire and saw a blue light which radiated from the bottom. The fire quickly became brighter as it lifted to the heavens. His eyes traced from the bottom to the tip of the tower, where he saw two peculiar traits which he did not know were possible. First, the ashes of the wood lifted to unknown heights and slowly drifted back to the surface; as the ashes fell, Dioni felt a sense of peace in witnessing how the tiny specs of burnt wood resembled harmless natural candles, which became dust as they touched the ground. Second was the radiant source of natural light, which Dioni would not have noticed had he not followed the flow of embers. It was the moon, which was in its fullest form, and larger and brighter than he ever remembered. Truly, this was a visual spectacle that very few outside birds were given the chance to experience. Dioni was the Omega – their guest of honor – and as such he knew that his place among these special birds was extraordinary.

"*Pavo cristatus!*" Deepa shouted.

The sound of the shouts, chants and movements became immediately silent. Only the fire was heard as it roared with fury.

"We are the guardians of the Earth's color," Deepa began. "We have a responsibility which was granted to us long before our existence. On this night, we celebrate the passing of another winter and the dawn of a new spring…as well as to honor the many lives we lost unexpectedly."

The peacocks raised their wings and voices to the sky. The birds who circled and observed from above lowered themselves and perched along the surrounding trees. They began to sing along with the peacocks. It was not a song of joy, but rather a cry of mourning.

"We face a new challenge with the start of the new spring," Deepa continued. "I am not here to mislead you, but rather to ask you to listen as we fight a battle which we may not live to see victorious in our favor."

Dioni was shocked by her statement. To which battle did she refer?

"I see us!" Deepa proclaimed, with greater emphasis in her voice. "We shout in the streets, begging to be heard. Our trees, our homes, our lives are destroyed and replaced with paved roads, factories, and buildings. Plants are of no match to the destructive force and endless amounts of waste produced by those who have the same intelligence and ability to prevent the destruction of our shared habitats."

Deepa looked at Dioni. He turned to face her and saw the reflection of fire in her eyes. She returned her attention to the assembled birds.

"For the first time in our history, we have experienced an event which we cannot explain. Each of you remember the day of the darkening of our land."

All of the peacocks and peahens in the circle bowed, an action of respect for the fallen. The birds who observed from the surrounding trees screamed in anger, in frustration, and in remembrance for the lives that were taken on that darkest day.

"We lost countless numbers of our friends, the Mynas, who were slaughtered by a force beyond our understanding." Deepa looked to the trees and extended her wings upward. "To our friends who join us here tonight, I beg you to not see this as a night of mourning, but as a celebration of the lives they lived. Tonight we honor their sacrifice, for they gave us all a final gift before their lives were inexplicably taken. They were chosen – as we all are chosen – and I pray that their sacrifice was a warning and not an act of retaliation for the gradual destruction of the balance."

Deepa's words captured Dioni's attention. If the balance of the Earth was the responsibility of all birds, then why would the Earth retaliate against those who worked to maintain it? Dioni walked to stand closer to Deepa to better understand what he heard. From the corner of her eye, Deepa noticed as he came near. She signaled for him to approach.

"Perhaps it is fate," Deepa continued, "that we have with us our next Omega bird, the first of his kind, among us tonight. The obligation granted to our friend Dioni, the blue quetzal, is unlike any challenge granted to those before him. I ask of each and every one of you – every bird on our land and every bird in the sky – to share with him the wisdom that is our natural birthright."

"Our future and the balance we work tirelessly to provide has been challenged, yet we prevail!" Deepa shouted. "Our Earth is alive and it breathes in living color. So tonight, we honor the many birds who were reclaimed by the land for which they gave their lives."

Manju bobbled on his legs as he carried a heavy object and approached Deepa.

"Now?" he asked her, a gleaming look on his face.

Deepa smiled at the youngling. He reminded her of herself at that age…so full of life, wonder, and enlightenment. No living bird should ever lose such a sentiment, no matter what trauma or inexplicable occurrence happens in its life.

Deepa recalled the fateful day when she was summoned to the fields outside of the sanctuary. She pierced through the sky as she followed the birds who had already seen what was once deemed impossible. In all her years of service, and despite her knowledge, experience and wisdom, nothing had prepared her for what she saw beyond the peace and tranquility of her home.

From a distance, Deepa saw a divot in the grasslands. She slowed her speed, lowered her altitude, and saw the sight which would remain forever engraved in her mind. Scattered about the grounds, and covered and blanketed by the tall blades of grass, was a mass gathering of hundreds of mynas. As if a sudden shock of force had struck violently and without warning of any kind, the field was covered in lifeless birds, scattered about on the ground and still in their flight formations. Their eyes were open, and they portrayed expressions of fear as they fled for their lives. The mynas, hundreds if not thousands of them, were purposely frightened just moments before their lives were taken from them.

Upon closer inspection, Dioni saw what Manju carried: a large collection of feathers. They were not heavy, but there were so many of them that the chick was barely able to see beyond the pile he carried. They were the feathers of the fallen.

"Now?" asked Manju. He looked to Deepa for approval. She nodded.

Manju smiled as he waddled until he was a safe distance from the heat. He stepped forward and used his chest to push every feather he held into the roaring fire. Almost immediately, the flames changed to a spectacle of various colors. Dioni observed as every color of the visible spectrum – and even more colors than he knew existed – flared from the fire of the wooden tower.

"We have defeated the winter, and we welcome the new spring!" Deepa shouted.

The many peahens and peacocks in the giant circle shouted with glee and danced in unison. They moved closer to tighten the circle, joined their wings, and tossed more fuel into the raging fire. The light of the fire was briefly drowned with the countless feathers of fallen mynas, which then further enraged the flames.

The perched birds among the trees, unable to join in the festivities from the ground, raised their voices and sang to the fire. As the celebration began, many of the visiting birds leapt from the trees and created a second whirlwind around the flames. The fire twisted in the wind created by their flightpath, which emanated light and color in every direction. The fallen ashes returned to the ground in just as many colors, which created an impression of the universe within the confines of a protected forest.

Dioni joined in on the celebration. The thought of an existence away from his present form had completely escaped his mind. Though a stranger in a land far from his home, he was among his own kind. They knew nothing of him – not of his past, not of his shortcomings, and not of his life as an orphan – yet they accepted him as one of their own. For the first time in his life, Dioni felt what it was like to belong to a family.

Only the peacocks of India knew the true meaning and importance of the annual ritual, which was as deeply embedded in their culture as were the radiant colors on their feathers. On this special night, it was the multitude of colors which arose from the dancing flames of the bonfire that forever changed the perception of all which Dioni understood to be real.

Chapter Twenty

Countless thoughts brewed in the mind of the Alpha bird. Of what he thought, however, was not clear to Mimidae. The Alpha was widely known to be absent for extended periods at a time, to be in deep thought, as he had the reputation of a mindful leader. Those who worked with him more closely knew an entirely different side to him. He was a vulture, and as such he lived according to the code of his kind. He personified the reputation that scavengers did not deserve, who would otherwise be much more valued members of the avian society.

Yet year after year, decade after decade, and century after century, as life transitioned and the tides of time brought forth new phases of history, there remained only one constant – a single Alpha who held the mantle far longer than any bird cared to wonder. Countless generations of birds had come and gone, and none had ever known a time when another bird controlled the balance of nature as did the vulture.

The Alpha looked down to his kingdom. His ego inflated as he absorbed the sights and sounds of the Earth's most powerful organization. His executive perch was outside of an open window, where he pondered for hours and studied the actions of lesser birds. The surface on which he stood was made of a transparent material which floated effortlessly with his every movement. Though he did not smile, the Alpha was not unhappy; he was in a profound state of mind that could not be seen but was instead understood by centuries of self-exploration – the likes of which few living organisms ever achieved.

From his vantage point, the Alpha saw both sides of his empire. With envious eyes he scanned the youth and vitality of the many birds who were blissfully unaware of their own foolishness. These birds were oblivious of the actions taken and of the decisions and sacrifices made by the birds of the past, and they were too ignorant to care or know any better. The vulture was not the Alpha because he was wise; instead, he was wise because he had lived through it all. No experience was new, no story had gone untold… and no foolish bird had ever dared to challenge his superiority.

Below and to his left was the Trading Floor, where he observed as hundreds of negotiations and transactions took place. He saw the many projected images and screens filled with data for confirmed negotiations, settlements, and amendments to live weather patterns on Earth. He noticed as orders were delivered by scores of hummingbirds, who zipped through the air to deliver their leaflets; he calculated their movements and searched for patterns among their flightpaths. The Alpha observed as two or more teams of birds debated passionately, which was a sight he particularly enjoyed. He was content when other birds felt as passionately about their sectors as he did of his own, and it made him proud to know that the end result would ultimately come to him for final approval.

Below and to his right was the Control Center – a massive technological marvel. The investment to produce the Control Center cost more lives than history cared to count, though there was a time when the need for such power was entirely unnecessary. The Alpha recalled a period when the art and science of the Earth's natural balance was less challenging than observing a plant grow over time. So long as the population of the presumed wisest beings on the planet was kept under control, there was no need for continuous restoration of the balance. As with all in nature, the design of the Control Center was engineered to perfection, though it was never used to its fullest capability. It was only a matter of time before natural selection created the catalyst for the Earth's next destabilization.

From his overhead position, the Alpha saw thousands of data points which provided him with the intelligence to know the exact weather detail of any location on the planet, with master accuracy and with historical records dated as far back as the start of time...the start of time. The Alpha was there at the dawn of its present version, when he proudly accepted his responsibility to do that which was best for all living species. It was a proud day when his global vision became the reality that he so passionately envisioned. The Alpha looked up from his perch and smiled at the large, bioluminescent letters that glistened on the massive wall opposite from where he stood: Department of Global Climate Control.

As he stood and looked over his empire, the thought of the next phase of his grand plan came to mind. His face slowly changed from a passive neutral color to an agitated shade of red, which was a clear indication that something was amiss.

"S...sir?" said Mimidae. She approached the window as carefully and quietly as possible, as to not startle the Alpha. "Sir?"

The Alpha realized the change in his facial pigmentation and quickly altered his dark thoughts to more pleasant ones. He lowered his head and shook his entire body, then forced a gleeful expression on his brow. He turned to face Mimidae.

"Mimidae!" the Alpha exclaimed, optimistically. "I was just thinking about you."

"Oh, sir?" Mimidae responded.

"Mim, I want you to take a vacation. Effective immediately."

"A vacation, sir?" Mimidae nervously asked. "Have I done something wrong?"

"Wrong? What? No, not at all!" said the vulture. "I'm not dismissing you, Mim. I don't want you to leave. It's just that...you work harder than any bird in this place. You're the first one here every morning, and the last one to leave every night. And frankly, it sickens me that you don't complain a fraction as much as some of these other birds. Lousy pheasants."

"Should I complain more, sir? I can start immediately."

"Mim, you're not getting it. I'm not punishing you. In fact, I am trying to reward you. When was the last time you were away from here for more

281

than a day?"

Mimidae stood silent. She looked at her feet and clutched a leaflet onto her chest.

"I don't remember, sir," she responded.

"That's exactly my point," said the Alpha. He stepped away from his perch and entered his executive suite through the large window. "You need to get out more. I want you to get away for a few days and see what you've been missing. Maybe you can go visit that one place in Paris with the chef."

"Chez Amadi."

"That's the one."

Mimidae opened her stance and lifted her head. She never considered the option to take time away from work, and now the decision was made for her.

"But...what about you, sir?" Mimidae asked.

"What about me?" the Alpha responded as he moved to his executive desk. "I've been around longer than you've been alive, Mim. Contrary to popular belief, I can handle a few days on my own."

Mimidae smiled. She had never known of any bird to be offered such an incredible opportunity, and she did not want to do or say anything to jeopardize it.

"When would you need me to return, sir?" she asked.

"What's with all the questions, Mim? Feels like I'm talking with a parakeet...annoying little birds."

"Sir?"

"Take a few days to recharge your batteries, so to speak," said the Alpha. "I want you to experience the world – go watch a show, swim in the Caribbean, enjoy a sunset, poop on a luxurious car just out of the carwash – do the many things that birds do. And when you come back, I want you to tell me all about it."

Mimidae changed her expression. Her timidity became joy the moment she was granted permission to go and see the world; it was a concept which was almost entirely foreign to her, except for what she was told by messenger birds. She placed her leaflet on the Alpha's executive desk, then took one pace back. It was nearly impossible for her to contain her excitement.

"Will you need me to complete anything before I go, sir?" Mimidae asked, her excitement evident in her voice.

"Mimidae. Seriously? Do I need to spell it out for you?" the Alpha rudely responded. "Just go! Really, I'll be fine. Besides, in case of anything, I can get Donna to help."

"Yes, sir! Will do! Thank you so much, sir!"

In her excitement, Mimidae lost her professional composure. Her small body trembled with glee and a wide smile was visible across her face. She turned and quickly paced away from the executive desk.

"Oh, hey…" said the Alpha, which caused Mimidae to return her attention to him, one step away from freedom. "Whatever happened to that friend of yours?"

"Which one, sir?" Mimidae asked, the shine of her smile visible in the distance.

"That little bird. The one from India. I'm thinking a…robin?"

The smile on Mimidae's face remained, though the emotion behind it was the absolute opposite. She knew precisely why he asked the question. He just could not help himself.

"A roller, sir," she responded.

"Yes, that's the one! The roller friend of yours. Where is he these days?"

"I'm not entirely sure, sir," she said.

Mimidae withheld a mixture of various emotions. The Alpha leaned back onto his executive perch and placed his wings behind his head.

"Well if you see him, tell him I miss those bad jokes of his. They call them rollers for a reason, you know. They have a reputation."

Mimidae sighed heavily, though a smile remained on her face.

"I'll let him know, sir," she said.

She turned away and exited the room.

The Alpha waited momentarily to hear the soothing sound of Mimidae's departure. He knew not where she would travel, nor did he care if she ever returned. All he needed was a few days of time, and with Mimidae gone there was no one to oppose his actions. As the projected image from his executive desk appeared, he took special notice of one particular statistic displayed before him: Average Global Temperature. The number was altered by an amount so small that it went entirely unnoticed. The Alpha smiled.

"I see what you're doing," said a voice from a short distance.

"You shouldn't be able to see much of anything, should you?" responded the Alpha. "Only *active* Omegas can do that."

He kept his attention on the projected image. He knew the source of the voice, and he did not want to provide her the satisfaction of his interest.

"You should've read the fine print in the retirement section of your contract," continued the Alpha.

"He will stop you, you know," said the voice. "He's going to see what you're doing, and he'll put an end to it once and for all."

"Who? The only, Dioni?" the vulture responded. He chuckled in amusement as he mocked the bird who spoke to him. "The kid barely knows his beak from his tail." Without moving his head, the Alpha looked up. "You sure knew how to pick him, Ally. Solid choice."

At the center of the executive suite stood the magnificent Alalā. Her appearance was not of a bird who lived an entire lifetime and aged accordingly. Instead, she was the stunning vision of a crow in her prime. Her stare was as intense as the darkness of her feathers.

"I like this look on you," said the Alpha. He lifted his head and looked at the crow who stood in front of his desk. "It says…'I've aged gracefully, though by the looks of me you'd think that I hatched a few days ago.'"

The vulture laughed at his own joke.

"Laugh all you want," Ally responded. "You're going to lose to a tropical bird."

"See, that's the thing," the Alpha said as he placed his feet on the floor and walked towards Ally. "I don't lose. Never have, never will. If you would've been just a tiny bit more diligent, you would've noticed that about me."

"Someday you'll pay for what you've done. For what you're doing to the planet."

"Yeah? Well, add it to my tab," the Alpha responded with a devilish smile on his face. "It's for the good of the planet. You agreed to it, remember?" He moved closer to her. "Oh, and by the way, nice job on choosing a successor. The color scheme doesn't bother me as much as the obliviousness, but coming from you that's not a surprise."

The Alpha towered over the black bird. Fearless, she held her ground. She looked up to him with feelings of disgust and repulsion.

"An orphan was chosen for a reason," Ally said.

"Then maybe you should've picked a better one," the Alpha responded. "You know he almost died in flight school? While trying to echolocate in the dark. How do you explain that one, *Qui-Gon?*"

"You have nothing on him," Ally said in anger to his insulting tone. "He has nothing to lose."

"That's what you didn't comprehend when you were the Omega, and what you *still* don't understand now," said the vulture. He turned his timeworn body toward a large window of the executive suite and paced forward as he spoke. "I don't go into business of any kind without knowing everything about my opponent. He has more to lose than you ever did, and I promise you, he is afraid to lose it."

The Alpha stood before the window and admired his reflection in the glass.

"You see that, Ally?" the Alpha continued. Ally failed to move; there was no need to satisfy his belittling demeanor. He lifted his wings. "It's like conducting an orchestra. A symbiotic symphony."

Ally rolled her eyes. She was in no position to argue or negotiate with him, and he was well aware of it. She knew better than to speak negatively of the Alpha bird.

"Only a decomposer would see it that way," Ally said.

The Alpha's enraged face turned bright red in color, an indication of his fury over Ally's insult. He instantly turned to scorn her for her insolence and for her lack of respect for a superior being. The room was empty; he saw nothing but his executive suite, untouched as if he was by himself the entire time.

"That's what I thought," he said aloud.

The Alpha turned his attention back to the open window and looked diligently at the Control Center. The pigmentation of his face slowly returned to its normal, dreaded color.

"Donna!" he shouted.

Immediately, five fast-moving hummingbirds entered the executive suite.

"I only need one," he said.

All but one of the hummingbirds zipped away.

"I need the coastal currents and negotiated trades for Central America for today and for the next seven days," the Alpha instructed.

The hummingbird nodded and immediately flew out of the executive suite through the open window.

The vulture looked down and observed the many birds on the Trading Floor. He could not hear a word they said, but from where he stood, he knew they were busy. His birds were loyal to him, as was customary of all who worked at the Department of Global Climate Control. Ally fell into his trap perfectly, and it was only a matter of days before Dioni did the same.

The hummingbird returned. She carried with her a glass device which projected a digital image. She presented the device to the Alpha, and she stood by as he reviewed the information he requested. The Alpha touched the glass and made motions and gestures to cause the images on the screen to rotate. He searched for a specific town; his face filled with glee the moment he located it.

"Oh, that's better than I thought!" the Alpha said with enthusiasm.

He moved his wing, which modified the images on the glass. He read a series of numbers, charts, and graphs, all of which he studied with fierce intensity.

"Yep...yep, that makes sense. It's springtime there also," he said as he moved his eyes to the various datapoints on the glass. He found a particular number and smiled at his discovery. "That. Is. Perfect."

The Alpha returned the device to the hummingbird, who held the transparent material with surprising steadiness.

"Thank you, Donna," he said.

The hummingbird turned and flew back toward the Control Center.

"Wait! Donna...one more thing," the Alpha instructed. "Relay a message to the Controller for northern Guatemala."

The hummingbird nodded. She gently tossed the glass device in front of her, where it remained suspended. She motioned for the Alpha to proceed with his instruction.

"Your region was selected as a test site for the Natural Anomaly program. Field testing is to commence immediately. Details to follow. All negotiations for your region are suspended by order of Alpha executive privilege." He looked at the hummingbird. "Did you get all that?" The hummingbird nodded. "Good. That'll be all."

The hummingbird took the glass device and flew away from the suite to transmit the Alpha's executive order. Within a matter of minutes, all of the regions selected for the site test were notified of the new directive.

The Alpha took a deep breath and stood proudly, confident of his control over the domain beneath him. He was not afraid of Ally, nor of her words of warning. He smiled. He had no reason to fear a child, especially one with so much to lose. To the Alpha, this was a game of space and time – both of which he easily manipulated.

Chapter Twenty-One

Mornings were never kind to Dioni. With over a decade and a half of battle experience in fighting the daily struggle to welcome each new day, every attempt remained a colossal failure. It was always the roughest part of the day for him, and the new start was no different than any other.

Dioni waddled out of a hole located at a high point of a tall tree. He sensed a unique smell in the air; not unpleasant, though it was unfamiliar to him. It was a sweet aroma, which despite his brain and body's slow adjustment to work at a limited capacity so early in the morning, he was intrigued.

He waddled further from the hole and onto a long branch. He looked down and saw a group of peafowl younglings who spoke among themselves. Dioni heard their chirps and voices, and he recognized the occasional chuckle of laughter which was ever-so-common among the youth of all living beings. He sluggishly opened his arms, fell back from the branch on which he stood, then glided down to meet the young birds at the ground level.

The sunlight caused him to squint. Combined with his tousled tailfeathers and a hairstyle which clearly indicated he favored to sleep on one particular side, Dioni's disheveled presence fueled the chuckles of the young peafowl. This was not a new experience for Dioni; an identical scenario occurred time and again with the many toddlers who lived at the orphanage. Dioni learned to ignore their laughter, and just as he did previously, he maintained his attention on what he smelled rather than what he heard.

A large pile of ashes and a small stack of mostly-burnt wood were the sole remains of the previous night's bonfire. The place where the wooden tower once stood was altered as a firepit, which contained a stove-like device that distributed heat from a small fire. Alas, Dioni discovered the source of the pleasant aroma. He slowly paced toward the firepit. The young peafowl observed from a distance as Dioni waddled his way closer to the stove. He knew not of the unexpected surprise just a few paces away.

Dioni gradually regained his sense of balance. His waddle became steps, his harsh squint became a deep stare, and his tousled tailfeathers flowed freely behind him. Once closer to the source, he saw the smoke that elevated from the stove. He approached the firepit in the same method he approached his favorite *pasteleria*: with awe and wonder, and with desire in his eyes. The peafowl became silent, a change in their behavior which Dioni failed to notice.

Before Dioni were stacks of flawlessly placed, perfectly symmetrical pancakes. As one of his favorite foods – regardless of time of day – pancakes were the fastest way to earn Dioni's good graces. This knowledge was advantageous for the birds of India. For the briefest of moments, Dioni recognized the benefits provided to him as the Omega bird.

He walked closer to the firepit. The extraordinary pancakes were unlike those he remembered from home. They appeared solid, almost toasted, and were not as flat as he recalled. He was so close he could nearly taste them. Only a short reach of his wing stood between him and total bliss. The younglings stood quiet and motionless, well aware of what was to happen to the unsuspecting quetzal.

Dioni barely lifted his right wing before he felt the mighty blow of the largest peacock in the entire sanctuary. The colossal peacock did not touch Dioni, but landed so close and at such high speed that its tailwind was enough to thrust him back and onto the cold ground.

The younglings watched in awe, as if time intentionally slowed enough for them to capture the moment and engrave it into their memory. Dioni's tailfeathers were tossed in every direction, which entangled him in his own body. The question as to whether or not he was fully awake was answered in that instant.

The large peacock stood at attention in front of the firepit. He sternly kept himself between the food and the Omega. Like a soldier on guard, the peacock gazed coldly at Dioni with a look of furor, and with a permanent scowl the likes of which few birds could recreate.

Dioni was defeated. He awakened only a few moments prior and had already experienced a knock-out. He struggled to get to his feet and coughed as he desperately attempted to find the air which escaped his small lungs. He then felt the wings of another bird on each of his shoulders.

"You tried to steal one, didn't you?" asked Deepa.

She assisted Dioni to his feet.

"I don't know what they are!" Dioni responded, comforted though still in shock. "I reached for one and then I was hit by a tornado!"

The younglings laughed hysterically as they witnessed the entire performance. Deepa immediately turned her head to the young peafowl and shifted her expression. She instantly became the peahen equivalent of judge, jury, and executioner, which immediately quieted the laughing younglings. They stood in complete silence even after Deepa returned her attention to Dioni.

"You mustn't be afraid to approach, Dioni, but you cannot take Shankar's food without asking his permission. Everyone knows this."

"Well I didn't know," Dioni responded.

The aroma remained in the air, yet his desire to chase it was long gone. He looked to the large peacock and pointed at him with a sense of fear. He felt safe with Deepa at his side.

"Shankar?" Dioni asked.

"Also known as the best 'pea-cook' in all of India," Deepa responded. "Today is actually a very special day for him."

"Why is that?" Dioni asked. He looked up to the mighty bird. "Is he going to chop me up and feed me to the others?"

"Who? Shankar? He would not hurt a butterfly. He's like a big pillowcase stuffed with exotic feathers."

The large peacock smiled and lowered his guard. He took a pancake from the top of a stack and offered it to Dioni. Though envious of what they witnessed, the younglings did not move or make a sound. Dioni nervously reached for the pancake and accepted it. He grasped the treat and took a few paces back to stand away from Shankar.

"This is called *malpua*," Deepa said. "It is a special treat Shankar prepares for us, but only on this day, every year."

Dioni smelled the treat then gently pecked at it. He tasted only a morsel of malpua and knew in that moment that it was the greatest version of pancake in existence. Dioni's manners drifted away as he stuffed as much of the malpua as his beak was able to hold.

Deepa turned her attention to the group of younglings who looked at her with big, pleading eyes. It would have proven difficult for a single chick to attempt this method of manipulation and be successful, but as a group their chances increased substantially.

"Malpua?" Deepa asked the younglings.

Each of them nodded their heads and lifted themselves to stand at the tips of their toes. One youngling lost her balance and fell on her face. Deepa smiled. She envisioned herself at their same age and recalled the emotions of her youth as well as the joy of special treats.

"We are blessed to have among us a bird with such extraordinary talent," said Deepa. She turned to the large peacock. "Shankar, will you please share the malpua with these birds, who will speak far and wide of your culinary skills and talents?"

Shankar raised his chest. He looked to his left then to his right. At long last, it was his moment to shine. He stood back then opened his tailfeathers, which displayed a landscape of intricate colors and patterns. His tailfeathers radiated with a detail so fine that they were undoubtedly painted by master artisans.

"It is my pleasure, Deepa," Shankar said with an expression of joy on his face.

He opened his wings and inhaled deeply.

"To my brothers and sisters!" Shankar shouted. "On this special day of Holi, I welcome you to enjoy the traditional morning meal of malpua, prepared for you as my gift to welcome the return of the greening spring. Please, come and help yourselves!"

The wind carried his words, which returned to Shankar in the form of a light breeze that drifted from the many trees of the sanctuary. The younglings, too young to understand what was to happen, stood nervously and wondered why there was no motion from any direction. Perhaps Shankar did not speak loud enough for all to hear.

"Quickly, young ones!" Deepa instructed the younglings. "Get your malpua before the others arrive!"

A young peacock, relieved of the burden of his timidity, ran to a small stack of fresh malpua. He immediately stuffed one in his beak, which was not large enough to fit the entire portion. The remaining younglings happily ran to the firepit and reached for the stacks of malpua. Their joy came to a sudden halt when they heard a roar among the trees.

Dioni looked up. The shadows of incoming birds danced along the tree barks. As they emerged from the tree line, the source of the roar came to full fruition; the wind brought forth scores of birds of all shapes, colors, and sizes. While most were peacocks, many were smaller birds who also lived in the sanctuary and were granted permission to participate. Not a single one of them missed the opportunity to taste the malpua made by the finest chef in all the land.

Each of the birds had marks or stains on their faces and bodies, as if they had attempted to wear a special type of makeup or a form of warpaint. In their beaks, many of the peahens held large, woven baskets, which were covered by leaves. The birds landed near one another, away from the fire pit, where designated peacocks acted as traffic controllers and instructed the masses to spread about the area.

"Hurry, young ones!" Deepa said to the younglings, who were distracted by the sights and sounds of the countless number of birds who surrounded them.

The chicks proceeded as directed. Shankar quickly distributed a single serving of malpua to each of the young birds, who were in absolute glee as they each stuffed their beaks with far more than they were able to chew.

The traffic controllers held the crowd for as long as possible. The colorful peahens, who landed with baskets in their beaks, bolted to the firepit. They had only seconds to enjoy their treat before the mass of birds ensued. Shankar became surrounded by the many hungry birds who began their day by feasting on the best malpua in India. It was the start to a much grander celebration, and though he observed from a distance, Dioni found every second of it to be incredible.

"Malpua is traditionally served for breakfast during Holi," Deepa said as she walked to Dioni.

"What's Holi?" Dioni asked.

He picked at the morsels that remained on the feathers of his wings.

"What are we peafowl responsible for on this Earth, Dioni?" Deepa asked.

"Color," Dioni responded.

"Yes, correct. Holi is a festival of color. Do you see those birds who carried their woven baskets?"

"Do they have more malpua?" Dioni asked excitedly. Deepa smiled.

"We must allow every bird to have one, Dioni."

"Understood," Dioni said.

"The baskets contain color packets which are made from the leaves of the sacred fig tree."

Dioni looked to where the peahens stood. Each of them distributed the contents of their baskets, which contained packets of meticulously woven leaves that held powders of various colors.

"The colors you see on their bodies are part of the celebration," Deepa continued. "We use various natural substances for color, and we make powders. In many places around the world, but particularly here in India, we celebrate the end of the winter and the arrival of the spring by spreading color to what was until recently, mostly dull and grey."

"How do you spread the color?" Dioni asked. "Does every bird just grip as much as they can hold and drop it from the sky?"

"You'll see," Deepa said with a large grin on her face. This was a surprise she wanted Dioni to fully experience. "Just one friendly word of caution: look out for Nabhitha."

"What's Nabhitha?"

"You'll see."

Deepa turned away from Dioni and joined the birds at the center of the malpua stacks. Beside her stood Shankar, who was pleased with the success of his work. Dioni was unable to hear what Deepa said to Shankar, though he saw how Shankar bowed to the ground and allowed Deepa to stand on his shoulders.

"Brothers and sisters!" Deepa shouted. She garnered the attention of every bird whose beak was either full or filling with delicious malpua. "Spring has returned to India! The evil beings and spirits have once again been eliminated! I invite all birds to celebrate this day by giving to the Earth the color it so desperately deserves!"

Deepa waved her wings to the peahens who reached into their woven baskets. The peahens tossed wingfuls of leaves into the air. The leaves opened and released powders of various bright, striking colors to all who stood beneath. As the colored powders fell, the many birds who feasted on the ground began to cheer; they opened their wings to have the colored powder paint their feathers. Additional color packets were tossed in the air, and soon, a cloud of powders was unleashed upon the grounds.

Dioni laughed at what he witnessed. He saw the happiness of the birds of the entire community, as a result of this tradition. There was so much commotion and movement among the birds that it was difficult to determine one from another, yet it was a sight Dioni enthusiastically enjoyed. Distracted by the festivities, he failed to hear the sound of a young, below-average-sized peahen who approached and stood beside him. He was startled when he suddenly noticed her, and she returned his look with a fierce gaze. Whoever she was, she meant business and was not there solely for her amusement.

The small peahen wore her colors in an extreme camouflage pattern. Had Dioni not witnessed the ways in which the colored powder effected the feathers of the many birds, he would have concluded that the small peahen was prepared for battle. Across her brow was the tailfeather of a dark-colored bird, who may or may not have willingly given it to her. Strapped across her side was a custom-made satchel, which held smaller sacks of powder. In her stance, she resembled a fully weaponized machine of war.

She did not blink or move in any way; the only motion of her body was the result of the wind which moved the feathers on her head. The young peahen stared intensely at Dioni. With robotic movement, she reached into her satchel and pulled a small sack of powder, wrapped eloquently in a fig leaf. Ever so carefully, she spread her wing to Dioni and offered him the sack of powder.

"Uhm…no…no, thank you," Dioni replied, unsure of whether the peahen offered peace or eminent doom.

In reverse motion, the peahen returned the small sack to her satchel, then slowly moved her head to face the same direction her body pointed. Dioni looked at her, with his eyebrow raised, and wondered what occurred in her mind. The peahen swayed herself back and forth. She neither breathed nor made a sound, and she stared deeply into the fog of color. She raised her wing and pointed directly in front of herself, then instantly disappeared into the crowd of birds.

Dioni's expression failed to return to normal as he looked to his left and to his right. He wondered if any other bird had witnessed what occurred. What an odd bird.

The birds who joined the celebration were drenched in the colors cast down from the skies. Their only refuge to escape one another was to fly away.

"To the sky!" Deepa shouted as she lifted her wings. "Today, we color the world!"

295

Every bird who was present amidst the chaos lifted from the ground. Their sudden movement reminded Dioni of his murmuration training, and how so many birds simultaneously knew where to go and how to prevent from crashing into one another. To them, this was instinctive; to Dioni, however, it required the use of his pathfinder.

"Dioni!" Deepa shouted as the cloud of color followed the birds who took flight. "Fly with us!"

She motioned for him to follow then spread her wings and chased after the crowd of birds who left trails of color behind as they flew further from the ground.

Dioni followed as closely behind the other birds as possible. For the first time since his Flight Academy training, he realized he had an advantage over other types of birds. Because of the considerable weight of their tailfeathers, peacocks were slightly slower in the air, though their size corrected the difference. Every bird whom Dioni passed – the teenagers who flew like young fighter pilots, the adults who controlled the direction of travel, and the elders who flew in longer strides and carried the younglings on their backs – displayed the same emotion: pure joy. The colors of their feathers were on the extreme points of the color spectrum, yet the birds flew together as they euphorically migrated toward a large temple in the distance.

Dioni looked at the city beneath him. At various points in nearly every direction he saw small puffs of multicolored powders tossed among the people. He noticed as they threw the powders at one another, and how they playfully laughed while they chased each other along the streets. The elders acted as children, and no one person was excluded from the country-wide festival. It was a celebration of epic proportions, and he had the best possible view of it all.

"Toward the mausoleum!" shouted a voice from the distance. It was Deepa, who was further behind than Dioni realized. "The other side of the mausoleum! On the grounds before the river!"

Dioni understood her instructions. He lifted his shoulders to increase his elevation and speed, and quickly flew to the front of the line. His unusual flight pattern made no difference to the other birds, who were excited for what was to come. He smiled and increased his speed, which placed him further away from the flock.

Dioni saw a large gate, which led to a park with a stretched walkway. In the middle of the walkway was a rectangular pool filled with water, and a garden located directly at the center. At the far end of the great pool stood a magnificent, ivory-colored mausoleum. Dioni's only knowledge of sacred structures was from the temples of Tikal, which were built and engineered to the aesthetics of the Mayan people. The mausoleum before him, however, created an entirely new level of architectural extravagance. The sight of such incredible workmanship made a profound impression on him. Though he maintained his speed and altitude, his eyes did not look away from the sheer magnificence of the structure. The mausoleum was pristine, with measurements, angles, and configurations that were designed to perfection. As he flew above and beyond the stunning building, he saw the perfectly balanced elements of color which were formed into the design.

Distracted by his attention to the detail of the temple's aesthetic beauty, Dioni bypassed the landing zone. Before he knew it, he had flown over a river, which caused him to worry. He looked in every direction yet failed to see where he was supposed to land. Dioni turned his head and saw the grounds behind the mausoleum, where a peahen waved to him as if she were anxiously anticipating his arrival.

The grass on the grounds behind the mausoleum was green and undisturbed. Dioni noticed how teams of peacocks and peahens lined themselves along a wall and busily worked as a large assembly line. He felt safe to approach and landed near the peahen who waved to him, though far enough away as to not disturb the other birds as they continued their work.

"Hello!" said the joyful peahen. "Welcome to Taj Mahal! You are with Deepa's group, yes?"

Dioni nodded.

"Would you like to help us until she arrives?" she continued.

Dioni nodded once again, smiled, and approached the assembly line.

To his amazement, Dioni saw a table-like platform stretched along the back wall of the grounds behind the mausoleum. The peafowl worked diligently to produce the many color packets to be used for the ceremony. One team of workers distributed fig leaves, while the others stuffed the leaves with powders of various ingredients and of various colors. They worked in near perfect unison to produce a stockpile of thousands of packets for all to use and enjoy.

"Here, take this," the peahen instructed Dioni. She gave him a fig leaf. "Hold it out and directly in front of you."

Dioni did as he was told. He held the leaf in front of his body and stretched it as much as he could without causing it to tear. The peahen then placed a small amount of red powder directly in the center of the leaf.

"Fold it from the right to the left, and from the top down," the peahen instructed as she guided Dioni's wings.

A slight gust of wind blew in from the river. The wind caused the powder to drift from the leaf and into Dioni's nostrils. He sneezed, which spilled a small amount of the red powder onto his chest. He looked at himself, then looked up to the peahen with eyes of worry.

"That's okay," said the peahen. "It looks good on you. No need to worry, it washes off."

The first of the peacocks and peahens from Deepa's group began to arrive. The peahen instructed and guided Dioni once more, and on his second attempt he successfully produced his own color packet. It was not the best, but he was proud of it.

"Did you learn how to make a color packet?" Deepa asked as she approached Dioni and the peahen.

"I think so," Dioni responded. "I got some of it on me, though."

"That's okay. It's kind of the point." Deepa turned to the peahen. "And I see you met my sister?"

"Oh, I'm so sorry," said Dioni. He turned to the peahen. "Hello, my name is Dioni."

"Hello Dioni," she responded. "My name is Lakshmi."

"Dioni is our special guest," Deepa said to Lakshmi. "This is his first Holi."

"Then you are most welcome here, Dioni," Lakshmi said. A large smile glowed from her face. "Just be careful with Nabhitha."

"What's Nabhitha?"

"You'll see," both peahens responded.

Dioni looked to the grounds behind the mausoleum, which slowly filled with a multitude of birds. They landed, greeted one another, and talked amongst themselves. Many already showed signs of exploded color from the various powders of the color packets.

"Dioni, as our guest of honor, will you launch the festivities?" Lakshmi asked.

"Umm...sure," Dioni responded. "What do I do?"

Lakshmi gave Dioni the color packet she helped him make. Deepa then turned Dioni to have him face the many birds on the grounds between the mausoleum and the river. The birds continued their conversations and enjoyed the beautiful day as if no different from any other. None looked at Dioni.

"This is perfect, Dioni. They don't suspect it's you," Deepa said, excitedly. "Throw the color packet as far and high as you can, towards the crowd of birds."

"Okay," Dioni responded.

He placed the color packet on his right wing, then reached back and put all of his force into the launch of the small sack of colored powder. A short distance away, the color packet burst midair, and spewed a bright, red color onto the unsuspecting flock of birds below. The chatter among them came to a sudden halt. Every bird turned to look at Dioni. He nervously looked at Deepa.

"Now what do I do?" Dioni asked.

Deepa looked at Lakshmi. They smiled at one another.

"Dioni…run!" the peahens shouted then immediately moved away from him.

Dioni looked up and saw two color packets in the air, aimed directly at him. He was struck on his chest and on his back, which surrounded him in a cloud of red and green dust. The act immediately prompted every bird to follow, and soon an epic battle was underway. It was a war of peace and celebration among birds, who utilized multiple rounds of color as their preferred weapon of choice.

Within seconds, the peaceful, naturally green grounds behind Taj Mahal were completely covered in a thick fog of colored powders. Feathers flapped, feet ran, voices sang, and every bird was in a euphoric state of joy as they drenched themselves in a display of color unmatched by any phenomenon in nature.

The youngest and smallest of the birds knew how to navigate at their level; they created paths along the grounds by which they splashed colors on the elder birds without the risk of retaliation. The larger birds threw the color packets further than the others; their preferred targets were the birds who attempted to flee as chaos ensued.

Color and light radiated from every visible angle. Unable to run far or run quickly, Dioni moved to the epicenter of the pandemonium, which placed him at ground-zero to remember every moment of the experience. He laughed with a joy he failed to remember. The pressures of his past and of his future drifted from his mind. He was in his element, with others like him, and he lived for the exact moment. Dioni discovered that utopia truly existed on Earth, and that the birds knew more about it than did any other beings on the planet.

Dioni was ambushed from every angle. Instead of acting on revenge for those who targeted him, he just stood and laughed, and enjoy the moment. As more packets hit his body, Dioni found himself in a cloud of smoke that slowly dissolved with a perfectly timed gust of wind. In the center of the chaos – where every bird stood and aimed color packets at one another – the flock stopped and stared at the Omega bird. The noise level dissipated as the fog lifted from around Dioni.

"What?" Dioni asked.

Every pair of eyes looked squarely at him. No sound was made by any living creature nearby.

"What?" Dioni repeated. "Did something happen?"

He searched in every direction for Deepa, who was lost among the crowd of extremely colorful birds.

Dioni failed to notice the incredible accuracy of the colors painted on his body. Each of his blue feathers was splashed in bright green, which released a glow unlike any the birds of India had ever witnessed. His chest, which moments ago was a solid white color, was almost entirely red.

For the first time ever, the fowl of India saw before them the most striking bird in the entire world. Before them stood Dioni – the live image of a resplendent quetzal – the likes of which was never seen beyond Central America. Every bird on the planet knew why the resplendent quetzals stayed only in their natural habitat. Though the birds of India failed to recognize him for what he was as a blue-colored bird, they quickly realized that it was a true Omega bird who stood before them. The momentum of the Earth temporarily froze around Dioni. There was no movement, nor a tick of time, nor an existence away from that moment.

In the near distance a battle cry was heard. Another bird approached quickly, and with no regard for the meaning of the moment. The sound was the shout of the small, militant peahen, of whom Dioni previously refused to accept her initial offering. She sprinted to him with only one goal in mind. Her voice was heard, though she was unseen. Dioni looked frantically in each direction to identify the location from where the sound came.

The small peahen emerged in a flash; not from the ground, but by means of an aerial attack. She somersaulted while airborne then landed heroically on the ground a few paces before Dioni. She looked up and smiled; Dioni nervously returned the gesture. She then leapt to be in vertical alignment with the light of the sun. The peahen screamed its battle cry while airborne, reached back, and launched the biggest color packet she had in her arsenal.

"Nabhitha! No—" were the only words Lakshmi was able to yell before the course of the peahen's actions were set in motion. Her decision was made before she became airborne; the peahen had patiently waited for the opportune moment, and it finally presented itself.

With no time to take defensive action, Dioni braced for impact. The strike of Nabhitha's attack battered Dioni so forcefully that it lifted him from the ground. His small, momentarily resplendent body crash-landed on the cold, powder-stained grass. The entire exchange occurred within the span of a few seconds, though it felt much longer to every bird who witnessed the event.

The young peahen landed on the colored ground. She raised her wings and once again screamed her battle cry, which was heard through the halls of Taj Mahal and beyond. Immediately, the paused action of the moment erupted into the continuation of the festival of color. Smoke clouds of colored powder created a haze on the grounds behind the mausoleum.

As he slowly regained his composure, Dioni saw blurred, red flashes of light on a projected image. It was his pathfinder, which appeared to have taken severe damage at the moment of impact from either Nabhitha's blatant attack or the hard landing that followed.

"Dioni...Dioni!" he heard.

The blur in his eyes slowly vanished. Above him stood Deepa, with a worried expression on her face and with feathers drenched in a multitude of bright colors.

"I think my pathfinder's broken," Dioni said to her.

"What?" Deepa asked. "How do you know?"

"It's really blurry and flashing red letters," responded Dioni.

Lakshmi landed beside Deepa, equally soaked in colored powder.

"That could be an important message for you," said Lakshmi.

"Is yours doing the same thing?"

Deepa and Lakshmi looked to one another. They reached down and took hold of Dioni's wings.

"No, Dioni. We do not use pathfinders," Deepa said as she and Lakshmi helped Dioni to his feet.

He attempted to read the letters that flashed before him.

"What? Why not?" Dioni asked.

He looked to Deepa. Lakshmi shifted her head twice, the universal sign to move to another location. Dioni followed the two peahens who walked away from the colorful madness of the festivities.

"Neither of you use pathfinders?" Dioni asked.

He bumped the side of his head with his wing in an attempt to fix his navigational device.

"None of these birds use pathfinders," Lakshmi responded. "There is no need for it here."

"That doesn't make any sense," Dioni responded. "It helps you to communicate. How else does headquarters know what's happening here?"

"The Alpha knows what happens here," Deepa responded. "He does not need us to be attached to his network. We communicate to our representatives on our own."

The letters which flashed before Dioni became legible, though were still slightly blurry.

"Wait, I think I can read it," said Dioni. "It's saying, 'Warning: Natural Anomaly Protocol Administered. Secondary Approval Required. Please Report to Headquarters'."

Lakshmi looked at Deepa as Dioni read the message from his pathfinder. A worried look grew on her face. Deepa motioned for Lakshmi to change her expression; her fear could spark the same within the inexperienced Omega.

"It's probably a standard test," Deepa said to Dioni though she faced Lakshmi. "No need to alarm or panic. They need the approval of the Omega in order to run it."

"That's it? Can't I do that from here?" Dioni asked. "I'm having a lot of fun and I was hoping to get more malpu—"

"—Listen, Dioni," Lakshmi said abruptly. "If nothing else, let them know that the birds of India are always watching."

"Watching what? Which bir—?"

"—They may ignore us, they may destroy our lands, and they may fail to see what they are doing…yet the birds are always watching, okay? The birds are *always* watching."

Lakshmi looked to Deepa, who noticeably altered her expression. Lakshmi mouthed a phrase to Deepa. Though it was inaudible and in another language, Dioni understood its apologetic tone. Lakshmi returned to the festival and disappeared into the roar and color.

"What did she mean by—?"

"—You have a responsibility, Dioni," Deepa stopped his question before it went any further. She collected herself and continued. "You will not find whom you seek in India."

"How did you know I was looking for something? Or someone?" Dioni asked.

His pathfinder began to work properly, and he was able to clearly identify the words which flashed before him. With his vision fully restored, he looked at his own body and noticed its many colors.

"Because if it were meant to be, you would have found it by now," Deepa responded. "Do you see these birds?"

She pointed at the array of feathers that peeked through the haze of colorful powders. Dioni looked at the commotion. Perhaps one of those birds would be willing to take his place.

"Can I ask any of them if they want to be the Omega bird?"

"You can try, but none will accept." Deepa responded.

"Why not?" Dioni asked.

"Dioni, you have to report back. Let me save you the trouble. The bird you seek will be in the place you most fear."

"What?"

Dioni did not care for her response. How could he find a bird in the place he feared most? How would she know where he was most afraid, and how did she know another bird would be there?

"Your pathfinder is flashing, is it not?" said Deepa. "Your immediate attention is needed, so you must go. But remember what you promised me."

"I promised you something?" Dioni asked.

Deepa rolled her eyes; he was younger than his tailfeathers claimed.

"The pilots...?"

"Oh, yes!" Dioni responded optimistically. "The best pilots in the world...right! Ha! Not falcons. Okay..."

Dioni's sarcastic tone drifted as he dusted the colored powder off his wings.

"I'm serious, Dioni."

"Oh, I'm sure you are," Dioni laughed.

It was ridiculous to acknowledge the existence of better pilots than the falcons who tamed the wind.

Deepa understood what it was like to be a young, sophomoric bird. It was her advantage over the new Omega, who could not possibly understand a wisdom beyond his years.

"Pathfinder," Dioni instructed. The flash of words paused. "Destination, headquarters."

Dioni aimed his face skyward, spread his wings, squatted his body, then pushed himself off the ground. He instantly surged to the sky; only an echo of colored powder preserved his direction of travel.

Deepa watched his departure and tracked his movement until she lost his location among the clouds. Lakshmi, covered in more colors, nervously approached Deepa.

"I'm sorry, Deepa," Lakshmi said.

She lowered her head as she stood beside her sister.

"Don't be," Deepa responded. "You did the right thing."

"What did you say to him?" Lakshmi asked.

"What he needed to hear. Nothing more."

"Oh Deepa. Please don't tell me that you filled the boy's head with hopes and dreams."

Deepa looked at her sister, a sense of sass made its way from Deepa's mind to her beak.

"I would not dare do such a thing!" Deepa exclaimed. A smile trickled from the side of her beak. "If the boy is old enough to have his tailfeathers, then he is old enough to make his own decisions."

Without warning of any kind, two color packets hit Deepa and Lakshmi, perfectly aimed at the backs of their heads. The two elder peahens turned and saw a small, lavishly colored roller. The worried expression on the small bird's face spoke volumes of its anxiety.

"Good shot, Taqhi!" Deepa said to the roller.

"That will be your last!" Lakshmi said as she wiped powder from her large eyes.

Taqhi immediately took to the sky. The two peahens chased playfully behind him.

Chapter Twenty-Two

The Alpha bird felt most in his element while in his power stance – his wings behind his back, his chest raised, his beak lifted, and his eyes intensely focused on the task at hand – the rightful image of a bird who knew he had no successor. He was known for his incredible ability to stand motionless for hours at a time, observant and studious of hundreds if not thousands of weather patterns. The Alpha's presence near the base of the Control Center and before the massive data screen was all too common. More so, however, was the inquisitive nature of why he was so attracted to personally oversee all natural anomalies.

The fourth and final work shift of the Control Center was naturally slower paced. The system ran automatically once all of the work orders were submitted and set, and a skeleton crew of misfit birds was all that was necessary to oversee operations after high traffic hours. The Alpha bird found that the late shift was the best time to stand proudly before his domain. The birds who remained in the Control Center during the later hours grew accustomed to the Alpha's usual stance and position, and ultimately cared very little over his presence among them.

The vulture was statuesque in that he did not move in the slightest. His eyes consistently scanned the immense map on the colossal screen, which was the sole action that proved he remained alive. No bird ever understood how or why he behaved in such a manner, nor did they question the intentions or motives for why he did so. For all the other birds, it was business as usual.

"Donna!" the vulture called. His shout immediately summoned three hummingbirds who hovered nearby and awaited his command. "I only need one," he said, which prompted two of the small birds to depart as quickly as they arrived.

"I need to run a simulation sequence," continued the Alpha, to which the hummingbird responded with a series of fast gestures of body language. "I'd like to run a storm sequence along the Gulf of Mexico."

The hummingbird made even more gestures. She spun rapidly in place.

"Yes, yes! Right! But from the east *and* the west," responded the Alpha.

The hummingbird halted her movements. Her facial expression told stories of her opinion for the Alpha's order, though it was in bad form to question his motives.

"A natural anomaly simulation, Donna. We need to prepare for every possibility."

The hummingbird shook her head then zoomed away in the opposite direction from which she entered.

"Oh, and Donna," the Alpha said. The small bird paused mid-flight then returned. "This one is on the hush-hush."

The hummingbird acknowledged the command and quickly exited the scene. The Alpha returned to his favorite pose. As he looked intently at the massive screen, a large shadow hovered over the Alpha. The shadow covered him momentarily, yet the vulture did not feel threatened enough to give the shadow his attention. A large bird landed a few paces behind the Alpha, with a strength and vigor that was given only to a select group of aviators.

The California condor who stood behind the Alpha was the textbook definition of intimidating, matched only by an ugliness that rivaled that of the elder vulture. To any other bird – and to most land-roaming pheasants, mammals or amphibians – a bird of such scale who stood just a few paces away and in a threatening manner was more than enough to cause a sense of deep fear. The Alpha, however, was too far in his train of thought to notice the larger bird who stood behind him.

"Hi Chuck," said the Alpha, his eyes on the large screen.

"Hiya boss!" said the condor, excitedly.

Though difficult to fathom because of its sheer size and intimidating demeanor, the bird's voice was inquisitively sweet and kind natured.

"Listen, Chuck, I called you here for..." The Alpha scowled. He turned to face the condor. "Did you say 'hiya boss'?"

"Yeah! What'd I say?" asked Chuck. His tone changed from innocent to apprehensive. "Did I say something wrong? What'd I say? Should I not have said 'hiya'? Or was it the 'boss' part you didn't like? Should I have flown in from the south side? I *knew* I should have flown in from the south side. Everyone said I should fly in from the south side but I didn't listen and now look what hap—"

"—Chuck!"

"Yeah boss?"

"You're at a nine. I need you at about a four," said the Alpha. He used his wing to demonstrate the vertical difference between a level nine and a level four.

"Oh. Right. Yep. I know what that means. Is it hot in here? Because I'm feeling a little faint."

"Chuck! You're fine."

"You're right. I'm fine," Chuck responded. He took a deep breath. "You called for me, sir?"

"Much better, Chuck. Thank you."

"You betcha!"

"I ask..." The Alpha abruptly paused. He became annoyed after just a few seconds into the conversation. "I asked you here because we're going to run an anomaly simulation."

"That is wonderful news, sir!" Chuck responded. He failed to understand the seriousness of the work order. "I remember my first anomaly like

309

it was yesterday. Me and a few of the fellas were watching the game at Candlestick Park when it hit. And a good thing we waited until traffic had gone down, otherwise we would've had a catastrophe! Did you know that would happen to the bridge? None of us did. We felt bad about it after. Freddy lost eleven bucks betting against Oakland."

"Chuck! I swea—"

The Alpha stopped himself. His face turned red, which clearly expressed his state of mind. The success of the anomaly was more important than his desire to scold the fast-talking condor. He closed his eyes and took a deep breath before he continued.

"No, Chuck…" continued the Alpha, more calmly though he remained irritated. "I was not aware that the bridge would collapse."

"Well, things happen, I guess," Chuck responded.

"They sure do, Chuck. Now listen, we're going to run a new program this time, and the wind off the Pacific is going to play a strong role in this."

"Sir, we are at your service the moment you give the order. Nothing would make the California condors more proud than to serve at the pleasure of the Alpha bird."

"That's nice to hear. Anyway, this order might seem a little strange for the Pacific, but it's for a new training protocol we want to test."

"Your very wish is my every command, boss!" exclaimed Chuck, whose voice returned to its state of innocence. "Hey, speaking of boss, have you met the new Omega bird? Word has it that it's a bluebird and that he went to the USA-Mexico border to talk to Makawee about auditioning for a musical. He's not here, is he? I was hoping I would see him here so I could audition in person! I've been working on my song choice for it. What do you think of "Memories" from *Cats*? It's not my favorite, like *Les Mis* or *Phantom*, but I thought I'd go for something less obvious. Have you watched *Sweeney Todd*? I still don't trust my barber after I watched it, and he's a bald eagle…"

The Alpha turned and looked at the large screen. He specifically searched along the center of the map.

"Why would he go talk to a bald eagle?" he thought. "It's "Memory"," the Alpha said aloud, cutting the flow of the condor's monologue while he maintained his attention on the screen.

"What was that, boss?' Chuck asked.

"It's not 'Memories'. It's 'Memory'. Singular."

"Oh," said Chuck. "I'm glad you told me. Last thing I would ever want to do is fail my audition because I didn't know the name of the song I was singing. Now that's embarrassing! You know, my cousin did that once at his niece's *quinceañera*—"

"—That'll be all, Chuck," interrupted the Alpha. "I wanted to let you know what we have planned. Now you know."

The Alpha heard enough. Fate opened a window, all because a condor could not close his beak.

"That's it?" asked the condor. "Well, it was a pleasure, sir. We'll be waiting for direction from headquarters."

The condor shifted his body and opened his wings to prepare for a ground takeoff. He bumped the back of the Alpha's head in the process. The clumsy action of the condor did not phase the Alpha, whose mind was far from the Department of Global Climate Control.

"And it's a quetzal," said the elder vulture.

"What was that, sir?" Chuck asked as he stood in his pre-flight posture.

"The Omega...he's not a bluebird. He's a blue quetzal."

"A *blue* Q?" Chuck momentarily paused to absorb the news. "That must be a strange-looking bird."

The condor pushed his giant feet against the stone floor of the Control Center then lifted himself away from the area. The Alpha waited for the talkative condor to be gone. Once Chuck was at a far enough distance, he returned his attention to the large screen. He lifted his wings and gestured to the global map displayed before him.

"Track pathfinder, Omega. Last location," the Alpha commanded, which prompted the screen to display a signal beacon in the region of

311

northern India.

"India?" the Alpha said aloud. "Deepa." He paused to recompose himself. "I see what you're doing. Nice try, kid."

The Alpha smiled. In this particular rivalry, Dioni was of no match.

The same hummingbird, who moments ago left the Alpha's sight, returned. She carried a mesh bag which contained a helmet-like device. She held the bag just above the Alpha, who graciously accepted it.

"Thank you, Donna. That'll be all for now," he said, which prompted the hummingbird to leave.

The Alpha reached into the mesh bag, pulled the headpiece, then dropped the bag on the floor. The object he held was an extraordinary piece of hardware designed to simulate hundreds of thousands of climate scenarios, instances and calculations, without the need to leave the comfort of the Control Center. It was custom built and designed to look like a helmet for the Alpha's specifications, with an added sense of security that only he was able to access.

With the device firmly in place, the Alpha was able to use the large map on the screen to sync actual weather and climate conditions to any scenario his eager mind desired; the device gave him full autonomy to design and run simulations of real-world scenarios. If he wanted to do so, he could produce an Earthquake in Japan while simultaneously creating a severe lightning storm in Argentina. All that was required was for him to command his headpiece to do so. Though the results of the simulation accurately depicted what could occur given the designed scenarios, the approval of the Omega bird was necessary in order to make the simulation a reality on Earth.

"Run simulation," said the Alpha.

He adjusted his headgear to better see the images on his screen. A series of letters displayed on a transparent surface, visible only to him: CONFIRM SIMULATION PROGRAM

"Natural anomaly program," said the Alpha.

The device displayed additional words: ENTER CASE NUMBER

"Run case number one one zero one zero…uh…what's the placed called? Ummm mumumumummm….Flores, Guatemala, Central America."

The letters disappeared from the transparent screen. On his display he saw a map which mimicked the grand map of the Control Center. From an outsider's perspective, the scenario appeared as nothing more than a vulture who stood alone, in the center of a large room, before a massive screen, who wore a ridiculous helmet and who shook his head while he spouted unintelligible banter.

An overtly colorful quetzal – one who was undoubtedly the target of an attack of exploding color powder – appeared by the bridge which separated the Control Center from the Trading Floor. From a distance, he saw as the Alpha stood in a trance-like state, with an emotionless expression, while he wore an odd machine on his head.

Dioni circled above the Control Center and found a place to land near the far end. He touched down onto the cold floor and slowly paced to the Alpha, as to not disturb him. With each step, specs of colorful dust released from Dioni's body. Since he did not know what to make of what he witnessed, Dioni thought it best to stand beside the vulture and follow along.

Dioni observed the images on the screen. He attempted to listen to the Alpha's words, which sounded more like random babel than an actual spoken language. Dioni looked at the map, which showed various patterns of extreme and violent weather spread sporadically across every continent. The screen flashed warning indicators at major population hubs on the map, though no letters were larger than the red characters displayed at the top.

"What is 'Natural Anomaly Program'?" Dioni asked.

The sound of his voice surprised the unsuspecting vulture. The Alpha instantly recognized his error; he completely disregarded the notification that was immediately sent to the Omega's pathfinder once the program was activated. While the approval of both the Alpha and the Omega was required in order to launch the sequence, any overrides or changes to a planned anomaly needed only the approval of one of the birds. This was a policy revision the Alpha personally oversaw decades prior.

He was caught red-winged, guilty as charged, by the one bird who could wreak havoc on his plan. His entire playbook was on full display, and he had only a fraction of a second to respond to Dioni to defuse the potential damage he had allowed.

"Standard procedure," the Alpha said, like a guiltless politician. He turned his attention to Dioni. "Hey kid, welcome back. The N-A-P is designed to practice for something beyond our control. We run these every so often to prep for potential crises created by the people."

"Humans can control the weather, too?"

"Ha!" responded the Alpha. "They only wish they could. No, they can't. But their behavior can cause chain reactions that we then have to go back and correct. It's all about the balance."

"That doesn't seem so bad."

"Oh yeah? How about you go tell the birds of the Pacific islands that they're going to have to redo all of their negotiations because of human behavior. Let me know how that works out for you."

"So what's the point of practicing for something beyond our control?" asked Dioni.

"It's a policy we put in place after World War II. Think of it as a training exercise to prevent them from creating a much bigger problem."

"Well, then…why don't we just tell them?"

The Alpha bird sunk his head lower than what was necessary, as an expression of his disappointment. No bird could possibly be so ignorant.

"We don't interact with the people, kid," he responded.

He struggled to maintain his calm composure.

"Why not?" asked Dioni.

"For one, safety," the Alpha responded. He raised his head and looked directly at Dioni. "If they knew what we do, there would be endless wars to try to control it. No people involvement, we maintain the natural balance,

314

and they are none the wiser. Make sense?"

"So the people can never know of this? Ever?"

"Ever, kid. Promise me that under no circumstances will you *ever* even think to tell a person about this. Not like they would understand you anyway – all they hear is random chirps or whistles or whatever god-awful sound it is that roosters make – but no interacting with people. You understand me? They're not ready for this."

Dioni nodded. He knew better than to question a practice that was set in place long before he knew it existed. The Alpha returned his attention to the helmet and to the simulation it created. Dioni stood by the vulture's side and quietly observed. Only a few seconds passed before the vulture grew annoyed by his unwanted sidekick.

"What brings you back to the office, Dioni?" the Alpha asked.

He did his best to withhold his frustration and once again lowered his headpiece.

"My pathfinder told me to come here. I'm not entirely sure why. Am I supposed to do something?"

"That's right," the Alpha responded. He was one step ahead and was well aware of it. "Pathfinder. Secondary approval. Almost forgot about that."

"Do I have to do anything?"

"Yeah, uhh…" responded the Alpha. His train of thought trailed away. "Need your approval…need your approval."

The vulture scanned the area and began to fidget, as if he searched for an object that was visible only to him.

"Should I go get a pen or something?"

"A what?" the Alpha questioned, angrily. "No…no you don't need a pen. Just tell your pathfinder you approve."

"What if I don't?" Dioni asked.

The Alpha's last ounce of patience ran dangerously low. With the most obviously forced smile he had ever displayed, the Alpha responded.

"It's in your best interest if you do."

"Pathfinder," Dioni said aloud. "Approved."

Nothing changed. The Alpha raised his wing over his face and once again shook his head. A scrolled message appeared on Dioni's pathfinder.

"I don't think I did this right," said Dioni. "It's saying, 'bad command or file name'. Did I break it?"

"Kid," the Alpha began. "I'm going to ask you a question, and all you have to do is respond by saying 'approved by Omega'. Can you do that?"

One, possibly two unintelligent questions was all the patience that remained before the Alpha would transform himself into the most ruthless bird Dioni would ever see. He envisioned blue feathers scattered everywhere around the Control Center.

"Approved by Omega. Yes. Got it," Dioni responded.

Dioni's words soothed the nearly enraged vulture. The Alpha returned his attention to the screen then touched the side of his headgear. The screen of the Control Center changed from a massive map of the entire Earth to a running list of thousands of simulated weather patterns.

"Natural anomaly case number one one zero one zero, commissioned by Alpha requesting approval by Omega. Do I have Omega approval?"

Dioni hesitated. His attention was diverted by the data and the colors on the screen. The Alpha coughed loudly, which released Dioni from his state of distraction.

"What?" Dioni questioned. "Oh, yeah…uh….what was I supposed to say?"

That was it. The vulture's rage knew no mercy after the last straw was officially brok—

"Approved by Omega," said Dioni.

He failed to understand how dangerously close he came to experiencing a wrath unlike any he had ever felt – as a bird or as a boy.

The huge screen flashed the letters A-P-P-R-O-V-E-D, then quickly transitioned back to the map of the Earth. The large display changed to show live weather data from every point on the planet. With his rage carefully under his control, the vulture returned to his work.

Dioni saw no difference from what was displayed prior to his approval. The same map showed the same data points, with no changes of any kind. He felt as though he was called away from the festival of color for no apparent reason. The Alpha was too entranced by the images displayed on his headgear to care for the thoughts of the Omega bird.

"So...?" Dioni opened after a few seconds of boredom. "Do I have to approve anything else, or...?"

"No. You're good. You're free to go," the Alpha responded, coldly.

"Okay. Good," said Dioni.

He looked around the room and noticed the other birds – the so-called 'skeleton crew' – who seemed entirely unphased by what occurred.

Dioni dusted the colored powder which floated around him with his every movement. The dust made him cough then sneeze. The sound of his actions echoed through the massive room. No bird in the Control Center moved in any way.

"So...?" Dioni opened. "Should I go anywhere or do anything...?"

"How about Antarctica, Dioni?!" the annoyed vulture stated.

It was the first thought that came to mind. His large eyes did not suppress his true sentiment for Dioni.

"Have you ever touched snow before?"

"No, but I've always wanted to!" Dioni said with excitement. "Can you really eat it?"

"Only one way to know for sure, right? How about you get out of here, shake the dust off those tropical feathers of yours, experience the cold, and make some friends with penguins. How does that sound?"

Dioni's excitement grew. His sole impression of Antarctica was that the continent existed as nothing more than a wasteland covered in snow and ice. The opportunity to discover a new territory and meet new birds would surely allow him to find a suitable replacement Omega bird.

317

"Yes! Antarctica would be perfect!" Dioni responded.

"Great! Now get as far away from here as possible and go discover it!" the Alpha responded, sarcastically.

Dioni shook his body, which created a colorful plume of dust around him. The action added to the Alpha's annoyance, which he expressed through a perfectly timed sigh. Dioni momentarily inspected his feathers; he searched for any specs of color that he may have missed, then took the time to lightly brush away any remaining powder. The Alpha observed and mumbled his disapproval under his breath. It was his time to be uninterrupted, and Dioni had made a mockery of it. Even Ally knew better than to disturb him when he was most in focus.

"Some of the birds that I met said I would be happy to have these long tailfeathers, but I don't see why," Dioni said as he carefully inspected and brushed the powder off his long feathers.

"Kid, if you don't leave in the next two seconds I'm going to rip those tail feathers off you and strangle you with them," the Alpha said, inaudibly.

"What was that?"

"Those feathers let you rip through air currents and better angle your body when you fly," the Alpha responded matter-of-factly.

He knew Dioni would believe anything he said if he made it sound like it were true.

"I guess that makes sense," responded Dioni. "They didn't explain that in flight school."

"They don't explain a lot of things. Are you going, then?" the Alpha's speech pattern accelerated.

"Yeah, I'm good now."

"That's nice. Now you go and fly from the Transportation Cen—"

"—Wait! How cold is it in Antarctica?" Dioni interrupted. "Should I get a sweater or something?"

His question was a legitimate one. A tropical bird would not have experience in such cold conditions, and under normal circumstances it

318

would not have been a problem for Dioni to ask. As it stood, however, the question was the final link in the chain reaction that caused a simulated meltdown within the Alpha's mind. An external expression of his emotional state would have revealed a similar anomaly to the many he had previously created – volcano explosions, violent tornadoes, earthquakes from deep within the sea – but in the moment, the wide-eyed vulture imagined the result of his own lack of control. He needed a naïve Omega and he knew it, and so it was in his best interest to contain his explosiveness.

"Use. Your. Pathfinder. DONNA!" the Alpha shouted. Six hummingbirds appeared almost instantly. "I only need one," the Alpha said, which dismissed all but the same hummingbird who stayed behind moments prior.

"Donna," the Alpha continued. "Show the Omega bird how to use the temperature regulator on his pathfinder…please."

The request came as a shock to the hummingbird; not because of the Omega's lack of knowledge, but in admiration of the Alpha's restraint. The tiny bird flew beside Dioni and used her beak to peck at the side of his pathfinder. After a few carefully entered commands, an image displayed before Dioni. The hummingbird moved to hover directly before Dioni, then she used her wings to ask him what he saw. The Alpha returned to his work, not to be interrupted.

"It's showing me a computer drawing of my body," responded Dioni. "It's giving me options for my internal temperature: 'maintain at current level, adapt to environment, go offline'. I think I have to pick one. What should I choose?"

The hummingbird strongly suggested he choose the first option.

"Maintain at current level. Yeah, so if I feel fine now, I should be okay if my pathfinder keeps me like this, even if it's cold. That's how this works, right?"

The hummingbird nodded.

"Good, then I have what I need," Dioni said.

His words were much to the delight of the Alpha, who made every effort to remain focused and not make eye contact with Dioni.

"I guess this is it, then. Off to Antarctica!" Dioni said excitedly.

He bent his body, looked to the high ceiling, and leapt a few millimeters off the ground before he suddenly remembered a question he almost failed to ask.

"Wait a second!" Dioni said to the Alpha. "What is the current temperat—"

The hummingbird used her tiny feet to close Dioni's beak before he finished the question. She shook her head – the universal sign for 'no' – then pointed her wing to the Transportation Center. Dioni immediately understood. The hummingbird released her grasp once she felt it was safe to do so.

"I'll see you later...?" Dioni asked.

His eyes remained on the hummingbird though his voice trailed toward the Alpha.

"Yep. See you later, kid. Have fun. Bye now," the Alpha responded, his attention squarely on his greater priority.

Dioni leapt then flew directly to the Transportation Center, away from the Alpha and the hummingbird. The Alpha's eyes followed Dioni until he was out of sight. He sighed, then lifted his eyes to the ceiling.

"Why...why a tropical bird? I just don't understand it," the Alpha said to himself though aware that the hummingbird remained nearby. "Ugh! I'm half-hoping he does find a replacement with the penguins. They don't ask...they just do."

The hummingbird held her position. She looked from side to side and wondered if it was the Alpha's intention to mention a replacement Omega bird. She became uncomfortably nervous. The small bird flapped her wings at a faster rate to make a stronger sound and gain the Alpha's attention.

The Alpha looked at the hummingbird. "That'll be all."

The hummingbird acknowledged the Alpha's command and departed from the area as fast as she had arrived. Instead of returning to base, the small bird flew to the Transportation Center. Her tiny wings became weary after the display she made just a few moments prior, yet her curiosity surpassed her fatigue.

The hummingbird flew through a small entryway, which led to a tunnel system designed specifically for the hyper-speed transfer of all hummingbirds to any area of the Department. By manner of a lifetime of experience and knowledge within the tunnel system, the small bird knew the fastest way to get to where she wanted to go. With minimal effort, she travelled at spectacular speed. She flew through tunnels vertically, horizontally, upside down, and through a structure of loops and lights which guided her journey.

She funneled through another small opening, which exited to the avian Transportation Center. Once she was out of the tunnel system, the hummingbird hovered momentarily. The Transportation Center was nearly vacant during the low traffic shift; only the skeleton crew and a few owls roamed the area. She searched in every direction with hopes to track the Omega bird. If he was nearby, it would not be difficult for her to see him.

The hummingbird looked and spotted Dioni in the distance. She placed all of her remaining energy into her small wings and dashed to the portal, dodging any roaming bird or automated cleaning equipment in her way. She flew as quickly as her small body allowed and almost crashed into Jelanni, who was shocked to see a hummingbird near the portal. Though she desperately hoped to catch the Omega before his departure, the hummingbird was too late. She saw the trail of Dioni's long tailfeathers as he was directed away from the portal, through space and time, to his destination in Antarctica.

Defeated, the hummingbird hovered momentarily. She searched nervously in every direction, as if to seek affirmation for what she witnessed. She turned her body and saw Jelanni, who viewed the small bird with bewilderment. The hummingbird flew to Jelanni and held herself a few inches in front of the much taller bird. She made a series of motions with her long beak and her wings. With her actions, the hummingbird communicated with Jelanni in a language that was known only to the birds of the Department of Global Climate Control.

"Antarctica," Jelanni responded. "He said something about meeting penguins and was excited about the snow."

The hummingbird shook her head. She turned her body to the portal exit then drifted away from the area. She flew at an unusually slow airspeed for a hummingbird. She avoided the few roamers who remained in the Transportation Center, flew beyond the automated custodial machines, then glided through the small entryway which connected her to the tunnel system.

Chapter Twenty-Three

The cold, the wind, and the ice-covered grounds were not enough to deter the birds who ruled the arctic. For centuries, these birds lived as the castaways of the avian kingdom, unable to soar above the land. Yet despite their lack of talent in the field of aerial transportation, their ability to adapt to the Earth's cruelest climate was unmatched by any group of aviators. Because of this, the penguins of the arctic became far more resilient to the harshest elements of nature than most other birds combined.

The recently completed summer months were recorded as a success, and the community had reason to celebrate. Unlike other birds, however, the Adélie penguins celebrated a unique custom with admiration and silence; no time of day was more important to them than the point in which the sun returned. In the weeks that followed, the sun would gradually stay away for longer periods of time, would shine and brighten the land a little less with each passing day, and would ultimately set and not return for months. For this reason, the Adélie penguins developed a daily tradition to witness the rise and gradual fall of the light. Regardless of age – whether a recent hatchling or an elder of the rookery – the dawn of each day was a momentous occasion for the birds who lived within the Earth's southernmost habitat.

An avian bird of any kind was a rare sight to behold for the Adélie penguins. With the exception of the occasional incursion from egg-stealing birds who were considered menaces of the arctic, or the emperors who felt the need to remind the others of their size and dominance, the Adélies had the majority of their land to themselves. Unlike other parts of the world where birds of all colors, shapes, sizes and abilities coexisted, negotiated and shared resources, birds of the arctic conducted their transactions amongst themselves. The penguins mostly worked in groups, grounded in strong traditions of democracy.

From the sky, Dioni saw the vastness of a white land with hills of ice which protruded from the frozen streams. It was the tundra, the absolute bottom of the Earth, yet such brightness blinded Dioni as he looked in amazement at the uniqueness of Antarctica. He squinted as he kept his wings spread as far as possible, and the intensely cold air passed above and below his body. The heat of the sun provided warmth for the birds below, all of whom were almost identical in size, shape, and even in their patterns of color. If Dioni was a stranger in places where intense color existed, his presence in a land void of color was remarkably welcomed.

The birds below grouped together as a massive congregation of spectators who observed the beautiful symphony of light, conducted by nature. Most were in a state of disbelief, and some showed signs of deep emotion as they felt the warmth of a new day. This was their home, their paradise, their utopia, and for a brief moment, only the awe of the light existed.

Dioni shifted his body to turn himself and land among the flightless birds, whom he saw as he admired the view from above. To avoid startling the birds, or being accidentally mistaken as a predator, Dioni glided around them and landed on the ground behind the colony. His decision to do so prevented a distraction from the event while it allowed him the opportunity to admire the same view. As he curved around the large group, one particularly observant penguin noticed an unidentified aviator who invaded the Adélie airspace.

"Well, would you look at that," said Wayne, a male Adélie penguin who spoke with an English accent. "Never thought I'd live to see the day."

Every bird stood at attention and looked intensely at the solar light as it slowly took its place in the sky. Wayne was the only bird who followed

Dioni's every move. As Dioni made landfall behind the colony, Wayne was the only of the hundreds of Adélie penguins who turned his entire body to see the visitor among them.

"Hey, Jeff, can you have a look at this?" Wayne asked the penguin beside him. "You're not going to believe what I'm seeing here."

"Hold on a sec, guv," responded Jeff, a male penguin who spoke with an Australian accent. "I'm in the moment here."

Wayne looked around. He hoped to find another penguin who was not as involved in the observation of the sunrise. He spotted a male penguin nearby, who used his wing to scratch an itch.

"Hey...hey Russ," Wayne said to the male penguin. "Can you look at something? I think my eyes are starting to get the better of me."

"Brotha, just give me another few minutes and I'll help you with whatever ya need," said Russell, a slightly smaller penguin with a surprisingly deep voice and who spoke with an American accent. "Sound good?"

"Oh for the love of—" Wayne responded. "I can't be the only one seeing this. I might be going mad."

Wayne searched for another witness nearby. He saw a female penguin who was distracted by the prism-effect of the light that reflected from melted ice.

"Kimberly, can you give us a sec?" Wayne asked her, unbeknownst whether or not she would acknowledge his existence. "Kimberly, did you hear me?"

"OMG, Wayne!" responded the young female, whose smaller stature hid a vastly larger personality. "Can you not see that I am appreciating nature here? Every second under the sun counts, you know. It's not like I have an eternity of sunlight bottled up somewhere that I can grab whenever I want. Ugh!"

"Right," Wayne responded. "Listen, sorry to bother, but do you see an odd-looking bird a few yards behind the rook?"

Kimberly rolled her eyes; Wayne knew better than to bother her during sunrise. She turned to look and saw snow, light, and the sky. By contrast and color, Dioni was camouflaged.

"The only odd bird here is you!" Kimberly said to Wayne, rudely.

"Yep, 'nuff said," Wayne responded, mostly to himself.

Wayne searched for a more reliable friend among the vast group of penguins who gazed into the sunlight. A few yards ahead, and slightly to the left, stood the only penguin among the entire colony who held his wings out and used the front of his body to capture the rays of light.

Wayne broke formation and waddled to the open-armed penguin. He hoped to not distract the others as he moved between them.

"Flay!" Wayne whisper-shouted at his friend as he came closer. "Flay! Are you with us, or are you somewhere in la-la land again?"

"I don't need to hear this right now, Wayne. I'm in my zone," responded Flay, who spoke with an accent all his own, though clearly North American. Flay kept his wings open and did not shift his stance. "If I don't get my daily dose of vitamin D, I'm gonna be the sorriest looking penguin in this group of castaways. Be gone, bird."

"Yep, sounds exactly what I thought you'd say. Still need your attention, though."

"I said be gone!" Flay exclaimed in return.

Wayne looked towards the sunrise once more. He became anxious to find a penguin – any penguin – who could verify his suspicion. The sunrise was sacred to the colony, and unless he knew of a distraction that was more powerful and beautiful than the light of the sun, he would simply have to wait his turn.

"Looking for something in particular?" asked a voice.

Wayne turned to look in the direction from which he heard the voice. He saw nothing but more penguins bewildered by the dawn.

"Well, it's official. I've lost it," Wayne said as he searched among the crowd of formally-dressed birds. "Serves me right, I guess. Mum always did say karma would catch up to me one day."

"What are you looking for?" asked the voice.

"Hoping one of me mates can see what I see. I just want to prove that I haven't gone mad."

"Oh, alright. So what do you see?" asked the voice.

"A tropical bird," Wayne responded. "One that has no Earthly business being here."

"Oh yeah? What did it look like?"

"Hey, mate!" shouted Jeff, the Australian penguin, from a distance. "Who's ya budgie friend?"

Intrigued, Jeff waddled toward Wayne.

"Beg your pardon?" asked Wayne.

"Your little friend standing next to you. Can't you see him?"

"Ice, water and light, friend," Wayne said to Jeff. "That's all I see right now. That and a silly penguin who spent far too much time in the cold."

"Welcome to Antarctica, budgie!" Jeff shouted with delight.

"Wait, did you see another bird?" Wayne asked. He searched for it in every direction. "What did you call it?"

"A budgie. Can't you see it, mate?" asked Jeff. "There's a budgie standing next to you."

Wayne looked to his left then to his right and saw nothing out of the ordinary. It was all ice and the reflection of the sky in each direction.

"Lean forward and turn your head to your left whilst looking down," Jeff instructed Wayne.

Wayne did as he was told; he leaned his body forward, tilted his head to his side, then looked back. This caused him to plop his head on the ground. Though upside down, he saw what was hidden in plain sight.

"Oy! I see it!" Wayne said with glee. "That's not a budgie, Jeff."

"It looks like a budgie, so I'm gonna call it a budgie," said Jeff. "A blue budgie, unusually large. Reminds me of one of me mates back in Melbourne."

"You're a tropical bird, aren't you?" asked Wayne, his head on the snow-

327

covered ground.

"I am," responded Dioni. "What's a budgie?" he asked Jeff.

"An avian bird. Looks like you, sometimes blue, somewhat smaller. Better haircut."

"Agreed," responded Wayne.

"Are there any budgies here?" asked Dioni.

"No chance, mate," responded Jeff. "Budgies are in Australia. Swarms of them, especially in the fields. I bet if we put you in a crowd of budgies you'd be completely invisible."

"I doubt that," responded Wayne, still upside down. "I doubt that very much. Look at him. He's twice their size. Plus those long tailfeathers."

"Got it, right. Budgies don't have the tailfeathers like you," Jeff responded. He leaned in closer to address Dioni only. "Don't lose those, mate. You're gonna be glad you have them."

"What?" Dioni asked.

"Why is this one on his head?" asked Russell, the American penguin with a deep voice.

"Looking at a budgie," responded Jeff.

"He's not a budgie," said Wayne.

"The blue bird?" Russell asked. "He looks like a budgie; like a big one, with a weird haircut."

"Right?" responded Jeff. "That's exactly what I said!"

"He's not a budgie," said Wayne.

"What's with all the insider talk, boys?" asked Kimberly as she waddled to the semicircle created by Jeff, Russell, Dioni, and Wayne, whose head was still on the ground. "Spill it!"

"Talking to this budgie," Jeff responded as he pointed at Dioni.

"He's not a budgie," said Wayne.

"What's a budgie?" asked Kimberly.

"A parakeet," responded Russell.

"Oh, gotcha," said Kimberly. "Kinda big for a parakeet, don't you think? Haircut's gotta go."

"It's confirmed," said Jeff. "He's definitely a budgie."

"He's not a budgie," said Wayne.

"Who's a budgie?" asked Flay as he joined the group and made the circle slightly larger.

"Blue bird, here," Jeff responded. He pointed at Dioni.

"He's not a budgie," said Wayne.

"If you're a budgie, then I'm the mayor of San Francisco," Flay said to Dioni.

"Thank you, Flay!" said Wayne. "At least one of you sorry sods sees it. This bird is definitely not a budg—"

"—Although I can see it," Flay interrupted. "Put him in a swarm and hide those tailfeathers, and I'd see nothing but budgie. But, oh, honey, that haircut…"

"That's it!" Wayne said, agitated by his fellow penguins. He stood and composed himself. "You poor excuses for Adélie penguins! Can you not see what is clearly in front of you, or did you all forget what tropical birds look like? This blue bird here," he paused and got a better look at Dioni. "My word, he really does look like a big budgie. And you weren't kidding about the haircut."

"Okay, stop!" exclaimed Dioni, which halted the fast chatter between the penguins. "What is happening right now?"

"We're all looking at a strange budgie," responded Jeff.

"Aside from that!" said Dioni. "What are all those penguins doing?"

"Watching the light show," responded Wayne. "It's a tradition we have here in the arctic."

"Is that an Omega-class pathfinder?" asked Jeff, who pointed his wing at Dioni's head.

"No way!" said Russell. He leaned closer to inspect the device. "I heard they upgraded these last year."

"Ooh, fancy!" said Kimberly, who followed Russell's lead. "I've never seen an Omega-class."

"Pah-lease, sister," said Flay. "Budgies aren't given Omega-class pathfinders." Flay leaned closer to Dioni to inspect the headpiece and saw that the device was indeed marked for the Omega bird. He gasped. "Oh can I please borrow that? I just have to make one call and I promise I'll give it right back to—"

"—He can't take it off, budgie-brain," said Kimberly. She immediately recognized her poor choice of words. "No offense," she said to Dioni.

"None taken," Dioni responded.

"Sure he can!" said Russell. "It's just as easy to take them off as it is to put them on. Watch." Russel raised his wing and looked at Dioni. "Hold still."

"Don't!" shouted Wayne, which interrupted the motion of Russell's wing. "These things regulate temperature for them, remember? Budgie or not, he is a tropical bird. He won't last a minute without it!"

"Good call, Wayne," said Russell. "I didn't even think about that."

"So mate," Jeff said to Dioni. "What brings ya to the tundra, then? Doing the 'Omega world tour'?"

"Nah," responded Kimberly. "Look at him. He's here on official business. You're measuring seawater levels, aren't you?" she asked Dioni.

"Water levels?" asked Russell. "Why on Earth would the Omega bird come all the way here to measure water levels. We've got way bigger problems than that."

The five penguins looked at one another. With Russell's comment, they realized the importance of the bird who stood before them.

"All the plastic and oil have to go," said Flay as he continued the conversation. "I have sensitive, delicate skin, and if my pH is off…let's just say you won't want to see what comes next."

"What does an Omega have to do with oil and plastic?" asked Jeff.

"Wait, what is pH?" asked Wayne.

"Acidity," responded Jeff. "Try to keep up."

"The iceberg placements are already scheduled, right?" asked Russell. "It's not like an Omega came here to override that order." He looked at Dioni. "It took us months to negotiate that."

"Can you do something about the orcas," asked Kimberly. "They're not as friendly as they used to be."

"How would a bird have anything to do with the behavior of the orcas?" asked Wayne.

"He's an Omega. It's worth a shot," Kimberly responded.

"Doesn't change the fact that he's still a bird, though," said Russell.

"A budgie," responded Jeff.

"He's not a budgie," said Wayne, more annoyed than he was previously.

"Sure looks like a budgie," said Jeff

"Okay, stop, stop, stop! That's enough!" said Wayne. He faced Dioni, "Forgive their ignorance…uh….puh….huh…sorry, I didn't catch your name."

"Dioni."

"The only what?" the five penguins responded simultaneously.

Dioni lowered his head and exhaled slowly. The fast-talking penguins were as infuriating as they were confusing. The five penguins looked at Dioni with bewilderment.

"How about we start over?" Dioni asked the group.

"Standard protocol," responded Wayne. He turned to his fellow penguins. "An official vote has been called to order. All in favor of starting over?"

"Aye," said the five penguins.

"The 'ayes' have it," continued Wayne. "Very well. The floor is yours, The Only."

"Dee-Oh-Nee," Dioni responded. He spoke louder and slower to better introduce himself. "My name is Dee-oh-nee. Dioni."

"Oh, Dee-oh-nee. Right, I get it now," responded Jeff.

"Where you from, Dioni?" asked Russell. "You seem a far ways from home."

"Guatemala," responded Dioni.

"I know where that is," said Kimberly.

"And how would *you* know where Guatemala is?" asked Flay, doubtful of Kimberly's knowledge. "It doesn't even sound like a real place."

"I *have* made friends with other birds, you know," responded Kimberly. She looked at Dioni. "It's in Central America, right? Two ocean coasts, south of Mexico, next to Belize?"

"Yes!" Dioni responded. "That's correct!"

"See, it's good to talk to other birds," Kimberly said to Flay, who still doubted her.

"You're penguins, and you live here, yet you each speak differently," said Dioni. "Is this common for penguins in Antarctica?"

"We live here, but we're not all originally from here," said Russell.

"We're Adélie penguins, Dioni," said Wayne. "We were brought here as part of an international Adélie wildlife rehabilitation program."

"What does that mean?" asked Dioni.

"It means we came from different parts of the world where we were kept for some time, then we were brought here to help increase our population," responded Kimberly.

"Oy, mates!" exclaimed Wayne. "Introductory lineup for the tropical bird!"

The five penguins immediately proceeded into a unit formation. They stood proudly in front of Dioni, like five naval officers who wanted to impress their commander. Each penguin took a step forward and displayed an electronic tag on one of their wings as they made their formal introduction.

"Wayne Pennyworth, Bristol Zoo Gardens, England, from her majesty's royal penguin conservation program."

"Russell Elzie, Aitken Sea Bird Colony, arctic restoration program, Bronx Zoo, New York."

"Jeff Blaire, Melbourne Zoo, Australia, joint collaboration between Melbourne and the San Diego Zoo's institute for endangered species."

"Kimberly Sarnav, Shedd Aquarium, Chicago, save the penguins program."

"Flay, from the one and only San Francisco Zoo by way of the United States Navy, arctic species rescue and revival program."

Dioni watched in awe as each bird spoke so eloquently. Once they completed their round of introductions, they all stood still. The penguins expected Dioni to introduce himself in the same manner. The six birds stood in an uncomfortably long silence.

"Who are you," Wayne coughed, which awoke Dioni from his distracted state.

"Ah! Uh…Dionisio Sedano, Flores, Guatemala, the …uhhhmm… ToursTikal ancient birds program…" Dioni responded. His voice trailed near the end of his introduction.

"Wow, mate, that sounds fancy," said Jeff.

"Are you really an ancient bird?" asked Kimberly.

"Like the Alpha bird?" asked Wayne. "I hear he's one of the original birds of the department. He's the roaming definition of ancient."

"They say he's been there at least a thousand generations," said Russell. "Is that true?"

"Now how can a vulture have lived over a thousand generations?" Wayne asked Russell.

"He's the Alpha. He would know better than I would," Russell responded.

"Ugh, vultures are such vile birds," said Flay. "They have zero sense of fashion and are in more desperate need of a makeover than any other bird on the planet."

"Now that's just silly," responded Wayne. "Have you seen every bird on the planet?"

"I met a Mandarin duck once," said Kimberly.

"That is too extreme of a makeover," responded Flay. He turned to Dioni. "Some birds take it way too far...and it looks hideous."

"Now, a bald eagle," said Russell. "That's what an iconic bird should look like. Simple color scheme, big feathers, no surprises."

"I met a bald eagle," Dioni chimed in.

"So did I!" responded Kimberly, excitedly. "He went on and on about how big his feathers were and how fast he could fly. We were like, 'okay, flyboy, we get it!'"

"I had a similar experience with an ostrich," Jeff said to Kimberly. "Went on and on about how long his legs were and how fast he ran. Was completely mum when me and me mate said those long legs still couldn't get those tiny wings off the ground. Tried to prove us wrong."

"What happened?" Dioni asked.

"He didn't," Jeff responded.

"Seems like there's one in every type of bird, isn't there?" asked Wayne.

"What about penguins?" asked Dioni.

His question brought the entire conversation to a halt.

"What about us?" asked Flay.

The attention of the five penguins immediately shifted to the Omega bird.

"Well, you don't really fly...and you don't really run..." said Dioni. He chose his words carefully.

"What're you trying to say?" asked Kimberly. "That we're useless birds?"

"N..n...No!" exclaimed Dioni. "No, not at all! It's just...you're the first penguins I've ever seen and—"

"—And what?" asked Russell, more curious than offended.

"And..." Dioni said slowly and quietly. "I...I don't know what you do..."

Dioni lowered his head between his shoulders. He kept his eyes on the penguins.

The penguins looked at one another then smiled at their fortune. They understood the uniqueness of their circumstance. It was rare to have an Omega in their territory, and even more so to have one who was a tropical bird.

"Look around you, mate." Jeff opened. "What do you see?"

Dioni raised his head, no longer in fear of retaliation. He looked at the colony of penguins.

"They're all looking at the sun," Dioni said.

"It's not just the sun," Wayne responded. "It's the light. We come out each day and watch as the light returns."

"It's bright now, but in the coming weeks it's only gonna stay light out for a few minutes," said Kimberly. "For us, this moment is extraordinary."

Dioni looked toward the light. He saw how it spread itself over the intensely cold ground. There were no plants for which the sun would be necessary, no farms or cities that would use the sun as a form of energy, and no viable reason why it would make any difference on this part of the Earth.

"Why is it extraordinary?" asked Dioni. "There's nothing special about it. It happens every day."

"Because it might be the last one we ever see," responded Kimberly.

Dioni understood her response all too well. It was more than just a daily ritual for the penguins; it was a preservation of the most beautiful scenery they would likely witness on that day. The penguin culture demanded that they overcome the most extreme climate conditions on the planet, and it was their sense of beauty which provided them with the inspiration to fulfill their responsibility to the natural balance.

When the sun arose to its full glory, the colony erupted with glee. The hundreds of Adélie penguins cheered for the light. It was an act of gratitude, which astounded Dioni. He joined the chorus of cheerful sounds made by every penguin in the colony. As the chorus of cheers came to a close, the mass of Adélie penguins waddled – in perfect unison – to the shoreline where the ice met the sea.

"Where are they going?" Dioni asked.

"It's off to the races, blue bird!" said Russell as he waddled by Dioni.

"Penguin races?" Dioni asked.

"It's just a phrase," said Jeff, who followed closely behind Russell.

"It's the daily hunt," said Kimberly. "Come join us!"

"What's your policy on krill?" Wayne asked Dioni.

"On what?" responded Dioni.

"You primitive birds will never understand how to properly treat special guests," said Flay. "Follow me, Dioni. These manner-less mongrels know nothing of krill gathering. Today, you're gonna learn how to *really* fly."

Flay's last phrase captured Dioni's attention.

"I already know how to fly," said Dioni, confused by Flay's statement. "And penguins are not flight birds, are they?" Dioni turned to Wayne. "Can penguins fly?"

Kimberly and Wayne looked at one another and smiled. If there ever existed a moment to make a lasting impression on the new Omega bird, this was it. The two penguins waddled behind the rest of the colony, which collectively moved toward the water. Wayne motioned for Dioni to follow.

Upon reaching the water, Dioni witnessed how the penguins easily dove in and disappeared into the ocean. It was as if the water absorbed them and ported them through another dimension. Dioni's five penguin friends stood in line, with Dioni in the center between Wayne and Kimberly.

"See ya on the other side," said Russell. He dove head-first into the water, then quickly disappeared to the depths. Flay and Jeff followed immediately behind.

"Dioni, what do you remember from flight school?" asked Kimberly.

"How to use my wings and feathers, wind patterns, how *not* to echolocate…" Dioni responded. "Oh, and murmurations."

"Yes, that's all right and true," responded Wayne. "But tell me, did you happen to see any penguins while you were there?"

Dioni paused and thought for a moment.

"No," he responded. "But penguins don't fly. Flight school would be unnecessary for them."

"But you did see all manner of birds at the Flight Academy, correct?" asked Wayne.

"Even flightless birds," chimed Kimberly. "Ostriches, emus, kiwis, and probably every bird who lives mostly on water, am I right?"

"Y…Yes," responded Dioni as he attempted to recall the many birds he saw at the Academy. "I think so."

"Then why not a single penguin, one does wonder," said Wayne.

Dioni paused, unsure whether or not Wayne's comment was a legitimate one, or if it was part of an elaborate game penguins played with their guests.

"Dioni, look underneath the surface," Wayne continued. "Just place your head down and look in the water. And don't worry, your pathfinder will protect you."

Dioni carefully walked to the edge of the water. He bent his body and dipped his head below the surface, which was detected by his pathfinder. Dioni opened his eyes and saw the most incredible display of subaquatic transport patterns created by the birds of the arctic sea. It was a completely random operation of traffic management, where each bird was in full control of its speed, direction of travel, and proximity to every other penguin. Unlike aviator murmurations where shifting winds could limit movements, the penguins were free to alter their direction, independently, with absolute ease. What most astounded Dioni was not only the ease in which the penguins could maneuver their environment, but a unique skill in which a sonic burst of energy pushed each penguin at speeds unlike any he had ever seen. The feat seemed impossible; even the most skilled flyers in the world could never have the advanced capability to perform the same actions in the sky.

Dioni lifted himself above the surface.

"It's like they are all flying underwater! It's amazing!" he said to Kimberly and Wayne, with an excitement almost too grand to contain. "How do they do that?"

"Could it be that the best pilots on the planet have no need to attend the Flight Academy? Hmm?" asked Kimberly.

She dove into the water and vanished from view.

Dioni once again placed his head under the surface, in an attempt to track her movement. He looked in every direction but lost sight of her among the depths and spirals created by the hundreds of other penguins. He lifted himself then looked at Wayne.

"Are you ready to try it?" asked Wayne.

"Absolutely!" responded Dioni.

"Follow us, then," said Wayne. He lifted his small wings and prepared to dive into the water.

"Wait!" Dioni exclaimed, which immediately halted Wayne's descent. "Are penguins really the best pilots?"

Wayne chuckled.

"Come see for yourself," he responded.

Wayne leaned the weight of his body forward then fell head-first into a crack within the ice.

Dioni had only ever leapt into a pool as a child. He would run, hoist himself into the air, grab the bottom of his legs, then would make the biggest splash his underweight body could create. As the Omega bird, however, he felt embarrassed to do the same. Instead, he attempted to recreate the actions he remembered from what he once saw on television. He stepped back a few paces, stretched his wings, paced forward as quickly as he could, then leapt into the air. Unfortunately, Dioni failed to shift his weight so as to dive perfectly into the water. The back of his neck was the first part of his body to break the surface. Instantly, Dioni's pathfinder recognized his present state and location, and it created an invisible barrier to protect him from the extreme cold.

The words "Submersion Detected" displayed momentarily on his pathfinder. Unbeknownst to Dioni, the action automatically sent an alert to the Department of Global Climate Control. The notification of submersion brought a sinister smile to the Alpha bird's ancient face.

Dioni saw the trails of air and water pressure created by the high-speed travel of the colony of flightless birds. Those who leapt from the surface dove to levels which Dioni was unable to see, as the light of the sun simply could not penetrate much further into the water. He tracked the movement of the birds by the waves that each penguin created, which resembled a trail of aftershocks that pierced through the sea. The birds did not require flight feathers in order to dash at unbelievable speeds.

Though it seemed like an eternity to Dioni, only a few seconds passed before his natural inclination for oxygen outperformed his desire to watch the penguins in action. Dioni used his wings to lift himself to the surface. As air filled his small lungs and the saltwater fell from his face, Wayne and Kimberly emerged from the water.

"You can swim, can't you?" Wayne asked Dioni as he treaded above the surface. "Never met a tropical bird who couldn't swim. It'd be a shame to break that streak now."

"Ye—"

"—I once met a duck who couldn't swim," chimed Kimberly

"Ducks aren't tropical," responded Wayne.

"Well, this one had a tan," said Kimberly as Russell broke from beneath the surface.

"What's going on?" Russell asked. "Don't want krill for breakfast today?"

"Dioni can't swim," responded Kimberly.

"Really? I thought all budgies could swim," said Russell. "They're tropical."

"He's not a budgie," replied Wayne.

Jeff and Flay emerged to join the group.

"We got a good krill batch today, gents," said Jeff. Kimberly coldly glared at him. "Sorry! *Lady* and gents!"

"Are we taking a vote on something?" asked Flay. "Because this krill isn't gonna catch itself."

"Dioni can't swim," said Kimberly.

"Actually, yes I—"

"—A budgie who can't swim?" asked Jeff. "But they're tropical."

"He's not a budgie," responded Wayne.

"I once met a duck who couldn't swim," said Flay.

"Was it a mallard with a tan?" Kimberly asked.

"Ohmygod, yes! Bill the mallard from Cleveland! Do you know him?" Flay asked excitedly.

"Is anyone else starving?" asked Russell. "Because I'm starving. I don't know about you guys, but I'm hankerin' for some krill this morning."

"Same," said Wayne.

"Same," said Jeff.

"Same," said Kimberly.

"Same," said Flay.

"Very well, then," said Wayne. He turned to Dioni, "Sorry guv, you're just gonna have to observe and follow from the surface. Maybe we can find you a straw or something so you can keep your head underwater. Though you really must learn how to swim. I think I know a pelican who teaches a class."

"I know how to swim," Dioni said.

"Well why didn't you speak up?" asked Jeff. "Here we are blabbering about when we could be krill hunting. Sunlight is limited these days, you know."

"How about this?" Kimberly addressed the group. "You boys go and hunt while I teach Dioni the basics of launching."

"Launch training could take hours," responded Jeff.

"And we're burning daylight as it is," said Flay.

"You can't teach old budgies new tricks," said Russell.

"He's not a budgie," responded Wayne.

"I know it can," Kimberly responded to the group. "Just trust me on this. You boys go. Dioni and I will catch up. Just save some krill for us."

"Don't have to tell me twice," said Flay.

Flay immediately dove into the water and out of site. The remaining male penguins shrugged their shoulders and followed closely behind.

"Okay, Dioni, just do what I do," said Kimberly.

She kicked her short legs and lifted herself out of the water to once again stand on a floating patch of ice. As instructed, Dioni followed.

"First thing you have to do is shake the water off and get as much air in your feathers as possible," Kimberly instructed.

"Air in my feathers?" asked Dioni.

"Spread those wings, shake off the water and feel the air. Then do the same with your back, your tail, and the rest of your body," Kimberly said. "It's easier to do this part while on land and not in the water. The next part is a little tricky. Just do what I tell you and you'll be fine."

The two birds shook their bodies in an effort to remove as much water from themselves as possible; doing so trapped small pockets of air in the tiny spaces between each of their feathers. This came naturally to Kimberly but felt strange to Dioni.

"Okay, good," said Kimberly. "Now when I tell you, dive into the water, spread your wings, face forward, then align your entire body. Got it?"

"Dive in, spread wings, face forward, align body," responded Dioni. "Got it."

"When you do those steps in that exact order, your pathfinder is going to display something like, 'activate launch' or 'wind tunnel active'. Just blink twice and look forward, okay?"

"Okay, yes, I can do that."

"Alright…here we go," said Kimberly.

She walked to the edge of the ice patch and once again dove into the sea. Dioni walked to the edge, paused, took the largest breath of air his small lungs could hold, then dove into the water.

Once submerged, Kimberly performed the same steps as she instructed Dioni. She spread her wings, faced forward, then aligned her body to perfection. As did all good instructors, she waited for her pupil to do the same.

Dioni spread his wings, which released bubbles that floated back to the surface. He lifted his head and faced forward, then brought his legs to his body as to align himself perfectly in his desired direction of travel. He felt as the sea carried his body, suspended in an environment with no visible barriers. As predicted by Kimberly, Dioni's pathfinder recognized his series of motions and displayed the words "Activate Launch". With his body in perfect alignment, Dioni blinked twice, which the pathfinder understood as a confirmed command.

Kimberly failed to inform Dioni that the sequence activation had a short delay, which Dioni had not anticipated. He turned his head to look at Kimberly, then used body language to question the lack of action. Kimberly noticed his misalignment and desperately motioned for him to look forward.

Instantly, Dioni's body transcended from motionless suspension to hypersonic overdrive. Because his head was slightly turned at the exact moment of launch, his face felt a drag which pushed his beak in the opposite direction of travel. He used all his strength to lift his head and realign himself. With his body in proper form, the ease in which he travelled at such incredible speed seemed unreal. From the corner of his eye he saw Kimberly zoom by and swirl around him; she playfully created a tunnel within a tunnel. He noticed how she shifted her body to change her direction of travel, all while she maintained perfect alignment. In an attempt to prove a point, Dioni did the same.

Dioni discovered a new state of euphoria. He learned that it was possible to fly while underwater. While the birds who claimed dominance of the sky were forced to battle both wind and gravity, the best pilots on Earth did not have the same limitations. Instead, penguins created the currents themselves, which enabled them to travel in any direction they desired. This was a freedom and force of nature which only the strongest of arctic birds understood.

Dioni followed closely behind Kimberly. With every movement of his wings and tailfeathers, he felt a drag which shifted him in different directions. He was submerged, though his navigation required the use of similar procedures as if he were in the sky. Dioni's mind drifted as he pierced through the arctic water, which was a sensation too wonderful to describe. He remembered the promise he made to Deepa in India; never again would he make a claim without first learning all of the facts.

In a sudden motion, Kimberly shifted down and plummeted deeper into the sea. Dioni lost sight of her. Before his sense of fear was able to take over, he saw as Kimberly dashed from the depths and lifted towards the brighter water near the surface. Her body was in flawless formation as she focused solely on her point of exit. It was an incredible sight to behold.

Wayne, Flay, Russell, and Jeff stood on a steady patch of floating ice, away from most other penguins. Each had a mouthful of krill which they pulled from a shared pile.

"Good krill catch today," Jeff said to Wayne, Flay and Russell.

"Yep," said Russell. "Good day for krillin'."

"Where do you suppose Kimberly might be? She's missing out," said Jeff.

"Her loss," responded Russell.

"More for the rest of us," said Flay. "What—"

Before Flay was able to finish his thought, Kimberly emerged gracefully from the water. She landed on her belly and slid directly in front of the pile of krill. She opened her mouth as wide as possible to grasp her share of the feast.

"Good catch today, boys," she said with a mouthful of breakfast.

"Those aren't free, you know," said Wayne.

"Where's your budgie friend?" asked Jeff.

"He's not a budgie," said Wayne.

"In the water," Kimberly responded. "He'll launch out soon."

"Well, how soon?" asked Russell. "Those budgie lungs can only hold so much air."

"He's not a budgie," said Wayne.

"Ahh!" complained Flay. "I can't do a rescue mission after what I ate. I get really bad cramps if I launch after breakfast."

"You need more potassium, mate," said Jeff. "You might want to change your diet."

"Is that what it is?" Flay asked. "Because I was thinking about what a vegetarian kororā once told me—"

Dioni emerged from the water. He grossly overshot the landing zone and drifted high into the sky before he realized he was far above the surface. His instincts and flight training took over. Too exhilarated to fly, Dioni allowed gravity to do most of the work as he drifted down to where his friends stood.

"Would you look at that," opened Jeff. "Dioni learned to launch. Kimberly must be a good instructor after all."

"Not that good," responded Russell. "He overshot the landing."

"Well, lucky for him budgies can fly," said Jeff.

"He's not a budgie," said Wayne.

Dioni's feet touched down on the ice shelf where the penguins enjoyed their morning meal. Kimberly stood up as Dioni approached. He breathed slowly yet profoundly.

"So...?" opened Flay. "How did it go...?"

"It...was..." Dioni responded. He thought of the proper word to describe the experience. "*Estupendo!*"

The five penguins stood uneasy; two of them stopped chewing though krill remained in their beaks. They looked at one another, confused by Dioni's response.

"Is that a good thing?" asked Jeff.

"That's a new word for me," said Russell. "I'm not entirely sure what it means. Do you think he enjoyed it?"

"Maybe it's an odd budgie language?" asked Kimberly.

"He's not a budgie," said Wayne, with his beak full.

"Well then ask him, but get clarification," said Jeff.

Wayne swallowed the half-chewed krill and turned to address Dioni.

"Dioni, we seem to have misunderstood your response just now," Wayne said. "We are humble Adélie penguins, you see, and we are not versed in tropical languages. Would you be so kind as to rephrase your... uh...response...please?"

For a reason he could not determine, Dioni thought of Alma. He thought of what he would say to her – the stories he would tell – upon his return home. She would likely find his quest as a bird to be highly unlikely. However, she would very much enjoy the Adélie penguins' response to the word *estupendo*. It was part of the story which she would likely find hysterical. Dioni smiled at the thought of seeing her again and hearing her laughter.

"It was," Dioni began. The five penguins leaned closer to listen intently. "The most spectacular, scariest...while at the same time....uh.... overwhelming rush of sensations! That. Was. So. Awesome!"

"Good on ya, mate!" exclaimed Jeff, excited that a portion of the penguin culture was embraced by the new Omega bird. "And that's considering the high likelihood that he has not yet taken full advantage of those tailfeathers!"

Dioni did not understand why his tailfeathers were mentioned, but he was too overstimulated to care.

"WOW!" Dioni shouted. "That was the most intense experience ever! What else can your pathfinders do? Can you shoot lasers at ice or something because that would be incred—"

"—Uhm...Dioni," Flay interrupted. "Penguins don't use pathfinders."

"Nah, mate…" said Jeff. He tapped the side of his head to prove he wore no form of aviator technology. "We're natural pilots."

"What're you saying?" Dioni asked, astonished by their natural abilities. "You just *know* how to fly?"

"Penguins don't fly," responded Wayne. "We launch."

"Some of us waddle," said Russell.

"Some of the lazier penguins just slide on their bellies all day," said Flay.

"But no matter the penguin, every one of us knows how to do what you just experienced," said Kimberly. "And here's the good news: if you can launch in the water, you can launch in the sky."

Dioni wondered how the birds of the arctic, at the southernmost point of the world, had greater talents as pilots than even the most skilled aviators. He was so certain that falcons were the greatest pilots; he understood beyond all doubt that no bird could match the first-class stealth of the elite rulers of the sky. Except it was not true, much to Dioni's disbelief. He had spoken too soon.

"Are you gonna have some krill with us, Dioni?" asked Russell. "We picked some up for you in case you were hungry."

"Yes, I'm starving!" responded Dioni. He bent forward and shoved as much krill into his beak as it could hold. He was too excited and too hungry to be picky over new foods.

"Well chaps, I'd say we did alright," opened Wayne, satisfied with his accomplishment for the day. "We had an excellent light ceremony, made a new friend, one of us taught an Omega how to launch—"

"—Thank you," said Kimberly.

"—And the krill hunt was a brilliant success," continued Wayne. "Which has been very unusual this year…again."

"That sounds like a productive day to me," responded Russell.

"So we're done here?" asked Flay.

"What about our budgie friend?" asked Jeff.

"He's not a budgie," said Wayne.

"Is this all you do every day?" asked Dioni. Krill dripped from his beak.

"Heavens no," responded Wayne. "We Adélie's have greater responsibilities than to watch the sunrise and hunt for breakfast."

"Like what?" Dioni asked.

He did his best to swallow far more krill than he was able to hold.

"Ice and water checks," responded Russell.

"You have to check the water every day? What for?" asked Dioni.

He once again dove into the pile for another big scoop of krill.

"It's more than watching ice melt, Dioni," said Kimberly. "We maintain a certain balance—"

"—Too much ice and not enough water could be bad for the natural balance," said Jeff. "And vice versa."

"We oversee ice production from the south pole to reintroduce as water from the south sea," said Wayne. "Is this making any sense to you?"

"No. Not…really," Dioni responded with his mouth full.

His appetite may have been larger than what his small body could sustain.

"It might be best if we just show him," said Kimberly. "I call for a vote."

Wayne turned to his fellow penguins.

"An official vote has been called to order. All in favor of taking our new Omega friend on a tour of the badlands and teach him the water-to-ice ratings system?"

"Aye," the five penguins responded.

"The 'ayes' have it," continued Wayne. He turned to Dioni. "I hope you are okay to swim after eating, because we have a lot of work to do and not a lot of time to do it."

"I'm fine," Dioni said as he swallowed his last gulp of krill.

He became distracted by the sound of dozens of Adélie penguins as they returned to the water and launched in a different direction from which they came.

"Penguins…balance water and ice…?" asked Dioni, a slight sense of skepticism in his tone.

"Adélie penguins," responded Jeff. "And yes, we do."

"At least we don't have to balance sea salt like the emperors," said Flay.

"Lady and gents…shall we?" Wayne said to the group. "The ice and water are not going to balance themselves now are they?"

Flay and Russel were the first of the group to slide into the water, followed by Jeff. Wayne gave Kimberly a signal of approval before he waddled a few paces forward, fell onto his belly, then slid into the arctic sea.

"Are you ready for this?" Kimberly asked Dioni.

"Yes! Absolutely!" Dioni responded, like a child who was asked if he would like to repeat a ride on the world's most exhilarating rollercoaster.

Kimberly sighed then waddled to the edge of the ice patch. Dioni followed behind as he did earlier. They jumped into the arctic water at the same time.

Dioni saw the air trails left behind by Jeff, Russell and Flay as they launched from the small ice patch near the krill hunting grounds to a location far beyond his field of vision. Wayne felt a sense of peace with Dioni's comfort while in the water. Omega birds rarely gave Adélie penguins a second thought, much less spend time among their colony and even learn to launch, yet Dioni was different. To gain Dioni's attention and to have him understand the importance of their work meant more to Wayne than the fact that Dioni was definitely not a budgie.

Wayne aligned his body then looked to his side. He smiled and winked at Kimberly. He turned his head to be in perfect alignment, opened his wings, then immediately launched into hyper speed. Since verbal communication was not possible while underwater, Kimberly used a series of motions to instruct Dioni to align his body. She was especially insistent to remind him to look forward and not turn his head before takeoff.

With experience came the knowledge of what to expect. Dioni aligned his body, spread his wings, looked forward and awaited the signal from his pathfinder. The same two words appeared as before, "Activate Launch". Dioni blinked twice to confirm the command. He remained motionless as he waited for the launch sequence to activate – no sound was made, nor did movement occur from any direction. For a moment in time, Dioni was all to himself, suspended in underwater animation in a part of the world which was a universe away from home. Before he became too comfortable with his state of peaceful bliss, Dioni's pathfinder commenced its directive and launched him to hypersonic speed.

In the same manner in which he swayed and easily changed his direction of travel by utilizing the wind, his wings, and his tailfeathers to guide him in the sky, Dioni discovered that speed and trajectory were controllable while submerged. He stretched his body, pushed his wings to their furthest extent, reached his head as far as it could go, and placed his tail as far back as possible; the result of his actions allowed hypersonic travel with less resistance. As he gained speed, Dioni drew close enough to see the air trails of the pod of Adélie penguins who launched before him.

With subtle movements, Dioni bypassed some of the more cautious swimmers. He did not care if they were too young to travel at such high speeds, nor if they were too old to worry whether or not they arrived at their destination before all the others. Dioni selfishly thought of his own talent; with only two experiences of underwater navigation, he already showed signs of superiority over the natural-born pilots.

Though it proved difficult to distinguish one penguin from another while on land, it was even more so while in the water, especially at such high speed. Dioni, on the other hand, was easily trackable. Kimberly, one of the superior pilots of the group, stayed close to Dioni and followed his every move. She ensured that the young Omega did not stray too far from the group, nor that he launched in the direct path of a predator.

Kimberly observed as the flock of penguins dipped further into the sea. When they reached their desired depth, the penguins shifted their wings, aligned their bodies vertically, then used their momentum to surge from the water and slide onto the icy surface. Their actions left behind a trail of bubbles as evidence of their speed and precision. Kimberly thought it best to lead by example as to prevent Dioni from repeating his previous experience, and so she navigated to position herself at Dioni's side.

Dioni noticed Kimberly's position, though he misinterpreted her guidance. He knew to follow the path set forth by every penguin in motion – to dip to further depths then align vertically to rush to the surface – and so he resolved that her movement was a way to challenge his abilities. Dioni, however, recognized his advantage; not only was he able to maintain his speed while underwater, he was less inclined to follow the strict laws of gravity once he broke the surface.

Kimberly and Dioni dove further into the arctic sea. They then used their wings to align their bodies vertically, toward the surface. Kimberly configured her body to absolute perfection, a skill which was developed over thousands of launches and recoveries. Dioni cared more for his ego and for the thrill of high-speed travel than what the best pilots on Earth knew all too well. He intentionally shifted his wings and slightly lowered his beak, which altered the direction of his momentum.

Kimberly's launch came to a perfect conclusion as she surged from the water, effortlessly, and slid on her belly until her momentum came to a complete stop; no part of her recovery was mismanaged in any way. Dioni's exit from the arctic water was not as free from dramatics. Instead of performing a successful surge – one in which he landed on his feet and recovered his balance while on solid ground – Dioni shot into the sky at a speed and angle that was as selfish as it was reckless.

"Wooooooo!" screamed Dioni as he lifted from the sea.

The penguins heard Dioni's shout and followed his inglorious exit from the water and into the sky.

"Well that seems unnecessary," said Wayne.

"Yeah, we get it," said Flay. "You can fly. We can't. What else can you do?"

Jeff turned to Kimberly. "Your budgie friend overshot the landing again."

"That's it!" shouted Wayne, the last of his patience entirely gone. "I give up! He's *not* a budgie, but if you saps want to call him one, then be my guest!"

Dioni looked down from the sky. He flew with a sense of pride and glee, and with the knowledge that he had an ability which the land-dwellers did not. He kept sight of his friends as he circled around where they stood. In doing so, Dioni failed to realize that he slowly reduced his airspeed and came closer to the surface. His momentum was of no concern to him, for he found it hilarious to see the penguins waddle on the snow. Dioni laughed, not at them, but at how fortunate he was to witness such an unforgettable—

WHAM!

Dioni slammed into an unknown object and immediately fell to the ground. Had it not been for his pathfinder detecting the danger which he ignored, his life could have ended at the exact moment of impact. The mysterious object was enormous by comparison, and to him it felt as though he had flown into an invisible wall. He was lucky to be alive.

The entire colony of Adélie penguins instantly took action. Many fell onto their bellies and pushed themselves to launch while on land, while others waddled to the site of Dioni's crash as fast as their webbed feet could carry them.

In a daze, Dioni stood and moved a few steps back. The object before him was a behemoth, with a near-frozen exterior which gradually eroded under the cruel, arctic climate. It was almost entirely black in color, with portions of pure white which faded to a dull grey. As Dioni's visual focus returned and his pathfinder completed the automatic reset function, he noticed movement near the front of the massive object. It was alive.

Dioni's immediate instinct was not a reaction of fear, but rather of curiosity. He paced forward, cautiously, to confirm whether or not he saw the object move. With each step, it became more evident that it was not a random object, but rather a live being that was out of its natural element. The object was a creature of the sea. It struggled immensely to retain its life, though it was in an indescribable amount of pain. Dioni paced underneath a massive dorsal fin, collapsed onto its side. He turned around. At the far end of the giant sea creature's body was the fluke of a titanic tail.

Dioni continued. The movement he noticed was from the eye of the massive creature. He moved back and was able to see it in its entirety.

The eye of the creature opened and came into focus. He saw his own reflection in the surface of the creature's eye, and in that moment, Dioni sensed its agony and felt compassion for a being which was larger than life itself. Though it was impossible for them to communicate, Dioni understood that the giant's life neared a slow and painful end. The creature's natural instinct was to hunt, yet it was not a threat to any of the birds nearby.

Dioni stood in the presence of an orca. The whale intentionally beached itself, which was a core indication that something occurred beyond the control of the Adélie community. Dioni approached the orca and placed his wing on the whale's face, near the orca's eye. The eye was clouded, though large and reflective enough for Dioni to see himself in full view. The orca blinked then used every ounce of energy it retained to open its mouth. It made a faint pitch of sound.

"No, I'm the one who should be sorry," said Dioni, just as softly. He brushed his wing on the orca's thick skin. "I flew into you. It's not your fault."

The penguins sprinted towards Dioni. They feared for the life of the Omega bird and for the significant damage it would cause to the entire community – not to mention to their reputation as hospitable birds. As the first wave of penguins reached Dioni and saw that he was unharmed, they collectively slowed their pace and approached more calmly. They stayed at a safe distance from the whale, yet were close enough to witness the actions of the Omega bird. Kimberly was the first to approach Dioni, albeit extremely cautiously.

"Do you know what happened?" she asked.

"No," Dioni responded. "He's in pain. So much pain."

Dioni looked at Kimberly. Behind her was the larger colony, all of whom looked in awe at what they saw.

"Adélie penguins control the ice and water levels, right?" Dioni said to the entire flock.

"Dioni, you misunderstand…" responded Kimberly.

"We can help him!" Dioni shouted. "All of us! We can help him!"

"Dioni," Kimberly said. She sighed. "We can't do that."

Wayne, Jeff, Russell and Flay waddled to join Kimberly.

"What? Why not?" Dioni asked. "It's a whale! He belongs in the water, not on land! If we work as a group we can get him back in!"

No penguin moved. It was a collective sign of respect, not of neglect.

"Mate, this is nature taking its course," said Jeff. "It is our responsibility for the balance—"

"—You don't balance nature by letting him die!" interrupted Dioni, a point which was made and taken harshly.

The penguins respected Dioni's emotions.

"Adélie penguins analyze ocean currents," opened Russell. "It's our job to determine how much of the ice is returned to the sea. What comes back to us is made into ice again, and the cycle repeats itself endlessly."

"Dioni," said Jeff. "Lately, the seawater is bringing something back with it. The color of the water is different in some areas."

"What you see here is the result of something far beyond our control, Dioni," said Kimberly, who acted as the voice of reason to the Omega bird. "Something is forcing an unnatural balance, and this is the result. There is nothing we can do for this whale."

"NO!" Dioni shouted. "He's still alive!"

Dioni used his wings to dig solid dirt and ice away from the whale. Though they witnessed his struggle, none of the penguins offered assistance; they stood and watched with their fins at their sides and their faces down.

Dioni fought to remove a large piece of ice beneath the whale. He shouted in anger. Unable to clear the ice, he moved towards the orca's front, inches from the whale's mouth. He dug as much of the ground and ice as his small wings could sustain. His frustration was evident with every scoop he pulled from the ground.

The orca opened its mouth and exhaled, which pushed Dioni away. The penguins understood the orca's deliberate action; they rushed to Dioni and created a barricade between him and the whale. Dioni stood up and shoved the birds who attempted to hold him back.

"Why won't you help me?" Dioni asked.

"Dioni," responded Flay. "He saw what you were doing, and he pushed you away."

"What? Why would he do that?" asked Dioni, bewildered by Flay's statement.

"You have to understand what's happening," said Wayne. "We are not hurting this whale more than what it has already endured. We are respecting his choice to end his path here. This is as far as he chooses to go."

"So you're just going to let a helpless whale die in the cold?" Dioni asked.

Tears formed in his eyes. He lowered his guard and saw the helpless orca behind them.

"There is nothing we can do," said Russell. "Even if we all worked together to somehow get him back in the water, he would not survive."

"You have to understand, Dioni," said Kimberly. "There are no resources for this whale. He sacrificed himself so that the rest of his pod could go on without him."

"That doesn't make any sense!" responded Dioni. "Why would an orca do that?"

He wiped the tears from his eyes.

"Something is happening in the water, and we can't explain it," responded Wayne. "There's less and less food and resources needed for their survival." He turned to the beached whale and lowered his head. "We simply don't know what's causing this."

"If their health is deteriorating, then it's a sign that the entire ecosystem is deteriorating," said Kimberly.

"What does that mean?" asked Dioni.

"It means that if they're sick, something is seriously wrong," responded Flay.

"We haven't discovered the reason for this, Dioni," said Russell. "We've done everything we know to do, and all we've learned is that it's not something we're causing."

"How do you know?" Dioni asked. He demanded answers.

"Because it was never negotiated," responded Wayne, to which Dioni reacted by manner of a harsh glance. Wayne used his wing to show the extend of what he spoke. "The land you see here, all around us…it was all icebergs and snow hills."

"It's flattening," interjected Kimberly. "We never asked for this. We know more about the natural balance of the arctic than anyone—"

"—Exactly," interrupted Jeff. "We've controlled ice and water levels for thousands of generations. We have no history of this ever occurring."

Dioni paused. He looked at the frozen orca, nearly void of life. He parted a path between Kimberly and Wayne, walked by his penguin friends, and stopped at a short distance from the orca.

"This has to be reported," said Dioni, a fierce look on his face. "The Alpha needs to know."

"We've done that, Dioni. Multiple times," responded Russell. "Ever since it started, a while back. Why do you think we're so happy to see the new Omega bird here?"

Dioni reflected on Russell's comment. Why would nothing be done even after multiple reports from the local birds? Despite his youth and lack of experience, Dioni was by no means ignorant of the world. He had the wisdom to know the difference between right and wrong, and when he was made a fool.

"What am I not seeing?" Dioni thought. "What am I not seeing?"

The Alpha mentioned Antarctica for a reason. Why? What was there to gain by visiting the arctic and talking to the Adélie penguins? If the strange occurrence was previously reported on multiple occasions, and still nothing was done, then clearly the Alpha knew and had ignored it. But for what purpose?

Dioni looked at the entire colony of penguins. He understood their truth, and they looked to him for help. By manner of desperation they did all they knew to do. They pretended to give Dioni the impression that all was well in the arctic. It was crucial for them to establish a bond with the new Omega bird, as the risk of not doing so meant a catastrophic failure of the balance. Their primary objective for the collective launch to the orca's location was not by accident; it was their one and only opportunity to ask for help. Regardless of how it occurred – whether it was by mistake or by sheer luck – Dioni's placement in the Adélie penguin territory was not a mere coincidence.

He knew he could not disappoint them. He had a responsibility – to the Adélie penguins, to the orcas, to the entire Arctic Ocean – and it was not within him to betray their trust. For the first time since he accepted his role, Dioni felt that crucial information was deliberately withheld from him. The birds with whom he had previously met had nothing to gain if they lied to him, so what was he *not* being told? What information did the Alpha keep from him? He had so little time to solve the mystery.

"The Alpha...think, think, think," Dioni thought. "He'll lie to me if I ask. I can't go back, otherwise he'll be suspicious." Dioni sighed. His train of thought continued. "Who can I talk to? Makawee? Wait...Deepa! But how do I get to India without using the portal?"

"Kimberly," opened Dioni. "The underwater flight technique you taught me."

"Launching?" asked Kimberly.

"Yeah, launching. You mentioned I can do it in the sky. Is that true?"

"Absolutely!" responded Kimberly. "It's the same sequence on your pathfinder. It'll be more difficult to navigate, and you will lose energy at a faster rate, but yes...yes you can."

"Okay, great. Thank you," Dioni responded. He turned to his five friends. "I have to go talk to another bird and ask some questions. This isn't the only place where strange things are happening. I need to know more before I go back to headquarters. I promise, I will help you."

"We understand," said Wayne. "We'll take whatever we can get."

Dioni looked at the orca. Its faded eyelid was shut. He approached the whale and felt its cold skin. If nothing else – if for no reason other than to wake up in a few days with the understanding that the entire experience was nothing more than a dream – Dioni wanted to remember the moment. It was a darkness unlike any he had ever seen, a cold unlike any he had ever felt, all of which occurred under the rays of the arctic sun.

Dioni looked to his five friends. They crossed their wings on their chest, a sign of deep respect among the penguins. He turned to the rest of the flock, who stood in the same stance as the others. Dioni became more than a boy trapped in the body of a tropical bird; he was the Omega, the one on whom the colony depended.

Dioni spread his wings, jumped, then flapped away with all his strength. The penguins observed from the ground as the Omega bird flew higher and higher. It soon became difficult to see him as his blue feathers merged into the sky. Only when they saw a small, perfectly formed circle in the sky – followed by a loud boom which launched him to airspeeds unlike any other – were the Adélie penguins able to feel at ease.

The penguins lowered their guard and waddled toward the open water. The sunlight had reached beyond its peak for the day. Though they still had important work to do, the penguins felt a sense of relief with the success of Dioni's visit.

"Phew," Wayne sighed, glad that the entire ordeal concluded peacefully. "That orca could have easily swallowed him whole. Lucky for Dioni, orcas don't seem to like budgies."

"He's not a budgie," said the other four penguins, simultaneously.

Wayne's expression changed from optimistic to annoyed.

"I hate all of you."

Chapter Twenty-Four

There were only a few times during the day – any day of the week, really – when the orphanage was at peace. Though most nights were relatively quiet and serene, the ambience of the daytime included a myriad of sounds from the outdoors as well as from within. Cars and buses strolled by, people walked along the roads and on the uneven sidewalks, and the elder children played in the courtyard or chased each other, which oftentimes resulted in a collusion of some kind. Occasionally, the faint sound of birds was heard in the distance. To Alma, it was home.

The children of the orphanage knew better than to become too attached to another child. Friendships were encouraged and bonds were formed between the children, but at any given point, on any given day, a visitor from afar could adopt one of them and take him or her to a new home. While this was a dream come true for those who were adopted, it was a heartbreaking process for those who were left behind. Some of the adopted children moved away to live in colder areas, some of them went on to live in the mountains and valleys of more developed nations, and the luckiest went on to live in buildings that were so tall they touched the clouds. Regardless of the parents who adopted them or of the foreign lands to which they were taken, all of the children who left the orphanage had one common quality: they did not return and were never heard from again.

Alma became accustomed to the cycle of creating bonds then detaching herself from the infants, as it was common to see the youngest leave as quickly as they had arrived. As a young child, she envied the cuter children who would undoubtedly live in riches beyond what she imagined. In her teenage years, she molded a new role for herself as a mentor. Her mindset was no longer to be gone from the orphanage once and forevermore, never to return. Instead, Alma felt she could accomplish more through education, to study and understand the development of the children in her care. More than anything, her desire in life was to become an educator and help her students learn all there was to know of the world.

Alma sat on a rocking chair and daydreamed of an existence beyond the confines of the orphanage. In one of her arms was a cradled infant, who drank from a bottle which was held to her mouth by Alma's free hand. The two were alone, and aside from the faint sound of a nearby television, the common room was tranquil. Alma smiled as she fed the child. She rocked back and forth to help the infant feel at peace.

"Hi, Penelope," Alma said to the infant, who immediately turned her attention to her caregiver.

Penelope's eyes were unusually large, and in them Alma saw a shade of blue color which was solely found in the Earth's most beautiful bodies of water.

"Someone is hungry this morning," Alma continued.

Penelope drank her milk with such vigor that Alma wondered whether a small dose of cacao was accidentally added and mixed into the bottle. There was only one way to determine if that was the case, and Alma had no desire to test her theory. She calmly inhaled the morning air, closed her eyes, and leaned her head as she continued to rock the chair back and forth.

A strange bird flapped its wings and landed on the nearby windowsill, which was mostly a divot on the concrete wall, covered by a hand-made curtain. The bird stared at Alma, almost as if it felt the need to learn and understand all there was to know about her. The bird made no sound.

Penelope noticed the unique object nearby. Her attention immediately drifted away from her morning meal. She released the bottle from her mouth and turned to face the small bird; Penelope's movement returned Alma from her distracted state of mind.

"What? What are you looking at?" asked Alma as the child's blue eyes focused on the strange object in the room.

Alma followed Penelope's line of sight and saw the receiver of the child's attention. It was a silver-colored mockingbird – a bird which had no business being near the orphanage, or in Flores, or anywhere near Guatemala. The bird was far away from its natural habitat, and although neither Penelope nor Alma knew enough to identify it, they both knew it was out of place.

The bird absorbed the contents of what it saw, as if it desired to record the moment. It moved its head slowly, not in quick, short bursts as was the usual behavior of a bird, but rather in long glances, the same manner in which an artist envisions a masterpiece on a blank canvass. The bird looked at Alma, then paced a few steps forward. It paused and glared at Alma with deep intensity.

The mockingbird tilted its head, a behavior of observation and of wonder. The bird was there for a reason, though it made no sense as to why it chose an orphanage in a remote town, away from natural resources. The bird chirped. Alma and Penelope looked at one another, confused by what they saw. Alma locked her knees, which stopped the sway of the chair.

As quickly as the silver mockingbird arrived, it shifted its body, opened its wings, and flew away. The bird left no evidence of its visit to the orphanage.

"Okay…" Alma said aloud. "That was odd. Did you see that?" she asked Penelope, whose attention returned in its entirety to her bottle.

"It's the little things in life, Penelope," Alma playfully said to the child. "They come and they go so quickly, but those are the things we remember. I have no idea what type of bird that was, but maybe it was here for a reason, and now it's gone. We both saw it, right? It'll be our little secret, okay? Don't tell the others!"

The child heard every word yet understood nothing. Penelope's expression did not change, though her attention shifted to the images and colors seen on the nearby television.

"What?" Alma asked. "Do you want to watch the weather? It's going to be hot, and it might rain. There, is that what you wanted to know?"

Alma smiled at Penelope, whose attention remained on the screen. Alma sighed and shook her head. Penelope was too young to hold her own bottle, yet she was more interested in the television than in her morning meal.

"Kids today," said Alma.

She looked at the screen and saw as a meteorologist made a circular pattern on a map of North America. The image on the screen changed to a map of southern Mexico, which then displayed a circular pattern near the easternmost part of the Gulf.

"Huh...what is he talking about?" Alma said.

She held the child and the bottle in place as she reached for a remote control. She aimed it at the television and increased the volume.

"...With winds increasing from both the north and the south," said the meteorologist. "This is not typical weather for this part of the world, especially for this time of the year, though it is certainly not improbable. The good news is that it will bypass us entirely. Our models do not indicate that it will amount to anything more than a severe thunderstorm, which will likely move north towards Florida by the afternoon."

"Now, speaking of unusual weather patterns," the meteorologist continued. The map behind him changed to display the west coast of the United States. "If the storm from the east was not unusual enough, we are also seeing a strong storm developing along the western side of the United States and Mexico, currently off the coast of California. Again, we have no reason for concern at this point, but we are seeing that this storm is slowly gaining strength and is moving south due to unusually strong winds from the Pacific..."

...

361

The Alpha bird stood proudly at the helm of the Control Center. His wings were at his side – a stance of dominance and of superiority over every bird who worked at the Department of Global Climate Control – and his attention was on the screen before him. He watched the same weather segment as did Alma and Penelope, though with an odd, almost joyful expression on his face.

"...And just like I mentioned about the storm from the east, south of Florida at this point," continued the meteorologist. "Our models are showing that this storm will likely miss the mainland and drift back into the Pacific Ocean as lower pressure comes in from the north. We'll certainly keep an eye on it for now. As for the rest of the day today, we can expect sunny skies and more humidity..."

"Yes!" exclaimed the Alpha, proud of the success of his plan; he saw what he needed to see. "Change the screen back to live weather, but show only North and Central America," the Alpha commanded the two white doves who sat behind a circular desk along the back wall in the center of the room.

With a few simple motions of their wings, the doves altered the display on the massive screen of the Control Center. The display changed from a news broadcast of a local weather segment to an actual, live weather feed of the American continent, from southern Canada to the southernmost tip of Panama.

Business carried on as usual. The Control Center was in full operation, with all scheduled initiatives set in place, strictly tracked and monitored. The Trading Floor was as busy as ever, with additional negotiations underway for the areas which would experience higher-than-usual rainfall as a result of the dual storms on the east and west coasts of North America.

Every bird in the Department paused to watch the progression of the simulated, natural anomaly. It was no secret that all anomalies were only modeled tests; while the tests usually resulted in increased wind, additional rain and longer weather reports, the simulations stopped before any creature on land, air, or sea, came to harm. This policy was set in place decades prior, after a simulation went horribly out of control and caused both a catastrophic volcanic eruption followed immediately by a typhoon. The birds of the Philippines never again agreed to any anomalies until a strict policy was adopted for all future tests. With no reason to fear any unscheduled changes for the anomaly in progress, all birds continued their work as they did on any other day.

The vulture, who stood near the control desk of the Control Center, opened his wings and lifted himself off the floor and towards his executive suite. The Alpha circled high in the air, under the bridge between the two divisions, to see the grandness of his empire. The wind that brushed his face allowed his eyes to open even wider, which enabled him to absorb the full spectrum of the experience. He cared not about the colors of the thousands of beautiful birds who flew in every direction, nor did he care for the extraordinary technology that he himself helped to create over the course of hundreds of thousands of years. All that mattered to him – as he flew above his kingdom – was the elevated sensation of superiority, of his sovereignty above all living beings on Earth.

He flew to the perch outside of his executive suite, where he overlooked his domain. It was perhaps his favorite location within the entire Department; it was where he stood above all other birds, and where he arrogantly looked down upon them.

"Donna!" shouted the Alpha. Five hummingbirds approached from his suite, their wings flapped in rapid unison. "I only need one," he said, to which all but the furthest hummingbird immediately flew away.

"Donna, I'd like everyone to see me working from here today," he said to the tiny bird. "I'm gonna need the portable unit brought to me, and I need it to be incognito to the main screen."

The hummingbird nodded to confirm it understood the Alpha's order. It turned its head then flew in the direction from where it entered.

"Oh, and Donna!" the vulture said loudly. The hummingbird stopped in its path and returned to him. "Bring me the tracker unit. And keep that last part to yourself."

The hummingbird once again nodded, then turned and zoomed away from the Alpha's sight.

363

...

Kimberly absolutely told Dioni the truth when she said that a launch in the sky was far more exhaustive than in the water. Though doing so dramatically cut the overall flight time to get from one point to another, Dioni discovered that it was difficult to maintain such airspeed for extended periods of time. What's more, sky launches did not provide accurate navigation from his pathfinder. It seemed that even the most advanced avian technology had its limitations.

Dioni was airborne for hours. In every direction he looked, he saw nothing but endless amounts of water, with the occasional cloud formation in the sky. Though he felt a collective exhaustion of his mind and body, the determination to make his destination – to ask for help from the wisest of all birds – outweighed his intense desire to surrender. Nevertheless, his body and mind were only able to sustain so much self-abuse.

By manner of trial and error, Dioni learned to release from an aerial launch and return to his natural flight speed, where he maintained his altitude and simply glided above the Earth without the need to land or unexpectedly crash into a large, foreign object. The reduction in his speed allowed Dioni to conserve his energy, and also enabled him to reconnect his pathfinder to request his location and position in accordance to his destination.

"Pathfinder," Dioni commanded, nearly breathless after a release from an extensive launch. "Detect current location."

The words *South Atlantic Ocean* once again appeared to Dioni, which annoyed him after hours of travel and multiple launches. The further north and east he travelled, the more he recognized that natural light would not last for the duration of his flight. His time was limited, and his destination remained so far away. Dioni continued his flight, determined to ensure that his next launch attempt would be his last. His plan was to maintain his speed until he was incapable of doing so any longer, which he hoped would place him where he needed to be.

Dioni aligned his body and once again instructed his pathfinder to push him through the sky. Launching at such high speed and at such great elevation meant his field of vision was limited. He flew blindly, with the light of the sun on his back, for hours, until he saw something other than ocean water. At long last, signs of life were visible once again.

In the distance was another bird, who flew at a much slower speed though it did so without the need to launch or by the use of its wings. As Dioni drew closer, he saw that the body of the bird reflected brilliantly against the light of the sun, and that a series of letters were drawn on its side.

Dioni travelled too fast to observe the full magnitude of what he saw, though he realized that the object was not a bird. He became perplexed by the aircraft, as it was the first airplane he had seen at such close proximity. The Flores airport had airplanes which flew in and out almost every day, but this was his first opportunity to see one without the need to stand behind a tall fence.

Dioni reduced his speed and flew closer to the side of the plane. He looked through the open windows and saw some of its passengers. With the exception of a person who sat near the tail of the aircraft, every passenger he saw was either asleep, in deep observation of something unseen, or was otherwise distracted. Dioni moved closer to the open window above the wing and saw a young boy who admired the view of the Earth from thousands of meters above the sea.

As Dioni slowed his speed to match that of the airplane, which was mostly to test the limits of his own curiosity, he became visible to the boy, who looked in awe at the mysterious object in the sky. The boy's eyes grew wide as he knocked on the window. He saw a bird which was far beyond its natural environment, both because of its species and because it was impossible for any bird to fly at such speed and elevation. The boy turned to an elder woman beside him and desperately attempted to show her what he saw.

Dioni shifted his body. He knew that doing so would cause him to disappear into the bright, blue sky. He failed to understand, however, that the action had an unintended consequence: it forced him to change his direction of travel.

At the urgent request of the boy, the woman looked out of the window and saw nothing but miles of cloudless sky. Dioni was camouflaged, which he found enjoyable though it meant the child was disciplined for needlessly waking his mother. Nevertheless, Dioni had larger priorities to address. He pushed himself once more to increase his airspeed, and soon the airplane was far behind.

Hours passed. Dioni thought of the orca that sacrificed itself so that the rest of its pod could continue. He wondered what caused it to get so sick, and why it was abandoned by its family. He thought of the penguins, and though he pondered dozens of scenarios, he could not conclude as to why their reports were ignored by the Alpha. Dioni resolved to help his newfound friends, even if it meant having to spend a few more days as a bird.

Dioni saw land in the distance. He smiled, inhaled and exhaled slowly, and exited the launch sequence. He momentarily glided above the land. With his airspeed within tolerance of the pathfinder's detection capabilities, Dioni confirmed his location and was pleasantly surprised by the pathfinder's response. The words *North Atlantic Ocean, Gulf of Guinea, Cameroon*, scrolled before him, which was a huge relief. With limited use of his pathfinder, Dioni was capable of managing his flightpath.

"Show on map," Dioni said aloud.

The pathfinder projected an image of his location. Dioni saw his airspeed, current wind velocity, and the trajectory of his flightpath, which confirmed that India was ahead, even if thousands of miles away. He planned the remainder of his flight: cut through the continent of Africa, over one large body of water, and continue in the northeast direction until he reached the sanctuary.

In an effort to regain some of his strength, he glided in the sky and used his wings and tail to guide him to lower altitudes. He was hungry and nearly drained of all his strength, yet he remained determined to achieve his goal.

"If I push myself one, maybe two more times, I could fly over the entire continent," Dioni thought aloud. "Just do one launch until I see water again, then take a break, and then once more, and then I'll be in India!" He paused. "I can make it before the sun goes down." He looked at the map generated by his pathfinder, which showed the vast distance to his destination. "Yes, I can do this."

Dioni launched and disappeared into the sky before the Cameroonian fishermen, the local birds, or any of the marine life who dwelled along the border of the African nation noticed a blue quetzal in their airspace.

...

"Track the Omega," the Alpha said to a translucent screen. He wore a unique device on his head, which was a larger version of Dioni's pathfinder though far more technologically sophisticated.

The words *Omega Offline* displayed on an image before him in bold, red color.

"Offline?" the Alpha asked. "That's unlikely." He returned his attention to his device. "Track Omega, see last broadcast."

The words *North Atlantic Ocean, Gulf of Guinea, Cameroon,* displayed, which also presented the exact coordinates of Dioni's last signal on a projected map, visible only to him.

"Cameroon?" the Alpha asked, taken aback by the image displayed. "Why are you in Africa?"

The vulture brought the tip of his wing to his beak, his preferred stance to ponder.

"Track Omega, flight path history, most recent," the Alpha instructed the device, which presented him with a series of connected broadcast signal points, detailed on the projected map.

A series of lines showed Dioni in Antarctica – which was expected – followed by a series of dots placed further apart from one another. The dots ended at the location of Dioni's last broadcast, in Cameroonian airspace.

"Would you look at that," said the Alpha. "Someone learned how to launch." He connected the dots of Dioni's flightpath. "Where are you going, kid? What are you up to?"

The vulture turned his attention to the main screen of the Control Center, which displayed live weather readings of the Americas. He smiled and lowered his wing.

"It doesn't really matter now, does it, Dioni?" he said. He spoke to his device. "Track Omega. Set alert notification for next signal broadcast."

. . .

Dioni remained in flight much longer than he initially anticipated, which took a strong toll on his body. Though his pathfinder protected him from immediate danger, there was no defense for careless aviation. It was an unnecessary risk for Dioni, whose determination to reach India outweighed the better judgement to be alive when he arrived. The light of the sun grew dimmer as he flew over miles and miles of topographical diversity, some of which was covered by a large blanket of clouds.

While in launch-flight sequence, Dioni failed to take into account the Earth's natural rotation. Had he paused between launches and taken the time to adjust his direction of travel, he would have easily discovered the fastest, safest, and most convenient route to India. As it stood, Dioni was far from his desired destination.

At the point where the clouds parted and land was visible, Dioni saw a large body of water. Nearby was a large island, which was his first indication that something was wrong. A second indication came shortly thereafter; he passed the island and flew over an endless mass of land.

"Where am I?" Dioni asked.

He reduced his speed and gracefully exited from the launch. Once Dioni's pathfinder connected to a broadcast signal, it immediately sent a notification of his location to the Alpha's device.

"Pathfinder," Dioni said, exhausted from his journey. "Detect current location."

Dioni's pathfinder displayed the words *Mediterranean Sea, Syria*.

"Syria?" Dioni exclaimed. "Where in the world is Syria?"

The pathfinder understood Dioni's question as a command. It displayed his flightpath – the same points that were displayed to the Alpha – with an additional point added in Syrian airspace over the Mediterranean Sea.

"Show map," he commanded.

The pathfinder displayed his location in relation to his destination. Dioni mouthed a phrase which his exhausted body exemplified.

"I can't do this," he said aloud. He looked ahead and saw that the night sky was too close to elude. He was beyond exhausted. "I'll try again tomorrow."

In an effort to remain undetected, Dioni spread his wings and glided high above the land. In the distance he saw the lights of a city, which was not ideal. He circled the entirety of the city from high above and noticed that its inhabitants had moved indoors for the night.

The light of the sun slowly faded. The clouds followed Dioni and soon covered the entire city. When he felt it was safe to do so, Dioni reduced his elevation and searched for a tree where he could maintain his cover and rest for the night. He did not want to take a chance to sleep in the rain.

Away from the city – far enough to not be seen in the light yet close enough to be near a source of food in the morning – Dioni located a tree where he could rest. The tree was tall enough to hide him from predators, with enough leaves to protect him from natural elements. He found an open point on the tree which was clear, and he set his fatigued feet on an inner branch. He felt as if he had carried a mountain across two oceans and over most of northern Africa; it was a level of exhaustion only few birds had ever known.

Dioni placed his feet beneath his body and rested his weight on the trunk of the tree. As he drifted in the odd state between awake and asleep, he noticed the birds who slept on other branches within the same tree. In the darkness, Dioni was only able to determine that the birds were smaller than him. They had dark feathers – perhaps they were finches or sparrows – and they posed no immediate threat. It was enough for Dioni to release his guard, close his eyes, and fall immediately into a deep sleep.

...

"Oh, ho hoh, Dioni!" the Alpha bird said excitedly as he received notification of Dioni's location. "Come on, kid! You're making this too easy for me! Syria? Of all places."

If there existed a single trait of the Alpha that was both respected and feared among all birds who knew him, it was his ability to instantly detect the weaknesses of his enemies. To the Alpha, the world was a small place where repetitive patterns occurred on a consistent basis, and where certain situations could easily be triggered by an element which he had the power to control. What he knew, more so than any other, was how to strike fear into the bird of his choice.

The vulture's ego was fed in that moment. He had no intention to eliminate his counterpart. Instead, he wanted Dioni to surrender his position. If Dioni chose to live as a bird without interfering in any of his plans, the Alpha would have full authority over the Department of Global Climate Control. Such autonomy had never existed, and because of his patience to oversee the Department long after scores of generations of birds had come and gone, the Alpha wanted what rightfully belonged to him. The dividends of his investment were long overdue.

The Alpha commanded his device to display its content on the main screen of the Control Center. He confirmed the weather patterns on display and was fully delighted by what he saw. The scenario was almost too perfect.

He lifted his wings and conducted a series of careful motions which were read and interpreted by the screen. The Alpha took it upon himself to override the conditions of what was previously negotiated and approved. He submitted a change order to a seemingly minor aerial wind pattern, specifically for the Syrian city where Dioni rested. The change was too subtle to raise a concern by the local birds, though if it had, the Alpha did not care.

A message appeared on the screen: *Modification to Scheduled Order. Authorization Required.*

The vulture smiled as he said his three favorite words.

"Approved by Alpha."

The system acknowledged and confirmed the command, which set in motion a simple alteration to the clouds over Syria.

Chapter Twenty-Five

Dioni loved the sights and sounds of his homeland – the blue of the mountains visible just before each sunrise; the ancient city which provided him with opportunities uncommon for many his age; the small street on which he lived, where everyone knew him; and Alma's laughter. Nothing in heaven nor on Earth was more profound than the sound of Alma's voice, the view of her expressive smile, and the knowledge that her joy was the result of a deep bond they shared with one another.

He held her hand as they sat at the end of a pier which overlooked Lake Petén Itza. The sky was cloudless, and the aquamarine water was as peaceful as the mountains in the distance. The light of the sun danced gracefully on the surface of the lake. It was a perfect afternoon.

Dioni leaned forward and noticed his reflection on the surface. The reflected image was that of a young man with a lifetime of experiences ahead of him. Alma leaned closer to him and looked down at the water. The two of them giggled as the water captured the perfect portrait of young love.

Dioni turned his head to look at her. The entire world moved slower. Alma turned her head to look at Dioni. The wind gently brushed a few strands of her hair onto her face. She caressed the side of his face then smiled at him.

He looked into her eyes; there existed nothing more beautiful. He gazed, longer than necessary, which forced her to laugh and turn away. There it was again! It was truly the most perfect sound he ever heard.

Dioni looked at his hand. Her hand rested in his grasp. She felt warm, and her hand was soft. He looked at his feet submerged in the water. He wiggled his toes. She moved her feet to be on top of his.

A gentle breeze carried with it the subtle sound of leaves in motion. No other living being existed. All which mattered in the world was present in the moment.

Dioni turned to search for something. The object was gone. He had to find it.

"What are you looking for?" asked Alma. The sound of her voice pulsated through his entire body.

"I lost something," Dioni responded as he searched all around.

"Well, maybe you don't need it."

"I remember having it with me."

"I didn't see you with anything, Dioni."

"I just don't want to lose it," he responded. A sense of worry came over him.

"It's just me and you here," Alma said. "I can help you find it. But if you don't have it with you, maybe it's not necessary to carry it everywhere you go."

"Yeah," Dioni responded. He abandoned his search. "It's probably not important."

"You know what is important, though?" Alma playfully asked.

"What?"

"This," she said.

She leaned into him and kissed him. She closed her eyes. He did the same. The sensation he felt in that moment was like no other. She pulled away. Her face glowed with delight. She opened her eyes. His heart raced tremendously.

Dioni saw a small boat in the distance. It drifted peacefully. It made no wake as it came closer to the pier.

"I want to show you something," Dioni said as the boat sailed to him.

"What?" Alma asked.

"I can't tell you," he responded excitedly. "You have to come with me."

He stood. He was taller than he remembered. He reached for the boat, which guided itself to the pier.

"Where are you going?" Alma asked.

A gust of wind blew from the opposite direction. A cloud formation appeared in the sky. Dioni entered the boat and extended his hand to her.

"It's for us. I have to show you what I—"

"—Dioni, I can't go with you," Alma interrupted. "It's not meant for me."

The sky filled with clouds. The sunlight's dance on the surface of the water came to an abrupt end. The wind grew stronger and colder.

"What?" Dioni asked in desperation. "Why not?"

"You have to go, Dioni."

A tree cracked loudly in the distance. The wind scattered dead leaves. The motion of the water became more intense. Alma stood. She leaned into the boat and pushed it away from the pier.

"Wait!" Dioni pleaded. "Come with me! Don't push me away!"

Alma looked at him. Tears formed in her eyes. She pushed harder, which forced the boat further into the water. She stood in the lake and observed as Dioni drifted aimlessly away from her. The intensity of the woodland noises grew louder and faster.

"Alma!" Dioni shouted. "Swim to me! I can pull you up and then we can go together!"

She blew him a kiss. She waived at him. The boat drifted further and further. The water shook the boat, which created ripples that stretched to the shore. The sky became dark. He heard a roar in the distance.

Dioni looked to the sky. It was angry. The wind grew stronger. Dioni looked towards the pier. Alma was gone. He searched frantically in every direction. His heart paced faster. His eyes swelled with tears. He shouted her name. He heard only the roar of the incoming thunder. He shouted her name. He was voiceless. The movement of the water became more intense. He clenched his hands into fists.

He shouted her name with all his might. No sound resonated from him as it was drowned by the crash and fury of a powerful bolt of lightning.

BOOM!

Dioni was instantly awakened from his deep sleep by the explosion of a mortar, which crashed against a concrete wall behind him. The blast was so intense that it shook the tree violently, though its strong roots enabled it to remain upright. Two of the smaller birds fell from their perched positions as a result of the impact. They froze in their state of fear.

Dioni moved towards the end of the branch to determine what had caused such a violent explosion. He looked down and saw a small trail of blood near the base of the tree. It flowed slowly onto a paved portion of the street.

Though the dawn remained hours away, the light from the moon was strong enough to provide visibility to the brutal acts which occurred below. Dioni looked up and saw the star-filled sky, perfectly clear, as if the clouds had purposely parted and moved themselves away from the city.

Dioni's heart raced faster with each moment that passed. In the distance he saw two men, each of whom held large weapons as they ran towards the base of the tree. The two men stopped nearby. One of the men walked towards the body of a third man, who laid on the ground, motionless, beside the tree. The man touched the back of the fallen man's neck, then stood up and ran in the direction of the loud sound. The second man yelled to the first to no avail. He hesitated momentarily then ran past the tree to follow his friend.

Dioni moved to gain a better view. He followed the men as best he could while he remained under the protection of the large tree. He heard the two men shout, though he could not understand what they said. Violent blasts were heard from the opposite direction.

The night sky illuminated with the brief flashes of light created by rapid gunfire. The two men quickly hid behind a damaged car on the street. Bullets rushed in every direction and struck the surface of the car, which the two men used as protection. The men shouted as they stood and returned fire, their bullets destroyed all in their path.

Dioni took cover. He hoped against all odds that the bark of the tree was strong and dense enough to withstand the punishment of gunfire. He placed his head down, crouched into the tightest stance he could hold, and used his wings to cover his ears as he inaudibly shouted for it to stop.

As quickly as it began, the attack came to a sudden halt. Dioni released the grasp of his wings over his ears, opened his eyes, then stood to his feet. He saw the other birds scattered among the many branches of the tree. They were much smaller than him – less than half his size – and they remained in a collective huddle. The branches were filled with small birds, who stood petrified in a state of shock. Every bird looked at Dioni.

One man shouted to the other. Dioni looked in their direction and saw as one of the men dropped his weapon and ran, as fast as his legs could carry him, to the concrete wall near the tree. The beam of a powerful light illuminated the scene below, which spotted directly on the man who ran away. The man sprinted for his life as the beam of light easily followed his every move.

Dioni was unable to determine the source of the light. He moved to a higher position in an effort to gain a better visual perspective on the actions below. He carefully secured his foothold with each leap from branch to branch; the small birds traced his every move. Dioni reached the peak of the tree, which was covered by a thick dust. The light of the moon was more powerful from his elevated point of view. He looked down and saw the source of the sound, the source of the light, and the source of the violence.

The beam of light that captured the man's movement was cut as he ran beyond the wall and hid behind the tree. The light shifted to be in perfect alignment with the base of the tree, which created a long shadow in which the man disappeared.

Dioni identified the reason why the man ran for his life. The source of the powerful light was a beast of war, and despite the cover of darkness, the moonlight allowed Dioni to see a massive gun barrel aimed directly at the base of the tree. At a speed faster than Dioni's ability to fathom the reason why it occurred, the barrel released a warhead; it took absolutely no chance to miss its intended target.

The warhead exploded. It instantly shattered the base of the tree and completely destroyed the concrete wall, which eliminated any chance of the hidden man's survival. The top of the tree, untouched by the warhead, was pushed several yards away, onto the street. As it fell onto the cold cement, the force of the fall violently shook the many birds who stood innocently in fear; the crash of the tree caused the small birds to drop from every direction.

Dioni, who stood atop the tree at the moment of impact, was spared from permanent damage. The hard fall forcibly thrust him from the peak of the tree. He rolled onto the ground, came to a stop, and laid motionless on his side. His pathfinder had the ability to warn him of incoming danger and to form a barrier of protection around his body in case of an emergency, yet it failed when he needed it most.

Dioni was hurt. He coughed, which released the build-up of air and dust that was stored in his lungs. His vision was intact, though his pathfinder suffered damage as a result of the impact. He lifted his head and felt an odd pain in his upper body. He looked down to his feet and wiggled his toes, which provided him with a slight sense of relief. He rolled onto his back and looked at the night sky. There were no clouds anywhere in sight, and no wind gusts from any direction. The moon was as bright as Dioni had ever seen. It cast its light onto a street nearly void of artificial illumination.

A faint sound distracted Dioni from his view of the star-filled sky. He heard a chirp, which derived from the fallen tree. He turned his head in the direction of the sound and saw a small flame at the top of the destroyed tree. He coughed once more. Dioni was angered by what he witnessed. The single chirp quickly became two chirps, then three, and were soon followed by many more. The chirps from the birds were cries of panic and despair.

Dioni grunted as he shifted his body and rolled onto his face and abdomen. He used his wings to push himself from the ground, ignoring the soreness that was felt by his every muscle. He brought his feet beneath his body and lifted his torso to once again stand upright. The chirps from the birds intensified.

The words *Pathfinder Offline* became visible to Dioni as he stood at attention. In an attempt to reactivate the device, he tapped the side of his head where his pathfinder was placed.

Acquiring Signal, Please Wait…

A small, red circle was visible to Dioni near the top of the pathfinder's projected screen. Dioni ignored it. He took a step forward in an effort to move closer to the fallen birds. He froze; he witnessed a sight no bird should ever live to see.

The lifeless bodies of the smaller birds were scattered in every direction. Dioni walked a few paces forward and saw a fallen, innocent rock sparrow, whose only crime was to be at the wrong place at the wrong time. The sparrow's life ended in brutal fashion; though it suffered briefly, the pain it felt was excruciating.

Dioni returned his attention to the birds within the fallen tree. The collapse of the tree created a cage which trapped the sparrows beneath a weight far greater than they could lift. Fear, anger, and adrenaline fueled his every movement as he sprinted to them. He reached the remains of the tree, where the flame on the higher branches provided the illumination to see into the eyes of the terrified, panic-stricken sparrows. Through the few cracks of the broken branches and fallen leaves, the imprisoned sparrows noticed as Dioni stood before them. They collectively raised their voices. The sound of their cries became eternally engraved in Dioni's mind.

Dioni lifted the first layer of branches, which allowed him to see the many birds trapped beneath the fallen tree. He saw their faces – the terrified look in their eyes, the desperation in their voices – as they screamed in agony for Dioni to save them. The sound was deafening, the unexpected byproduct of birds who fought for their chance to survive. The flame atop the tree grew larger. Though it provided more light for Dioni's rescue efforts, it created an even greater threat. He knew the fire would soon grow out of control.

With every ounce of energy in his body, Dioni lifted the smaller branches; he stretched his body and used his feet to push other branches down. His tactic enabled him to move closer to the sparrows but made no difference in his ability to lift the larger and heavier branches which barricaded the birds within. The fire grew larger.

A symphony of violent sounds surrounded Dioni from every direction. It was the sound of war, of two enemies who targeted one another with artillery created for the sole purpose of death and destruction. The noise originated from multiple sources, though from opposite sides of the fallen tree. Men shouted at one another as the thunderous explosions of rapid gunfire were heard from every direction; thousands of bullets obliterated anything they touched. The fire grew larger.

Dioni moved further into the fallen tree. He fought with all his might to come as close to the sparrows as possible; if he managed to free one, it would be possible to free them all. The branches grew thicker and heavier as Dioni came closer to them, until he reached the branch which proved beyond his abilities. The sparrows screamed in agony – a combination of both pain and fear – which Dioni was helpless to suppress. Try as he may with every last degree of strength, the branch which caged the sparrows was too heavy for him to lift, push or pull away. The fire grew larger, the battle intensified.

The light on Dioni's pathfinder changed from red to green.

"Help me! Help me! Help me!" shouted every sparrow.

With his pathfinder online, their voices became audible and understandable to Dioni.

"I hear you! I'm trying!" Dioni yelled in response, his voice muffled by the chaos of the scene.

Unable to lift, pull, push, or break the large branch, Dioni fell to the ground and crawled through a labyrinth of gaps between the branches and leaves. The smaller twigs stabbed him repeatedly, though in his state of mind he felt no pain. Dioni tangled himself within the branches. He crawled as far into the fallen tree as was possible. The fire grew larger, the battle became louder and moved closer.

"Help me! Help me!" the sparrows cried, with no break between their shouts of agony.

With no alternative, Dioni reached his wings through the branches, towards the terrified birds. He heard them, he saw them, and he felt their pain. He stretched his blue wings as far as they could go, in hopes to save even a single bird. The sparrows did the same; they reached from within their imprisonment towards their final chance at salvation. The fire grew larger, the battle became louder and moved closer.

Dioni felt a tremble which shook the fallen tree. He paused to briefly collect his thoughts and to search for the cause of the vibration. He looked in the direction from where he entered. In the distance he saw a large object that reflected the moonlight. Dioni pulled himself away from the sparrows. He immediately discovered what caused the tremble.

An instrument of destruction slowly approached the tree. It moved with no wheels but rather with two continuous tracks on each side. As it approached, the moonlight enabled Dioni to see the massive war machine – capable of destruction far beyond his comprehension – whose primary weapon was aimed directly at the tree. The fire grew larger, the battle grew louder though mostly from a single direction.

Dioni pulled further away. The cries of the sparrows slowly ceased, and their sense of hope faded. He looked at them through the fallen branches. As the intense fire raged, their eyes reflected the light of the flames. The sparrows looked at him and saw not a chosen bird, but rather a child who was far from his nest.

"I'm sorry!" Dioni's voice cracked.

He turned his back to the birds who stood in silence as the rage of the fire reigned upon them. Dioni quickly escaped through the same path he created to get to the sparrows. He dodged the embers and dust particles that fell from the sky. He reached the peak of the tree then leapt from the pile of broken branches to land on solid ground. With tears in his eyes, Dioni spread his wings then lifted himself far above the violence, as quickly as his wings could carry him.

"Dioni!" shouted a nearby voice. "You have to go back!"

"Get away from me!" Dioni shouted in return, unsure from where the voice originated.

"You can save those birds!" said the voice.

Dioni shifted his body to fly in a different direction and escape into the darkness. He looked to his side. The light of the moon created an aura around the body of a Hawaiian crow.

"You can still help them!" said the crow. "It's not too late. Go back!"

"Then *you* go down there, Ally!" shouted Dioni. Tears streamed down his face.

"Dioni, listen to me," said Ally. "You have to be brave! You have to be the Omega bir—"

"—I never asked for this!" shouted Dioni. "You did this to me! I don't want to do this anymore!"

Dioni dipped his head, lowered his tail, and perfectly aligned his body. Ally knew his next move.

"Dioni, NO—"

BOOM!

Dioni's launch broke the sound barrier and knocked Ally from her flightpath. She stabilized herself, looked up, and saw the perfect circle he created followed by faint trails which faded into the darkness. The loud explosion, however, was not caused by Dioni's launch, but rather by the actions on the ground.

The sound of rapid gunfire, of the horrors of warfare, came to a crescendo and then fell to thunderous silence. Neither honor nor victory existed in the actions which took place. No one would grieve the mass of lives lost. No one would remember the names of those who perished, nor would their memories be passed to future generations.

Ally looked down and saw as a large fire consumed an entire block of destroyed structures. What was a fallen tree on a small street became a display of fallen ashes, exploded shards of wood, and the charred remains of innocent rock sparrows.

Chapter Twenty-Six

"So the little brother was already in the room, right?" said a small bird.

It resembled a parrot, though in miniature form. The front of its body was covered almost entirely in green feathers, with yellow feathers on its top and back. The bird's head was rounded, as was its small beak, and it had dark stripes that extended from the back of its head to the base of its tail. It spoke with an Australian accent.

"Yah, yah…no, I got that, I got that," responded a second bird, which was nearly identical to the first in almost every way, including a matching accent.

The two birds sat along the bank of an inland body of water surrounded by tall blades of grass. Trees were visible in the distance.

"Yah, right, forgot I had mentioned it," said the first bird. "So the little brother was in the room, right? And the mum, for a reason I will never understand, completely redid the entire design of the room."

"What does that mean, mate?"

"Well, she moved everything around, see?" the first bird responded. He used his wings to create gestures for the various objects he attempted to describe. "So the elder one's bed was like this all winter long, ya follow? The two beds was straight with one another."

"They was parallel?" asked the second bird.

"Yah, yah…they was parallel. All winter long, one bed was on one side of the room, the other bed was on the opposite wall."

"Well that's kinda sad, innit? I mean, they're only two brothers. Why did they have to be on opposite sides of the room?"

"Caleb, are you gonna let me tell this story or not?" asked the first bird, upset over the unwanted commentary.

"My apologies, Dom! I try to set the scene as to get a better sense of it all," responded Caleb.

"Thank you," continued Dominic. "So as I was saying, the beds were parallel all winter long, right? And so the older brother would come in at night, but would do a whole run-and-leap routine every night at lights-out."

"Like a dance? Seems a bit much, especially before bedtime," commented Caleb.

"Well, it wasn't like a performance or nothin'. Not like he was trainin' for the Olympics. It was just something he did every night," replied Dominic. "The little brother was tucked in his bed, nothing extraordinary for a Wednesday."

"And where were you, mate?" asked Caleb.

"I was in the cage, on the nightstand."

"Okay, the scene is set. Continue."

"The younger sibling had turned off the light, see, and what he failed to inform the older brother was that their mum had moved things about the room."

"Well that seems like an invasion of privacy, doesn't it? Why would she do that?" asked Caleb, further interested in Dominic's story.

"Best I can tell she just wanted to play mind games with her kids, you know? Keep them on their toes and let them know she's in charge."

"Makes sense. Me mum did that to me once. Pushed me straight out the nest. Told me I had to learn to fly or I'd be buggered. I learned to fly right there on the spot."

"So now the beds weren't parallel, right," Dominic continued, ignoring Caleb's commentary. "She moved them so they were perpendicular."

"Oh mate! I think I know where this is going!" Caleb responded excitedly.

"Well let me finish, let me finish," said Dominic. His wings transformed from objects he used to accentuate his gestures to visual aids to help tell his story. "So for months, the design of the room was younger brother's bed, nightstand, older brother's bed. Simple, easy to remember. But now, the mum had changed it around to younger brother's bed, just the same, older brother's bed – at a perpendicular crossing – followed by the nightstand."

"Wait," Caleb cut in. "Where was you during all of this."

"I already told you! I was kept atop the nightstand, in a cage. It was the only place that could support the weight."

"Oh, no no, yah, I remember now. Carry on," responded Caleb.

"Thank you. So here I am, minding my own bizzo, right? The younger brother is in bed, and I'm pretty sure the older brother is seconds away from his nightly ritual."

"Oh, this is going to be good, mate! I can feel it!"

"I hear the drongo coming up the steps," continued Dominic. "Which was the queue. And I look up, and from a distance I see him in the doorway. He's going for it. Just like he did every night all winter long, he locks into position and goes for the gold."

"But wasn't the light off at this point? The little brother was going to sleep."

"Would you look at that, the budgie is paying attention after all!" Dominic said to Caleb, sarcastically. "Yes, the lights were off, but that was of no matter to the drongo. He had the routine memorized to a science: run, leap, land on the bed, tuck himself in like a pair of tight grundies."

"Ha!" chuckled Caleb. "Tight grundies. You're a dag, mate."

"And so with the fury of a roo from hell, he sprints towards his bed, see. He's easily 10 clicks deep at this point, so there's no turning back. And as he does every night, the drongo takes a giant leap. But here's the kicker:

384

midair, this *galah* completely forgets that the room had been rearranged, right? So instead of landing on the bed, he's point blank headed for the nightstand."

"Wait, weren't you on the nightstand? In the fancy cage?" asked Caleb.

"Right! So because of that, I see him in the air and I'm bracing for impact, you know? I'm thinking, 'This is it! This is as far as this budgie's gonna make it! Hooroo, boys, I'll see you on the other side!'"

"And then what happened?"

"The overgrown meat-locker lands hard, squarely on the nightstand, completely smashing it to oblivion. I mean, the tree that was used to make the nightstand was in better shape than this stand itself, you know?"

"And the cage?" asked Caleb.

"Might as well been made of foil, mate. Didn't stand a chance. But the kid's atop the cage, and I'm here checking myself for life-threatening wounds. It's not every day a budgie survives an impact of that magnitude."

"And you was okay?"

"I was trapped under the shrapnel and the kid," responded Dominic. "Now, the mum was downstairs, see, and she would normally come up the steps one at a time: 1...2...3....4, all the way to 14. I only heard her feet touch steps one, six, and maybe eleven. Before any of us could make a sound, she's at the door. She immediately turns on the light and sees the drongo, spread out like a boomer in the bush, broken wood and glass everywhere. The little brother jumps out of bed and looks at what the elder had done."

"Bloody catastrophe, mate," responded Caleb. He shook his head in disbelief. "Exy furniture, gone to waste over a drongo's ill-timed landing."

"So the lights are on and the mum is seeing this, and the first thing that comes out of her mouth is, 'what happened?' And you know what the drongo responded?"

"What'd he say, mate?"

"He looked at the mum dead in the eye and said, 'I...I...I missed my bed.'"

385

The two birds laughed together, hysterically.

"I missed my bed!" Dominic repeated. Tears streamed down his face from such excessive laughter.

A female bird, nearly identical to Caleb and Dominic though slightly smaller, overheard as the two birds laughed. She hopped from the edge of the water to where they stood.

"Hey Dom, Caleb. What are you boys laughing on about?" she asked them.

"I.........I......." was all Dominic was able to say between fits of laughter.

"Oh, Dominic. You didn't tell Caleb the 'I missed my bed' story, did you?" The two male birds laughed with even greater force when they heard her say the title of the story. "The two of you must be the lamest ducks in this entire pond."

"Oh now, Maddie!" Dominic responded, his laughter slowly subsided. "There's no need for name calling. We was just having a laugh, that's all."

"Wait, mate!" shouted Caleb, his laughter slightly calmed. "What happened next? How did you escape?"

"Oh yah! I didn't finish," responded Dominic.

"Oh lord, here we go," said Maddie.

"So the mum gets the drongo up. Meanwhile, the little brother is in hysterics. He's like one of those tin toys all wound up. He's laughing and laughing. The mum gets the drongo off the floor, then picks up the cage. Only that the top of the cage is detached from the bottom now, so I'm as free as the Omega at that point. It's now or never for your boy Dominic. I go for it, and fly out of the room."

"Good on ya, mate!" responded Caleb. "Way to take advantage of the sitch, especially after a near-death experience, mind you."

"I fly out of the room, which makes the younger lad laugh even harder. The kid can't breathe he's laughing so hard. So I make my way down to the first floor, through the living area, through the kitchen, and out the open back window."

"Classic maneuvering, mate," said Caleb.

"Whatever prevents me from the barbie, right?" said Dominic. Maddie rolled her eyes. "And it's night out, so I figure I go onto the roof and wait it out until lights up. And you wanna know what happened after that?"

"What, mate?" asked Caleb.

"That little joey of a younger brother laughed almost non-stop for the next two hours. I could hear him from the outside! The mum had to separate the two because the little one wouldn't stop laughing."

"Okay, that's a bit much," interjected Maddie. "The drongo part, believable although a stretch. The broken cage, makes for a good story so I'll allow it. The joey of a younger brother laughing to the point he had to go, that's just theatre, Dom. Now I'm positive none of that actually happened."

"That's the whole truth!" said Dominic. "At lights up I left and flew back here."

"Seems furphy, Dominic," responded Maddie. "A total exaggeration of the truth."

"Erroneous!" cried Dominic. "If I am telling even the slightest bit of a lie, then may I be struck by the fury of the flock, right where I stand!"

—CRASH! BOOM! SPLASH!—

An unidentified object relegated itself to subsonic speed and quickly lost both altitude and momentum. It struck the surface of the water, which forced it to bounce and ricochet like a smooth rock thrown at a precise angle. The object flew beyond the shore of the small lake, zoomed at incredible speed in the centimeters of open space between Dominic, Caleb, and Maddie, then rolled forcibly onto the tall grass. Its forward thrust came to a sudden stop after it rebounded repeatedly on solid ground.

The three small birds looked at one another. Dominic's eyes were opened widely, as were the mouths of Caleb and Maddie. They looked in the direction of the fallen object.

"On second thought," Dominic opened. "Maybe parts of that story are not as accurate as I originally remember."

The three birds immediately flew to the crash site. They brushed through the tall blades of grass and saw the divots left behind by the object as it struck the ground with intense force. A small trail of blue-colored feathers led the birds to where the object came to a stop. They approached cautiously. The birds saw that it was not an unidentified being which fell from the unknown, but rather a bird who crash-landed from an extraordinary altitude and at ridiculous speed. It was blue in color, with two long tail feathers that extended beyond the length of its body.

"What is it, Maddie?" asked Caleb, nervously. He stepped closely behind her.

"I don't know," Maddie responded. "But whatever it is it's bigger than the three of us so don't do anything stupid. That goes double for you, Dom."

"I neither did nor said anything and already I'm being wrongfully accused," responded Dominic.

The three small birds stepped slowly towards the crash-landed body. The two male birds kept themselves a few paces behind the female. She brushed away a few of the taller blades of grass, which revealed the face of the foreign flyer. It was unconscious, though it breathed heavily. On the side of its head was a small, circular object, where a red light flashed repeatedly.

"Is it dead?" Caleb asked as he saw the full length of the bird on the ground.

"Nah. Can't be," responded Maddie. "It's still breathing."

"What's this on its head, then?" asked Dominic. He reached over Maddie and extended the tip of his wing toward the circular object on the fallen aviator.

"Dominic!" exclaimed Maddie. "Don't—"

Maddie's warning came fractions-of-a-second too late. Dominic tapped the object, just once. There was no response from the unconscious bird.

"This one's done for, mates," said Dominic.

Caleb gasped and brought the tips of his wings to his beak.

"How do you know?" Caleb asked, his voice hidden behind his wings and closer to a faint, high-pitched whisper.

"I've seen this before," responded Dominic. "Me and a mate of mine. In Sydney."

"Oh, shut it, Dominic," said Maddie. "You and your tales."

"It's not fantasy, Maddie! Honest! Me and my flatmate, Joe, was puckering about the town when we see a lorikeet—"

"—One of them rainbow colored ones?" interrupted Caleb. He lowered his wings as he became interested in yet another of Dominic's stories.

"Yah, one of them," responded Dominic. "So this lorikeet must've taken in one too many pints of amber fluid and then made the unwise decision to take flight while inebriated."

"Then what happened, Dom?" asked Caleb.

"The sorry stirrer lifts off the ground, makes a single-way into a tree, head-first with no helmet, then nose-dives straight to oblivion."

"Did he die?" asked Caleb, worried over the fate of a bird he had never known prior to the story.

"Not before spewing a liquid laugh all over hisself," responded Dominic. "He was pushing daisies by later that afternoon."

Caleb respectfully bowed his head. He mourned for the loss of a fellow bird. Maddie stared harshly at Dominic.

"You're telling me," Maddie opened. "That you witnessed a rainbow lorikeet—"

"—Me and me flatmate, Joe," interrupted Dominic.

"Right...you and your flatmate, saw a rainbow lorikeet. In Sydney."

"Yah, so far so good."

"Who was so buggered, that he flew head-first into a tree and died on impact?"

"You left out the liquid laugh portion, Maddie," said Caleb.

"And you expect me to believe that?" Maddie asked Dominic.

"Well…yah. That's how it hap—"

The large blue bird instantly raised its upper body. It was completely out of sorts, lost in both space and time, confused as to what occurred just moments prior. Maddie, Dominic and Caleb immediately froze in fear. Even from a seated position, the blue bird was significantly taller than them, and they had no intention to discover whether or not it was a friend or foe. The blue bird turned its head.

"Where am I?" the larger bird asked.

His eyes looked directly at the small trio, with an expression as cold as arctic ice. The light on the blue bird's circular device changed from red to green.

"You're in Australia, mate," responded Dominic. His fear was evident in his voice and in how he stood before the threat of the larger bird. "The Outback. In the interior. West of the Great Divide."

"Are you gonna give him directions to the nearest servo or something, Dom?" responded Maddie.

Her eyes remained on the large bird as she addressed Dominic's stupidity.

The blue bird changed his expression. It looked at each of the three small birds in the same manner a predator examined its forthcoming meal.

"Who are you people?" asked the blue bird. His voice was rough and barely audible.

"We're birds, mate. Not people," Caleb responded.

"Oh my g…" Maddie said aloud, mostly to herself. "These two idiots are gonna get me killed."

She cautiously took a step forward to address the taller bird.

"We're budgies!" Maddie said, loudly and slowly. "This is our lake. You're in Australia."

The tall bird stood. He looked at the panorama of the scene. His eyes were emotionless and his face became expressionless. He was in the middle of nowhere, far from civilization or anything he found even remotely familiar.

"Hey, mate," began Caleb. "Why the long face?"

"Matches that tail," said Dominic.

Maddie's gaze threw daggers at Dominic.

The blue bird looked down at the three small birds. His balance was off, and one of his eyelids was more open than the other.

"Wait," the tall bird said, a hint of delight evident in his tone. "You're budgies!"

"Oi, our reputation precedes us," responded Caleb, who earned the same response from Maddie as did Dominic's last phrase.

"What's your name, mate?" Dominic asked, loudly and slowly.

"Dioni," he responded, the sound of his voice difficult to comprehend.

The look in Dioni's eyes informed the budgies that his mind drifted far from where his body physically stood. The budgies looked at one another and shrugged their shoulders.

"The only *what*, mate?" asked Caleb. He spoke as slowly and loudly as the others.

Dioni looked at the vastness of the empty field. A faint hint of clouds was visible in the distance. The land itself was completely untouched and undisturbed.

"Huh," Dioni responded.

Dioni's eyes rolled to the back of his head. His legs gave out, and he flailed in the breeze like a fragile plant whose leaves far outweighed its roots. The budgies cautiously stepped back. They did not desire for their final resting place to be beneath the weight of the larger bird.

Dioni snapped upright, in perfect posture and at full attention. He opened his eyes, though his pupils were smaller than before. He made an abrupt, forward motion with his head, as if he choked or had an object trapped in his throat.

"Oh sweet mercy. This is it!" shouted Dominic. "Cover yourselves, mates! Liquid laugh!"

Dioni lowered his head, opened his beak, and projectile vomited what was only describable as an array of colorful, transparent fluid. He drenched the budgies entirely in a disgusting, goop-like substance too vile to describe.

Immediately after doing so, Dioni's eyes once again rolled to the back of his head. His legs were no longer able to sustain his weight, which caused his body to collapse backwards. The back of his head crashed against the vomit-soaked ground.

The three budgies witnessed the entire ordeal, petrified in their protective stances and saturated in a foul-smelling liquid.

"Ugh!" shouted Maddie. "My mouth was partially open!"

Caleb approached Dioni and saw that his eyes were narrowly exposed. He crouched to be as close to Dioni's eye level as possible.

"Hey, mate," Caleb said to Dioni. The light of cognizance faded from Dioni's eyes. "Welcome to Oz."

The last object Dioni saw was the large smile of a budgie – up close and personal – with two other budgies behind him; one of the budgies gagged in disgust while the other desperately attempted to clean herself. Dioni lost his ability to focus as his mind drifted to a new state of exhaustion.

…

An empty house – adjacent to an unpaved trail which was far from the nearest city, village, town, neighborhood, or any nearby civilization – stood amidst a forest of tall trees which further barricaded it from any point on any map. It was peaceful and quiet, serene, where no living creature – woodland or otherwise – knew of its existence. The four walls of the home were held by a small roof, which further hid the house within the trees. The house itself was almost entirely empty, save for a wooden chair, a matching table, and a far-outdated television.

A tiny dot of light projected from the center of the small television screen, which sat atop the wooden table. The voice of a woman was heard as the small light grew larger with each second.

"...And for more on this story we go to our chief meteorologist to further explain the details of the absolutely strange weather pattern in southern Mexico," said the woman's voice, calm and collected. "Scott, what do you make of this?"

"Thank you, Helen," a man's voice responded.

The image on the screen grew larger. Ever so slowly, the screen showed a man who stood behind a digitized map. The picture came into focus, although the color was difficult to correct as the television struggled to display a clear shot.

"Folks, you know how we tend to complain that winter's here in Chicago last for nine months?" said Scott, the meteorologist on screen. "Well, after you hear more about this, you're going to be glad you live this far north."

The picture on the elder device slowly revealed a man who stood before a large map of North and Central America. He wore a silver colored suit, with a red shirt and tie. Behind him was another screen, which he used as a visual aid. Two sets of animated arrows pointed in one direction, while another series of arrows pointed in a circular motion. A white, cloud-like image was animated to move in a circular pattern which repeated consistently as the man spoke.

"We've followed this storm path in the Gulf of Mexico here," continued the man as he pointed on the screen. "We can officially confirm that this is a category three hurricane. Now, while Florida and most of the Caribbean islands were spared the brunt of this storm, it appears that southern Mexico and parts of Central America are not going to be so lucky."

The man turned himself. He used body language along with the surrounding digital images to further explain the weather phenomenon.

"Our storm indicators and expert trackers are telling us that winds pushing down from the north are literally changing the trajectory of this hurricane, forcing it further south, while the hurricane's path is consistently west. The good news of this comes from our hurricane prediction models that are showing us that the high north winds will likely push this storm further south and weaken as it travels out of the Gulf of Mexico, though parts of Mexico, Cuba, and maybe even the Cayman Islands could be affected by torrential rain. We're definitely keeping a close eye on this storm."

The map behind the man shifted from the Gulf of Mexico to a considerably sized animation of a second storm, hundreds of miles west of Baja California.

"If this weather pattern was not strange enough, then take a look at what we are seeing on the other side of Mexico. This large, tropical storm formation that you see here is the result of odd wind patterns pushing south from the northern Pacific, while warmer winds from as far south as the southern hemisphere push north. Once again, all signs point to a hurricane, though this storm is building and travelling considerably faster than most tropical storms, or faster than most hurricanes for that matter, in this region. Should this storm also continue in its current path, it will likely make landfall somewhere around the central region of Mexico, or maybe further south. The good news from the Pacific side is that the storm seems to be pushing further south and going further west, which tells us that while it is gaining strength, it will likely pass over any of these populated regions and die down somewhere in the Pacific."

The image behind the man changed to display the entirety of the region. On the screen was the meteorological presentation of two massive storms as they occurred, simultaneously, along both coasts of southern Mexico.

"So as you can see here, two major storms are forming on both sides of Mexico, at the same time. This weather pattern is now being called the Twin Hurricane System, which is extremely unusual. In fact, there has not been a recorded instance in which this has occurred since we began keeping track of these storms from our weather center. Earlier today, the World Meteorological Center released the names of these twin storms, which are Hurricane Elijah in the Gulf, and Hurricane Eliza in the Pacific. We'll keep you informed as these storms continue to develop."

The images on the screens behind the man transitioned to an animated display of the skyline of the city of Chicago. A series of vertical blocks and numbers appeared on the television.

"Back here at home, we are looking at a steady couple of days with highs in the —"

The television suddenly turned black. Its source of power was cut, which rendered its visual and audio capabilities to complete darkness.

The eerie sound of faint laughter was heard. A pale reflection was seen from the glass of the television. Only the silhouette of a man was visible.

"That's perfect," said a mysterious, low-toned voice.

...

"You suppose those long tail feathers do anything for him?" asked Caleb. He sat on a self-made perch. At a close distance was Dioni, who remained in deep sleep, unmoved from his last position.

"They do more for him than you know," responded Dominic as he paced back and forth in front of Caleb.

"Like what, Dom?"

"Well, if he's a northie, then he'll likely need them for navigation. Gives him an odd flight pattern, you know?"

"Oh, yah, makes sense. And what if he's not?"

"If he's not a northie, then he's definitely tropical. Which means that those long tailfeathers tell the girl birds of his kind that he is...uh...how shall I say? Um...open for business..."

Dominic stopped and looked at Caleb. He wondered whether or not Caleb understood the subtlety.

"Open for business?" asked Caleb. "What type a business do you suppose he's running, Dom? Like a coffee shop or something? You think he sells boogie boards to nippers?"

"Mate," Dominic responded. He sighed then turned to Caleb. "You couldn't run a chook raffle in a farm, could you?"

"Sure I could," responded Caleb. "It's a raffle! I'd just be reading numbers!"

Dominic looked up and saw as Maddie flew in from the distance, trailed by over a dozen smaller budgies who looked nearly identical to one another.

"Brace yourself for incoming," Dominic said to Caleb. The two birds watched the small flock of budgies as they landed nearby.

"Hey boys," Maddie said to Dominic and Caleb. "Did you saps miss me?"

"Not particularly, no," mumbled Dominic.

"What was that?" asked Maddie.

"Dom said, 'not particularly, no'," responded Caleb.

Dominic shook his head and rolled his eyes.

"Be that as it may," Maddie said as she scowled at Dominic. "How is 'the only'?"

The younger budgies gathered closely behind her. They hoped to see the phenomenon but did so from a safe distance.

"Hasn't moved," responded Caleb.

"Same place he's been this entire time," said Dominic. "Still alive, though."

"Perfect!" Maddie responded, optimistically. She turned to address the younger budgies. "Class, lets gather around the blue bird so you can all see what it looks like."

The younger budgies did as they were told and vigilantly surrounded Dioni as he lay coldly on the ground.

"Miss Madison," said one of the young budgies, nervously. "Is it safe? Does the blue bird eat budgies?"

"He's harmless," Maddie responded. "Plus, he has a small beak, not very pointed, and it's not hooked. So what does that mean?" she asked the class.

The students were too nervous to recall the correct answer.

"Emily," she directed one of the younger students who stood further from Dioni. "What does it tell us if this bird does not have a hooked bill?"

"That it doesn't eat other birds?" Emily responded, timidly.

"That's right. So if this bird is not a predator, then we are perfectly safe. Come now, move around it," Maddie instructed her class.

The young budgies moved slowly and carefully to form a tight circle around Dioni. Caleb and Dominic observed, though they remained on alert should the larger bird suddenly awaken.

"Now, what type of bird is this?" Maddie asked her students.

"Is it a big Aussie wren?" asked a young male.

"Why would you say that, Billy?" responded Maddie.

"Well, it's big and blue."

"Yes, that's a good observation. But other birds can be blue, can they not?"

"Miss Madison?" asked a female student. She raised her wing high above her head.

"Yes, Isla?"

"It's a crimson rosella."

"Interesting guess, Isla. Why do you say that?"

"Because it looks like one."

"Yes," Maddie responded. "But a crimson rosella is…well, crimson, isn't it? This one's all one color from the back and most of its front. It just has white feathers on the front side. Why do you suppose that is?"

"Miss Madison?" said another young male. He had an unusually large head for his small size.

"Yes, Joseph? Do you have an answer for the class?"

"This bird looks an awful lot like a Guatemalan resplendent quetzal," responded Joseph. "A male resplendent quetzal. It has the exact same structure, roughly the same height, size and length, and those long tail feathers indicate he's old enough for mating."

Caleb immediately turned to Dominic.

"I thought you said those long tail feathers meant he was running a business."

"Caleb," Dominic said. He stood before his colleague and placed his wings on the other's shoulders. "You're the pride of all Australia. Never forget that, mate."

"Aww," Caleb responded, a smile beamed on his face. "What a nice thing to say."

"That might be correct, Joseph," Maddie spoke over Caleb and Dominic. "But then how do you explain his color? What makes this, 'the only', so unique?"

"Dioni," responded the blue bird on the ground, in a harsh voice which momentarily stunned the younger budgies and alarmed the elders. His eyes remained closed.

No sound nor motion was made by any of the birds. Only the breeze which brushed against the tall blades of grass gave notice that time had indeed not ceased in that moment.

"Come…come again, sir?" asked Maddie.

She stepped back slowly and mouthed and gestured to instruct the young budgies to raise their wings for sudden takeoff.

"Dioni," he responded, his voice rasped though slightly more audible than before. "My name. It's not 'the only'. It's Dee-Oh-Nee. Dioni."

Maddie looked to Caleb and Dominic.

"Right. Dee-Oh-Nee. Got it."

She gestured signals to the older males to protect her and the younglings from any potential harm, none of which either of them understood.

"Uh…sorry for the mix-up, sir," said Maddie. "You mentioned it just before blacking out and we couldn't quite gather what you had said."

Emily gradually paced closer towards Dioni's head. She leaned closer. Dioni's eyelid flashed open. His large, black eye came into focus. He looked directly at her. Emily screamed in fear, which caused the rest of her classmates to do the same. In a panic, the students lifted from the ground and flew away.

Dioni lifted his head and followed the younglings as they fled for their lives.

"Where are they going?" he asked. "Was it something I said?"

"Well, that's the last time they're gonna trust me, I'll tell you that," responded Maddie as she watched her students flee in terror. "They're gonna tell the headmaster what occurred here."

"What happened?" asked Dioni.

He lifted his head, which exposed his pathfinder.

"Oh, nothing much, really," responded Dominic.

"All's you did was make a grand entrance," said Caleb. "Introduced yourself, then buggered out right in the spot you're in now."

"But not before spewing a vile liquid from your mouth," said Dominic. "Like a bloody geyser."

"I did?" asked Dioni. "I don't remember any of that."

"Well then, what do you recall?" asked Maddie.

"I remember being in the sky," said Dioni. His brow moved up as he attempted to recall the actions which led to the present. "Then I remember hitting the ground, and then you saying you were budgies, and then I fell asleep."

"Fell asleep?" Dominic said, harshly. "Mate, you were far from just 'fell asleep'. That state of slumber left you hours before you landed in the Outback."

"Yah, mate," chimed Caleb. "We thought you was dead. We did everything we could to wake you, except maybe pull your tailfeathers, and you didn't move at all."

Dioni lifted his wing then rolled his body to free the other wing trapped below his own weight. He stalled for a moment to gain the energy to push himself from the ground. The three smaller birds stepped back to protect themselves. They provided ample room for Dioni to stand.

"How long was I out?" asked Dioni.

"Just shy of a whole twenty-four," responded Caleb.

"I lost a whole day?" Dioni asked, shocked by Caleb's response.

"I wouldn't say *lost*, mate," said Dominic. "More like misplaced."

Dioni pushed his upper body from the ground, which provided enough leverage for him to bring his legs beneath himself. He stood, though without the proper strength in his legs to hold himself upright. His body tipped. The three budgies sprang into action and used their wings to hold him vertically.

"Find your balance, Dioni?" asked Maddie. "It might take a sec."

"Yes," Dioni responded. "I'm up."

"Good," said Dominic. "The three of us is gonna let go and slowly walk away. You ready, mate?"

"Yes...yes, I can hold myself up. Thank you."

The budgies kept their wings high as they slowly paced away from him. Dioni remained on his feet, which allowed the budgies to feel enough at ease to lower their guard.

"Right then," opened Dominic. "He's awake. He's vertical. What now?"

"Can we keep him as our pet?" asked Caleb. "I bet his business closed down, seeing as how he's not there to manage it and all."

"What?" asked Maddie, snarkily. "Wha...no! He's not a pet! He's a bird! Look at him. He may as well be one of us."

"Him? A budgie?" asked Caleb. "Awful big budgie."

"With an awful haircut," chimed Dominic.

"Dioni?" Maddie asked. She ignored the statements made by her fellow budgerigars. "Are you hungry? Would you like to eat?"

"Umm," responded Dioni. "That would be great, actually. I'm starving."

"No surprise there, mate," remarked Dominic. "You must've left at least two days' worth of meals on the grass. Did you eat krill or something?"

"Dominic!" sneered Maddie.

"Yah, in liquid form," remarked Caleb.

"Caleb!"

"I...I don't remember that," responded Dioni. "But food would be great."

"Good," said Maddie. The cold scowl of her face changed entirely as she turned to Dioni. "What'll it be? What do you eat?"

"I...uh...I don't know," responded Dioni. "What do budgies normally eat for breakfast?"

"Brekky?" asked Dominic. "Mate, brekky passed us hours ago. You missed first light."

"I did?" Dioni asked.

"You did, Dioni," said Maddie, in a gentler tone. "But you are welcome to join us for lunch."

"Uh...okay," responded Dioni. "What do budgies eat for lunch?"

"We don't really eat lunch," responded Caleb. "We's eat once a day. Brekky. By the water."

Dioni's facial expression changed to visually express his misunderstanding.

"I apologize for the confusion, Dioni," said Maddie. "Lunch to us is not typical to what it might be for you."

"So there's no food?" asked Dioni. "Only at first light?"

"Oh, there is, but not here," responded Maddie. "We go as a large group to find it. Seeds and grain have been scarce around the Outback lately. This time of year in particular."

"So you hunt...seeds?" Dioni asked. The two male budgies chuckled.

"No, Dioni," said Maddie. "Seeds and grain must be found, not hunted. We fly as a group to find where there is enough food for all of us."

"Yah," said Dominic. "Big group. Really big!"

"Yah," said Caleb. "We had a group so big once that it knocked a grain truck off the road in Queensland. Had grain and insects for nearly a whole season that year. Remember, Dom? We didn't have to murmurate nearly that entire summer."

"We did, but it was mostly for fun," responded Dominic.

"You murmurate to find food?" asked Dioni.

"Yes, Dioni," responded Maddie. "But not solely to find food. Sometimes we do it for sport. You know, just to keep up our instincts. Other times it serves as a distraction."

"When you do murmurate to find food, what then?" Dioni asked.

"We feast, mate!" responded Dominic. "It's not every day one finds enough to feed five thousand budgies."

"I'm sorry?" Dioni said to Dominic. "How many did you say?"

"Five thousand," responded Dominic. "At the very least. We haven't done this year's census."

Dioni became stunned. He was trained to murmurate with only a couple hundred birds, and they were simulated starlings. A flock of thousands was enough to overwhelm him.

"Does your kind know how to murmurate?" asked Caleb.

"Caleb! That's incredibly rude!" shouted Maddie.

"No, it's okay," responded Dioni. He turned to Caleb. "I learned how to do it in school. As long as my pathfinder is connected to yours, I should be able to stay within the group."

The three birds looked at one another, confused by Dioni's words.

"I'm sorry?" Dominic said to Dioni. "As long as your which-is-what is connected to our what-in-the-who, now?"

"What's that, then, mate?" asked Caleb.

"My pathfinder...this," Dioni responded. He turned his head to show the device to the budgies. "It helps me...hold on, you don't use pathfinders?"

"No," responded the three small birds.

"What does it do?" asked Caleb.

"I've seen one of them before," said Dominic. Maddie rolled her eyes. "It's a communications device. A tracker tool. It lets him connect back to the office at any time. Probably senses and translates for him too."

"Yes, that's right!" responded Dioni. Maddie's expression changed as she became surprised by Dominic's knowledge. "How are you able to murmurate with so many birds?"

"Instinctually," responded Dominic.

"Yah," said Caleb. "We've always known how. We was born with it. I can fly with a hundred thousand budgies with my eyes closed, and I won't crash into a single one."

"With your eyes closed, ey?" said Maddie. "That's not the song you were singing when you plowed into the side of that seed truck."

"There was seeds painted on the truck, Maddie!" exclaimed Caleb. "That wasn't my fault! Any budgie coulda done it."

"And yet none of us did," said Dominic.

"Dioni," said Maddie. "You are welcome to join us for our flight. The rest of the group is on the other side of the lake. If you're hungry, there might be a few leftover scraps near the brekky grounds. But when we get to the grain fields, you can have as much as your heart desires."

"Yah, mate," said Caleb. "Stick with us and you'll never be hungry again."

"Not with those tailfeathers, he won't," said Dominic. He leaned over and inspected the long feathers on the ground, behind Dioni. "You better find a way to tuck those in or something. It's bad enough you're blue."

"Is it a problem? That I'm blue?" asked Dioni, worried over a characteristic beyond his control.

"Nah," responded Caleb. "We's got blue budgies in the group. Not a lot of them. Me mate Simon is a bluey."

"He's right," Maddie chimed in. "Your color is not a problem, but those tailfeathers will be. They'll change your flight pattern and you won't be able to keep along with us."

"What should I do?" asked Dioni.

He reached behind and pulled his long tailfeathers towards his lower back to conceal them beneath his wings.

"Just try to hold them in place," responded Dominic. "But don't you dare lose them!"

"Okay..." Dioni responded. He rolled each of his tailfeathers into a ball and held them in place with his lower wings. He stood up and successfully concealed them. "Does this work?"

"That's perfect, mate!" responded Caleb. "You could absolutely pass as a big bluey!"

Dioni smiled. He felt better to be away from danger and in a place where he was welcomed. The budgies failed to mention or even notice his status or responsibilities; if they had, they did not show it. The budgies cared more to treat their guest as one of their own than to report problems to him. If life for these birds was so simple, Dioni would certainly choose a lifetime as a big bluey rather than another day as the Omega bird.

"Good," said Maddie. "Follow us, then."

Maddie shifted her body to face the direction in which she intended to travel. She spread her wings, leapt, then lifted herself from the ground. Dominic and Caleb followed suit and remained closely behind Maddie, one at each side.

Dioni bent down and opened his wings. The ball of his tailfeathers fell, rolled onto the ground, and extended to the full length of each feather. He sighed and grunted. He reached back and rolled each feather into its own ball, then grasped each ball with both feet. Doing so not only looked and felt strange, it also prevented Dioni from proper lift-off.

Dioni unraveled his tailfeathers and held one in each wing. In an act of brilliance, he crossed the feathers and wrapped them around his lower body, which created an odd fashion statement though it addressed the problem. He then tied the ends of the feathers to make a tight belt around his waist.

Dioni looked up and saw as his new friends travelled further into the sky. He secured his tailfeather-belt, spread his wings, leapt from the ground, and became airborne.

The three budgies landed near the outer bank of the local waterhole, where hundreds of other budgies, all of whom looked nearly identical, stood in groups and shared in small conversation. Dioni landed behind them, seconds afterward.

"We're on time," said Dominic. "I thought we'd have to catch up to the group, but we're on time."

"I could ask Simon if he knows when we're lifting," said Caleb.

He craned his head in search of his friend, who was hidden among the scores of birds.

"Have some water, Dioni, and grab all the berries you'd like," Maddie said. "There's not much left, but whatever you find is yours."

"Thank you," Dioni responded.

He looked on the ground and saw the remains of what was likely a feast. He searched through the crumbs and found scraps that were only partially touched.

"There he is," Caleb said excitedly. "Hey Sy!"

Caleb gained the attention of a blue budgie who was in the middle of a conversation, hidden perfectly in plain sight among the others. By a method which was possible only to budgerigars, Caleb identified the sole blue budgie in the large group. It was a talent limited to birds with a lifetime of experience.

Simon saw Caleb, who waived his wings and craned his head back and forth. He ended his conversation and walked towards the outer bank where Caleb, Maddie, and Dominic stood.

"What's this about, then?" asked Simon. "You buds find a fallen falcon of some sort? A group of younglings flew in a few minutes ago claimin' Miss Madison took them to the outers to get eaten by some killer tropical bird. Oh Maddie, the headmaster is looking for you."

"I knew it," responded Maddie.

"He's not a killer, Sy," said Caleb.

"What is it, then? Not another one of your 'brilliant discoveries', ey, Maddie?" Simon asked.

Maddie scoffed at the blue budgie's arrogance.

"He's a new friend," responded Caleb. "Some sort of tropical bird.

Runs his own business, sells boards to nippers. We made him an honorary budgie. A bluey, just like you, mate."

"Ha! That's good for a laugh," responded Simon. "Honorary budgie. Where is it, then?"

Simon's eyes followed as Dioni raised himself from the ground where he pecked for scraps, to full height, where he stood with a mouthful of berry morsels. Dioni towered behind Caleb, Maddie and Dominic.

"That's a *big* bluey!" exclaimed Simon. He glared in awe as Dioni attempted to chew the food stuffed in his mouth. "No wonder the younglings fled. You can't bring that thing with us! Oh, and Maddie, the headmaster…"

"I know, Simon!" said Maddie.

"What? Why not?" asked Dominic. "He's not gonna harm no one. He's not a hunty."

"Looks like one," responded Simon.

The four small birds looked at Dioni. A red liquid poured from his beak and onto the berry-stained ground.

"Nah," said Caleb. "This budgie's big, but he's harmless. Aren't you, big fella? He kinda looks like you, Sy."

"Like me?" asked Simon. He stepped forward and looked up to Dioni. "No self-respecting blue budgie's gonna have a haircut like that. I don't care how big it is."

Dioni, mid chew, rolled his eyes.

"Big fella you got here," Simon said to Dioni. Simon turned his attention to the others. "Can this one murmurate? If he can't he's likely to crash the flight."

"Yah, he can," responded Caleb. "He's got a findpather. It tells him how to fly."

"Well, good then," said Simon. "The flight's gonna leave any second now and I don't need no foreign bird sullying my good bluey name."

Dioni chewed and managed to swallow the mouthful of scraps he found on the ground. He wiped the remains from his beak, took a deep breath, and extended his wing to Simon.

"Hi," he greeted. "My name is Dio—"

Dioni's introduction was cut by the sound of thousands of small birds who lifted from the ground. They communicated by action and not by spoken word, and like a tidal wave, the thousands of small birds lifted in increased numbers until they were able to temporarily darken the Australian sky. Dioni was astonished.

"This is it, Dioni," said Maddie. Her body was bowed with her wings spread widely. "Stay close and stick with the pattern. I'll come find you if you break formation."

Maddie, Simon, Caleb, and Dominic took to the sky. Dioni wiped the tips of his wings, bent his body forward, spread his wings, then leapt and joined the flight formation as close to the others as possible.

Unlike the murmuration simulator of the Flight Academy – where every bird was accounted for and which was programmed to outmaneuver predators – the real-life version of a murmuration was far different than how Dioni was taught. Whereas the simulator held him in place and enabled him to track the movement of each bird in the group with relative ease, the non-simulated version lacked the same qualities. Dioni's pathfinder calculated the individual flight patterns of thousands of birds, simultaneously. While it successfully highlighted each bird in the flock, it also attempted to predict thousands of individual motions, which was impossible for a single pathfinder to do, even if it was an Omega class.

Shortly after he joined the group flight, Dioni broke formation. His pathfinder navigated his every action and directed him to fly in pre-calculated movements, which did not match the flight pattern of the murmuration. He became frustrated and confused. The budgies did not fly in predictable patterns, but rather in completely improvised formations which each one of them simply understood without the need of verbal commands or instructions. The budgie method of murmuration was purely instinctual, an adapted ability which was passed from generation to generation.

Dioni recalled how he struggled with his first attempts at murmuration in the simulator. He momentarily glided away from the formation, regained his focus, then reengaged into their flight pattern. On his second attempt, Dioni focused more closely on the directions given to him by his pathfinder.

As it struggled to maintain perfect calculations of the actions of such a vast quantity of birds, Dioni's pathfinder instructed him to fly in three different directions, simultaneously. Confused by the navigation, Dioni once again broke from the formation. He glided toward the ground and lifted his wings as he drifted away from the mass motion of the budgies. In a single turn, thousands of small birds moved in perfect unison.

Dioni failed to understand the nature of the danger which headed directly at him; the murmuration changed direction, which placed him squarely in their flightpath. Moments prior to a midair collision – which was far less forgiving than a failed simulation – Dioni pushed his head down and instantly dove. Had Dioni hesitated for even a fraction of a second longer, his actions would have caused a chain-reaction of catastrophic proportions.

Dioni's heart raced faster as he glided to the ground. He set his feet down, then looked up to see how the budgies were able to murmurate with such ease. He observed and noticed there were no patterns – no method to determine their aerial behavior – nor could he understand how they were able to communicate, individually and as a group, without the use of navigational equipment.

Maddie looked to the ground. She saw as Dioni studied a skill which could not be taught. Maddie safely broke formation and drifted away from the mass of budgies. She looped around the motion of the birds then glided to Dioni.

"Oi," Maddie said as she hovered near Dioni then carefully landed beside him. "Can't murmurate, can you? No need to feel shame. It happens to a lot of birds, especially the bigger ones."

"No, but I know I can do this," responded Dioni. "I really can. I've done it before, in a simulator."

"A simulator? For a budgie murmuration? Highly unlikely."

"Not for budgies. It was for starlings."

"Then there's your answer!" said Maddie.

Dioni turned his attention from the cloud of budgies in the sky to the single bird who stood beside him.

"What is?" he asked.

"You studied starling but you're speaking budgie!"

"Speaking budgie? I thought—"

"—And therein lies your problem," Maddie interrupted. "You're overthinking it. Budgies don't fly like starlings, mate. It's unpredictable."

"Even by you?"

"By me, by you, by anyone. Just go up there and fly for the joy of being a free budgie…well, an honorary budgie in your case. Pay attention to what your mates are doing and fly accordingly."

"How do I do that?" asked Dioni.

"Well, ignore your findpather, for one," replied Maddie. "Use your instincts. Fly as one bird, not as one in thousands."

Dioni looked up. He followed the murmuration's consistent motion.

"Think you got it?" asked Maddie.

She observed him as he stood and studied the action in the sky.

"I think so," Dioni responded.

"Good! Let's get up there before you go and ruin everything by thinking again."

Maddie and Dioni leapt and lifted from the ground. The two birds reengaged into the active flight formation created by the thousands of budgies. Within seconds they reached the large group, and Maddie became lost among the crowd.

Dioni took Maddie's advice to heart. He ignored the calculations and directions given to him by his pathfinder. Instead, he looked beyond what he observed and sought to connect to a live unit of birds in flight.

Their individual formation depended on their location within the group – whether they were in the center of the pattern or at the edge – and each budgie acted as an entity of a greater whole. As if to form a massive bird in the sky, the budgies were aware of their individual positions as well as their role in the grander formation.

Dioni maintained his direction and airspeed because he paid especially close attention to the birds who immediately surrounded him. The approached proved unsuccessful; Dioni did not take into account his size in relation to wind gusts. Nonetheless, he did not falter. Dioni rejoined the formation and moved in their aerial pattern. He was mindful of his position and location within their movements, and he observed how it was a game of chance as opposed to a strict set of rules. No one bird was in charge. Though they had no set destination, their contribution to the entire company allowed them to search the ground as a team. The budgies mastered the art of murmuration – in a method that was as visually stunning as it was personally gratifying – which enabled them to search the entire Outback with relative ease.

Within minutes, Dioni was hooked. It was a form of flight unbeknownst to any other bird. More importantly, however, was how Dioni became one among the larger mass. On land and in almost every scenario in the sky, Dioni was clearly not like the others: he was taller, he was larger, and his plumage was of a completely different color. But within the murmuration, every bird was one and the same. Dioni loved every second of it.

Time went by, though to Dioni, it felt as if the rotation of the world ceased while he was within the group. As the winds shifted and the cloud of budgies hovered over the Australian sky, the mass of birds identified their designated target in the distance. With the necessity to feed the entire group, the murmuration ended as the birds gathered and hovered above a large wheat field. Thousands of small birds spread across the golden field, where the food appeared as though it had been brought forth from the ground specifically for their enjoyment.

As was their long-standing tradition, the flock of murmurating budgies hollered with joy and delight as they hovered over their newfound source of food. The collective sound of the birds echoed and was heard from miles away. Dioni felt as one among them and joined the chorus of budgie celebration.

The murmuration transformed into a large, blanket-like formation that swayed over the wheat. The budgies landed in the fields — some plucked along the ground while most found places to perch along the stalks. There was plenty of food for all, and they made it abundantly clear that the embarrassment of riches was theirs to take.

Dioni made himself at home. He found a thicker stalk near Maddie, Caleb and Dominic, and began to pluck away at the wheat. It was more food than he would ever be able to finish in a season, yet his nearly empty stomach demanded he make the attempt to do so.

"Oi!" shouted Simon. "Looks like you were able to chase the chum," he said to Dioni as he landed on a nearby stalk.

"What?" Dioni asked with his mouth full.

"Ride the tide?" responded Simon. "Make the morsel? Pie the piper? Land the lot?"

With absolutely no knowledge of what Simon attempted to say to him, Dioni stood motionless on the stalk. He turned in every direction in search of any bird who was able and willing to translate for him.

"He's saying you kept up with us and found this field," said Dominic.

"Oh," responded Dioni. "I wess tho."

Dioni once again stuffed his mouth with more food than he was able to chew.

"Hungry, aren't ya, big fella?" said Maddie. "No matter, there's plenty for all."

"Not if he stuffs it all first," said Simon. "We only eat once a day, you know. We're supposed to start on this at first light."

A mysterious sound was heard from beneath the flock. It was not loud enough to cause any reason for worry, though it sounded as though a large being exhaled loudly. It created a small puff of air that emerged from the ground. The budgies ignored it. As birds who lived in the Australian Outback and had experience with predators of all abilities, shapes, and sizes, a small gust of wind was the least of their concerns.

"He might be bigger than us, but he can stay," continued Simon. "He didn't sully the good bluey name, so we'll accept him as one of ours."

"Oh, that's great news, mate!" Caleb responded excitedly. He turned to Dioni. "That means you're one of us, then, officially."

"Not officially, Caleb," said Maddie.

She flew from her stalk and landed on the ground.

"And why's that?" asked Caleb. He turned his attention to her. "He's already been drafted by the tribe."

"All we know of him is that he can survive a crash landing, spews waterfalls, scares children, and can murmurate," said Dominic.

"Plus he runs a small business and has a findpather," replied Caleb.

"That's not..." Dominic sighed. He turned to look at Dioni. "Sorry about him. He's three feathers shy of a full-course, if you know what I mean."

"Wahs okay," responded Dioni. His beak overflowed with food.

"Does anyone feel anything strange on their feet?" asked Maddie.

She lifted one of her legs and inspected the surface on which she stood.

"Not any more strange than usual," responded Dominic.

"What's that you're stepping on, Maddie?" asked Caleb.

Maddie took a few steps back and saw a strange pattern on the ground. Millions of tiny squares were installed across the length of the wheat field.

"I'm not entirely sure," she responded. "Seems like some kind of protective coating or something."

"For the ground?" asked Simon. "That's a stretch. You might wanna tell that to the headmaster when you see him."

"Fine then, Simon," Maddie responded, her tone changed as her annoyance of Simon's presence grew. "If you know everything, then what is it?"

"How should I know?" Simon responded. He peaked his head and followed the pattern on the ground. "From here it looks like netting."

"Netting," Maddie said. "Like what the people use for fish? That's ridiculous! Why would there be netting in a field?"

A harsh thump was heard a few aisles away. It was loud enough to capture the attention of the small birds, though not loud enough to distract Dioni from his meal.

"What was that?" asked Dominic.

"Bird fell off a stalk," responded Caleb. "Probably Lawrence again."

A second, third, fourth, and fifth thump was heard. They turned in the direction of the sounds. In the near distance, two budgies suddenly fainted and fell to the ground.

"You sure it was Lawrence?" asked Maddie.

She searched in every direction for the cause of the sudden change in their behavior.

"Not anymooooorrrrr—" replied Caleb.

He instantly fell asleep and lost all sense of balance. He fell from his perch and dropped to the ground.

"What's this, then?" Maddie asked Caleb, who lay motionless. "Caleb? You having a laugh?"

"Hey Maddie," Dominic said. "I'm not feeling so—"

Dominic fell from his perch in the wheat, followed closely by Simon. Both birds became motionless as they landed coldly on the ground.

"What's going on with you silly birrrr—" were the only words Maddie was able to muster before she lost consciousness.

Dioni looked down and saw his friends, paralyzed on the ground, lifeless. He used his pathfinder and quickly scanned the area from his perch among the wheat. The pathfinder did not detect any of the budgies nearby. He swallowed the food he had stuffed into his beak.

"Umm," Dioni said. "What's going onnnnnnn—"

The light faded from Dioni's eyes. His body lost all sense of strength, which forced him to fall from his stalk and land beside the other budgerigars.

Chapter Twenty-Seven

Chaos reigned supreme at every level of the Department of Global Climate Control. Birds of all sizes, shapes, colors, speeds and abilities moved frantically about the Trading Floor. A few birds paused every so often in front of any one of an endless supply of projected screens that displayed global weather reports of the largest natural anomaly in recorded history. Rumors flew faster than the birds themselves, and no bird knew what to expect as a result of the fury of the twin hurricane phenomenon.

The elder and experienced birds knew, more or less, the predictable behavior of their counterparts during anomaly simulations. The shiftier birds – such as sparrows, woodpeckers, and the occasional seagull – planted seeds of ideas in the minds of inexperienced negotiators, then sat back and waited for their harvest. Some birds took advantage of the naiveté of their fellow aviators, and then used the chaos of the phenomenon to make negotiations in their favor. This was considered insider trading, with no rules, laws, or policies set in place to prevent them from doing so.

The more knowledgeable, veteran birds knew better than to give any attention to the younger birds who tried desperately to make a name for themselves. They knew, beyond a shadow of a doubt, that all anomalies ended in the same fashion: the scheduled weather would reach a certain peak until it was retreated, and most everything went back to normal. Periodically, there were instances where collateral damage did occur – such as a simulated tornado aborted moments longer than scheduled – which resulted in shifted winds to nearby territories, higher rainfall than expected, and the occasional destroyed barn. The elders knew it was meaningless and unnecessary to participate in any negotiations until the anomaly cleared, which motivated the youth to target their territories.

Mimidae paced on the Trading Floor. She dodged the many birds who ran in every direction, while she paid little attention to those who flew above her. She walked quickly, as if on a mission to audit and maintain order among a society in disarray.

"Mim!" shouted Nestor, an overgrown New Zealand parrot who had better things to do.

"I'm a busy bird, Nestor." Mimidae responded. She remained on task. "What do you want?"

"I wanted to ask you something," Nestor responded. He ran in front of her in an attempt to slow her speed, which resulted in failure. "Can I ask you something?"

"Walk and talk, Nes. I have things to do."

"I know, I know. Okay, I'll be quick," Nestor said. He stayed one step behind her. "You know how this nat-phen is happening in the Pacific? Well, the keas have reason to believe that the rise of the storm system will require rainwater to be diverted from our territory to cover the magnitude of the hurricane that's closer to us. So we want to know, would it be possible for us to have that rainwater returned to us after the nat-phen?"

Mimidae abruptly stopped. She turned around and looked at the much larger bird.

"Two things, Nestor," she said, a disdain for him evident in her tone. "First, don't call it a 'nat-phen'. Like, ever. It's a 'natural phenomenon'. Either say the whole thing, or don't mention it at all. I don't know where you younger birds are getting this, but it has to stop. And second, if you looked at any one of the hundreds of weather reports or maps we have in any direction you see, you would've noticed that the twin system is heading for Central America. Central America, as you may remember, falls within the region of the Atlantic Ocean, the Gulf of Mexico, and the Pacific

Ocean in the northern hemisphere, which is far from your territory. And even if by some strange marvel it was in the South Pacific, this would still not affect your territory, would it?"

"No ma'am," the large parrot nervously responded.

"I didn't think so," she said with a sarcastic smile. She turned in the opposite direction and walked away. "So go back to the keas and let them know that I see what they're doing and I don't appreciate it."

Mimidae continued on her path. Every screen she saw – between the gaps created by the frantic birds – showed various images of weather reports broadcast over hundreds of television networks on Earth. The meteorologists recognized and tracked the storms, though none of them understood more than their technology could tell them. The only common factor among every projected screen on the Trading Floor was the repeated flash of the names of the storms: Elijah and Eliza.

Mimidae was nervous, though she would never admit to it. She despised natural phenomena for such reason. It was always the same chaos, the same known unknowns, the same ridiculous questions, the same politics, the same unnecessary panic, and the same results. There were a few notable exceptions, none of which occurred throughout her time with the Department.

Other birds attempted and failed to gain her attention. Some went so far as to offer bribes or use scare tactics to persuade her to address their selfish concerns. She heard every one of their excuses yet remained unphased by their many attempts to get what they desired from her. She was the one and only bird who had immediate, untethered access to the Alpha. While Mimidae had the power of persuasion, the Alpha had the authority to divert the resources of the natural phenomenon in any direction he desired.

Mimidae entered through a passageway hidden in plain sight. She passed between a partition of liquid plasma which was fitted to her silhouette, as if the barrier between one division and the next had created a method for her to cross. The liquid which flowed from the partition provided her with the security she needed; had any other bird attempted to follow, the plasma would immediately transform from liquid to solid and trap the intruder for all the birds of the DGCC to observe. Many birds learned this lesson the hard way.

Mimidae rested in the space which separated the two divisions of the Department. She closed her eyes and leaned her back against a wall, where she looked up and took slow, deep breaths to calm her nerves. The chaos was beyond the usual scope of a normal natural phenomenon. Prior to this occurrence, she was never asked to leave or be away from the Department during scheduled anomalies. The fact that it occurred while the new Omega bird was still in early transition meant something was negotiated without her knowledge.

A few days prior, Mimidae visited the origin home of the new Omega bird. She had witnessed numerous Omega birds come and go, but the uniqueness of the blue quetzal made her want to understand the reason behind Ally's decision. Why him? Why an Omega from a small town in Guatemala? What did he have to gain, and what could he not lose?

The answers to Mimidae's questions came at the moment she saw the young woman in the orphanage. The young woman sat in a chair and rocked back and forth as she held and bottle-fed an infant. Mimidae looked around the room and noticed the details of what Dioni left behind. It was not a home of luxury, nor did it house any item of particular value or importance. Here lived the children forgotten by their own kind, of whom little to nothing was expected of their lives. If after ten days of absolute freedom – and of learning the many secrets and benefits of his position – Dioni still felt the desire to return, then surely there was far more to his home than bricks and mortar.

Mimidae saw it immediately. If there existed a reason for Dioni to do the impossible, it was not for the things he left behind, but rather for the person. It was for Alma. It was always for Alma. Mimidae understood that she was Dioni's greatest source of strength as well as his greatest weakness. She knew it was only a matter of time before—

Mimidae snapped out of her daydream. She took one final deep breath,

417

shook the nerves from her body, then continued down the short hallway. The far wall had a second liquid plasma security system, which identified her as the assistant to the Alpha bird then granted her permission to access. On the Control Center side, the chaos was far better managed.

The hummingbirds took charge of the demands imposed by the Alpha's commands. That which Mimidae endured single-handedly on the Trading Floor was done so by dozens of teams of hummingbirds, who circled the entirety of the Control Center. Work requests came from many directions, and the hummingbirds were the best in the world to stay on track, to maintain order, and to prioritize their workloads according to the needs of the Department.

Each bird who oversaw a particular territory – or who overlooked their control screen and regulated any one of thousands of factors which created a physical change to the weather on Earth – was on high alert. The stakes of the natural phenomenon were extraordinary; there was simply no room for error or failure.

The massive screen by which weather and climate negotiations were made visible to all aviators, across every territory and sector of the Earth, was entirely focused on the Americas. Eliza and Elijah were by far the main attractions – two superstorms that were, individually, powerful enough to devastate an entire city, and when combined, had the power to decimate an entire continent. The storms were on track as planned and scheduled; only the order commanded by a single bird prevented the twin hurricanes from unleashing their strongest, most destructive capabilities.

What struck Mimidae as extremely odd was not the rushed flightpaths of the dozens of hummingbirds who dashed simultaneously, nor the sheer amount of noise made by the commotion of a global control system that oversaw one of the largest weather experiments the world had ever known. It was the stance of a single bird – the vulture who stood at relative ease, perched on his favorite location in the entire universe – which captured her attention. He looked down upon his creation with pride and arrogance. He knew that his reward was not to the benefit of all who served under him, but to the power which was bestowed upon him after generations upon generations of lesser birds had tried and failed. He was the one and the only Alpha, a bird whose deeds were not the result of wisdom and intelligence, but rather the end product of old age and experience.

…

Dioni lay motionless on a cold, hard surface. His mind was active, as were his ears, though none of his other senses functioned. He was unable to smell, unable to taste, nor did he possess the strength to open his eyes. He was, however, able to hear his surroundings. His sense of sound was not fully intact, though he gradually heard faint sounds nearby. He heard the sound of a steady grunt, a noise consistent in both pitch and tone, which sounded familiar.

The sound of happy budgies was faint, yet audible. Dioni heard the flaps of their wings as the budgies made short flights from one end to another. An odd, vague rhythmic sound played ambiently. It was music, though not something he recognized.

"What do you reckon of this song, then?" asked Dominic.

Dioni heard Dominic's voice, though it echoed as if he spoke from a distance.

"It's a good song," Simon responded. "I like this new-age music. It makes a bird like me want to get up and dance."

"That's just nonsense," said Maddie. "This new-age stuff can't hold a candle to the boy bands of my day. I don't even know what these kids are saying nowadays."

"You birds like this sound?" asked Caleb. "It's all a bit too much for me. I prefer the golden oldies. You know, the classics."

"Classics, Caleb? Like what?" asked Dominic.

"Oh, you know…what's the name of that one song about a free bird by that old quartet? I believe they was from Liverpool. Now that's good music, mate."

"A song about a free bird sang by a quartet?" asked Simon. "That could be any one of a million different songs. What say we narrow it down a tick.

What year were you born in, mate?"

"What's my age got to do with it?" responded Caleb. "I know a good song when I hear it!"

"Well then let me finish listening to this one," said Dominic. "I like it and I can't hear it over you budgies flapping about."

"Sorry, mate," responded the three budgies.

Dioni's senses gradually returned to him. He was almost able to move his face, though his body felt stiff. His lost sense of smell reverted. He smelled something familiar, though he could not determine what it was nor from where it came.

Dioni moved his eyes but remained unable to open his eyelids. The ground shifted slightly, which caused him to bounce; it was a sensation he was glad to feel. He slowly moved his extremities – first his wings, then his toes, then his head – none of which came easy to him.

The song he heard in the distance faded and was replaced by the voice of a woman, who spoke eloquently. She sounded like a news reporter, which informed Dioni that he was near a television or a radio. He listened attentively to the sound of her voice.

"...For your local weather report at half passed the hour," said the woman's voice. "It's hot out there now, just as it was yesterday, just like it's going to be tomorrow. No major changes expected for the rest of the week, really. Though if you think the weather is bad here, be glad you're not in Central America. If you haven't heard, reports are saying that they're going to get hit with a phenomenon called twin hurricanes. That's new. And get this, the storms are named Eliza and Elijah. Whoever has the job of naming these things isn't particularly creative, is he? We'll be right back with more of today's hits and yesterday's favorites. You're listening to the power hour radio on mix one oh three point five."

"I knew a bird named Elijah," spoke Dominic, over the sound of radio commercials.

"Oh yeah?" asked Caleb. "Was he a twin?"

"Nah," replied Dominic. "At least I don't think so. A kookaburra. Used to just laugh and laugh at everything. Even if it wasn't funny. For no reason, he'd just laugh."

Dioni further regained his abilities. He moved his body, including his wings and his feet, which enabled him to shift himself to his side. He opened his eyes. Upon doing so, he was only able to see a brightness and subtle contrast between light and dark, though all remained out of focus.

Dominic looked down from where he stood, on a perch made of artificial wood.

"Well look who decided to join the rest of the bandwagon," said Dominic.

The budgies looked down to see Dioni as he struggled to get to his feet.

"Oi, Dioni," said Simon. "Welcome back, mate."

Dioni coughed. He placed his wings beneath his body then pushed himself from the floor. He managed to stand, though he struggled to stabilize himself vertically. He felt as though he was in continuous motion.

"What happened?" Dioni asked as he balanced himself.

"We was gassed," responded Caleb. "Happens more often these days."

"Gassed?" asked Dioni. "What does that mean?"

"Landowners," responded Maddie. "They don't want us eating their crops no more, so they created a system to gas the fields. I'd only heard about it until now. That explains the nets on the ground."

Dioni regained more of his sight. He saw shapes and colors. Despite his lack of ability to visually focus, he was able to see the silhouettes of dozens of budgies who drifted from one side to another, in short distances. Dioni noticed a series of vertical and horizontal lines.

"Are we moving?" Dioni asked. "I feel like we're moving."

"Can't you tell, mate?" replied Dominic. "Of course we're moving. We're on our way to the biggest pet shop in all Australia."

"We's gonna be someone's pet, Dom?" asked Caleb.

"It's not an actual pet shop, Caleb," responded Maddie. "It's more of a budgie sanctuary."

"Where are we now?" asked Dioni.

"Filthy liar!" Simon said to Maddie, disgruntled. "How would *you* know anything about the pet shop?"

Maddie turned to Simon.

"This isn't my first rodeo, Simon, thank you very much. Unlike you, I'm a travelled and well-versed budgerigar."

"So what're you saying?" asked Simon. "You've been there before and miraculously escaped? I don't believe that for a second!"

"The audacity!" responded Maddie. "I've forgotten more things than you've seen! You honestly believe that this is my first time in a truck?"

Maddie's response struck a chord for Dioni, who almost immediately regained his eyesight. Everything came into focus. He looked in every direction. He was caged within a cage – in the cargo trailer of a truck – separate from the budgies. He had sufficient space to move, to breathe, to stretch, and even to fly. Instinctually, his mind went entirely blank. Dioni's heart began to race uncontrollably. He vaguely heard as Simon and Maddie argued. His face turned pale and his body temperature increased. It became difficult for him to breathe.

"I have to get out," Dioni said, his voiced muffled by the flaps of the many airborne budgies and by the heated argument between Simon and Maddie. He swallowed the emptiness in his dry mouth.

"I have to get out!" Dioni shouted.

His voice was weak and unable to travel further than his own ears. He placed his wings on the wire mesh which surrounded him. He gripped tightly then shook the wiring as best he could. His attempts proved futile. He quickly moved to another area of the cage and repeated the actions, to the same results.

Dioni entered a state of panic. He ran along the perimeter of the cage and pushed the wired mesh with all his strength. He searched for a weakness in the design of his enclosure. There was no escape, at least none he was able to identify, which furthered his anxiety. He was imprisoned. His heart raced faster and his eyesight returned to a blur. Dioni gripped the side of the cage then violently rattled the wires. He was desperate to break through the impenetrable barrier.

"Let me out! Let me out! LET ME OUT!" Dioni shouted. His screams echoed and silenced the thousands of birds in the trailer. "AAAAAHHHHHHH!"

Simon and Maddie paused their argument. The four friends flew down to be at Dioni's level.

"Mate, what are you doing?" asked Dominic.

"Dioni, calm down!" shouted Maddie. "This isn't so bad. We'll be there in no time."

"I have to get out! Let me out!" Dioni cried.

He pushed and pulled the wire with every degree of strength within him.

"It's not that long of a ride, man," said Simon. "No need to get all flustered."

"AHHH!" shouted Dioni.

He rallied every muscle in his body to try to free himself.

A small bump in the road forced the truck to briefly lift. Dioni's force, along with the bump, caused him to hit his head on the wire, which created a small yet visible indentation within the cage. Dioni discovered hope as he noticed the dent he created. He repeated the action and hit his head at the same point where the wire dented. He felt pain but completely ignored it.

"Dioni! You have to stop!" shouted Maddie.

Her voice, his shouts, and the harsh sound of his head repeatedly hitting the side of his containment echoed throughout the trailer. No bird made a sound, nor did they look in any direction other than where Dioni stood.

Dioni's pathfinder beeped with each strike. The device protected him from any potential irreparable damage he made to himself. Every blow to his head was traced, recorded, and reported to headquarters.

Unable to further expand the dent he made, Dioni pushed away from the wires and created a distance between himself and the edge of the large cage. He bent down, jumped, then struck his head and shoulder against the inside of his container. The force of his attack occurred with such great vigor that it pushed him back and caused him to fall. He felt the pain as he struck the cage, yet nothing changed. Dioni stood, moved further back, and repeated the process.

"Dioni! This is madness!" shouted Maddie. "You have to stop!"

Dioni ran as far back within his cage as possible. He pushed himself from the end, sprinted to the side of the cage, and forcefully hit his upper body against the wire mesh. He fell back yet he remained on his feet. He once again moved far back within his cage, then used all of his energy to gain enough speed to burst through the side. It was of no use; the bars simply did not move. He fell to the ground. His heart beat madly. Tears formed in his eyes and his breath slowly escaped him.

"Dioni, listen to me," said a feminine voice. "You can't do this to yourself. You have to calm down."

The voice was familiar. It was not any one of the thousands of budgies who glared at him with fear, but rather the one voice he never wanted to hear again. He escaped from her during the darkest night of his life, and he thought he made himself perfectly clear: he hated her.

Dioni looked up. A prodigious crow stood before him, on the opposite side of the wired mesh. She looked down to him. Dioni's facial expression proved he no longer cared for her opinion. He stood and looked at Ally, as close to eye-level as possible, then slowly walked backwards to the furthest end of the cage. He felt the cold wall on his back. Dioni sprinted forward, opened his wings and used the force of his momentum to crash his head against the wires. The bars refused to move. He kept his eyes on Ally as he repeated the process.

Every budgie in the trailer locked eyes on Dioni's actions with shock and disgust. They were witnesses to the death of another bird – done so by his own accord – and were powerless to stop it. The younger budgies looked away and covered their ears; some sobbed as they witnessed Dioni's selfish act.

Dioni repeatedly crashed his head and body against his cage, in shorter and faster cycles. Ally knew she was powerless to a quetzal's natural instinct.

She looked up to see the many budgies who glared in her direction.

"Make him stop!" shouted Caleb as tears streamed down his face. "He's gonna off himself!"

"He's a quetzal!" Ally shouted to all the birds in the trailer. "They can't be captive! He's doing it on instinct!"

She looked in every direction, desperate for a solution. Dioni continued to hurl himself against the side of the cage.

"Help me! We can free him!" Ally shouted. She raised her wings. "I need all of you to get to this side of the trailer," she shouted, then pointed to the side where Dioni was contained.

No budgie moved.

"Please!" Ally shouted. "I can't do this alone! We can save an Omega bird!"

"Do as she says!" shouted Maddie.

She jumped and flew to the side of the truck where Ally directed. Within a few seconds, the elder and braver budgies followed her lead.

"When I give the signal, you have to dash from this side of the truck to the other, and hit that far wall as hard as you can!" Ally instructed.

The budgies prepared themselves. This was a rescue mission unlike any they had ever experienced. Individually, the budgies were small, powerless birds with no special talents or capabilities. As a team of thousands, however, they had the power and strength to pull their collective minds as one, and to overcome any obstacle which presented itself. Their mission was to save the life of the honorary budgie, the Omega bird, and not one amongst them desired to have a dead quetzal on their conscience.

Ally lifted her wings then instantly dropped them, which queued the budgies to run as fast as possible and push against the side of the trailer. The truck briefly swerved from its lane. The driver of the truck felt a strange movement but was able to quickly and easily regain control of his rig.

"Again!" shouted Ally.

The directive caused a stir among the flock, who struggled to return to the far side of the trailer. Some were hurt, others limped in pain, yet every budgie in the trailer returned to their position. Ally raised her wings and dropped them, which queued the second rescue attempt.

The truck swerved from its lane and nearly struck a bus that travelled in the opposite direction. The driver, though shaken, kept control of the rig and was able to stay in the proper lane. He checked every gauge on the truck's dashboard and saw no indication of what caused it to suddenly deviate from its path.

"Again!" shouted Ally.

She looked at Dioni. His energy faded with every strike he made against the side of his cage.

"The strongest flyers to the top!" Ally shouted. "This time, when I give the signal, push off and hit the side wall from the top! If we can't swerve this rig off the road, then we'll tip it over!"

Hundreds of larger, more prominent budgies did as instructed and flew to the top of the trailer. Like elite soldiers on the verge of battle, they held themselves in position with one wing placed on the side of the trailer while their feet were pressed firmly against the wall.

Dioni shouted and sprinted towards the side of his cage. He lowered his head and used his face to strike the wire mesh with excessive force. He wounded himself just above his right eye. A small drip of blood fell from where his face came in contact with the cage.

Ally raised her wings. Every budgie in the trailer – including those who were previously too afraid to move – was in formation. She shouted a battle cry for the life of the Omega bird, which was mimicked by the budgie formation from above and below. She dropped her wings, the signal for the attack. With desperation as their motivation, the flock of thousands of budgerigars struck the side of the trailer. The force of their thrust caused the truck to swerve then tip to its side, which lifted half of the truck and trailer from the ground.

The driver franticly attempted to regain control. He turned the large steering wheel in the opposite direction, which caused physics and gravity to take hold of the cargo; the truck crashed onto its side and the rear gate swung open. The collateral damage as a result of the interior strike created havoc within the trailer. Sparks erupted from the weak points of the structure as the fallen truck momentarily slid along the road. The attack proved successful, though it came at a cost.

The force of the impact freed Dioni from his cage, though he remained trapped beneath the flock of budgies. Dioni struggled to free himself; he pushed and pulled the many budgies who surrounded him but was only able to lift his head. He looked to the back end of the trailer and felt a sense of peace as he saw the light of day. The gap was large enough for every bird to escape and once again be free. Dioni saw the blue sky, which was more beautiful than ever before.

The truck and trailer came to a stop near a road sign. Other motorists, who witnessed the truck collapse onto its side, quickly came to the aid of the fallen. The driver of the truck was stunned. He remained in his seat and was strapped tightly by his seatbelt; his hands were unable to release their grasp from the steering wheel.

The budgies – some hurt, some dizzy, some shocked, and some surprisingly unscathed – stood and collectively moved toward the back of the trailer. Those who were unable to fly escaped by foot, then took to the sky once they felt the wind on their feathers.

Dioni pushed and pulled his way to the back of the trailer. He ignored any bird in his path and moved as fast as possible, desperate to liberate himself from forced confinement. He smelled the air of the Outback, heard the sound of birds in flight, and felt the light of the sun on his body. He wiped away tears of joy, as well as the evidence of his self-inflicted wounds, from his face. Still partially in the trailer, Dioni leapt above the budgies, spread his wings, and aligned his body to perfection. His pathfinder, in good condition after the harsh treatment it received, immediately recognized Dioni's request for action.

From the outside, Maddie, Caleb, Dominic, and Simon stood in a huddle as they waited patiently to see the honorary budgie exit the trailer. Neither of them spoke, though they were happy to have survived, relatively unharmed. Maddie looked up and saw the top of Dioni's head tower over the others as the birds exited the trailer. She lifted her wing to gain his attention, which he failed to recognize. Caleb, Simon, and Dominic turned their attention to the inside of the trailer.

The four budgies kept their eyes on Dioni as he leapt, perfectly aligned his body, then launched and disappeared into the cloudless Australian sky.

Chapter Twenty-Eight

Dioni soared in perfect alignment with the endless amount of water beneath him. He was entirely alone, accompanied by no other bird, no false mentor, not even a cloud in the sky.

Never had Dioni experienced such raw emotion, as if panic struck him and seized every fiber of his being. His immediate thought was not of those he loved, nor of anyone he left behind, nor of the thousands of birds who were trapped alongside him and who made the collective effort to free him. Dioni thought only of himself and of the freedom he nearly lost; nothing meant more to him in that moment than his liberty. Even if it meant death, it was a risk he was instinctually inclined to take.

Dioni flew high above the sea. He searched for a place to rest that was as lonesome and tranquil as the cloudless sky. The last two days had taken a severe toll on his mind and body, and he was far beyond the point of exhaustion. His heart no longer raced, color returned to his face and body, and his eyes returned to their normal state of focus. With decreased levels of adrenaline and with energy reserves lowered with each flap of his wings, Dioni wanted nothing more than to sit away, alone, and wait for the remainder of his negotiation to expire. Even if it meant a lifetime of loneliness on a beach – perched in a tree and hidden from the nearest resemblance of a life of duty and responsibility – it was far preferable than to continue as the Omega bird.

Dioni saw the first sign of land among an entire world of water. He needed rest, he needed sustenance, and he needed to be away from other birds. In an effort to not attract the attention of potential predators, he withdrew from launch speed. He hovered and spotted an oasis of green which floated on the Indian Sea.

Dioni kept his wings spread widely as he drifted above the land. From his elevation he saw that the oasis was not one large island, but was instead a consortium of smaller islands which created an odd formation above the sea. The water that ebbed and flowed was neither deep nor dark, but rather a bright turquoise color. The transparency of the water created the impression that the ground itself gave way to endless streams of peacefulness and tranquility.

Dioni circled the islands and drifted in the sky to remain invisible to the land-dwellers below. He gradually lowered his altitude as he glided in a large infinity pattern. One of the larger islands had vehicles, road signs, and people who went about their various activities. Another island contained a large stretch of flattened land, where paved lanes were constructed to allow for the departure and arrival of small aircraft.

Dioni maintained his air speed and altitude while his sky-colored feathers kept him invisible. He circled over a small island – a part of the culmination of the greater whole though so far removed from the rest of the islands that no form of life seemed to reside there. He briefly circled above the land to inspect as much of the island as possible. He gradually descended once he felt it was safe to release his guard and give rest to his depleted body.

Dioni made landfall on the beach. The small island held the remnants of what was once a thriving landscape, though there was no evidence of life anywhere nearby. A few small waves briefly made their way to the shore then retreated back from where they came. Dioni took the time to search for any sign of life which could prove to be of danger to him. He found none. For the first time in his life, Dioni was entirely alone, as if the Earth had rid itself of anything to do with the scrap of land on which he rested.

Dioni sat, not how a bird knew to sit, but in the manner of a child. The water was close enough to call to him, to distract him from the thousands of thoughts which clouded his mind, but not so close as to claim him back to the open sea. The sun remained in the sky, with no clouds to cover it or to provide shade from its strong rays of light. It made no difference to Dioni; his mind drifted, and his body was too weak to feel much else.

He sat and watched as the water came to him then quickly receded – a pattern which repeated indefinitely. He looked at his feet. His toes were replaced by small claws. He looked at his lower body. His once strong legs and developed torso were two skinny sticks and a front covered in white and blue feathers. He raised his wings before his eyes. His arms, hands, and fingers were two wings with blue flight feathers so flawless that even the most noble of birds would slay others just to obtain them. Dioni came to his feet and walked to the sea. He looked down. He wished to see anything to remind him of a previous life, from which he felt so far removed.

The transparent water reflected an image, albeit faintly, of his present state. The waves presented Dioni with the depiction of a resplendent bird, an incredibly unique blend of the natural with the supernatural, balanced perfectly in the form of the most advanced transformation the world had ever known. Dioni squatted to get a better look at himself. His face was different, though the color of his eyes reflected as he remembered. Above his eye was the injury he gave himself as a result of his effort to escape his containment. He saw the small, dried specs of blood above his eyelid, then dipped his wings in the water and used them to cleanse his face.

With his wings in the water, Dioni noticed a foreign object in the reflection. A green light flashed from the device on the side of his head. The device, though able to provide him with incredible stealth, safety, and abilities far from that of any person, came at the cost of his independence. It was known as a pathfinder, but in reality, its purpose pushed Dioni further and further from the path he pursued.

Dioni lifted his wing to his head then removed his pathfinder. He felt no physical pain in doing so, though it briefly disoriented him. He held the pathfinder in his wing. He noticed its detail and the intricacy of its design. He momentarily thought of the incredible amount of ingenuity housed in such a small device, and how so many people could benefit from access to such advanced technology. The green light began to flash; it likely provided a warning or some form of communication to inform headquarters that the Omega bird was offline. It made no difference to Dioni. His mind was set.

Dioni looked to the calm waters of the Indian Sea. He closed his eyes, sighed, and absorbed the light of the sun. He reached back and pitched the pathfinder into the ocean, then observed as the waves pulled the device to claim it as its own. The pathfinder drifted away until it was no longer visible on the surface of the sea. He sat with his legs and feet spread before him while his spine remained unsupported. His long tailfeathers drifted aimlessly in the gentle breeze.

Dioni thought of the birds he met in his short yet meaningful journey over the last few days. He had convinced himself that he could live the remainder of his life hidden among a group of thousands, which he learned was too good to be true. He thought of the world's greatest pilots, who oversee and manage the balance of the Earth's most powerful resource. He then thought of the beached orca, whose presence on the icy shores of the arctic was as mysterious as the unknown cause for the fallen birds in the United States as well as in India.

Dioni thought of India. He looked at his feathers and paid particular attention to their color. He looked up and saw the light of the sun; it radiated purity and provided the visible spectrum by which so much color is possible. Dioni turned his body and looked at the palm trees behind him. Not a day went by where he did not see a palm tree in his native land, though he had taken them for granted. No tree was more magnificent than the one which stood, gracefully and powerfully, above all others on the island.

Dioni's attention returned to the shore. He thought of the small birds in Syria who he abandoned and left to die. He wished he would have chosen an act of bravery and had died a hero, which was better than to live the remainder of his days with the guilt that he could have taken action yet fled in fear. This was the primary lesson of his transition – not the transformation from boy to bird, but from child to adult. This was regret, a state of being so powerful that it requires no physical form yet has the ability to consume and outlive the mind which hosts it.

Dioni felt a rumbled sensation in his gut, a clear indication to replenish the energy he burned when he escaped the Outback. A mouthful of berries and grain could not sustain a bird of his size for very long, especially after the experience in the trailer and the launch that immediately followed. Dioni searched the ground for berries, seeds, or even for the remains of a fallen coconut. He did not know how to hunt for fish, but if it were mandated by hunger, he would learn to do so. Dioni came to his feet. He saw an object flail nearby, visible because of its shadow but indiscernible by the light of the sun.

He walked towards the object. He wished for it to be food or at least a tool which he could use to find his next meal. Dioni approached the object from the same direction as the light; it was not food, nor was it an object of any use. He had found a plastic bottle which discovered a way to balance itself between the water and a few carefully placed shells on the beach.

Dioni sighed. He kicked the bottle and observed as the wind carried it away. He once again looked down and saw that the objects which held the plastic bottle were not seashells, but rather a countless number of plastic items that drifted from endless miles away. Plastic waste littered the entirety of the shoreline, inconspicuously covered by a thin layer of sand. He found bags, food containers, shoes, markers, bins, baskets, wires, glasses, beach balls, toys, and a full assortment of indistinguishable, non-perishable items, all of which had claimed the land as their own. None of the objects had decomposed beyond their faded labels, bleached by the light of the sun. In every direction he turned, Dioni discovered more evidence of an ecosystem of beauty destroyed by plastic waste contamination, which penetrated every open pore of the island.

"The Cocos Keeling Islands, huh?" said a familiar voice. Dioni recognized it immediately. "Seems fitting."

Dioni did not want to turn to see her. He had no desire to hear a lecture from the one and only bird who could have prevented his entire misadventure.

"The budgies felt bad about what happened," Ally said. "They asked me to give this to you."

She tossed an object just to the side of Dioni, who kept his back to her. From his peripheral view, Dioni saw that the budgies gifted him a banana. Under other circumstances, he would have gratefully accepted the fruit, likely eaten it by grasping entire mouthfuls at a time, then showed his appreciation for the meal. Instead, he turned and walked away from the banana. He knew what it was – an offer of peace – which he refused to accept, as doing so meant he forgave Ally for the burden she placed upon him.

Ally sighed. She paced forward and grasped the banana in her beak, then carried it with her as she followed behind Dioni. He stopped at the point where the waves were not large enough to go further inland. He stood with his wings tucked neatly at his side. Ally remained close behind. She dropped the fruit then stepped back. She observed the setting of the distant sun, as if it were the last image she wanted to remember.

"You know what it is about being the Omega bird?" Ally opened. "It's not a job anyone wants. Actually, it's not a job at all; we don't get paid to do it. It's a responsibility that no bird would ever want the burden to have. It amounts to a lifetime of endless dedication to something far greater than you will ever know, only to never be remembered for the countless lives you helped. You're forgotten into the tides of time. I know what you're thinking, Dioni, and you're right. Who would *want* that responsibility?"

The waves continued to drift and retract on the sand. Dioni remained calm and motionless.

"I chose you because I thought you would have nothing to lose," Ally continued. "I thought you could literally fall off the face of the Earth and not a living soul would care or make much of a fuss. Just another kid who was at the wrong place at the wrong time."

Dioni briefly bowed his head then returned to his stance.

"But I was wrong, Dioni. You have people who remember you, who have made an impact in your life. They miss you. They think about you just as much as you think about them. Well, one in particular. She hasn't lost hope."

434

Dioni's eyes swelled with tears. He slowly closed his eyelids, then opened them to return to his stance. Ally carefully stepped forward though she kept herself at a respectable distance from Dioni.

"Somewhere inside of you there's something you can't fully understand or explain. It's a sense of adventure. You want to be more than just an orphan tour guide for visitors from other countries, yet you have no idea how to make that happen. You want to be remembered, not for your greatness but for your contributions for helping others, even if it means no one will know the name Dionisio Sedano. But the world is so big, and you are so small, and nothing you will ever do will be enough to make a difference to anything or anyone. So it's much easier to do nothing."

Dioni heard enough. There was no reason to listen to her. He spread his wings and bent his legs.

"Fly away, Dioni," Ally said. "You'll do that for the rest of your life. Whether you ever see me again or not, you'll always choose the easier path, won't you? Before you go, though, keep in mind that there's a massive storm that's going to destroy Flores and probably all of Guatemala. But you know what? It's not your problem, so go and do what is best for Dioni. Let the birds deal with it. Blame the Alpha."

Dioni stood down. He tucked his wings at his side then stood to observe as the sun touched the water.

"You've lived more life in fifteen years than most people do in a hundred and fifteen," continued Ally. "You've felt the full spectrum of emotions. You've seen blue mountains at dawn, and the path created by light as it drifts on the very same sea you're looking at now. It's beautiful, isn't it?"

Dioni looked up.

"Only now, you've seen so much more. You've seen the same mountains from the sky. You celebrated the festival of color with those who have painted the world. You learned to communicate with thousands without saying a single word. You learned of a balance, and how the birds of the Earth work tirelessly to control and maintain something so grand yet so delicate. You witnessed birds negotiating weather in their areas, and you saw how it's controlled. You learned that all birds have their own jobs and responsibilities, although no one obligation is greater than the one that was given to you. And you learned to soar, when you weren't even born to fly."

Ally paused. She looked at the beauty of the sunset and absorbed the gradual fade of the light for one final moment.

"Just imagine, Dioni," she said. "Imagine what you could do, what you could learn, what you could accomplish, and how many living beings you could save...if only you would believe it for yourself."

Dioni lowered his head. A small wave made its way to his feet and buried the tips of his toes in sand. He heard as Ally opened her wings.

"What ever happened to that eagle?" Dioni asked.

He refused to make eye contact.

"What eagle?" asked Ally.

She raised her posture and retracted her wings.

"You told me a story about an eagle who thought it was a chicken."

"You remember that? I didn't think you were paying attention."

"I remember everything you've said to me," responded Dioni.

He lifted his head to look at the sea.

"He died," Ally responded. "He lived his entire life thinking he was a chicken." She sighed. "He was born for so much more."

The two birds stood in the sand. They heard only the sound of the waves.

"I told you that story because it has stayed with me every day since it happened. *That's* regret, Dioni. Not a day has gone by that I didn't regret not telling the eagle that he was far greater than he thought himself to be. Maybe he would have doubted me. Maybe he would have ignored me or laughed at me or called me a fool. But maybe he would have believed me. Maybe he would have believed in himself. Maybe he would have felt what it was like to be an eagle, to fly and feel that sense of freedom unlike anything else. And maybe he would have died knowing that he belonged in the sky. But I'll never know that, will I? I could have given that bird everything, and I chose to fly away."

Dioni gazed into the light. Ally lowered her head. There was nothing more she could do for him, and nothing more she could say for him to understand his importance to the natural balance of the Earth. A lifetime with the burden of a single regret was more than enough for her, and she knew better than to repeat her mistake.

"Goodbye, Dioni," said Ally.

She spread her wings, leaned forward, and leapt toward the sky. She flew over Dioni and gradually lifted herself further away from the island. Dioni watched as she gracefully soared away. Her flight was immaculate, as if the winds far above the land carried her and delicately caressed her every move. He held his view until he lost sight of the Hawaiian crow, who disappeared into the light.

The sunset was not blocked by hills nor by volcanos as it was in Guatemala. Dioni had witnessed more sunsets than he could remember, though there was nothing more mysterious to him than where the sunlight went after it drifted beyond the horizon. At long last, the mystery was solved. Dioni looked behind him and saw the banana which rested on the surface of the sand. He was hungry, yet his conscience eclipsed his appetite.

He felt that he was of neither one world nor of the other. As a young man, Dioni was an orphan – a child abandoned by parents he never knew, to live in a home filled with others with similar fates. Life in Guatemala was simple, but he would never belong there. The Earth simply would not allow it.

As a bird, he was 'the only'. He was unique, yet unaccepted by his own kind. His appearance resembled that of a resplendent, mystic bird. Among other birds, however, he felt as though he did not belong within their communities. Dioni was neither hated nor envied, neither loved nor feared; the birds understood he was a child who was far from home and who would likely collapse under the pressures of his responsibilities. Failure was the expectation.

The world, as he saw it, cared little for his existence. He was not special.

He had no more business in the sky than did a man with wings made of feathers and wax. He felt alone, a member of two worlds but who belonged to neither. He was just another bird, albeit one with an odd culmination of ancient plumage mixed with a contemporary color palette.

The Blue Q.

Dioni bent down and pecked at the banana but struggled to peel it. He used his claws, his beak, and the weight of his body to force the peel off the fruit, to no avail. He kicked it, which hurt him more than it hurt the banana.

"Ow," Dioni said as he limped and circled away from the scene.

He approached the fruit once more, bent down, and chipped away at the tiny fibers of the outer peel. After a few instances of trial and error, Dioni pulled a string of the peel. The small victory excited him, and he repeated the process until he was able to remove larger strips of the outer surface.

Dioni scooped as much of the fruit as his small beak could hold. He closed his eyes and smiled. His eyes opened and he looked to the sun, the lowest part of which nearly touched the endless sea. As he feasted on his meal, Dioni thought of nothing. He lived only in that moment. He tasted the sweetness of the banana, felt the gentle breeze of the cool wind, heard the waves crash against the sand, smelled the salt and the sea, and saw how the light of day fell with every passing moment.

He scooped more of the banana until only an empty peel remained. As Dioni bent his body to grasp the final morsels of fruit, he paused when he noticed an odd item in the sand. It was red in color, square-shaped, and it did not appear as if placed with any specific intent. Dioni removed the peel then lifted the item from the sand. It was a piece of broken plastic. He looked around the beach and noticed as the light reflected an infinite supply of similar, odd-shaped items in the sand; they surrounded every inch of the beach.

Dioni looked in every direction in search of a safe place to take cover for the night. He saw how the land was littered with plastic sandals, straws, cups, and a variety of other objects he did not wish to identify. The plastic bags had made their way to the branches of the palm trees, where they waved in the breeze with infinite complacency. He returned his attention to the dusk.

"Huh," Dioni thought aloud.

He wondered if it would be possible to fly and stay in the sunlight. Perhaps it was possible for a bird to always remain in flight, to disprove the notion or law of physics of that which goes up.

"What if…?" he asked himself. He sighed.

Dioni lowered his body, spread his wings, then leapt from the sand. He returned to the sky and flew higher and higher, until the grains of plastic disappeared beneath the waves of water. He wished to see the point where the sun ceased to set, and where he could drift aimlessly for the remainder of his life.

Dioni learned that his altitude made no difference to the light. As the sun peaked over the horizon, he turned and saw the incoming darkness. The moon was visible, and it looked larger and more mythical than it did from the ground. Dioni smiled. He flapped his wings and moved closer to the faded sunlight. He saw streams of light which briefly created a multi-colored sky. He looked up once more.

"What if…?" he asked himself.

Dioni flapped his wings with all his strength. He flew even further above the sand, above the sea, and at a higher elevation than what was known by his fellow aviators. There was a sense of peace among his solidarity in the deep blue sky; this was the greatest advantage of the Omega bird.

Dioni stopped his climb. The Earth, as he saw it from a perspective known to no other form of life, was a place which deserved to be protected. The birds of the world discovered the absolute power of the Earth's natural balance, and how the resources provided by the planet could suffice for all who lived, and for generations to come. Dioni looked down; all the life that had ever existed in the world was beneath him.

"Keep your eyes open and look toward the ground," he directed himself. "If the ground gets too close, just open your wings and pull your head back."

Dioni pushed his head forward and granted permission for gravity to do what it does best. From such extraordinary elevation, he plunged at a speed much faster than a launch from his pathfinder. The wind that pushed against him was cold, which once again caused his eyes to water. The reaction was the same from his first such experience.

Dioni had a responsibility to himself and to the balance of the natural world. If this was his final act in life, then he would crash onto the ground with the understanding that his fate was settled when he fell into the crater lake of *el Volcan de Ipala* on that stormy evening. If not, then from the ground would emerge the reflection of his own image, a system by which he was granted access to his home base, and where he would learn – once and for all – whether or not he was the Omega bird.

From far beneath him, an object of tremendous brightness emerged. The object was another quetzal, which flew at his same speed though from the opposite direction. The quetzal who climbed towards Dioni was made entirely of light, which was far brighter in the darkness than it appeared upon their first encounter.

Dioni stayed on course. He held his position as the quetzal of light lifted at the same rate in which he fell. This was it; this was his last chance to escape and live an ordinary life as an ordinary bird, or to take wings against a planet in peril and oppose the bird who had outlived his usefulness. Dioni chose the latter.

The brightness of the quetzal of light forced Dioni to close his eyes. At the exact moment of impact, an overwhelming sense of warmth surrounded him. The two birds collided in the night – an unstoppable force struck an immovable will – which created a blue flash in the sky. Dioni left behind only an aura of blue energy, which was gradually absorbed by the moonlight.

Chapter Twenty-Nine

While the attention of meteorologists from around the world was on the natural phenomenon, the working birds of the Department of Global Climate Control were diligently focused on the administration of their respected territories. The scene was the sum of all fears, where little attention was paid to the reason why the anomaly was scheduled to take place. Every bird wanted a piece of the action. No negotiation was off the table, though the final say belonged to the bird who oversaw all work order requests.

Mimidae had unlimited jurisdiction when it came to where she was allowed and welcomed, yet she knew better than to get in the way of the hummingbirds. She grasped a semi-transparent device as she flew over and around the commotion of the Control Center. The birds whose territories fell within the path of the twin storms were hard at work. They frantically attempted to maintain control of the storms while they adhered to the rules of the Earth's natural balance. Of all the workspaces she saw from her perspective as she circled around the workstations below, only one station was vacant. As if abandoned by the bird responsible for that respective territory, the workspace was void of a Controller who oversaw operations for that region. This was highly unusual, especially for that particular station.

The Alpha noticed as Mimidae approached. He was in his power stance, a position of confidence which created an aura of superiority over all birds who worked beneath him. He was invincible, and nothing could make him feel otherwise.

"Mim!" said the Alpha, a forced cheerfulness evident in his tone. "Don't you absolutely love these things?"

"What things, sir?" asked Mimidae.

She landed beside the Alpha, on the solid surface one step behind the Alpha's perch.

"Anomalies, Mim! What else would I be thinking about?"

"Seems like a normal Thursday to me, sir."

"Oh that's just nonsense," the Alpha responded. He turned to face her. "Just listen to how loud it is."

The Alpha raised his head and smiled as he put his wing to his ear.

"Sir," responded Mimidae, uninterested in the Alpha's unusually optimistic behavior. "On my way up I happened to notice workstation 06-01-10B8 was vacant."

"Oh yeah? What station is that?"

"The quetzal station, sir. The Mayan city in northern Guatemala. It seems odd that the most affected region has no Controller. The station looked abandoned."

"Yeah, well, these things happen, Mim. Not my problem," responded the Alpha, cold-heartedly. "The job's not for every bird. If it was that easy we'd still have dodos, wouldn't we?"

Mimidae sighed. She powered her communications device and made motions to reveal a smaller version of the gigantic map displayed on the wall of the Control Center.

"Sir, the storms are close to making landfa—"

"—I know! Isn't it great!" the excited Alpha interrupted.

He returned his attention to the scene beneath his executive suite.

Mimidae grew agitated. She quickly read the warnings displayed on her device.

442

"Sir, we only have a few hours in which we can redirect the weather patterns and push the hurricanes back. The high winds and rainwater are already starting to impact the region. Reports from the toucans indicate damage to villages and trees. They're worried about unexpected flash flooding."

"Nothing they can't handle, Mimidae," he responded, unphased by her concern. "Proceed as planned."

"Sir, one more thing."

"Make it quick, Mim. I'm a busy bird."

"The Omega, sir."

"What about him?" asked the vulture.

He kept his back to Mimidae, though was fully attentive to her every word.

"We seem to have lost his signal by the Cocos Keeling Islands. That station has been unoccupied since the contamination levels increased to—"

"—I'm sure he's fine, Mim," the Alpha responded, his voice slightly somber. "We have bigger things to worry about than a tropical bird going on vacation just after his orientation."

"Sir," Mimidae said. "I know it's none of my business, but—"

"—No, it isn't," the Alpha interjected. He turned in her direction and changed his expression to that of intimidation. "So how about you stay in your lane before we reassign your precious Indian roller friend to permanent night duty on a forsaken island in the arctic."

Mimidae stood down. The Alpha knew how to hit his opponents where it would hurt them most, and despite their work-based relationship, Mimidae was not immune to his strikes against her.

A burst of energetic light emitted in the distance. The light was blue in color, and while it made no difference to the mass of Controllers who worked diligently in the Control Center, it caught the attention of the mockingbird who hoped for the Omega's return. A faint yet visible stream of blue light followed the flightpath of an object in motion. Though the source of the energy was not clearly identifiable, the Alpha knew exactly who had made a grand entrance to the Department.

"See, Mim," said the Alpha. "There's your precious Omega." He looked to the trail of light. "And you were worried."

The Omega bird flew closer. The light he emitted gradually faded as his physical form became more prominent. The moment she saw him, Mimidae felt both a sense of relief and a sensation of worry. She wanted for him to be alive and well, far from the chaos of the twin storms, yet she knew that his presence was mandatory. Ally was never forced to undergo such an event, especially not when she first learned to be a bird. There was nothing coincidental as to why the Alpha chose the moment for the phenomenon to occur.

Dioni set his feet on the luxurious floor of the executive suite. He flapped his wings to burn his excess energy, then turned to look at the two birds beside him. Mimidae's face gave Dioni the impression that she was worried for his safety, while the Alpha's face displayed a hypocritically forced smile.

"Just the bird I wanted to see!" the Alpha said in a gleeful tone. "How was your trip? Those penguins, huh?"

"I need you to change me back to who I was," Dioni demanded.

He shook away the remnants of excess energy.

"Ohh...kay," responded the Alpha. "That wasn't exactly the warm, 'hello...nice to see you...how have you been...I met a peahen...,' that I was expecting, but it's good to see you too, Dioni."

"I'm done living like this," Dioni said.

He paced closer to the Alpha and failed to acknowledge Mimidae's presence.

"Would you look at that, Mim," said the Alpha. "We give the boy a flying lesson, a few days of freedom and an automatic translator, and suddenly he's calling the shots. I love it!"

Dioni looked at Mimidae. Her small body trembled with nervousness. She did her best to keep her emotions from the Alpha, who would not

444

have cared one way or another. Dioni paced toward the ledge to stand within closer proximity to the Alpha.

"Come, Dioni. Have a sit with me," the Alpha said.

He opened his wing and extended an invitation for Dioni to share his perch.

Dioni did not move. He was not there to negotiate, but rather to get what he wanted and then leave, once and for all, on his own terms. The Alpha lowered his head. He sighed as he looked down upon his empire.

"Did I ever tell you that this is my favorite spot in this whole place?" the Alpha said, with his back to Dioni and Mimidae. "It's what I imagine a conductor must feel like. It's a beautiful symphony, Dioni. Do you hear it? It's absolutely beautiful."

The Alpha lifted his wings and began to sway his arms and body to mimic the motions of a symphonic conductor. Dioni stepped forward.

"I don't care," said Dioni. "I want to be me again. I want to go home and see Alma and live my life and never be a bird again."

"It offends me that you're not paying attention to what I'm saying, Dioni," responded the Alpha. He lowered his wings and returned his attention to the scene below. "So if you're not going to listen to my words, then maybe you'll listen to reason."

The Alpha lifted from his perch and flew into his executive suite. Both Dioni and Mimidae stepped back to shield themselves from the wings of the much larger vulture. He turned to face Mimidae.

"Leave us," the Alpha said to her, a command which was not to be ignored.

Mimidae did as she was told. She walked away from the executive suite and into her administrative office. She stood behind a wall, where she was not visible to the birds in the suite but was close enough in proximity to overhear their conversation.

"The answer is no," said the Alpha. He turned away from Dioni and walked to his executive desk. "We had a deal, kid. Ten days, no more, no less, unless you find a replacement. Did you find a replacement?"

"No, but—"

"—No, that's all you had to say, 'no'. Sorry kid, the deal's off." The Alpha leaned on his desk and faced Dioni. He slowly turned his back to the inferior bird. "You lose. I don't know what else to tell you. Enjoy those tailfeathers, I guess. I don't know. I'm not entirely sure what your plans for the future might be..."

It was not the response Dioni expected. In a fit of anger, Dioni ran, lifted his wings to the height of his shoulders, and charged at the vulture. He struck the Alpha and pushed him violently into his own desk. The Alpha felt the strike against his back, then felt the pain of where he hit against his desk, on his chest, which forced him to release his breath. Dioni stood his ground, motionless, with rage visible in his eyes.

"You ungrateful little primate," the Alpha said.

The vulture's face became red with fury. He lifted his wing and placed all his strength to strike Dioni with a back-winged blow. The Alpha's wing struck Dioni with so much force that the hit lifted Dioni out of the executive suite entirely. He reacted quickly and opened his wings at the moment he was thrust out of the office and far above the Control Center. As a quetzal – an expert in flights that begin with a fall from an elevated position – Dioni's fast reaction prevented him from a long drop which would have undoubtedly done irreversible damage. Mimidae witnessed it all.

The Alpha looked out of the window of his executive suite and saw Dioni, with open wings and who momentarily glided a few meters away from his executive perch. The Alpha immediately ran to the open space, extended his mighty wings, and bolted out of his suite. He rushed towards Dioni in the same manner a falcon blasts from the sky and sees nothing but its intended target.

Dioni saw the Alpha rush toward him, then instantly dove. The chase was on. The screams of the vulture echoed throughout the entirety of the Control Center, where the birds who worked diligently below disregarded his sound. The commotion of the natural phenomenon took priority over that which occurred just above them.

Like two fighter pilots who dodged shells of explosive rounds in an airburst above a war zone, so too did the Alpha and the Omega swish through the air. Dioni carefully evaded the many hummingbirds as he navigated through the large space above the Control Center. With each flap of his wings, Dioni desperately attempted to further himself from the clutches of the Alpha. His wingspan was significantly smaller than that of the vulture's, which placed him at a great disadvantage. His saving grace was the presence of the many hummingbirds who zipped in every direction, with little regard to their surroundings; while Dioni flew above, below, or to the side of the tiny birds, the Alpha charged through anything that came in his way.

Dioni dove as close to the floor-level as possible, to the surprise of the scores of Controllers who sat at their workstations and became awestruck by the two birds who engaged in aerial battle. Dioni locked eyes with a bird whose head stood above the others; he nearly slammed head-first into a completely unsuspecting emu, who was so distracted by the management of his station that he failed to notice the incoming threat.

"Look out!" Dioni shouted.

The emu instantly pushed its head forward and narrowly avoided a crash that could have resulted in serious injury to both itself and the Omega bird. The emu attempted to regain its posture, only to have a second near-death experience with the enraged Alpha.

Dioni lifted his shoulders and pulled up to raise himself further above the workspace level. The Alpha bird remained a short length behind. The upward motion placed Dioni in perfect alignment – the primary requirement for a successful launch – to escape by utilizing the technique he learned from the world's greatest pilots. Dioni aligned his body with absolute precision, not a single feather out of place, in perfect configuration to prepare for launch. He failed to realize, in the exact moment his body ascended immaculately to escape the fury of the vulture, that he no longer wore the most important piece of technology essential for launch activation.

Dioni closed his eyes. He recalled the moment he removed his pathfinder and tossed it to the abyss of the ocean. His momentum, though in flawless vertical form, slowed enough for the vulture to easily capture him. Time itself came to a near standstill as he suddenly expected the inevitable. The entire Department became silent.

Dioni looked back and saw he was alone. He noticed as the eyes of every bird in every workstation, including the many hummingbirds, were directed solely upon him. In the distance, Dioni saw a pair of hummingbirds whose attention was elsewhere. One of the small birds closed her eyes and turned her head away as if to shield herself from witnessing the next event; the second hummingbird lifted one of its wings and repeatedly pointed upward, which was the only assistance Dioni received from any of the thousands of birds in the Control Center.

Dioni once again shifted his shoulders back. He looked up, for the briefest of moments, and saw only the flash of a deep, dark color, before he felt the full strike of the Alpha bird's mighty wing. Without his pathfinder to provide external protection from known or unforeseen threats, Dioni absorbed the full impact of the Alpha's rage.

Dioni's body immediately descended. The impact forced him from perfect vertical alignment to a weak ball of blue feathers. He struck the front of the control deck and came to a stop, faced down, at an open area between the workspace of the white doves and the surrounding workstations. The doves, in shock to witness such a violent occurrence in their presence, looked over their workstation to determine whether or not the tropical bird survived the impact. They saw only his back and his rattled tailfeathers, with his head positioned away from them.

Dioni was in pain though still very much alive. He coughed, which resulted in a sting that was felt by his entire body. He collected the strength to place his wings beneath himself and pushed his body off the floor. He mustered every ounce of energy that remained to get himself to his feet. Dioni opened his eyes and saw only a series of blurred lights. He lifted his head and suddenly felt the clasp of a giant talon squeeze around his neck. Dioni's body was lifted and violently pushed against the front of the control deck, which cleared what little breath remained in his lungs.

The Alpha maintained his grasp on Dioni as he pinned the smaller bird between the front of the control deck and the floor. The vulture lowered himself to be at eye-level with the Omega. He tightened his grip on Dioni's neck.

"I'll give you the choice, right here, right now," said the vulture, the tone of his voice as dark as the primal feathers on his body. "This is a one-time deal, and the offer expires immediately, so take it or leave it. Option A: you go back to being you – to the normal, useless orphan life you so desperately want – but you don't do so until after my twins finish their job and we give the world a performance it will never forget. Option B: you agree to remain the Omega bird for as long as I say you are. We call off the twins and save your disgusting little village and the rest of the vile creatures that live there."

The blur in Dioni's eyes slowly cleared to allow him to fully focus. He saw the leg which held onto the talon that so forcefully gripped his neck. He saw the full frame of a once mighty vulture – a respected aviator whose very existence proved that birds were indeed the greatest living beings on Earth – infected by an overwhelming sensation of hate. He looked into the eyes of his opponent, where the Alpha bird housed both fear and chaos, and where a minute reflection of white light mirrored from their surface.

Dioni looked beyond the vulture who towered before him. With his eyes in full focus, Dioni saw the images displayed on a screen of such great size that its light radiated heat for the entire room. In that very moment, Dioni understood the sheer magnitude of his opponent. In flashes of repetitive animations, Dioni saw the vastness of two colossal superstorms on the verge to annihilate all which stood in their path. On display was a massive map of the American continents of the Earth – a region which contained islands, mountains, canyons, and massive cities. Yet despite all that existed within the confines of that which was displayed on the map, only one location was labelled. Beneath the repeated images of the scheduled path for the twin hurricanes, Dioni caught the sole mistake made by the otherwise perfect plan of the Alpha. Someone changed the display on the mighty screen, which provided Dioni with the only evidence necessary to make his decision.

Dioni saw a circle around a small piece of land in northern Guatemala, with a single word shown beside it: Flores. Nothing could survive. The damage was likely underway – lost power, flash floods, overflowed riverbanks – a culmination of the worst of the worst. To the poorest people who lived in Flores, it was armageddon, the apocalypse…the fulfilled promise of the end of days.

The Alpha had no intention to negotiate with Dioni; the decision for the destruction of Dioni's homeland was finalized the moment Ally chose him to succeed her. The Alpha wanted Dioni to accept his proposal, then use the excuse of nature's fury as his means to justify the destruction of an entire country. The decision would live on Dioni's conscience for the rest of his life – for an eternity – if he agreed to the Alpha's proposal.

Dioni's eyes returned to the Alpha. The vulture tightened his grip, which forced Dioni to open his beak and desperately grasp for air. Dioni's eyes watered and he began to lose sensation in his extremities. His entire body was cold, though the vulture's talon radiated heat. The Alpha pulled his talon back while he maintained his grip. He hoped to hear the desperation in Dioni's final words.

Far above the scene on the ground level, Mimidae watched in horror. She was well aware of the Alpha bird's temper, and she knew that he would not hold himself back from causing permanent damage to the Omega. He would do whatever it took – for his legacy, for his reputation, for his pride – to ensure that the natural balance of the world remained under his control. She stood on the Alpha's perch and looked down as the scene unfolded.

"Don't give into him, Dioni. Don't let him win," said Mimidae, unheard by any bird but herself.

Streams fell from Dioni's eyes. He clenched his beak and did all he could within his limited abilities to not show defeat at the mercy of a more powerful bird. His tears ran down his beak and landed on the clenched claw of the Alpha. With his last gasp of breath, Dioni muttered a single, painfully spoken word:

"Nnn….ooo."

Dioni coughed, which sprinkled teardrops onto the vulture's face. As if spat upon, the Alpha felt the gross disrespect that projected from a far inferior fowl.

"You're a disgusting waste of life, kid," said the Alpha.

The Alpha took to the air with Dioni in his clutches. The strain on Dioni was unbearable; he was lifted off the cold ground by the talon around his neck, which rendered the rest of his body almost entirely useless. His arms and legs trailed, defenseless against a far superior authority, and drifted as effortlessly as his long tailfeathers.

The Alpha gained speed and altitude. He rushed toward the immense screen of the Control Center; he knew that he had the attention of every bird on this side of the Department. It was his opportunity to make an example of any bird who dared cross him. He was the Alpha, the one and only Alpha, and may the birds of the future remember this occurrence as the legend of the blue quetzal, the foolish bird who – for a brief moment – believed he was greater than the dust from where he came.

The vulture flew as fast as his wings could carry his ancient body. He halted his momentum and released his grasp on his victim, which permitted gravity to finish the rest of the job. Dioni drifted aimlessly from the grasp of the mighty bird's claw. He glided in the air like a ragdoll tossed across a gigantic room. Dioni's body crashed onto the large screen, which created a series of shattered cracks that flowed outward from the point of Dioni's impact. His body collapsed onto the cold floor, beyond the visibility of the Alpha. The only evidence of Dioni's presence was a small blue feather that rested within the crater produced by the collision of his body with the screen.

Not a single bird in the entire Control Center made a motion of any kind. It was the very nature of shock and awe, a military tactic all too familiar to the bird who had lived through every possible scenario on Earth. The Alpha swooped up and gained momentum as he swerved and soared over his empire. The attention and fearful respect of every bird was solely on him. Regardless of how it came to be, he embraced the attention.

The Alpha made one final swerve over the far side of the Control Center, then lowered his speed and altitude to land precisely at the scene of the crime – a few paces before the main control deck. The two white doves stood at attention, afraid to share in the same fate as the Omega bird. The Alpha lowered his wings and shook his body to release the excess energy

451

created by his fit of anger. He approached the terrified doves.

"Proceed with the anomaly," the vulture commanded as he paced closer. "Override non-compliance of protocol. Approved by Alpha."

He turned to face the screen and gave his back to the doves he confidently knew would not disobey his direct order.

The two birds failed to move. Whether paralyzed by fear or by the defiance of a rule that was set in place long before either of them existed, the wide-eyed doves only glared at the much larger vulture. The pause was too long. The Alpha turned his head and gave an ominous look to the unsuspecting doves.

"What are you waiting for?" asked the Alpha. "Proceed with the natural anomaly as planned. Override non-compliance of protocol. Approved by Alpha."

Once again, the doves failed to move. The Alpha's face, which had momentarily returned to its normal state, glowed red with anger. He turned his body and paced toward the main control deck. The two birds cowered in fear with every step in which the Alpha came closer. He paced to the edge of the control deck and lifted his mighty wing; if he had not proven his authority by what he had done to the Omega, surely he would not hold back from doing worse to any of the others. The male dove, the larger of the two, threw himself before the female in an effort to shield her from a bone-crushing blow.

"I…refuse…" said a cracked voice in the distance. "Declined…by… Omega."

The Alpha lowered his wing and turned to the source of the sound. At the bottom of the screen, badly beaten and nearly unable to balance himself, stood Dioni. His body leaned to one side, and he used his right wing to caress the ache of a hurt left shoulder. Every syllable he spoke was done so with incredible amount of pain; as such, Dioni carefully chose his every word. He breathed heavily.

"Once wasn't enough for you, huh?" said the Alpha. "Stay down, Dioni. You'd be better off if these birds thought you were dead."

Dioni looked in every direction. He saw a massive room filled with birds, each of which looked at him with both awe and pity. He was made a fool by the Alpha, though his resilience gave him a credibility and respect which few birds lived to achieve. Dioni inhaled as deep as he could. He ignored the pain from his chest.

"Help me!" he shouted. His sound was barely heard beyond the birds nearest to him. "Help me! Help me! Stop him! Help me!" he continued, each spoken word slightly louder than the one before.

The Alpha smiled; this was drama in its finest form. Before him and all the others, Dioni had made a mockery of himself and of his position as the Omega bird.

"You lost your pathfinder, remember?" said the Alpha. He did not withhold his amusement over what took place. "They don't understand a word you're saying."

"Help me! Please, help me!" Dioni babbled.

Every sound he made was incoherent.

"Stop it, kid," said the Alpha. "You're making yourself look even worse."

"I know you understand me! Please, help me!" Dioni pleaded.

No bird in the entire Department moved a feather.

"See Dioni, you didn't think your plan through," said the Alpha. "To them, you're nothing more than a…squawking chicken…on the ground… where you belong."

Dioni's exhaustion got the better of him. He regained a portion of his voice with every plea and attempt for help, though it was all for naught if the other birds heard nothing but the random chirps and sounds of a quetzal. Dioni lowered his head in defeat.

"Proceed with the natural anomaly as planned," said the Alpha. He spoke to the doves though he faced Dioni. "Override non-compliance of protocol. Approved. By. Alpha." He turned to the doves. "I am not going to say it again."

Dioni raised his head. He looked at the larger of the two doves and hoped beyond all doubt that his eyes spoke the words his voice could not. Over the shoulder of the vulture, the male dove saw the battered quetzal.

He noticed the expression on the quetzal's face, a plea that was recognized and understood in every language.

The larger dove turned to the other. He made a motion with his face in the same idiom in which he understood Dioni. The smaller dove took one pace to stand beside him. They looked at one another then turned their attention to the Alpha. Together, they lifted their wings, pushed from the ground, and abandoned their workstation.

Every bird in the colossal room watched as the two doves gracefully departed. Dioni followed their flight from his place on the cold floor. The notable symbols of peace on Earth had left the room and disobeyed a direct command in doing so. The smaller of the two doves looked down from the air and saw Dioni. She maintained eye contact with him until she and her companion circled around the mighty wall and flew out of the Control Center.

"Commendable," said the Alpha as he watched the two doves flee. "But grossly mistaken."

A nearby cardinal stood on the top of his workstation. The redness of his body exuded a natural color which could not go unseen. The cardinal looked at Dioni. He made a sound which Dioni neither understood nor recognized. The cardinal then looked directly at the Alpha, opened his wings, then leapt to follow the same flightpath as the doves.

Along the far side of the Control Center wall, a blue jay stood on his workstation. Near the center of the room, a snowy owl jumped to stand on her workstation. On the opposite side, a keel-billed toucan jumped from his perch to stand atop his workstation. A few rows below, a kingfisher stared angrily at the Alpha as it took a large step forward to stand on her workstation. A mere few meters away from Dioni, a woodpecker jumped from the ground to stand on his workstation.

From across the room, dozens of birds repeated the action of the brave cardinal. Each bird turned to look at Dioni, then made a sound which he could not comprehend. They turned toward the vulture and regarded him with resentful eyes. One by one, the birds spread their wings and took to the sky. They formed a mass exodus in the air as they swirled to the far ends of the room and circled around the mighty wall which divided the Department.

Dioni ignored the pain he felt through his entire body. He corrected his posture and dropped the wing that embraced his injured shoulder. He nodded at each of the birds who looked down to him as they exited the Control Center.

"Thank you," Dioni mouthed to the many birds who turned their attention to him as they left the scene. His voice was muted against the uproar of the thousands of birds who took flight simultaneously. "Thank you."

The commotion of the Trading Floor came to a sudden stop as the birds who busily negotiated looked up and saw the migration of birds who flocked from around the wall. The birds in the air circled above the ground in perfect coordination; the realization of a flawless murmuration. The Traders stood in awe as the Controllers circled the Department.

The vulture stood alone at the top and middle of the Control Center, just before the operations control deck. He brought the tip of his left wing to the top of his face, then looked down and exhaled loudly. Dioni, with his back to the giant screen and at a lower position, stood his ground. He was prepared for the Alpha's next move.

"What you did here is to make things worse," said the Alpha. He slowly raised his head to look directly at Dioni. He took one step forward. "Oh, but not for me." He took another step forward. "I'm right here…" Another step. "…with the empty stations your friends left behind." Another step forward. "Your worthless village, however…that's another matter entirely." Another step.

Mimidae moved from the executive perch and flew into the suite, behind the Alpha's desk. With a series of motions, she powered a projected image which rested on top of the desk. After decades, if not centuries, of countless hours invested to perform the tasks which were beneath the Alpha, Mimidae was well versed in the many ways she could grant herself executive-level access to the control deck. With her wings and body motions as guides, Mimidae navigated to the control platform of the countless screens on the Trading Floor. She activated the video signal in the Control Center and redirected it to a new source.

The screens of the Trading Floor flickered as they switched from global news and weather broadcasts to a live feed of what occurred on the other side of the large wall. Every bird in the room, including the Controllers who found empty zones among the Traders, turned their attention to the screens.

Dioni watched as the Alpha drew closer, though he remained at a safe enough distance.

"Do you know what two hurricanes can do to an underdeveloped country, Dioni?" the Alpha asked. His movements towards Dioni continued. "Your despicable town will be completely destroyed."

The Alpha looked up to admire the two storms on display.

"And here's what I find amusing," he continued. In a few days, no one's going to remember it. It'll be gone and buried, completely abandoned and left to rot."

The Alpha stopped in his tracks. He remembered something just then.

"Oh that's interesting," he thought aloud. He once again faced Dioni.

"Wait a second! This was how we buried the Mayan city!" the Alpha said excitedly. "Of course we started with a volcanic eruption and a drought and then worked our way up to a hurricane…hurricanes…but you get the idea." The Alpha resumed his walk toward Dioni. "You can't make this stuff up! Isn't this fantastic?" He looked to Dioni. "And to think, you could have saved Alma."

The final two syllables that drifted from the vulture's beak were enough to cause an implosion within Dioni. He disregarded his pain, along with the limitations of his physical being, and hurled himself forward to run towards the Alpha. From a position of inferiority, Dioni jumped and spread his wings. His momentum was fueled by the fire of vengeance, which he used to direct his attack on the much larger vulture.

Dioni screamed; it was the war cry of an ancient bird whose mythical existence stemmed from history's bravest warriors. He set his sight on the vulture, who stood stoically from an elevated position and who hoped for Dioni to do his worst.

Dioni placed all of his energy into a charge aimed squarely for the

Alpha. He felt the tip of his wings hit the vulture with full force, yet no damage was done to his opponent. The Alpha launched out of Dioni's path and immediately took to the air. Dioni ran through a translucent trail left behind by the Alpha's rapid movement. Before he collided against the front of the control deck, Dioni felt a tight clutch around his entire body.

In a flash, the vulture dashed above Dioni and grasped his body with its powerful talons. If the pain and helplessness Dioni felt during the Alpha's first attack served as any indication of what to expect the second time around, he was grossly mistaken. The Alpha was a much elder bird, whose abilities to hunt were far out of practice but whose strength remained intact. Dioni screamed in agony as the Alpha's talons gripped tightly around his body. Dioni desperately fought for his life, in accordance with his natural instincts. He was trapped, worse than caged, at the literal hands of his opponent.

Mimidae frantically motioned her wings before the projected screen to make every possible known attempt to assist Dioni. The images on her screen moved like mad until she found the command for which she so vehemently searched.

"Please work please work please work!" she exclaimed, at a faster rate than she had ever spoken before.

The screen before her came to a halt, frozen from a dramatic overload of commands. A single word flashed in front of her: Confirmed. Mimidae immediately flew back to the open bay of the executive suite and looked down at the battle between the Alpha and the Omega.

With only the blue quetzal's head beyond the grasp of the vulture's mighty talons, the Alpha aimed directly at the crater that Dioni's body created on the massive screen just moments prior. Since the momentum of a sudden stop and a harsh drop were not enough to eliminate Dioni the first time, a much more severe impact at a far greater speed would undoubtedly terminate whatever life the smaller bird retained.

The launched flight of the Alpha came to an abrupt halt as he collided with an invisible force which pushed the vulture and released the quetzal from his grasp. The Alpha fell back. He lost his navigational balance in the air and landed harshly on the cold ground.

Dioni's near-lifeless body penetrated through the force that withheld the Alpha. His frame glided in the air at an incredible speed, projected to crash at the same point and against the same surface as before. At the moment of impact, Dioni passed through the colossal screen, entirely unharmed. The solid structure was overridden to plasma form, which enabled Dioni to pass through it, to transpose through the wall on which the screen was constructed, and to reemerge on the Trading Floor, unscathed. Though away from the clutches of the vulture, Dioni's momentum forced him from one side of the Department to the other, and he came to a stop with the assistance of the many birds who caught him on the other side.

The Alpha was alone. He came to his feet and shook his head, then walked to the mighty wall. With all the strength he possessed, the Alpha punched the wall repeatedly but was unable to breach its solidity. He yelled at the wall and repeated his actions. He used both wings in an attempt to break the screen which displayed a live broadcast of the phenomenon over Central America.

Unable to make even the smallest dent, the Alpha stepped back, turned his body, and flew to the control deck at the back and center of the room. He landed and took his position behind a series of switches, buttons, and controls, all of which created a multitude of operations in accordance to his every command. He made a sequence of gestures with his wings, which instructed the operation of the control deck.

"Donna!" yelled the mighty Alpha. His voice echoed across the empty Control Center.

From far above the room, near the tunnel system utilized by the most efficient birds in the entire Department, emerged a single hummingbird. It paused just before it reached the control deck and kept itself at a safe distance from the vulture.

"Only one?" asked the Alpha.

He exhaled a loud grunt and swung his wing at the lone messenger.

The hummingbird dodged the vulture's attack, then immediately dashed out of the Control Center. The Alpha continued his gestures until he orchestrated the proper command. A wicked smile flashed across his face as he approved the execution of Isolation Protocol.

A violent sound rattled the ground. At the base of the wall, from above and below, two large spaces opened and released an enormous shield. Every bird on the Trading Floor observed as a colossal barrier was lifted from below and dropped from above; this was an event that neither the Controllers nor the Traders ever knew was possible. The two halves of the shield appeared as storm clouds, where bolts of red lightning passed between one end and the other. Though it was slow to close, the birds looked in shock and amazement as the barrier gradually covered the entirety of the wall and separated one half of the Department from the other. Within a matter of seconds, the Alpha successfully locked and isolated himself inside of the Control Center.

Dioni was brought to his feet with the help of the birds who caught him. Though his every breath came with significant pain and discomfort, he was physically and emotionally strong enough to hold himself upright. Dioni looked up and saw the storm shield which the vulture used to barricade himself on the Control side. He then turned his attention to the many screens that displayed a live feed of the Alpha's every action.

"Can we stop him?" Dioni asked, a question which no other bird understood.

He noticed how they looked to him, as if they questioned whether he hit his head too hard to communicate in an understandable language. Dioni repeated himself and used his body as a form of sign language in an effort to communicate with the thousands of birds in the room. It was to no avail. He scanned the Trading Floor to find another bird who could be of assistance. In every direction he turned, Dioni was met with the same response. The aviators did not understand him, and his actions did not translate as he intended.

"AHH!" Dioni yelled in frustration.

He searched the room once more, desperate for a translator. He looked up, and there she was. In the distance, Dioni located his watchful protector.

It was Mimidae, perhaps the only other bird who could help him in his time of need.

Dioni kept his eyes on her. With his right wing, he tapped on the side of his head. With his left wing, he made back-and-forth motions in front of his beak. He hoped she understood, despite the distance between the two of them. Mimidae looked down with curiosity at the motions made by Dioni.

"What is he doing?" she asked herself aloud. "What do you need? Something for your head? Are you feeling sick? What is it, Dioni?"

She shrugged her shoulders, which Dioni saw from below.

"No, no," Dioni visually responded.

The many birds of the Control Center were intrigued by Dioni's effort to communicate with Mimidae. Dioni lifted his wing to his brow and mimicked the motion to search for something. He then repeated his previous actions; he tapped the side of his head and motioned in front of his beak.

"Looking for something? Is that it?" Mimidae asked. "Looking for…? Looking to find…? Find…on your head? A speaker…? Talking…find… searching…? A pathfinder? A PATHFINDER!"

Mimidae launched out of the executive suite. She zoomed passed her office, through the long corridor which led to the bridge, beyond the artwork displayed to stroke the ego of the Alpha bird, and into the small office which previously belonged to Ally. She immediately went into the desk and searched through every drawer to find what she needed. Each storage space, however, was cleared, an order issued by the Alpha to Donna the moment Dioni was transferred to the Flight Academy. Mimidae paused to think. She looked around the room and saw the framed feather on the wall.

"That's it!" she said excitedly.

She stepped onto Ally's perch and used it for leverage. She reached to the framed feather and pulled it back, which revealed a small storage space in the shape of the frame. Mimidae stretched as far as her body allowed. She reached for a small, triangular box near the far corner of the secret space. She opened the box to confirm its contents and verified that it was precisely what she needed: Ally's former pathfinder. Mimidae firmly grasped the small box then immediately launched away from the office.

"Come on, Mim…what are you doing up there?" Dioni asked aloud.

He faced up and kept his eyes on the window to the executive suite. Within moments, Mimidae launched from the open window. As she made her way out, she looked to the Control side and saw that it was completely barricaded, sealed entirely, with no method for her or any bird to get in or out of the Control Center. She continued on her path and quickly reached the ground level of the Trading Floor.

"Mim," said Dioni, grateful to see her. "I need a new—"

"—Here," responded Mimidae. She removed the small box from her grasp and opened it to reveal an older-generation pathfinder. "This goes on the back of your neck, not on your head like the other one."

"Is there a difference?" Dioni asked.

He kneeled to be at an easier height for the installation of the device.

"Yes, this one is different," Mimidae responded. She placed the device on the back of Dioni's neck and pressed it to hold in place. "It's not as advanced. This one doesn't calculate murmurations."

"That's fine, I'll figure it out. Thank you, Mim."

Dioni turned to the first bird he saw, a cebu flowerpecker with unusually ruffled feathers.

"Can you understand me?" Dioni asked.

"Yes, I understand you," responded the flowerpecker. It spoke with a strong Filipino accent.

"Good," Dioni said. He turned his attention to address every bird on the Trading Floor. "Can everyone in this room understand what I am saying?"

"Yes!" "We hear you, Omega!" "Loud and clear!" responded the many birds.

Dioni corrected his posture and looked at the scores of Traders and Controllers gathered in the room. He had the attention of the entire Department.

461

"The Alpha is going to force the hurricanes to pass through," Dioni addressed the crowd of birds.

"How do you know?" asked a Trader.

"Because he wants to destroy my village," Dioni responded.

"It's true," said the larger of the two white doves from the Control side. "He commanded us to override standard anomaly protocol. Once the anomaly is set, all it needs is the approval of the Alpha to proceed."

"Can I do anything to stop it?" asked Dioni.

"The Omega bird does not have that authority," responded the smaller of the white doves.

"Then can we get inside the Control Center and change everything he put in place?"

"Override the system?" asked an unseen bird.

"Yes," said Dioni. "Can we do that?"

"No, Dioni, we can't," responded Mimidae. "He activated Isolation Protocol."

"What is that?" asked another bird.

"It's a containment system for the Control Center," Mimidae responded to the large crowd. "It was put in place before any of you were here. We created it as a way to protect the Control Center after the explosions in Japan in 1945. It ensured we could still maintain operations even under extreme conditions."

"Why did we not know about this?" asked a bird who stood near the far back wall.

"It's privileged information," Mimidae responded. "Only the Alpha and the previous Omega knew about it. With Ally gone, the Alpha didn't need her approval to activate Isolation Protocol."

"Then how do we get back in?" Dioni asked.

"He has to let us in from his side," said Mimidae.

Dioni grunted.

"Think, Dioni, think," he said aloud. "He can't stay in there forever, can he?"

"No," responded a Controller. "No one bird can control global climate by his or her self. That's how the system was designed. He needs us in there."

Dioni looked to a screen above the masses. He saw as the Alpha worked frantically behind the control deck.

"It's me he wants," said Dioni. "If he can't get me, then he's gonna go for her."

"For who?" asked a bird lost within the crowd.

Dioni scanned the room to find an elevated position where he could address the thousands of birds on the Trading Floor. He saw a perch near a sign which pointed towards the Transportation Center, and he immediately flew to it. He stood above the others as he looked to the sea of birds. In that moment, he became their leader, their symbol of hope.

Dioni became incredibly nervous; his body trembled with both fear and anxiety. He closed his eyes and briefly saw a faded image of Alma. He opened his beak but was unable to utter a single sound. His voice ceased its ability to function.

"If we can't override it from the Control Center, then we're going to have to do it manually!" shouted Mimidae.

Every bird who faced Dioni turned to look at her. She paced forward and jumped onto the perch where Dioni stood.

"The land of eternal spring is in danger!" she addressed the group. "This is bigger than anything that can happen to any of your territories! We may not be able to stop the anomaly, but we can protect the living!"

Chatter began within the crowd. This was no ordinary anomaly, but rather a unified call for action. Mimidae turned to Dioni. She placed her wing on his shoulder.

"What do you need us to do?" asked a large owl, who shouted from the back of the room.

The chatter ceased. Mimidae paused to see the many birds who gave

463

her their attention. No matter how great, how fast, how fierce, how strong, or how mighty, the birds who ruled their territories turned to her for leadership. Their utmost admiration was addressed to the mockingbird who – for so long – stood just a few paces behind such responsibility.

"Every bird who has wings, every bird who can swim, every bird who has a voice, and every bird who has a place to call home!" Mimidae shouted. "No matter where you dwell, what your abilities may be, what you negotiated on this side or what you controlled on the other, get to Guatemala and stop this storm!"

Mimidae opened her wings.

"If you think you are incapable of doing this, remember you were born a bird, nature's most perfectly engineered being! It is because of you that the natural balance of the world is possible!"

The thousands of birds on the Trading Floor cheered such validation, especially because it came from Mimidae.

"A threat was made against us! The Alpha is just on the other side of that wall, doing whatever he knows to do for the purpose of destruction, all for the sake of his pride!" she continued. "The Omega bird needs our help! Someone is threatening to destroy his home and to devastate the natural balance. This is not the act of a hero, but rather that of a desperate coward. It is our responsibility as birds to restore the balance, no matter how great the threat is against us. And we *will* restore it!"

A mighty cheer erupted across the entire floor. Every bird in the room became inspired to take immediate action, regardless of the consequences they faced against the supernatural storm. Mimidae took a deep breath.

"Go out there and get every bird that has wings, every aviator with feathers, and every pilot in the water. Get to Guatemala, immediately! The Alpha's target is a village called Flores, so that's where we'll stop it!"

With her final word, every bird with a voice shouted, sang, or called toward the sky, fully engaged to fight the strongest opponent they had ever confronted. The order was given, and by no means was failure an option. Scores upon scores of birds moved in every direction – some launched, some dashed, and some headed to the Transportation Center – all in a unified effort to do what no avian generation had previously performed.

Mimidae jumped from her improvised perch, followed closely by Dioni.

"Ricky! Jackie!" Mimidae shouted over the sounds of thousands of birds who actively mobilized. The two white doves turned and paced to her. "We have to find a way to get in there," Mimidae addressed the doves as she pointed to the barrier between the Control side and the Trading side. "Whether he gets out or we get in, I need the two of you to get to your post immediately after the wall opens. Let all the other birds go out. You two stay here with me."

"Yes, ma'am!" the two doves responded.

Dioni's attention drifted along with the commotion of the birds who rallied in every direction. He was dumbfounded by the spectacle of what he witnessed. The birds knew nothing of him – he was nothing more than an odd-looking bird with a peculiar name – yet they came together as a unified front during his greatest time of need. They cared not about his external being, but rather of what he represented to the balance of the natural world.

Another image of Alma flashed before Dioni. He came to his senses and turned to Mimidae.

"Mim, what about me?" Dioni asked. "What should I do?"

Mimidae looked at the Omega bird. She placed one of her wings on his chest, just below his neck. This was an action of respect, one of significance known to all living beings. Mimidae placed her opposite wing on his shoulder. She blinked, slowly. There was a chance for the worst, and he should be where he belonged. She looked directly into his eyes and saw the soul beyond Dioni's blue exterior.

"Go to her."

Chapter Thirty

The sounds of the Alpha's movements echoed in every direction across the Control Center. For the first time in known history, the Control Center was sealed with only a single bird at the helm. The Alpha became responsible for the oversight of climate control for the entire Earth, all while he maintained a delicate balance for hundreds of thousands of local territories across the globe. It was by no means a simple responsibility, nor one which could be single-handedly operated by even the most skilled bird of all time. The Alpha created a solid seal between the two sides of the Department, and he was very well aware of his only option to escape.

It made no difference to the mighty vulture. His attention was solely on the execution of the order which he himself created; one he was determined to oversee until its very conclusion. He had ample work experience with Omega birds of all personality types – overzealous falcons, excessively talkative tropical birds, arctic wanderers, birds of the day, hunters of the night, birds of wisdom, birds of justice, birds of prey, swimmers, gliders, climbers, runners, nesters, decomposers, one philosopher, and finally, one who was well out of his league. The Department was the only existence he had ever known, and in his infinite wisdom, he was not afraid to sacrifice it all in order to ensure that the natural balance of the Earth would forever remain according to his will.

The Alpha moved around the control deck. He utilized his wings and body to produce a series of motions in various patterns which were understood as commands by the operating system. With full control and with no opposite authority to override his wishes, the vulture made true on his promise.

He stepped back and observed as an image repeatedly flashed on the massive screen before him. The two hurricanes were in route to destroy and physically alter the land, to forever transform the Central American landscape. The bridge between North and South America was to suffer the same fate as history's greatest civilization. If the Alpha was able to successfully execute the command which sunk the greatest metropolis ever known into the depths of the deepest, darkest sea, then the repetition of the process was not difficult for him to do. Flores, however, was not Atlantis. It was a lesson mankind would learn once and for all, and dare not mythicize the second time around.

"You did this, Dioni," the Alpha thought aloud. "May history remember this as your fault, not mine."

The Alpha raised his wings. He made a series of circular motions that dictated the actions to take place in accordance to his commands. On the great screen of the Control Center glared the sole word which flashed in bold, red lettering, and which gave him a tremendous sense of relief and satisfaction: CONFIRMED.

On the opposite side of the great wall, beyond the sealed Control Center in which the Alpha barricaded himself, stood three birds – a worried mockingbird who paced back and forth while she continuously observed a nearby projected screen, and two white doves who each stood behind improvised workstations and made a series of motions towards the sensors of digital projections.

"Anything yet?" asked Mimidae.

"No ma'am," responded Ricky. "An override was never programmed from this side of the wall. Each side acts independently of the other."

"I'm trying to find a way to break into that side of the network," said Jackie. "Operations weren't shared, but we might have saved previous files on their servers."

"What about Donna?" asked Mimidae. "Do you think Donna would know?"

"I doubt it, but it wouldn't hurt to ask," responded Jackie.

"Donna!" shouted Mimidae.

The normal, instantaneous response from the hummingbirds was not up to the usual standard. A few seconds went by with no hummingbird in sight.

"Now that's *two* things I've never seen before," said Ricky as he diligently searched for a solution. He used his wings and his body as signals by which he commanded the workstation. "Normally you'd get about half a dozen of them."

"Yeah, I know," responded Mimidae. "They can't all be gone." Mimidae lifted her posture and impersonated the voice of Dioni as best she could. She hit the tone almost to perfection as she once again shouted the name, "Donna!"

The room stood quiet. Mimidae looked at one of the dozens of nearby screens which displayed a live broadcast of the colossal storms just a few hours away from causing irreparable damage to the Earth. She sighed and faced down, then continued to pace along an open space near the white doves.

From a tiny gap on the far, upper deck of the main wall, a single hummingbird appeared. It's body, though mostly dark in color, had iridescent wings which glowed in a fluorescent indigo as it zoomed in the air. As it passed beneath the beaming lights of the Trading Floor, its wings displayed a prism-like color which provided a unique effect seen exclusively by those fortunate enough to witness the flight of a black jacobin hummingbird.

The small bird landed behind Mimidae, a few paces from her path, and a few yards away from the doves. The hummingbird went momentarily unseen, until Mimidae turned and paced back. Mimidae stopped immediately when she noticed the small bird who casually stood between her, Ricky and Jackie.

"I don't think I have ever been happier to see you, Donna!" said Mimidae.

The hummingbird responded with gestures of her wings, a well-known sign language among birds of her kind. She indicated her appreciation for the acknowledgement.

"Donna," continued Mimidae. "Is there any way to open the security gate from this side of the wall?"

Donna looked up. Unlike the rest of the hummingbirds of the Department, her eyes were a unique shade of blue. They appeared as if the sky itself had given them their color, which provided her with an ability no other hummingbird could claim. She looked around the room then zoomed to Ricky's workstation to quickly study the commands he inputted. She searched but was unable to find what was needed. The hummingbird then zoomed to Jackie's workstation and immediately read through hundreds of lines of aviator computation codes.

"The system cannot be overridden from one side without the permission of the other," signed Donna. "It was designed as an emergency measure."

"Yeah, we know that," responded Mimidae. "After what happened in Japan, 1945."

"Right," signed Donna.

"Can the permission be disobeyed?" asked Jackie. Donna turned to Jackie, who continued to make motions before the digital sensors. "Can we use a shared network to gain access to the mainframe of the Control Center?"

"You can only do that via the main control deck on the other side," signed Donna. "The Control Center can access the servers and the mainframe of the Trading Floor, but it does not work the same in reverse without the permission of the Control side."

"AHH!" Mimidae shouted in frustration. "What brainless bird would design a system like this?"

"He's on the other side of that wall," signed Donna. The four birds turned to look at the mighty barrier which divided the Department. There had to be a way to break in.

...

Thousands of meters above the ground, at an altitude far above the height in which any tropical bird was able to fly, soared a blue quetzal. The portal released him as close as possible to his chosen destination, though extreme precautions were taken to ensure he remained at a safe distance from the powerful storms. Dioni squinted and protected his eyes as he glided through the clouds, his wings held in perfectly balanced alignment. In the distance he heard the loud roar of rolling thunder. Strong gusts of wind pushed Dioni upward, which he dodged and continued on his path. The roar grew louder. He noticed a vast space in which the sunlight was able to pierce through the clouds.

Dioni thought only of Alma. Even if the local authorities ordered the entire area to be evacuated, Alma had nowhere to go. Who would accept the children of an orphanage? Who would willingly take responsibility for what most considered the problems of others? Why would anyone care when they had to save themselves?

The many questions that circled Dioni's mind came to a sudden stop at the precise moment the clouds parted. He saw what no other living soul had witnessed from such a perspective. To his left, Dioni saw the powerful light which radiated from the sun. Its beams provided him with the warmth that was immediately removed by what he saw below. As if in a dream – or perhaps a nightmare of epic proportions – Dioni attained the very first look at the forces which slowly, yet confidently, drew plans against all in their path.

The massive cyclones existed solely for the purpose of total destruction. Beneath Dioni and to his left was Eliza, a storm so large and so angry that its cyclonic span branched a series of storms of its own. Beneath Dioni and to his right was Elijah, though apparently smaller than his twin sister, Elijah's fury drew from the depths of the warmer waters to block the sun and leave nothing but darkness in its wake.

Between the two mighty storms was the Central American terrain. Dioni saw the streetlights as they flickered as a result of sharp winds. From an incredible distance he witnessed how the twin hurricanes – though yet to actually touch the land – caused the trees to sway in unison in almost every direction. It was perhaps his one and only chance to see the full gravity of the Alpha's master plan, which was programmed to absolute perfection.

Dioni lowered his altitude to search for the safest path to Flores. He feared not the pain caused by the wind, which struck him with raindrops that felt like tiny shards of glass. He feared not the thunder, which roared with rage at the crash and strike of each bolt of lightning. What Dioni feared most was the loss of his opportunity to see Alma before the storms took what remained of her. His objective was to save her life and the lives of every orphan, even if it meant a trade for his own.

From miles above the land, Dioni descended to a point where he saw dozens of long streams of white mist created by odd behavior in the ocean. It was not a reaction from rogue waves, nor was it a result of strong winds that pushed the shallow waters away from Guatemala. Instead, the streams appeared as if they travelled from the south, along each coastline, headed north.

This intrigued Dioni. He used the force of gravity to descend towards the source of the streams. With each moment, as he gradually lowered his speed and altitude, Dioni further regretted his decision to toss his pathfinder into the sea. His ability to launch and cut through the sky was a talent he completely took for granted, a lesson he learned just once. Dioni dove close enough to the ocean and saw rows upon rows of objects which dashed in and out of the water, and who moved in impeccable unison. The creatures at the front of each stream launched under the surface of the sea and leapt from the water to grasp air and return to their formation. With each leap they replaced one another as the leader of the pack.

Dioni descended further and saw that the creatures who dashed below and jumped above the surface were not birds, but rather pods of dolphins. Beneath the streams and waves created by the dolphins were perfectly symmetrical streaks of air bubbles, created by the world's greatest pilots. Dioni was familiar with the formation of the bubbles, which gave him a sense of relief to know that the mass group was the result of two completely different species who joined forces against a common enemy.

471

Dioni raised himself as he came within a few meters above the sounds of the dolphins who lifted above and dove below the surface of the ocean. They were gleeful and playful as they raced one another through the water, and they maintained their speed while they remained at a safe distance from the further submerged penguins.

The pods of jumpers noticed Dioni as they leapt from the water, and they whistled to him as if to gain his attention. Despite the abilities of his pathfinder, Dioni was unable to understand their form of communication, yet their actions were loud and clear – the dolphins were ecstatic to see the Omega bird. Dioni further descended to be at eye-level with the fastest of the dolphins as they continuously leapt from the ocean then splashed into the water and dashed at incredible velocity. The cycle of their actions repeated over and again.

A particularly strong and overly-playful dolphin lifted from the water and purposely brushed against Dioni's long tailfeathers, which forced Dioni to look down. In doing so, he saw that one precise stream of air bubbles separated itself from the mass group and headed toward a small patch of land. The same dolphin repeated his action and once again jumped out of the water to bump Dioni in the direction of the streak that led away from the parallel rows of launchers. The two beings communicated in completely different languages, yet the dolphin's actions conveyed the message his words could not.

Dioni followed the solo streak until it reached its end on an uninhabited spec of land within the waters of the Caribbean Sea. The streak of air bubbles momentarily disappeared, though Dioni was able to follow the submerged motions of the object which created them. From beneath the water emerged an emperor penguin, who launched from the sea and landed perfectly on the sandy shore of the islet. Dioni circled above the penguin then landed a few yards away. He made sure to leave ample space between himself and the much larger bird. The penguin waddled towards Dioni.

"Sir, are you the Omega bird?" asked the penguin as he approached.

"I am," said Dioni, who lifted his head to address the mighty bird.

The penguin raised his right wing to his brow, a sign of respect to salute the Omega. Dioni responded by doing the same in return.

"Sir, you were spotted by our naval comms team while you were in flight. I'm here to confirm the operation," said the penguin. He lowered his wing to his side.

"I was under the impression only flight birds would take part in this," responded Dioni. "I thought penguins were only going to help communicate the mess—"

"—Can I speak freely, sir?" interrupted the penguin.

"Yes, absolutely!"

"Sir, our team analyzed the data provided to us by the quetzal station in the Mayan city of northern Guatemala."

"The Mayan city?" asked Dioni. "Wait…when did this happen?"

"Three days ago, sir. Their message said they saw this coming. They said they had known an event such as this occurring in the past. Their ambassador at headquarters abandoned his post and relayed the message to us."

"To the penguins?"

"The emperors, to be more specific, sir."

"That doesn't make sense," said Dioni. "Why would she do that? And under whose authority?"

"Ambassadors do not require authority from the Alpha or the Omega when their home territories are under the threat of a natural phenomenon. They must have seen something the other stations did not."

"Huh," responded Dioni. He questioned whether or not he should have known to do the same. "Then why would they reach out to the penguins before asking for help from other territories?"

"The emperors, sir," said the penguin.

"Right, the emperors. Why you?"

"Sir, if they have indeed seen this before – and if they knew what to expect – then they likely knew the greatest impact of the storms would be from the water and not from the wind. This was conveyed to us as a rescue mission."

"That still doesn't make sense."

"We presume they needed the assistance of the world's greatest pilots. We may not be practical in the sky, sir, but our troops are unmatched in the water. No offense."

"None taken," said Dioni. "Well, the mission is already underway. A signal was sent to all territories to send birds to help stop the storms from the sky. How do you plan on stopping two hurricanes from the ocean?"

Dioni raised his eyebrow as if to question the penguin's knowledge.

"We can't, sir," responded the penguin. "At least not from the sea. We were asked to concentrate on collateral damage."

"Collateral damage?"

"The crashing waves, whirlpools, and keeping the pressure off the land, sir. We'll monitor the water so the airborne teams can concentrate on the sky."

"So what are you going to do?" asked Dioni. "Hold the water in place?"

"No, sir, that would be impossible. Our plan is to push it back. It's how we fight the cold in the winter to protect our kind. We huddle as one, then push out in waves. Same concept. It's the only way we can beat this. All or nothing, sir."

Dioni smirked. He never considered how flightless birds could take part in an event of such magnitude. Even if his time with the Adelie's was brief, Dioni was grateful for what he learned from a different group of penguins. He turned his head toward the vast ocean.

"What about the dolphins?" asked Dioni.

"They volunteered, sir," responded the penguin.

"Volunteered?"

"Their communications systems are far superior than even our best tech, sir. They saw us migrate from the Antarctic and joined us out of sheer curiosity. Once they learned what we were doing, they sent a mass broadcast to their kind. They joined us on the Peruvian side of the Pacific, and on the Brazilian side of the Atlantic. They call themselves the 'Phins of Fury', sir."

"Phins of fury? What does that mean?"

"We're not entirely sure, sir. We can communicate with them, but we don't speak their language. Our intelligence tells us that this is some type of game to them. It's almost as if they're looking forward to the challenge of the waves created by the storms, sir."

"Well then let's not get in their way," Dioni said, a smile flashed across his face. "If we can't stop this, we're going to need every last one of them to act as lifeguards." Dioni looked directly at the taller and larger penguin, then raised his right wing to his brow. "Good luck out there."

"Yes, sir. Thank you, sir," responded the penguin.

The emperor raised his fin to once again salute his superior officer, then turned his body to waddle toward the ocean.

"Wait!" Dioni shouted to gain the penguin's attention. "Can I ask you one last thing?"

"Sir?" the penguin turned and responded.

"Launching," said Dioni.

"What about it, sir?"

"Can it be done by an aviator without a pathfinder?"

The emperor smiled and lowered his guard.

"It would take a very special type of aviator to do so, sir. It's a skill that can't be taught."

Dioni shook his head.

"That's what I thought," he responded, disappointed by the penguin's response.

"Sir, can I offer a suggestion?"

"Yes, by all means," Dioni said, excitedly.

"Your tailfeathers," said the penguin, aware of Dioni's dilemma.

"What about them?"

"They do more than send a signal to the female birds your age, sir."

"They do *what*?"

"It's why you fly in a wave pattern," the penguin continued. "Why not just fly in much larger waves? Use gravity and the wind to your advantage. You lose speed on the rise, but you gain it on the descent."

Dioni stood dumbfounded. He was unsure whether he was more annoyed at himself for not having thought of the solution on his own, or because the suggestion came from a bird who had no business in the sky.

"Good luck, sir," said the emperor penguin.

He waddled a few yards forward and disappeared into the water shortly after he submerged himself and launched into the Caribbean Sea.

Dioni looked to the sky. Behind him was the warmth and kindness of a perfect ecosystem, one which provided ample sunlight and long life to countless beings. It was peaceful, and happy, and far from the threat of danger. In the opposite direction, the light was drowned by the ferocity of nature. The twin hurricanes approached with vigor, and they dared all forms of life to make even the slightest attempt to curtail their destiny. It was only a matter of hours before the storms reached the shores of Guatemala and released a wrath matched by no other force on Earth.

...

A strong breeze brushed Alma's hair as she looked attentively at the cloud formation in the sky. The mega storms had yet to make their grand entrance, though the elements of their rage made landfall. Alma stood in the street, alone. She was grateful that the one her young heart loved was not present to experience what she saw. If by a great storm Dioni was taken from her, then by the same fate would she face nature's wrath and welcome the chance to once again be united.

"Alma!" shouted Oscar from a distance though loud enough to be heard over the rumble of the wind. She turned her attention to him as he ran from the orphanage to the street. "The electricity went out. On the radio they said that we have to stay inside, away from the windows, and wait for it to pass us by."

Alma once again directed her attention to the clouds.

476

"You can't be out here," Oscar continued. "We can't stay in the orphanage either. It's too old and has too many windows, so we're going to the church. It's big enough and strong enough to hold everybody, plus it only has the one big window—"

Oscar's words drifted away as Alma turned her head and looked in the opposite direction. She saw a small patch of cloudless sky, a blue oasis between two mighty storms. It seemed as if the world itself was after her, to finish what it began with Dioni. She secretly wished for the storms to do their worst; it was no act of bravery, but rather one of desperation. She accepted her fate, to live an entire lifetime without him, though she wanted nothing more than another opportunity to see him. Then she could tell him everything she always wanted to say. Then she could properly say goodbye.

Oscar lost his patience. Though he did not feel it himself, he understood his sister's pain. He knew she would gladly remain outdoors and battle the elements on her own. It was his responsibility to get her to safety. He gently grabbed Alma's arm then led her away from the emptiness of the lonely street.

…

Mimidae's paces evolved into a circle-eight flight pattern above the impromptu workstations of the two white doves. Flight was traditionally difficult for her to do while on or even near the Trading Floor; to be able to do so with no interruption was a serene, almost peaceful experience. With each circle she made, Mimidae looked down to the doves with hope to witness their achievement of the impossible.

Donna stood on Ricky's shoulder as he searched through an endless list of historical documents – centuries upon centuries of global climate and weather information – to discover the possibility of a clue. The files were calculated by the millions, and after hours of search, not a single one provided instruction for a backdoor entrance to the mainframe of the Control Center.

Jackie knew, beyond a shadow of a doubt, that the system was imperfect.

In one way or another, a flaw existed – a weakness yet to be discovered. To prevent an endless search through countless documents, to find a microscopic needle buried within the largest digital haystack in the universe, Jackie looked to find a method in which she could reconfigure principal control over the entire Department. She learned that while the birds of the Earth held the power and the responsibility to control the climate of the planet, they were powerless against the automation which regulated the environment for the Department of Global Climate Control. The system knew to protect the Alpha bird at all costs, even if it meant harm to other birds. As if programmed by the Alpha himself, the firewalls simply could not be breached.

With every loop she made, Mimidae replayed thousands of conversations between herself and the Alpha. As a mockingbird she had the natural gift of superior memory, and though historically she used her talent of recollection to mimic the calls and sounds of other birds, the same talent allowed her to remember a lifetime of conversations. As she looped from one side of the Trading Floor to the other, the sound of Dioni's voice echoed in her mind.

...

With the lack of his assigned pathfinder, Dioni's ability to launch – or to achieve rapid flight of any kind – was limited to what he could physically perform, with calculated exceptions. Ally's pathfinder was inferior to the one he willingly donated to the Indian Ocean, yet it was far greater to what he was able to do without it.

Dioni knew better than to question the information he received from the emperor penguin a few hours prior. The Earth's greatest pilots carried their distinction with honor and with pride, though also with full recognition of their earned reputation. Despite the physical limitations, their uncanny ability to study flight was second to none.

Dioni soared in enormous wave patterns, which enabled him to utilize the laws of physics to his advantage. It cost him physical strength to elevate himself with each rise. He flapped his wings with all his strength to attain the highest altitude his small body could achieve, then aimed each descent to gain a speed arguably equal to that of a launch.

The deadline for Dioni to reach his hometown was fast approaching. In the near distance he saw the first effects of the horrendous storms: houses leveled, streets flooded, cars carried away by water, and trees ripped from their roots. It was the first phase. Merely a matter of hours remained before the full ferocity of the superstorms annihilated what remained of northern Guatemala, to leave behind only a faint memory of what was once the land of eternal spring. In a repetition of history, a single bird would once again be responsible for the aquatic burial of an advanced, ancient civilization.

With limited navigational abilities, Dioni followed the seemingly endless coastline from the shores of Nicaragua and Honduras to the beaches of his home country. He dodged the cyclonic winds of Hurricane Elijah and flew towards a large bay, where he saw a town not too dissimilar from his own. The mighty storm's valiant effort to destroy the coast had proven successful, though fragments of coastal villages remained intact. The first town he saw along the bay was one which displayed proof of life; it was the only location that retained electric power. The light emitted by a single bulb enabled Dioni to read a sign atop a small chocolate shop: *Bienvenidos a Puerto Barrios.*

He made it! Dioni was vaguely familiar with the city of Puerto Barrios. Once in Guatemala, only a short flight further inbound and northbound remained for him to reach his final destination. If the pathfinder was able to get him within range of locations he recognized, Dioni could easily navigate himself to Flores.

"Pathfinder!" Dioni shouted over the roar of fierce waves and powerful wind gusts. The device on the back of his neck emitted a beeping sound which confirmed its availability to receive orders. "Navigate northwest, towards the Mayan kingdom!"

Immediately after it received the command, the device navigated Dioni over a river that was protected by a vast topography. The only landmark he was able to identify was a centuries-old castle on the bank of a river, which held strong against the unnatural weather.

"That's *Río Dulce*," Dioni said aloud.

He finally understood why Mario insisted he learn to read maps as opposed to relying so heavily on electronic navigation. Had he not previously invested countless hours to study road maps of the area – as all good junior tour guides must do – he would have been completely oblivious to the fact that his path home was paved and free of traffic. Dioni circled the castle to find the road that directed him to Flores.

His flight through the storm became increasingly difficult. It was as if the twin hurricanes had familiarized themselves with his plan and worked together to prohibit the Omega bird from achieving his goal. With almost no visibility, Dioni was forced to rely on his instincts and his memory of the natural landscape, which was slightly less difficult to do at a higher elevation. Dioni pushed his wings as best he could to lift himself above the first layer of clouds. The higher altitude provided him with the first full view of his opponent.

Dioni became awestruck. Separated by only a flicker of space large enough to allow a glimpse of blue sky and sunlight, were the supernatural creations designed by the Alpha. They appeared as suspended islands – massive structures in motion that consumed all which stood in their path. Eliza, though derived from an ocean whose very name defines tranquility, was as merciless as her twin brother. Independently, each storm had the capacity to level an entire forest. Together, they could consume mountains.

Dioni dove and returned to the unnatural chaos. His enemies were the wind, which pushed him violently in every direction; the rain, which was cold and struck mercilessly against his frail frame; and the light of the sun, which found a way to hide itself as it, too, feared the power of a scorned mother nature. Dioni fought through the elements and through his pain as he followed the road that guided him home.

...

The bird at the helm of the Control Center took his stance of pride as he tracked his creations on the massive screen. In his mind he heard a symphony. Like a deranged conductor, he moved about the vacant Control

Center to create disorder to the weather in various locations around the Earth. As he danced and hummed his own tune, he took control of the smaller workstations and reprogrammed the commands that were submitted by the birds of each station.

"Just a little here, and a little there," the Alpha said aloud. "Paris could use a little rain right about now." He performed a series of motions before a monitor surrounded by Parisian decorations. "Approved by Alpha."

The residents and tourists of the French city enjoyed a beautiful afternoon before they noticed an odd, sudden formation of rainclouds above them. To the Alpha, his actions were hysterical. He continued his mischief as he strolled from workstation to workstation to create a series of minor anomalies: a heavier-than-usual fog over San Francisco; a completely unexpected snow shower in Montreal; an unusually sunny day in London; an incredibly windy night in Sydney; massive waves off the coast of Rio de Janeiro; a surprising cold front upon the entire island of Madagascar; and an unexpected avalanche in the mountains of Afghanistan were among the dozens of strange and inexplicable weather phenomena which occurred simultaneously around the globe. So long as his twins remained undisturbed and were allowed to proceed as planned, the vulture could not care any less for the consequences of his actions.

The Alpha reached workstation 06-01-10B8 and paused his tune as he gleefully entered the abandoned space.

"The quetzal station, huh?" he said with a large grin on his face. "Why on Earth would this station be empty? If anything, this is the only bird who should be here."

The vulture took his position within the workstation. He opened the controls and saw that the list for scheduled weather orders was entirely blank.

"Strange…" he said aloud. "Well I guess that makes sense. If none of it's going to exist after today, there's no point in scheduling for the future."

He turned his attention to the massive screen. A hurricane reflected in the glimmer of each of his eyes; Eliza and Elijah were harmonious objects of beauty.

"You should've been here, bird," the Alpha spoke to an invisible adversary. "Then you could've helped me find your friend. Doesn't really matter now, does it?"

The Alpha turned to address the rows of empty workstations.

"You're all fired!" he shouted with glee. "Unless one of you foul fowl can track the location of the Omega, none of you are of any—"

As a requested command from the Alpha, the massive screen immediately displayed the exact location of the Omega bird. The gargantuan map revealed a black triangle as it moved toward northern Guatemala. The vulture howled with delight; in his wildest dreams he never imagined it was possible, and so simple, to solve multiple problems simultaneously.

"Young man, who gave you permission to use Ally's old pathfinder?"

The Alpha smiled as his face transitioned from freakishly pale to gleefully red.

"How ignorant can a bird be?" he said between fits of laughter. Tears formed in his eyes and rolled down the sides of his face. "I'm crying! I'm crying!" he shouted with delight.

The sound of laughter echoed through the halls of the Control Center. For the Alpha, it was a euphoric sentiment which could not be forced, replicated or duplicated. He looked at the tracker on the screen and almost burst with happiness.

The Alpha quickly took to the air and sat on the perch of the control deck. He opened the controls and used his body movements to continue the command of the twin superstorms to his desire. He suddenly halted his actions.

"Wait a second," he said, his large wings pointed vertically. "Not yet." He slowly lowered his wings. "Let it simmer…let it simmer."

The Alpha looked at the screen, placed his wings behind his head, then leaned his body against the back wall of the workstation.

Chapter Thirty-One

Few aspects of flight are more stressful to birds than the skill and precision necessary to remain airborne under conditions of zero visibility. While the pathfinder Dioni wore was programmed to protect him, it was far from its programmed capabilities to navigate him through a torrential downpour. He was struck from every direction, pushed and pulled violently through the air, with only sheer willpower to guide him through the storm.

The road which led to Flores was barely visible. The wind carried the debris of all it destroyed, which amounted to the obliteration of entire fields of sugarcane, tropical trees, tin-roofed homes, and countless pieces of plastic and garbage. For moments, Dioni had no idea which direction was up or down, north or south or east or west. He was far removed from his element, which Eliza made every effort to exploit.

Dioni swerved in the sky to avoid a series of wooden blocks and other heavy items that attacked from every direction as if aimed directly at him. Ally's pathfinder was intelligent enough to defend Dioni against threats from above or behind, but to dodge the many objects that were hurled at him was a skill he was forced to acquire on his own. In doing so, Dioni lost the road below. No matter the strength he used to direct his flight closer toward the ground, Eliza simply refused to allow it.

Dioni noticed a large object that swirled beneath him, though still attached to the ground. The object fought desperately to hold itself in place but was ultimately unable to fight a far superior enemy. Dioni opened his eyes just enough to see a large palm tree ripped from its roots and spin out of control as it was involuntarily lifted to strike him. The pathfinder signaled loudly to warn him of a great threat headed his way. He shifted himself a mere instant before the palm tree permanently removed him from the sky. The move forced Dioni to lift his head and his body. In the distance he saw a flicker of light which beamed at him from an invisible source.

With every ounce of energy his small frame could muster, Dioni fought against the storm to gain a better view of the light. Between strikes of lightning and flashes of clarity, he saw a white glow which highlighted over his entire body and followed his every move. Like a ray from a lighthouse in the distance, the source of the light gave Dioni a moment of visibility among the darkness and destruction.

Dioni raced toward the brightness as best he could. With every degree of strength he placed into each stroke of his wings, Dioni discovered he was of no match against a force of such grandeur. The light in the distance grew brighter as it followed his every movement; it was a welcomed blessing to Dioni, who was unable to navigate any further than the length of his wings as the wind and the rain prevented greater visibility.

Dioni was exhausted, yet he remained determined. The weight of the water made his wings increasingly heavier, and no matter of flight made his treacherous journey any less difficult. The light that followed him flickered and created a strobe-like effect which caused him dizziness. In an effort to escape the searchlight, he elevated himself and forced his body to drift aimlessly to a higher altitude.

"Dioni!" he heard, faintly, over the madness of the downpour.

He looked in every direction, unsure whether the sound he heard was the voice of another bird or a severe malfunction of his borrowed pathfinder.

"Dioni!" repeated the voice, more audibly. "Your wings are too heavy!" Dioni searched again and saw nothing but drops of rain and elements of debris. "Dive down and keep your wings as level as possible!"

Dioni did as instructed. He squinted his eyes, pushed his head forward then shifted his body, which allowed gravity and the mighty wind to take command. He was instantly forced down by the storm's fiercest element. The source of light tracked and followed his movement. He opened his eyes and saw the silhouette of a large structure in the near distance.

Dioni felt a sudden, powerful grip on his shoulders. It was another bird, who pulled and lifted him away from the madness of the storm. He kept his wings as level as possible. His body became limber as he surrendered control to an aviator who was far better prepared to navigate under such harsh conditions. He looked up and saw a deep red color, which emerged beneath the brightest green feathers he had ever seen. Dioni's rescuer was completely unphased by the unnatural elements under the command of a greater authority. With utmost ease, the rescuer pierced through the wind, the rain and the debris, and through the many artifacts that relentlessly attempted to remove both birds from existence.

The green bird navigated to the source of the light, which became increasingly brighter as the two birds approached. Dioni squinted to block the brightness, as well as to clear some of the raindrops which impeded his vision. He suddenly felt a sensation of warmth, then the beam of light completely disappeared.

The two birds breached an invisible barrier. Instantly, Dioni was removed from under the threat of an aimless flight within a hurricane. The sky became calm and peaceful, and despite his ability to see the effects of the external storm, no immediate threat existed on the opposite side of the barrier. Dioni's vision came into clarity. He looked up and once again saw the same colors as before; he distinguished his rescuer in its resplendent form. The bird who held Dioni by his shoulders was a mighty quetzal – a fellow aviator to whom Dioni would remain forever grateful.

Beyond the barrier through which he was carried, Dioni saw the destructive force in all its splendor. The wind and the rain did not falter, yet he remained entirely untouched by nature's fury. As if held back by an invisible energy, neither Eliza nor Elijah had jurisdiction among the great Mayan city of Tikal, nor were they welcomed within the Great Plaza. Though he initially overpassed his intended destination, Dioni had successfully returned.

The green quetzal navigated to a door-like opening at the peak of the large stairwell, which Dioni recognized as the Temple of the Great Jaguar. A series of green lasers appeared from within the entranceway of the temple, a security measure by which the quetzals detected foreign birds or beings who did not belong. The green quetzal gained speed and flew directly into the laser field. He held Dioni as close to himself as possible, then yelled a battle cry which was heard and recognized by a force within the ancient structure.

The two birds crossed the threshold of lasers, a system by which their bodies were scanned from beak to tailfeathers. They glided from one habitat to another, from the modern world to that of an ancient civilization, where natural light was held back in exchange for an ultra-sophisticated manner of illumination. As the two birds further entered the security field, Dioni heard the soothing, feminine voice he vaguely recalled upon his first entrance into the quetzal kingdom: "*Pharomacrus* identified, *mocinno*. Approved for entry".

The green quetzal released Dioni the moment the two birds were completely away from harm. With full illumination to enable him to see the vastness of the avian sanctuary, Dioni returned to the grandeur of the city hidden beneath the Great Plaza. He remembered the colors, the hieroglyphics, the light, and the energy he sensed from the mythical birds. Dioni felt welcomed and appreciated; no longer was he a boy trapped in a bird's body, but rather the known Omega bird who had earned his place among his kind.

Dioni looked down to an eager audience in waiting. Whereas he was previously a trespasser within their habitat, he had since become their beacon of hope. The collective sentiment of the thousands of quetzals who gathered at the base of the mighty tree – where the mystic river met the ancient trail – was evident. Even from afar, Dioni felt their fear. The birds of the quetzal kingdom feared not the pressure to host a controlled natural phenomenon in their territory, but rather the possibility of absolute annihilation. The Department of Global Climate Control relinquished their right to exist and made every possible effort to ensure the complete and total destruction of their sacred territory.

Dioni landed near the base of the river, where he was immediately surrounded by hundreds of anxious quetzals. He looked up and saw hundreds more perched among the mighty walls, along with others who observed from their positions within the massive tree. From every solid surface large enough to sustain them stood scores of resplendent quetzals. He was approached by a younger quetzal who offered Dioni water from the river, carefully wrapped in a banana leaf. Dioni's body rejuvenated with every gulp of the mystic liquid.

"Are you here to help us?" asked a nervous, young quetzal.

The bird spoke with a native accent which borrowed from Spanish. Dioni turned to face the youngling, who trembled with fear.

"Yes," responded Dioni, "but I need your help."

He walked to the young quetzal and lowered his stance to be at eye-level with the smaller bird. It reminded Dioni of how he soothed the younger children of the orphanage when they, too, were frightened of that which they did not understand.

"Señor Omega," said a female quetzal, a few paces behind Dioni. He stood and turned to face her. "We lost communication with the main station. We sent a broadcast signal to request for help, but we did not receive a response. Can you tell us what has happened?"

"Where is the representative from headquarters?" asked Dioni. "The one who works in the Control Center…is he here?"

There was no response, save for a single bird in the distance who raised his wing.

"I'm here, sir," said an elder quetzal, whose once bright colors had slowly faded; only one of his tattered tailfeathers remained.

"Your workstation was empty," Dioni responded. "I was told you knew this was going to happen. How is that possible?"

"All of the proper elements were in place, señor Omega," responded the elder bird. "This is a repetition of history. I left my post once I determined my involvement would be of no use. I choose to die among my kind than to live at the mercy of the vulture, sir."

Dioni looked around the massive complex. It was impossible for him to believe that the vast empire remained entirely unscathed by the wrath of the two hurricanes.

"How can this be?" Dioni asked, loud enough to be heard by every bird in the vicinity. "How is this temple protected from the hurricanes?"

"All of *La Gran Plaza* is protected, señor Omega," responded an elder female quetzal.

"How is it done?" Dioni asked her.

"This was negotiated long ago," responded the elder male. "Our kingdom was to be protected by the Department, but the people were forced to leave."

"The drought?" Dioni responded. "Did the Alpha force the people to abandon the city?"

"Yes, to restore the natural balance," responded the elder male. "*La Plaza* is protected from the elements of the sky, but not from the sea. A flood from two hurricanes will leave us at the floor of the ocean, to remain forever lost. He has done this before."

Dioni sighed. He was at a complete loss as to what could be done to save the ancient birds of the Mayan kingdom, though he did not lose sight of the main objective for his return to Guatemala. Every second meant more destruction caused by the twin hurricanes.

A faint sound was emitted from a signal detection system housed on the ledge where the projection screens of the quetzal kingdom communicated with headquarters. Dioni turned toward the direction of the sound and saw a small dot glide across a large screen.

"What is that?" Dioni asked.

Every bird within the mythic sanctuary turned to the screens.

"An unregistered bird, señor Omega," responded the elder female.

"Unregistered? What does that mean?"

"The sound is a signal source. It indicates when a foreign bird is within the vicinity. Our kind is endangered outside of these walls, so we use this as a failsafe method to protect—"

A second sound interrupted her explanation, followed by a third, a fourth, a fifth… What began as single sounds quickly transitioned to hundreds, which grew exponentially with every passing second.

Worry intensified among the resplendent birds. They spoke amongst themselves – some filled with fear, others prayed to their creator – while many huddled together and looked to the sky as if they expected an aerial attack.

Dioni smiled. He turned and kneeled to directly face the young quetzal.

"The rescuers are here," he said. The youngling smiled.

Dioni returned his attention to the screen and noticed the additional dots. Hundreds of thousands of unregistered birds created a formation above the Mayan airspace.

"Is there a simple way out?" Dioni asked. "One that will not put me directly in the storm?"

"Si, señor Omega," responded a large, male quetzal. His green and red colors were as prominent as his warrior physique. "I can take you."

"Perfect. Let's go," Dioni responded. He paced toward the larger quetzal.

"What shall we do here, señor Omega?" asked the elder male.

Dioni faced the elder bird and sensed a glimmer of hope, evident in his eyes and in the gaze of every bird who looked to him as their hero. Dioni opened his beak but was unable to utter a single phrase. He looked around the mighty temple and observed how he was one among the ancient birds, not an outcast of a different color who did not belong. Regardless of the color of his feathers, he had earned his distinction as a member of the world's most elite beings. The words *blue* and *go* were not mentioned by any bird in the entire kingdom.

A singular thought came to Dioni. He recalled the wise words said to him by two of his friends, who wanted for Dioni's success more so than he wanted it for himself. They were right; no matter where he travelled, the fact remained. Though separated from one another by two oceans and a grand continent, the wise birds ingrained the idea which transcended the elements of fear and doubt within him: the birds are always watching.

"Get ready," said Dioni. He smiled as he saw the eyes of every quetzal who looked to him for strength. "We are the birds of this land, and we will fight against anything or anyone that tries to destroy it! If history does repeat itself, it will not be over this territory!"

Dioni faced the elder quetzal.

"The birds are always watching, right?"

Dioni and the warrior quetzal spread their wings and lifted from the ground. A third quetzal, the most skilled aviator among them, followed closely behind. The three birds circled around the mighty tree at the center of the quetzal kingdom then flew directly toward a light on a high peak. It was the same light that guided Dioni through the storm, and which would once again direct him to the path he narrowly escaped.

The three birds rushed out of the temple as the energy of the mighty structure thrust them to the sky. Immediately after they surpassed the protective barrier, the three birds felt the merciless anger of the storm. The wind was cold and unrelenting, and the clouds released a cascade of rain and hail to deter the Omega's attempt to engage in a battle he could not possibly win.

The two accompanying quetzals flew adjacent to Dioni, to protect him as best they could. They were far more experienced aviators and were better prepared to absorb the fury of the storms. Their actions were not acts of bravery nor of chivalry, but rather that of service. Their presence made the flight significantly less complicated for Dioni, who led the trio above the clouds.

The three birds reached an elevation far above that which the two experienced aviators had ever attained. They glided momentarily as the view above the clouds displayed a murmuration too grand to describe; Dioni looked in awe at the largest gathered formation of birds ever assembled. As they circled above the mighty storms, thousands upon thousands of birds flew as a single flock. In mass unison, the birds remained oblivious to each of their differences. There existed no predators, no prey, no birds of beauty in color nor of splendor in sound. Their dissimilarities were of no importance, for their objective was not for the benefit of their individual territories. The murmuration was for the benefit of all birds, where the victors would rise far beyond the legacy of every aviator who had ever felt the freedom to soar in the sky.

Dioni flew toward the center of the mass formation. Followed closely by his guardians, he joined the massive murmuration to fly in unison with the countless number of birds engaged and ready for battle. The three quetzals navigated through the aerial traffic. Dioni dodged and weaved through the small crevices of available space as he searched for the single bird in command over the vast collection of Earth's bravest aviators; in his mind, only one bird was capable of such respect and distinction.

Dioni looked to his left and saw a familiar face. He briefly smiled. Dioni assumed the encounter on the beach of the small island would be the last he would share with his mentor. The thought that he would never see her again slowly drifted from his mind with each flap of his blue wings. He spotted a glorious Hawaiian crow, whose lack of physical color did not deter the natural light which radiated an aura of authority among all birds. Dioni flew through the collection of birds who slowly circled high above the ground.

"Ally!" Dioni shouted. His voice landed on deaf ears. "Ally!" he repeated, with no reaction from the crow or from any of the birds near her. "Ally!" he shouted a third time, from a distance he knew was close enough for her to hear.

The crow failed to notice him, nor did she make any gesture to acknowledge his presence. Dioni glided to position himself beside her, where she would undoubtedly see him.

"Al—"

Dioni quickly acknowledged his error and stopped himself before he was able to say her name. He mistakenly misidentified the Alalā, who turned to Dioni and glared at him with eyes seemingly void of life. Dioni was taken aback; not only was he under the impression that Ally would be the bird responsible for the unification of millions of aviators who came to battle the creations of the Alpha, he also became startled by what he saw in the eyes of the crow.

491

The brightest stars of the deepest, darkest night sky reflected in the eyes of the crow he mistook for his mentor. The bird's eyes were both full of life yet completely lifeless, and they manifested the formation of the galaxy as if derived from a universe far beyond any natural environment which Earthbound organisms could comprehend.

Dioni turned to his opposite direction. A much smaller goldcrest flew beside him. It flapped its wings with all its strength to remain within the greater formation. To Dioni's amazement, the goldcrest's eyes displayed in the same manner as the crow: a vast darkness which reflected an infinite number of stars in the galaxy. The same was evident in the geese behind him, in the whooping cranes above him, in the cardinals beneath him, in the mallards in the distance, and in the swans who pierced through the sky with utmost ease. Each minute brought scores of additional birds of all shapes, colors, sizes, strengths and abilities. As they joined the murmuration, their eyes transitioned from their natural colors to a state beyond the realm of possibility.

Dioni pulled himself away from the large formation, which gradually gained speed though slowly lost altitude. He was followed closely by his two guardians, who kept themselves at a safe distance from the Omega should there be a need to protect him. As if pushed by an unseen force, Dioni reengaged with the greater formation by no act of his own. The two guardian quetzals attempted to follow but were powerless against a threat they could not identify.

The wind pushed and guided Dioni beside a large snowy owl, whose eyes were as supernatural as the rest of the birds in the mighty formation. The owl noticed Dioni – the only bird within the murmuration to acknowledge Dioni's existence – and drifted to maintain its flight beside the blue quetzal. The snowy owl then extended its wing to Dioni, as if to offer his assistance while they remained in flight. Dioni touched the extended wing of the owl with his own.

A force of both darkness and light immediately struck Dioni's being. His vision transcended the universe, which enabled him to link his energy with that of the grander formation. Dioni envisioned an alternate version of the Earth; he was blind to the light of the sun, yet was able to see an illustrious planet filled with colors so vast and so rich that they were indescribable by written or spoken word. Every bird – regardless of how it appeared under the spectrum of visible light – displayed a vast array of radiant energy which surpassed the pureness of the sun.

The Omega bird became united unto a dimension known only to the beings responsible for the balance of all that is natural to the Earth. Below him were the twin hurricanes, which he saw in all their might and fury. However, he saw the energy beyond the storms themselves – beyond the wind, the rain, the hail, and the fury – and was able to feel them in the same manner in which he sensed another living being. They were not creations of nature, but rather two organic energies who felt, who saw, and who breathed, as did all creatures of the Earth. Just as all forms of life fought for their survival when under the threat of extinction, so too would the mighty twins.

Connected as a single formation as opposed to a multitude of birds that circled in the sky, Dioni acknowledged the unspoken plan guided by the murmuration. The birds were unable to block the two storms or divert them from their paths, for the magnitude of their strength was far too great to overpower. Instead, the ingeniousness of their counterstrike was in the creation of a rival force; with the whirlwind created by the flight formation of millions of birds, the storms were to be attacked through the removal of their source of strength until all that remained were streaks of cirrus clouds in the sky above the Guatemalan landscape.

Dioni looked up and saw a vast collection of stars and constellations from galaxies near and far. To him, the planets of various universes appeared as sources of light, which radiated with vast amounts of life that stretched from his place within the murmuration to the vastness of infinity. He saw the immensity of infinite space and time, and he saw the lifeforms of other worlds who were responsible for the natural balance of their home planets.

"Dioni," said a muffled voice which echoed in his mind. He looked down, beyond the chaos of the storms, to the source from where the voice originated. "Dioni," the voice repeated, more clearly.

He recognized the sound immediately. It was the voice of Alma, who was sheltered and confined within a small space. She did not speak a single word, her thoughts powerful enough to reach him.

Dioni turned to the snowy owl, who acknowledged what he felt. The owl nodded then retracted its wing and returned to the formation. Dioni's eyes were restored to their normal, natural color. He returned from a place void of a name and back to the physical Earth, where he once again focused on the immediate threat below. He lifted his shoulders and spread his wings, which forced him to push back and away from the murmuration. He flapped his wings and glided away from the massive group, where he was quickly met by the two guardian quetzals who had followed him thus far. He hovered at their level.

"I'm going to Flores," Dioni said to his protectors. "You can either stay here and join the formation, or you can return to the temple and help protect the kingdom. The choice is yours."

"What about you?" asked the warrior quetzal.

"I'll be where I belong," responded Dioni. "If these two storms cross paths, Flores doesn't stand a chance. Track my pathfinder."

"Yes, sir," said the two quetzals.

Dioni pushed down and dove through the natural chaos. The larger of the two quetzals joined the mass formation, while the younger bird momentarily glided in the sky before he dove to return to the ancient city.

…

Mimidae intently studied a screen which displayed the internal operations of the twin hurricanes. She thought of the people of Flores and of the small orphanage beside the church she visited just a few days prior. It was unreasonable of the Alpha to target the small town for the sake of his ego; by no choice of their own, the inhabitants of the town would be the collateral damage of a natural phenomenon far beyond their control. Mimidae analyzed the calculated configurations of both Eliza and Elijah, who cared little for the havoc they wreaked on the Central American landscape.

Ricky was hardly able to keep his eyes open after he searched through thousands of files and digital records in an effort to discover the method to open the security wall which separated him, Jackie, and Mimidae from the Control Center. The names of each of the documents blurred as he scrolled through the system, which meant that his usefulness to the project quickly faded.

Jackie focused attentively on the projected screen. She used logic to rule-out scores of unnecessary files and documents. In doing so, she stumbled upon a particularly well-hidden file folder buried so profoundly within the digitized organizational system that it was likely overlooked as a prehistoric record.

"Mim," Jackie said.

She leaned closer to the screen to inspect her discovery.

"Yeah?" responded Mimidae, who directed her attention to Jackie though not enough to release her focus from the data she studied.

"What is ice?" Jackie asked.

"Water...at or below zero degrees Celsius," responded Ricky, mostly sarcastically from sheer exhaustion.

Jackie was not amused by his response. He was too fatigued to recognize her unspoken reply to him.

"No, like the letters: I-C-E. It's on this folder I found," said Jackie. "Mim?"

"I'm not entirely sure," responded Mimidae. "It's an acronym for something."

"I figured that was the case, but for what?" asked Jackie.

"India-Canada-Ethiopia for all I know," Mimidae responded. She turned to face Jackie. "I-C-E...what else is in the folder?"

"It just says 'I-C-E', and the files inside are numbered one through nine."

"Huh," said Mimidae. "Ice one through nine? It can't be containment operations...all of those files were transferred to facilities."

"Well, whatever this is, it hasn't been updated in decades," said Jackie.

"It looks like this was one of the original files built into the system…or something."

"Really?" asked Ricky. "I couldn't find anything before the fourteenth century."

"I-C-E…I-C-E…" Mimidae repeated.

The correct answer suddenly struck her. Hidden in plain sight, Jackie discovered a document so profoundly buried that it was possible that even the Alpha did not know of its existence.

"In case of emergency!" Mimidae shouted. "Open the folder for 'ICE one'!"

Mimidae dashed to inspect Jackie's discovery. Her eyes grew wide as she read through scrolls of ancient code.

"What is it?" asked Jackie as she and Mimidae looked at the thousands of ancient records.

"Go all the way to the end," Mimidae instructed Jackie.

With the use of her wings, Jackie commanded the workstation to display and list the digital codes contained within 'ICE one'. She was taken aback as she read the final entry.

"Omega One," Jackie read aloud. She turned to Mimidae. "What does that mean?"

Mimidae cheered from where she stood. It was by pure fate and coincidence that the correct record was found, purposely buried from anything or anyone who could destroy it. If there ever existed a single document that was likely unknown to the Alpha, Jackie had serendipitously discovered it.

"It's source code from the first Omega bird," said Mimidae. "It's a fail-safe…emergency protocol. She was there when the system was created. Our answer is going to be somewhere in that folder."

Ricky attained his second wind and joined the two birds at their workstation.

"That can't be right," said Ricky. "The security wall wasn't built until after 1945. How would the first Omega bird have known about it?"

"Jackie, when was the I-C-E folder last updated?" asked Mimidae.

"June tenth, 1948," responded Jackie. Mimidae looked at Ricky.

"Why would a folder containing pre-historic code have last been updated in 1948?" asked Mimidae. "Especially the folder specifically labelled for emergencies. Someone saw the chance that this could happen and purposely left a trail."

"Who?" asked Ricky, confused by Mimidae's logic. "Who was the Omega bird in 1948?"

Jackie and Mimidae looked at each other.

"Ally," the two birds said, simultaneously.

"Look at all of this," Jackie said. She stared at the detail of the written text. "It'll take us months to decipher it."

"If you were able to find this, then between the three of us we can figure it out," said Mimidae.

Jackie looked at Ricky. The chance of her making such a significant discovery was marginal at best, and she had come too far to fail. Ricky sensed her determination; he knew better than anyone that his spouse was fully determined to achieve her goal.

"Well then we better get started," said Ricky.

...

The fierce strength of the wind forced the clouds to drop entire waterways worth of rain onto the land below, only to push it back to the sky and repeat the cycle with even greater intensity. As he dove further towards the ground, Dioni felt the rush of the twin storms that conspired against him, desperate to deter him from his goal. The strength of the opposition was of no difference to the Omega. His determination to reach Flores was far greater than the pain he felt from the elements of nature's fury.

Dioni reached a level low enough for him to distinguish the buildings and streets. At long last, he had returned. While still airborne, Dioni identified the brick road which led from the small park where his childhood memories were buried, to the structure he fondly remembered as his home. He landed on a small patch of exposed dirt, where his feet left imprints on the mud-stained ground. Dioni was grateful to once again feel the land he so passionately missed. Though no longer in flight, the wind and rain cared not for his safety and continued to drench his body. With poor visibility, Dioni ran towards the main entryway of the orphanage.

As the heavy drops of water continued to fall, Dioni heard a crash which repeated itself and grew louder with every step he drew closer. He lifted his left wing to shield his eyes from the elements of the mighty storm, then he discovered the source of the sound. He ran closer to the entryway and noticed that the main door was open, though was repeatedly and forcefully jostled by the wind. Dioni remained on the ground. The entryway was the safest manner in which to enter the building, yet a strong gust of wind could push the door and crush him. He paused. If she was on the other side of that door, it was worth the risk; if he accomplished nothing else, he just had to see her.

Dioni timed his entry to a sudden instant in which the wind forcibly opened the large door. He ran inside the structure and shook his body to remove excess water. He briefly saw the inside of the orphanage before he was hurled back onto the street by the reverse motion of the large door. Just as the wind enabled his access into the building, it quickly changed its mind and pulled Dioni away to once again place him among the cold, wind, and rain.

The force of the door struck him unexpectedly. He was hurt, more so physically than emotionally. Dioni stood up, which was a struggle as he battled his pain and the harsh wind in order to do so. With his energy severely depleted, he once again used his wing to cover his face and took a moment to examine the door that blocked his entrance. Dioni's face showed his anger. He lowered his wing, pushed his head down and bravely rushed forward.

Dioni heard the cry of a young child, a sound which was carried by the wind and the rain. He turned around, his face soaked with rainwater, and he searched for the source of the noise. He closed his eyes...it was the cry of an infant, which came from the adjacent structure. Dioni opened his eyes and faced the church. If the orphanage was unable to provide a shelter from the storms, then the only other option was to move to the closest logical safe space.

Dioni ignored the many aches of his body. He lifted his wings to cut through the wind, which provided him with a brief opportunity to run to the church. He looked at the much larger doors of the elder building. The entryway was sealed to protect those on the inside from the brutal strength of the severe weather. There was no way for him to push through the much larger and heavier doors.

Dioni hesitated before he took action. He recalled his childhood and of how simple it was to sneak in and out of the church. He remembered how he and Oscar would purposely burst through the doors in an attempt to frighten the nuns and startle those who prayed in quiet solitude. This produced a negative disciplinary effect for the two boys, who were then forced to perform a number of grueling tasks as punishment for their behavior. Still, it was not nearly as bad as the time when he chucked a rock through the stained-glass window...

The window!

Dioni ran to the side of the building to return to the scene of his long since forgiven crime. He ignored the flashbacks of the price he paid for the damage he caused and looked up to see the rock-sized, unrepaired portion of the window just above a small ledge. He pushed his wings out and shook his body as vigorously as possible to extract the additional weight of the water. He then lifted himself from the ground. The wind pushed Dioni against the side wall, which knocked him onto the solid concrete. Dioni fought harder, every flap of his wings done so with utmost pain. The sound of the infant's cries grew louder, as did the voice of the young woman who attempted to comfort the child. Dioni pushed himself from the wall and redirected his wings. With one final attempt, Dioni lifted himself onto the ledge then thrusted forward and through the small, rock-shaped crevice he created so many years prior. Though the cold remained, he was finally out of the rain.

The interior of the building was entirely dark, except for the candlelight which flickered in the distance. To the best of Dioni's recollection, the building had always been dark – even on the brightest of days. The present darkness brought forth by the hurricanes hindered his ability to navigate in parts of the building he had never known. His knowledge of the interior of the church stemmed from the doorway through the alter, and the hall in between. Dioni paced forward in search of the light source. He was anxious to see her again…so anxious, in fact, that he failed to notice the lack of ledge beneath his feet. Before he was able to open his wings or brace for impact, Dioni fell and crashed against the cold floor. The harsh sound he made drew the attention of everyone in the church, with the added benefit that it also quieted the wailing infant.

The children of the orphanage sat at the front of the hall near the base of the alter, enclosed in a tight circle. The elder children sat toward the outside of the circle, along with the elders of the church. Some among the elders were the seniors of the village, who had no other place to go.

"What was that?" asked Oscar, who nervously broke the tension created by the sound of Dioni's fall.

"Probably something the wind pushed in," responded one of the nuns.

"Like what?" asked a younger child.

"Like nothing," responded the nun. "Just a sound the wind makes, nothing more."

Dioni groaned as he stood to his feet. Elevation awareness was a lesson he learned on his first day as a bird, though it had yet to become instinctual. The fall helped him remove the excess water from his wings, which made him feel much lighter than he did before he dove into the building. He stepped a few paces forward and noticed as the elders looked nervously in his direction. The light of the candles provided him a limited vision, which was just enough to faintly see the lines and shadows of each of their faces. Dioni stepped to his side. He stood in awe as he recognized the face of the person he so dearly missed.

Alma sat at the outer rim of the circle and held an infant who rested safely in her arms. She looked every bit as beautiful as Dioni remembered, and he was finally close enough again to see her, to hear her, and to feel the warmth of her embrace. He pushed himself from the cold concrete to once again become airborne. The sound of his flaps echoed through the small cathedral.

"What was that?" asked Oscar, more fearful than when he previously spoke.

"I don't know," responded a nun.

Every member of the circle searched in all directions for the object which created the sound.

"But you did hear it, right?" asked Oscar. "I'm not going crazy, am I?"

"Not because of that sound, no," responded the nun. "It's flying."

The children looked in terror as the airborne creature made its way about the hall. The candlelight flickered against Dioni's body and created a series of long, frightening shadows, which made his movement appear as that of a carnivorous, winged beast. With every flap and every pass, the children shrieked in horror.

Dioni came into the light. He saw her face then immediately returned to the shadows.

"It's a bat!" shouted another nun.

She removed herself from the circle and ran to a small closet behind the alter.

Dioni circled and momentarily glided above the pews of the church. He thought of the best way in which to present himself as to not frighten the children or anyone else. He was likely larger than what they would recognize, but surely they would not be afraid of a harmless blue bird. The accusatory nun returned from the closet with a long object in her hands.

Dioni circled the hall once more then lowered himself to make his final approach. He opened his wings at the exact moment a strike of lightning illuminated the entire church. To the children, Dioni appeared as the monster of their nightmares. Though the flash of light was instant, it was long enough for the nun to pinpoint Dioni's exact location. If he were to

501

land just a few meters in front of the children and slowly walk into the light, they would all see that he was just an innocent quetz—

WHAM!

With the force and shout of a world-class athlete, the relatively small nun released her fear on the unsuspecting Omega bird. Dioni was struck by the brush side of a broom. While the initial impact to his chest did not cause physical harm, the blow forced him from his intended path. He stabilized himself in the air and continued his flight, though more cautious of the impending doom brought forth by the nun who clearly had anger management issues.

The nun swung the broom in every direction as she attempted to knock Dioni away from the children. With each swing, the children ducked, more fearful for their safety from the broom than of the threat of the unidentified flying object.

Lightning struck once again, the light of which lasted long enough to allow the children to see the blue bird in flight. Alma, who more tightly held the infant in her arms, looked up and noticed the bird's distinctive features. The luminance emitted by the lightning did not provide enough detail to enable her to see its true colors, though she noticed that the bird looked directly at her; a familiarity existed in its eyes.

"It's a bird!" Oscar exclaimed as he dodged the broom. "Chase it out!"

Oscar jumped to try to catch the bird with his hands, only to feel the tip of the quetzal's tailfeather brush against his arm. Two other children stood and did the same, each with no success as Dioni lifted to distance himself from them. The other nuns shouted at the children who broke the circle formation, then rushed to pull them back and away from danger. Dioni circled above them then flew to the back of the church, at a safe enough distance from the overzealous nun and away from the light of the candles.

...

Though she was the second of the twins to make landfall in Guatemala, Eliza was the first to arrive in Flores. While the penguins and dolphins worked tirelessly to hold the two storms, their best efforts only stalled the inevitable. Elijah, the more hesitant of the twin hurricanes, lost some of its strength as a result of the empathy it felt for the lives it destroyed. Eliza, on the other hand, subscribed to no such niceties; she yearned to make a lasting impression.

As she easily brushed beyond the first line of defense from the shores of southern Mexico, Eliza unleashed that which she initially withheld: the relentless and merciless power of hurricane-force winds. Slowly and steadily she moved beyond the shoreline and began the second act of her destructive performance, through the cities, towns, and villages of northern Belize. Cars were leveled, homes were destroyed, and objects of all shapes and sizes were carelessly hurled to the sky. What had taken centuries of time and generations of people to build was destroyed in its entirety within a matter of minutes. This pleased Eliza, though she saved the worst of her wrath for the hometown of the Omega bird.

. . .

Evidence of Eliza's arrival in Flores slowly came to fruition. The rain fell with greater force, the thunder roared with grander vigor, and the winds blew with utmost fury – the combination of which shook the foundation of the small cathedral. The walls were stable enough to withstand tremblors and minor Earthquakes, but its stability against an overly-aggressive natural phenomenon was never designed to withstand such opposition. Objects of various sizes hit against the concrete walls of the church's exterior, which created a series of frightful sounds to those who remained inside.

The hurricane acknowledged the resistance by the small structure. The wind further increased its intensity. Cars were tossed aside as monstrous stones rolled effortlessly along the empty streets. The trees – those who acted selflessly as protectors for the lives beneath them – absorbed the majority of the pain caused by the fierce wind. Their leaves and branches acted as sails, which hurled them violently in every direction. Many of the trees were able to stand their ground, their roots buried deeply in the

Earth; the mighty tree which stood in the courtyard adjacent to the church was not as fortunate.

Those within the building felt their shelter tremble as the wind lifted the tree and launched it against the church. Though the four large walls withstood the mighty blow, the clay tiles of the roof were not able to do so. Dioni was only a few steps away from the point where the tiles dropped on the concrete floor. While on the ground, a short distance away from the objects which could have crushed him, Dioni looked up and saw an opening which permitted a cascade of rainwater to pour into the church. The children and the elders huddled in fear; the infants wailed in utmost distress.

Dioni's time was limited. With the top of the structure in peril, it was only a matter of minutes before another large object struck the church and finished what the tree had begun.

"Pathfinder!" Dioni commanded, which activated the triangular device on the back of his neck. "Contact Mimidae!"

The pathfinder generated two high-pitched beeps, followed by a third sound of a much lower tone. A projected image came before Dioni's eyes, where in bold, red letters he read the words, *Signal Not Available.*

Dioni looked across the room, through the cascading rainwater which separated him from the huddled orphans. It was because of him that this occurred. He looked down and felt as the cold water streamed by his small feet. His body shivered, briefly. He was desperate for help – from any living creature nearby – and he had neither the knowledge nor the time to experiment by trial and error.

"Pathfinder," Dioni said. "Broadcast a message to all birds in the sky."

The device beeped twice to acknowledge Dioni's command. The letters of the projected image changed from red to green, which enabled him to relay a message as far as the signal could carry it.

"This is the Omega," Dioni said as he faced the stream of water which poured from the ceiling. "I need help! If anyone can hear me, I am at the church in Flores. There are people here with me. Please, we don't have much time!"

The message was instantly recorded and broadcast as an audio signal, with waves that weaved through the storm and lifted towards the sky. Far above the clouds, within a murmuration so massive that the clouds below feared its existence, a quetzal heard a faint sound. Though the sound of high-altitude winds faintly interrupted the signal, the quetzal received Dioni's communication. He heard a voice in distress, broadcast from a nearby source. The quetzal broke from the formation and flew away from the vast assembly of birds.

The quetzal's eyes opened wide; a single bird was powerless against an anomaly of such magnitude. Whether it was the Alpha, the Omega, or any bird who willingly placed itself in danger for the lives of others, no bird was too far gone to receive help from his peers. The quetzal curved in the sky and returned to the mighty formation in search of birds who could withdraw from the murmuration without abandoning the greater goal. A short distance away were a macaw and a toucan – two tropical birds from the nearby jungle – to whom the quetzal flew immediately.

The quetzal lowered his altitude to hover beside the toucan. As it partook in the great murmuration, the toucan's eyes were glossed and filled with both darkness and light. The quetzal reached to touch the top of the toucan's wing, which instantly connected the two birds. The quetzal relayed Dioni's message of distress to the toucan, who acknowledged and understood the command from the Omega bird.

The quetzal once again broke from the formation and dove towards the foulest facets of the storm, to risk his life in an effort to save the Omega bird. The toucan in the sky touched the nearby macaw and transmitted the message, then broke formation and followed behind the quetzal. The macaw repeated the action to another nearby aviator, who repeated it to another, who repeated it to yet another. Within moments, Dioni's broadcast message transferred from the ground to the thousands upon thousands of tropical birds in the sky, hundreds of meters above him. Scores of aviators broke from the formation – not to abandon their post or to leave the responsibility of their fight on the wings of others, but rather to attack the enemy from within.

505

Dioni stood on the cold concrete, his legs and tailfeathers wet from the water which flowed from the gap in the ceiling.

"Come on…come on…" Dioni anxiously said aloud, unto himself.

There was no change, no movement of any kind other than the remnants of Eliza's malevolence. There was absolutely no time to waste. At any given moment the entire structure could collapse under the pressure of the wind, which would crush those who attempted to flee from the storm's intensity.

"Pathfind—" Dioni began.

He stopped short as he saw a large, winged creature quickly pass through the line of site made possible by the gap above him. The creature was of similar size to Dioni and had his same lengthy tailfeathers. It was another quetzal. Dioni smiled; his call for help was received.

Just outside of the large doorway entrance to the church, Dioni heard a solid thump, the sound made by a bird who landed harshly on the ground. Moments later, he heard a second, similar sound of another bird, though a few meters away and closer to the side of the building. Almost immediately, a third sound was heard, which came from the opposite side of the church along the far exterior wall.

Dioni looked up. Beyond the falling water he saw as a wave of birds dropped from the sky, who aimed directly towards the exterior of the church. As the scores of birds landed – pulled by the wind and pushed by the rain – they struck the ground with such force that each of their landings emitted a harsh noise. The sound caused greater fear among those huddled within the church, who stood and positioned themselves in a tighter circle. The children in the center of the circle lowered their heads and braced for the worst.

Dioni heard a sound from just above where he stood. He saw a proud, green quetzal, who stood on the roof of the church near the edge of the broken tiles. The green bird looked down to Dioni. It made visual contact with the Omega bird, then motioned for Dioni to join him. Dioni stepped to the side of the waterfall. He could not see Alma, yet he knew she was protected within the circle. He spread his wings, lifted himself from the concrete floor, then flew through the gap.

Dioni returned to the wind and the rain. He flew to stand beside the green quetzal, who patiently waited for him. Dioni looked down from his position atop the roof of the church. As the many birds struck the ground, they quickly positioned themselves along the perimeter of the structure, which they themselves reinforced. The larger birds, able to sustain greater weight and pressure, positioned themselves along the base. The smaller birds slowly gathered and positioned themselves on the shoulders of the larger birds. Together, they linked into their place within the formation, opened their wings, then held onto one another as best they could.

"What are they doing?" Dioni shouted to his green companion, over the force of the wind.

"Protection protocol, sir," responded the quetzal, calmly.

"What?" asked Dioni. "What does that mean?"

"It's how we defend our flocks," responded the quetzal. "We're building a nest, sir."

"A nest? What do you mean, 'a nest'? How?"

"Think of it as a wall of birds," responded the green quetzal. "With enough of us we can hold the effects of the storm, at least momentarily." The quetzal used its wing to point at the gap in the roof. Dioni saw the circle created by the adults in the church. "What they are doing in there, we are doing out here, sir. Protection protocol."

Dioni watched in amazement as scores of birds dropped from far above the land and wasted no time to position themselves within the nest. The spectacle was an entirely collaborative effort, which required no negotiation nor instruction of any kind; the birds knew, instinctively, that a supernatural threat was decreed against the Omega, and they did not question the notion to sacrifice themselves under the protocol of protection. It was not solely an act of valor, but also of greater responsibility to the natural balance of the Earth.

Within moments, the windows of the church grew darker from the shadows of the birds who worked together to create a protective barrier.

The strong winds which damaged the structure slowly subsided, as did the sounds created by the large objects which crashed nearby. The adults inside the church looked to the gap and stood in disbelief as they witnessed how the birds battled the storm in an unusual, impossible manner.

Alma slowly lifted her head. She protected the infant in her arms as she witnessed the actions of the birds along the perimeter. She looked up to the gap from where the rain entered the church and noticed the draped tailfeathers of a strange bird. She looked with great intensity at the tailfeathers as they flailed aimlessly in the wind. Through the drops of rain she saw a bird who stood proudly, as if unphased by the fury of the storm. Alma carefully placed the infant in the arms of her brother, then put her hand on the floor and balanced herself as she came to her feet. Though her view was blocked by the droplets of water, she saw the unmistakable magnificence of a resplendent, blue quetzal.

Chapter Thirty-Two

The Alpha stood with unease as he looked at the main screen of the Control Center. His plan was executed to perfection – two hurricanes, one destination, no survivors, no remorse. Even in his most imaginative and wishful thoughts, he never would have predicted how Ally made it all so incredibly easy for him. To have chosen a successor from a small nation with two oceanic coastlines was almost too perfect. As the Alpha, he could maintain control without an Omega, just as it was possible for an Omega to oversee the operations of the Department without the necessity of an Alpha. However, in one way or another, the balance had to remain.

The ancient vulture did not worry over the actions underway to stop him, nor of the whereabouts of the Omega. The intensity of his gaze was targeted at the anomaly within the anomaly. A force beyond his control hindered the programmed, destructive path of Hurricane Elijah. The storm was commanded to pummel the mainland, to destroy as much as possible of the Guatemalan topography. Instead, Elijah's intensity gradually faded as the storm slowly retreated to the Caribbean Sea.

"What are you doing out there, Dioni?" the vulture said aloud. "You're making me look bad here, kid." He turned his attention to the side of the aerial map that displayed the progress of Hurricane Eliza, which proceeded as planned. "Ah, my beautiful princess…my pride and joy. Look at how much you've grown!" he said with a sense of pretentious sarcasm. "I'm so proud of you."

The Alpha's mood changed as he looked again to the prodigal storm, who seemed to dishonor his authority.

"Why can't you be more like your sister?"

The vulture moved away from the main screen and returned to his self-appointed post behind the control deck.

"Control one," the Alpha commanded. "Show me the ground-level view of the eye of Hurricane Elijah."

The significantly smaller display of the control deck projected three words as a response to his request: *Signal Not Available.*

"Ahh!" the vulture shouted angrily. His voice echoed across the vast, empty space. "How am I supposed to destroy the place if I can't see what's blocking my—"

He paused. With the Alpha at the helm of the control deck, and with no other Controllers at their workstations, the only method in which a storm of such magnitude could be altered is if it was done so from...

"Control one," the Alpha commanded. "Show me all birds along the Atlantic coast of Guatemala. Show on screen."

The mighty map promptly changed to display the exact positions of the thousands of emperor penguins who launched to and from the beaches and into the sea. With the use of their world-class skills as pilots, the emperors successfully reinforced the levees and limited the access of the seawater through the production of massive waves launched in the reverse direction of the storm. The penguins, with the assistance of the undetectable dolphins, utilized the power of their combined efforts to disperse the cyclonic winds and direct the waves to the north and south. The valiant counterstrike was coordinated to perfection.

The Alpha shook his head in disappointment. His anger was not directed at the emperors – who worked bravely to protect a foreign territory – but rather at the treasonous bird who undoubtedly and deliberately disobeyed his command. He never expected such behavior from his most trustworthy assistant.

"You shouldn't have done it, Mim," the Alpha said aloud. He raised the tip of his wing to his face, his favored stance when deep in thought. "Control one, show me all the birds above Flores, Guatemala. Show on screen."

As instructed, the map on the mighty screen transitioned to display the town of Flores. The display was unable to successfully detect and track such an immense quantity of birds. The Alpha saw a conglomeration of thousands of detected aviators in a vortex, which was the combined motion of every Trader and Controller whose pathfinder remained traceable. The formation encircled Flores, at an elevation greater than the reach of the twin storms. With every moment, the formation of birds steadily increased in size.

The Alpha inhaled deeply and placed his wings behind his head.

"AAAAHHHH!" he shouted.

The vulture slammed his wings on the control deck, which struck with the force of two furious fists and caused severe damage to the equipment. He repeated the process, the sounds of his anger echoed within the vast chamber. In his fit of fury, the Alpha shattered the small screen utilized by the birds who oversaw the control deck workstation. His wings remained on the ravaged control deck as he looked to the larger screen.

"Control one," he commanded, in a deeper and more somber tone. "Track the Omega."

...

Jackie, Ricky, and Mimidae remained attentive to their main priority: to disable the barrier which separated them from the Control Center. Mimidae paced on the ground, nervously.

"Control two," Mimidae said to a series of interconnected screens. "Track the Omega." The projected images changed to display Dioni's exact location, made visible on a digital map.

"None of these files make any sense," Jackie said aloud. She was exhausted from the hours she spent searching through centuries of ancient code. "I went through I.C.E. seven and eight, and nothing. I found some weird commands on nine."

"What do they say?" asked Mimidae, with her back to Jackie.

"I'm probably reading this wrong," Jackie responded. She leaned closer to her small display. "It's showing something about a big comet or meteor, but it's in a completely different language."

"Then how do you know it's a comet or meteor?" asked Ricky, who searched diligently through additional electronic records.

"I don't," responded Jackie. "I'm just guessing from these hieroglyphic-looking drawings on the file."

"That's probably not what we're looking for," Mimidae addressed Jackie. "Just leave it for later and search another folder."

"I'm still on I.C.E. two. I'm not seeing anything," Ricky said. He turned to Jackie. "I'll check three and four if you check five."

"Fine," Jackie responded.

The two doves returned their full attention to the electronic documents displayed on their screens.

Mimidae continued her infinite pace in a bi-directional, circular pattern. She was noticeably worried, unable to recall the method by which the security wall was deactivated. She ignored the many screens which flashed live broadcasts from hundreds of news outlets around the world. She looked up and noticed the vastness of the vacant Trading Floor. For her entire life, she was loyal to the constant transformations of the Department of Global Climate Control. She sacrificed an entire lifetime of experiences and memories, just to sit at the incessant beck and call of the most detestable bird of all time. Yet her loyalty to him remained strong...even after he sent her away; even after he failed to treat her as she deserved; even after he banished her one and only friend from the Department.

Mimidae paused before a series of screens.

"Control two, track the Omega."

...

Dioni watched in awe as countless birds appeared from all directions and found their place among the unbreachable barrier they created with their bodies. What began as a single line of birds transitioned into a base around the perimeter of the church, which then evolved into a mighty dome-like structure made entirely of the birds who answered Dioni's call for help without hesitation. No bird was too large nor too small to contribute, for their role in the creation of the mighty nest ensured the safety of the Omega.

The wrath of the wind and the rage of the rain descended upon the land as the hurricane mercilessly accumulated in intensity. The protection provided by the birds disabled the wind from passing beyond their bodies; while the wind was rendered powerless against a defenseless church, the rain remained another matter entirely. Though the barrier of birds withstood the harsh conditions, the size and scope of the nest was limited to the perimeter of the actual structure, which left much of the roof almost entirely exposed to the rain. As additional birds placed themselves among the formation, they expanded outward and pushed against their unnatural adversary.

Dioni felt a sense of peace as he witnessed the true power of the birds. Raindrops fell from his face. The weight of his tailfeathers pulled him as they fluttered effortlessly through the gap of missing tiles. With the perimeter of the structure surrounded by birds, the sole source of light within the church derived from the hole in the ceiling near where Dioni stood. A puddle of rainwater formed from the drops which fell from his tailfeathers and onto the floor of the church.

To be in the presence of a quetzal – whether by circumstance or by accident – was a sacred spectacle to behold. The resplendent bird represented far more than just liberty; its life was the symbol of an ancient civilization, an honor and responsibility which all quetzals proudly accepted as their birthright. Of every story Dioni ever narrated, of all the tales he ever told, and of all the fables he likely created just to try to impress Alma, none were more memorable than those which included the extraordinary, wondrous bird.

Alma focused intently on the blue quetzal. She momentarily ignored the angry whispers of the nuns who repeatedly instructed her to sit and stay within the circle. She kept her eyes directly on the bird's tailfeathers as she slowly and carefully sneaked to better see it from a closer distance. With each step, Alma observed the bird in greater detail. He was larger than what she envisioned a quetzal to be, though his tailfeathers were shorter than those of the stuffed quetzal on display at the museum which she and Dioni visited during their elementary years. Alma cautiously took a larger step toward the blue quetzal. She paused and straightened her posture. With her arms at her side, she whistled a soft tone – a poor attempt to mimic the song of a resplendent bird.

Dioni's attention was entirely on the actions outside of the church. The droplets of water, which moments ago fell from the sky with great intensity, gradually calmed to a temperate rain shower. The ferocity of the storm slowly faded and created an odd sensation as the change occurred unexpectedly. The altered behavior of the wind and rain did not fool the birds within the flock, for they knew better than to trust the eye of a merciless hurricane.

Dioni felt the warmth of sunlight on his back. He looked up and saw the presumably impossible sight of a circular patch of blue sky. With no knowledge of the interior conditions of a hurricane, nor the life experience to understand how a vast amount of energy was controlled and operated, Dioni's thoughts concluded to his desired outcome: victory. Against overwhelming, impossible odds, the birds not only suppressed the storm from causing catastrophic damage, but were able to defeat it in its entirety.

Dioni smiled and wiped droplets of water from his brow. He laughed and shook his head. He looked to the beautiful, clear blue sky, where the clouds kept their distance. The nightmare was over, and all had survived. Far above the height of the clouds, Dioni saw the murmuration that hovered in a perfectly coordinated circular flightpath. He raised his wings and cheered towards the sky.

From within the church, below where he danced and celebrated, Alma saw the peculiar movements and sounds made by the blue quetzal. She froze where she stood, directly beneath the large hole in the ceiling, and hoped to not frighten him away.

"You did it, Mim!" Dioni shouted. "I don't know how, but you made it happen!"

Dioni opened his wings. He jumped back and momentarily fell from the rooftop hole before he lifted himself towards the tranquil sky.

Along the steeple-side of the exterior barrier, where the thousands of birds held in their protective formation, the faithful guardian quetzal saw as Dioni became airborne and flew away from the safety of the nest. The quetzal immediately panicked. He broke formation from the barrier, which created a gap that was quickly filled by a nearby macaw.

"Dioni! Come back!" the quetzal shouted.

He took flight to desperately chase the Omega bird.

. . .

Two sets of eyes were certainly better than one, even if both of those sets aimlessly searched through the same evidence to find a clue hidden within millions of lines of code. Mimidae stood on a portable platform beside Jackie, which allowed them both to be at eye-level with the projected images on the small display. Together, the two birds sifted through thousands of mathematical formulas, scientific models, and three-dimensional electronic code, all encased within a sophisticated sequence of symbols. Jackie controlled the computerized system via her actions and movements.

"Wait wait wait! Go back!" Mimidae said to Jackie, abruptly.

"What?" asked Jackie. "Did you see something?"

"Maybe, I don't know. Go back."

Jackie motioned her wings, which shifted the images displayed on her screen.

"Stop there!" Mimidae instructed the dove. She moved her face closer to the screen then used her wing to point at a small, insignificant icon buried within the code. "Zoom in on that."

Jackie motioned her wings to enhance the size of the icon.

"Did you find something?" asked Ricky.

"An icon," responded Jackie.

"I've seen about a million of them in the last hour," said Ricky. "An icon of what?"

"Make it bigger," Mimidae instructed Jackie while she ignored Ricky. The image grew bigger on the screen then came into focus as the resolution cleared. Jackie and Mimidae looked at one another. "A hummingbird."

"A what?" asked Ricky. He looked away from his workstation and moved to see what was on Jackie's screen. "Like Donna?"

"Not exactly," responded Mimidae. She turned to Jackie. "Break it apart and run the decryption program."

"Yes, ma'am," Jackie responded. She immediately did as instructed.

"On a hummingbird icon?" asked Ricky. "Why would there be anything there?"

"I'm not sure," responded Mimidae. "What icons did you see in the other folders?"

"Hieroglyphics mostly…of random objects and animals," said Ricky. "Cars, horses, books, lots of dogs and cats, rivers, a spaceship, something that looked like a lightning bolt and a wand, seashells, buildings, a lightbulb, three wooden ships, different telephones, I thought I saw the Eiffel Tower, a radio and a television, a ring, musical instruments of all kinds, a bridge, an odd-looking mouse—"

"—But no birds, right?" Mimidae interrupted. "Not one icon of a bird."

"No…none. Why?"

"In every location we've searched, that's the only indication of a bird," Mimidae responded, her eyes pasted to the screen. "All the others were of live or inanimate objects on Earth. This is the only bird."

"So?" asked Ricky. Mimidae looked at him with disappointment.

"When this was all established, after the big asteroid strike, the first assigned Alpha was a vulture," Mimidae said. "The same vulture, might I add, that is on the other side of that wall. The first Omega was a hummingbird."

"Donna was the Omega?" Ricky asked. Both Jackie and Mimidae sighed.

"You seriously should've paid more attention in history class," said Mimidae.

"Agreed," Jackie chimed.

"Donna stayed on in her capacity as part of an agreement that was made between the Alpha and the second Omega, but the very first Omega was a hum—"

"—I found something!" Jackie interrupted. Mimidae and Ricky rushed to stand beside her. "It's a code hidden within a program. The hummingbird icon is an encrypted application. There's a message written in some ancient text. I can't read what it says."

"Let me see it!" said Mimidae.

She brushed Jackie aside to get a full view of what was discovered. Her eyes opened widely.

"Pathfinder," Mimidae instructed. She paused to wait for her device to illuminate a secondary screen, visible only to her. "Translate text. Display on workstation."

The device immediately took action. As it scanned the three-dimensional, digital object, the pathfinder analyzed the series of shapes, colors, and patterns found within the ancient text. Within moments, the results were displayed to the three birds, who beamed with joy the moment the screen displayed the words, *Master Operations – Control.*

"How in the world..." said Jackie, in a state of both shock and wonder.

"Decrypt the code and run a full search for term, 'security wall'," Mimidae directed her pathfinder.

The two doves and the mockingbird looked at the screen, optimistically, as the entirety of the hummingbird code was searched for two specific words. If the instructions to enable and disable the security wall were created and left to be found by future birds, it was undoubtedly the only location where they would be hidden. Three words flashed on the small display.

"Term not found...what does that mean?" Ricky asked as he read the message on the workstation screen.

"It means it's not here," Jackie responded, disappointed in herself for her overexcitement.

"No, no…" said Mimidae, an evident sadness in her voice. "It couldn't find the term. It wasn't known as a security wall back then. It was called something else."

"How would we know that?" asked Jackie.

Mimidae placed her wings on her head as she turned and walked away from the doves.

"Where did you hide it, Ally?" Mimidae thought aloud. "Okay, recap. What are the clues? An icon of an encryption, ancient code. Modern language would be too easy…anyone could discover that. But the code is in pre-dated text. How would you hide a security wall in predated text or ancient code?"

Ricky smiled.

"And you said I should've paid attention in history class," he said, sarcastically. "Search the term, Jericho."

"Jericho?" asked Mimidae.

The device searched for the keyword as instructed by Mimidae. Seconds passed, followed by a change on the screen seen by the three birds. The mockingbird and two white doves shouted with joy as the screen displayed a multi-dimensional model of the entire Department. The word 'Jericho' was displayed as the name of a command, which showed an image of the Control Center's security wall.

Jackie turned to Ricky. She lifted her wings to his face then pulled him close and kissed his beak. Ricky blushed.

"How did you know that?" Mimidae asked.

Jackie immediately returned her attention to the workstation.

"Ancient text, right?" Ricky responded. "It was the world's first security wall, and it's the only one that was brought down by sound. Every bird of peace knows this."

...

The Alpha's angered eyes stared in fury at the triangle icon displayed on the map, projected in full view on the main screen of the Control Center. The ends of his wings throbbed with pain, though he barely felt anything other than the furious sentiment he shared with the storm he commanded on Earth. The Alpha bowed his head in defeat. He breathed heavily. His face became a deep, dark red.

"Wait a second," the Alpha said to himself. He lifted his wings from the damaged deck and motioned his command. "Show Hurricane Eliza and track the Omega. Display both on screen."

The image on the primary screen changed from a map which only displayed a triangle, to a three-dimensional projected image, in accordance with his command. The Alpha saw the same triangle and its coordinates in relation to the position of the storm. The triangle was in motion; its elevation climbed as it flew within the only part of the storm which was not covered in clouds and rain. The Alpha smiled.

"I couldn't make this stuff up if I tried," he said, excitedly.

He performed a series of motions in front of the control deck, which altered the behavior of a small cluster of clouds within the hurricane.

"Strike target on my command," the vulture said.

The small cluster of clouds moved slowly above the displayed flightpath of the triangle.

A sudden, thunderous sound reverberated from every direction; a gigantic hydraulic mechanism shook the entire Control Center as it retracted the barrier between the two sides of the Department. The Alpha looked up and became surprised as natural light trickled from the retreating wall.

"Nice job, Mim," said the Alpha. "You figured it out...Jericho."

The Alpha's smile remained undeterred. Defeat was not a part of his character, and after a supereon of service, he had no intention to retire under circumstances beyond his control. The barrier continued to retract.

The vulture looked around the mighty room, proud of his accomplishment. Life owed him a debt of gratitude, regardless of how he chose to live it. He turned to the main screen then lifted his wings.

"Goodbye, Dioni…you ridiculous blue bird!"

…

Dioni flew excitedly towards the clear sky. He wanted nothing more than to fly above what remained of Eliza, and to witness as the storm harmlessly perished before his eyes.

With every stroke of his wings, Dioni climbed further into the sky, near the circular opening where the clouds were mysteriously absent. He heard a faint sound from behind him, which he ignored. Dioni pushed harder, anxious to see the result of his victory. He failed to notice a small cluster of clouds which repositioned itself just above him, as commanded by the Alpha bird from the Control Center.

"Dioni!" he heard a voice shout, which caught his attention mid-flight.

Dioni paused his climb. He looked back and saw another bird. It was a green quetzal, his voluntary guardian, who flew to Dioni as fast as his wings could carry him.

"Dio—"

A blinding bolt of pure light flashed in the sky. Dioni looked up. For the briefest of moments, the world came to a sudden halt; time stood still, and the means by which life was possible ceased to exist. The energy discharged from the cluster of clouds with a strength and magnitude unmatched by the fiercest strike ever recorded, which pierced through Dioni's frail frame with utmost ease. A tremendous rush of both cold and heat consumed his entire being, and the colors of the Earth faded unto the depths of the cruelest darkness.

The green quetzal screamed in agony. He felt powerless against the attack and flew in a mindless state of petrification as he witnessed the Omega bird return to the dirt from which he came.

As designed and engineered for all birds who carried one, Dioni's pathfinder surrendered itself in exchange for the life of the Omega bird. The device absorbed the full force of the bolt which struck Dioni, and though saved from instant vaporization, Dioni's small body – unable to withstand such an intense amount of pain – became limp and lifeless, and rapidly fell from the sky.

The green quetzal dove in chase. Despite his talent as the fastest aviator in the entire Mayan kingdom, his best effort only enabled him to helplessly observe from afar as the Omega bird fell at a faster rate than he could reach it. The intensity of his flight caused tears to form and trail along the side of his face. A gust of wind pushed the wailing quetzal in another direction. He became blinded to the trauma of having to witness the end result of the Omega bird's falling body.

. . .

The security wall which separated the Control Center from the Trading Floor slowly retracted, enough so that it provided the necessary space for Mimidae to rush into the massive room as fast as her small wings could carry her. She stopped short of the master control deck, placed her feet solidly on the ground, then looked around the room. The Control Center was completely vacant.

The security wall further retracted to allow Jackie and Ricky to enter the room, where they headed toward the center of the enormous space. Mimidae launched to the executive suite. She hovered near the Alpha's perch, entered his office, searched behind his workstation, and dashed as far as the mighty bridge. No trace of the vulture was anywhere to be found. She immediately dashed from the executive suite and returned to the Control Center.

"He's not here," Mimidae said to the two white doves. She positioned herself between the control deck and the massive screen. "He's gone."

"How could he have left?" asked Ricky. "The entire Center was sealed."

"That doesn't matter," responded Mimidae. "We have to stop the hurricanes."

The three birds turned their attention to the main screen, which displayed evidence left behind by the Alpha. They saw as Hurricane Elijah remained held in position along the Caribbean coast, unable to breach beyond the beaches protected by penguins and dolphins. Hurricane Eliza, however, graciously accepted and fulfilled her promise to conquer all that stood between her and total annihilation of the Pacific coast. Mimidae pointed to the center of the screen.

"Her first, then him," Mimidae commanded. She looked at the two doves who were in disbelief of what they saw on the screen. "Let's go!"

Mimidae monitored the screen as the doves broke from their trance-like state and rushed to their assigned workstation. Ricky noticed the pieces of broken glass and destroyed equipment, and he used his wing to protect Jackie from the sharp objects that remained.

"He broke it," Ricky said to Jackie.

"He did it on purpose," Jackie responded. "Mim! The control deck is offline!"

Mimidae turned to Jackie.

"What do you mean, offline?"

"He destroyed it," Jackie responded. "It looks like he slammed it with something. There's shattered glass and broken parts all over. It's useless."

"Come on!" Mimidae shouted. She turned to the main screen and focused deeply on Eliza. "I know you have a weakness. What do I do... how do I stop you?"

Mimidae closed her eyes and took a deep breath. She exhaled slowly, lifted her head, then once again opened her eyes. She faced Jackie and Ricky.

"We'll use the workstations," Mimidae commanded. "Pick a territory and start changing the weather in that part of the Earth."

"The workstations?" Ricky asked. "Three birds can't control every territory simultaneously. We run the risk of making it even worse."

"Not just the three of us. We have backup." Mimidae responded.

"From who?" Jackie asked. "Every Controller is out there fighting this thing."

"Not all of them," said Mimidae. She lifted her head and placed her wings beside her beak. She inhaled as deep as she could then shouted as if to reach the furthest walls of the Department. "DONNA! OMEGA ONE!"

The room remained quiet and motionless. There was no sound nor movement from any direction.

"Mim…" said Jackie, solemnly. "It's just us."

"I had to try." Mimidae sighed and lowered her head. She felt defeated. She raised her head and turned to Jackie and Ricky. "We can't just sit here and watch it happen. Let's just each grab a station and start—"

A fierce roar arose from the far walls of the Control Center. The rumble grew louder and louder, which shook the broken pieces of the control deck. Jackie and Ricky stood closer to one another as they glanced in every direction above them. The roar emanated from the sound created by the rapid movements of thousands of tiny wings – a buzz made by an immense flock of aviators who moved in rapid unison.

Scores upon scores of hummingbirds descended from above, which created a mighty cloud of miniature birds who drifted in perfect formation within the Control Center. Their collective attention was given to the sole hummingbird who hovered closest to Mimidae.

"I need you all!" Mimidae said, enthusiastically. "The control deck is offline! We have to use the workstations to bring down the two hurricanes!"

The flock of hummingbirds turned their pointed beaks to the main screen. They showed no emotion of any kind. Simultaneously, the scores of birds looked again to Mimidae.

"Pick a territory!" Mimidae shouted to address the flock. "Change the weather in that area so that it offsets and pulls resources from Central America! This has to be coordinated perfectly so that we do not create something worse in any other part of the world! Ricky will help coordinate operations on the Pacific side, and Jackie will oversee the Atlantic!"

Mimidae turned to the two white doves. They nodded in agreement as they looked at the bird who flawlessly filled the role left vacant by the spineless vulture.

"Let's get started!"

…

Alma fell back as the rigorous crash of thunder resonated through her body and reverberated through the foundation of the church. The smaller children, along with three of the nuns, shouted in fear as the echoed vibrations of the thunder slowly subsided. The tremble of the structure caused the dust to lift from its state of rest, which cascaded translucently through the sole light source from the ceiling of the church.

Alma remained on the cold floor. Her back became wet as she fell on a puddle created by the rainwater which cascaded from the gap in the ceiling. She looked up and saw the same blue sky that a mysterious blue bird attempted to reach just moments prior. The wind was calm, though it worked in secret to diligently finish what it started. Drops of rainwater fell from the ceiling and quietly joined the puddle that reflected the beam of light provided by the sun.

Alma placed her hands on the floor then brought her knees closer to her chest to boost herself to an upright position. As she pushed down with her arms, she heard a harsh sound, which immediately caused her to cease in place. She looked around the sanctuary and saw no change of any kind. The sound came from something just outside of the church, near the entryway.

A mourning dove and a dark-colored toucan stood on the roof of the church. From a safe distance, they looked down through the broken tiles to see the inside of the structure. A scarlet macaw appeared next, followed by a golden eagle and a blue jay. They stood along the perimeter of the gap, and quietly observed from above. The birds were joined by a falconet, a pelican, a sooty tern, a pair of lovebirds, a canary, and a golden pheasant. The last bird to join and stand along the perimeter was a green quetzal.

Three gentle knocks were heard from the outside of the large entrance doors, located at the far end from where Alma stood. The large door handle moved, and a mysterious object carefully opened the door. With no desire to take any chances and face a potential threat, Alma slowly crawled back towards the others and maintained a direct line of sight with the entrance of the church. The large door closed. Alma scooted back. She paused her movement when she noticed the peculiar silhouette of the object. All that separated her from the mysterious being was an empty space, broken tiles, and the natural light which beamed from the damaged roof. The object came closer. Alma pushed herself to a seated position, her arms rested at her sides. She followed the movement of the mysterious being as it slowly came into the light.

"Alma?" said a gentle voice.

She immediately recognized it. Her facial expression told stories of how she felt in that moment.

Dioni, the beautiful young man she remembered – the one whose memories she buried yet who she knew deep inside was still alive – came into the light. His feet were bare, and his clothes were of a silk-like material which flowed effortlessly in the mild breeze. He was dressed almost entirely in a shade of blue, with only his face, neck, and most of his arms left uncovered.

The light of the sun created an aura around the young man, which accentuated his flawless complexion, his tender face, his dark brown hair, and the depth of his dark eyes. To the younger children, who remained seated in the circle and looked in wonderment, Dioni appeared as a beacon of light, the personification of an angel.

Dioni smiled. He stood in the light, the embodiment of life in its most innocent form, with his hands cupped and held out as if to present a gift. Alma came to her feet. She took one step closer then moved to see him from a different angle; if it were a dream, or if she had unknowingly succumbed to the storm, surely the image of Dioni would appear as a figment of her imagination. Oscar stood, as did some of the elder children, yet remained at a cautious distance.

"Dioni?" said Alma.

She paced closer to him, fearful that his presence was not real. Dioni nodded. He extended his left hand to her while he placed his other hand closer to his body.

She touched his hand; it felt exactly as she remembered. He grasped her hand and felt the smoothness of her soft skin. He touched her wrist, felt her palm, and intertwined her fingers with his own. Gently, he pulled her closer.

"Look," Dioni said to Alma, who could not remove her stare from his eyes.

He lifted the object he held so delicately in his right hand. She saw the lifeless creature.

"A bird?" Alma asked.

"A special bird," Dioni responded.

She inspected the bird more closely and noticed its long tailfeathers. A gust of wind blew within the church and gently wrapped the lengthy tailfeathers around their clasped hands.

"Is it a quetzal?" Alma asked, excitedly.

To see a quetzal was rare. To be so close to one was surreal. The emotion of the present moment was beyond her wildest dreams.

"Yes," Dioni responded.

He chuckled at her innocent question.

"Is it alive?" she asked. She raised her free hand to touch the small bird. "Will I hurt it?"

"He's alive, but not like you think."

Alma gently petted the tattered feathers of the quetzal's head. It was incredibly soft, almost to the point where it tickled her to touch. She gently caressed the bird's head, neck and face, which Dioni felt on his own body. Alma smiled.

"What's his name?" Alma asked.

"Dioni," he responded.

Alma chuckled.

"Why would you name your pet bird after yourself? That's a little arrogant."

Dioni quietly laughed. In her innocence, it would be impossible for her to understand what he had experienced since he last saw her.

"Let me show you something," Dioni said.

He placed three of her fingers on the chest of the unconscious bird, then took her other hand and placed it on his own chest.

"What am I supposed to do?" asked Alma. "Is it a trick?"

"Do you feel it?" said Dioni. Alma's facial expression showed her confusion. "It's very subtle."

The tips of her fingers felt the beat of a tiny heart, which matched the exact heartbeat she felt on the hand she placed on Dioni's chest.

"How are you doing that?" she asked, dumbfounded.

"That's why his name is Dioni," he responded. He hoped she would understand. "He's me. He and I are the same. It's difficult to explain."

Alma looked at the bird. Her deepest fear had come true. Her eyes swelled with tears.

"Then…are you de—"

"—No," Dioni responded. "I'm here. I'm alive, but not like you see me. The day of the storm, something happened, and I woke up as this bird. A quetzal. I learned so much and saw so many things, but I never stopped thinking of you.

Mystified, Alma looked at the bird in his grasp. With her same three fingers, she petted the side of the quetzal's face.

"I can feel that," Dioni said, happily.

Alma shifted herself to get a better view of the resplendent bird.

"Why is it blue?" she asked.

"I'm not entirely sure," Dioni responded.

She gently combed the small, tattered hairs on the top of the bird's head. To Dioni, this was heaven on Earth.

"Alma, I'm sorry..." Dioni whispered, hardly able to say the words.

"For what?" she asked.

"I wanted to come home. I wanted to see you but there was this vulture that tricked me and now I—"

"—Dioni, it doesn't matter," she responded.

She lightly brushed his hand aside and embraced him. She held him close and felt the warmth of his body on her own. She felt his heartbeat. Alma placed her head on his shoulder to fully absorb every aspect of his being. Dioni was alive, and in that moment, nothing else in the world mattered.

...

Mimidae nervously tapped her foot as she scowled at the large screen of the Control Center. She saw the animated movements of the twin storms, which displayed on a repeated cycle. She looked to her sides. Not a single workstation was empty. Though the birds worked tirelessly to disarm the massive threat over Central America, little progress was made.

"Excuse me, Mim?" said Jackie. "Can I talk to you?"

Mimidae turned her attention to Jackie. She joined the white dove along with two hummingbirds who hovered at her side.

"What's the status?" Mimidae asked.

"Bad news," responded Jackie. "We're doing everything we can but Eliza's not giving up. We can't stop her from here without creating an even bigger storm in South America. The hurricane was too far inland by the time we regained access."

Mimidae turned away from Jackie. She was aggravated, not by the thousands of small birds who acted as interim Controllers to stop the storm, but by the one bird who created it. Had she never left, none of this would have occurred.

"Ricky," Mimidae said to the other white dove who stood a few meters away. "What's the status on Elijah?"

"Under control," he responded. "Japan is gonna get a lot of rain, and it's going to be unusually windy in South Africa, but its manageable. We caught it in time, though I have to say we can't thank the emperors enough for whatever it is they did to stop this thing. They held it in place long enough for us to go in and take it down."

"What are our options?" Mimidae asked Jackie.

The two hummingbirds at Jackie's side dashed to hover before Mimidae. With a series of body gestures, the two small birds communicated their idea for the best logical option to terminate the unstoppable hurricane.

"That's a lot of moving parts," Mimidae responded. "Is it doable?"

"It is," said Jackie. "We calculated it seven times and checked the simulators. They have to weaken it and disperse the wind. We can take over the rain from here once the wind is under control."

"But you're saying we have a tiny window of opportunity," Mimidae addressed the hummingbirds. "And the signal has to come from a single source, so we can't broadcast it from here, correct?"

"Correct," responded Jackie. "It has to happen at the exact, precise moment. If we send the signal from here, we run the risk of them receiving the command at different intervals. Even if the counterstrike happens just a few seconds apart, they would only weaken the storm and we lose our chance."

"What about the Caribbean?" Mimidae asked.

"We received word from the emperors that they can handle it. They're working with some sort of volunteer navy, but they were unclear as to who they were."

"Okay, good," said Mimidae. "As long as it's under control. Fine. And how do we get the murmuration to disperse?"

"Dioni is already down there," Jackie responded. "He can take the lead. Once he is up in the air we should be able to regain his signal. We can relay the command to him directly."

Mimidae turned her attention to the map on the main screen. Eliza's intensity grew as her brother's slowly dissipated. Left unrestricted, the Pacific storm was likely to create a far worse scenario. The balance was in peril.

"It's a small window, Mim," Jackie said. "And we only get one chance. If the eye passes beyond Flores, that's it…we lose."

"Make it happen," directed Mimidae. "Broadcast the message to all the birds in the formation above Guatemala. Let them know it's on Dioni's command."

"Yes, ma'am," said Jackie.

Jackie followed behind the two hummingbirds as they returned to their workstation. Mimidae kept her attention on the large screen, primarily on the signal source of the triangle which flashed at the center.

…

The wind gradually increased its intensity as rainclouds slowly returned above Flores. The brief moment of sunlight and blue sky was quickly replaced with cold and darkness as the eye of the hurricane continued its path to the east. The ground shuddered from an explosion of thunder.

The many birds who encircled the perimeter of the open roof simultaneously looked up. An urgent message was broadcast from the Department. The signal reached the land; all birds were given detailed instructions on how to neutralize the natural anomaly. Dioni remained offline, thus unable to receive the message.

The green quetzal shouted at the scene below in an attempt to capture Dioni's attention. Dioni failed to look up; his mind and body were at peace, alive in a precious moment. The green quetzal repeated his call, which was heard by Alma. She looked up to see the various birds assembled around the gap.

"Are they with you?" Alma asked.

Dioni looked to the birds.

"Yes. They're helping us. They're telling me I have to go." Dioni nodded at the quetzal.

"Birds can talk?" Alma asked.

"Not like you and me. They have their own languages, and they speak in accents but I can understand them because I have a pathfi—" Dioni paused. There was no way she would understand what he described. "Birds do so much more…" He looked into her eyes. "I'll show you! Come with me!" he said, excitedly.

"Where?" Alma asked. She lowered her arms.

"Anywhere…everywhere. The world has so much for us to see and do. We don't have to stay here for the rest of our lives! We can go anywhere we—"

"—Dioni, I can't." Alma interrupted. She turned to look at the others in the church, who looked at her in a peculiar way. She smiled at her brother. "This is my home…our home. Oscar is here, my family is here. I can't leave them." She faced Dioni. "This is my life."

"We can make a new life anywhere we want! I can show you—"

"Dioni," Alma began. "I knew there would come a day when you would leave the orphanage and that I would never see you again. It's what you've always wanted, and I've always wanted you to have it. And you would go on amazing adventures and you would see so many places and meet so many people…and I wouldn't be there with you."

"Alma, wait…you can come with me. There is no reason why you can't—"

"My life is here, Dioni, and that's okay." Alma placed her hand on Dioni's chest. She placed the fingers of her free hand on the chest of the small bird he held in his grasp. "I want you to follow your heart. This bird's tiny, beautiful heart." She looked into his eyes. "All I ever hoped for was a chance to say goodbye."

The green quetzal called to him once again. Dioni looked to the gap above him. The force of the rain increased, and the wind gradually returned to an intensity even greater than before. Dioni lowered his head.

531

He looked at the bird which rested peacefully in his hand, its lengthy tailfeathers wrapped around his arm. He closed his eyes. The birds who looked down from the roof lifted from their positions and returned to their formation far above the clouds. The green quetzal stayed behind and momentarily waited.

"I will see you again," he said to Alma. His eyes watered. "I am *not* saying goodbye. I *will* come back. I promise you I will come back. I'll never say goodbye."

Alma's eyes swelled with tears. She forcibly smiled then lifted Dioni's chin with her hand. She looked deeply into his dark eyes.

"Tell me all about it someday, okay?" she said. Her voice cracked with each syllable. "Go, Dioni."

Alma hugged him, if only to feel his embrace one last time. Dioni held her close. He fought against his emotions as best he could. Alma released her embrace then took a deep breath. She looked at Dioni once more. His eyes swelled. She placed a hand on each side of his face, then gently pulled his lips to her own. They closed their eyes and embraced one another with the love expressed by their very first kiss.

The green quetzal took to the sky. He knew that the moment shared between Dioni and the young lady was not intended for him to witness. The quetzal ascended further into the sky to rejoin the massive murmuration which patiently circled above the hurricane. From a greater elevation, he saw the devastation Eliza left in her wake. As the primary representative for his territory, his priority was to rejoin the formation and fight for what remained of his land.

The eye of the hurricane passed over the town of Flores and continued along her destructive path. Eliza was no ordinary hurricane, but rather a cyclonic superpower which improvised as she moved. She had a mind of her own, calculated to utmost precision and to absolute perfection. She was aware of herself and knew the full extent of the power she had over the land, over the birds, over the Department of Global Climate

Control…and she refused to willingly step aside for the sake of those responsible for her creation.

The green quetzal battled against the wind, rain, and hail as he fought a series of storm clouds. He felt a difference in the air; it was colder, it pushed down while it simultaneously lifted large objects from the ground, and it whistled in various tones. The quetzal flew above the heavy clouds and reached the point where he saw and felt the light of the sun.

Birds of all sizes, of all flight abilities and capacities, and in quantities too large to accurately fathom, ascended in a huddled formation far above the land. They formed a colossal murmuration, a vast collection of birds the likes of which the world had never experienced. Free from the chaos of Eliza's fury, the birds flew according to their collective will. They continuously shifted from side to side and stayed within proximity of one another, with no technology to instruct them on how to successfully navigate as both individual entities as well as a greater whole.

The green quetzal rejoined in the mighty murmuration. He touched a nearby aviator, and within moments, his dark eyes glazed, covered entirely by a darkness matched only by the deepest galaxies of the universe. The eyes of every bird in the formation displayed in the same manner. It was their duty – a voluntary submission to all living beings on Earth – for which no bird was too small, too large, too old, too young, or too important to withdraw; none of their differences mattered in their greatest time of need.

In their formation, the flight pattern of the murmuration began to shift. The birds flew in unison and slowly created a wave-like effect by shifting their wings to lift or dive in perfect coordination. This was the flight pattern known and recognized by the resplendent quetzals, who developed and mastered the technique thousands of years prior. The waves in the sky slowly grew in size and intensity. The dives went deeper, the lifts went higher, and the birds steadily generated a wind pattern of their own.

Eliza fought back. The large drops of rain which punished the ground below were suddenly lifted up and aimed to disperse the mighty avian formation. The birds were pelted by the rain, which surged like projectiles and struck nearly every point of their bodies. In their unity, the birds remained undeterred by the water. The attack only served to unify the grand murmuration as they progressed the retaliatory attack into its second phase.

The waves of birds dispersed to create a colossal loop in the sky, counter to the direction of Eliza's circular movement. Their waves grew larger and larger as their flight formation raced faster and faster. The billions of brave birds within the murmuration created a secondary cyclonic wind pattern, a whirlwind, to counterattack Eliza's ruthless power.

From the Control Center, Mimidae saw the formation of the birds and the impact of their unified defense against the Alpha's final creation. The primary display screen presented the intensity of the hurricane as well as the full force of the murmuration. At the very center of it all, a small, black triangle flashed repeatedly. It failed to move.

"Mim," Jackie said from a nearby workstation. "They're nearly at max-Q. This is it...our one and only shot—"

Mimidae stared keenly at the triangle on the screen. "Come on, Dioni."

The counterstrike was nearly at maximum intensity of both altitude and wind pressure created by the aerial waves. The final strike had to occur at the exact moment the enormous circle reached an airspeed which Eliza would be powerless to withstand.

While the transmission of the command came through a mass broadcast as directed by Mimidae from the Control Center, the command for billions of birds to simultaneously launch an airstrike required the signal of a single aviator from within the murmuration. If dispersed by even fractions of a second, the mighty formation would prove to be a colossal failure. Though they would likely weaken it at various points, the hurricane would remain, and would immediately gather any strength it lost to retaliate against any and all lifeforms who dared defend themselves.

The wind, the rain, the lightning, and even the roar of the thunder were powerless to penetrate the mighty formation of birds in the deep sky. The murmuration lowered its altitude and continued its rotation to counter the cycle of the hurricane. So strong was the combined force of the avian pilots that a secondary eye gradually developed, though not remotely strong enough to alter Eliza's natural rotation.

From the ground, far below the formation of the birds, a funnel-shaped cloud of unimaginable size ascended to the sky. It moved at incredible speed and in a circular motion, at a force greater than the source from where it came. A cyclone of rage created a windstorm which effortlessly lifted objects of substantial weight and aimed them at the murmurating aviators. A large gap in the center of the cyclone became visible, as if purposely established for a reason known only to the birds.

Mimidae looked intently at the primary display of the Control Center. The black triangle did not move. She turned to Jackie.

"What's happening?" Mimidae asked, anxiously.

"Eliza's defending herself," Jackie responded. "He programmed this natural phenomenon to fight back if threatened." Defeated, Jackie looked to the screen then once again faced Mimidae. "Mim, what do we do?"

Mimidae brought the tips of her wings to her face. She closed her eyes, ever so briefly, then opened them to return her full attention to the black triangle on the screen.

"Jackie, send him the signal!" Mimidae commanded.

"We're trying!" Jackie responded. "Nothing will go through to him until he's in the sky!"

The murmuration reached the precise speed, force, and location by which the counterattack was to be successfully executed. The window of opportunity for the strike would close just as quickly as it had opened; to miss the opportune moment would result in a catastrophe of epic proportions.

From hundreds of meters beneath the murmuration – beneath the wrath of Eliza's reckoning, the pain she inflicted on all beneath her fury, and from the cyclone she formed as a mechanism to her defense – emerged a single bird. With all its strength, the bird weaved and dodged every attack of the unsympathetic hurricane; the fierce winds attempted to push it in every direction, the lightning attempted to strike it with bolts powerful enough to vaporize it, and the thunder sought to blast the bird out of the sky by the vigor of its uproar.

Amidst the clouds of rage arose a resplendent quetzal, blue in color. The entirety of its small frame was coated in light, as if protected by an aura of unknown origin. As the resplendent bird pushed beyond the clouds – beyond the reach of any harm Eliza was capable to inflict upon him – he saw the incredible formation of birds. The quetzal's eyes transitioned from their natural, dark color, to a profound darkness which matched the gaze of every bird in the murmuration. The blue quetzal launched toward the epicenter of the titanic flock, where it momentarily hovered.

"Send the signal!" Mimidae directed Jackie, who instantly turned to her workstation.

The dove made a series of physical movements then clapped her wings. The sound emitted by her wings was carried throughout the entirety of the Control Center. The many birds who filled the workstations immediately dropped their tasks to look intently at the principal screen.

The blue quetzal stretched his wings, held in his current state by the invisible energy of every bird which called the Earth its home. He paused. The quetzal took a moment to fully grasp the magnitude of what was to occur. He smiled.

"Now, Dioni! Now!" Mimidae shouted.

Her voice penetrated the enclosed walls of the entire Department.

Dioni inhaled deeply. With his wings stretched in perfect alignment, his tailfeathers pointed perfectly toward the ground below, and his head raised towards the limits of the Earth's furthest atmosphere, he opened his beak.

Dioni shouted the call of a billion birds; the sound of his voice echoed through space and time.

The sky above the clouds trembled at the overwhelming explosion of sound created by the billions upon billions of birds who simultaneously launched in every direction. The sudden supernatural force created a sonic blast heard by birds around the world. With the use of their wings as wind traps, every bird within the mighty murmuration carried with it a fractal portion of Eliza's energy; when divided by the immeasurable number of birds who executed the command, the hurricane was powerless to overcome such an overwhelming counterattack.

On the ground, a wave of invisible energy pushed down then immediately erupted towards the heavens. The dark clouds, which moments prior unleashed a torment of wind, rain, and hail, completely vanished. The cyclone within the hurricane instantly fell to the ground and evaporated as the energy of the winds dispersed in every possible direction. A haze of humidity momentarily lingered on the surface level, which then lifted to reveal the peaceful bliss of a cloudless afternoon sky.

By the strength and unity of billions, the birds of the Earth earned their victory; they celebrated as they launched in every conceivable direction and carried the remains of a once powerful adversary. They sang and cheered, their sounds reverberated by the birds who were unable to join the airstrike. The penguins and dolphins rejoiced as they launched and leapt out of the ocean and raced one another to playfully challenge themselves to determine who among them could leap the highest.

The echoed cheers were copied by the birds who remained at the helm of the Department of Global Climate Control. Mimidae, Jackie and Ricky screamed, danced, and cheered with joy and gratitude, while the hummingbirds used their rapid wing movement to create a unified song by which they expressed their happiness.

Mimidae became overwhelmed with emotion over what transpired. She took a moment to sit at a nearby perch, where she sobbed with tears of joy. For the first time in her life, the mockingbird was speechless.

The storm cleared, and all that remained were a small number of clouds which hid nervously behind the distant mountains. The light of the sun returned to Flores, to all of Guatemala, and once again the land of eternal spring was free from total annihilation.

Alma was the first to emerge from the church, followed closely behind by her brother. She looked up to the sky as she walked onto the rain-soaked street. She lifted her arms, closed her eyes, and smiled. The nuns, the elders, and the children slowly exited the church. They looked up to the heavens as witnesses to the impossible. The sky above them was blue, with gradience to yellow and red at the point where the sun turned to rest for the remainder of the day. Oscar approached his sister, who praised the heavens with a dance of gratitude.

"What were you talking to in there?" Oscar asked Alma. "It looked like you were talking to a bird."

Alma's dance subsided to a series of jovial bounces. She was unable to contain her joy. She faced her brother and looked at him with the biggest smile she was able to make.

"I wasn't talking to anybody," Alma responded. She turned away from him then howled towards the sky. "Woooooo!"

A bird rested elegantly on the branch of a nearby tree and observed the scene of the young lady as she danced in the street. The bird grinned and laughed as he witnessed how poorly she danced, yet how excitedly she did so. He was at peace – a sentiment which had negated him for as far back as he could recall.

"Woooo!" the bird shouted, in response to the cheers of joy which emanated from the young lady.

He turned and saw the people of his town slowly exit the homes and the many places where they took refuge against the storm.

The bird opened his wings, fell back from the branch, then lifted his body forward to push against the wind and elevate to the sky. He circled above the town and slowly passed over the church. The bird circled one final time around the orphanage before he flapped his resplendent wings and lifted himself far from the ground.

Dioni's long tailfeathers drifted aimlessly in the wind. He flew in a wave-like pattern as he gained altitude, as he looked down to observe what survived, and as he disappeared into the blue-colored mountains, painted by the light of the Guatemalan sunset.

Chapter Thirty-Three

"Human life, in and of itself, is a paradox; paralleled by no other form of life in terms of complexity and sheer brilliance, yet a colossal failure as defined by purpose."

A middle-aged man stood before a bright light, half his face covered by the luminance of a screen projector, the other half hidden in the shadows. He wore a dark business suit, perfectly tailored to his elder yet virile physique. His skin was smooth and pale, his eyes as dark as the elegant tie which hung from his collar, and his rust-colored hair impeccably groomed to the fondness of every administrative assistant he met earlier that day.

"So, what're you saying?" asked an elder man, whose thinned, white hair contrasted the business suit he wore. "Eliminate all humanity? Doesn't that leave us with no customers?"

"What?" responded the middle-aged man. "No, that's not what I'm suggesting at all."

"So then what are you suggesting?" asked another elder gentleman, who sat at the helm of a large, oval-shaped table at the center of an impressively sized boardroom.

The elder man's look of impatience was evident, though he listened to every word said by the presenter at the opposite end of the table.

"I'm suggesting we cut the middle man," he responded. "I'm saying we have to enhance humanity, gentlemen. I'm saying everything that breathes becomes a customer of ours, so to speak."

"That's absurd," chimed a third elder man, who sat near the center and at one side of the oval table. "Look, Mr....whatever-you-said-your-name-is...we're a middle-sized engineering firm. Our clients expect quality products and services from us, and that's been our bread and butter for decades. We sell trust and dependability—"

"—I couldn't agree with you more," interrupted the middle-aged man. "And that's what puts you in the unique position at the forefront of perhaps the greatest piece of innovation ever developed. You're on ground zero of the light bulb, gentlemen, and I'm presenting you with a switch. All I ask is that you answer one simple question: what if?"

The man stepped away from the light of the projector and pressed a button on a remote operator. The ceiling lights illuminated to reveal a large boardroom, where thirteen elder men sat around a large oval table and talked amongst themselves. The screen behind the man slowly raised into an opening in the ceiling, and the projected image powered down and faded away.

The man walked towards a wall of large windows which were covered in shades that automatically lifted to further brighten the impressive room. The windows revealed a large metropolis, which the man observed from a high elevation. He placed his hands behind his back. He felt comfortable in his surroundings. The man glared at the city beneath him; the sun radiated both heat and light, which allowed the large city below to enjoy a beautiful day. An indistinguishable bird quickly dashed from one side of the exterior to the other, which the man followed as it flew by until it disappeared from sight. He sighed.

"Oh, Dioni, Dioni...Dioni...Dio...oh-ho hooooh...that's perfect!" the man said to himself, gleefully.

He returned his attention to the men seated at the large table.

"What I'm saying is that, if we have the means and the technology to give people better options, *our* options, it will ultimately make life far easier for everyone. Just imagine what I'm telling you – an interconnected, global system that improves lives at a greater rate than anything mankind has ever achieved. It's not just selling trust and dependability, we're selling our customers time and freedom, across every sector, every industry, every market, and every demographic of every nation on Earth. My belief, gentlemen – members of the board – is that you are at the forefront of changing the world."

The man at the helm of the table leaned closer. He placed his clasped hands to his chest.

"What did you say your name was, again?" he asked.

The middle-aged man looked to the far end of the table. He smirked, which released every bit of charm stored in his hypocritical face.

"Victor Setrysorcen, Alpha Consulting."

...

"Do you understand what I am saying, Dioni?" asked Mimidae.

She sat at a perch, located at the helm of the recently renovated executive suite. Placed before her was a large screen, shaped in a semi-circle which surrounded her executive perch. From her perspective, Mimidae could monitor and track every assigned territory of the Department of Global Climate Control.

"No," responded the Omega bird, whose face was visible on Mimidae's projected screen. "Not even a little bit. Can you run that by me again?"

Mimidae sighed.

"Okay, let's explain it another way," Mimidae responded. "Heat protocol was established at the time when the Earth was completely frozen; we found this under a protocol called I-C-E Nine. At the time, the Alpha created a new program where he was able to implement a slow-rising heat to help thaw the planet and thus restore life. However, it was implemented at the time when the Omega bird's approval was unnecessary. The Alpha created and implemented the program on his own, and it was designed so that only he could disable it."

Dioni looked puzzled.

"So it's heat? That's it? That doesn't seem like a big deal. We can bring in cold air from the arctic…it shouldn't be so complicated. You said we still have control of the territories, right? Then let's just shift winds from certain parts to—"

"—That's not how it works, Dioni," interrupted Jackie, who walked into the room as Dioni spoke. She stood beside Mimidae. "It's a heating element that only he can shut down. The people will start feeling it within the next few years, but they won't know what's causing it. They'll just see it as a series of strange weather occurrences in different parts of the world."

"Then what's so bad about making the Earth a little warmer?" asked Dioni. "Shorter winters? Longer summers?"

"Irreversible worldwide destruction, Dioni," Jackie responded. "It's what we're calling I-C-E Ten.

"With *heat?*" Dioni asked, shocked by Jackie's response. "How?"

"Think of it as a biological response to fighting an infection," responded Mimidae, who spoke before Jackie was able to do so. "You know how the forests keep getting cut down and how there's all that plastic gathering in the Pacific and all the pollution in the air? Well, the Earth is going to fight back. Like when you became ill as a child and your body ran a fever, the Earth is sick and is also going to run a fever until it destroys the infection. Then it'll have an infinite amount of time to repair itself without people or birds or any living creature. I-C-E 10."

Mimidae turned to Jackie.

"Have we identified the source of the heating element?" she asked.

"Carbon, ma'am." Jackie responded. "According to the last entry by the Alpha, the directive from his protocol was submitted and approved as carbon. We also learned that this was put in place years ago."

"This can't be happening…" Mimidae said.

Mimidae stood to her feet and walked away from her perch.

"Carbon? What does that mean?" asked Dioni.

"It means that the only clue the people are going to get is a series of unusual levels of carbon in the atmosphere," Jackie responded. "Carbon dioxide. C-O-2. It will slowly acidify the ocean, which will make it increasingly difficult for us to control and maintain the balance."

"And they won't learn about this until a few years from now?" Dioni asked.

"If they're lucky," said Jackie. "They'll see signs, though: increasingly hotter summers, colder winters, polar ice melting, massive typhoons, tornados, hurricanes, earthquakes, tsunamis...the worst of the worst, Dioni."

"I...I don't believe it. How could he do that?" Dioni asked. "Can we stop it?"

"We're not entirely sure," said Jackie.

"Alright, let's move on," Mimidae said in frustration. "We're not going to resolve this today." She returned her attention to her screen. "Dioni, what else did you have?"

"What are the results of the tests from the birds in the United States and India?" Dioni asked. "Did we determine a cause?"

"The results were inconclusive," responded Mimidae. "We ran dozens of tests on location, and even more tests with the bodies that were brought here, and the only thing we learned is that it happened in the same manner in both locations. Something must've caused them to panic, and then they instantly dropped. That's all we know."

"Birds don't just randomly fall out of the sky," Jackie added. "But we can't determine why it happened."

"Okay," Dioni said, disappointed by their response. "We'll keep monitoring the territories from here and see if it happens again."

"Sounds good," said Jackie.

"Dioni, one last thing before you go," Mimidae interjected. "How are the recovery efforts in Guatemala?"

"After six weeks? Well, at least the news reporters are finally talking about something other than the hurricanes, but they still can't seem to agree or explain how it all happened. The capital and some of the bigger cities are back online, but there is a lot more to clean up, especially in the smaller towns. It's going to take us a few more months to clear it all, so we'd really appreciate it if you kept rainstorms away from here for the next few weeks. At least during the day."

"Understood," responded Mimidae.

"Thank you, both. Alright, I'm signing off," Dioni said.

"We'll talk to you later, Dioni," said Jackie.

She turned and walked out of the executive suite.

"Jackie…" Dioni nodded to her. "Madame Alpha," he said as he nodded to Mimidae.

"Dioni, hold on," said Mimidae. She looked to ensure Jackie left the room. "I know you're busy with the rebuilding efforts, but there's something you and I need to discuss. It's about the Alpha and the Omega. I don't think Ally talked to you about a crucial detail."

"Can it wait?" Dioni asked.

"Yes, of course it can," Mimidae responded. "When you're ready to come back to the Department, we'll talk then. Stay safe, Dioni."

"Will do, Mim."

The projected image in front of Dioni powered off. He sighed. He looked up and noticed a female quetzal who circled at a close distance then landed beside him.

"How did it go?" asked the female quetzal.

"Yeimi, it looks like we have a lot of work to do," responded Dioni, a look of determination evident in his expression.

"Oh," Yeimi responded. She shrugged her shoulders. "Well then, we better get started, huh?"

"Yeah," Dioni said. He smiled.

Yeimi grinned at him. She opened her wings and then lifted away.

Once in the sky, she turned and looked at the Omega bird as he stood at the peak of the Great Jaguar temple. It was known by all members of the Mayan city that it was Dioni's favorite place to be when he was home, and where he stood to decide his next move.

Dioni looked to the plaza as he absorbed the sights and sounds of the ancient kingdom and its surrounding jungle. He opened his wings and leapt forward, and momentarily fell before he swooped and lifted himself toward the open sky. He circled over Tikal – a tradition of his which brought him both peace and joy – then further ascended far above the sacred grounds of his homeland. Dioni's blue tailfeathers swayed in the open sky. From far above the land, he gracefully hovered.

Dioni instantly disappeared; a sonic boom and a trail of airwaves pointed in the direction of his launch.

The World As I See It

The world as I see it…is an absolutely beautiful place.

From where I have been to what I have seen and experienced, I can only come to the conclusion that our Earth is unlike any other planet in the universe. We are surrounded by life anywhere and everywhere we go, and there is so much vibrance and color to all that is our home.

The birds were with you at the dawn of civilization. We guided you as you stepped away from the caves, hills and mountains, and as you built the massive structures which reach higher than the clouds. We witnessed as you grew in numbers, how you have evolved as a species, and how there are so many of you who find joy in all that is provided by the natural balance of the Earth.

We share a responsibility towards our home, and for the first time since the existence of life on this planet, we come to you for assistance to help us restore that which neither you nor we can afford to lose. Our natural balance can be repaired, and our magnificent planet can once again provide for all, but it can only happen if we work together.

We will always do our part and never will we fault on our responsibilities. Though we may suffer losses, and though we may never live to see the results of our sacrifices, we forever carry with us the knowledge that we gave all we had so that the Earth of the future can generously provide, and that the lives of tomorrow fulfill the lives that were lost along the way.

We are here with you, and we always will be. Enjoy life to the fullest, but please help us by not causing further damage than what we are able to control. The birds of the world will forever be grateful to those of you who work tirelessly for the benefit of life – for all life – which is the foundation upon which the natural Earth is balanced.

And never forget…the birds are always watching.

- Dioni

About the Author

Dennis Avelar's mission to become a published author began while he was in middle school, where he developed a passion for telling compelling stories. Born and raised in and around the suburbs of Chicago, he drew inspiration from the people, places, events, and experiences he shared with friends and family.

As a graduate of Columbia College Chicago's film and video program, Dennis further developed his passion for storytelling by incorporating elements of cinema into the universes created by his mind.

His lifelong goal remains the same as it was when he first sought to achieve it, and he hopes that the opportunity to help others with his words and writing continues to inspire his future works and stories.

He currently resides in Addison, Illinois.

Learn more about the author and view his other creative works at
www.DennisAvelar.com.

Made in the USA
Monee, IL
20 January 2023

25676755R00305